MW01133518

THE DIARY

A novel
Frances Potts

First edition, February 2010
Printed in the United States

THE DIARY. Copyright © 2010 by Frances Potts
All rights reserved.

Hardcover edition published 2010.
Paperback edition published March 2010.

Cover from original diary,
and digitally manipulated by Rod Smith.
Author photo by Bob Story.
Cover design by Creative Consulting.

ISBN: 978-0-557-27050-7
www.allawaybooks.com
www.lulu.com/content/8189720

For my children Robert, Melodie, Daniel, David and Theresa

Lives of great men all remind us,
We can make our lives sublime,
And, departing, leave behind us,
Footprints on the sands of time

Footprints, that perhaps another,
Sailing o'er life's solemn main,
A forlorn and shipwrecked brother,
Seeing, shall take heart again.
— Longfellow

Prologue

He seated himself in the camp chair beside the dead fire and waited.

Alvin was the first thing Emerson saw when he emerged from his tent.

He ignored his son, walked to the wash basin and scooped water over his face. With his back to Alvin, he toweled his face and arms, taking his time. Then he turned, tossed the towel over his shoulder, and stepped to face Alvin over the cold ashes.

"Well, let's have it then. What's on your mind?" Emerson said.

"You know damn good and well what's on my mind. What I want to know is what the hell you've got on yours."

"Watch your mouth, Alvin. This is your dad you're talking to."

"Some dad!" Alvin was dismayed to hear his own voice crack.

"Listen, boy. That girl just wasn't right for you. She's got a weak streak in her, and you might as well know it now as later."

"You don't even know her!"

"I knew her the minute I laid eyes on her. What I did, I did for your own good. I did you a favor, son."

"Bullshit," Alvin said in a voice devoid of emotion.

Before his father could react, Al strode away from camp.

Chapter 1

It was a warm Saturday in August of 1932. The air hung heavy with the scent of new mown grass and, more faintly, of dung from the cow pasture across the creek. Zinnias added their color to scattered flower beds that were in the blowsy stage of a fading summer.

Oblivious to it all, a young man sat on a wood-planked stoop, doing nothing and enjoying it. He sat bent over, head in his hands and elbows on the knees of his gray flannel pants. He was intent on watching a ladybug climb a milkweed stalk.

If he stood and stretched to his full height, anybody who was interested could see he was just shy of six feet. A good guesser might put his weight at one hundred forty, but a shrewd one would know that was five pounds too light. The slight mistake could be blamed on the vulnerable look his frame gave him.

The young man went by the name of Al, officially as Alvin Ezra Potts. In March he had seen his twenty-first birthday, celebrated without fanfare. The scale he was forced to step onto each week had finally reached one hundred forty-five. He had worked hard for the last twenty of those pounds. When he could manage to tip the scale at one fifty, he likely would be allowed to pack his bags and leave this place he had, with tongue in cheek, called *home* for the past year.

But, at this moment, he was just sitting on this scrap of a porch at the front of this unpretentious hospital in Washington state, watching this persistent little bug, and feeling his oats, as the farmers would say. It was called marking time.

Al was deliberately not thinking. And he had plenty to not think about.

He was not thinking about the county's tuberculosis sanatorium adjacent to the hospital where he was all too familiar with a white, iron bed and a strict routine that never varied. The poorhouse with its back-end directly in front of him, was also on his avoidance list. The massive, two-story building housed the indigent and homeless. To Al, the poorhouse stood as a symbol of man's final inability to provide for himself in these trying times. That sure wasn't something he wanted to think about.

Al was specifically not thinking about all the county-supported people in these three buildings because, if he did, he would have to admit that he was one of them.

Walla Walla County's complex, generally called the County Farm, was spread over rolling acreage that lay between two cities, Walla Walla and College Place. It was a nice spread, Al had to admit, green with grass and dotted with shade trees. The three buildings sat on a rise that gently sloped down to Stone Creek, where the water ran clear and fast and gave up trout nearly as long as your arm.

Well, as long as your fore arm, but that wasn't counting the head or tail.

The land smoothed out beyond the creek, providing boggy pasture for the farm's herd of dairy cows. The pasture, fed by numerous springs, was hell on the hooves of the animals. Al couldn't help wincing every time he caught sight of the cows plodding uphill to the bright red barn at milking time. Their hooves were so deformed by the wet, the cows looked as if they were walking on skis.

The complex was entered from a road that ran right into the circular parking lot of the largest building, the poorhouse, and then angled left to cross the creek and dead-end at the barn. The road was used not only by staff and visitors, but by milk trucks that came to pick up the surplus milk and cream produced by the county farm. Al had traveled over it twice in the past year, once when he arrived as a patient and again to get a tooth filled in town.

From where he was sitting, Al could also see, in the distance, a graveyard. On one of his good days, he had been allowed to wander that far. He had walked through it, reading the markers. One especially had caught his eye. It was dated 1854. Its message was: *Far from home in a strange land.* Not a thought to get embroiled in when you are a young man caged in an unfamiliar place yourself. But he had entertained it, for the brief time he had run his hand over the elaborate headstone and traced the engraved words with a pointed finger. It had conjured up images of an immigrant seeking a better way, and finding disappointment at the end of the trail.

It was exactly that kind of thinking Al was avoiding today.

Chapter 2

It really was too nice a day to spoil with dreary thoughts.

For once, although he had his fingers tangled in them, Al was not even thinking about his head of curls, which sometimes drove him so crazy he'd like to shave them off and start over. For special occasions he settled for sticking the sandy brown ringlets flat with what he called bear grease.

Right now the ladybug had all of his attention.

Her shiny red shell was perfectly polka-dotted with black, and she paused every few inches to test the faint breeze which lifted her wings slightly. Al put out a finger to hurry her along, but she clung tenaciously to the stem refusing to progress beyond the pace she had set for herself.

"Go on. Get out of here," he whispered to her.

She ignored his nudgings. When he persisted, she crawled onto his finger and continued her march.

He grinned at her passive resistance, and remembered the days when he could have saved himself a few bloody noses if he had learned that lesson when he was a kid growing up in the back woods of Daisy in northern Washington.

Instead, it had taken Alvin more than half his twenty-one years to overcome the hot temper which led him into playground fights from which he and his favorite opponent would emerge bloody but never bowed. At least not until the day the teacher gave all the kids bushy switches and turned them loose on the warriors in a last-ditch effort to exert some control over her wayward charges.

That unprecedented attack put a stop to the school fights, but the anger inside Al continued to well up and burst out at unexpected times. His elder sister, Alta, and young brother, Murray, would try to shame him out of his tantrums by calling him a poor sport.

No one ever asked the boy why he was so full of anger.

The mail box at the end of the lane became Alvin's talisman during this time. His mother's letters a lifeline that helped ward off the darkness that filled him. Even though he wanted to, he couldn't seem to talk with his mother about that darkness or his anger. Maybe it was because their time together was always short. When Ora came from her rented room in Colville to spend a few hours with her children in the two-room log cabin on Pine Flat, the allotted minutes had to be divided among five. Or maybe the words Alvin so desperately wanted to spit out could not be forced past the lump in his throat.

An outbreak of influenza in 1923 robbed him of any chance to seek her help. Two years after his mother died, at the age of thirty-two, Al put his anger to rest.

After all, by then he was a boy of fourteen on the verge of manhood. He could better understand the situation with which his mother had struggled. He never doubted her love for her husband, Emerson, and her children. Alvin finally faced the fact that his mother had left their home because the man who had promised to love and cherish her refused to protect her from his mother. Alvin remembered that Grandma Potts had not only tried to dictate to her son's household, but had treated Ora as if she did not exist. Ora's mother-in-law carried her animosity to the point of extending her dinner invitations only to her son and his children. Her exclusion of Ora was never addressed by Alvin's father.

Emerson seemed content to leave his young wife at home with baby Pearl while he walked the other children over Huckleberry Mountain to sit down to his mother's chicken and dumplings. Al dreaded those meals. It was Grandma Potts who was always consulted by Emerson when there was a decision to be made, even though it was Ora who had to live with those decisions.

The two homesteads were among only a handful scattered like wood chips throughout the Daisy area, but the isolation served to alienate the two women, rather than draw them together. The older never tired of trying to subjugate the younger. Alta, Ora's eldest, was caught between the two like a fly in a spider's web. Alvin simply walked into the woods where he could not hear or see the abuse his grandmother heaped on his mother. Murray and Lily took refuge in the cellar where they played among the stored goods and carved pictures in the walls that were made of a soft chalky stone that drifted over them like snow. They emerged like little, white ghosts after Grandma left.

Grandma Potts' heavy hand was often felt in their cabin, especially while Emerson was away. And he was away often.

Although Emerson had fulfilled the requirements of homesteading when he built the cabin, developed a spring for water and lived on the property, he was too busy providing for his brood to break land, even for a garden. His search for work might take him north to a mine in Lead Point to haul ore from there to a smelter at the Canadian border, or much farther south for harvest on the Palouse near the Idaho border where ranchers were doing their damnedest to turn two million acres of prairie into wheat fields. Anywhere roads were being built was another job opportunity.

When Emerson returned home from one of these lengthy working trips, his truck would be packed with staples—flour from a mill, sugar and canned goods to last the year out. But it was beyond the provider's power to reclaim the reins from his headstrong mother and turn them over to his wife, who was seventeen years his junior.

It wasn't until after Ora's death that her angry boy finally came to understand that it had been less painful, or only equally as painful but in a more tolerable way, for his mother to finally walk away.

When Ora left her home in Daisy to live alone in a rented room in the nearest town, there was no question of taking even one child with her. Grandma Potts would not hear of it. And her word was law, as she had proven many times over.

Nancy Kennedy, Ora's mother, had also married a man older than herself. John was in the last years of his life when his daughter chose separation as the only way to settle her marital problems. His poor health and disinclination to lend himself to such a drastic solution prevented him from interfering. Nancy hesitated to act on her own. The Kennedy homestead was also just over the hill from Pine Flat, so she, too, did not reproach their headstrong neighbor. Without reinforcements, Ora was forced to surrender to the winning general. She compensated for her sacrifice by spending every dollar she could save from her waitress wages on what she called "my five precious babies."

Ironically, Grandma Potts died in 1924, just a year after Ora's death. On the day of her funeral, Nancy Kennedy, recently widowed, stepped resolutely forward. She took Ora's three-year-old by the hand, and said, "Come, Pearl, you're going home with me." Alta, Alvin, Murray and Lily remained with their father.

It took his first fourteen years, but Al Potts learned that hitting out seldom gained him anything and usually left him with scars.

He gave up his anger with a sense of relief.

Now, as a man, on the rare occasions when he felt it perking below the surface, he was able to clamp a lid on it. He might still feel the red hot throb of it, as he did a year ago when the doctor said "It's TB", but he knew the futility of giving voice to it. He considered himself an unlucky young man to whom unfortunate things kept happening, but he would never say or do anything that might give others a reason to label him a bad sport.

Like the ladybug that still clung to his finger, Al preferred to avoid confrontations.

He lifted the persistent ladybug to eyelevel so he could study the tiny eyes no bigger than the head of a pin.

"Hey, lady, don't you know you are free to fly anywhere you want?"

When she didn't seem interested in contributing to the conversation, he tossed her into the air and leaned forward intently, almost anxiously, to see how she would handle the dilemma he had created.

Her wings cracked open and fluttered wildly as she adjusted to this new situation. When her flight leveled off and carried her toward the next milkweed stop, Al couldn't resist calling out an almost forgotten nursery rhyme, "Ladybug, ladybug, fly away home. Your house is on fire, your children are gone. All except Nan, and she hid under the frying pan."

It was then he caught sight of a girl watching him from the back porch of the poorhouse.

Chapter 3

She was a slip of a girl, and what there was of her was wrapped up in a Mother-Hubbard, one of those voluminous cotton aprons the women who worked at the poorhouse wore. Hers went almost from her chin to her ankles.

Al couldn't help but notice they seemed to be trim little ankles. The sun filtering through her hair turned it into a golden halo. "Soft, like the down on a milkweed blossom," Al thought. And she appeared to be young, a novelty in this place.

He saw that she was looking right at him.

He felt his cheeks flush with embarrassment. Good god, a grown man talking to bugs. He wondered if she had noticed. He couldn't sink into the ground or disappear into thin air, and he really didn't want to. He hadn't been this near a woman under thirty in a year, so he damn well wasn't going to let her get away without at least a hello.

He hoisted himself up with all the nonchalance he could muster, stuck his hands in his pockets, pursed his lips into a whistle and began to close the space between them. He used a step that was somewhere between an amble and an outright footrace.

He was right. She was well under thirty.

He'd be surprised if she'd seen her twenty-first birthday yet. And she was a tiny little thing. He bet he could tuck that wavy, blonde hair of hers right under his chin. And he was thinking he might like to try. He let the fluted tones of bird-like warble die on his lips.

"Pretty day, isn't it?" he called up to her.

It wasn't the most original of openings, but weather was always a safe topic.

"Oh yes. Real pretty. And it's nice out here on the porch. There's a breeze."

She was right. If there was even a whiff of stirring air to be caught, this hilltop captured it. Little beads of perspiration dotted her upper lip. Al noticed that her lips seemed to be a natural rosy red. He had an urgent desire to lean over and lick the drops away.

Louis Armstrong's sultry voice, singing *All of Me*, drifted out from somewhere inside the house.

"Hello there. I'm Al Potts, and I'm a patient right in there, in the TB san," he said, flicking a thumb back over his shoulder.

Better get that out of the way right at first.

"That's nice."

Nice? Did this kid have anything under that fluff of hair?

"Well, I don't mean it's nice that you're a patient. I just mean…" She ducked her head, just like the shy girls did in the Saturday night movies down at the Liberty. But not showy. No, she looked like the real McCoy.

"I mean…it's nice to meet you, Al Potts."

She had bright blue eyes that were so luminous they were a surprise.

With eyebrows of feathery golden arches, the eyes were definitely her best feature. Her mouth was generously wide in her narrow face and those rosy lips were soft and full.

Al knew what he wanted to do. But what he did was climb the steps up to her, gently withdrew the wire rug beater she clutched in her hand, and walked back down the stairs to a rug hanging on the nearby clothesline and gave it the first of several tremendous whacks.

As he sent the dust flying, Frances Kerr wondered what kind of man this was who would so quickly lend a hand with one of the many jobs she had been told would be hers here at the poorhouse, where she had come this day to work and board.

Chapter 4

It wasn't long before Frances found out.

When she wasn't setting the tables in the dining room, washing dishes or churning butter from the cream of the county farm's own crazy-footed cows, Frances wrote letters for one of the poorhouses's residents. The old codger was incontinent as well as unable to read or write. He got to smelling pretty high on a hot summer day as they sat in the stuffy, but public, dining room, which was considered the proper place for a young girl of twenty to conduct charitable services.

"Let me do this for him," Al said when he heard about it. "I have to stay outside when I'm not in the TB ward and he can just come out here with me. It won't be so bad in the fresh air, and I think I'd enjoy writing his letters."

It was then she began to think seriously about this tall fellow with the curly hair.

The chores in the creamery, located in the basement, could be heavy work, but were ones Frances especially enjoyed because she could work unsupervised, even though the cook's watchful eye from the adjacent kitchen was often upon her. The solitude wasn't always convenient. A helping hand would have been welcome when she struggled to set the ten-gallon cans of milk to cool in two, six-foot long, concrete vats into which fresh spring water was piped.

She had been on the job less than a week when help did come, in the form of Lizzie's son, a young man who seemingly took no notice of Frances, but did pause to help her lift the cans as he passed through the creamery. Frances' words of thanks were short, but were accompanied by her usual smile from those rosy red lips. This brief exchange was noted by Lizzie, whose beady, black eyes held a malevolent gleam as she stared at her son and Frances from beneath a frizzy fringe of bang. Frances was aware of the cook's eyes on them, and was relieved when Lizzie's son left the creamery.

Frances was not exactly afraid of the cook, wary more likely. She had already heard of Lizzie's reputation as probably the best cook the poorhouse ever had, which might not have been saying much, but it was her strong point. The staff agreed Lizzie was not long on good judgment though, and that, the gossips warned, was saying the very least on a bad subject. While Frances did not indulge in the small talk among the other employees, she did have ears, and she did hear it. So, she had been careful to try to avoid offending the cook.

What Lizzie thought when she saw her son lend Frances a helping hand was anybody's guess. Whatever it was, it drove Lizzie to pick up the butcher knife, with which she had just sliced the dinner liver, and make a run at Frances. The unsuspecting victim was removing the last empty milk pitcher from the dumbwaiter that serviced the residents' dining room upstairs. Frances became aware of the charge when she heard Lizzie's thundering footsteps coming at her across the concrete floor.

Frances' first thought was that the cook looked like an avenging angel.

Lizzie, all dressed in white with her hair crammed into a mesh net that had a stiff, white band across the front like a halo, uttered not a word. When Frances saw the knife Lizzie was swinging, her only thought was to run, and run as if the devil was after her.

The short flight of steps to the outdoors seemed like her best bet, and Frances sprinted for them. She concentrated on digging in her feet in an effort to keep her leather-soled shoes from slipping on the cement floor still slick with water from the shallow, open drain that ran the length of the room from the cooling vats. Her path to the stairs was wide open, and she skimmed past the long counters filled with drying milk cans, pitchers and butter churn.

She heard the tinny rattle of a pitcher overturning, evidence that Lizzie's bulk was not far behind.

Ahead loomed the short flight of stairs that stood between Frances and the open yard where she hoped to lengthen the lead that was closing fast. She took the steps, two at a time, pulling herself upward with a hand-over-hand grip on the iron railing. The top step was in reach. A last pull on the rail propelled Frances up, her foot slapped onto the landing, and then she was on level ground.

She did not dare to risk a look behind, but she heard the swish of Lizzie's heavy, starched skirt and the rasp of coarsely woven rayon stockings rubbing together as Lizzie pumped her thick legs in pursuit. The brick root cellar with its heavy wooden door was just in front of Frances.

Could she leap down its steps, wrench open the door and slam it shut before Lizzie was upon her? Just in time Frances remembered the padlock that protected the cellar's store of home-canned food. Locked tight! Which way to go?

To the right would take her around the house and past the hospital and sanatorium. Left led to the front of the house. In a split decision, she chose left, and raced on across the green grass toward the poorhouse's parking lot. There were no cars in the lot; no help forthcoming there. The firmly shut double doors on the adjacent garage announced too clearly that no one was working in there today.

Frances' breath was coming in short bursts now, burning in her throat, but, if she was beginning to hurt, surely this race was taking a toll on the older and very hefty Lizzie. Frances was panting like a dog, but behind her Lizzie's gasps sounded like a wheezing bellows. But close, still too close.

As she rounded the house, Frances risked a look, and it was her undoing.

A pair of startled ducks catapulted out from the cover of a gnarly grapevine at the corner of the porch, and ran squawking directly in front of her. Frances managed to leap over one, stumbled over the second, and bird and girl went flying head over wings. Frances scrambled up, spitting feathers, and ran on. Lizzie, close on her heels, found herself entangled with the same duck from whom she had collected eggs just this morning.

Now Frances was leaping, great leaps that closed the distance to the back porch stairs from which she could again gain entrance to the house, this time the main floor and safety, she hoped. She was at full stride when she hit the stairs, but the only sound was her own rapid footsteps and Lizzie's approaching clop. The residents' dining room was empty, and the rest of the house was still.

Frances headed for the fourteen, steep steps that led back to the basement. If she was lucky, very lucky, someone might be in the staff dining room there. It was a chance she had to take. Someone had to be somewhere. She bounced from one step to another in a downward spiral that was half fall, half flight. She burst through the dining room door about ten jumps ahead of Lizzie.

Lo and behold, a burly orderly was dawdling over a tuna sandwich. She had never been so happy to see anyone in her life.

The lead she had gave him scant time to assess the situation. The butcher knife made the decision easy for him. He jumped up and snatched Lizzie around her generous waist as she came hurtling through the door.

He disarmed her with such ease Frances had a suspicion that this was not the first time Lizzie had given chase. As the orderly hustled a puffing, panting, red-faced Lizzie off, Frances sank into a chair, trying herself to catch a breath.

The story of Frances' flight from the half-crazed cook was quick to make the rounds and filtered to Al in the tuberculosis sanatorium before the evening meal. The highlight, told with either chuckles or awe, was the silence in which the chase had taken place. Neither Lizzie nor Frances had uttered a sound. Lizzie's silence, perhaps, was understandable, but for Frances to flee in total silence was the talk of the staff.

When Al asked Frances why she had not screamed for help, she said, "I didn't want to disturb the old people and patients. They have enough problems."

'Now that's the kind of stuff a good wife's made of,' Al thought. But he didn't say it aloud. What a man might want and what was practical were two different things. He had a feeling you moved slow with this kind of girl.

Chapter 5

Their courtship over the following months was an undeclared but public event the patients treated as their own special entertainment.

If Alvin caught sight of Frances shaking a dust mop and hurried across the lawn to say hello, it was a diversion for the bored tuberculosis patients sunning in their lounge chairs. The first time they saw him pick up that rug beater and help her send the dust flying, a few eyebrows were raised. When it became a regular Saturday routine, amused looks were exchanged.

Eventually, the staff and ambulatory patients entered into an unspoken conspiracy when they gathered to gossip on the poorhouse's wraparound front porch after sunset. They knew these hours before curfew gave the young couple another opportunity to be together, so often they prolonged their conversation. Nurses, too, sometimes cooperated by not hauling Alvin and the other patients off to bed at the required time. The talk was always general, but Alvin seldom contributed to it and Frances never.

She sat on the railing, in the dark, with her back to the grape vine that clung to the trellis at the end of the porch where it rustled and sent off a fruity, dusty perfume.

He sat at the opposite end of the porch. So they sat night after night, separated, but painfully aware of each other while they listened to the others. He always nodded a 'goodnight' in her direction at the end of an evening as he left the porch. Sometimes he politely shook her hand in a formal farewell. Once she offered him a few of the small, green grapes that tasted like sugared grapefruit. Their fingers touched briefly as the grapes changed hands.

On a Saturday night the porch-sitters were interrupted by a baritone voice emerging out of the dark. The unseen man asked the shadows on the porch if Frances Kerr was there. When she rose and joined the man, an awkward silence fell.

The crunch of their feet on the gravel driveway as they walked away together was loud in the stillness. The murmur of their voices floated back, then an engine roared, and car headlights outlined the circular drive. Everyone listened as the car drove away.

Someone cleared his throat.

Then the gravel crunched again. Frances stepped out of the night and returned to her place on the porch. Alvin's sigh of relief was lost in a babble of voices.

The gentleman caller spurred Al to action.

The very next day he intercepted her at the clothesline. He wasted no time with preliminaries. He leaned across the wash she was pinning to the line, covered her hand with his, and bluntly spoke his piece.

"When you got up and went with that fellow last night, I felt real bad to think you had a boyfriend," Al confided.

"I told him I couldn't go out with him because I already have a beau."

"You do?" Al asked, stricken.

"Well, maybe it was a little white lie." she said, cutting a coy look at him.

He got her message.

"No lie at all." His relief was obvious. Without considering the consequences, he kissed the tip of her nose, the only part of her he could reach over the clothesline.

"I think my nose is too pointed," she murmured.

"It's the perfect nose," he said.

It was their first kiss.

Whenever they found two chaperones willing to play, Frances and Al set up a game of croquet on the reasonably level lawn alongside the poorhouse. The supervision was an expected requirement. In the middle of one of these approved games, while Frances stood with feet firmly planted apart as she attempted to knock her yellow striped ball through a wicket, Alvin walked off the field without a word of explanation. She thought he was feeling ill and had returned to his room.

Later, Al told her that their male "chaperone" had leered at

Frances' shape, poked Alvin in the ribs and asked, "How'd you like to lie down between those legs?"

"I'm just a ladybug," Alvin said, when he told her about it. "I don't sting like a bee. I just climb along and keep going. That day I felt like climbing right over that fellow, but punching noses doesn't put weight on bones and I want to get out of this hospital."

Al put in his time over the next three and a half months, but his release could not have come at a worse time, weather-wise. December was no time to be looking for farm work. He did not know where he would even begin. Discharge was three days away when Miss Gillis, the sanatorium supervisor, approached him.

She carried an armful of papers and wore her no-nonsense expression, Al noticed, as she steamed down upon him and ushered him to her office.

"Come! Sit!" she said. She plunked herself down in a chair, and pulled another up for him. "We have paperwork to do before you abandon us."

Gillis was scratching out the last bit of information on the last form when she asked the question he had been dreading.

"What do you plan to do when you leave here, Alvin? Have you a place to go, a job?"

"No to both questions, Miss Gillis, I'm sorry to say. I've been thinking on it, but haven't found a solution yet. My sis's fiancé is looking around for me, checking out who might need another hand."

"So! No definite plans for work or lodging, correct?"

"You aren't going to write that down, are you? We're still looking and I have three more days to find something, don't I?"

Alvin thought his voice sounded awful whiney, pitiful and whiney. *Well, I feel whiney and my situation couldn't be much more pitiful.*

"Just checking with you, because there is a possibility I thought you might be interested in…"

That evening it was a confident man who sat down to write a letter to his sister.

Dec. 29, 1932
Dearest Sis,

I received your letter some time ago but just failed to answer it. Your Elwin has been in to see me a number of times since you went up to Daisy. His mother is in pretty bad shape he said.

I am getting along fine. The commissioners decided to let me stay until Spring. I have an idea Elwin told you I passed my exam.

I won't be staying in the hospital any more. They will move me out to the bunk-house with Sundae. He is my best friend on the poor farm.

How is Uncle Charlie and Aunt Orpha? I got more presents this year than ever before. We had duck for Christmas and plenty of it. I heard from Lily, Murray and Pearl lately, so must answer all of them rite away. It has been awfully nice here lately. Last night it snowed about six inches in 5 or 6 hours.

The big brother, Alvin

His sister Alta was actually older than Alvin, but today he was feeling mighty big. He drew a rapid sketch of the bunkhouse— kitchen and large living and dining rooms on one side, three bedrooms on the other. He marked with an X the bedroom that would be his. He tucked letter and sketch into an envelope. Let Sis see where he would be living until spring.

It wasn't a bad deal Gillis had arranged for him. He could spend the cold, sterile winter months here, live close to Frances. It would give him time to know more about this girl of his. He wondered if all that glittered really was gold.

Chapter 6

One of the first things Al did when he moved into the bunkhouse was catch a ride out to the Kent ranch with the hope of hiring on for the spring season. He also wanted to retrieve the old, black Ford coupe he had bought with his last earnings there.

Al was optimistic about getting the job. The Kents were good people. While their ranch wasn't in competition with the big wheat growers in the valley, it was still big enough to need a spring hand willing to weed the summer fallow and stay on for wheat and hay harvest. They set a good table for the crew, too, Al remembered, and Mr. Kent had not hesitated when he had asked to store the car in a shed at the ranch more than a year ago.

His optimism was not misplaced.

"Ready to go to work, boy?" Kent greeted, as he clasped Alvin's hand in a firm grip.

'As if he'd seen me just yesterday', Al thought. He was grateful for the understated welcome. He really would rather not rehash the past year, and this man seemed to know that.

In typical farm fashion, that handshake sealed their deal for the coming season. Business out of the way, Kent and Alvin pulled away the gunnysacks covering the Ford's hood.

"Maybe could use a little polishing, but she runs," Kent assured Alvin. "We started her up now and then, even ran her down the drive a time or two, so she should just purr along for you."

When Al climbed behind the wheel and rolled the Ford out onto the road, he knew he had really re-entered the land of the living.

The Ford brought a considerable amount of privacy into what was now a full-blown courtship. Now it was Al's footsteps that crunched across the gravel on the nights he drove out with

Frances. That was not a frequent occurrence. They still conducted most of their courting on the porch, but the gallery had thinned out considerably. They even dared to retreat together to one of the porch swings where their conversations, conducted in low voices, could not be heard by others. Al tried, but Frances still would not allow him to coax her into the swing that hung in the most secluded spot.

"I'm glad that's behind me," Alvin said at the start of one of their driving dates. The lighted windows of the complex he was talking about disappeared in his rear view mirror. Living in the bunkhouse proved to be an altogether different proposition. Al no longer felt like a patient.

Usually they took just a short spin, but this night Al pulled off the road and parked under a big, weeping willow tree. Its drooping branches surrounded them so they seemed to be in their own private living room. It made Frances a little nervous when he turned off the motor, but he just tapped her lightly on the shoulder, and got out of the car.

She heard him walking around the back of the car. He opened her door, and motioned to her to scoot over.

"Do you know why I did that?" he asked, settling in beside her.

"Because of this," he told her, pointing to his right cheek that was now turned away from her. On it was a puckered arc that stretched from his right nostril to the outer edge of his upper lip, pulling it into a perpetual grin.

She didn't know what to say. Of course she'd seen the scar many times. She hadn't given it much thought. It was just part of Alvin.

"It doesn't bother me," she finally said.

"Didn't you ever wonder how it happened? Do you want to know?"

"If you want to tell me. But I want you to know it's not something that bothers me."

"That's good...if you really mean it. It used to bother the hell out of me, but not anymore. I do know it isn't pretty. I've lived with it since I was eleven years old."

"Well, I really mean it, but what did happen?"

"Had a little run-in with a milk cow. I startled her when I

went to feed her. Before I could get out of her way, she tossed her head and her horn caught me right inside my mouth. She carried me around that stall pretty good before I shook loose. Left me with this souvenir."

"Were you alone?"

"No. It was a pitch black night, so my little sis Lily was holding a lantern for me to see by. I was blood all over, but she steered us up to the house. A doctor from Colville came out and sewed me up right on the kitchen table.

"He took me back to his house, and his wife nursed me for about a month before I could go back to Pine Flat."

"I bet you missed your family."

"Well…you see, my mother boarded at the doctor's house, so I saw mother every day. In some ways, it was even better than being home," he said.

"The doctor said no one would ever know from looking at his work how bad it had really been and I should never let any doctor touch it, but some day I'd like to have it fixed up a little more."

"Maybe that would be nice…" Frances said, and hesitated.

Nice? Alvin gave her his lopsided grin and waited, because now he knew there was something more than fluff under her golden hair.

She placed the cool palm of her hand on the smooth cheek presented to her. She raised her other hand to cradle his head and gently turned it to trail a finger over the scar that puckered his face.

…but I think the doctor was right," Frances finished, as she pressed her lips to his.

That kiss sealed the bond between them.

Chapter 7

Saturday, March 4, 1933 found Alvin and Frances in the sitting room of her mother's home on Chestnut Street in Walla Walla, waiting to hear the broadcast of the new president's inaugural speech.

Alvin tried to hide his worry. He did not want to miss one word of Roosevelt's talk, but Ida's old Montgomery Ward Airline was snapping and crackling with static. Frances' brother, three-year-old Herbie in his droopy, wet pants, also threatened to turn the evening into a fiasco.

As he listened to the radio squeal, Alvin vowed if he ever had a brand new radio it would not be an Airline. Frances made her own vow as she scooped up the soppy baby brother she was tending. Any baby she had would be potty trained way before it was two.

The radio and Herbie settled down by the time Franklin Delano Roosevelt spoke his first words to the nation as its president:

"This great Nation will endure as it has endured, will revive and will prosper. So...let me assert my firm belief that the only thing we have to fear is fear itself—nameless, unreasoning, unjustified terror which paralyzes needed efforts to convert retreat into advance. The people of the United States have not failed. In their need they registered a mandate that they want direct, vigorous action. They have asked for discipline and direction under leadership. They have made me the present instrument of their wishes. In the spirit of the gift I take it."

That was their new president speaking.

His words of hope in a time of depression were the prod for which Alvin had been waiting. If the president of the United States had hopes for the future, things were bound to get better. And it had to be only a little better before a man could afford a wife and family.

That night, with Herbie tucked in bed out of the way and Frances nestled close to him on the divan, Alvin took the plunge. In all the previous months he had seen nothing in Frances that had dissuaded him from his early opinion of her. He valued the loving, trusting nature she showed to him in so many ways. He hoped to offer her the same. He was sure she was the one for him. He had been sure almost from the first. Now, if she only felt the same! He had reason to believe she did.

There was no hesitancy in Frances' reply when he took her in his arms and asked her to be his wife.

She had to wait until the following day for Alvin to place on her finger an ivory ring that was a legacy from his father's trip to Alaska. It was not gold or silver, but Al considered it his sacred pledge to her until he could replace it with a gold wedding band. Because her knuckles were enlarged by the hours she spent rubbing clothes on a scrub board, Frances could wear it without worrying that it would fall off her otherwise slender finger.

When prohibition ended nine days after Roosevelt took office, Frances and Alvin toasted its demise and their new engagement with loganberry wine flips at a friend's Saturday night house party. They danced to Eddy Duchin's *Night and Day*, joined the others in singing another new song, *Lazy Bones*, and dined on sandwiches and coffee at midnight. In honor of the president, Ida banged out *Happy Times are Here Again* on the piano before the party broke up.

The happy times weren't immediately noticeable.

Chapter 8

For the next seven months Alvin worked for room and board and a dollar a day at the Kent ranch, while Frances kept her job at the poorhouse. Their time together was limited to weekends since Al boarded at Kents and Frances at the county farm.

A weekend off during the spring work wasn't a problem for Al, who tootled into town in the Ford to continue courting his girl. As the weather and work heated up, he was lucky to have a spare Sunday.

He learned that, when he did get a Sunday off, Frances' parish priest was going to claim a piece of it.

"If we're getting married, there are things you need to know. Things you need to promise," she told him.

"Like what?" asked a startled Al.

"Our children will have to be raised Catholic, just as I was," said Frances. "And that's something you have to promise. And, before you can marry a Catholic, you have to learn about our religion. You sit down with Father Gallagher and he'll talk to you."

"What's there to know that you can't tell me?"

"Well, of course, I could tell you. But you have to meet with the priest."

"Why?"

"You just do."

There didn't seem to be any answer to that except to make an appointment with the Reverend Patrick Gallagher.

Alvin didn't know what to expect. He'd never had any dealings with priests or even clergymen. When the likes of them made the rounds at the sanatorium, they skipped his room and that was fine with him. Just hearing their preachifying at a distance set his teeth on edge.

So, when the housekeeper held the door of the rectory open on that first Sunday evening, led Alvin down a hallway and showed him into a room she called the parlor, he entered a curious man. Silence was the first thing he noticed, then the scent of beeswax. He'd never seen such shiny tables. He figured if all the furniture in this place had the same deep shine as the parlor tables, whole hives of bees must be kept busy for years. An equally highly waxed, hardwood floor framed a plush carpet in jeweled tones.

Al sat gingerly on the edge of the straight-back chair, legs spread, hands hanging between his knees. He nervously twirled his hat round and round.

He heard the priest coming before he could see him. Heavy steps marked his progress down that long waxed hallway. Then there he was in the doorway. Robust to say the least. The last time Alvin had seen cheeks that rosy they were on a department store Santa.

"So, me boy, what's this I hear?"

And an Irish brogue.

"You think you're going to get away with Ida's little girl, do you? Well...we'll chat about that, won't we?" The priest wagged a pointing finger at Alvin.

"Come along. Come along. We'll just step into my office. It'll be a bit more cozy."

No waxed surfaces here, unless they were hidden under the mounds of paper stacked everywhere. Swiping one pile to the floor and giving it a shove with his foot, the priest cleared a chair, waved a hand toward it and said, "Take a seat, Jocko." Father Gallagher settled himself behind the desk.

The priest seemed to be in no hurry to get down to business. He proved to Alvin that he knew enough Irish jokes to easily fill the hour and, no doubt, Alvin thought, have some left over. He did interrupt his joke-telling to jot down the names of Alvin's parents and a few statistics about the family.

"Baptized were they? Only your mother on her death bed and her wee babe, who died so young? Hmmm."

Since the topic of Alvin's suitability to mate with a Catholic girl had not yet been mentioned at the end of the hour, Al thought it must be up to him to put it on the table.

"So, Mister Gallagher..."

"Call me Father, me boy."

"Oh, yes sir ..."

"It's not necessary to sir me, Al, me boy. Just Father will do."

"Yes, well, Father...are there some things I should know since I am marrying Frances? Some things a non-Catholic needs to know?"

"Non-Catholic? What foolishness are you talking now? No, no, Ida's girl isn't marrying a non-Catholic. Wouldn't hear of it. Wouldn't do, not a'tall. No, Alvin, we'll start instructions and see how it goes. But you can't just jump into it, you know. We can't just take anybody into the church. There be things you need to know, to believe. It's a matter of faith, me boy. But don't you worry, I'm thinkin', in time, you'll make a fine, Catholic husband."

Alvin couldn't believe his ears.

Before he could frame a response, the priest banged open a desk drawer, pulled out a bottle and said, "Now, a young lad with grandparents named Kennedy wouldn't be refusin' a little tot of good Irish whiskey, would he? Just a wee one for the road?"

The Ten Commandments, the seven sacraments and various precepts of the Catholic Church were eventually squeezed in among the priest's jokes, tall tales and tots for the road. Somewhere along the way, Father Gallagher discerned that faith had grabbed hold of Alvin. He gave Al the good news, along with a poke in the ribs and the stern warning "to remember where the seed comes from and where it should be goin'. Don't be scatterin' it where it won't do no good."

The first sip of the farewell tot was on Al's lips by the time he figured out Father Gallagher was not advising him on next year's crop, but had just given him the final lesson: *Good Catholics have big families.*

With the way clear before them, Frances and Alvin set a wedding date, which he immediately fired off to his sisters. To Alta and Elwin, who had been married in August, he wrote:

November 1933
Dear Sister and Brother-in-law,
We extend to you a very cordial invitation to Our Wedding. It

will take place at St. Patrick's Church at 8:00 o'clock, Friday,
November 3rd. I should say Friday morning.

We were afraid we wouldn't see you before the fateful event
took place, so decided to drop a line or two.

As that is the cause of my writing, I close with unlimited
respect.

Expecting to see you.

Your brother, Al.

He had to send a second letter correcting the date. *There was a*
slight mistake, he wrote. *It will be on Saturday, one day later. It*
will be the same hour in the morning. Sorry I made the mistake or
we made it. I do hope you come to see us before the wedding and
then we can tell you all about it. Hope to see or hear from you
soon. Al.

Frances found a white gown of slipper satin which fit over her
slim form like the proverbial glove. The only adornment on it was
a ribbon belt fastened with a clasp set with crystals.

The wedding veils were all too dear, she told Ida, as she
rejected first one and then another, reluctant to part with such a
large amount from the money she had saved for this occasion.
Mother and daughter put their heads together, and decided they
would make the veil together. They shopped the yardage counters
at the Beehive, and Ida chose a fine mesh net that they agreed
would do very well for the veil. Frances picked a lace that
matched nicely to use for the headpiece. Ida fashioned an oblong
piece from a triple thickness of the lace, and they took turns
sewing seed pearls onto it, leaving a small trim of ruffle all around
it. Ida then attached it to the net. When finished, the pearls
glistened in an arc across Frances' hair, and the veil puffed up in a
cloud exactly as they had envisioned.

Eight o'clock seemed early for a wedding, but that was the
regular time for the Saturday morning mass. "Good thing the
guests are all farmers," Al said with a laugh. In addition to their
families and a few friends, all of the regular, weekday church
goers were in attendance, so the huge church on West Alder did
not appear too empty.

When Alvin and Frances exchanged wedding vows that

Saturday morning, they were not starting out on just a new life together, but new careers. Al wanted Frances to be a full-time housewife, and he started a new job as an orderly at St. Mary's Hospital. He was also a newly baptized Catholic.

Work at the Catholic hospital was a year-round position, not seasonal, and paid more cash money than he earned on the ranch. Of course, it did not include room and board, but he was entitled to one meal a day in the hospital's kitchen. He would have the other two meals at home. He welcomed the change.

St. Mary's Hospital, an imposing brick building on Chase Street, was under the direction of a Mother Superior. The woman had her own ideas about running a hospital. Al especially liked the one that ordered all her orderlies to wear starched, white pants, at least on Sundays. The rest of the week she allowed them to wear gray pants that didn't cost as much, but Al loved Sundays.

He liked the feel of the crisp, white linen against his legs. He liked the way the white pants crackled when he walked down the hall. He felt professional. He wished he could wear them every day of the week. They were far different from the bib overalls that caked with dust from the fields.

'Marcelline would be proud if she could see me in these,' he thought, as he turned and lifted patients, settling them into more comfortable positions. He knew Frances was proud of him. Heck, he was proud of himself. If accused, he might deny that he *strutted* on his way to work each day. But he would have to admit that he sure carried himself tall as he walked past the Blessed Virgin's grotto at the St. Vincent Female Academy, from which Frances had graduated, and through the hospital's rose garden, which joined the two Catholic institutions.

He could perhaps be forgiven for the extra minute he took in the middle of the rose beds to pose over the sundial so he could admire the crease in his pants while seeming to consult the hour. It had been a long time since he had reason to delight in a good garment.

There came a day when Al inherited *four* pairs of the white pants, gifted to him by a friendly, former orderly, who moved away to take a job provided by the Civil Works Administration. The CWA was a project that President Roosevelt initiated after Harry Hopkins, his right hand man, convinced him it was needed.

Hopkins was at the top of Alvin's list from then on, in spite of what the Republicans said about him later.

In those first days of their marriage, Alvin confided things to Frances as they cuddled together against the November nights which sometimes surprise Washingtonians with their crispness. He could never bring himself to talk about the angry parts of his childhood or the parental separation that ended in death not divorce, nor about stern Grandma Potts who had moved in to fill a gap she'd created.

Late one night, he did summon up the courage to tell Frances about the day his dad, Emerson, went hunting squirrel for Pup.

"Pup was my bird dog. I was nineteen and we were living in a tent up at…"

"Oh, did you live in tents, too," Frances interrupted.

"Mom and Dad and us kids lived in tents a lot. Once, when Dad owned a garage, we lived in a house and stayed there longer than we ever stayed anywhere. Did you know I went to twenty-four schools in twelve years? I was so glad when we moved to Walla Walla and I could go all four years of high school at St. Vincent Academy with the nuns. Of course, Dad didn't live with us then. They were divorced and he was off exercising his itchy feet. Isn't it nice that I ended up in Walla Walla, so I could meet you?" she said, squirming into his arms and snuggling her head onto his shoulder.

"Now, go on, tell me about Pup."

"Well, it was summer and Dad pitched a tent because Alta had to spend every summer in the mountains after they found out she had TB. But all of us kids stayed there, Alta, Lily, Murray, Pearl and me. Our brother, Arlie, wasn't with us anymore. He died of kidney problems years before. We had a cook stove and our cots. Alta even had a gas-powered washing machine. Since she was the oldest, she did all the cooking for us, but Lily and Pearlie helped her out and it was kind of like a vacation. Dad was working as a ditchrider on the Burlingame Canal down at Lowden and he'd drive back and forth to work every day. The girls would stay home, but usually Murray and I would go along and help Dad.

"This day I'm talking about Dad went home a little early, and me and Murray said we'd get a ride up later. Alta told me she was still cooking dinner when Dad got there. Dad asked her if he had time to make the circle…"

"What do you mean, make the circle?"

"That's what Dad called walking a certain path through the woods. It was a pretty and peaceful walk and, in the right circumstances, could even be a romantic walk.   One of us made that walk every day to shoot a squirrel to feed to Pup. Alta said she told Dad he'd have just about enough time to do that. She called it right because just as he came back and was hanging his single shot .22 up on a nail hammered into a tree, Alta called out dinner was ready.

"Dad hung that rifle up by its trigger every night. We all did. But this time something went wrong. Maybe the gun misfired. Maybe the trigger pulled against the nail. Anyway, there was just one shot and Dad crumpled to the ground. Alta said it wasn't but a minute before she was all over him. She had a dishtowel in her hand, and, when she saw blood coming through his shirt, she stuffed it against his chest. She told us later it didn't look too bad, so she ran back to the tent to get a rag soaked in water. She washed him off, and then she got into Dad's truck and took off for the nearest ranch to get help.

"She said that old truck was just bouncing over the meadow, lurching along. I bet it was, too. Alta had never driven a car before.

"It turned out that Dad's wound wasn't serious. But he died in St. Mary's the next day. He lost too much blood. It's a pretty long way from the foothills to Walla Walla."

"You never said before, but I wondered how your father died. That's just terrible."

"And all because of a squirrel. I don't know if Pup ever ate it."

Chapter 9

"What did you kids do then?'

It was a whisper in Al's ear that woke him up. Through sleep-fogged eyes he could see the gray light of early morning seeping around the edges of the green shade.

"What?"

"I said, what did you kids do then? After your dad died?"

The whisper was accompanied by the tickle of warm breath on his neck and an arm wrapped snugly around his waist, fingers drifting idly across his stomach.

"I can think of something I could do right now."

"Ummm. But what did you kids do?"

He wrapped his hand around the moving fingers until they stilled. He then moved her hand to his chest and held it there, right over his heart.

"We did what we had to do," he said. "Do I get a cup of coffee?"

"Later, after you tell me," she said, and, when he sighed, she added, "With toast and an egg, I promise."

"Ok, pal, you do love a story, but it's a hard way to start the day," he complained.

"It was like I said last night. We did do what we had to do. I tried to do Dad's job on the Burlingame Ditch in Lowden, in hopes that I could keep the family together, but I wasn't up to it. There was the irrigation needs of a lot of rural customers to oversee, and the flow of the water to be controlled through all these canals, flumes, pipelines, gates and ditches. It was a twenty-four hour a day job, Sweetheart. Dad's shoes were just too big for me to fill. His dying split us all up.

"Alta went all to pieces. Dad's death was just too much of a shock for her. She was kept in the hospital until our aunt and uncle in Spokane sent for her. Pearlie went to Spokane too. A family in Roseburg, Oregon took Lily. Murray went to live with a family in Echo. Dad's foreman found me a job in a dairy, and I boarded with the dairyman and his wife. That's where I started having nosebleeds. Marcelline—that was the wife's name—Marcelline sent me to Doc Campbell, who told me I had tuberculosis.

"You would have liked Marcelline. I liked her." Enthusiasm crowded out the sleepiness in Alvin's voice.

"I liked her a lot," he continued. "Marcelline was a special lady. She had an elegance and a natural kind of wisdom. And her ideas! Gee, pal, she had some tremendous ideas. She made me kind of disappointed in myself. I know I should have finished high school. Alta tried to tell me that. I had only a year to go when I quit. I wish now I had stayed it out. Maybe I wouldn't have grown up to be a poor, old, dumb farmer earning a dollar a day and tobacco. Maybe I'd be somewhere on the ocean sailing to an island full of palm trees where the sun is always shining and the pineapples and coconuts are yours for the picking."

Fingernails dug into his back.

"Alvin Potts! You're an orderly now, but you know you loved farming. And you aren't dumb and you aren't old. You don't smoke either, so you could have asked Mr. Kent to give you a nickel instead of the tobacco."

The bed shook with Al's silent laughter, and he was still laughing when he ducked his head under the sheet and gathered her in close. When she filled her hands with his curls, his laughter faded into a smothered groan.

It was quite awhile before he sat down to bacon and eggs.

Chapter 10

They laughed a lot in those first months of marriage. Frances was a full-time homemaker now. Alvin just would not stand for her to work outside their own home. It was a point of honor to him to provide their livelihood, he told her.

They laughed the first time she ironed one of his shirts. He teasingly promised her a walk downtown to buy her favorite vanilla ice cream cone at Duff's Creamery, if she would iron a clean shirt for him. She wanted to do such a good job she turned the sleeves round and round so they wouldn't have creases running up the sides. He looked askance at his smooth sleeves as he pulled the shirt on and remarked, "I usually have creases. I think you're going to have to settle for chocolate."

They laughed out loud and until their sides ached when he tried to rig a clothesline and it collapsed under the first load of her clean wash. If truth were told, he didn't want to bother with it in the first place, but she smiled up at him when she asked. Seeing those white sheets tangled in rope and dragging across the ground tickled his funny-bone and, fortunately, hers too. "The damn thing failed," he roared as they hugged each other and staggered around the yard, drunk with laughter.

He came back later and got the job done right. He couldn't remember when he felt such satisfaction. After that, whenever he saw white sheets flapping in the breeze on Monday wash days, he felt what he called "tremendous joy". Tremendous was one of his favorite words.

Their first home was a two-room cottage in a row of cottages on Seventh Street in Walla Walla. The bathroom was at the end of the row and everyone shared it. It became a familiar sight to see Frances, loaded down with cleaning supplies, on her way to or from the communal facility. For Alvin, who had grown up in a two-room log house with three sisters and a brother, the house was more than adequate. For Frances, who had always shared her bed with at least two of her four sisters and a bathroom with all of them, plus four brothers, two rooms all to themselves was a mansion. Cleaning up after others was no problem; she had been doing that for a number of years.

The newlyweds scarcely knew a depression was going on outside.

On a morning a month after the wedding, Alvin drew Frances away from the table she was clearing and led her into the bedroom. He put his hands on her shoulders and bent down to kiss her.

"I love you very much," he told her.

Then he gently turned her head so she could see, reflected in the mirror of their dressing table, the red stain that dotted the back of her dress. It was her last menstrual period until the following year.

The pregnancy, when it made itself known, was not unexpected by this Catholic wife. While it slowly turned her small figure pear-shaped, it did nothing to upset her routine. By ten o'clock every morning the breakfast dishes were washed, the floors mopped and waxed, furniture dusted, windows shined and, on Mondays, the laundry sorted and ready to trundle to her mother's in a big, old, wicker baby buggy for which Ida no longer had any use.

Frances used her mother's Maytag to do the washing for both households. It was a fair exchange, because Frances had no machine and Ida could use the help since she cleaned other people's houses every day.

Ida had been her children's sole support since her husband, John, had left her and the kids behind when he went in search of, he said, gold in California. At the time Ida had not reminded John that his youngest was still an infant in a crib and the gold rush was ancient history. She had heard too many times his argument that there was still gold to be had, if one had the patience to look.

The car John drove away in was registered in his name, but Frances had paid for it from her earnings, as John had expected his dutiful, unmarried daughter to do. As one of the three eldest in the family of twelve, Frances was accustomed to helping support the family.

During John's absence, Ida worked and waited, receiving a letter every now and then, but no money. When John returned a year later to announce he had found a woman in Sacramento instead of gold, Ida removed her wedding ring, tucked it away in a drawer of her Singer sewing machine, and went on working.

While Frances could no longer help Ida financially now that she was married, she did what she could.

On Saturdays Frances spread homemade bread with deviled meat, which cost her four cents a tin, or hand-picked and home-canned strawberry jam and invited her mother in for lunch. Ida's job on Saturdays was cleaning the Catholic church just a block from Frances' cottage, so lunch together was not only fun, but convenient.

On Sundays Ida herded her starched and shiny clean brood into the same church for nine o'clock mass where Frances and Alvin shared the same pew. Ida always returned at eleven to enjoy another service by herself. When people teased her about being "so holy", Ida told them she went to church twice as much as most people because she was twice as bad. Frances thought it might be the extra hour of peace and quiet without her kids that was the drawing card, but never said so.

Saturday night brought its own routine. Invariably the newlyweds walked to town where they strolled the streets, shoulder to shoulder with other people doing the same thing. Saturday was farmers' night in Walla Walla. The farm owners and laborers, along with their wives and kids, shared the hustle and bustle of the streets with the town folks.

Alvin and Frances were drawn to the brightly lit windows of the store people affectionately called Monkey Wards. Although the dime store was more likely to attract any business from the new Mr. and Mrs. Potts, they did own a pair of real silver salt and pepper shakers Al had purchased at Martin's Jewelry Store while they were courting.

He had spent the princely sum of seven dollars and fifty cents for them, more than a week's pay. Now on Saturday nights they leaned on the window ledge and compared their shakers and plain gold wedding bands with Martin's current glittering display. They agreed their rings were prettier than any there, but they never expressed their disappointment with the silver shakers that gave the salt an odd taste.

No Saturday night downtown was complete without joining the crowd in front of Walgren's drugstore in the middle of skid road to listen to the Salvation Army band.

The band made quite a show with the ladies in their tight-fitting bonnets and long, blue serge skirts and the men dressed in military preciseness. The trumpets and drums acted as magnets, and the band played until it had a crowd six deep at the street corner. The speechifying began then, and Alvin usually dropped a couple of pennies, sometimes a nickel if he had it to spare, into the tambourine as it was passed around. The sermon weeded out a few, but the tambourine was sure fire to thin out the crowd. The last stop before they headed home was at the ice cream parlor where the ice cream was good, but not quite as good as the vanilla at Duff's over on South Third Avenue.

The walk home was a hand-in-hand, leisurely affair they didn't want to trade for a round-trip in the Ford. Besides, said Frances' resident orderly, walking was good for mother and baby-to-be. The stars overhead, the soft breeze that stirred the leaves on the overhanging trees were all a part of their new life together. If it was a simplistic life, it suited them.

The very predictability of Frances' weekly routine, Alvin's job at the hospital, a new baby on the way, all seemed to be the fulfillment of the promises made in Roosevelt's speech the night Al proposed.

Chapter 11

The good times just kept rolling. By the time Easter arrived, Alvin and Frances had moved to a house in nearby College Place. It had a bedroom, a dinky living room, a kitchen just big enough to hold a table and four chairs, and a screened-in back porch. Their luxury was the bathroom with its stool, commode and tin-lined shower stall. A bathroom all to themselves.

Frances was wrist-deep in soap suds and losing her race with the clock. There was no way the breakfast dishes were going to be done in time for her to drive to Walla Walla, pick up Herbie and get him to the Active Club's Easter egg hunt at Wildwood Park. She hated to break a promise. The egg hunt was to be his reward for not wetting his bed in the past week. It looked as if she was going to have a disappointed kid brother.

Then she felt a kiss on the back of her neck. Fingers pulled loose the bow of her apron.

"Just leave them. You get that kid to the egg hunt. The dishes will keep," Alvin said.

She hurried into the bathroom, rinsed her hands and ran a comb through her hair.

'What a luxury to be just steps away from water and a mirror,' she thought.

An anxious Herbie waited on Mom's front porch. A big smile spread over his face when he saw Frances' Ford pull up. His big sister hadn't come to a full stop before Herbie was tugging at the door.

"Go tell Mom we're leaving," Frances commanded her too eager brother.

"She knows! She knows! Let's go."

"Not before you tell her I'm here and taking you."

Ida saved Herbie by stepping outside and waving them off.

The weather was typical of most Saturdays before Easter Sunday. Dark clouds airbrushed the sky and threatened rain, but the iffy weather had not discouraged Walla Walla's upper set. Their Packards and Hudsons and even several Auburn convertible cars converged on the park at Boyer and Division Streets. The young mothers flocked across the grass in their high heels, billowy skirts and hats adorned with ribbons and flowers. A regular Easter parade. The children they had in tow were almost secondary accessories, shining brightly in new Buster Browns, the girls in frills and the boys in crisp, store-bought shirts so new they crackled.

Herbie's brown paper bag did not quite match up to the beribboned Easter baskets these children carried, but he didn't seem to notice. He was too busy scoping out possible hiding places, impatient to get at those colored eggs.

Frances was glad he wasn't comparing his well-worn overalls to the Easter finery around him. She was sorry she was so aware of her ballooning belly primly covered with an ordinary cotton house dress. Well it was crisply starched. Her sensible, low-heeled shoes felt like clodhoppers.

Frances took a stance near two matrons, who were deep in conversation under their broad-brimmed straw hats. They scarcely noticed when the word was given and their children broke loose and pushed and shoved in a mad dash to be first into the hunt. Frances had her eye on Herbie, who was scrambling under bushes and searching every long tuft of grass. He looked awfully cute.

"What's that?" Frances heard one of the women say.

She turned to look, and saw them sniffing the air as if they smelled something bad.

"Do you smell bleach?" one asked the other, wrinkling her nose.

"Yes! But where on earth would it be coming from out here?"

Frances was afraid she knew all too well, but she raised her hand to her nose just to double check. Yep! Soaking the dishtowels that morning had left her a marked woman.

She discreetly moved downwind of the matrons, but she suspected they knew too. She hoped the trace of her morning chores would soon evaporate. She fought a desire to either laugh or cry, she wasn't sure which. Most of all she wanted to get away from these young…and slim…ladies.

When she returned home, not only were the dishes washed, but all the pans hung on nails Alvin had hammered into the wall of the porch. It looked like a little pantry. In that moment, Frances knew exactly how it felt to be rich. And it had nothing to do with silk dresses or fancy perfume. She wrapped her arms around her husband's waist and laid her head against his chest.

"How did it go?" Al quizzed.

"Herbie found two prize eggs, but I'm the lucky one."

The last four months of Frances' pregnancy passed swiftly for Alvin, slower for her. By August she was wishing for the figure she'd had at Easter.

Alvin reveled in the work at St. Mary's. His organization of the supply room earned him a Valued Employee award. He never stopped with one coat of wax for the floors assigned to him. He had the rectory's example in mind when he slapped on the second. Two were better. He liked reassuring fathers-to-be, who paced in the maternity waiting room. A cup of coffee or a little conversation calmed them right down. Seemed to take their minds off what might be happening behind the closed doors of the delivery room.

One expectant father, on hearing that Al would soon be a father, teased him. "You'll be right here, walking and worrying yourself one of these days."

"No, I won't," Alvin countered. "I'll be right in there with her."

Sister Superior had promised to stretch the rules for Alvin, based on his status as an employee of the hospital. He had her promise that he could be with Frances from first pain through the delivery.

True to his word, that's where Alvin was on August 22 when the pains twisted through Frances. He hadn't realized what he had asked for. The labor did not proceed well. Frances' body strained uselessly all of Wednesday and through the night.

"This little lady has the narrowest pelvic bones I've ever seen, and a little hook that's caught the baby's head and isn't letting it drop down naturally," said Doc Campbell, after one of his examinations.

Frances did not scream once throughout the difficult labor, for which Al was grateful, but she bit her lips until the skin broke and bled. Half-moons dented the palms of Alvin's hands where Frances' fingernails had dug in. He repeatedly mopped sweat from her face, sliding the cool cloth around the back of her neck. Always, he received a sweet smile in return.

Alvin was still beside her early Thursday morning when Frances was rolled into a delivery room that was starkly bright with its glistening white paint and glaring lights overhead. Her fingernails still bit into the hand she kept tightly clenched in hers. She relaxed her hold only when the ether took effect.

Their daughter finally battered her way into the world with the aggressive help of Dr. Campbell's forceps.

"It's a girl," Campbell said. He handed the baby off to Al as soon as he spanked a cry from her. Alvin held her in his arms. She was still sticky and slimy. Bruises marred her forehead and cheeks. *And besides that her face looks like hell.*

"Why does her face look so strange?" Al asked.

A nurse took the baby from him.

"We'll clean her up now. Then she'll be ready for a nice visit with her mother when she wakes up."

The nurses wheeled Frances back to her room, but Dr. Campbell took Alvin aside.

"That was quite a struggle your little girl went through."

Alvin thought he was talking about Frances, so he didn't comprehend Doc's next words.

"The left side of her face is paralyzed."

What the hell did that mean?

The longer Doc talked, the more confused Al became.

He finally realized it was the baby's condition that was being described.

"It may be permanent. It may not. The next twenty-four hours will be a wait-and-see period," said Dr. Campbell. "You can see your wife any time now, but it will be awhile before she awakens."

Al walked wearily along the corridor to the elevator. A cup of coffee from the cafeteria would taste good about now. When he had it in hand, he went back upstairs.

Ether fumes still clung to the unconscious Frances. When Alvin bent to kiss her cheek, the cloying anesthetic set his head to spinning briefly.

Not as tasty as loganberry flips, but much the same results.

He flopped into a chair to wait for his wife to wake up. It wasn't long before her eyes fluttered open. Her reaction to the anesthetic was immediate. Bile spewed forth, and then tears. She mumbled something about not wanting him to see her like this. Al had to laugh. After what they had been through since yesterday, a little spit-up would be a cinch to deal with. He wiped her lips with his handkerchief, and stripped the soiled sheet from the bed. When she was comfortably settled, he took her hand in his and told her the bad news.

It was with apprehension that Alvin and Frances waited for Dr. Campbell to come to them. Tired, they still could only catnap between bouts of worrying. They were aware of nurses in and out, of offers of food, but the handclasp between them was their only reality. Exhaustion overtook them in the wee hours of Friday morning, and they were sleeping when Dr. Campbell entered the room. Frances woke first and shook Alvin awake. They searched the doctor's face for the answer they hoped to see. Campbell did not waste words.

"All's well. The baby's face is perfectly normal now. No paralysis at all," he said. "She may not look a beauty. There's still bruising because it was an extremely difficult delivery, but I do assure you the bruises will soon fade. You'll be pleasantly surprised to see how good she'll look then."

As he left the room, Doc Campbell quietly said to Alvin, "Your wife will soon be good as new."

"I won't put you through that again," Alvin whispered to Frances when they were alone. "We are not going to have any more babies. We have our Frances Pearl and that's enough."

Whenever Alvin was asked for whom his new daughter was named, he always answered, "For my wife Frances and my youngest sister, Pearl." He never mentioned that Pearl had also been his mother's middle name.

Chapter 12

John Kerr came back to Walla Walla from his wanderings in time to attend his granddaughter's impromptu, first birthday party. Never one to hold a grudge, Ida showed up at the College Place house with her three youngest children, Herbie, Ray and Agnes, the only ones who wanted to see their father. Herbie received slight attention from his father, but John bounced Frances Pearl on his bony knees, ran his fingers through her blonde ringlets, admired her big blue eyes, ate a piece of chocolate birthday cake, and then excused himself because, he said, he had an errand to do.

"Well, what do you think of that?" Ida asked of no one in particular.

"I think I'll have another piece of cake," the intrepid Herbie offered.

The laughter he caused dispelled the tension John had brought into the house with him, and the little party took a gayer turn.

The next morning when Alvin arrived at the hospital, there was a message asking him to report to Mother Superior's office. She sat at her desk, her usual perfect posture even more rigid to Alvin's eyes. He didn't like what he saw. She looked braced for a storm.

"Your father-in-law is John Kerr, is that correct," she asked.

"Yes, Sister." *Now what's this about.*

"That man, that John Kerr, was here, here in my office, yesterday. He told me you had TB and have been a patient in the county tuberculosis sanatorium. Is that true?"

"Yes, it's true," Alvin answered. *Hell, this wasn't a storm, it was a hurricane.*

"I'm sorry to have to tell you this, but our rules state very clearly that we can not have hospital employees working in the wards if they have, or have ever had, TB."

She paused, as if waiting for him to say something, but then seemed to decide there was no way that was going to happen.

"I would make an exception in your case, if I could, Alvin, but I can not. You have been one of the very best orderlies we have ever had. You take pride in your work and it shows. I wish I had another place for you in the hospital, but there are no openings whatsoever at this time."

"Not even in the laundry?"

"Not anywhere. I checked this thoroughly before I asked to talk with you. If a position should become available in which there is no contact with patients, I will be sure to let you know."

"Thank you, Sister. It's been a pleasure working here," Al said in words that sounded scraped up from a raw tunnel.

Mother Superior sighed, shook her head from side to side, and her spine lost a little of its steel.

"I'll miss you, Alvin. I will pray for you and for your little wife and baby. Tell your mother-in-law I will continue to pray for her, too."

"That's dad, making trouble just for the sake of making trouble," said Frances when Alvin told her why he was home from work before the morning was half over.

"There's no apologizing for him. He probably thinks he saved the whole town from TB," said Frances. "Now what will we do?"

"It just means we'll have to look a little harder for work."

A month later, Alvin thought he might have found a job on a farm.

"But it's an opening for a couple; the woman would cook. Shall I go see about it," he asked Frances. Her answer was an enthusiastic yes. Frances' eldest sister, Angie, who was temporarily calling their couch her bed, agreed it would be a good opportunity.

It took Al two days to find them a ride out to the job. He had sold his car the day after he lost his job, but he hadn't really missed it until now. He might as well have saved them the trip. It took the foreman two minutes to hike his boot to the running board of the borrowed car and tell Alvin and Frances the job was filled.

When Angie didn't come back to sleep on the couch, it wasn't long before they found out she and her fiancé were the new employees.

"There's no use crying over spilled milk, but I sure do feel bad. We really needed that job," said Frances.

"I guess Angie and Roy did too," Alvin said.

"Well, that farm got itself a good cook, but we got our couch back," said Frances.

Chapter 13

By October not only were they without a car, but had moved back to Walla Walla where job hunting was easier without transportation. Frances missed her little pantry, but they had gained a larger living room. They reluctantly applied for relief, but it was a necessity without money coming in.

It was called 'relief', but being handed staples from someone else's list at the welfare office applied an uncomfortable pressure Frances had never felt when she made her own selections at Ode's Grocery on Chestnut Street or at the Red and White downtown. She learned to cook around whatever was in the box they were handed every two weeks. Sometimes they were given a sack of oranges, and once a pineapple was even handed over the counter. Frances couldn't help but remind Alvin that this pineapple had just dropped into their hands, as he had once fantasized it happening.

"All that's missing is your tropical island," she teased.

"And the sunshine," he answered.

Because his name appeared on the welfare rolls on Oct. 31, 1935, Alvin was eligible for a WPA job on the Mill Creek flood control project. According to the rules of the Works Progress Administration—another of Harry Hopkins' ideas—only those who were on relief on that specific date would be eligible for WPA jobs.

In Walla Walla jobs were available because the government was willing to invest $834,000 to curb Mill Creek, which often overflowed its banks, raising hell with the town and countryside. The people of Walla Walla had paddled canoes up their streets more than once over the years when the waters of Mill Creek and the Walla Walla River overflowed their banks. The valley town's Indian name translated to 'many waters,' and the snow-fed streams of the surrounding Blue Mountains did raise havoc.

At first the flood control project was handled by the county, but, when a majority of the voters approved formation of a flood district, the district took over the work and agreed to put in $255,000. Men were set to work building wire revetments, which they filled with rocks they dug out of the creek bed with shovels and their bare hands. They also started excavating for a settling basin and bulkhead underpinnings.

In December Alvin stored away his five pair of white pants, put on his bib overalls and joined about three hundred men who were working for forty-four dollars a month in icy water, which kept Al wet to his knees. A few of the men had rubber boots but more, like Alvin, had only leather work boots. By the end of every day he could wring water out of his socks and his feet were wrinkled and white.

Alvin read in the newspaper that four men in Seattle were employed by WPA to catch rats on the Seattle docks. The article said they had caught three hundred eighty-seven rats in two weeks. Alvin didn't know whether to envy them or feel sorry for them.

The same day the newspaper reported the rat-catching efforts, another article reported that a hundred of Walla Walla's upper crust were "tripping the light fantastic" at a Masque Ball at the Marcus Whitman Hotel, a ten-story building on the corner of Rose and Second Streets. Constructed in 1927 as an answer to the community's need for a 'first class' hotel, the Marcus Whitman lived up to the designation. It now towered over the other city buildings. Its top four stories were inset from the bottom six and were topped with a pointed cupola, built in two layers, which gave the entire building the look of an ornate, tiered wedding cake.

According to the newspaper article, on this night the ballroom was decorated with great clusters of brightly colored balloons, palms and ferns. At intermission, it was reported, a huge snowball was rolled into the ballroom where it burst open to reveal smaller snowballs which the costumed guests tossed about in restrained frenzy. It was real snow hauled in from the intake up Mill Creek where it had fallen during the night of January 2.

Al and Frances had read the article together. Her comment was, "I wonder who cleaned up that mess?" Alvin thought the snowfall, which the weatherman promised would move into town, would be an improvement over the thirty-two degree temperature and inch of rain that had fallen on the workers in the creek bed.

On January 28 WPA workers requested supplemental food orders for men who had six or more in their families. Concerned inspectors, visiting the work site, opened one man's lunch box and found only a cup of cooked prunes.

"They just aren't making it," Alvin told Frances while she toweled his feet dry and propped them to warm on the open oven door of their wood stove.

On Valentine's day Frances ladled hot stew into Alvin's thermos bottle and put it into his lunch box along with an unbuttered slice of homemade bread and two heart-shaped cookies wrapped in waxpaper. He tucked the box under his arm and tried to get out of the house before she became aware of the wracking cough, which he had been trying to hide from her, without much success, for some weeks.

His chest was burning and his feet were already cold when he climbed off the truck that brought the men to work. He made his way down into the creek's cold channel between Marcus and Palouse Streets. For an hour the crew pried rocks from the mud and dumped them into the wire revetment to form a stable wall along the creek bed. The work progressed in silence so the shout, when it came, was heard by almost all of the men.

"Why should we work?" a voice demanded.

A few heads turned to see who was yelling.

"Why should we work? We can go home and still get our pay!" the voice asserted.

Pay without work. That caused a few more heads to turn.

The speaker was standing, two cold feet on a box in mid-stream with hands stuck inside his vest to keep warm.

"Come on, fellas, let's go home," he cajoled. "It's cold and wet out here. The temperature must be zero. We can go home and still get paid."

Now that he had their attention, his voice took on a strident note.

"Haven't you heard WPA will pay us, if the weather stops us from working?"

When several men moved closer to hear what more he might have to say, the rest of the crew followed until the speaker was surrounded.

"In yesterday's *Bulletin* it was right there in black and white. It said WPA will pay us if the weather stops us, or will pay us if we're sick or if we can't get materials to work with. So, what do you say?" he shrilled.

"I say I got something to work with," called out a tall, skinny man, waving his shovel in the air.

His words brought laughter from the men gathered around, but then muttering broke out, turning to more vocal grumbling. It was cold. It was wet. The fellow had made a point.

The orator stomped his feet impatiently and yelled, "So, what do you say? Are we going home or stay here and freeze to death?"

At that, a big, broad-shouldered man pushed his way through the crowd, knocked the speaker loose from his perch and took his place.

"All right, you guys, as the foreman of this project, I'm the one who calls the shots around here. So listen up! Pay without work? That's a pipe dream! Any of you who don't want to work, can walk. Those who don't believe everything they read in the newspaper can get back to work—and I mean right now!"

The agitator pulled his vest closed around his chest, punched his fists into his pants pockets, and climbed out of the creek channel without a backward glance at the foreman who had usurped his place. He was followed by several men who kept their heads down as they scrambled over the slippery creek bottom. They were joined by others who left, in twos and threes, until the ranks were depleted by about thirty.

Alvin was among those who returned to scrabbling at the rock, which seemed even more resistant.

It was a disgruntled group that worked, silently for the most part but with an oath or two flung out in frustration. The rest of the day passed uneventfully. The next day, the foreman welcomed the thirty workers who had straggled back when they learned there would be no pay for no work.

"Shouldn't believe everything you read in the papers," he joked with them.

He received rousing whoops and hollers from all of them when he announced that everyone would receive a ten percent pay raise beginning with the first paycheck in March.

Before March arrived, Alvin was so sick he couldn't get out of bed.

Chapter 14

"I think I have the flu. I can't seem to get warm," Alvin told Frances.

He shook and shivered under the great mound of blankets and quilts she piled on him. Each day he thought he would be well enough to return to the creek. Frances became alarmed at the way his ribs showed through his skin and his eyes seemed too bright and his cheeks too red. But he said he was fine, just fine, and would be up in another day or two.

The flour, sugar, oatmeal and potato sacks began to sag, and there hadn't been fresh meat in the house for weeks. Frances took a quick inventory of a closet she had turned into a pantry, and decided to invite Alvin's sister and her husband, Elwin, to dinner because she needed to talk to someone who loved Alvin as much as she did. She decided she would make soup, again, and homemade bread.

She was sorting the dirty laundry when she found the five-dollar bill in Alvin's pocket.

"Oh, Al, look. Look what I found!" she exulted, running into the bedroom where he lay propped on the pillow. She waved the money at him and threw herself down beside him, hugging him in glee.

"Al, we can buy a chicken for supper. It's a whole five dollars!"

She was so excited that it was a few minutes before she noticed his silence. Finally she became aware of how rigidly he was holding himself.

"Why were you going through my pockets?" he asked her in a voice heavy with accusation and tight with restrained anger.

"Why, Al! It's something I do every wash day. Aren't you happy I found the money?"

"Oh, Frances. I was saving that money to buy you a pair of shoes." His voice broke as he turned his face to the wall.

She climbed onto the bed, pressed her length against his back and wrapped her arms around his waist.

"Al, sweetheart, don't be mad at me. Right now I'd rather have a nice slice of white meat more than new shoes. But you are my own true sweetheart for thinking about me. I love you dearly and for always."

They lay quietly side by side until she asked, "How do you want the chicken? Roasted or fried?"

He was still laughing when she kissed his hot lips.

They had the chicken roasted.

Alta and Frances put their heads together in the kitchen after supper, and Alta slipped into the bedroom to have a quiet talk alone with Alvin. When she came out, she pressed a cool cheek to Frances', kissed the air and said, "He definitely has a fever, but I can see you are taking good care of my brother. Don't worry. We had a good talk and it's going to be all right."

Alvin and Frances were lying in each other's arms the next morning, listening to the March wind whip around the corners of their little house when Alvin whispered to her, "I think I better go back to the hospital today."

It was March 16, 1936.

Chapter 15

Diary and Daily Reminder
Lives of great men all remind us,
We can make our lives sublime,
And, departing, leave behind us,
Footprints on the sands of time.

Footprints, that perhaps another,
Sailing o'er life's solemn main,
A forlorn and shipwrecked brother,
Seeing, shall take heart again.
—Longfellow

Alvin put his toothbrush, comb and razor into a drawer in the table beside his bed. At the back of the drawer he placed a book with a red, leather cover on which was stamped *Diary and Daily Reminder*. Its sole entry was dated February 26. It showed Al had parted with ten cents for toothpicks, thirty-four cents for soup, fourteen cents for toilet tissue, four cents for a yeast cake, thirty-two cents for eggs, sixty-nine cents for fifty pounds of potatoes, fifty-three cents for sugar, thirty-nine cents for oats, thirty-eight cents for milk and forty-seven cents for vegetables.

On the flyleaf of the little book was a quotation from Longfellow. The words *"And, departing, leave behind us, Footprints on the sands of time"* caught his eye.

Hmmm. Footprints, huh, footprints that someone might take heart from. Well, right about now I could sure use a set of footprints to put a little heart in me!

He had been hospitalized before. He knew how slowly the days crawled by. The little book might help while away the hours. It had two hundred pages waiting to be filled. Alvin would make the diary his daily responsibility.

He sank back on the bed, stretched out and closed his eyes. He was tired—all the way to his toes. Tired over the entire frame of his body.

He was tired of worrying about where the sixty-nine cents for potatoes were coming from, tired of eating potato soup for lunch and dinner, tired of watching the weight melt off his bones, tired of the hacking cough, tired of drawing each breath through a fiery furnace, tired of the pain that seemed to invade every ounce of his now one hundred nineteen pounds.

He was just plain tired, in body and soul.

Frances had stayed long enough to see that he was safely admitted and assigned this bed in Ward One, but left as soon as she saw the nurse was ready to shoo her out. Al didn't want to be alone. He wanted his wife. But, even more than wanting his wife, he wanted to sleep. Oblivion was his immediate need.

Behind closed eyelids Al reflected on the changes in his life since his stay at the county farm four years ago. First, of course, was this Blue Mountain Tuberculosis Sanatorium in which he was now bedded down. He knew this new building was a project of the Washington Emergency Relief Administration (WERA). He had watched it going up. It beat the old one all to hell. Just one wing of it was larger than the county TB san that hadn't been more than eighty-feet in length over all.

Just before Frances Pearl was born, he and Frances had sat in the car right here, alongside the Dalles-Military Road, and watched the carpenters at work. He never thought then that two years later he would be living in it. But here he was.

This new sanatorium had two one-story wings flaring out from a two-story hub that held administration offices on the first floor and staff living quarters on the second. The admitting nurse explained that the left wing was for female patients and the right for the men. She did not have to say '*and never the twain shall meet*'. Just the tone of her voice made that obvious. Al had seen a community recreation room between the men's wing and the offices. *A big layout, all right. And only opened a year ago.*

The building was called the Walla Walla Tuberculosis Sanatorium while it was under construction, but, upon completion in 1935, it underwent a name change. WERA turned the building over to the county, and it took on the name of the mountains that could be seen from its windows.

When Frances had driven up to the Blue Mountain Sanatorium, its white exterior and rows of windows, one or more to every room, gleamed in the sunshine. And the mountains were there, like a backdrop. Alvin had what he considered, from the quick glance he had taken before lying down, one of the choice rooms. It was the room nearest to the recreation room where the telephone was. 'I'd have to be pretty damn sick before I couldn't make it that short distance to call my girl,' he thought.

The room had other compensations. His bed was next to a window from which he could look out onto the circular drive and the road. He had stood there and waved goodbye to Frances a few minutes ago. He watched until Ida's car was out of sight. *It was decent of Ida to loan Frances the car to bring me out.*

Two tall shrubs framed the window, and, if he opened his eyes, he could see a maple tree from his bed. It was a small maple, being just two years old, but it was the fullest of the seven that landscaped the front grounds.

Love that tree. Loved trees ever since the days in Daisy when me and Alta would run wild through them with that neighbor boy...what was his name...Pete, no, that's not right...Pete, P-something, Perry. Yeah, that's it. Perry. Run through those woods like wild Indians. Surely do love trees. The rustle they make in the wind. Peaceful those trees.

It was the last thought he had before he fell asleep.

Chapter 16

Alvin's first waking thought several hours later was of trees. He lay with eyes closed, almost hearing the swish of wind through them. This was a comforting daydream to wake to. He let the carefree days of childhood play behind his closed lids.

As if it were yesterday, he saw Perry, Alta and himself playing gypsies in the woods, building little fires over which they propped water-filled tomato cans to boil the little birds they caught.

A grin crinkled Al's lips as he remembered how he and Alta would sneak a live coal out of the kitchen stove and blow it into a blaze for these clandestine outdoor fires. The firebugs always had an eye out for a way to steal a light.

The time Emerson, Alvin's dad, had stopped at a tree stump to strike a match to light a roll-your-own cigarette was an opportunity they didn't miss. Emerson thought he had doused the match by sticking it in a wormhole in the stump. Three pairs of eyes saw otherwise, and Perry, Al and Alta jumped on the hot-headed match and pampered it into a satisfactory blaze. When Emerson returned from the barn with a foaming pail of milk, the stump was on fire.

It wasn't the only time the trio ran afoul of fire. Boiled frog legs led to sparks flying out of the circle of rocks they'd laid around the usual tomato can. They watched wide-eyed as fire crept over the dry meadow grass. Finally spurred to action, they stomped, until the flames were taller than themselves and then they ran. They stood at the edge of the trees and watched as the fire consumed the hillside. It was extinguished when distant neighbors saw the smoke and flames, and rushed to beat it out.

Emerson confronted the trio with the blackened tomato can and demanded an answer to who was responsible.

"Perry did it and we tried awfully hard to put it out," Alta claimed.

Their plea of innocence did not deter a harsh sentence. The 'gypsies' were told in no uncertain terms not to play with matches or fire ever again. But, Emerson didn't tell them to stay in their own backyard because they didn't have one. They had the whole forest, and they continued to play in it and with the things they found in it.

Once, great spools of wire were the day's treasure. It took them awhile to roll all of them down the hill…but not as long as it took to roll the sixty-pound spools back up the hill when Emerson discovered their game.

"I couldn't do that today," Alvin murmured aloud.

"What's that?" asked a voice.

Alvin, jerked abruptly out of daydream, opened his eyes, and saw he was being addressed by a man he assumed was his roommate since he was occupying the next bed.

"Sorry. I was just talking to myself," Al said.

"You don't want to be doin' that too much, young fella, or…" He paused. "…Or you'll be just like the rest of us around here!" he added with a guffaw that rocked the bed.

The man swung his legs over the edge of the bed, sat up and offered his hand to Alvin.

"Call me Leo," he said. "Because that's my name," he added with another laugh.

"Al Potts here. Pleased to make your acquaintance, Leo."

"Likewise, but it'd please me more if we were meetin' somewhere else. Is this your first time out here?"

"In the new building, yes it is," answered Al, "but I was at the TB san over at the county farm in 1932."

"Then you know the routine. Breakfast at seven-thirty, lunch at noon, supper when it gets here, and bedtime at nine. Wednesdays and Sundays are visiting days, two-thirty and seven-thirty. Friday's fish day, which is OK if you're a cat-licker, but hard on those of us who aren't because it's usually stale salmon and we can't even offer it up as a penance. And saltpetre doesn't make it taste any better. Tuesdays and Fridays are bath days, and you better get there early if you want hot water. Weigh day's Saturday. Doc comes through once a month and says 'ummm'.

"Sound as if anything's changed?" Leo grinned.

"Maybe. I think doc used to say 'hmmm'," Al said.

Leo laughed and fell back onto his pillow. "It's gonna be OK, Al. We're gonna get along just fine."

When Leo's chuckles faded away, Alvin said, "And I am a Catholic."

"Oh damnation, 'scuse me and my big mouth. But, Al, the salmon really is pretty damn bad," said Leo.

"What did you mean by saltpetre not making it taste better?

"That's a new one on me," Al added.

"You know what saltpetre is, don't you?" asked Leo, casting a quick look at him.

"It's used to make gunpowder and even cure meat, isn't it?" Alvin said hesitantly.

"Yeah, that too, I guess. But around here it's slipped into the food to take the zip out of our zippers, if you know what I mean," said Leo.

Since Alvin still looked perplexed, Leo added with a grin, "Things may get difficult around here, kid, but they'll never get hard, not if you eat your saltpetre like a good little boy."

Alvin's face registered both understanding and embarrassment. A side effect of tuberculosis was an almost constant sexual desire, an annoying and frustrating physical reaction to the disease.

"OK, OK. I just never heard of that before," he said.

"And I'll bet a good lookin' young man like you is sorry you heard about it now. They usually don't even ask if you do or if you don't want it. But if you raise a stink about it, they won't salt your food with anything but salt. For an old fella of forty, like me, who isn't goin' anywhere anyway, it don't matter too much but you might have other ideas."

"The only idea I have right now seems to be more sleep," said Alvin.

"How 'bout I pull the curtain closed between us so's I don't bother you," Leo asked.

"Thanks, Leo, that'd be fine," said Al.

The afternoon light filtered over the bedspread and sent dust motes dancing in the air.

But sleep wouldn't come.

I wish I could dance free like that. Just drifting through the air like a sailboat on water. But if I were a sailboat, I wouldn't be in the air.

He wondered if he was delirious. He felt a little dizzy, even lying flat on his back, and his stomach was queasy. He decided if he could wonder about delirium he probably wasn't experiencing it. The thoughts that danced in and out of his mind were crystal clear, not hazy like the stuff of which hallucinations are made, he concluded. But he wished he could push a button and turn them off.

To the nurse who peeked around the curtain to check on her newest patient, Alvin appeared to be relaxed and resting, but, if she could have looked within, she would have seen a seething caldron.

The pounding of his heart was loud in his ears and heavy in his chest. It fluttered against his ribs like a bird beating against the bars of a cage. He folded his arms above his heart and pressed gently down in an unconscious attempt to hold it in.

Could this frantic racing be what the Jews in Germany felt when that edict came out several months ago? Hell, it took away their government jobs, and turned them out of their offices overnight.

The correlation between his predicament and theirs was not lost on him. Forced out of jobs—check! Outcasts, him by disease, them as if they were diseased—check! The warnings were there for the Jews, if they had heeded them. Especially last year when they were stripped of their German citizenship. Al got his warning in '32 when he was first told he had tuberculosis. *Wonder if they expected it to come to this, or if they are as surprised to find themselves untouchables as I am to be one.*

While he lay with closed eyes, Al's thoughts continued to gnaw away at the German puzzle, which he was aware of only from the bits and pieces that came to him through the pages of the *Walla Walla Bulletin.*

The idea of an entire nation condoning the anti-Semitic measures he read about appalled, yet fascinated, him. He would like to be able to crawl inside one of those nationalistic Germans and wear that mentality as he did his skin in order to experience for himself what must be a tremendous driving force. *But only if I could crawl out as soon as I wanted.*

He wondered if the little, white-haired, German grandmothers were content to sit in their German living rooms, rocking and darning grandchildren's stockings just like Frances' German-born Grandma Hempe did in Ida's living room. He wondered if those little old ladies ever thought about what was happening to the Jews outside their doors.

Somehow Al could not imagine Grandma Hempe anchoring her bun with her ivory hair pins and pulling her good black cloth coat on over her dumpling shape to go out and do verbal battle with an Adolph Hitler.

But he bet, if little old ladies like her did unite the world over, they would be a stronger force than even Hitler. German mothers and grandmothers just might be the height of passive resistance if organized, he thought.

But maybe all the little old grandmothers in Germany were of one mind...and that brought his thoughts full circle on that subject.

He tried deep breathing to slow his heart beats and clear his mind so the oblivion he craved could creep in. He knew from experience the effort would probably be futile and bring only sharper pains.

When the pain got this bad his mind usually ranged over a wide variety of topics and worries before sleep released him. It could be the price of potatoes plaguing him in these hours, or the threat of a city-wide epidemic when it was reported that a Whitman College girl broke out in smallpox after the Christmas holiday. Nothing was too small or too large for Al to ponder or worry about when sleep was illusive.

In the wee hours during these past months he had tried to figure out how the Corning Glass Works made its new glass frying pans and why his hair curled up into tight little balls when it got rained on while his sister's equally curly hair only waved. He had imagined himself at the Winter Olympics in Garmisch-Parten-kirchen, and, in his mind's eye, he had seen the cocky, little fuehrer as he declared the games open in the village nestled below the Alps.

He remembered that the Olympic games in February had even carried over into his dreams where he felt himself struggling in knee-deep snow up a steep slope with skis on his shoulders. There had been a downhill run in which he had careened madly around curves only to be confronted abruptly by a lake from which there was no escape.

Now that he was back at the san, he figured the dream had been an unconscious warning to let him know he was in an uphill physical battle, out of control and rushing toward the inevitable. *Whether I wanted to admit it or not.*

He reached over, pulled open the drawer in the bedside table and removed his little red book and a pencil. He turned the pages to March 16 and read the daily reminder inscribed on that page: *"Search thine own heart. What paineth thee in others, in thyself may be."—Whittier.*

"Words to live by," Al whispered. Then he made the first entry in his diary.

> *Monday, March 16th, 1936. Entered*
> *Blue Mountain Sanatorium.*
> *Weight 119 feeling like hell.*
> *Just able to get around.*

Chapter 17

*Tuesday, March 17. Spent a long
night awake. Too tired to sleep.
Sure hope wife and baby spent
a better night.*

The diary was the first thing Al reached for when the gray light of dawn finally announced daybreak. It had been a long, sleepless night. He was glad it was over.

As he wrote the entry for his second day in confinement, he took note that there were 18 lines on each page, with each page dedicated to two days. *Nine lines to squeeze my day into. Not to worry. Used up only four today.*

Al watched the sunrise spread across the patch of sky framed in his window. The rattle of basins finally broke the hospital quiet. He recognized the activity as ward clerks carrying wash water to the patients not allowed out of bed. It was the official signal that morning had arrived at the san.

Alvin didn't wait to find out if he was on the list of bedridden. He climbed out of bed, knotted the cord of his hospital robe around his waist, gathered up his toilet articles and went in search of the shower rooms. Since it was Tuesday, a legitimate bath day, according to Leo, Al was determined to have an all-over wash.

Someone was splashing in one of the stalls when he went in, and Al was glad to see steam drifting over the partition. He laid his razor and shaving soap out, worked up a lather and scraped away light stubble. He was one of the lucky ones. He didn't have a heavy beard, but, to save Frances whisker burns, he had gotten into the habit of shaving every day.

"I could save myself the trouble now," Al grumbled.

"Don't tell me. Let me guess," Leo called out. "It's that new fellow who talks to himself! Right?"

Al laughed. "Good morning, Leo," he said, throwing his robe on a bench.

"I see you took my advice and got here before the icicles formed. You feelin' better this morning?" Leo asked.

"I think so."

Al reached in, turned the tap and tested the water before he unbuttoned his pajama jacket and removed it and the bottoms. He gave them a quick fold, tucked them under his robe and stepped into the shower. Backing into the spray, he stood with head bent, arms dangling at his sides and let the needles of hot water massage his neck and shoulders.

The water coursed freely over a frame that could only be called skin and bones. Shoulder blades poked out like wings and ribs, collar bones and vertebrae stood out like knobs on a cabinet. Beads of water glistened on his brown curls which spray and steam were already turning kinky. His chest was broad and covered lightly with hair the same color but not as curly. A silky thin arrow of it extended downward over his concave stomach, as if pointing to his masculinity which hung uncircumcised between his legs. His buttocks, though mere suggestions of the pads which had rounded out his white linen pants last summer, were still firm. It wouldn't be true to say that most of his height was in his legs, because he was well proportioned, but today their thinness emphasized their length. His feet were long and almost delicately slender with the second toes on each foot longer than his big toes. He had called it "a Potts tradition" when he took his newborn baby's small foot in the palm of his hand and gently uncurled the pink toes to show Frances the infant's inheritance.

He turned to let the water pour over his face and into his upturned mouth. He ran a bar of soap over his chest and armpits, down his sides, across his abdomen and then under the scrotum he lifted gently but indifferently. Pushing the foreskin back from his penis to cleanse around it, he felt it stir reflexively. *I'll have to talk to someone today about that saltpetre.*

When he heard Leo leave the room, he turned off the water and stepped out. He toweled quickly before another patient entered and caught him nude. He was a modest man and preferred privacy, but didn't expect to get a great deal of it here.

Dressed, he turned his attention to his hair. The crinkly waves weren't helped by a cowlick which refused to lie down. He was not a vain man, but his comb was often in his hand trying to tame the head of hair the creator had seen fit to give him. His brother, Murray, had a cap of tight curls which held their place and were much admired by the girls. Alvin felt that his waves were not that much of an asset, although Frances did love to thread her fingers through them.

Alvin walked toward his room. He tried not to look into the rooms on the way, but couldn't avoid eye contact with some patients propped high on their pillows waiting for breakfast. When one would smile or nod, Al returned the greeting self-consciously.

The small burst of energy which had carried him through his shower evaporated suddenly. His legs and arms became lead weights. Sweat sprung from his armpits and slid down his sides. There was a roaring in his ears and the wide hall became a narrow tunnel extending forever. The antiseptically smooth white walls offered no support.

I wonder what they'd think if I just slumped down on the floor and waited for someone to come drag me away.

His stomach turned over at the odors rising from the covered dishes on the food wagons as he passed outside the rooms. He held his breath against their onslaught and concentrated on putting one foot in front of another.

"It'll be over soon," he whispered, urging himself on.

He almost walked past the door of his room, but, when he recognized it through the mist before his eyes, he entered with relief. He clutched at chair backs and bed frames until he was back in his own bed. He fell onto it and began to shake with the exertion. He wanted nothing so much as a pair of giant hands which would lift him up, wrap him in a warm quilt and hold him close.

Instead he shivered on the cold counterpane as his body flushed first hot and then cold.

"Are you all right," Leo asked anxiously.

His words were only echoes in a tunnel to Alvin, who couldn't answer.

"Still a little weak, huh?" Leo asked. He came to stand by Alvin's bed.

"Here, you just slip under the covers and warm up a bit and rest. Breakfast will be along soon and that'll put some strength into you."

Al grimaced.

"Oh, I know food doesn't sound so good to you right now," Leo said, seeing the look of disgust. "But it'll do you a lot of good, you'll see."

Leo pulled the spread from under Alvin and drew it up over him. He tucked it in awkwardly around his shoulders. "Just close your eyes and rest until it gets here," he advised.

After a few minutes, the world stopped spinning and Alvin began to feel drowsy. He was half asleep when a cheerful voice told him to sit up. A ward clerk slid a tray onto the bedside table.

"Mr. Potts, here's your breakfast," said the cheery voice.

"I think I'd rather just sleep," he said.

"Oh, no, Mr. Potts. The nurse said you didn't eat your supper last night so I was to make sure you had a nice breakfast. Just sit up here and swing your legs over the side of the bed. There's some real good oatmeal here and we've got brown sugar for on it."

Alvin looked at the smiling, round face of a plump little woman who was trying to entice him and decided he couldn't say no to her.

"Thanks. Brown sugar sounds fine," he said.

The oatmeal was rather gluey, but Alvin finished it, plus a slice of toast, a cup of coffee and a glass of prune juice, which was served for a specific reason he was pretty sure. He put the cover back over two greasy looking fried eggs.

Leo and Al both had coffee refills when the ward clerk returned and offered it to them.

"Feeling better now?" asked Leo.

"Some. I guess I just got a little too ambitious," said Al.

He took a sip of coffee. "Say, what's her name? The woman who brought us breakfast."

"That's Flora. She's a pretty good Joe."

"She seems real friendly."

They drank together silently, Leo sitting on the edge of his bed and Alvin stretched out on his.

"Is Miss Sanders still here?" Alvin asked.

"She's the lab technician, but does just about everything else.

Was she here when you were here before?"

"Yes, and she was always real good to me. But she just worked on the wards then. Does she still take time to come around and visit?" asked Al. He remembered that Miss Sanders had often been among those who gathered on the hospital porch when he was was trying to get up his nerve to court Frances.

"Sure, sometimes she visits and even brings us things once in awhile. See that plant? She brought it in," said Leo. "Was Miss Gillis the supervisor in—what year was it you were out here?"

"It was 1932 and Miss Gillis was the supervisor then too. She kept things running smooth. I bet she likes supervising in a brand new hospital," said Alvin. "Did you ever see the old county hospital?"

"I believe I missed that pleasure," said Leo.

"It had rooms like dormitories. Nothing at all like this one with only us two in a room. The rooms were all crowded. You could reach out and touch each other practically. This is a real improvement."

"Yeah, I guess if a guy has to be in a place like this, it's good to be in one that has some benefits. But don't get too used to all this luxury," Leo said, laughing, "because sometimes we have three patients in here, not just two."

Flora came back with a copy of the morning *Union*, which she gave to Leo. "Here's some reading material for you two. You can catch up on the news," she said. She took their dishes with her, leaving them to share the paper. Leo kept the front pages and handed Alvin the sports page.

The newspaper soon dropped from Al's hands as he fell into the sleep he had been waiting for since yesterday.

Chapter 18

"I'm hungry as a bear!" Al roared when he opened his eyes.

"Hey, you're awake, finally! Do you realize you slept the clock around? You missed yesterday's lunch and dinner. No wonder you're ready to eat," said Leo.

"Best sleep I've ever had. Surprised that Flora wasn't shaking me awake for meals yesterday."

"You can thank your old friend Gillis. It was her who told the ward clerks not to disturb you. Said you needed rest more than food. From the looks of you this morning, I'd say she was right about that. You're looking right dapper compared to yesterday."

Alvin gave Leo a faint grin.

Flora did not have to coax Alvin to tackle the breakfast tray she delivered. Even the questionable fried eggs disappeared this morning. By noon Alvin was ready for the meat sandwiches Flora brought around, and he had no trouble doing justice to the rest period that followed. But at quarter past two, he was sitting up, watching out the window for the first visit from his wife.

He picked up his red book, and puzzled over the daily reminder for this day.

"I have always said and felt that true enjoyment cannot be described."—Rousseau

Al wasn't sure just who Rousseau was, but thought he had it dead on. It would be difficult to put a name to the fuzzy, warm feeling that came over him when he wrapped Frances up in his arms or that almost fierce protectiveness he felt when he walked the floor with his crying baby.

He picked up his pencil, tested the lead. Sharp enough.

Wednesday, March 18. Slept very well and feel rested today. Appetite very

good. Took a second helping.

With one eye on the road, Al sneaked a peek at the pocket watch he held in his hand. Frances was due in fifteen minutes.

Unconsciously, as he waited, he rubbed his thumb over the smooth back of the Surety timepiece in much the same way an ancient Chinese gentleman might have stroked a worry stone to ease his tensions.

The watch, a legacy from Emerson, was worn through its silver nickel finish down to its base metal which deceptively glowed gold. A rim of the nickel metal still framed the face on which silver numerals stood out on a black circle. Through habit Alvin avoided disturbing its face from which the crystal was missing. It had broken one day when he fell on a slippery rock in the creek bed. He had never wanted to spend the money to have it repaired. Usually it was tucked away into his overall pocket, anchored securely to the pocket's loop by a thin leather cord.

Here the watch had a new home. Alvin kept it within reach on the bedside table. It bore the marks of the days when his father had carried it as he cleared debris from irrigation ditches to let the water flow free to the fields. Maybe because of that, or because it was one of only two things his father had left him, Al cherished it. The other item of his inheritance was the ivory ring he had given Frances in lieu of an engagement ring. It was carved in the shape of a seal. Emerson had brought it from Alaska after delivering a load of cattle there by sea long before Alvin was born.

Al was lifting the watch to check the time again when a Model A came into sight. Ida was at the wheel and Al could see Frances leaning forward eagerly to catch a glimpse of him through the windshield. He got out of bed, leaned on the window frame and waved at her. She saw him and waved back. Ida wheeled into the drive and pulled to a stop directly in front of Alvin's window.

"You're early. I hope they'll let you come in. I've missed you," Alvin called.

"I missed you too. How are you feeling?" Frances asked.

"Top rate, now that you're here!"

"Come on, you love birds, let's get this show on the road," said Ida, herding Frances off toward the entrance.

Alvin smiled at his mother-in-law's gruffness. Since marrying

Frances, he had learned that his mother-in-law took refuge in harsh words as cover for sentimental emotions. He chalked it up to her German background, which, he'd observed, lent itself more to pragmatism than tenderness. He had found that Ida had far less difficulty in giving the sharp edge of her tongue to anyone when she thought they needed it.

When Frances entered the room, Alvin was reminded of the first day they met. Her shyness was as obvious now as it had been then. He stepped forward to ease her past the pajama-clad Leo whose interest in Alvin's company was equally as obvious.

If Leo's eyes had been a Brownie camera, the first picture from it would have shown downcast eyes, a perky size thirty-four bust neatly and modestly encased in a crisp cotton print housedress, and a trim waist circled with a white belt. The second would have moved on to a pair of shapely calves and ankles, which were the only part of Frances' legs that showed beneath her hemline. A third shot from that Brownie would have revealed that Leo hadn't missed even the wedgies from which toes peeked.

The picture might also have shown, slightly out of focus, a figure in the background whose demeanor was that of a mother hen who has its feathers ruffled.

"When you get your eyes full, fill your pitcher," Ida snapped as she brushed past Leo's bed.

Al saw that his roommate had not gotten off to a good start with Ida. As for himself, he was willing to give Leo the benefit of the doubt, and attribute his blatant interest to curiosity rather than to lust.

'Every man deserves one chance...but only one when it involves my wife,' Al thought, as he made the introductions, which Frances acknowledged graciously and Ida almost totally ignored. Leo seemed to recognize that Ida was a woman one would do better to deal with carefully. He turned his back on the little group.

At Frances' urging, Alvin laid down. She fluffed the pillows under his head and then perched beside him on the bed's edge. Ida pulled up a wicker chair, ostentatiously closing their circle, a gesture that was wasted on Leo's back.

Husband and wife held hands and exchanged looks while Ida set about to pry from Alvin every last detail of all that had transpired since he checked in.

"Are they feeding you good? Are you getting enough sleep?" she quizzed.

"Has the doctor been in to see you? Have you still got a fever? What are they doing that's going to help you get out of this place?" Ida demanded.

Her rapid fire questions caused Leo to ask Alvin: "How long have you had that machine gun in your family?" But he asked only after Ida left.

Chapter 19

Frances had scrubbed the kitchen floor so many times since Alvin entered the hospital, she'd be afraid the pattern was going to come off if she didn't know it was inlaid linoleum and bound to last forever. 'But,' she thought as she set soapy rag to scrubbing, 'that red squiggly does look a little more faded than yesterday.'

She dug at it with a vengeance. She had never particularly cared for red as a color anyway. Blue was so much more restful, or a brilliant sunny yellow to pick up your spirits. She hadn't noticed the linoleum pattern much when Alvin was home, but now this black and red on cream was about to get to her.

At least something was.

She told herself the floor needed mopped every day because the baby played on it, but in her heart she knew it was busy work. And she needed to keep busy. She hadn't grown accustomed to all that cool, empty space in her bed and she didn't think she ever would. She missed Alvin's shoulder under her head and the soft tunes he whistled for her before they fell asleep.

He had been a whistler since he was a little kid, he told her.

In fact, the first thing an uncle of his had said when he heard about the cow splitting Alvin's lip was: "That's a real shame because he could whistle so good." But when the stitches were removed and Al puckered up, the notes he whistled were still clear as a bell. His mother had smiled her pleasure and, when that song was finished, she had leaned forward to trace the angry welt with her forefinger.

Sometimes in the night, just before sleep overtook them, Frances would trace that same feathery soft, almost ticklish, trail across his lips. She would end by plugging his puckered whistle with a fingertip, and he would kiss the tip and draw it into his mouth until he could wrap his warm tongue around it.

It was that closeness and the feel of his soft waves under her fingers when she reached out in the middle of the night that she missed now.

The first two days Al was in the sanatorium, Frances kept busy adjusting to the change. There was the special trip to the store to buy the Camay soap he preferred because other soaps irritated his skin. She picked fourteen cents out of his flat, worn, brown billfold and splurged on three cakes of Camay. One she set out to carry to him on the first visiting day. The others she put aside as special surprises for later. Then there was the walk into town to the welfare department. Ida told her she had to swallow her pride and ask for more help.

"Temporary help for sure, but help for you and baby until you can get back on your feet," Ida insisted.

Frances learned that, in addition to the staples they had received several times after Alvin could no longer work on the Mill Creek project, she would now be eligible for a rent payment and clothing as it was needed. She was glad there was no immediate need for clothes for herself and Frances Pearl. She was not looking forward to standing in lines, as she had seen others do, waiting for a dress or pair of shoes to be handed over the counter in what was clearly charity no matter what name it was called by. She would do it. No doubt of that. The day would come when she would take her place in line and accept what was given to her, just as she had taken the flour and oats and oranges and, yes, even the pineapple.

"But I will not stand in line dirty with stringy hair and shoes untied. Some of them just seem to want to look poorer than they are," she told Ida.

She wished Alvin could be there beside her when she did go in for help, beside her to find something to laugh about as they had laughed and teased when the pineapple had been handed to them. She had a feeling that standing in line was going to be just one of the things she would be doing alone for awhile.

But arranging these things had kept her occupied. That and floor scrubbing helped the first two days pass quickly. It wasn't until her first visit to the san at night that Frances became aware of what the separation really meant.

Ida didn't accompany her on the evening visit.

"Take the car and I'll watch Frances Pearl. If that weasel in the next bed minds his own business, you might get a chance for a word or two alone with Alvin," Ida said, handing the car keys to Frances.

Most of their visit was spent in silent hand-holding and the exchange of long looks, all of which the "weasel" studiously ignored.

When the nurse came around and announced the end of visiting hours, Frances wanted to cry out 'So soon?', but she put on her brightest smile.

They did not kiss goodbye. What they had done so fervently just three days before was not allowed now. She squeezed his hand instead, and got a squeeze in return. She took the bar of Camay from her purse and slipped it into his table drawer.

She didn't look back when she walked away. She was scarcely aware of the drive home. And she watched with dry eyes when Ida pulled out of the driveway. It was then, as she stood with forehead resting against the frosty windowpane watching the taillights fade away, that the cold grip of loneliness became a reality.

Back at the san, Al fought loneliness in his own way. He pulled his little red book out to finish his diary entry for Wednesday, March 18:

> *Frances and her mother*
> *were out to see me. Frances*
> *came again in the evening.*
> *God how I love my wife*
> *and baby.*

Chapter 20

Frances let the loneliness drain the marrow from her bones and fill them with an icy flow of despair. She wanted to raise her head to the moon and howl like a coyote, throw herself on the floor and kick her heels like a baby. Tear her hair and shred her garments like the tragic biblical characters of old.

Instead she stuck out her tongue and put its tip against the icy pane which held it fast.

She stood there, silent, welded by that tiny link. She could feel the strong attachment, painful in its coldness. Carefully—very carefully—she breathed a small circle of warm air around her tongue to release it. Then she went into the bedroom to peer into the crib to check on baby Frances.

The room was dark, the only light a thin stream from the overhead bulb in the kitchen. The baby lay on its stomach, a spit bubble on her pursed lips. Sweat-dampened curls had turned to ringlets around her ears. Frances pushed them back and lifted her baby's head to let the air dry them. She pulled the pink and blue cover Ida had quilted over the baby shoulders and tucked in the edges to ward off the air, which would grow colder once the fire was banked in the kitchen stove. That done, she returned to the kitchen where she took pencil and tablet from a drawer and seated herself at the table.

She put the pencil's sharp tip between her pursed lips, frowned and then bent over what would be her first letter to Alvin. She filled two lined pages with words of hope, love and encouragement. At least she hoped they were. She conjured them up to hide emotions too strong to name. Finished, she folded the pages, creased them with a brisk stroke of her thumbnail and slipped them into an envelope she addressed with Alvin's new address. She licked the three-cent, purple stamp, laid it precisely in

place and gently, but firmly, pressed her palm over George
Washington's image.

Rising briskly, she shook the clinkers out of the stove, put in
two fresh pieces of coal and adjusted the damper.

Frances was in bed, lying on her back, when the tears finally
fell. They slipped down her cheeks and puddled in her ears.

The next morning, before the baby awoke, Frances was on her
hands and knees vigorously scrubbing the kitchen floor. By the
time the child called out from her crib, the floor had dried and the
stirred-up fire in the stove had raised the temperature in the house
to a comfortable level. She pushed a pot of oatmeal to the back of
the Monarch range to keep warm, and went to lift Frances Pearl
from her crib. She pulled down the baby's sleepers and deposited
her on a potty chair.

Frances Pearl wasn't yet two years old, but was well on the
way to being toilet trained. It was a promise Frances had made to
herself, and kept. While the child sat, slumped sleepily but
uncomplaining, Frances poured boiling water from the tea kettle
into a galvanized tub on the counter. She added enough cold water
to make it pleasantly warm when she dipped her elbow into it.
When Frances Pearl staggered up from the potty, Frances swiped
the dampness from her bottom with a bit of tissue and popped her
into the bath water. The sudsing began to rouse the child from her
sleepy state.

"Daddy," she asked, looking from under her mother's arm in
an effort to see if he was there.

"Daddy's in the hospital."

"Daddy?"

"Daddy isn't home, but he will come home."

"Da..."

"Daddy's not here!" Frustration tinged her words.

"Daddy." The baby's voice was insistent now.

"He *will* come home, probably soon."

Before Frances Pearl could repeat her demand, Frances said in
a soothing tone, "Soon is not today and not tomorrow, baby. Soon
is sooner or later. Usually later than we want and not soon enough
for me!"

That was too much for baby. Her growling stomach now had

her attention.

"Eat?"

"You betcha. That's something I can give you right now, but wouldn't you like to get some curls first?"

Frances didn't wait for an answer from baby's limited vocabulary. She toweled her off, sprinkled her with Johnson's baby powder, gave it a rub in, and pulled an undershirt and shirt over her head.

A pair of striped, bib overalls and high topped shoes freshly polished white to cover yesterday's scuff marks finished the morning's toilette. Frances ran a comb through the baby's silky strands, wrapped a whisp of the blonde hair vertically around her finger, anchored the curl with a bobbypin and then slipped her finger out of the corkscrew she had formed. Frances proceeded with dexterity to make sausage curls in Shirley Temple style around the child's head, anchoring each curl to its neighbor. When they dried, she would remove the pins, and the curls would hold their shape to bob up and down like steel springs with the child's every movement.

It was a morning ritual. Sometimes, on special occasions, a candy striped, grosgrain hair ribbon was knotted into a crisp bow, given a bobbypin backing and planted firmly and perkily over Frances Pearl's right ear. This morning, Frances skipped the ribbon.

"Now for some oatmeal with brown sugar. How does that sound?"

"Eat."

"Oatmeal with brown *sugar*. Frances Pearl will have oatmeal with brown *sugar* for breakfast. Can you say *sugar*?"

"Shh…"

"That's right. *Sugar*. And you will have it right now. No waiting. Not soon, but right now! And Grandma left us some cream last night, so we'll have cream on our oatmeal, too. Aren't we two lucky girls?

"You bet we are," Frances answered herself. "We are two lucky girls. Just like the little girl in your nursery rhyme book. *She will sit on a cushion and sew a fine seam and dine upon nothing but strawberries and cream.*

"Well, no berries today, but lots of cream, little girl. And, when we are finished with breakfast, we are going out to mail a letter to Daddy so he knows we love him."

> *Thursday, March 19. Spent another wakeful nite. Can't seem to sleep at all at nite. Sleep very good during day.*

Chapter 21

Friday, March 20. Another sleepless
nite to my credit. I wish to god I
could sleep. Feel pretty good.
Had a letter from Frances
and Murray. Sure looking forward
to seeing Frances and baby Sunday.

"You philosophers are sages in your maxims and fools in your conduct."

—Benjamin Franklin

When Flora handed George Washington and his twin to Alvin during the morning mail call, Al added 'ten o'clock mail' to his mental schedule of routine activities.

He felt a foolish grin beginning to curl his lip and was amazed that Frances' penciled name on an envelope could cause the tremendous surge of happiness and excitement that was filling his chest. He slit open the letter from his brother, Murray, first. *Save the best to last.* He read the few lines Murray had scratched.

"Dear Al. Tough luck. Sure can't be for too long. Will get out to see you as soon as I can. Hope your stint is short. What does the doc say? I'll keep an eye out for Frances and the kid. Is there anything you need? Love, Your brother Murray"

Alvin smiled at the thought of his nineteen-year-old brother taking care of his serious little Frances. Carousing and hell-raising were more his style. What Murray couldn't think of to do, Frances' brother, Will, could. They were the same age and great chums. Murray slept as many nights at Ida's house as he did in his own bed at Alta's, he and Will tiptoeing in long after Ida's imposed, but often ignored, curfew.

Al turned his attention to the thick envelope from Frances. Just feeling its bulk beneath his fingers filled him with warmth. He bounced it on his hand, weighing it with anticipation.

He read and re-read the letter from Frances throughout the day. That night as he tossed and turned in sleeplessness, the letter crackled under his pillow where he had put it for company. Though it was narrower, he found his hospital bed as empty as Frances was finding their bed at home.

"I caught a little cold last night," he told Leo the next morning.

His head ached. A cap of congestion was drawing its band tight around his forehead when Flora brought their breakfast trays. As Al lifted the dome from his tray, blood gushed from his nose and splashed over the staring yellow eyes of two sunny-side-up eggs before he could divert it.

He spent the next few hours with a wad of cotton under his upper lip and a pack of ice tucked behind his neck.

The flow was staunched by the time Flora distributed Saturday's mail. He received the same thing he had for breakfast—nothing.

Saturday, March 21.
Slept a little better last
night but caught a little
cold. Had a nose bleed this
morning at breakfast time.
Lost out on breakfast, so look
forward to lunch. Tomorrow is
visiting day. Hurrah. Something
else to look forward to.

What visiting day had in store was more than he could imagine.

Chapter 22

The time by Alvin's watch was ten minutes before the visiting hour when a vision flounced into the room.

"Ta dum!" She signaled her entrance.

Hands on hips and elbows thrust forward, the visitor stretched a long, left leg out to her side and struck an exaggerated model's pose. Her stance threw into bold view glossy red lips, pointy breasts and jutting hip bones that framed a pelvis shouting challenge. She spun on one foot in a dizzy circle which sent her shoulder-length red hair swirling in a pink cloud and revealed flashes of bare skin and frothy lace. She came to a dramatic stop at the foot of Leo's bed, flinging her arms wide, palms turned outward.

"Well, what do you think?" she asked.

"That's Ruby," said Leo, turning to Alvin and grinning at the incredulous expression he surprised on his face.

"Damn right, that's Ruby! And I'm asking you what you think of my straight-from-New York, brand new, tropical garden print as shown at A.M. Jensen Company's style show yesterday."

She smoothed the green and coral pattern over her hips and down her thighs.

"Well?"

"Great. You look just great, honey," Leo told her.

"Well, you ain't seen nothing yet," she said, tossing her head.

She slowly stripped off a jacket of the same print material and turned around to reveal a broad expanse of bare back.

She gave them only a quick look at the creamy white skin, with which only lucky redheads are gifted, before she whirled to face them and hiked her calf-length skirt high over her knees.

"And take a gander at these. Chiffon!" she said, running red enameled fingernails down a very long leg.

"Clear, ringless chiffon hose, they call them. Classy, huh? And with reinforced toes and heels."

She slipped off one spiky, sling back, white shoe and wiggled her toes enthusiastically.

"No toenail is gonna pop through there, daddy. What do you think? Is this outfit class or is it class?"

"You look really great, Ruby. That green and pink is your colors. Looks really fine," Leo praised.

"Pink? That's coral, you dumb bunny," Ruby said, slapping at Leo.

"Well, it looks pink to me," said Leo, catching her hand and drawing her closer so he could slip an arm around her waist.

"Don't it look pink to you, Al?" Leo asked without even glancing at Alvin.

He slipped a finger inside the collar of Ruby's jacket and let it slide toward the curves.

"Hey, don't get fresh," she said, moving slightly out of his reach. "And ain't you got no manners? Aren't you gonna introduce me to this fella here?"

"To be sure. Let me mind my Ps and Qs. Queen Ruby, I'd like you to meet the man who has taken your place in my life, my bed fellow, so to speak, Al Potts. Al, this vision of loveliness is my wife, my *young* wife to be sure, Ruby, queen of all she surveys," said Leo.

He turned to Ruby with a grin. "Does that take care of the introductions to your satisfaction, Your Majesty?"

"Pleased to meet ya, I'm sure," Ruby said primly with a nod in Alvin's direction and an elbow in Leo's ribs.

"Don't mind this yahoo here, Al. He likes to think he's a comedian, a real comedian. Don't you, daddy?"

"A few laughs is about all I can give you anymore, so enjoy them," said Leo.

"Oh daddy! Honestly! The things you say and in mixed company." Her tone was one of embarrassment, but she was digging in her purse while she said it.

The thought crossed Alvin's mind that the embarrassment was probably feigned, and this act between husband and the wife who looked half his age had played before.

Ruby found the pack of cigarettes for which she'd been

scrabbling, pried one out and placed it between her lips.

"Got a match?" she asked Leo.

"You know smoking's not allowed in here," Leo said.

"Allowed. Schmallowed. Who's gonna stop me?"

"Miss Gillis can smell a weed a mile away and, when she does, she'll be in here so fast it'll make your head spin," said Leo.

"Well, whoopty doo. Look who's afraid of the big, bad witch. Not me!" she sniffed. She jabbed the air with her cigarette to help make her point. Further rummaging in a purse the size of a small suitcase produced a match. Fitting her thumbnail over the head, she was about to strike it when she turned to Alvin.

"What about you, Curly? Do you object to me lighting up?"

Caught by surprise at being brought into the skirmish and with casually being baptized with a nickname, Alvin found himself stammering and turning red.

"Well, will you look at that, daddy! Migawd, when was the last time you saw a full grown man blush? Is that a yes or a no, Curly?"

"I guess it's a no, M'am. I mean a yes," Alvin said, still flustered.

"What I mean to say, M'am, is, if you're asking me what I prefer, I guess I'd have to say I'm comfortable with keeping to the rules."

"Sounds mighty dull to me. I thought rules were made to be broken," Ruby said, laughing. But she put the cigarette back into the pack and tucked it into the recesses of her purse.

"And for gawd's sake could you just call me Ruby and not m'am? Makes me feel about a hundred and one years old, and I'd venture to guess I'm not that much older than you, Curly Locks," she said, as she carefully picked a piece of tobacco from her lips.

Definitely uncomfortable now, Alvin looked out the window and was relieved to see Frances approaching. She was carrying Frances Pearl. He thought his wife, wrapped in an ankle-length coat, looked like a soft, brown wren compared to Leo's colorful bird of paradise. He decided to meet his wife and snow-suited baby at the door and take them into the recreation room if it wasn't crowded with visitors.

He kept his eyes averted as he squeezed past Leo's bed, but he had the feeling they had completely forgotten about him.

'Wrens and their chicks are comfortable, reassuring little things', he thought, as he gathered his wife and baby into his arms once they were alone in the rec room. Then baby surprised him by kicking free of his embrace and pushing him away.

"She doesn't feel very well today. She doesn't know what she's doing," said Frances when she saw how upset Alvin looked.

In spite of his coaxing, the child ignored him. She turned to her mother and buried her face against Frances' shoulder. When Al tried to peek at her playfully, she cried.

"She acts as if she doesn't even know me," said Al.

Their visit limped along. When it was time for them to leave, Alvin held Frances' coat for her and bent to kiss the back of her head. He held her tight against him for a minute. "Don't worry. She just doesn't feel very well," Frances whispered.

When she returned for evening visiting hours, Al sneaked her into the rec room again even though Leo had told him it was off limits without permission. Frances had not brought the baby with her. They avoided talking about her, and Alvin tried to entertain Frances by describing Ruby for her.

"She sounds lively and fun," said Frances. "Is she in there with Leo now?"

"No. She didn't come back this evening, at least not yet. Today was the first time she's been here in the week I've been here," Alvin said.

"I bet you were surprised I have a wife like Ruby," Leo said to Alvin when they were lying in their beds after lights out."

"She seemed…lively and fun," Alvin said.

"And young?" Leo retorted. "Well, she is young. She's twenty-eight to my fifty. I was a good friend of her dad's. We logged together when we were just young bucks."

The darkness of the room seemed to unloose Leo's tongue.

"Ruby was fourteen when her dad was killed in a logging accident. She was the oldest of seven kids. Her ma was cook at the camp. They was just barely makin' it before her dad died, and after they didn't have a pot to piss in. I didn't have much else.

"Even then, kid that she was, Ruby had somethin'. And I couldn't take my eyes off that somethin'." Leo's sheepish laugh was hidden in the dark.

"But neither could a lot of other fellas. There were more guys hangin' round their cabin than there were flies that summer. Finally I sat down and had a talk with her mom. I told her I knew I was more of an age for her than Ruby, but I just couldn't get that kid out of my mind. I told her I didn't have much, didn't expect to ever have much, but anything and everything I ever had would be Ruby's if she'd trust her to me.

"I don't know how she talked Ruby into takin' a thirty-six-year-old bachelor over all those young hellions. I can tell you I didn't question it. I didn't know then and I don't know now what Ruby saw in me. Or if she saw anything at all. I might have just been the most familiar face around. God knows I bounced her on my knee when she was only five years old.

"Am I boring you?" Leo asked.

"I don't know what's got me wound up. Maybe it was watching you watch Ruby bounce into our room this afternoon. Sort of made me see her all over new again, you know? She sure is somethin', isn't she?

"I bet I coulda scraped your eyes off your face they were stickin' out so far when she made her grand entrance. I don't blame you. Sometimes she is a little hard to believe. It's been that way through all our married life. And that's been fourteen years now. She's been knockin' guys off their feet all along. Either they're bowled over by her sheer brassyness or, like you, they're nice quiet family men stunned to see something that foreign wander into their little world. Either way, she makes herself felt.

"When we were first married, I couldn't do anything wrong. She liked our little old cabin, havin' it all to ourselves without a bunch of little kids underfoot and into her stuff. She liked fixing it up and was always begging a nickel for a pair of curtains or a quarter for some doodad or other. "When I came in at night I never knew what I'd find. It might be a little bunch of flowers stuck in a syrup bottle or a pile of pretty rocks soaking in a saucer of water. She said the water brought out their colors. It was more often rocks and flowers than it was hot grub. She was still like a little girl in a lotta ways, not anxious to get into the serious side of cooking and cleaning. She wasn't a little girl, though, when we blew out the lamp.

"She's been like that all through our marriage, liking the play pretties. I've been able to give her few enough of those, so it makes me feel good when she comes in all happy, like she did this afternoon, looking 'classy', isn't that what she said?

"I noticed your wife has been in to see you afternoon and nights on both visiting days you've been here. Ruby doesn't get out with that kind of regularity. I never know when she'll come popping through that door, but most usually, when she does make it out, it's in the afternoon. I can understand why she doesn't come oftener. This place depresses her. And then Walla Walla is a stretch from Dayton and us without a car. "

There was silence from Leo's bed, unbroken by Al.

"Ruby, she likes a good time. Happy faces. A good laugh. Some people might get the wrong idea about Ruby. Her smoking and kind of freewheeling attitude might lead some people to think a few things that aren't true. But she's a good kid. I try to make allowances for her now. Don't get me wrong. I'm no pantywaist pushover. But I know where that girl came from and, if she can kick up her heels without falling over on her back, I'll go along with it. I'm not about to stand for any funny stuff, but I don't mind her havin' herself a good time if it's on the up and up.

"Is that hard for you to understand?"

Alvin didn't think it was long answers Leo was looking for.

"Nope," he said.

It was an honest answer, but Alvin knew he wouldn't be able to apply Leo's kind of understanding to his own wife.

All talked out, Leo fell silent. Lying there in the dark, Alvin remembered that he had not made a diary entry as he had intended to do every day.

"Hey, Leo, would you mind if I turn the light on for a minute?"

"Sure. Go ahead. Forget to scratch in your little red book?"

> *Sunday, March 22. Started out*
> *feeling fine today because I*
> *knew I'd see my wife and baby.*
> *Really felt worse. Baby hardly*
> *knew me but she felt bad. Leo*
> *and I both had company.*
> *Frances came back tonight.*
> *I sure love my family.*

Chapter 23

*Monday, March 23. Slept very well
last nite. Am rested this morn.*

*The broad-minded see the truth in different religions, the
narrow-minded see only the differences.—Chinese Proverb.*

After making his diary entry, Alvin spent a few minutes
meditating on the proverb at the bottom of the diary page for
Sunday and Monday. This brief, morning meditation had already
become something of a habit. He found it a thoughtful, if not
always peaceful, way to begin his day.

Today's reminded him of Leo's revelations the night before.
In the dark, the differences between their philosophies of life had
loomed large. In morning's light, and in view of today's proverb,
Al promised himself to try to broaden his own narrow view. He
wondered if the subject of religion would ever come up between
them and how far apart they might be on that. 'First, I'd have to
find out where I stand,' he thought ruefully.

It was good to wake up rested. There was nothing on today's
schedule, so he and Leo spent it lounging on their beds, Alvin
reading his way through a book and Leo listening to his radio.

As evening shadows were making their way into the room,
Alvin was surprised to hear a playful, shave-and-a-haircut rap at
the door and Frances calling out, "Can we come in?" The "we"
was Ida carrying Frances Pearl.

How they had talked their way in on a non-visiting day was
not discussed because as soon as the baby saw Alvin, she threw
out her arms and said, "Daddy!" She wasn't content until Ida
deposited her beside him on the bed. Then she was all smiles and
giggles. She wrapped her chubby arms around his neck and

ignored their warnings not to kiss him on the lips. Her wet kisses landed in his ear and on his neck and chin as Alvin dodged them. She unraveled one of his corkscrew curls and laughed when he did the same to one of hers.

She was still throwing her daddy kisses when they left the room. He laughed to see her go, dangling over Ida's arm with her pink-checkered ribbon tipped at a cockeyed angle after their rough-housing.

> *Temperature was down four*
> *degrees tonite and sure feel*
> *swell. Frances, her mother*
> *and baby were just here.*
> *Was I glad to see them.*
> *Oh, 'God', Baby knew me.*
> *What a blessing that is.*

He closed his diary, snapped off the bedside light and turned his face to the window. The lilting tune *All I Do Is Dream of You* from Leo's radio lulled him to sleep.

Chapter 24

"The Nazis are using x-rays now to build their master race," Leo greeted Al the next morning from behind the front page of the Walla Walla *Union*.

"It says here the Nazis are using x-rays to sterilize the 'unfit' and to 'eliminate biologically unsound persons.' Do you think the Germans would consider us 'unfit', Al?"

"The way this tooth is hurting this morning, I think I'd classify myself unfit," Al replied.

"Well, the way I understand it, it's not their teeth they're treating with x-rays," Leo said, flicking his eyebrows up and down in a suggestive way that made Al laugh in spite of himself.

"It says they're giving 'special attention' to women over thirty-eight and men whose doctors say they can't undergo operations. I wonder if these people are standing still for that? Or do the Nazis do the picking and choosing?" Leo questioned.

"I don't know. What does it say there?"

"Doesn't say. That's about all there is. It's just this little piece here," Leo said, waving the paper in Al's direction.

"Say, that Howard Hughes is going to try to break a record. It says he's going to try to fly to Miami from Los Angeles. You know, he's the guy who holds the transcontinental air speed record. You ever been up in a plane, Al?"

"No. And I'd just as soon keep my feet on the ground. I do like a fast car and boats hold a real attraction for me, but I haven't sailed on one of those either," said Al.

"I took one of those airplane rides they used to give at the fairgrounds. People looked just like ants from way up there. It was quite an experience.

"Hey, here's a strange thing," Leo continued. "Police arrested a man and his son up on Blue Creek Ridge between Blue and Mill

Creeks. You ever been up there? Good hunting up there. We used to go up and get a deer once in awhile. This guy they're tellin' about here in the paper, looks like he got a deer too, but forgot it's not hunting season. Slapped him in the jug for having deer meat. It says here he claimed he killed it just to make himself some fresh meat broth because he'd been sick a month and didn't have nuthin' but canned stuff to eat. Says it's his first offense…but he's still coolin' his heels at the county jail. What do you make of that?"

Alvin grinned.

"Makes me think he should have met up with the same game warden who visited us once when I was a kid," he said.

"Dad always used the game warden as a kind of boogie man to keep us in line. It was either the game warden or the gypsies who were going to get us if we didn't behave."

Leo laughed with Alvin, then asked, "They ever get you?"

"The game warden was a real threat even though we really didn't understand why. When we'd be playing with deer's feet, Dad would say 'The game warden will get you'.

"I don't think we were aware that dad shouldn't be shooting our food out of season, but we knew you had to walk light when the warden was around. One day the warden came to the house while mother had venison in a boiler on the stove getting it ready to can. He came in, looked around that one room cabin and all us kids staring and just left. Never said a thing.

"But we held our breath when he walked away down the path we'd shoveled out of the snow. He walked right between those snow banks. Under that snow were stone jars full of venison. Whenever we took a jar out, we always smoothed the snow back, but, like kids will, we'd left the top edge of one jar sticking out. That warden just walked right along that snow bank with mother's meat stash inches away. When he was almost out of sight, he called out, 'Mrs. Potts, better do a little shoveling. Don't want good meat to go to waste.'

"After that, the game warden wasn't quite the boogie man he'd been in the past."

"I don't know any man who wouldn't shoot a deer, season or no season, if his family was hungry," said Leo, and added, "Wouldn't be no kind of a man, if he wouldn't.*"*

"Amen to that."

> *Tuesday, March 24. Am sleeping*
> *better now. Today is bath day.*
> *Feels good to have a bath.*
> *Am looking forward to seeing*
> *my family tomorrow.*

Chapter 25

Wednesday, March 25. Here it is
visiting day and cold as
blazes. Sure having bad
weather. Frances was
here. Coming back tonite.

Al's morning toothache reached gigantic proportions by evening, and seemed to pulse in rhythm to the wind blowing in gusts against the window. It was still throbbing when Frances arrived at seven-thirty.

Their visit was punctuated with Alvin's complaints and Frances' murmurs of sympathy until she finally had enough.

"Al, honey, I'm going to find a nurse. Something has to be done."

His attempt to stop her was on the feeble side.

It was a triumphant Frances who returned to his room.

"Tomorrow! Someone from the welfare department will come to take you to the dentist. And, Mr. Potts, Miss Gillis said she'd use the trip as an excuse for them to bring you by the house to see baby and me! So, how about that?"

Alvin's grin said it all.

The promise of being together in the privacy of their own home made both their hearts pound and also made saying goodnight easier. They were almost anxious to separate as if that would hurry their afternoon together.

If they had known the visit was to be a brief stop at the curb in front of their house while Frances held their baby up to the car window, they would have lingered over that goodnight. But they didn't know.

When they were able to touch only fingertips surreptitiously while the wind whipped her hair and Alvin's escorts looked on, Frances could not conceal her disappointment. Alvin was left with a picture of eyes bright with unshed tears.

He carried that image to bed with him Thursday evening, and his penis throbbed along with the space left by the extracted tooth.

His diary entry summed up the visit.

> *Saw baby and mother.*
> *Baby sure is getting sweet.*
> *Frances seemed rather*
> *lonely. I am too.*

He had to laugh when he saw the quotation for the day.

"Give not reins to your inflamed passions, take time and a little delay; impetuosity manages all things badly.—Status.

"Hey, I hear we're having fresh oysters for dinner tomorrow night," Leo called out as Alvin rolled over to turn out the light.

"I don't know if I can stand that," said Al.

Chapter 26

The wind that had blown for three days continued to whistle around the corners of the sanatorium. As it increased in velocity, a ripple of excitement spread throughout the building. Patients left their beds and crowded around the windows to watch tree limbs bend to the ground and dust clouds blot out the sun.

The lights were turned on at noon. They burned all day as dust kept the skies dark. Leo's afternoon *Walla Walla Bulletin* called it 'a black blizzard' and reported winds up to twenty-eight miles an hour. A cloud burst mixed with a second storm front and the cars that passed the san were plastered with mud. It made quite a show for the patients.

The oysters were served at Friday's dinner without fanfare. While their texture talked queasily to his stomach, Al felt no residual effects on his libido.

> *Saturday, March 28. The dust is still*
> *blowing with the wind.*
> *I guess it will never*
> *quit. Tomorrow is visiting*
> *day, sure look forward to*
> *that. Am feeling not so*
> *good. Two teeth are in bad*
> *shape and ache all the time.*
>
> *Sunday, March 29. Here it is, visiting*
> *day at last. Frances*
> *was out and she is*
> *gone again this eve.*
> *Frances has gone home*
> *and it is time to go*
> *to bed. Good night.*

Chapter 27

"You're sure an early bird. What the hell time is it?" Leo asked, groaning and stretching.

"It's only six o'clock, and snowing to beat hell. It's been coming down since midnight," Al said from his place at the window.

Leo pulled himself out of bed and padded over to lean on the window sill next to Alvin. Companionably, side by side, they looked at the unusual spring scene in front of them with tulips and daffodils peeking through almost four inches of snow. That eerie silence that accompanies a heavy snowfall extended into their room, and they stood enveloped in it. The glass frosted over with their combined breath.

The slap of shoe soles on the linoleum of the hall broke the quiet, and they could hear windows being raised in rooms along the way.

"Now what's up?' Leo asked.

Miss Gillis provided the answer when she strode briskly into the room and started throwing open their windows. The chill wind that swirled in drove Alvin and Leo back to their beds where they crawled under their Pendleton blankets.

The snow and wind howled through the ward, and the two were still seeking protection in their beds when the breakfast trays came around.

While tuberculosis patients were no longer relegated to live in the open air cottages of the early 1900s, rest and fresh air, preferably cold, were still the core of accepted treatment. When Nurse Gillis opened the windows Monday morning she was following a method of treatment introduced in England in 1840 by George Bodington, whose ideas of rest and fresh air were considered so radical and were so criticized he ended up closing the institution he had established. In 1859 Hermann Brehmer, a German physician, took up the fight, opening a tuberculosis sanatorium in the Black Forest that was keyed around rest, life in the open and supervised exercise. It took 20 years for the innovative treatment to cross the ocean and be taken seriously in the United States.

Basically, it was Bodington and Brehmer's treatment that the patients at the Blue Mountain Sanatorium in Walla Walla were receiving. "Whatever it takes to let your lungs rest," the doctor had told Alvin when he was first diagnosed with the disease. "The constant motion of your lungs keeps the diseased portion from healing, so make bed rest and fresh air your friends."

Knowing that the snowflakes the wind was wafting over him were for his own good didn't make the bed any warmer, though. He huddled under the blankets and comforted himself with the news his Aunt Mary had brought to him yesterday during visiting hours. At least his sister, Lily, had been released from the sanatorium yesterday. *Seems like the whole family's going to end up with the damn disease.*

Alta and Aunt Mary, who was sister to his mother, often discussed how TB had crept its way into their family. Alta favored the theory that a visiting uncle, who later died of the disease, had carelessly coughed without covering his mouth in their presence. Aunt Mary tended to lay the blame at Bossy's door.

"It was that unpasteurized milk. Some of those cows probably had tuberculosis, and you know we all drank raw milk from those cows," Aunt Mary would argue.

"Yes, *we* all did. So why didn't *any* of you Kennedys get TB?" Alta's retort always put an end to their debate, but Alvin never could see any sense in pointing fingers of blame. It didn't change anything. Alta, Lily and even Pearl were, like him, hosts to the disease. Only Murray had escaped...so far. But it was good news that Lily had recovered and was back home. He hugged that thought close, even while feeling a twinge of envy that he wasn't the one set free to join family.

Alvin braved the cold at the end of the day to reach tentatively out of his cocoon of blankets to reel in his red book and record the storm.

Monday, March 30. Have five windows

open and the snow and wind howls in pretty good. My Aunt Mary came to see me yesterday. Lily has left the san.

Chapter 28

*Tuesday, March 31. It is still
snowing but it is an awful
wet snow. I think it will quit
pretty soon. Tomorrow I
will see my wife again. I
sure enjoy these visiting days.
Am 25 years old today.*

"Hatred does not cease by hatred at any time, hatred ceases by love; this is an old rule."—Buddha.

"You tell 'em Buddha."

"Now, who you talkin' at?"

"No one in particular, Leo, my friend. Just this Buddha fellow who thinks you and me should love TB."

"Well, to hell with that!"

Chapter 29

Wednesday, April 1, 1936. Visiting day
It is snowy and cold this morning.

"If we live truly, we shall see truly. It is as easy for the strong man to be strong, as it is for the weak to be weak."—Emerson

"What words of wisdom does fat, old Buddha have for us this morning," Leo asked when he saw Alvin hunched over his Diary and Daily Reminder.

"Nothing from him today. Today it's Emerson encouraging us to live truly so we will see truly."

"Whatever in hell that means!" Leo grumbled.

"Well, he also says it's as easy for a strong man to be strong as it is for a weak man to be weak."

"Did Emerson make money writing obvious stuff like that?"

"Now don't go picking on my daily advisors, especially this one. I think I may be partial to the thought for today, if for no other reason than Emerson was my dad's name …Emerson Alvin he was."

"Weak or strong?"

"Now that is a matter of opinion, Leo. Depends on who you'd be talking to. No harder worker than my dad. Went all over looking for it, too, when he couldn't find it close to home. Once took a load of cattle to Alaska. Wouldn't that be something? Seeing something outside of this state? I could go for that."

"Still could happen. You're a young fellow."

"Don't know. Getting older by the minute! Yesterday was my…"

"Shh…what's that? Listen!" said Leo, turning up the volume on the radio by his bed. The voice of the announcer on KUJ filled the room.

"...who was 25 years old yesterday. This request for...*The Drunkard's Song* comes from Mr. Potts' sister. Hey, she must know something I don't. So, here you go, Al. This is for you. Happy birthday and stay out of the snow!"

"For gosh sakes. That's you!" said Leo. "I didn't even know yesterday was your birthday."

They laughed as the music rolled into the room. On April Fool's Day, too. Leave it to Alta to come up with *The Drunkard's Song*. But hearing his name on the radio sure made the day begin to feel like a birthday.

The real birthday celebration began at two-thirty when Frances picked her way through the snow drifts, galoshes flapping. Al watched her progress. She precariously balanced a cake in one hand, her purse in the other, and attempted to wave when she saw him watching from the window. The cake did a teetering act, but she managed to keep it upright.

There was a great glob of chocolate frosting on her thumb when she finally got it to his room, but no real damage was done. It took more than a little coaxing, but Frances finally talked Leo into joining her in singing the *Happy Birthday* song. After a sheepish false start, Leo got into the swing of it and they belted out the song together, both off key. Their birthday serenade ended with the three of them in giggles. Al blew out all twelve of the red candles Frances had poked into the thick frosting in the shape of the figure twenty-five. They dropped crumbs on the beds, licked frosting from their fingers, and Al proclaimed it "a tremendous party".

Before she left, Frances slipped a Powerhouse candy bar from her purse and gave it to Alvin, along with one of the kisses she wasn't supposed to exchange.

"From baby and me, to our twenty-five-year-old daddy," she told him.

Flora came by at the end of her shift and left a magazine on his bedside table.

"It's hardly read," she said, then added, "But don't be expecting to find a bottle hiding in it, Mr. KUJ Celebrity."

Before the lights were dimmed, Alvin pulled out the diary and finished the entry he'd begun in the morning.

*Frances was here and brought me a
birthday cake and a Powerhouse.
Sis had a request piece played for
me. Called it The Drunkard's Song.
There ain't no justice. Never could
drink more than a gallon.*

Chapter 30

*Thursday, April 2. Am going to town
and have some teeth fixed or
pulled.—Well had them pulled and
it took Bill almost two hours to
get them out—just two of them.
Broke the roots off and had to
drill them out.*

*Friday, April 3. My jaw is sure sore.
Didn't sleep at all last night.
Hardly able to eat. I guess
they will quit hurting one
of these days. Mrs. Spence has
left the san. A day or two ago. The
news just drifted over to us.*

*Saturday, April 4. Couldn't sleep
last night and am getting pretty
tired. Wish they would do
something for this sore jaw of
mine. Tomorrow is visiting day
sure hope Frances can find a
way to come over.*
*Sunday, April 5. Jaw is no better.
Haven't slept since Thursday. Damn
such a pain. Here comes Frances.
Bless her heart. Sure is a fine
little kid. Hope some day she
can be happy.*
Monday, April 6. I still have the

sore jaw. A hot water bottle
helps for a while and then
nothing does any good. My head
aches too. We are having a fine
dust storm. Had a blood test
this morn. Damn a needle.

Tuesday, April 7. Another day and
still no relief from this pain in the
jaw. Frances will be here tomorrow
and I suppose it will hurt all the
time she is here. I am too darn
cranky to be around.

Chapter 31

Frances always started her walk to the Blue Mountain Sanatorium by counting her footsteps. Her intent was to measure the distance from their house at 902 West Poplar to Al's window with her size four shoes. Although, she'd been making the trip for several weeks, often on foot, something always interrupted the count. Today she was determined to count every step.

It wasn't a bad two-mile walk, most of it on sidewalks along South Ninth Street until she turned onto Dalles Military Road, a narrow county road that connected Walla Walla to College Place. And even that wasn't bad, especially now that the weather had lightened up. There was always something to see. Today it was tulips and daffodils in yards she passed and violets peeping out of the tufts of grass on the last leg of the trip.

It was always a good day when stray dogs in the county left her alone, and she hoped this was to be one of those days. Just in case, she pulled a stick out of the dry leaves in the ditch alongside the road. She swung it several times to test its strength and gave it a whack on the road. *Nope.* It broke, so she kept her eyes on the ditch until she spied another that looked as if it might do.

Now, well armed, Frances marched on.

"*I only have eyes for you,*" she sang softly under her breath. She had the words of this comparatively new song down pat, but she was more than a little off key. A singer she was not. But her ears didn't know it, and a song was usually on her lips. The dishes in their suds were never affected by her renditions and Frances Pearl often fell asleep to her mother's gentle, if not melodic, monotone.

Today the song Frances had heard for the first time at a house party a little more than a year ago was accompanied by the trill of a robin sitting on a branch of a tree she was passing. "A true sign of spring, you are," Frances interrupted her song to call out.

She'd learned that song and many others, and sung them along with family and friends, who gathered most weekends at one house or another to sing and dance away an evening. Babies were tucked in among coats piled on the bed, and children nested on the floor as they fell asleep. Rugs would be rolled back and whoever knew how would play the piano. Often it was Ida, and, when there wasn't a piano available, there was always someone who had a guitar or an accordion.

For a woman who couldn't carry a tune, Frances was a surprisingly good dancer. At these get-togethers, no woman who wanted to dance ever sat out a dance, but Frances was a favorite partner. But even the girls with two left feet were pulled into the fun, and children were often balanced on toes for a spin around the room. The dancing would go on until midnight, and then sandwiches and coffee were served before the party broke up.

Now it seemed that house parties for Frances would be put on hold. For how long remained to be seen. Even though they were family affairs, and her mother would probably still attend, it wasn't something Frances felt comfortable doing without Al.

"*I only have eyes for you,*" she sang as she walked.

Darn! She'd forgotten to keep counting. And the san was in sight.

Frances heard a car approaching and moved farther onto the shoulder of the narrow road to get out of its way. A sleek—and big—car swished by her, throwing up road dust and pebbles. It had three windows on each side and fenders that reminded her of ocean waves. *What a car!* It began to slow and pulled off the road just short of the driveway into the san.

'Oh how I wish it had pulled up a little further so Al could see it from his window. He does so love cars,' Frances thought.

But the four-door vehicle with an impressive gleaming grill had stopped short of the driveway. In fact, it had stopped in a position that put it just out of sight of the windows of the men's wing. Frances could see two people in it, but no one seemed to be getting out. As she drew near, she saw a slice of sky with clouds floating in it reflected in one of the car's shiny hubcaps. *Just like a mirror.* There didn't seem to be a scratch or a speck of dust on the vehicle's entire bluish-gray surface.

She threw her stick down, noting where it landed so she could pick up her weapon for the return trip, and then crossed the road. When she walked in front of the car, she noticed the front bumper came to a sharp dip in the center, forming a vee similar to the wave pattern on the fenders.

Frances was almost to the door of the sanatorium when she heard the thunk of a car door and footsteps crunching gravel. She looked over her shoulder and saw a pretty red headed woman hurrying up the drive. She waited for the woman, then opened the door.

"Classy, huh?" the woman asked.

Frances didn't have to ask what she meant. The woman had just gotten out of the sleek car that was now hidden from their view.

"Beautiful car," she said.

"But classy, don't ya think?" the redhead insisted, but didn't wait for a response. "Hey, it's a Hudson Straight Eight. *That's* class! I mean it's a 1934, but, Sis, didja see the lines on that car. And it's got a baggage compartment as big as my kitchen. Looks brand new, too, doesn't it? Class, that's what it is. Straight class! Don't ya think?"

"It is beautiful. My husband loves cars. I wish he could see it. That's his room right there," said Frances, pointing to the window of Al's room.

"There? That's his room? That window there?"

"Yes. That's it."

"That window right there, huh? Oh migod, is Curly Locks your husband?"

"Curly Locks?'

"Well, I don't rightly remember his name, but the fellow that's my husband's roommate has a head full of curls. Is that your husband?"

"It is, if your husband's name is Leo."

"Oh, migod. Wouldn't you know it? Wouldn't you just damn well know Ruby Pritchard can't fart without it being heard round the world. Just my luck, Sis, and it ain't good luck today that's for sure," she said, slamming through the door ahead of Frances.

"So Leo is your husband?"

"Darn tootin'! And he's gonna be real upset if he knows I

drove up here in this car. And you know these guys can't get upset. Hell, it rips their lungs all to pieces or something, doesn't it, if they get upset? They like to keep them cold as Thanksgiving turkeys in an ice box and trussed up just as tight and quiet."

"So, Leo might be upset?"

"Oh yeah. Oh yeah. He's gonna be real upset...*if* he knows about that car. See that car belongs to...to my girlfriend's boyfriend. And he done me a real big favor by givin' me a ride. See, he's just gonna drop me off and then he'll pick me up on his way back to town. See, it's a favor for his girlfriend, who is this friend of mine. He's not really doing *me* a favor. He's doing it because *she* asked him to give me this lift. But it's not something Leo's gonna understand. See, Sis, there's nothing wrong with this friend of my friend giving me a ride, now, is there? But it's just too much to explain to Leo, do you see?"

She turned to face Frances, who noticed that Ruby had a smear of lipstick on her front tooth.

"So, Sis, could you maybe not mention seein' me in that car?"

Frances ran her finger over her own front tooth and raised an eyebrow at Ruby, who quickly ran a finger over her teeth.

"So, about the car? Huh? What do you think?"

"I usually visit just with Al. That's my husband. Al. Alvin's his name."

"Sure. Al. I remember now. Al."

"Well, usually it's just Al I talk with. I usually just say hello and goodbye to Leo. Most usually, that's what I do."

"That's good. That's good, isn't it? Just a hello and a goodbye. That'd be good for me."

"That's what I usually do. I s'pose that's what I'll do today, too."

"Thanks. You're a good Joe. You understand. Don't want to upset these lung-ers, do we?"

Frances turned and gave Ruby a look that anchored her to the floor.

"I don't know about *you*. But I certainly don't want *my* husband upset. And it isn't their *lungs* that get 'all tore up' if these patients, *who have tuberculosis*, get upset. The only way these *TB patients* can get rid of the tubercule bacillus is to get it walled off in the lungs. And the fibrosis that walls it off is as delicate as a spider's web. The slightest activity can tear that fibrosis away. So, Ruby, that's why these *TB patients* have to stay so quiet if they want to heal.

"And they're *TB patients*, not lung-ers. Do you hear me?"

"Gotcha. But I didn't mean nuthin' by it. Just wasn't thinkin', was I?"

Ruby curled back her upper lip.

"Did I get it all off?" she asked as she exposed her front tooth and swiped her finger across the orange smear.

Frances was still shaking her head in exasperation when she entered Al's room. Then, from behind her, she heard a soft whisper. "But it sure is classy, ain't it?"

> *Wednesday, April 8. Frances was here. My dentist came out and washed my gums out. He pronounced two dry sockets. The most painful pain known to human science. He gave the nurse some medicine for them.*

> *Thursday, Boy! Oh! Boy! I slept almost all nite. That stuff sure has done wonders. I feel like a new man. Thanks to Bill my dentist.*

"He's not valiant that dares die, But he that boldly bears calamity."—Massinger

Chapter 32

Friday, April 10. Another nice nite.
Am feeling lots better. The weather
is a little cool and windy, but
pleasant. Everything is running
smoothe. Evidently everything is
under control. Rest period is upon me
so by! by! Al.

"That which is everybody's business is nobody's business."—
Izaak Walton

With his dry sockets now under control, Alvin's spirits were on the rise. But he was still puzzling over Frances's visit on Wednesday when she seemed so enthused about a car she had seen on her walk out.

A Hudson, she said, and she even knew it was a Straight Eight. Al was surprised Frances knew the make, let alone the model. But it gave him the opportunity to talk about a subject dear to his heart—cars. He had always owned a car, even in the tightest of times because there was always someone with an emptier pocket than his own who was willing to fob a vehicle off in exchange for some folding money or a little extra work. It had been a blow when his Ford coupe had to be sold off in the same way. *And damn inconvenient for Frances, too, to be on foot.*

So, the talk of cars Wednesday, while entertaining and unexpected, also tickled a sore spot.

Frances hadn't raised the topic until they were alone in the rec room. Al had suggested they move out of his room, not only to give Leo some privacy since his wife had finally showed up for a visit, but, he hoped, to avoid the familiarity Leo's wife seemed to breed. They had found a corner in the rec room where they settled in without being disturbed, and were not detected. The Hudson Straight Eight had given him and Frances something new to talk about.

Alvin knew Frances avoided mentioning expenses when she visited, and he avoided, or tried to avoid, talking about how frustrating it was for him to be so idle. Usually it was enough just to be in each other's company even when there wasn't much to say, but the Straight Eight had opened up a new conversational possibility. Not that he ever expected to own a new car, like the Hudson, that would take a hefty chunk out of seven hundred dollars, but it had been fun kicking the idea around with Frances. She hadn't seemed bored, actually had even seemed interested in hearing about the Hudson's one hundred and eight horses—113 horsepower if you got the bigger one—the three-beam headlights and the Hill Hold that kept the vehicle from rolling back on hills. "Now that was an innovation, although I believe Henry Ford came up with a similar technique earlier," Al had told her.

He recalled that when it was just about time to return to his room, Frances changed the subject and reminded him that Easter was this coming Sunday.

Now that he was feeling better, Alvin was even looking forward to the holiday. God knows it would be a welcome change from the tiresome routine here, which was nothing short of boring. But he knew he was luckier than some. He wasn't confined to total bed rest and was allowed to get up to shower, although an afternoon rest period was mandatory. He knew the importance of rest from his previous stay, but Gillis had been around to give him and Leo her little speech about what he liked to think of as 'the care and feeding of the animals in the zoo'.

Gillis had told them what they already knew, that stars in front of their eyes, whirls, flashes and black dots were normal side effects of this contagious disease, that indigestion would be a loyal, if not constant, buddy, and nervousness and restlessness were to be expected as poisons were sloughed off by the tubercular sores in the lungs. She advised them to drink lots of water to help wash the poisons out of their systems, to keep the windows open wide, to breathe less often and less deeply and, most important, avoid excitement which could cause their lungs to work faster and wash out more poisons.

"Singing and reaching over your heads are absolutely forbidden," Gillis said sternly. "And don't make me remind you of this again."

She then touched on the delicate subject of saltpetre.

"Tuberculosis is not a pleasant disease," she had said, which caused a rather rude comment from Leo which she pretended not to hear.

"It *is not* a pleasant disease, and its side effects can be disturbing," she continued. "In addition to the ones I've mentioned, TB often interferes with basic biological urges, increases them, that is. While it is not mandatory, most patients find the occasional use of a compound we provide helpful in alleviating that condition. I cannot order you to take it, but I do recommend it.

"It will be administered automatically." Gillis said sternly.

Reluctantly, she added, "But, if either of you prefer not to have this compound administered to you, either now or at a later date, you may so inform me. And, of course, at any time you can change your mind."

Leo's answer was a laugh. Al reserved his answer to give to her later. His preference was to have his preference *not* to receive saltpetre discussed privately.

He had come to regret that decision in the days since, but felt it was the one normal function he could still call his own. But some days the itch he couldn't scratch was almost too much to bear, especially on visiting days with his pretty little wife within touching distance.

Touch, but don't touch, that's our motto.

It was easier to deal with the rotten salmon that made its appearance on Fridays, just as Leo had foretold. *And God knows that was hard enough.*

Chapter 33

Easter Sunday, April 12, 1936.
Boy what a pretty day it is
starting out to be. We may
have anything to eat that we prefer.
I'll see my wife and maybe the kid.

"It is appointed for all men to enjoy, but for few to achieve."—Ruskin

A sharp rat-a-tat-tat on their window startled both Leo and Alvin, but it was only Alvin who recognized the face pressed against the pane. The nose was pushed flat, the mouth stretched into a leer, but the mop of curls marked the prankster as his brother Murray.

Alvin pulled himself off the bed, walked over and threw open the window. "Wipe your slobbers off the glass and get yourself in here, you boob!"

Murray laughed and ducked away.

"What's this we've got coming to visit, another Curly Locks?" asked Leo with a teasing grin.

"Don't be calling me that in front of my brother or I'll give you my share of Friday's stale fish," Alvin threatened.

"Murray can think up enough trouble for me without you giving him ideas."

Frances entered with Frances Pearl in her arms, and Murray close behind. He had a small sack with him that he laid on Alvin's table. "For you, bro. Let's see if you're farmer enough to make that grow!"

Al pulled a little pot and a carrot out of the bag. "I'll rig it up for you so it can hang right by your bed and you can watch it sprout," said Murray.

Alvin knew that Frances always had something sprouting on the kitchen window sill. It might be a carrot, an Idaho spud or a sweet potato with roots dangling in a glass of water and its head held up by a collar of toothpicks resting on the rim of the glass. He thought he knew whose Easter gift this really was, but he settled back to admire Murray's installation.

"It'll be fun to watch it grow," Al said, winking at Frances over Murray's shoulder.

After hugs were exchanged, the baby admired, and the carrot plant settled into its new home, Murray and Frances pulled chairs up to the bed and put on serious faces. It seemed that Al's visitors had more on their minds than a carrot plant or a casual Easter visit.

"We've been talking," Frances started.

"And thinking," Murray added. They looked at each other.

Murray nodded his head toward her in encouragement.

"Well, yes. We've been thinking and talking and, since Murray needs a place to stay and I could use some help around the house, we thought it would make sense for him to move into our house for awhile."

"Thinking. And talking, huh? And sensible? That's what the two of you think, huh?" Al said.

"Of course, it's up to you, Al. I don't want to be no bother, but if I could be a little help to Frances, well, I'm willing. But, of course, it's up to you," Murray said.

When silence was his only answer, Murray dipped his head and added, rather sheepishly, "Of course, it'd be a good thing for me, too."

"I can see that. It would be a good thing for you. Give you a place to headquarter 'til you can get settled, wouldn't it?" asked Al.

"Sure."

"But, Al, honey, it would be good for me too. Sometimes I can't get out to visit, if I can't borrow Mom's car, because I can't carry Frances Pearl all that way. This way, Murray could bring me," offered Frances.

"Or she could use my car and I could watch the kid at home, if it was too cold to bring her out," Murray said.

"But, of course, it's up to you," Murray and Frances said at the same time, and then laughed awkwardly as their words tumbled over each other.

"So," Frances said, looking directly into Alvin's eyes, "So, what do you think?"

Murray fidgeted, waiting for an answer.

Alvin looked at first one, then the other, and said, "I think you two have come up with a tremendous idea!"

"You do? You really do, Al?"

"Can't see why you two wouldn't know I'd be all for it. The more family we have around, the better I like it. And it's going to take a load off my mind, knowing Frances and the kid won't be by themselves. Never know when she might need another clothesline strung up or something," Al said, throwing a wink in Frances' direction.

> *"The day is practically done.*
> *I saw my wife and baby and*
> *am happy tonite. Happy*
> *to be alive, able to see*
> *them at all. May god*
> *bless them. Al.*

Chapter 34

*Monday, April 13. It is a little
cooler today. Although
very nice. I slept all
day today so don't
know much. Outside of
my jaw hurting I feel
pretty good. The days are
going by but awfully slow.*

*"A little knowledge is a dangerous thing. Drink deep or taste
not the Pyerian spring." —Pope*

*Tuesday, April 14. Am looking forward
to seeing Frances tomorrow.
Had a letter from her today.
Poor kid, lonesome for
an old stick like me.
I know she will be
happy some day. Al.*

*Wednesday, April 15. Frances and
Baby and Murray were out
to see me. They are
coming to have an
examination tomorrow.
Dear God let her pass
her examination. Clear
her of T.B. for my sake.*

Thursday, April 16. One month in

confinement. Frances was
out and had an exam. Thank
God she is all right so is the
Baby. I would willingly
give my life to keep them
that way. May God bless
them and keep them.

"He whose virtue exceeds his talents is a good man; he whose
talents exceed his virtue is a mean one."—Chinese maxim

"I guess I'll have to think on that one. My talents haven't been put to much use lately and imposed virtue may not count."

"Talking to yourself again, young man?"

"Uh huh."

Chapter 35

Frances and Murray had settled into a routine within their new living arrangements. She was the chief cook and bottle washer. He split and hauled the wood, raked the yard and looked for work. Welfare kept the little family afloat, but most of the time Frances felt like she was sinking beneath the charitable waves.

"A person likes to do something for themselves," she would repeat over and over to Ida. "And you will, all in good time," was always Ida's soothing reply.

It had been a relief when not only she, but the baby and Murray passed their TB exams. It was a routine ordeal for family members of tuberculosis patients, but still a dreaded one until the positive results were reported. She had schooled herself in the days before it to hide her anxiety from Alvin. She had received her first lesson in anxiety prevention from Nurse Gillis. In fact, when Frances had given her little lecture to Ruby on the importance of keeping patients calm, she had really been repeating what Nurse Gillis had told her, big words and all, to prepare her before her first visit to Alvin.

Since Gillis' private talk with her, Frances had done her level best to keep their visits on the light side, not too much laughing, no scuffling, certainly no kisses. But most of all, she kept her problems to herself. It seemed as if their home knew the man of the house had left and immediately started falling apart. But it would do no good for Alvin to know about the leaky faucets, the toilet that overflowed or the cold draft that blew in under the ill fitting door. Anyway, that last one was an easy fix, just stuff a rolled up towel against it. Problem solved. Putting food on the table was a little more difficult to figure out.

But the biggest hurdle, now overcome, had been this first TB exam. She didn't know what she'd do if she came down with it.

What would happen to Baby? Or, worse, what if Baby got it? But, thank God, they were all OK. Still, the worry had been there. She was pretty sure Alvin had done his own share of worrying, probably trying to protect her by not mentioning it, just as she tried to shield him.

Frances thought she even had Al convinced that the four-mile walk twice a day on visiting days was a stroll she enjoyed, no matter whether the dust was blowing or rain falling. "Good exercise and time to myself," she insisted when he would, reluctantly, suggest she not come unless she could catch a ride or borrow Ida's car. But she counted on their time together on Wednesdays and Sundays as much as Al did, and she wasn't about to give that up. 'It is nice having Murray's Ford in the family,' she thought. Another problem solved. And Murray was proving to be handy with repairs around the house, so things were improving. If only she could get a job, but Al was just dead against it. Maybe things were leveling out, and there wouldn't be such a need for keeping so much to herself.

Alvin had been away only a month, but she missed the closeness they had before, telling each other everything, and working together to get things done. And she missed his body next to hers, but that was something she just wasn't going to think about *at all*. Her focus was going to be on putting a little protein on the table, along with the starches from Welfare. If only she had space here for a few chickens, but they had talked long and hard just to get the landlord to rent to a couple with a baby, so she wasn't about to bring up the subject of chickens.

One thing she regretted being unable to talk to Alvin about was Ruby. As Ida would have expressed it, 'the redhead protested too much'. Frances was pretty sure Ruby hadn't been worried about an innocent ride, but, when all's said and done, it was really none of her business any way. She just hoped Leo wasn't going to be hurt. He seemed like a good guy. At least, Alvin was enjoying him as a roommate, maybe too much.

Al told her Gillis had already warned them several times about hearing too much laughter coming from their room. "A man can't have any fun around here," Al had protested good-naturedly.

Chapter 36

The threat of mortal sin hung over Alvin every Friday when the cook chose to put meat on the menu instead of something compatible with the Catholic Church's fast and abstinence rules.

April 17 was one of those temptation Fridays. The first two meals of the day posed no problems, but mystery meat sandwiches arrived on the supper tray, and Al wasn't happy about it. It wasn't ignorance about what lay between the slices of bread that upset him, but that he so much wanted to eat whatever it was. Just the thought of protein made him salivate.

This being a Catholic is taking its toll. He just hoped a missed meal now and then wouldn't register on the scale Saturday. His goal was to reach one hundred fifty pounds. That was still a magic number at the san. It often meant a patient was well enough to return home if he could tip the scales at one hundred fifty. To be called "fat and sassy" would be even better. That was a sure ticket home.

Was there really any reason to forego the sandwiches? Who would know if he ate meat? And how great a sin could it really be? A *mortal* one, according to Father Gallagher, who had put Friday fast and abstinence at the top of the 'Good Catholics Do Not' list, as in 'Good Catholics do not eat meat on Fridays.' *A mortal sin. That was pretty serious business.* It would be a definite stain on a soul that, Al figured, already was not lily white.

There wasn't just one sandwich, Al noted. No, there were two, made with white bread and sliced diagonally. Thick, too. And arranged nicely on the plate which held...nothing else.

So, decision time. Was it to be an empty stomach or a new black stain on an invisible soul?

"Hey, Al, see that tray? No stale salmon on it tonight. Looks pretty good, huh?"

The devil spoke in Leo's voice, the temptation loud and clear. Couldn't be clearer, if he had said 'Eat up!'.

It wasn't so much Father Gallagher's dire warning of mortal sin that turned Al away from the tempting sandwiches, but his hesitancy to give an outward sign to his own wobbly convictions. Al knew his belief on this particular church teaching stood on shaky ground, along with several others he hadn't been able to wrap himself around completely. Like having a half dozen kids or more. That was one that threatened to carve faith right out from under him. And right now having terra firma beneath his feet seemed more important than a sandwich in his belly.

> *Friday, April 17. It has been a*
> *nice hot day. We had a nice*
> *breakfast and oysters for*
> *dinner. Meat sandwiches*
> *for supper, so I was out*
> *of luck for supper. But feel*
> *fine after all. Al.*

Saturday's scale was good to Al, registering a gain for the week of just a quarter shy of three pounds. "Makes nine and three quarters I've gained since I came in here," Alvin told Leo, trying not to think about how much it might have been if he'd eaten those sandwiches.

Alvin was happy to share news of his weight gain with Murray and Frances when they visited Sunday. Frances greeted the news with smiles that Murray thought actually looked sincere. How anyone could be happy with the skeletal figure his brother cut stunned Murray. But then he hadn't seen Al at one hundred nineteen pounds in March. *That must have been one scary looking six-footer,* Murray thought. He attempted to manufacture a smile of his own when Al looked to him, seemingly for approval.

"Good job, bro. You're going to turn into a dumpling, if you aren't careful!"

"Don't think there's much danger of that just yet, especially if the rotten fish and meat sandwiches become a habit out here on Fridays," Al said.

"Maybe we need to order you up a Wimpy Special and have it sent out if the grub's no good, huh?"

"Sometimes the food's not bad. We had some good fresh oysters for lunch this Friday, but, you know, us Catholics can't eat meat on Fridays and that's what we had for supper."

"No meat. How come?" Murray asked, puzzled.

"It's a Catholic no-no. Get Frances to tell you all about it. But if you do, before you know it you'll be having a little chat with Father Gallagher."

"I don't think so. I'm allergic to religion," Murray said, laughing.

> *Sunday, April 19. Frances and*
> *Murray were here, so was Baby.*
> *Sure enjoy seeing them.*

Chapter 37

"Man, look at this day," Al called over to Leo. "Look at that blue sky and the breeze feels so good," he added, as he stood at the open window. "This is my kind of day, Leo. Almost as good as a visiting day!"

Nurse Gillis put a damper on their perfect April day right after breakfast.

"Well, men, you're in for a change in this room. We're going to shuffle things up a bit," she announced, walking briskly into the room, followed by Flora.

"Time for a new roommate for you, Mr. Potts, and a new room for you, Leo Pritchard," Gillis announced.

It was two quiet patients who watched as Leo's belongings were quickly and efficiently gathered up and his bedside table tipped onto its top at the foot of his bed. With scarcely a goodbye, Leo, bed and all, was wheeled from the room.

Since it wasn't the policy in this tuberculosis sanatorium to explain motives behind change, Al never expected to be enlightened as to what prompted his separation from Leo. And he wasn't. A change of rooms was not a major issue. It happened all the time. It just wasn't always pleasant. In this instance, it definitely wasn't, as far as Al was concerned. But, without an explanation, Al was left with a nagging doubt. He wondered if Leo had requested a change. But, no, he seemed as surprised by the sudden move as Al had been. *Still...one always wondered.*

Before nightfall, Al had a new roommate.

He didn't quite know what to make of him. The new man said nothing. He just stared. At Al. Stared and stared with big round eyes that reminded Alvin of the words in a song: *"Barney Google with his goo-goo-googley eyes"*.

Yes, by god, this was Barney, for sure. When a smile and

greeting weren't returned, Al rolled over on his side, picked a book out of his bedside table and settled down to read with his back to Barney. But he could feel those eyes. Right square in the middle of his back. Like a spotlight. Or a knife. He sneaked a peek over his shoulder. *Yes!* Right square in the middle of his back.

"So, oldtimer, how are you feeling?" Alvin asked.

No answer.

"Getting settled in, are you?" Al persisted.

No response.

"A new room's a little strange at first. You'll get used to it, I'm sure."

Nothing.

"Well, I'll let you rest. Maybe you'd like to just close your eyes. Have a little shut-eye?"

Silence, and eyes still boring in. *Barney Google with his goo-goo-googley eyes. Dammit to hell!* Alvin tossed his book back into the drawer, snatched the red Diary and Daily Reminder out of the drawer and sent his pencil racing over the page.

> *Tuesday, April 21. It looks like rain*
> *and I believe it will rain tomorrow.*
> *If I don't get changed out of this room*
> *pretty soon I shall go crazy. It is*
> *Frances' birthday today.*

"*Tell me where is fancy bred, Or in the heart or in the head?—Shakespeare*

Al slapped his diary shut, stuffed it back in the drawer, and rolled over to turn away from the Barney eyes.

"I suspect we laughed too much," he muttered.

Chapter 38

Visiting day was a rainy one, but for once the weather wasn't uppermost in Frances' mind since Murray's car made thoughts of it unnecessary.

"Warm and dry," she sighed and wriggled into the seat. "Gee, it's sure great to have a ride out every visiting day. I like having you around, brother-in-law."

"And I like being around, Sis. But, not to change the subject, what do you find to talk to Al about for a couple hours at a time? It feels kinda awkward to me," said Murray.

"Visiting days mean everything to me," she replied. "I wish we had them every day! Alvin and I don't do a whole lot of talking. Just being together is real nice. I know he likes to talk fishing with Carl Spence, and he and Elwin always talk about what's happening with the crops. You know Al loves farming. Out here he hasn't had much chance to talk with anybody about those things."

"Still it feels kinda awkward."

"Alvin is interested in most everything, you know that. Hey, you went to Lutcher's yesterday. You can tell him who you saw there. He played pool with a lot of the men there and would like to know what's going on with them. But, Murray, don't worry about it. Just be yourself. Just because he's lying in that bed doesn't make him a stranger. He's your brother, and you probably know him better than anyone. He's just happy to see us. We don't have to entertain him."

Conversation was ready-made as soon as Frances saw someone else in Leo's bed. She wanted to know what had happened to him. Alvin could tell her only that Leo had been moved, but there were still no explanations about why for Alvin to share with her. He was quick to get her and Murray out from under

Barney's eyes, which hadn't quit googling since he arrived.

"I'm going to go crazy, if that guy doesn't say something pretty soon," Alvin complained. "I can't figure him out."

They were sitting in the recreation room that faced onto the driveway. This time Al had begged permission. From here, they could watch visitors come and go. The circular driveway was always lined with cars until three o'clock. After that, the visitors thinned out. Maybe, Frances thought, they were like Murray and felt uncomfortable after an hour. For her, even two hours wasn't enough.

Their attention was caught by a long car that pulled up just outside the rec room's windows. Frances recognized the sleek lines of Ruby's ride. It was the Hudson Straight Eight. The passenger door swung open and a trim ankle was extended, then an umbrella was unfurled. They watched as Ruby got out, sheltered by the umbrella, and bent over to look back inside at the driver. She was laughing, and her red hair was a bright cascade over her shoulders. She waved merrily and walked toward the entrance, stepping delicately over the puddles.

"Who is *that*?" Murray breathed.

"That, brother, is trouble," said Alvin.

He looked across at Frances and silently mouthed, "A Hudson Straight Eight?"

She blushed.

They watched Ruby until she disappeared into the building. Evidently Ruby knew that Leo's room was now on the back side of the building, out of view of the driveway. Alvin gave Murray a short version of Leo's marriage arrangement. He had seen Murray's obvious interest and, like the big brother he was, he wanted to set the record straight. "I get it," was all Murray said.

The Hudson Straight Eight led them to a discussion of cars, and Murray complained that his Ford was bearing the brunt of road work being done on unpaved streets in town. "You can't get around it. The streets have already been graded, but the oiling and graveling they're doing now kicks up. It's making a mess out of the car," Murray said, adding, "Looks like that big bruiser out front knows the secret of staying out of their way though. Some shine on it, isn't there? Do you mind if I go out and get a closer look at it?"

When Frances and Alvin were alone, he slipped a folded paper into her hand. "Happy birthday," he said. It was a little hand-made card. Al had drawn a picture on it, a sign on a post plunked into a tuft of grass. The hand-lettered sign wished Frances a happy birthday from her loving husband. Murray's absence wasn't noticed for the next half-hour. When they did notice, Al suggested they take a little stroll down the hall.

They found Murray standing in the covered alcove outside the front door. He was leaning against the wall, puffing on a cigarette and admiring Ruby, who was also leaning and puffing in the sheltered space.

Al rapped sharply on the door and motioned for Murray to come in.

"Come on. Let's all go down and see Leo for a minute," said Alvin, obviously including Ruby in the invitation. Murray entered, but Ruby shook her head.

"Got to run, hon. Places to go, things to do, people to see. I already told Daddy goodbye. Take care now," she said and was gone.

"She's flash, isn't she? Really flash, and she does have cute little ways," said Murray, watching Ruby sway her way to the waiting Hudson.

"Know what she called me?" he added, as he ducked his head and looked sideways at Alvin. "She called me…"

Alvin raised his hand in a stop sign gesture, and said, "Let me guess. Could it have been…*Curly Locks*?"

"Now how in hell did you know that?" Murray sputtered.

"Wise up, little brother. That is one girl that is not, definitely is not, for you. Understand me?"

"Got it!"

"No, you haven't and you better not even think about getting it!"

> *Wednesday, April 22. It is raining*
> *just as I said it would. Frances*
> *and Murray were here. Has*
> *been a very nice day. Visiting*
> *day always is a nice day*
> *to me. Al.*

"Thought once awakened does not again slumber."—Carlyle

Chapter 39

"I know you!"

The words screeched in Alvin's ear like a screen door swinging on rusty hinges.

"I *know* you!"

The words were heavy with accusation. And, even though half asleep, Al recognized the threat they held.

"I know *you*!"

Alvin struggled up from sleep in a panic. He couldn't move. His arms were held fast to the bed. He fought to free himself. The more he thrashed around, the tighter he was held. When he finally became fully aware, he realized it was only a blanket tangled around him that was holding him fast. But there were those googly eyes, just inches from his face.

"I know you, you *sinner*, son of a whore dog! I know *you*."

Al felt spittle hit his face, and he pulled back against his pillow. Still struggling, he pulled himself upright, and tried to put some space between him and his roommate. But Barney hovered over him. He wasn't giving an inch. His face was twisted into a mask of hatred, and he continued to spew invectives at Alvin. Al saw no solution, short of shoving the ranting man out of the way, but it wasn't something he wanted to do. Barney's voice rose to a shriek, and, before Alvin had to take action, Flora came rushing into the room.

She took in the situation at a single glance. Al pinned to the bed, his roommate poised like a vulture over his prey.

"Just what's going on here, gentlemen?" she said, attempting to strike a casual tone.

Al had no words for Flora.

Barney had more than enough for both of them, but none that made much sense. Then he whirled on Flora, advanced on her and pointed a bony finger. "You know. You know. You know!" he chanted.

Flora's bland expression did not alter. Nor did she give ground.

"Now, Mr. Baker," she said, "that is entirely enough. Come over here. Come here to your own bed, and let Mr. Potts get ready for breakfast. Guess what we're having this morning. One of your favorites," Flora coaxed.

Mr. Baker, who would forever be Barney to Alvin, turned meek as a lamb under Flora's continued ministrations and docilely followed her to his own bedside. He turned to Alvin with a smile, nodded happily and said, "I know you."

And I know you, too, Barney Google, and I ain't impressed.

From that minute on, Alvin's goal was to transfer out of his room even if it meant giving up his window, the tree beyond and the view of the driveway. He started his campaign with Flora, who had witnessed the worst of it. He carried his plea to Nurse Gillis, who, after all, had the authority to make a move a reality. He didn't feel it would be right to ask that Barney be moved out, although having Leo back would be tremendous, as far as Al was concerned.

The only fair thing would be to ask for a transfer so that's what he did. Of course, he knew that a transfer without displacing someone else would depend on a bed becoming available. So, there was nothing to do but wait. Although, he felt, it couldn't hurt to issue a daily request, just to let Gillis and Flora know he was entirely sincere about getting away from old Barney.

However, Mr. Baker seemingly settled peacefully into the san's routine. Still never spoke much, still stared, but the rant and rage seemed to have drained out of him. He would lie like a lump, both day and night, staring and staring. Sometimes at the wall, sometimes at the ceiling, but most often at Alvin. With those goo-goo-googly eyes. He lay so still and his breathing was so shallow that his chest barely rose with the feeble effort.

Sometimes Al couldn't help but sneak a peek at him, just to see that there was still life in him. *That's one pair of lungs that's getting a lot of rest!*

Or, maybe, Al admitted reluctantly, maybe he peeked to make sure Barney wasn't going to leap up and attack again.

But for the most part, Al tried to ignore his new 'bed partner'.

He concentrated on tracking the weather from his window. Cloudy and cool, April showers, weather that prompted him to jot in his diary: *The rain has stopped and the sun has set behind the hills. Everything is green and in bloom.*

One of the innovations at this new san was greatly appreciated now by Al.

A radio system piped into all the rooms helped Al's attempt to blot out Barney's presence. Even though Leo had taken his radio set with him, Alvin could still listen to programs, though not always ones he would have chosen, if he had a choice. Still, he was totally oblivious to Barney during an especially interesting program that came out of Salt Lake City, and stories that came across the air waves were as good as reading a book. Actually better, because he didn't have to hold up a book—another physical no-no in this world of tuberculosis.

There were days in April when his spirits would be high enough to scrawl a whimsical *"Potsy"* as a sign-off to a day's diary entry, but most days just flowed into others, marked only by the rain or absence of it. Sometimes the outside world intruded briefly like when the wind carried the sound of a fire siren to Al's room. Then he would speculate on how much damage was done and to what. Bath days when he could *"wash himself and start all over again"* left him both refreshed and exhausted. A nap, a welcome escape, always followed.

Wednesdays and Sundays were still the two days he lived for, visiting days. Frances never failed to come, often bringing Baby. These were what he termed *"jolly"* days, but it was becoming difficult to relate to a world outside of his room. Weigh days made him suspicious. He didn't know if he could trust them when he was told he had gained, but not how much. He suspected very little, or none at all.

The little red book he wrote in every day was his safety valve. He could confide anything in it—fears, hopes and secret yearnings. But he tried to be cautious, to not offend if someone else should read his words. He could think of only one instance in which that might happen. And it was a thought on which he tried not to dwell.

Sometimes holding thoughts like that at a distance was

difficult when his heart pounded and pains stabbed through his chest and back. But he tried.

Alvin used everything at his disposal in April to disregard the depressing roommate with whom there was never going to be any rapport. But there were still days when Barney's stare-down would elicit a terse: *"Ho. Ho. And a loganberry highball"* notation in Alvin's diary.

Chapter 40

*Thursday, April 30. Nothing of importance
to tell. I guess I feel pretty good in
some places. Some day maybe I will feel
good all over.*

*"It is well men should be reminded that the very humblest of
them has the power to fashion after a Divine model."—
Maeterlinck*

*Friday, May 1, 1936. Fish day. Bath
day. And a nice day. Am feeling
pretty good. My heart is bothering
me some. –Evening-Was outside
awhile this afternoon. Don't feel
so good as I could. Al.*

*Saturday, May 2. We are having
a smattering of rain and
sunshine. It seems all I do is
lay here and wait. Wait for
something to happen. What,
pray tell me, am I waiting for.*

*"Oft fire is without smoke, And peril without show."—
Edmund Spenser*

*Sunday, May 3. Waiting for my wife
to come out to see me. Am lonely
and sure will be glad to see her.—She
was here. Bless her heart. I love her*

and baby so much. May God bless
them and keep them.

Monday, May 4. Have been
laying in bed waiting
for that unknown "something"
to come and get me or claim
my soul. Will "it" never
come or am I doomed
to wait two or three years.
Well! Here am I. Let it come.

"I hold the maxim no less applicable to public than to private
affairs, that honesty is the best policy."—Washington

Tuesday, May 5. Here am I, feeling
sorry for myself. When one
isn't worthy of death, one
shall suffer untold misery
for one's sins. I would to
God I soon get paid up.
I fear I am slipping off
the old track.

Wednesday, May 6. A short
time spent in the company
of my baby. A longer time
with my wife. Oh God to be
well and work for and
support them. Will it ever
be?? I fear the cards are
"stacked"~~~~Poor Al.

"A field becomes exhausted by constant tillage."—Ovid

Thursday, May 7. Pray tell. Dear
God how long is this supposed
to last? This waiting and
confinement. Does one die

of old age? Or of a broken
heart, already weakened?
I pray it comes whatever
it is.—Longingly, Al.

Chapter 41

Friday, May 8. Dr. W. F. Rossiter
here for six hours. A nice clear
shiny day. Am expecting a
change out here. Maybe
better surroundings from
here on out. Sure hope so.
Will know by morn—
Nite nite Little Pal.
Your Al.

"I can look sharp as well as another, and let me alone keep
the cobwebs out of my eyes."—Cervantes

Saturday, May 9. Have been moved
to another room. Hot as
Hell but better boys.
Sure glad to get away
from that "crazy man". Ha Ha.

Chapter 42

Sunday, May 10. Hello! Sweetheart.
Sure glad to see you.
Here is baby too.

Alvin was waiting at the window in his new room when Ida's Ford pulled into the driveway for the Sunday afternoon visiting hour. Not only Ida and Frances, with the baby in her arms, got out, but Al was surprised to see Grandma Hempe being helped out of the car by Frances's sister Jenny.

Not one, but five visitors. I've hit the jackpot!

He was glad to see them, but, being Al, was worried about where he was going to put all of them in this room filled with three beds. *First things first.*

He pulled the one chair allotted to his visitors close to his bed so it would be ready for Grandma. Frances and Baby could perch, as usual, on the end of his bed. *Jenny will be better off in the corner away from the eyes of these young guys and Ida can stand guard.*

The thought made Alvin grin, but there was some truth in it. Jenny was in high school now, and Ida did watch over her like a hawk. Ida already had successfully graduated three girls, Angie, Miriam and Frances, and the eldest boy, John, out of the house. Will, Ray, Agnes and Herbie, in addition to Jenny—the sixth in line— were yet to be launched. Ida depended on a vigilant eye and a stern set of house rules to keep her remaining brood on the straight and narrow. *So far she's batting a thousand, and I don't think these two yahoos in here are going to be a match for her.*

Alvin really was not worried about his new roommates, unmarried though they were. He had enjoyed brief visits with them on his way to and from the shower room before his move to their room yesterday. He had come to know them to be young men well acquainted with manners.

Phil was a real sports fan, who always had the latest on the American League results. It was Phil who passed the news around Ward A when Monte Pearson, the former Cleveland pitcher, held his old mates down to four hits as the Yankees downed the Indians 8-1 on May 30th. That was a trade that was turning out to be good for the Yankees, even though Johnny Allen had boasted that he'd make the Yankees sorry for handing him off to Cleveland in exchange for Pearson. "That was a boast he didn't live up to," Phil had said when he brought them the news of the Yankee win.

Not only would Alvin now be right next to a baseball fount of wisdom, but he could also indulge his passion for a lively political discussion because both Phil and Laurence were as interested in politics as Al was. Things were looking up, and Al didn't foresee any problems between today's visitors and the boys.

Although none of the three were confined to complete bed rest, they all were expected to stay stretched out quietly on their beds and carry on sedate conversations with their visitors, if any. But both Phil and Laurence slipped off their beds to stand up and be introduced as Alvin's company arrived. They gave Jenny only the slightest of courteous nods and saved their handshakes for Ida and Frances.

Grandma Hempe was an obvious source of curiosity for the boys. It wasn't just that her hemline was several inches lower than Ida's and brushed her shoe tops, or that her hair was knotted neatly in a bun at the back of her head that caught their attention. Her entire essence claimed her as something a bit out of the ordinary. Someone that, perhaps, didn't quite belong. *Haus frau* came to mind. Yes, her German ancestry was obvious even before she opened her mouth to greet Alvin. Her words, while clearly English, came forth only after they had fought their way over, around and past the guttural in her throat that came from learning German at her mother's knee.

Al had a soft spot in his heart for Frances' Grandma Hempe, who was the hearth stone in Ida's home. It was this little lady he had in mind while contemplating the effect a troop of irate German grandmothers would have on German's chancellor, if they dared to confront him. Widowed and no longer the strong farm woman, Caroline Hempe found refuge with her daughter, but gave as much to Ida's family as she received. She could almost always be found seated in her small rocking chair, from which she dispensed stories and a never-ending supply of freshly darned stockings. She could also turn out racks of fragrant loaves of bread when she was having one of her good days. But even on her weakest days, she always had time for the children. It was never too much trouble for her to lay aside her current project if one needed a bandage, a hug or just rocked to sleep. She was sometimes caregiver for Frances Pearl when the weather was too cold or wet for Frances to bring the baby to the san. Alvin was grateful to her for helping his wife.

Now, with these thoughts in mind, Al wrapped his arms around the dumpling.

He was careful to turn his face away from grandma's as he gave her a gentle squeeze and then settled her into the chair he'd made ready for her. Ida had a surprise for Alvin, which she couldn't wait to produce. Like a magician pulling a rabbit out of a hat, she swung Frances Pearl out of Frances' arms and plunked her down to stand beside his bed. And there was Al's girl, outfitted in an old-fashioned, flower-sprigged cotton gown with a poke bonnet on her head, thumb stuck bashfully in her mouth.

"So, what's this? What have we here?" Al asked.

"Now what do you think she looks like, Alvin? Take a guess!" Ida urged.

"Hmmm. You don't see many of those hats around these days. She looks like something that might have come off the prairie and over the Oregon Trail in a covered wagon. That'd be my guess."

"Right! That's right! She's going to be in Walla Walla's Centennial parade this summer."

"Looks like you've got her all dressed up in plenty of time."

"Oh you! It takes time to sew these outfits. We're making three of them. This is the first. Jenny and I are going to have the same kind of dresses and bonnets. I made Frances Pearl's out of sugar sacks I got for a nickel apiece. Isn't that a pretty print? I thought it made up real nice. Frances made a nice heavy starch and look how crisp the dress turned out. Same with the bonnet. And...we are going to ride in a covered wagon! Docey's fixing one up for us, but there's going to be a whole wagon train of them."

"And what's the little mother going to be doing while these three are riding the trail?" Alvin asked Frances. "Standing on a corner, waving at them," Frances said, settling down beside him.

"So, will Docey be driving the wagon?" Al asked.

"Yes, and it'll be his team that'll pull it. Jenny, Frances Pearl and I will ride right up on the seat so we can see and be seen. He's got it all planned out and is working on it. The parade committee has all the details on how these wagons go together. It's a big do, Alvin, a really big do for Walla Walla. One hundred years!"

Alvin smiled to hear the enthusiasm in Ida's voice. She was the doingest woman he'd ever seen. She was a member of the Eagles Auxiliary and always involved in one thing or another. If it wasn't marching in the auxiliary's drill team, it was making quilts for her kids, or off on some do-gooder errand with Docey.

It had taken Alvin awhile to figure out just how Docey fit into the Kerr family picture, and he still wasn't sure he had it right. If there was a family picnic, a tree to be cut down or a campfire to gather around, Docey was right there. But when it came to the Saturday night house parties, no Docey. A roly poly fellow with big, bright eyes and a happy smile, he was often in Ida's company, but no one seemed to consider them a couple. Certainly there was never a hint of impropriety. Alvin knew Docey did have some acres, kept some horses and maybe, just maybe, had a wife at home. Never saw her, if there was a her. It was never an issue in the family that extended itself to include the friends of all its members. There was always a crowd at the Kerr home. Over time, Alvin had come to see Docey as all the rest seemed to see him, as just one of the family.

Everyone knew there was no place for a man in Ida's life, being tied as she was by indissoluble church strings to the man who had abandoned and finally divorced her.

"It's a complicated world we live in," Al thought.

He ended his day thankful that the boys behaved themselves, as, *of course*, he knew they would, and that his visitors had been so pleasant. Of course, with so many, it left little time for just him and the wife. He hadn't even had a chance to ask her if Murray was behaving himself.

Saw Grandma and Ida
and some of the kids.
Am feeling top rate.
Al

"*Truth from his lips prevailed with double sway. And fools, who came to scoff, remained to pray.*"—*Oliver Goldsmith.*

Chapter 43

Murray slid his thumbnail over the penciled numbers scribbled on the inside of a cigarette pack. He had called that phone number three times now. He tapped the pack against his lower lip. He was deciding whether to call it again.

The other calls had led to innocent enough get-togethers, coffee at the doughnut shop, a couple of beers at the Green Lantern, chow mein at the New China. OK so it was escalating, and he was thinking of asking Ruby if she'd like to go dancing. That would crank it up a notch. *But how smart exactly would that be?*

Murray had no doubt about how Al would answer that question. But he was having difficulty making a decision, and there was no doubt about that. Sure, he wanted to call her, give her a twirl and get to know her better. But Alvin seldom interfered in his business, so he had to seriously consider his brother's warning about this particular woman. *And what a woman she was!*

That was the problem. Ruby wasn't just any woman, not just a run-of-the-mill kind of girl. She was…peppy. Peppy and full of life. Could really show a man a good time, he bet.

But where was it going to lead? *Face it, Curly Locks, nowhere, if you know what's good for you.*

Ruby wasn't an easy to please sort of girl either, he'd found out. He'd shown up at the doughnut shop right on their agreed upon time and hadn't minded waiting for her at all. Well, not for the first twenty minutes anyway. He was afraid she wasn't going to show, but he held out and was darn glad to see her when she did sashay in. Dressed to the nines, she was, too. Something red and tight that fit in all the right places. *A real looker, Ruby.* At first she was all smiles and fast talk, but then she seemed to get a little bent out of shape. It took him awhile to understand that she had expected something out of him besides a cup of coffee. "A little token of your esteem," she had called it.

It didn't take him long to wise up and throw a few compliments her way, in lieu of something of a more materialistic nature. He felt he was doing all right when she agreed to meet him again. In fact, he thought he was making strong headway when she accepted his invitation to go for a drink, and even agreed to let him pick her up at her house. Well what else could he do? She lived way out in Dayton, and she didn't have a car.

That time he was prepared. He had a little plant ready to give her after he helped her into the car. He knew Al had really appreciated the carrot plant Frances had given him for Easter, so he was pretty sure he'd made a good choice. Ruby didn't say much when he gave it to her. And he didn't think it was a good sign that she was quick to set his gift in the back seat. He noticed she slipped a lacy handkerchief from her purse and dusted her fingers off, delicately, one by one as if they had come in touch with something unclean.

After her brief toilette, Ruby then flipped the hanky briskly through the air before returning it to her purse.

He knew he had wiped the pot off really good, so maybe it was just that pansies weren't her thing. She was a lot of fun over the beers though, laughed a lot, flirted a lot…sometimes even with him. At the end of that evening, she was out of his car and almost to her front door before he could even turn off the motor. And that was probably all to the good. *I wasn't really expecting anything. Well, I wasn't! Well, maybe a bit of a snuggle. Or something.*

Murray thought their third date went better. She hadn't been too enthused when he called her, but she warmed up when he suggested a Sunday dinner. "I'm usually pretty busy on Friday nights and always on Saturdays, but, gee, Sunday dinner sounds spiffy. Let's not make it too early, OK, Curly Locks? And can we dress up?"

Murray felt more confident when he drove up to Ruby's this time around. He had listened carefully last time, and now fully understood that what a girl *really* appreciated either glittered or smelled good. Since his budget didn't stretch to include diamonds, Murray settled on buying what the drugstore clerk had assured him was "a very nice perfume, a scent to please any lady". He sure hoped so. The little bottle had hardly left enough money in his wallet for chow mein.

Murray remembered that night. The perfume had been a success. Sort of. If *"I didn't know they made such precious, teeny, little bottles"* was a compliment. Of course, she had added, "Exquisite scent!" He was pretty sure she wouldn't have sprayed a cloud of it over herself, if she hadn't really liked it. His car still smelled like a flower shop. But dinner definitely was not a big hit with Ruby.

"I was expecting the Marcus Whitman, not a bowl of noodles in a Chink joint," she had said.

Ruby's penciled phone number was getting kind of faded. Murray rubbed his thumb over it again. Should he or shouldn't he? No harm in a little dancing. Her old man couldn't see anything wrong in that. Al said Leo wanted her to have a good time.

Well, *I'm ready to show her a good time.*

But Al had also said this was one woman who wasn't for Murray. *But is big brother always right?*

Chapter 44

"I think that went all right," Ida told Frances as she steered her Ford away from the san. "He seemed in good spirits to me," she added.

Frances had responded to the call from Nurse Gillis by enlisting Ida's help in bringing visitors to distract Alvin, who, Gillis had said, was being moved to another room because he had gotten so depressed. "Down in the dumps," was the way Gillis had worded it.

Frances knew that Alvin hadn't been his usual self ever since Leo had moved out of his room and the newcomer had moved in. She had attempted to lift his spirits with stories about the cute things baby said or the mischief Herbie got into, but nothing she tried lightened his mood.

In the past 20 days she had seen Alvin slide into a dark place, a place so dark there seemed to be room for only one. When Nurse Gillis had called, it was almost a relief to hear that she, too, was worried about Alvin's state of mind. At least Frances now knew it wasn't her imagination that Alvin seemed to have retreated from all of them. Dressing Frances Pearl in the newly made centennial costume and bringing Jenny and Grandma along had been Ida's idea. "I think it did do him good to see all of us," Frances told Ida. "But, you know, I believe his new roommates are going to make a big difference. Al seemed more like his old self. I saw it as soon as we went in."

"Now what was it you said that bothered him about the old roommate?" Ida asked.

"Like I told you all along, nothing really. Nothing that I know of. Alvin never said that Mr. Baker *did* anything. Al said Mr. Baker stared a lot and didn't talk, but he never really complained about it. I thought he was just missing Leo's conversational bent, but he never really said. That's what made it so hard. I didn't know, and still don't know, what came over him. He just got quieter and quieter, wasn't his usual joking self. Moody like. And, you know, that's not Al. He's not the moody type."

"Well, let's hope he's back on the right track now," said Ida.

Frances's efforts to cheer Al up had led her to deliberately avoid telling him of her concern about Murray. He wasn't as helpful around the house as he had been, and she was pretty sure he was keeping something from her. There'd been those evenings he hadn't come home until late and hadn't told her where he'd been, which wasn't like the kid at all. Usually he was anxious to pull up a chair in front of the stove in the evening and re-hash what he'd done that day and ask her what was new with her. They hadn't had many of those evenings in the past three weeks.

She worried that Murray and her brother, Will, might be up to something. Between them they could usually scare up some trouble, trouble that too often started out with too much beer. Lately, Murray seemed jumpy, couldn't sit still a minute. He wasn't having much luck finding work. He and Will picked up some spending money by caddying at the golf course, but both wanted to find something that paid better and was steadier. Murray had talked about enlisting in the Navy, but, so far, he hadn't done anything about that. Too much time on the hands of kids their age just wasn't good.

She wished she could share her concern with Alvin, but that wasn't the kind of diversion he needed right now. Not now when he was just coming back into the light.

Chapter 45

May 12. Open house.
Red Letter day.
The one day when
the "animals" are open
for inspection to the
public. Oh what a
"trill". Anyway I'll see
my wife.

"What a man thinks in his spirit in the world, that he does after departure from the world when he becomes a spirit."—Swedenborg

Alvin's diary entry clearly expressed his feelings about the event planned for the day. He did feel a certain excitement at an extra visiting day with Frances, but it was tempered with reluctance at being put on display for the public, a display over which he had no control.

What he was calling a 'Red Letter day' was the brain child of all of the hospitals in Walla Walla to commemorate National Hospital Day, which fell on May 12, the birthday of Florence Nightingale, known as the Mother of Modern Nursing. Walla Walla General Hospital and its Sanatorium and St. Mary's Hospital planned to be open to visitors all day, and the Veteran's Hospital at the end of Chestnut Street had scheduled a morning and afternoon public reception. The most formal program for the day was to be held at the Grand Hotel where St. Mary's School of Nursing would hold an alumnae dinner followed by graduation exercises in the Spanish Ballroom for twelve young women. That celebration would include remarks by the chairman, an address by a noted physician and musical and vocal numbers.

Alvin expected the two to four o'clock reception at the Blue Mountain Sanatorium to be a more modest affair. Members of the Walla Walla County Tuberculosis League were going to come out to help staff members put it on. He expected a weak, but bright red, punch, store-bought cookies and a lot of nosey parkers.

It was the nosey parkers he resented. From past experience he knew it was difficult to pretend not to see them when they poked their noses in the door. When he had been hospitalized before, this particular event had been a major hurdle for him to leap. He sure didn't like being stared at, especially by people wearing more clothes than he had on.

Although it was still early in the morning, he could hear preparations being made. Flora had told them the recreation room was going to be turned into a reception area where the refreshments would be served and a slide show presented. Some of the patients, who were allowed the luxury of working with crafts, could display their work on tables being set up for that purpose. But even those patients had to stay in their rooms during the reception. *No mingling with the animals.* Phil already had billfolds and key chains he'd made packed up ready to take as soon as the tables were ready. He was the only one of the three in their room well enough to make the crafts that were deemed to be too energetic for most TB patients. While Al was waiting for the breakfast tray to be cleared away, he lay back on his pillows and contemplated the day's meditation in his diary.

He read the words several times, then closed his eyes and let them run through his mind. It seemed to him that Swedenborg seemed to be saying that a guy didn't change much when he left this world. Sounded like if you thought you were better than someone else, then you acted like that when you were dead and gone. Was Swedenborg saying that what you thought in the here and now was what you became in the hereafter?

I don't know. Maybe I don't have it right. Anyway, problem for me is, I'm not sure there's anything except the here and now.

The past few weeks all Alvin had thought about was leaving the world, and anxious to do it. Now things were looking up, and he thought he might like to stick around a little longer.

That was the trouble with this disease. It kept you on an

emotional roller coaster, up one day, down the next. When your heart wasn't pounding and your stomach wasn't roiling, a fella could actually enjoy himself somewhat. It was then that the nurses all seemed to smile and had time to stop by your bed and chat. Of course, Alvin knew these little talks were part of the treatment, a technique the nurses used to keep the patients calm. It did keep them from hopping out of bed and trying to roam the halls. A limited amount of visiting from room to room by patients who were not bedridden was tolerated, but there were always some patients who tried to break away from the beds they'd been told not to leave.

Alvin hadn't felt well enough, in body or spirit, these past weeks to room-hop. He was feeling better now, and, in spite of the unwelcome visitors today, he realized he was looking forward to a change in routine. *I might even have a glass of that red stuff with my little wifie. We can pretend it's a loganberry flip.*

Frances was one of the first visitors to arrive. She came prepared to stay the full two hours and didn't want to miss a minute of it. She would have Alvin all to herself. Baby was home with Murray, who had surprised and pleased Frances by offering to keep her.

Frances had no intention of sitting through a slide show or prowling through the halls and rooms. She did glance over the crafts on her way in. A wallet with a pine bough design caught her eye. She was pleased to see that one of Alvin's roommates had made it. She thought some of the punch on the refreshment table would go good with the sack of homemade oatmeal cookies she had brought. She had enough for Al and his roommates. They could have a nice little party.

It was an enthusiastic and happy woman who entered Al's new room. The first thing she noticed was that the room was stifling hot. The temperature outside was in the mid-nineties, but in this room it was well above that, she was sure. The window was cracked open, but there was no cross ventilation. There wasn't a hint of wind or rain to give relief. The pungent odor of sweat silently spoke to the discomfort of the three men lounging on their beds.

"Oh, aren't we a pretty sight," Al jokingly greeted her, swabbing sweat from his forehead. "Drowned rats, we are!"

"I wouldn't say that, but it is hot in here. Hotter than outside. Have all of you got ice water?" She was answered with a negative groan from all three. "I was thinking I could get some punch to go with these cookies I brought."

"Do you have a fan in your purse?" Al teased. "That's what's needed here, a good electric fan. A big one!"

"Well, since I can't produce a fan, I'm going to get all of us some punch," she declared. "And I think I'll take a closer look at the crafts. You have some lovely leatherwork there, Phil. I especially liked the wallet with the pine bough."

Phil's smile showed his pleasure at her compliment, but the aura of calm in which Al, Phil and Laurence had spent the cooler morning was not evident now. All were restless, and each expressed it in different ways. Phil was impatient at being confined to bed during the reception. He wanted to go to the rec room so he could see for himself how his work was going over with the visitors. The hand tooling on the wallets he'd put up for show was some of his best, all his own design. He couldn't sit still, was up, then down, peering out the door. Laurence was making an obvious effort to lose himself in a book, but it wasn't working. He read a page, put the book down, picked it up, turned pages.

Al was just as restless. When Frances returned with the cold drinks, he teased and joked and laughed in a too exuberant way.

It was the heat. Tuberculosis patients always had this reaction to heat. It made them restless to the point of too much activity. Frances wished she did have a fan in her purse. Maybe she could see about getting one in town, if this heat wave kept up. It seemed too early in spring for such weather. Maybe she could give them something else to think about.

"Yesterday morning I took Baby in the stroller down to Fourth Street to watch an Army regiment go through town. They were making a thousand-mile march through three states and ours was one. There were trucks and cars full of men. They drove down Main Street before they turned on Fourth, then headed out to the highway."

She had captured their interest. They were all sitting quietly now, listening, eating cookies.

"What were they doing here?" Laurence asked.

"Friends of ours, Nita and Carl Spence, went with us, and Carl said it was a new motorized regiment, the Tenth Field Artillery from Fort Lewis. Showing off, I guess, how fast they can go now that they've given up their horses."

"I remember that," Phil chimed in. "I remember hearing they discarded horses and tractors just last year. And I saw the Third Signal Company from Fort Lewis when its new motorized army units camped overnight here at the fairgrounds. They're really something."

"Carl said these were two battalions with 500 men. He said they really zip along the road, but he didn't know exactly how fast they could go. They had some big guns, too. Let me see..." she stopped to think, trying to remember what Carl had told them. "I think he said there were 75 millimeter guns and I know for sure he said some were machine guns and some were guns that could shoot down airplanes."

"Anti-aircraft guns," Alvin said.

"That's right. That's what Carl said. And they had all their supplies with them, tents and what Carl called 'field equipment'. Carl said you could tell this was the Tenth Field Artillery because of the insignias. It was a broken flag, what Carl called a broken guidon. He said it commemorated a time when the regiment recaptured its guns in France. I don't know much war history, so I really didn't know what he was talking about."

"World War I, I expect," Phil said tersely.

"Did you hear the sirens early Sunday morning?" Frances said quickly.

"The fire department was called out because there was a leak in an ammonia tank at The Villa. That's the restaurant on the corner of Ninth and Main Streets," she added for the benefit of Laurence, who was from Dayton and might not know places in Walla Walla.

"Can you believe this heat?" she then asked thoughtlessly. She tried to make up for reintroducing a subject she'd been trying to help them all forget by saying, "Fresh strawberries have been on the market for several weeks. Will took Jenny and Ray out to the strawberry fields to pick so they could earn some money."

"Did Murray go with them?" Alvin asked.

And there was another subject to avoid.

"Not yet," she answered, but didn't pursue the opening he'd

given her. She did not want to discuss Murray with Alvin, not now, not in this hot room, not with visitors lingering in the doorway from time to time.

She shook cookie crumbs from the paper bag into a wastebasket, folded the bag in half and once again. She fanned it across her face. Her fingers undid the top button on her dress, then the second. Her eyes closed, and the paper bag fan pushed a small whisp of hot air over her exposed collar bone.

When she opened her eyes, she saw Alvin's following the movement of the fan. The color was high on his cheekbones and the gleam in his eyes was feverish. Frances thought she wasn't doing so good at avoiding topics better left alone.

Al reached over for her hand and drew her closer to the bed where he lay. She felt his breath, hot and moist, against her ear. And then, as if read her mind, he whispered, "It's hard to tame the animals in this zoo."

Chapter 46

*Wednesday, May 13. Visiting
day again today. It sure is
hot. Am figuring on
being changed back to
my old room again.
It is cooler there.*

Frances was reluctant to beard the animals in their den the next day. The mercury was still soaring. The ward would be like a steam bath. She was sure the three men in Room Four would be just as unsettled as they had been yesterday.

As hesitant as she was to step into the same situation, she would not miss a visiting day. Besides, she had bad news that had to be given to Al today.

She planned to ignore Phil and Laurence and deal only with her husband.

She arrived fifteen minutes after the start of visiting hours. She was hot and red-faced after the two-mile walk.

"You're late today," were Al's first words to her.

She pulled her sticky dress loose from under her arms.

"It's so hot in here, I'm thinking of moving back to the old room," he said.

"I believe I can stand old Barney better than this heat."

Frances walked to the window, leaned on the sill, and bit her tongue. Hard.

Hot? Sure. But *everybody* was hot. And *everybody* had a lot more worries than just keeping cool, or changing from room to room to avoid unpleasantness.

It frustrated her when Al used the few hours they had together to complain.

She wouldn't have to look far herself to find something to complain about. The landlord had cornered her yesterday when she got home from the san, hinting, strongly hinting, that she might be wise to start looking for another place to live. Mr. Woods didn't say why. She guessed his reluctance to rent to a family with a child was resurrecting itself. Well, she wasn't going apartment shopping any time soon, and she sure wasn't going to spoil this visit talking to Alvin about it.

This, too, shall pass away.

Landlords could wait. The bad news could not.

Frances dreaded telling Alvin his sister, Alta, was being admitted to the sanatorium today.

Alta had stopped by the house to tell Frances the disease that had been put to sleep in 1930 was back again, gnawing at her lungs. Alta said Doctor Campbell seemed hopeful they had caught it early enough to cure again. Last time Alta was just a kid. She hadn't even had to be hospitalized. Rest at home had robbed her of several months of schooling, but rest, along with summers spent outdoors in the foothills, had done the trick.

Maybe she could remind Alvin of that happy ending before he got too upset over Alta today. Frances had tried to talk Murray into coming out with her today, to sort of be a buffer, but he had wanted no part in breaking bad news to an already cranky brother.

Murry told her he had to caddy today, but she thought that was probably just a convenient excuse.

Ida always said good news could be strung out, but bad news was like being poleaxed anyway, so just hit 'em with it.

So, when an opening presented itself, Frances plunged in.

"Alta is being admitted to the sanatorium today."

"Is that right? Well she couldn't have picked a worse day to come into this blast furnace. Did you see the weather report? Supposed to get even hotter!"

Frances was stunned. She could not believe that was all he had to say.

She had been prepared to hold his hand and make comforting noises. She was not prepared for this reaction, whatever it was. Stoic? Apathetic?

It wasn't as if she expected him to leap out of bed and go charging off to Alta's bedside, but his apparent indifference astounded her. It seemed as if Alvin was becoming self-centered, uninterested in anything outside of his room, this hospital.

She knew he had always had the ability to listen to the problems of others without becoming involved himself. She admired that in him. She felt it was a strength that he could wall himself off from someone else's pain, but still be open to listen and, when asked, even give advice or help. With her, he had always shown compassion and understanding.

Today, he brought none of those attributes to bear. It shocked her, but it also saddened her. This just wasn't Al.

Frances knew Alvin would have no direct contact with Alta, that the patients in the two wings were not allowed to mingle. Before his sister Lily was discharged from the women's ward, Alvin had kept in touch somewhat, but he didn't know she was gone until Aunt Mary told him a day later. Some ward clerks were willing to carry messages, if patients cared enough to send them. Then, of course, there was always the grapevine, which was rampant with rumors, some of which were even true.

It was through the grapevine that patients had heard about a supposed romance between a nurse and patient. The redheaded Miss Sanders was said to be involved with a tall, skinny patient who quickly came to be known as "Lucky".

Sanders, who had been a ward nurse during Alvin's first stay, was a trim looking thirty-year-old whose legs were much admired whenever she left the lab for a stroll through the men's wards. A visit from her was a real morale booster for all the patients, and, if the gossip was correct, especially for that tall fellow. It was said that the hospital administrators were frowning heavily upon the friendship. Nurses were expected to remain aloof from their charges, while at the same time visiting at bedsides in a chatty, impersonal, but friendly way.

Alvin always enjoyed these social visits from Flora and Supervisor Gillis and the occasional treat they would bring into the rooms, perhaps a plant, a book or newspaper. Miss Sanders had always been a favorite, and not just because of her good looks.

If Frances but knew it, Alvin recognized an empathy in Sanders that he knew was missing from his own character. He could easily see how the nurse might have become involved with one of the patients. It didn't stretch the imagination to think a patient might be interested in her in more than a friendly way.

So, maybe the grapevine rumor was true.

It gave the ward something to talk about anyway.

Principally, it would be this grapevine that would keep Alvin tied to his sister in the coming months. It remained to be seen to what use he would put it.

.

Chapter 47

"Hey, Al, I saw you made the papers!"

"Leo! Who let you out of your cage?"

"Cage is right. I slipped away from my keepers, old son. It's been too many a day since I saw your ugly mug. Thought I'd better come and give you the latest news. Well, it's not really the latest, but I thought of you a couple weeks ago when I read that the G-men caught *Alvin*, Public Enemy Number 1!"

"If it were me, I'd be pretty easy to catch, penned up as we are. Alvin who?"

"You'd think all America would know the name of a desperado the G-men tagged our number one enemy. I didn't know it, but I do now. Alvin Karpis. They nabbed him the first of this month. Don't ask me what he did to gain the honor. That I don't know."

"I do miss your regular news bulletins. Haven't seen a paper since you moved out. Phil's our sports man in this room, and Laurence gives me the Republican view of the world. How you doing, Leo?"

"Nothing new. Resting, resting, resting. Open house was a change, wasn't it? Some old beer buddies from Dayton came in, and Ruby dropped by."

"How is your wife?"

"She's a shining example of frustrated womanhood, Full of piss and vinegar. Other than that, she's doing good. Looks even better. And Frances and your baby?"

"All's well on the home front, near as I can tell. Except my sis was brought in to the hospital yesterday. Thought she'd beaten it, but…"

"Tough luck."

"Without tough luck, some of us would have no luck a'tall."

"Got that right. How you standin' this heat? This room seems a tad on the hot side. Why'd you check out of our deluxe accommodations? Your choice or were you ousted like me?"

"Let's just say my new roomie wasn't you. After rooming with the best, I was hard to please. I think I would like to transfer back, if Gillis will work it out, because it is too darn hot in here. Can you remember a May as hot as this one has been?"

"It's been a scorcher, for sure. Hey, I think I better be skeedaddling before the ladies with the nets catch me out of bed. You take care, you hear?"

"Sure. And you too, Leo. Thanks for coming by."

Leo made his way to the door, putting a hand out to rest it against the ends of the beds as he passed. When he got to the door, he looked back over his shoulder and gave Al a grin. Al saluted him with a flip of his finger to his forehead.

Leo didn't look so good. Bet he'll catch it, if they find he skipped out.

> *Thursday, May 14. It's raining a*
> *drop or two. Has cooled off*
> *some. Frances was out*
> *yesterday. Sure is a*
> *good kid. I love her all there is.*

"What a happy mortal am I for being unconcerned upon this occasion! For being neither crushed by the present, not afraid of what is to come."—Marcus Aurelius

Chapter 48

Mrs. Gillis approved Alvin's request for another change of rooms.

"But this is a hospital, not a merry-go-round, Alvin, so be sure you want to do this," she warned him. When he assured her this would be his last request, she told him they would move him in a few days.

As soon as he got the go-ahead, the weather turned cooler. "Wouldn't you know!" he said to Laurence. His hot weather excuse seemed feeble now. He also was a bit embarrassed to be leaving the boys behind to suffer the heat when it came, and come it would.

He spent a lazy Friday and marked it in his diary as *Just another 24 hours.* At any other time a day that dragged by could be almost intolerable, but anticipation gave him patience. Saturday was a milestone, two months at the Blue Mountain. He posed a question in the red book: *Weigh day—I wonder if I can break the scales?*

The answer was a total weight gain of ten pounds, which looked good on paper until one realized only a quarter-pound of it had been gained in the second month.

Barney Google was not on hand to greet Alvin when he moved back to his original room on Sunday. But he was not alone. A whiskery face poked out from blankets pulled up to a scrawny neck. A line of slobber drooled down the chin, and a thick tongue protruded from a gaping mouth.

That was Alvin's introduction to Bud, his new roomie.

> *Sunday, May 17. Frances and*
> *Murray were out to see me*
> *today. Am back in my old*

room now. Am not so
hot about this new patient.
Is pretty dirty at his cleanest.

Bud's major offense, in Alvin's mind, was being careless with his sputum cup. The containers that patients had to spit into were less than desirable, but necessary. The nature of the disease required saliva and mucus to be spit out rather than swallowed. Swallowing, they were told, could cause the disease to spread to internal organs.

Sputum cups were unavoidable, but considerate patients tried to be as discreet as possible. One as fastidious as Alvin completely shielded the process from anyone in the room. Not so Bud. Alvin considered himself lucky if Bud even hit the target.

"A regular swamp in here," he muttered to Murray, who had looked alarmed, then laughed, the first time during their visit that Bud hawked noisily and spat in the direction of the cup. Frances blocked out the sight of Bud by swiveling her chair into a corner, but the sound effects painted their own picture.

This time Frances thought Alvin had a legitimate complaint.

"But I intend to remain mum," Al said, as he pinched his thumb and forefinger together and twisted them in the middle of his lips, saying, "Tick-a-lock," which made Frances and Murray laugh. "At least," he added, "it is much cooler in here."

May seemed to take a leaf from March's reputation of 'coming in like a lion and going out like a lamb'. The heat wave broke three days later with *a wind howling like hell*, Al noted in his diary. And the cold settled in. Since it hit on Wednesday, a visiting day, he took it in stride, but when wind, rain and dust storms alternated days the following week to send cold blasts through the hallways, he turned *nice and cranky*, writing:

Thursday, May 21
It isn't hard to stay in bed
these cold days. One just
covers one's head and
sleeps or tries to. Maybe
after so many years in "exile,"
I may be turned out. Hope so.

Chapter 49

This afternoon's cootie party just might be the opportunity Frances needed to find a solution to a problem that nagged at her. Nita Spence was hosting the get-together for a group of women, and it was Nita that Frances wanted to talk to. The party would give her an excuse to do that in a casual way, she hoped.

Nita had been a patient at the Blue Mountain until her release some time in late March or early April. If anyone would know what went on in a patient's head, it should be another patient. At least Frances thought Nita was probably her best bet. She definitely would go to play cootie today.

She set about baking a batch of oatmeal cookies to take along to contribute to the refreshments. Frances Pearl would go too. Frances could always depend on her to behave. She was a good baby, but a mama's girl that clung too closely most people would say. Ida was one who voiced that opinion. "She's not a spoiled child, but she's a clinger," Ida chided Frances more than once. Frances couldn't argue that, not with the cotton of her skirt clutched in Frances Pearl's damp hand. Still, all in all, no one could deny the good behavior of the almost two-year-old.

Even with the baby along, a private conversation with Nita would be possible, especially if she stayed to help with clean-up after everyone left.

Nita's house was a pleasant two-story clapboard, white with black trim, on Chestnut Street. The freshly mowed lawn that surrounded it showed that Carl had spring yard work well in hand. Frances knew he would not be home during the party. When the ladies sat down to play pinochle or cootie in the afternoons, the men disappeared. Evening card games were another matter. Then the entire family—men, women, and children old enough to learn the game—joined in. If the men sought out a card game during daylight hours, it was usually downtown at Lutcher's, where poker reigned supreme.

Nita already had the card tables set up, but Frances was in time to place pads of paper and pencils at each place. She sharpened any blunt stubs before putting them out. The women began to arrive, singly and in twos and threes. Ida brought two of her friends from the Eagles Auxiliary with her. Right behind them was a stunning redhead.

Frances was surprised to see Leo's wife, Ruby. She seemed hesitant to step in among the chattering women, but Nita came forward quickly, hand outstretched to welcome her. Frances couldn't hear what Nita said as she took Ruby around the room to introduce her, but, when they finally stood in front of her, Frances told Nita they'd already met.

"Do you remember we bumped into each other at the san?" she asked Ruby. Ruby grinned, winked, and said, "Sure do."

There was no time to say more. The five tables were filling up and the women were ready for play to begin.

Cootie was a fast and mindless, but popular, dice game in which the winning player was the first to complete a drawing of a cootie, or bug. It was also a noisy game, and today's was no exception. The first woman who threw the number that allowed her to draw the head of the cootie gave the first shout. From then on, shouts, catcalls and laughter arose to announce the addition of a body, a leg, an antenna or an eye. Each body part had to be earned in the order prescribed by the rules, and the rules caused more uproar when contested by players anxious to win. No one wanted to be the booby, although a booby prize was always given to the one who won no games at all.

When the last prize had been awarded, Nita gathered up all the pictures of cooties, made a judgment, and gave a small, wrapped package to the 'artist' who had produced the funniest picture, It was a surprise twist to today's game, and brought a roar of laughter when a ceramic red and black ladybug was unwrapped by Ruby.

The cootie in the drawing that had won Ruby the prize wore a quizzical expression as if to say *'what am I doing here?'*

The room began to clear out, but Nita had many offers of help. Ida and her friends stayed on to clear away coffee cups and sweep up crumbs, others folded up tables.

Frances, who was gathering up pencils and pads, caught sight of Murray's car pulling up in front of the house and quickly stored them away. She had told Murray she would walk home, or catch a ride with Ida, but he must have decided to come for her anyway.

She hurried to the door, intending to tell him she'd be along later. She really did want time alone with Nita. She started down the steps, then stopped. The passenger door stood open, and Murray was waving a come-along in Ruby's direction. Without hesitation, the redhead scurried to the car, bounced in and slammed the door shut. The last Frances saw of them Ruby was laughing and leaning over to ruffle her fingers through Murray's hair.

What was that all about?

Frances slowly returned to the house.

"Are you riding along with us?" Ida asked.

"No thanks, Mom. I'm going to help Nita wash up and put things away."

"We'll all stay and help. Then you can come with us," Ida said.

"I'm going to stay," said Frances. She gave her a look that all mothers worth anything understand.

"Guess you don't need us," said Ida, and began to gather not only her own passengers together, but any others still lingering. She ushered them all out without appearing to rush, but the house was still and empty within minutes.

"Whew, that was fun," said Nita, "but there's nothing like the lull after the storm. How about you and I sit down and have a quiet cup of coffee before you leave?"

"That sounds super," said Frances.

Coffee poured, they sat across from each other, hands wrapped around warm cups. Frances Pearl was asleep on a couch where she'd been put down for a nap at some point during the party. This was the moment, but Frances wasn't sure how to begin.

"So, what is it you want to talk about?" Nita asked.

She laughed then at the look on Frances' face. "Hey, I can read your expression just as well as Ida can! I know you've got something on your mind. So come clean!"

"There is something I want to talk with you about, something about Alvin."

"You have the sweetest husband in the world, but go ahead and tell me what the bastard has done now," Nita said.

"Nita!"

"I'm only joshin' you. Trying to cut through all this ice you're building up. We've known each other for a long time. There isn't anything we can't talk about, so spit it out!"

"I'm asking you because you've been in the san. You know what it's like to be out there day in and day out, never getting to come home. So I thought maybe you could help me understand something I'm not understanding about Al."

"And that is?" Nita asked.

"Well...well, he doesn't seem to think too much about anybody except himself. His sister Alta became a patient this week, and you wouldn't think it even bothered him, the way he took it. And he doesn't ask about his sister, Pearlie, whose TB is in a leg bone and causing her all kinds of problems. She still goes to Wa-Hi, but she's got an awful limp."

"And, let me guess, it doesn't bother him a bit that you have to walk four miles twice a day to visit him. All he cares about is that you show up. Am I right?"

"I'm not complaining about that. I'd walk twice as far before I'd miss a visiting day!" Frances said.

"I know that. What I'm saying is that no one comes before him. Is that right?"

"Pretty much. Or so it seems."

"Sure. I can understand that. What Al is doing is trying to get well. Bed rest is only part of the treatment, you know that. To get well, his mind needs to rest too."

"But you weren't like that. You still cared about people, still worried about them."

"When I was in there, I had my own little trick for keeping the world outside my head," Nita said. "I just let whatever anyone said go in one ear and out the other. I refused to let any of it stick inside me. Nothing I could do about it lying there in bed, Frances, so I just said 'it is what it is' and let it go.

"But it *really* wasn't that easy," Nita continued. "Sometimes my mind just would not shut down. Seemed two o'clock in the morning was a favorite time for it to pull out something Carl had done or said, and play with it until it was in tangles. Drove me nearly crazy some nights, imagining this, imagining that. Some patients turn to the Bible for comfort. Others try to lose themselves in sleep. I think Al is one of the deep ones. But I also think he's one of the smart ones. I think he puts the problems he's really worried about on a little shelf somewhere far away where his mind can't wrap around them until he gets to a place where he can do something about them."

"So, you think it's natural. Natural for him to worry so about himself and not so much about others?"

"Honey, there ain't nuthin' natural about us TB patients after we've been locked up a month or so! But, yeah, I'd say how Alvin is handling his time in there is pretty normal. At least as normal as it gets out there. And, Frances, remember, when all you've got is four walls around you, it does become pretty normal to limit your living to what goes on inside those walls.

"Now *you* tell me something, if you can. Why in hell was Ruby Pritchard getting into Murray's car?" Nita demanded.

"Because the Hudson Straight Eight wasn't available?" Frances questioned innocently, but with a lifted eyebrow.

She threw her hand over her mouth as if to stop her impulsive words. Then she pressed harder, to hold back the laughter she felt bubbling up, but it wouldn't be contained. Frances laughed and laughed until the tears ran down her cheeks. And the laughter was such a relief.

Chapter 50

Saturday, May 23.
We will find out
how much we weigh
today. Weighing is over
and I weigh 130 lbs.
Figure one pound a week
for about four or five
years, I should be
a nice looking lad
when I "emerge" from here.

Sunday, May 24. I saw my wife
and baby today.
Baby was too sleepy to
visit with her daddy.
She and her mother sure
are sweet. Oh God I sure
love them.
May God be kind and let
me out of here.

"Remember this—that there is a proper dignity and proportion to be observed in the performance of every act of life."—Marcus Aurelius

Monday, March 25. Wash day at
home and general work day for
every one. Here I sit night and day
and let someone do my work for
me. I hope they do it as well as I

would like to have it done.

Tuesday, March 26. It is hot or
hotter than "hell" could
possibly be. A damn good
time to run a big temperature
this hot weather. Mine is not
bad considering everything.
About 99.4. I am average.

   "In the spring a young man's fancy lightly turns to thoughts of
love."—Lord Tennyson

Chapter 51

Wednesday, May 27. A visiting day that I always look forward to. In fact that is about all one has to look forward to. One day is practically the same as another in a place like this.

"I have an idea," said Alvin as soon as Murray and Frances walked through the door. "You can take turns visiting me and Alta. Murray, you can run over to her room now and, when you come back, Frances can go. What do you think? Good idea?"

"Sure. I guess," Murray agreed. "We were going to go see her when we left here anyway." Frances just nodded.

"The real idea was to get you alone, all to myself," said Alvin when Murray left, whispering so Bud wouldn't hear. He wiggled his eyebrows suggestively, and stroked the palm of her hand. She pulled away. "OK Mister Funny Man, what's up?"

"Methinks you know me too well," Alvin said. "I have been cogitating and…"

"You've been *what*? Methinks my husband is being a silly-billy. That's what methinks!" Frances interrupted.

"All right, honey. Serious it is. I was reading in my Daily Reminder last night and something I read stuck in my craw. You know that saying about a young man's fancy turning to love in springtime? I did a lot of thinking about that proverb last night before I went to sleep, and I think it's Murray I need to get alone. I think we need to have a brotherly talk."

"All this from one little saying?" asked Frances, not convinced.

"Docey was out getting some grass clippings for his rabbits

and he stopped by. He just sort of let it drop that he's seen Murray a couple times around town with a redhead. Asked how he was doing. Said maybe he'd have a little clean-up work for him. Just friendly like. But the only redhead I know Murray's shown any interest in was Leo's wife, and I sure don't want little brother mixing into that. So, when he comes back, I hope you'll take a powder and leave us alone to hash this out, if there's anything to hash."

"It's all yours, Sis. Alta is waiting for you," Murray said, waving his arm toward the door when he returned.

"Alta's her usual cheerful self," he informed Al as he dropped into a leather chair backed against the wall away from the bed. He wiggled until his rump settled on the edge of the chair and his spine slouched along the seat and his head rested against the back.

"Nothing gets that girl down," he continued. "She said she's treating this like a vacation and she's sure she'll be home soon. She's got everyone in her ward laughing, I think. Our sis is a real cut-up."

"Speaking of cut-ups..." Al began just as Flora entered the room.

The ward clerk bustled in energetically, clipboard under her arm and a bundle of newspapers and magazines in her hands.

"A little reading material, gentlemen?" she asked, just as her feet skidded out from under her.

Flora went windmilling across the room as if she were on a slab of ice. Papers fluttered like a snow storm around her. A crash seemed eminent until Murray leaped up, grabbed her under the arms and pulled her into a bear hug until she regained her balance.

Embarrassed, Flora shrugged free and lifted her shoes, one by one, to examine the soles. Her nose crinkled up and her lips curled with disgust. She wadded a page of newspaper and scraped it vigorously across one sole, then the other. An angry shove deposited it in the wastebasket. She moved over to Bud's bed, stooped and scrubbed at the floor. Thrusting herself upright, she glared at Bud, but bit back a comment.

She scurried around the room picking up the scattered papers and magazines. A ruddy flush suffused the cheeks and neck of the usually unflappable Flora, whether from anger or embarrassment it was hard to say. She glanced over at Murray and dropped her eyes, now obviously embarrassed. Her "thank you" was a mere mutter.

"Hey, kid, think nothing of it. It's a swamp in here," said Murray, laughing.

A grin that threatened to crease her lips disappeared under a stronger emotion, and Flora whirled out of the room.

"Now that's one mad lady, don't you think?" said Murray.

Both men looked over at Bud, who seemed unconcerned at the storm his lack of hygiene had raised.

"Don't know what all the fuss is about," Bud said, and turned his back on them.

Al's planned heart-to-heart went by the wayside. He didn't feel up to engaging the attention of Murray, who was slouched back in the chair, laughing uncontrollably.

Maybe tonight, if Murray comes back.

An orderly came in to swab the floor, and the odor of disinfectant was strong in the air. When the last afternoon visitor left the building, it was a silent and grim pair that appeared in the room occupied by Al and Bud. Nurse Gillis and Flora scooped up Bud's table, positioned it at the foot of his bed and prepared to roll him from the room.

"What's goin' on? Where you takin' me?" a startled Bud asked.

Gillis exchanged a look with Flora.

"Let's just say it's time for some rehabilitation around here," said Gillis.

Chapter 52

Only Frances showed up at seven-thirty. And she was the bearer of more bad news. The landlord could no longer be kept in the bag. She told Alvin that Art Woods, had asked her to be out of the house in thirty days.

This bolt from the blue pushed all thoughts of Murray and his transgressions, if any, out of Alvin's mind. At least for tonight there was no need to worry about that kid. Murray had stayed home with the baby.

Alvin used the privacy awarded to them by the ouster of Bud to coax Frances onto his bed where he cradled her in his arms. He smoothed back her hair, twisted little locks of it over his fingers and tugged gently until her face tipped up to his. He pressed a kiss onto her temple, her cheek, her neck. Then, to avoid taking possession of her lips as he so wanted to do, he nestled her face into his own neck, and felt the gentle nip of her teeth. He eased her away and smoothed a hand over her back, sliding it easily over her curves, but in a manner to comfort not to arouse. Arousing her was a risk he dared not take. Difficult enough to control his own desire. If she gave way, he would be lost.

"Ready to talk about it, little pal?" he asked her, putting space between them.

"All right."

"Did Mr. Woods tell you why he wanted you to move?"

"Not really."

"He just came over today without a by-your-leave, and gave you the thirty-day notice?"

"Not exactly. He kind of hemmed and hawed before that it might be a good idea for me to start looking for another place."

"Did you ask him why?"

"No."

"Why didn't you tell me, Frances?"

"I didn't want to bother you with it, sweetheart. I thought ...well, I don't know what I thought."

"Have you been looking for apartments?"

"No. I guess I thought he was just talking, would forget about it."

"Well, looks like he didn't. But we can handle this, can't we?"

"We can, can't we?" Alvin repeated, giving her shoulder a little shake when Frances didn't answer him.

"Sure. Sure we can," she said. But she knew there would be no "we" involved in a solution.

Chapter 53

Thursday.. My wife was so
unhappy and sad last
night. I sure feel sorry
for her. Oh God I wish
I could go home and
help her to find a place
fit to live in. They get
a man down and walk
on his wife and baby.

Frances woke up Friday morning determined to do something, even something drastic if she had to, in order to keep these walls around her and this roof over her head.

Art Woods had rented this house to them and she had kept the promises they'd made to him. She hadn't let the baby be a bother. They had kept the grass watered and mowed. The tulip and daffodil bulbs Ida had given her last fall had filled in the bare spots around the porch with blooms early in the spring. Murray had finished any repairs Alvin hadn't gotten to before he went into the hospital. The rent was paid on time.

"He should be happy to have us living here," Frances said to Murray on her way out the door to do battle with Mr. Woods, who lived right next door.

"Do you want me to go with you?" Murray asked.

"No. That's all right. I can handle this," she said, but some of the starch was leaking out of her backbone by the time she knocked at Woods' door. When she received no answer, she took a deep breath and rapped again even louder.

"What can I do you for?" Woods asked as he came around the side of his house and saw her standing on his steps.

"Oh! I thought you were inside. I…"

What a time to be at a loss for words.

"Nope. Here I am. What's on your mind, *Mrs.* Potts?" said Woods, putting a sarcastic emphasis on the Mrs.

Frances gathered her courage together.

"I think you're being unfair to ask us to move."

"Oh, you do, do you? Unfair am I? How so?" The wattles on his neck wobbled and the color began to rise in his cheeks.

"The yard looks nice, doesn't it? All mowed and green. The screen door's been fixed and that broken window replaced. We've kept it up real nice, I think, and we've been good neighbors. Couldn't you reconsider?"

"I *reconsidered* my rule about no kids when you and your *husband* practically begged me to. I think I'm about *reconsidered* out!"

"But baby hasn't been a problem. I'm sure she hasn't, has she?"

"It's not *baby* that's the problem, *Mrs.* Potts."

"Then what is? What is the problem?"

"All right. You asked for it, so I'll give it to you! I rented that there little house to you and your *husband*. I didn't rent it out to a string of fellows. And ever since your *husband* got put in the hospital, there sure has been a string of them in and out. When that fella moved in a couple weeks ago, that, that *Mrs.* Potts, was the last straw!"

"Why, Mr. Woods!"

The shock on Frances' face was not the reaction Woods had expected.

Then came the tears. A torrent of them. She sank to the steps, stabbed her elbows into her knees, and dropped her head into her hands. Her shoes were pressed tightly together, knees obviously braced against each other but completely hidden by a plain cotton housedress, the only kind he'd ever seen her wear.

Woods had to admit that she made a mighty sorry looking shady lady, if that is what she was. *Doesn't even wear rouge or lipstick. But how 'bout all those men? And this new fella what moved in. What about him?*

The tears had turned vocal. Frances wasn't just sobbing. She was bawling right out loud, shoulders shaking with the effort. It was making Woods nervous, and it showed. He paced in front of her, turned and retraced his steps, stopped, looked over his shoulder at her, and turned back to face her.

"All right, all right. Turn off the water works and we'll talk about it."

Boohoo-ing was his only answer.

"You reckon that would be fair? If we talk?"

Pitiful wails.

"Let's talk about it." He was practically pleading, and then he was.

"Please. Please, little lady. Let's talk about it."

Sobs punctuated by hiccoughs.

"That's it. That's the way. No more tears, now. We'll be reasonable, shall we?"

The sobs faded to a murmur. Frances, her head still bowed, pulled a hanky from her pocket, raised her tear-stained face, blotted her nose, then her eyes, which she set accusingly on the landlord.

"How could you, Mr. Woods? How could you think such a thing, that I would ever do anything to hurt my Alvin?"

"Then who the heck are all these fellas runnin' in and out, and, come to that, who is that in there right this minute who's been living over there day and night?"

"That's my brother, Murray. Well, he's *our* brother, Alvin's brother, who has come to help me. I don't know what other men you're talking about."

"There's that tall, tow-headed guy that comes around a lot, almost always on Saturdays, sometimes sleeps over."

"My brother, Will. Murray's best friend."

"And the little fat guy that picks up the grass clippings and then goes inside for and hour or so?"

"Our friend Docey. I give him lunch in exchange for hauling away the grass."

Woods was quiet, eyes downcast.

Frances eyed him. Then asked, "Any more?"

Woods turned his back on her, walked to the edge of his house and, without turning to face her, said, "I'm reconsidering. You can stay."

She pulled herself to her feet, wiping away the last of the

tears, and went back to her house, shutting the screen door gently behind her.

"How did it go, Sis," Murray asked.

"Brother, you won't believe it."

Chapter 54

It was going to be a grand weekend. How could it not be after this morning's victory?

"How much trouble I could have saved myself, if I had just asked Mr. Woods two weeks ago why he thought I should start looking for a house. It's the first thing Alvin asked me last night. Did I ask Mr. Woods, he said."

"Don't blame yourself. I should have gone over and introduced myself when we decided I'd stay here with you. It would have been the polite thing to do," said Murray.

"Can you imagine him thinking Docey and me..." She giggled.

"Can't imagine that. Don't want to either! Won't Al get a laugh out of it though?"

"I'd like to be able to call him up and tell him it's all settled, but it will have to wait until I go to Mom's. Unless...do you think Mr. Woods would let me use his phone?"

They fell into a laughing fit, like silly school kids.

"When you came home, you were a soggy mess, Sis. Were all those tears for real?

"Oh, they were real all right. Felt like a dam broke." She paused, made a funny little face by drawing her top lip over the bottom one, and looked up at him through lowered eyelashes. "Maybe toward the end the bawling and carrying on got a little out of hand," she admitted.

That set them off on another round of giggles.

"It's funny now, but it wasn't funny this morning," she said. "It made me feel sick inside, that someone thought I'd treat my husband that way, that I was that kind of woman. Made me feel just sick."

"You don't have to worry, Sis. Everyone who knows you

knows what kind of woman you are. Al sure does."

"But it's the appearance of the thing, Murray. I was careless and gave Mr. Woods wrong ideas."

"Hey, he's just a nasty minded old codger out to make trouble, Sis. Don't take it so hard."

"Maybe he is, and maybe he isn't. It's a woman's responsibility to protect her reputation, so I bear some of the blame. But it's over and done with now, and we have a great weekend ahead of us. You said you're taking a girl out tomorrow night, and I have a suggestion. You know that old, rotten cherry tree that Mom's been wanting to get rid of? Tomorrow's the day. Docey, Will, a whole gang are going to cut it down. Even Angie and Roy are coming in from the ranch to help. They're going to burn the stump out and we'll roast potatoes, wieners and marshmallows, have a real feast after dark. This girl you're going out with, why not bring her? It will be fun."

"Oh, I don't know about that, Sis. She doesn't seem like a wienie and marshmallow girl to me."

"Pooh, everybody loves a bonfire, Murray!" She tossed an arm over his shoulder.

"Come help cut the tree down tomorrow anyway. We won't have the food until it gets dark. That old tree trunk will be burnt down to a nice bed of coals by then."

Friday, May 29. It has been nice and cool today. Cool enough to appreciate a few blankets over me. I like this kind of weather if I have to stay in bed. I guess I have to stay in bed all rite. Al

"Oh Wind, If Winter comes, can Spring be far behind?"— Shelley

The gnarly cherry tree was trimmed of its branches, sawn into logs and stacked in Docey's truck. A fire was laid in the stump as soon as the tree was felled. The old wood caught, and whisps of smoke curled up, the fire just a thin yellow thread in the bright sunshine.

Ida's yard was full of leaves and woodchips and people. The work had drawn a crowd. Neighbors up and down the block had come to throw ropes around the limbs and ease them to the ground as Roy, high above in the tree, sawed them off. Will and Murray spelled him from time to time, but Roy, Angie's husband now, was considered the expert when it came to tree work. There was plenty for everyone to do. Even the girls were put to work trimming off the small branches.

The women were just beginning to rake up the debris when Murray made his escape. Or tried to.

"Say, boy, where you headed out to? Can we come along?" Will teased.

"Not this time, old soak. Hot time in the old town tonight!"

When she saw Murray preparing to leave, Frances hurried over.

"Don't forget, food soon. You come on back. Everyone loves a bonfire."

Murray made her no promises.

Docey was already tuning up his fiddle, and Will's girlfriend, Esther, a tall gangling blonde, pulled her accordion out of its case. There would be music tonight, and at this Saturday party Frances knew she would give no false message if she stayed. She went in the house to place a call to Alvin to tell him the good news about the house, but also in a small way to make him part of this evening. A kitchen crew headed by Ida and Angie were washing potatoes and patting them dry.

As dusk fell, the fire glowed brighter, and drew people to it. Docey struck up *Turkey in the Straw* and, when he grabbed Ida for a one-handed do-si-do grand finale, anyone who hadn't known before now had an idea why he was called Docey. When Esther and a neighbor's guitar joined in, they had everybody singing *Roll out the Barrel*.

The coals, a bed of rubies, were ready for baking. Ida's Ray stirred up a thick batch of mud under an outside faucet. Herbie, a seven-year-old enthusiastic about the job assigned to him, smeared the mud over the potatoes. Frances Pearl squatted beside him. She watched every move made by the young uncle who was fast becoming her hero. The potatoes passed on to older hands who stuck them in among the hot coals. Men whipped out pocket knives and sharpened cherry sticks, making fine points on ones sturdy enough not to bend under the weight of a wiener.

Dusk had deepened into night, and the only light came from the glowing tree stump. Neighbors and relatives were merely shadows milling through the dark, identity revealed only when they stepped into the ring of firelight. Will and Frances were pulling hot potatoes out of the fire and cracking off their clay-like shells when one of the shadows sidling up to the fire's warmth and light wore Murray's face.

Frances punched him on the shoulder and said, "Where's the girl?"

"That's a question, Sis, that's no longer relevant. Tonight I found out *I'm* a wienie and marshmallow kind of guy."

Will reached over, handed Murray a stick with a wiener on it and said, "Good choice. Have one on me, *Kemo Sabe.*"

Chapter 55

When Gillis and Flora wheeled in Al's new roommates, they brought him a surprise. In addition to a new patient to the san, Oscar Lodi, Leo was returned.

Al and Leo, of course, had their established relationship to fall back upon, but it wasn't long before Oscar fit right in. He was a quiet bespectacled man whose moon face seemed ready to break into a smile at the least provocation. There were tentative feelers and working out of the kinks that came along with having three grown men in close quarters, but that was eased by the parade of visitors that flowed through their room in June.

Alvin had the greatest share, with his sister Lily and his friends Carl and Nita Spence as the leaders on the last day of May. Lily divided her visit between Alta and Alvin, and, perhaps, it was Alta that prompted Lily's visit to the san. Lily had not been back since her own discharge, but Alta had taken the place of a mother for so many years in Lily's life that a duty visit was almost mandatory.

If Alvin realized he was only a secondary consideration, he gave no sign of it. He enjoyed teasing this younger sister, who was on the shy side. She wore the new marcelled hair style, cut short. He liked the look. "Smart, very smart," he told Lily. "Free at the beauty school," she said, touching her waves gently with her finger tips. *Free, huh?* Alvin tucked that piece of information away.

Carl was always a welcome visitor. Nita, too, of course, but Carl knew cars and liked talking about them. Since they were a passion of Alvin's, a visit from Carl always brought new information. It might be discussion of the Auburn's ride stabilizer that prevented the car from side-sway and roll or the Bendix controlled-vacuum power brakes and five-speed heavy duty transmission on the Studebaker three-ton trucks.

Why just exploring the research being done in Packard's Precision Laboratory took up half the visiting hour. Nita and Frances laughed at them, but Al figured women didn't understand the magic of a light-ray machine that could search out infinitesimal inaccuracies. That could be mighty important when turning out precision gauges the company used to check the parts that went into the making of a car.

"Do you ladies know how wide red is?" Carl asked after they had laughed.

"I don't even know what you're talking about, mister," Nita parried.

"Well, Al and I know!" said Carl.

"So, tell us. How wide is red?" Nita played along.

"It's a scientific fact that red light has a wave length of twenty-five one-millionths of an inch. And that, ladies, means that Packard can detect a deviation in a gauge as small as five one-millionths of an inch."

"And this here," said Al, plucking a single hair out of Frances's head, "is five hundred times thicker than that!"

This amazing information received only an "ouch" and a slap on the wrist.

The women were more interested in talking about the break that had finally come in the weather. Walla Walla had wilted, literally, in the heat wave that had begun the first of the week. Baked by the sun, wheat crops in the surrounding fields had wilted.

"We need the rain for sure," Carl commented, when the ladies raised the issue of how difficult it was to keep the grass green and the children free of prickly heat rash in temperatures that had reached ninety-nine degrees.

"Hottest weather for Walla Walla in May since 1897. Paper said it was 100 degrees that year. This has been the hottest we've had since August of last year," Carl said.

"What are they predicting for this year's wheat crop now," asked Alvin.

"It looks gloomy," said Carl. "Farmers need rain. The wheat straw is short, exceptionally so. Some of the wheat is heading out less than a foot above ground."

"That must be the wheat in lighter soil," said Al.

"Right. The heads that are developing in richer soil are still barely two feet high. I took a run out to have a look in my cousin's field, and the heads look poorly filled and like they're going to be on the small side," said Carl, adding, "And he's got good soil."

"Then there's the dust. The dust storms are taking their toll. That high wind we had lifted clouds of dust you wouldn't believe. Couldn't see anything through it. Stopped traffic all along the west side for awhile. It's bad, Al. Not good at all."

Yes, visitors were more than welcome that spring. It gave one things to think about, other than fevers, weigh day and sputum cups.

It still did not take much to irritate Alvin, especially when anything in the routine was changed. When a new woman was put on as ward clerk, Al was moved to jot her presence into his diary: *I like Flora a lot the best. Sure hate to see them break in a new girl. They are "so" dumb.*

Alvin felt sunshine directly on his skin for the first time in two and a half months when Gillis picked an evening to usher him out to a lounge chair on the lawn. He stretched his length out, and basked in the air that flowed over him. *It made me feel so fresh and a lot younger. I wish I could always feel well* he wrote in his red book that night.

The daily reminder for that Thursday gave him something more to ponder after the outing: *"But to know that which before us lies in daily life is the prime wisdom."—Milton*

'I might be happier,' Al thought, 'if I could see the wisdom of what's happening in my life. But there doesn't seem to be much sense to it.'

It was raining to beat the dickens when Frances and the baby ducked into the room on the following Sunday. Even though Frances had run from the car to the entrance, rain glistened on her hair and strands of wet hair were plastered to her forehead. A good time, maybe, to talk about marcelling.

"There's someone else waiting in the car who wants to come in to visit with you," Frances said after she pecked him on the cheek.

"So? Why is this mysterious visitor sitting in the car?" he

asked, swinging his legs over the side of the bed. He walked to the window. He clearly saw Murray's Ford, but the driving rain hid the occupants.

He could see that there were two, not one, waiting in the car.

"Jenny's out there. But Angie is too. She wants to come in, if it won't upset you."

"Migosh, why would that upset me!" Al said loudly.

"Now, Al, don't get excited."

"I'm not excited!"

"Well then, why are you talking so loud?"

"It will not upset me to see my sister-in-law. There. Is that clear? Is that tone of voice low enough to convince you?"

A sarcastic Al was not a pretty thing to see.

"And *why* did you girls think I couldn't handle a little visit?" he asked

"It isn't that we didn't think you could *handle* it. Angie knows she and Roy pulled a stunt on us when they took the job we were after, and she hasn't seen you since then. She's really sorry about it. I was glad she was at Mom's the night we pulled the tree out. It gave us a chance to clear the air. Now she wants to have the same chance with you. I thought maybe Jenny and I could go over to see Alta and give you two a little talking room, if that's all right with you.

"Is it?" she persisted, when Al kept silent.

"Send her on in," he said.

The exchange between them had not escaped Leo and Oscar. They looked at each other and immediately turned their blind eyes and deaf ears, a skill patients readily learned in tight quarters. But Leo couldn't leave it quite alone.

"Excitement on the way in, Curly? Do we need to evacuate the premises, hightail it for the hills?"

"I think you'll be safe enough. It's an old issue and time to be forgot," said Al, grinning.

It was a Monday when Dr. Smith made his rounds in Ward One. He scheduled Al for a complete exam. He was also supervising Alta's care in the women's wing, and had ordered some aggressive procedures for her that included collapse of a lung to let it rest. He was worried about Alvin, who wasn't making the progress he had hoped for.

Smith's findings were reflected in Alvin's diary entry after the examination.

> *Monday, June 8. The Dr. Smith*
> *made of me today a bed patient.*
> *Freedom for three months but*
> *at last captivity. It is a hard dose*
> *but I can take it. I have been*
> *taking it for a long time.*

Chapter 56

It took Gillis and Flora a week to tie Alvin to his bed.

He used every day before that to do all the things he would no longer be allowed to do. He continued to sneak to the shower room on Tuesday and Friday. He defiantly washed his hair, an arms-above-the chest exertion that strained the lungs.

I haven't felt good for two or three weeks, he admitted on a diary page, but he jumped out of bed to stand at the window and watch for Frances on Wednesday, and held little Frances on his lap when she was brought in.

"There's no keeping him down," Flora complained to her supervisor.

"We just have to keep trying," said Gillis. "It is almost always a week-long process before we can convince a patient that complete bed rest means complete. Alvin will get used to eating his meals sitting up in bed and no reading or writing. He won't be getting out of bed on his own to shower, and he surely will not be washing his own hair!"

"You're not going to keep that man away from his little red book. I don't know what he writes in there, but he's got it in his hands most mornings when I bring his tray and most evenings when I make my rounds."

"We can overlook a little hen-scratching, I suppose, but no more letter-writing," said Gillis. "What is most important for Alvin is learning what a rest period is. I saw him reading *The Last Light* during rest period instead of sleeping. When I challenged him, he was gracious enough to offer to loan the book to me after he finishes it."

"Isn't he a caution though?" Flora laughed.

"I have to admit he is one of my favorites, but it wouldn't pay for him to know that. He takes enough advantage as it is!"

Al continued to press those advantages through Sunday, going down the hall to visit the 'better boys' in spite of, as he wrote, *feeling like hell* and then being dismayed Saturday when the scale revealed he had lost a half-pound.

The weight loss did the trick.

Monday Al settled into his bed.

I expect it to get pretty darn tiresome before I am out of here, he confided to the red book, which he would not give up.

Frances, his aunt Mary and Carl and Nita had stopped in to chat the day before. Even a brother-in-law of Alta's had come by. *This having a sis out here has its benefits.* While he was sure Aunt Mary would still visit, she did seem to come around more frequently when one of the girls was hospitalized.

Murray had poked his head in the door, took a quick look around and then proceeded in the rest of the way, skirting Leo's bed a little cautiously, Alvin thought. He had heard from Frances that the interest in a certain redhead had petered out, but Murray must still be leery about bumping into Ruby.

Fat chance as little as she shows up around here.

Chapter 57

Anticipation was running high in Ward One. Phil popped in and out of rooms several days running to give the latest on what he was calling "The Big Night".

"This one's the big one!," Phil reported. "Winner gets a chance at the title, gets to take on the Jersey Irishman. They expect sixty-thousand people to watch, and each of the fighters gets thirty percent of the take! They're saying the gate could be seven hundred thousand. That's foldin' money, boys!"

Phil's "Big Night" was first scheduled to be held on a Thursday, June 18, a boxing match between Max Schmeling of Germany and the Brown Bomber, Joe Louis, out of Detroit. The winner, as Phil reported, would get a crack at the heavyweight title in a match-up with Jimmy Braddock, the reigning champ.

Set to go 15 rounds to a decision at Yankee Stadium in New York, the fight was cancelled by rain. Groans and catcalls greeted Phil's announcement of the postponement.

"But tomorrow is the night. For sure, tomorrow is The Big Night." Phil's prediction was given like a promise.

"Believe it when I hear it," said Leo.

The men were depending on the sanatorium's radio system to bring the fight into the ward over the speakers that reached every room. The individual headsets the Tuberculosis League had tried to raise money for had not materialized yet, but Gillis had promised that no one would miss the fight, even those who might not want to hear it.

"And I'll believe *that* when I hear it," Leo had grumbled.

The system often sputtered with static, cutting in and out, and generally irritating the listeners. "I don't mind when it cops out in the middle of that symphonic crap," said Leo, "but I really hate it when it louses up Maggie and Jiggs."

"Maggie and Jiggs aren't on the radio. They're in the funny papers," Oscar protested.

"Oh, so that's why I never hear them!" said Leo, which set all of them to laughing.

"Really, guys, tomorrow is The Big Night for sure. Get your bets down, if you haven't already," Phil urged. "This fight's going to give the winner a chance at the title. Whoever wins this is going up against…"

"We know. We know. J. J. Braddock, the Jersey Irishman. Give us a break, Phil, we might not be sports geniuses like you, but we didn't just fall off the hay stack," said Leo.

Phil was not deterred from his goal of providing them with a complete run-down of everything he had gleaned from the *Walla Walla Union*.

"All right, already! I hear ya, but the experts all agree Louis will polish off Schmeling like an Irish maid dusts off your momma's piano. Say he's gonna do it even faster than he downed Primo Carnera and Max Baer last year, same place. Louis is only twenty-two years old and Schmeling is an old man of thirty. Hey, at odds of eight to one, there's almost no money on Schmeling. What about you guys? You putting any on that German?"

"That *German*, Phil, used to be the heavyweight champ. Did you forget that?" Leo razzed.

"You sayin' eight hundred newspaper writers are wrong, Leo? That's how many have gone on record to predict Joe is gonna put old Max down in four rounds. A KO in just four, Leo. Whadda ya say to that?"

"I ain't said I'm putting money on anyone," said Leo. "But I got two-bits to squander, if you want to put your money where your mouth is."

"I'll take that bet, if you're saying Louis is going to lose to Schmeling. Heck yeah, I'll take that bet."

"Done!" said Leo, slapping a quarter on his bedside table. "Toss yours in the pot there."

"No need to see cash today. I'll just drop by tomorrow and collect," said Phil, grinning as he backed out the door.

"Leo, what are you doing? You've already got a bet on Louis," said Alvin.

"Hedging my bets, Curly, just hedging my bets."

Tension was still high Friday night as time for the fight broadcast drew near. For the first time, Al was glad Friday wasn't a visiting night. Propped up with a stack of pillows behind his back, he was more than ready. Next to cars, he loved a good fight. *Guess I proved that in Daisy.* He smiled at the memory.

The speakers crackled to life right on time. "Is that corn popping I hear?" said Leo. Al grinned, but flipped his hand in a pipe-down gesture.

The voice that came through was loud and clear.

The combatants are climbing over the ropes. They're in the ring here at Yankee Stadium. That's a black sky overhead, and it's estimated there are 40,000 souls who have braved the weather to watch this fight.

Al could see them. The Brown Bomber in his corner bouncing lightly on the balls of his feet. Schmeling weaving rhythmically from side to side, waiting, ready.

Here's Round One! Both fighters are coming out slow, sparring to mid ring. Louis jabs a left to the jaw. Schmeling crouches, retreats.

"Got him on the run this early in the game," Leo harassed.

Both Al and Oscar waved him off.

Louis moves in again, Schmeling clinches. A light left finds Louis' head. Schmeling comes off the ropes, takes both hands to the head. Louis shoots a right to the jaw. A counter catches him with a right to the body. A Schmeling left hook to the head.

Light body blows from both fighters, and they go into a clinch along the ropes. Schmeling gets in a body punch. Joe backs off and Max tries for a connect to the jaw with his strong right, but misses. Now Max is backing off. He crouches. Joe feints for an opening. They're in a clinch...and there's the bell!

"Who did that round go to?" Leo asked.

"Didn't catch it, if they said," Al answered.

"Sounded pretty even to me," said Leo.

Oscar offered his opinion, "Sounded that way to me. Listen! Here's Round Two."

Schmeling is still carrying his left shoulder high as Round Two opens. He swings a hard left, misses!

Louis uses both hands to give Schmeling a few cuffs on the jaw. Joe is fighting methodically, looking for an opening. He scores with both hands to the German's head. Schmeling plants a hard right on Joe's jaw. Max ducks a right and Joe's uppercut goes wild. Wait! A straight left from Schmeling stops Joe as the Bomber forces the pace, pumping his left twice to Schmeling's nose. Is he making his move here?

Wait! What's happening? The referee is herding the fighters to their corners, but the gong hasn't sounded. It's a mistake! The referee thought he heard the bell. There, they're back sparring but not much action before the bell sounds. This time for real, folks.

"That sounded like Schmeling's round by a shade," said Oscar. The announcer proved him right.

It's two wary fighters that are coming to the center of the ring. Schmeling sees an opening and goes for it. He smashes a hard right to the Bomber's jaw. That jarred Joe, but he rallys. Now we're seeing the Bomber's first real burst of fighting. Max is driven to the ropes, covers, is back in the middle of the ring. He's steadily giving ground, but he's blocking most of Joe's punches.

Louis' left pumps a dozen times to the head, without Schmeling getting in a single return! Joe follows with a hard right to the cheek. It's an aggressive fight Louis is putting on, but he's finding it hard to get past Schmeling's defense. And there's the gong. That round goes to Joe Louis.

"Here it comes. This is the round it's supposed to happen in," said Leo, winking in Alvin's direction. "If it ends here, Curly, you're gonna be out some money."

"It ain't over until it's over, my friend," said Al.

Round Four. They're coming out. Some sparring mid-ring. Louis gets in the first blow, a hard left to Schmeling's head. He follows it with a right uppercut that has Schmeling spitting blood...

"Like that's something new around here," said Leo.

"Can it, Leo!" snapped Oscar.

Leo flinched at the reprimand from the usually easy-going Oscar, but kept his mouth shut.

...cautiously, and he's missing a few opportunities to use that right. But there it goes! He smashes a hard right to Joe's jaw. Doesn't make the Bomber blink! But here's another! It's another hard smash to the jaw. It's got Joe staggering! There's a right to the jaw and Louis is down, down by a hard right! He looks

stunned. No, he's up!

The Bomber's on his feet and now they're slugging, slugging, slugging it out! Hear that crowd roar! They're still slugging away. There's the bell and the referee is breaking it up. The crowd is on its feet.

Ladies and gentlemen, this is some fight, let me tell you. The punch that put Joe down was a short right hand, but there is no official count on it. This is Max Schmeling's round all the way.

"Schmeling saved your money for you, Curly."

"Those Germans have to be good for something," said Al.

Schmeling's starting the fifth round with a rush, fighting along the ropes and smashing all the way…It's a desperate Joe Louis that's trying to cover from the rain of blows….Joe's staggered…he's blinking…he's dazed, but the Bomber is still punching! There's a sharp right to Schmeling's chin that lets Joe fight his way out of a corner. A hard right hook from Max that Joe ducks. They're in a clinch. Schmeling fires his right hand twice and there's the bell!

And Schmeling throws another right! That's after the gong, folks. Looks like Joe's handlers are going to claim a foul…They did. And…denied! The foul has been denied.

"That sounds more like the German way we're beginning to hear about in the newspapers," Oscar said.

Round Six is also starting with a Schmeling rush…he's finding Louis too often with his right…Joe's hanging on but it looks like his defense is gone…It's a dazed Joe Louis here tonight, folks, punching aimlessly at close quarters, along the ropes. Schmeling's right can't seem to miss its target. It's his round by a wide margin.

"He just might win it," Leo said.

"I don't want to hear that," said Alvin.

"Me either!" Oscar agreed.

Round Seven and Louis is coming out slow…his left eye is still blinking. It's a careful Schmeling we see in this round. There's two hard lefts from Joe catching Schmeling in the body and forcing him to a corner…The Brown Bomber is on the attack. A cross by Max lands on Joe's chin. There's a left from Joe that hits Schmeling on the beltline. That brings a complaint from the German…There's more snap in Louis' blows, and he's looking better at the end of this round. And it goes to Louis.

"There may be light at the end of the tunnel yet," said an enthusiastic Al.

"Toot! Toot!" Leo retorted.

Oscar barked a laugh, but shushed Leo with a finger across his lips.

We're seeing a more confident Joe Louis in this eighth round...he's using his left, to the body, to the head... but Max fires a right that jolts Louis and brings a roar from the crowd. Here's an exchange of punches. Schmeling's left eye is partly closed, but he still looks good. There's a low left hook. And there's the bell. Schmeling is wincing in pain. He's not happy about that low blow...he's complaining. It's a blow that's going to automatically give him the round.

By now the roars over the air waves were joined by either whoops and hollers or moans and groans from patients all along Ward One.

It's a battered Joe Louis that comes out in Round Nine. He's trying to wipe away the fog from that left eye...Louis' left cheek is badly swollen...Schmeling lashes with a right to the chin, moves out of range...he rocks Louis with a beautiful right hand to the face. The Bomber fails to counterpunch...Louis' left isn't dead, but there's no steam in his right...It's a groggy Joe, and this is easily Schmeling's round.

"I got nuthin' to say," Leo muttered.

"It's better that way," Oscar said, providing them all with a much needed laugh.

We're into Round Ten with five more rounds to go, ladies and gentlemen, and the crowd here at Yankee Stadium is getting its money's worth. Schmeling is taking the fight to Joe as the referee opens this round. He's two-thirds the way across the ring and Joe's still backing...there's a smash to the head...Schmeling's on a two-fisted attack and he's not stopping...Louis is taking heavy punishment...A couple rights to the head of Schmeling. He counters with a right to the chin...Is that a grin?

Yes! Schmeling's grinning as he brushes away Louis' uppercuts like he's flicking off a fly...It's a downcast Joe that walks to his corner. The round goes to Schmeling.

Alvin could see the Negro walking to his corner, head down to avoid the stares of people who had come to see him win. He wondered where this fight was going. It was a humdinger. He prayed that it wouldn't end in the next round.

Round Eleven is underway. Schmeling and Louis are meeting in the center of the ring. Schmeling's crouching. It's a defense Joe can't seem to get through...a little light exchange of lefts...Louis trying to find an opening. He has it! A right to Max's head...and Max Schmeling is laughing! He's bobbing and weaving. The Bomber can't find a place to unload. Looks like he doesn't know what to make of this German's defense. Joe digs in a light right to the ribs and cuffs Schmeling briskly on the chin...and there's the bell! The round is given to Schmeling.

"What the hell is happening?" said Leo.

"Beats me," Al and Oscar said at the same time.

"Beating Louis feels like," grumped Leo.

Here's Round Twelve coming up, folks. And Schmeling looks like he means business...Joe takes a right cross to the head and doesn't give anything back...no, wait, there's a terrific left to the ribs of Schmeling. Schmeling backs off, claiming it's in foul territory. Referee doesn't agree. He's ordering them to continue.

Joe is on the attack now, backs Max to the ropes, but seems to have done no damage...now it's Louis on the ropes and taking smashing rights to his head! Joe is staggering! He takes a right to the chin...it barely connects...he's down!

Joe Louis is on the canvas! He's in a heap. He's shaking his head. He's rolling over onto his side. And the referee starts the count. One-Two-Three... It's over, folks, it's all over. Two minutes and thirty-nine seconds into the round and it's a knockout!

"Can't ask for a better fight than that," said Leo. "Might could ask for different results, but not a better fight. Are we agreed, gentlemen?"

"Agreed."

"Agreed."

"Here you go, Leo, you lucky son of a gun," said Phil as he burst through their door. He flipped a quarter onto Leo's bed.

"Luck had nothing to do with it. It's all in knowing your fighters. It's skill, boy, pure skill."

"Skill my ass!"

"Now, now. There's no shame in an old codger like me knowing a bit more about this fight game than you do," said Leo, picking up the quarter and shining it on his pajama sleeve. "I thank you and my pocket book thanks you."

The lights dimmed, a warning that patients were expected to retire for the night. It was a signal that carried Gillis' weight behind it. In recognition of that, Phil cocked his chin up at the lights, waved a hand goodnight and left.

"Hedging the bets, it's called. Now I've got the quarter I owe old Hymie Schmidt. He's the only one I could find that was willing to put any money on the German," said Leo.

> *Friday, June 19. Well the fight is*
> *over and what a fight.*
> *I bet 50 cents with Miss*
> *Gillis that the fight would*
> *enter the fifth. I won.*
> *I bet 25 cents with Leo that it*
> *would enter the sixth. I*
> *won. I bet 25 cents with Leo that it*
> *would end in an even round. It did.*

Chapter 58

Saturday, June 20. I won a dollar
on the fight yesterday.
Boy it sure was a fight.
I believe it was the best
fight I ever heard.
The radio worked
absolutely perfect. I am
feeling pretty well today.
I gained ¾ lb. this week.

The ward was subdued, for the most part, on the day after the fight. The men had exerted their energy the night before and seemed content to rest or even sleep.

"Nothing like a good fight to take the starch out of our patients," Gillis had said when Flora reported after her rounds that all was quiet.

"It will give them a good rest before visitors come tomorrow. We always get more on Father's Day," Flora noted.

Sunday was a scorcher of a day, and at least one woman was dressed for the hot weather. Ruby's arrival was watched by more than one pair of interested eyes. Although screens kept the men from actually hanging out their windows, several were pressed up against them to watch her walk up the driveway. Skirts had fashionably dropped from knee to mid-calf, but Ruby was resisting the fashion trend.

Her show of legs was being much appreciated when Leo finally caught sight of her. He hurried across the room and bellowed out the open window. "Stop your gawking, you lazy gobs. Haven't you ever seen a *lady* before?"

Ruby stopped still, stood on tiptoe and waved her fingers cheerily over her head in Leo's direction. "Hi, daddy," she called.

A chorus of whistles answered her.

Leo slammed his hand down on the window sill, turned angrily and tromped out of the room.

"Our mate seems on the war path. What's up?" Oscar asked.

"His wife's on the way in and I guess he's not appreciating the attention she's attracting," said Alvin, disinclined to sort through Leo's marital issues with Oscar.

It was no wonder Ruby was the center of attention. Her red hair was enough to draw the eye, but today's raiment made of her a moving picture. Her sheer dress, cut low in the front, exposed a creamy expanse of flesh framed by a soft billow of ruffles. Her slender arms were uncovered except for ruffles at the shoulder line that revealed, more than covered, when a vagrant breeze lifted them. The effect was of a sunbeam bursting forth from a frothy cloud.

Leo was all smiles when he returned with Ruby on his arm.

"Oscar, I don't believe you've met my wife. This here is Ruby," he said, putting an arm around her and urging her forward.

"Pleased to meetcha, I'm sure," Ruby said, extending a dainty hand.

Oscar hesitantly took it into his big paw.

"And Al you already know."

"Sure. Hi there, Curly Loc…Alvin. How ya doin'?"

"Doing great, Ruby. Your visits always bring us pleasure because we like to see Leo smile."

"Oh you! You're just a big, old flatterer, you are. But guess my daddy does like to see his girl. That right, Daddy?" she asked, turning in his arm to look at him.

"You got that right, Baby," said Leo. "You're looking mighty pretty today, too."

"You like it?" she twirled, which caused all the ruffles to flutter.

It's like watching the wind carry away those puffy dandelion seeds after the blossom has died. It was a disturbing image. Al shook his head as if to clear it away.

"I had this made up special, just for you, Daddy," Ruby said. "This is ripple sheer georgette. Bought it at the Beehive, and had a seamstress make it to a pattern I had just in my head. I love a full skirt, don't you?" she asked, twirling once again. "It goes right on over a satin slip."

"Beautiful, Baby. It's beautiful and so are you."

"It's your Father's Day present," she said, spreading the skirt out on both sides to its full width.

Leo, Alvin and Oscar just stared as the sunlight pouring through the window backlit Ruby, turned her hair into a red sunset and etched in soft lines the curves of her hips and smooth length of her legs.

A very audible gulp from Oscar broke the silence.

"Jesu Christus," he muttered.

Alvin grabbed a drink of water to dampen down a throat suddenly gone dry, shook his head again, this time as if to shoo away dangerous thoughts, and rolled over to face the wall.

Leo said, "Enough with the fashion show, Baby. Come sit down over here and tell me what you've been doing."

"Whatcha mean what I've been doing? I ain't been doing nuthin'!"

"I mean what's going on out there in the big world? What am I missing out on, Baby? Except the obvious we already know about, of course."

"Piff, tiff, you dirty old man!" She squeezed his arm and settled down in the chair, a look of relief on her face. "Well, I have had a few adventures. I don't think I've seen you since the circus was in town. Have I?"

"Nope. That was sometime in May, right around that heat spell and dust storms we were having."

"In May? Oh, it can't have been that long ago, Daddy! But it is hard to get into Walla Walla from Dayton when I don't even have a car, so maybe it was May. It was hot that night. Almost a hundred, and inside the tent it was even hotter! I fanned myself about silly trying to keep cool.

"During the day was better, cooler anyway. We went down and watched these huge old elephants pushing big red wagons all around to set up the tents. Big white tents, Daddy, and those elephants just knew exactly what to do. Of course, there was a man there with a big, long iron hook that directed them.

"I was afraid I was going to get stepped on! And, Daddy, you shoulda smelled that coffee and bacon and eggs. Those dusty old workers sat right down to a breakfast!

"Made me hungry just to watch! We went down to the Coffee Cup afterwards and had ourselves a big feed. That night there was a big show with European riders. Called themselves the Great Christiani Family. They rode every kind of horse from Shetlands to Arabians. It was spectacular."

"Sounds like it. Whose the 'we'you're talking about?"

"Well, Daddy, you don't expect me to go places by myself, do you? It wouldn't look good, a lady going to places alone."

"No, course not. Just wondered who you had for company."

Friends. Friends, Daddy. You don't know them, but good friends to me."

"That's good. I wouldn't want you to be alone."

"Oh, and we've been out to Graybills too. The pool opened with free swims about two weeks before the circus came to town, and we got in on that. I've got me a summer ticket. Just six dollars. They say that water is fresh spring water. It just sparkles with the sun on it, Daddy. There's showers and footbaths full of chlorine so you don't get rot between your toes. This year they've got new diving boards. Spectators still get in free, and were there ever a lot of Nosey Parkers. I was so self-conscious I almost didn't even use those diving boards. But I overcame, yes, I did. I wasn't going to let a lot of big-eyed bozos keep me from having fun."

"That's good that you're having some fun. You deserve to have a good time."

"Well, my life isn't all just fun, Daddy," Ruby protested, pursing her lips into a pout.

"I mean without you at home, there's a lot for me to do. I have to do all my own work and yours, too, you know."

Somehow Leo could not imagine Ruby stringing fence wire, tilling up garden space and planting the vegetables that were supposed to see them through a winter. Not Ruby, who never seemed able to pick her own clothes up off the floor. But he didn't say anything. There was no use picking a fight. She was going to do what she wanted to anyway. A man has to know when to pick his battles. Leo did find it odd that Ruby could make the trip from Dayton to Walla Walla to go to Graybill's swimming pool and the circus but couldn't get to the san. 'We go where the greater attractions are,' Leo thought.

"I saw your wife in town a couple days ago," Ruby said, calling across to Alvin.

"Now, Ruby…" Leo cautioned.

"Don't you 'now Ruby' me. I did so see Alvin's wife."

Alvin rolled over to hear what she had to say.

Just then Frances and his sister, Pearl, walked in.

"We were just talking about you," Alvin said, giving her a big grin.

"I was just telling your husband, *Alvin*, that I saw you downtown a couple days ago. I waved, remember?"

"I do, and actually you saw my sister-in-law here, too. This is Alvin's sister, Pearl," said Frances, making the introduction a general one to include Ruby, Leo and Oscar. Pearl walked carefully over to give Alvin a hug, and then took a seat on the far side of the bed. Her leg, which was never a reliable support, was giving her extra trouble today. Shy, partly because of the lurching walk that was forced upon her, she preferred to be out of the limelight, even at the risk of seeming a wall flower.

"So was this a momentous occasion or just a chance encounter?" said Alvin, bringing the conversation back to Ruby's meeting with Frances.

"I think you've already heard about it," Frances said. "The Eagles state convention was held on a Saturday, June 13, and we went down to watch Ida's drill team perform."

Alvin nodded, indicating he remembered, but Frances could see from the expressions on the faces of Leo and Oscar that they hadn't heard about the event.

"It was a pretty big day in town," she said. "Teams from Seattle, Tacoma, Bremerton, Everett and I forget where else, came to compete, both men's and women's teams."

"Roslyn and Wenatchee, too," Ruby chimed in. "I have friends from Roslyn that came down from the club there."

"That's right, and they were all very good, very precise. They performed on Alder Street between Fifth and Sixth Streets at nine in the morning," Pearl offered from the safety of her corner.

"They had a band competition on the courthouse lawn just after lunch," Frances added.

"We skipped that, but we saw the parade in the evening. It

went all the way from Palouse down Main Street to Fifth Street and then straight out to the fairgrounds," said Ruby.

"They had a wonderful pageant there, and fireworks that were *tremendous*," said Pearl, giving her brother a conspiratorial wink as she used one of his favorite words.

"Now that you mention it, I do remember the fireworks, hearing them at least," said Oscar.

"Yeah, damn things keepin' us awake," Leo grumbled.

He said it as if being free to go out into the spring night and watch fireworks, holding your best girl's hand, held no interest for him.

When Pearl and Frances had a quiet minute alone with Alvin, they told him the news they had come to deliver. Pearl was scheduled to have an operation on her leg. The doctors thought they could repair some of the damage done by tuberculosis in the bone.

"It's not as if my leg will ever be right again," said Pearl, "but I should be able to move about easier and that will give me a chance to go on to college when I finish high school. And I'm almost to that point now, you know. I'll graduate and then go to Spokane for the surgery in September."

Al looked at his youngest sister. Her golden brown hair was pulled softly back with a grosgrain ribbon tied in a large bow that lay flat against the nape of her neck. It framed a round face that was a satiny sheen of palest ivory and old rose, a face that truly reflected her name. She was a beautiful girl, with expressive, clear eyes that had laughter hidden in their depths.

To look at Pearlie was to be at peace, Al often thought.

He felt a strong sense of responsibility for Pearl, even greater than what he felt for his own wife and child. His Frances was a survivor. She was tough, and he knew she could manage most anything. He wasn't sure about this little sis of his. She was so young and had already had so much to bear. He knew she was his responsibility, but it was one that he was unable to shoulder.

Dear God, when was this nightmare going to end?

An hour into the visiting, Ruby announced her intention to "fly off," and, as Leo escorted her from the room, it was as if an exotic bird had taken flight. This time Alvin kept his eyes firmly on his own visitors, but he could hear Oscar breathing heavily and hoped Frances and Pearl wouldn't notice.

> *Sunday, June 21. It sure is hot.*
> *Pearl and Frances were out*
> *to see me. Frances brought*
> *me a Father's Day present.*
> *An outfit of shirt and shorts*
> *and socks. All white, sure sweet.*

"So far as anyone shuns evils, so far he does good." — *Swedenborg*

Chapter 59

Monday, June 22. Sure hope
I get well so I can wear my
new present. I showed it to
Flora and she said it was
lovely. I know it is.
I love my wife and baby.

Tuesday. It is evening.
"Death Chant Harry" is
in. I hope and pray to our
dear God that he will stay
out of here. I am about
crazy with him talking
about dying. Pray dear God
help to keep him out.

"Oh my gawd, look who just landed!" Leo said.

Alvin and Oscar looked to where Leo was pointing out the window. A flapping black raincoat was all they saw at first. The figure coming out of the early evening gloom was lost inside the voluminous folds of the coat that was being battered by the breeze. An equally floppy hat was pulled down low over the brow of what appeared to be a man. It was a sight all too familiar to Alvin and Leo, but new to Oscar.

"Who is that?" Oscar asked.

"You mean *what* is that." The sarcasm in Leo's voice spoke volumes.

"Oh no," Alvin said, with a groan.

"Oh, yes. Prepare ye self. It's *Death Chant Harry* in the flesh," said Leo.

"Now what does someone have to do to earn a moniker like that?" said Oscar.

"Just wait. You'll see," Leo warned.

Alvin turned his eyes away from the approaching figure. He dug his diary out of its drawer and slowly opened it. With a faraway look in his eyes, he selected a page, rubbed a thumb over it thoughtfully, and bowed his head to put pencil to paper.

Leo aimed a thumb in Al's direction, and gave Oscar a meaningful look accompanied by a jerk of his head. His look said that whatever was on the way in couldn't be any too good for any of them and, most especially, maybe not for Al.

"He takes it hard," Leo muttered under his breath.

Just then a raucous voice was raised down the hall by the entrance.

"Are ye saved, brethren? Have ye heard the word of the Lord? And hearing, do you heed that word?"

"Oh," said a subdued Oscar. "A fire and brimstoner."

"All the way," said Leo.

"Do they allow him to come in and shout like that?"

"It's not what you'd call 'allowed'. It's more like catching up with him and corralling him. Takes time. And, if he confines himself to preaching in the rooms, not the hallway, he can make pretty good headway in here before they get him rounded up," Leo explained. "But, like now, there's always some spillover we get to listen to. Old Harry Pratt ain't what you'd call a quiet sort by any means."

As if to prove Leo's point, another shout was heard.

"Sinners will be cut off from the land. Those who aren't faithful will be torn away! Proverbs. That's Proverbs, boys! Are you listening?"

"Who the hell can escape that screeching?" Leo grumbled.

"He who will not listen shall burn. Are there boys in this room ready to listen to the word of the Lord?"

The volume lowered a notch as he entered a room, but his words still carried enough power to reach them.

"What about those who have taken paths that are crooked?" the voice asked.

"What path are you boys on? What path have you taken? Are you on the straight and narrow or are you dancing down that

crooked path? What about those who have taken paths that are crooked?

"The Lord will drive them out I say. Along with those who do what is evil.

"Repent! Repent!"

Having met no resistance to his message, Harry moved on to the next room.

"I bring you a message from your master, young sirs. Will you open your ears to hear?"

"Bring it on!" a gruff voice called out, cracking with laughter.

"You may laugh now, sir, but there comes a day when tears will fall. Will you be found wanting before the judge?"

"Hey, Harry, I'll tell you what I'm wanting!" another voice shouted.

"I stop my ears against you, sinner. I will not watch you make sport of the Lord's word," he screeched. Evidently a patient's disrespect was accompanied by gestures.

Undeterred, the self-ordained preacher plunged on. *"Even though people are very rich, they don't live on and on..."*

"Here it comes," Al murmured.

"No. They are like animals. They die! No one can pray enough to live forever and not rot in the grave. Everyone can see that even wise people die. Foolish and dumb people also pass away. All of them leave their wealth to others. Their graves will remain their houses forever."

Al was pulling his pillow over his head as the next shout came.

"Their graves will be their homes for all time to come!

"That's in the Psalms, boys. You've got to believe it, if you read it in Psalms. Do you read the word of the Lord, boys? Turn your eyes to the good book and be saved."

Message delivered, footsteps echoing in the hall marked the progress of Death Chant Harry.

"Sounds like he's next door to Phil's room," said Oscar.

"Two more then before he gets to us. Flora will be sure to snag him before then," Leo predicted.

"Listen to the word, boys. Isaiah tells us when they go out of Jerusalem they will see the dead bodies of those who refused to obey. The worms that eat the bodies will not die. The fire that

burns them will not be put out. It will make everyone sick just to look at them!"

"It's makin' me sick just hearing about it. Where's Gillis when we need her?" Leo asked. "What's keeping Flora? Someone better come and shut that old man up."

Leo cast an anxious look toward Alvin.

That look led Oscar to believe that Leo's protests were not so much on his own behalf as they were for Alvin, who lay with head buried under not one, but two, pillows.

Pratt's next words were drowned out by an even angrier voice than Leo's.

"Get the hell out of my room, you old fart! And take your cockamamie messages with you. We don't need and we don't want your kind around here. Move it!"

Scarcely missing a beat, Pratt continued, *"The Lord will bring everyone into court. He will use fire and his sword to punish those he finds guilty. He will put many people to death. Are you guilty, brothers? Are you ready to go into court? Are you ready to meet your judge? Repent! Repent!"*

"He's on the move now," said Leo, as the voice grew stronger, obviously moving closer to their room.

"I believe he's right next door," Oscar whispered.

"Well, that S.O.B. ain't comin' in here!" Leo threw off his blanket and stomped to the door. He closed the door and shoved a chair under the knob.

"There. That oughta do it!"

"But suppose you don't obey the Lord your God and you aren't careful to follow all of his commands and rules I'm giving you today. Then, then, you sinners, then he will send curses to you..."

The voice came through the walls, muffled, but still distinct enough to make out the Old Testament warnings.

"...He will send all kinds of sicknesses on you. He will send them until he has destroyed you. The Lord will make you sick and very weak. He will strike you with fever. He'll send burning heat. The hot winds will completely dry up your crops.

"All of these things will happen until you die..." His voice broke off.

The ranting began again.

"You do well to shed tears, my son. Are those tears of sorrow or tears of repentance? Answer me, boy, the tears you are shedding may be the cleansing water you need to become pure!"

These last words took the grin off Leo's face.

"Now what in hell has he done?"

"Heed the words, brothers. Heed the words. Anyone who touches a dead person's body will be unclean for seven days. He must make himself pure and clean with special water. He must..."

"*You* must leave the premises, Sir!" Flora's stern warning interrupted Pratt's harangue that had brought tears streaming down Laurence's face.

"Sir, you must leave *now*. I insist. Our patients need their rest."

"Well, the Lone Ranger rides again! About time Flora got here," said Leo.

"Sister, have you heard the word of the Lord? And having heard it, do you heed it?

Flora's answer, if any, was swallowed by the walls.

"Is she going to be all right? Will he hurt her or does he go quietly?" Oscar asked.

"Death Chant Harry never does anything quietly, but he isn't the violent type. At least not up 'til now." Leo responded. "But let's see if she needs a hand."

He went over to the door, moved the chair away and poked his head out the door.

Flora's arm was hooked securely around an arm that was still trying to emphasize garbled comments with gestures that Flora wasn't allowing.

"She's got him in an arm lock and is marching him out," Leo announced.

"She's got the situation well in hand, looks like. By gosh, nobody fools with our Flora, or they're a darn fool, if they do!" Leo said.

They heard the front door clang open.

"Repent, you sinners! As clumps of dirt are left from plowing up the ground, so our bones will be scattered near an open grave!"

They heard the door bang shut.

"Damn fool's got to have the last word," said Leo.

The squeak of Flora's shoes sounded loud as she walked the corridor. They could hear her voice speaking softly as she paused at each door. She was a long time in the room Laurence shared with Phil. When she reached their door, she stepped inside and moved to stand between the three beds, which put her at the foot of Oscar's bed.

She knew Oscar had never been exposed to the ranting and raving of Harry Pratt before. She wanted to be sure he had come out of it unscathed. She knew Alvin's reaction to the doom and gloom the old man preached, and regretted she had been too slow to divert Pratt tonight. If there was one thing these men didn't need to be reminded of, it was sickness and death. Some, like Leo, seemed to take it in stride, even made jokes about it. But others found the unannounced visits from Pratt to be devastating. No matter how Pratt's diatribe was received, it was always disturbing, and that was something to be avoided in this place.

Flora decided to tune in a radio program as soon as she finished her rounds of the rooms. Maybe some soothing music before lights out.

She soon had Fred Astaire's *A Fine Romance* and Eddy Duchin's *Lights Out* serenading her 'boys'.

"Well, we're done with his shit for awhile," said Leo.

"I can do without it forever," replied Oscar.

"Amen to that, brothers," Alvin mumbled from under his pillow.

His last thought that night was of the wheat wilting in the fields of Walla Walla.

Chapter 60

Complete bed rest robbed Alvin of taking up his favorite post on visiting day. No longer could he lounge at the window and watch for his wife to tootle up the drive. He could still catch a glimpse of her arrival, but the full sweep of the drive and part of the Dalles-Military Road were no longer his to enjoy.

On this Wednesday afternoon, the window still had his attention. So much so that he did not even notice Flora come in and hold a quiet conference at Leo's bedside. When she left, Leo climbed out of bed and started gathering clothes out of the closet. That Alvin did notice.

"What's up?" he asked.

"Trouble at home," Leo said curtly. "Gotta go home."

It was the last word he and Oscar had out of Leo. Their unasked questions went unanswered, and soon Frances' presence drove them out of Al's mind. He had something else to take their place.

"Frances, there's something I want you to do for me, and, before I ask, I want your promise that you will do it."

"A promise without knowing what it is? That's a tall order, isn't it?" she asked with a grin.

"I know you too well, little pal, so I want the promise beforehand."

"Oh, all right. Whatever it is, I promise, but you be fair and don't ask something I can't deliver!"

That put a thought into Al's head that made him grin and cock his eyebrow in a way that put a blush on Frances' face.

"Nothing like that, I promise," he whispered to her. "No, what I have in mind is a new hair-do. I was really taken with that wavy look Lily had done at the beauty school, and it would please me mightily if you would get yours marcelled too. It's about time you do a little something for yourself," Al said, adding, "And buy a new dress."

"A new dress! What do you think I have on? This dress is brand new, and I was just waiting for you to notice it. Mom sewed it up for me right after she finished making the centennial dresses. It's my favorite color, pink."

It was pink. It was also another cotton house dress made in the same open collar, straight skirt, button-down-the-front style Frances favored. And no wonder. Ida had one pattern and, with her expertise, she adjusted it to fit whichever woman in the family needed a new dress. Colors and prints did vary, of course, and this new model was pink. A pretty petal pink. Frances' favorite color, Al reminded himself, so tread lightly.

"Isn't it all right?" she asked, her insecurity showing.

She was standing in front of the window where Ruby had stood to show off her custom-made finery. The sun was streaming in behind Frances. It backlit her, just as it had Ruby, and turned her hair golden, but the opaque threads of the sturdy cotton dress defied even a lone ray to shine through. Frances was an impenetrable silhouette. A silhouette awaiting an answer.

Alvin and Oscar both looked at her there, sunlight streaming around her.

"It's a humdinger," said Alvin.

"Thank the Lord," said Oscar, drawing a puzzled look from Frances.

> *Wednesday, June 24. One of the*
> *patients left today, Leo Pritchard.*
> *Trouble at home. Thank God*
> *I have a good true wife.*
> *Frances was out and am*
> *waiting for her now. She*
> *would come if she had*
> *to crawl. Bless her heart.*
> *God have mercy on her.*

Chapter 61

Friday, June 26. We had sausage
for breakfast this morn. I am a
darn good Catholic, I ate some.
Before I thought. I thought about
it about an hour after breakfast.
I am heartily sorry. Honest.

Oscar was the first to see the shiny, gray-blue car float up to the entrance like an iridescent bubble atop an ocean wave. Or, perhaps, with all those curvy lines, like the wave itself. Whichever, it was some car.

"Lay your peepers on that, Potts," Oscar invited, waving at the sight just beyond their window.

Alvin was surprised to see the Hudson Straight Eight he had come to associate with Ruby.

It was only the second day since Leo had left them to go home to Dayton, to straighten out whatever trouble existed there, he supposed. Now here was this new development. Did Ruby not know that Leo had left? And, if she thought he was still here, would she really be so bold as to bring her ride right up to the door?

As Oscar and Alvin watched, the front door of the Hudson swung open.

A tall man, impeccably dressed in sharply creased trousers, shirt, tie and sweater, stepped out. *That's sure no farmer.* He moved with languid grace to the back door. His posture was attentive as he opened the door.

Alvin was surprised to see Leo step out.

"Now who do you suppose that is bringing Leo back?" Oscar asked.

Leo bent over to peer into the back seat of the vehicle. He stretched out a hand, but no one reached out to take it. He waved his fingers forward in a coaxing gesture. Still no takers. Leo's head and shoulders disappeared into the car, only his legs and upturned rump visible. He withdrew and made the coaxing motion with his hand again. Nothing.

"What's he got in there that don't want to come out?" Oscar asked.

Alvin had no answer for him, but he thought of the image Ruby had made with her flounces fluttering around her and the thought that had come into his head at the time...*like the fluffy seeds of a dandelion flying away after the blossom had died.*

The man holding the Hudson's door open put his hand on Leo's shoulder and gave him a gentle nudge away from the car. Displaced, Leo hung back, watching as the man took his place in the doorway and bent to look in. After a minute, the man straightened, hiked the legs of his trousers up with a pinch of fingers at each crease, and squatted down beside the car. He kept his attention directed inside the car and leaned closer, apparently deep in conversation.

"Now the other fella's taking a turn. Looks like he's talking up a storm," said Oscar.

"But it's doing no good either," Oscar noted, as the man withdrew.

The man went back to his position on door duty.

He tapped a foot against the pavement, staring off into space.

Leo stepped forward, climbed into the back seat, and pulled the door closed behind him.

"Pow wow time," said Oscar. "Leo's bringing out the heavy artillery."

"There's a bag of mixed metaphors for you," said Alvin.

"Well, you know what I mean. Something's going on out there and Leo's right smack dab in the middle of it. Can't help but wonder," said Oscar.

The door stayed closed for a long time. With each passing minute, the driver's foot tapped a little faster on the pavement until he had a nice drum roll going.

When the car door did open, it swung open abruptly and caught the tall man on his butt.

He swung around and looked ready to take offense, but Leo paid him no attention. He reached into the back seat, and this time his proffered hand came out holding a hand. Leo drew it toward him slowly, reached out and wrapped his other hand around an arm hidden inside a violet sleeve and carefully half pulled, half lifted Ruby out of the car.

"Well, I'll be damned!" Oscar exclaimed. "It's his wife."

Her feet on the ground, Ruby sagged and half leaned into Leo, her face pressed against his chest. He patted her back, and seemed to be whispering into her hair. Her head wagged back and forth, slowly at first, then faster as she began to beat on Leo's chest with her clenched fists. She lifted her head, tilted her face upward and howled at the sky.

"My gawd, it sounds like a wild animal," said Oscar.

"I'm afraid that's just what she's about to become, one of the animals," said Alvin.

He wanted to turn away, but the scene had him riveted.

Leo had his hands full as he clutched Ruby to his chest and tried to still her flailing hands. The tall man stepped around them in a sudden burst of energy. He drew a small bag out of the car and set it on the pavement. The Hudson's door slammed shut with a solid thunk.

That's how you can tell an expensive, well-made car from a rattletrap.

Alvin's thought was apropos of nothing that was playing itself out before them, but he just could not help admiring a good car.

It looked now as if the driver wanted to dodge the drama and get on the road. He was shifting from foot to foot. He grabbed up the bag, tried to thrust it into Leo's hand where it rested on Ruby's back, finally carried it to the entrance and set it down. He returned to the car, patted Leo on the back and winked at Ruby over Leo's shoulder before he climbed into the Hudson's front seat. Almost apologetically he pulled the door quietly shut.

"And away he goes," said Alvin. He listened to the luxury car's purr fade until it was only a throb in the distance.

Leo and Ruby were left standing alone in front of the sanatorium.

Now she was just a limp bundle of violet silk in Leo's arms, red hair straggling down her back. They saw Leo lift her away from him, kiss her cheek, and give her shoulders a little shake. He said something to her that they couldn't hear. Tears were streaming down her face as she turned from him, but Ruby bent down, picked up the bag and let Leo lead her through the entrance.

Alvin and Oscar waited in silence to see if Leo would return to their room. It was a good hour before he did, and it was a changed man that walked through the door.

At fifty, Leo laid no claim to looking young, but there had been a vibrancy about him that Alvin felt transcended the age difference between him and the twenty-eight-year-old Ruby. Today, Leo's age was spelled out in slumped shoulders and deep wrinkles across his brow, wrinkles that Alvin could not recall seeing on his face before. A snowstorm seemed to have fallen on the black hair that, before Leo's trip home, had only been frosted with white.

No one would have any trouble now believing Leo was Ruby's father. Even grandfather wouldn't be a push. *He looks empty and rumpled, like a paper bag filled with air and then popped.*

In unspoken agreement, Alvin and Oscar waited in silence for Leo to speak.

Leo slumped in the arm chair, chin on his chest. Alvin lay propped on his pillows. Oscar sat on the side of his bed. There was no awkwardness in the room. The silence seemed to be an armor donned, and shared, by all three. When Leo did speak, his voice was that of a creaky hinge.

"I tell you, boys, be careful what you wish for. How you get it may not be to your liking. And that's all I'm going to say on the subject."

> *It is hot as the dickens*
> *and I feel pretty tough.*
> *Leo came back. He*
> *brought his wife with*
> *him. She is a patient*
> *now. Nothing exciting*
> *to tell about. Sure hope*
> *Baby is better. Al.*

Frances Potts

"O, beloved Pan, and all ye other gods of this place, grant me to become beautiful in the inner man."—Socrates

Chapter 62

In spite of Alvin's wishes, written almost as an after thought in his diary on Friday, his baby was not better. In fact, she was a great deal worse, and Frances was getting worried. The child was fretful, cranky and down right ornery, all behavior that Frances was loathe to admit about her two-year-old. But it could not be ignored. Frances Pearl was not herself.

Frances had kept the baby home on recent visiting days because of the change in her personality; an irritable child had no business being in the san. Now it was more than irritability that curtailed the visits. Frances Pearl was running a fever. No matter how hard Frances shook down the thermometer, once it was placed under the baby's armpit the mercury slid rapidly into what was becoming the danger zone.

She decided to bundle her up in the buggy and take her to Dr. Campbell's office. Like most doctors, he held Saturday office hours, at least until noon, or would make a house call, if summoned. Since there was no phone in the house, it was as easy to stroll Frances Pearl to his office as it was to walk to Ida's to place a call. If Murray were home, his Ford could cover the distance faster, but he was at Lutcher's playing pool with Will. Frances hadn't decided a doctor's visit was necessary until the boys had left. It was certainly warm enough to take even a sick child out, so Frances didn't hesitate, but did throw a light blanket over Frances Pearl, just in case.

Dr. Campbell's office was near St. Mary's Hospital and the church, all within easy walking distance. Nothing like the tramp she had to make out to the Blue Mountain. Frances was pleased to see an almost empty waiting room. There was nothing worse than sitting in a crowd when you had a fussy child on your hands. She was sure the handful of people waiting would also be thankful to have limited exposure to Frances Pearl's whimpering. No amount of shushing helped, and the little body in her arms grew increasingly warmer as they waited.

"What have we here?" Dr. Campbell asked when Frances was finally escorted into his examining room.

"A fussy baby and a fever that's making me nervous!" Frances said.

"Well, let's take a look."

He swung Frances Pearl out of her mother's arms and perched her on the edge of the table. He pushed aside the bib of the child's overalls and unbuttoned her blouse far enough to allow him to place his stethoscope on the little chest. He tipped his head, covered with a thick shock of white hair, to one side, and listened. He moved the stethoscope to her back. Listened.

"Good. Good. Sounds good."

His huge hands moved surely, but gently, over Frances Pearl's neck. She whined and swatted away his hands. The Doctor ignored her, pried open her mouth, and shone a light down her throat while he held her tongue down with a wooden depressor.

That invasion brought squalls of rage, which he also ignored.

He turned to Frances and said, "We've got something going on here, but I'm not just sure what it is. Time will tell, though. Time will tell.

"You take her home. Put hot packs on her neck, morning, noon and night. I say hot packs, but not too hot! Make her drink lots of water. You can put her in a soda bath to keep that temperature under control, as many times a day as it takes. You just take her home. Keep her as comfortable as possible and bring her back to me on Tuesday. Call me before, if she gets worse. Any time, day or night, you hear?"

"Yes. Thank you, Doctor. And I am so sorry she misbehaved. Usually she is so good, but lately…"

"It's understandable. The little lady isn't feeling well. Just give her what she wants until we get this straightened out. Ice chips and ice cream might be just the thing for her."

Ice Frances knew she could manage. By the time she walked ice cream home from the nearest store to the house, it would be soup. She would check the piggy bank when she got home to see if she could scrape up fifteen cents for a pint of Duff's ice cream.

Shc would send Murray and Will after it when they came home. If they had been lucky at pool, there might even be enough for a quart.

She hoped they wouldn't hang out downtown too long. She was sure the romantic comedy with Jack Oakie and Frances Langford at the Liberty wouldn't tempt them to spend any of their winnings, but *Stormy* with Noah Beery Jr. and Jean Rogers at the Roxy might be another thing all together. It was advertised to be an outdoor drama, and, if there was anything those two liked more than the outdoors, Frances didn't know what it was. Well, maybe Lutcher's with its card games and pool tables…and beer. Then, being Saturday night, the farm crews would be in town. Will and Murray were sure to know some of the men whose bosses would drop them off on lower Main to take in the sights. Frances remembered when Alvin would leave his car at the ranch and be dropped off by Mr. Kent on a Saturday, along with the rest of the crew, to spend the day and overnight in town.

Yes, it might be awhile before the boys returned.

> *Saturday, June 27. This day is termed*
> *as Farmers Day in town. Sure*
> *hope to be able to spend*
> *a few more days in town.*
> *I don't seem to be ready*
> *to leave this world yet.*
> *Alvin, Ezra, Peter, Patrick Potts.*
>
> *Sunday. My darling wife was*
> *here to see me. My sisters*
> *Lily and Pearl were out also.*
> *Sure had a fine time. Frances*
> *will be out again tonight.*

Chapter 63

Tuesday, June 30. Am looking
forward to the coming day.
Visiting day and my dear
wife. We have a real sick
man next door. His folks
are staying with him tonight.

Ward One was unnaturally quiet. Every footstep in the hall
echoed off the walls and spiraled down to the ears of men tuned to
hear the slightest variance in routine. Every cough, every throat
that was cleared, every raised voice were processed for hidden
meanings. A door that opened or closed could cause consternation.

It was always this way when a patient was isolated. Either the
seriously ill patient was quietly rolled away to a room by himself
or his roommate was removed to provide the isolation. Isolation
was never good news. Too often isolation was a death knell.

A bed had been rolled out of the room next to the one
occupied by Alvin, Oscar and Leo almost at the crack of dawn.
The noise of the bed on the move woke Leo and Oscar. Alvin had
awakened when Gillis and Flora had first entered the room next
door.

The three of them listened to the bed being rolled away.

They exchanged gloomy looks but no words. Was it Phil or
Laurence being moved?

They listened intently for a clue. They heard Gillis
murmuring, but it was only a murmur. No words of enlightenment.

The squeaky wheels on the bed so early in the morning,
accompanied by the unmistakable click of Gillis' white nursing
shoes, were the first alert for the Grapevine. The word went out
quickly that something was up, then the silence settled in like a

pall over the entire ward.

Phil had gone along with the established routine, riding his bed to his new quarters, but he wasn't about to stay there. He waited for the chance to dodge Flora and Gillis so he could make his way back down the corridor. As stealthy as he was, waiting ears caught the soft slap of his slippers.

"Sounds like Phil," Oscar whispered.

The footsteps of the bearer of sports news were familiar to everyone along the hall. A kind of slap and glide, slap and glide, as if his carpet slippers were too large and threatening to fall from his feet.

They heard the steps pause just beyond their room.

Phil stood for a minute, ear pressed against the closed door. He heard both Gillis and Flora inside. "Time to call," he thought he heard Gillis say.

He shuffled past, as quietly as he could, and slipped into his neighbors' room. He recognized the unspoken question on their faces.

"This time the bell's tolling for Laurence," Phil said in a low voice.

The death knell, delivered in an uncharacteristic formal tone.

"That bastard!" Leo blurted in a gruff whisper.

Not one of the three who heard Leo's shocking judgment was in doubt about whom he was speaking. They all remembered Laurence's reaction to Death Chant Harry's tirade at his bedside a week ago.

"Yeah, the old guy got to him," Phil acknowledged. "He wasn't doing so well then, spitting up a little blood that was scaring him, too. It's down to the wire now. I think they're sending for his mom and dad."

Phil sidled to the door, took a cautious peek around it, and slipped away to carry his grim message to other waiting ears.

"Two peas in a pod, those two," said Oscar.

"Whatcha mean?" asked Leo.

"Phil and Laurence, as alike as two peas in a pod, don't you think?" Oscar replied.

Alvin thought about the 'better boys' next door, both with their brown hair slicked back flat to their heads without a part or a wave, both about the same age, both slim and tall, both wearers of

rimless spectacles, both burdened with this contagious disease.
Yes, two peas in a pod.
"Yes, they are very alike. Good boys, both of them," said Al.
"Damn good boys," agreed Leo.
"Two peas in a pod," said Oscar.
Breakfast was a solemn affair. They ate their oatmeal and toast
in silence, kept one eye on the driveway. They expected to see
Laurence's parents arrive at any time. The   silence from the next
room was broken now and then by a rasping cough. To a man,
they winced each time they heard it.
The silence among them today was uncomfortable.
Alvin was relieved when Leo tuned in his radio. At first, he
kept the volume so low only he could hear, but Oscar asked Leo to
turn it up. After first glancing at Alvin to see if he approved and
getting a nod, Leo adjusted it. If they weren't listening, at least
they could pretend to be. It saved them from trying to find words
when there were no words appropriate for this day of waiting.
And that's what they and the entire ward were doing. Waiting.
Today was a bath day, but only for those allowed to be out of
bed. That excluded Alvin, but Leo and Oscar made the trip to the
shower room. While they were gone, Laurence's parents arrived.
Their Ford touring car caught Alvin's eye while he was
writing in his diary. It pulled into the space nearest the entrance.
Alvin slipped out of bed and moved to a chair by the open
window. He wrapped the thin cotton of his blue and white striped
hospital robe around him, a slight shield against the breeze that
still held the morning's chill. He watched a gray-haired man alight
from the car. His erect bearing and slim frame were an older
version of the young man who lay next door. Laurence's mother
stepped out of the car. She stumbled, and her husband caught her
by the arm, providing quick support. They stood together for just a
moment, he holding her arm, she braced against his hold. Then
they parted. She smoothed down the skirt of her calf-length dress
of gray stuff. From the pocket of her matching sweater, she
produced a handkerchief, and brought it to her eyes, patting
gently.
*Lose that, little mother. Tears are only going to make it harder
for him.*
As if she heard the words that were only in Alvin's head,

Laurence's mother straightened her back and stuffed her hanky back in her pocket with a determined thrust.

Hand in hand, Laurence's parents entered the sanatorium.

Alvin heard Gillis greeting them at the door. She, too, must have been watching and waiting. The footsteps of the little group moved closer. Gillis spoke in quiet tones that Alvin thought conveyed skillful competency, as if the nurse knew words of sympathy might be the undoing of the couple she was escorting to what would be their son's death bed.

Wise woman.

Alvin crept back into bed before his transgression could be found out. He promised himself he would spend the rest of the day flat on his back to make up for the time-out.

Leo and Oscar returned, and were given the news of the parents' arrival.

"Taking up the watch," Leo noted quietly.

Leo hadn't had much to say since he brought Ruby into the san four days ago. His usual jokes, which sometimes fell flat with Oscar and Alvin, had not even arisen for their consideration. He had spent a lot of time tuned in to the radio and tuned out to his roommates. Alvin could just imagine what Leo was going through. He knew how he would feel if Frances or the baby contracted the disease. Having his sis in here was bad enough. He planned to have Frances carry a message to Alta, asking her to check on Ruby from time to time, for Leo's sake. It looked as if Leo's wife had taken her admittance hard. Maybe Frances could even take messages back and forth for Leo. Alvin decided he would ask her if she was up to the task when she visited him tomorrow.

Lunch, the largest meal of the day, was a welcome distraction. Oscar scared up a little conversation over the meatloaf until they saw Laurence's father pacing in the hall.

He glanced in the door at the trio, nodded curtly and went back to his pacing.

"Probably got no smokes," Leo remarked.

"Maybc he isn't a smoker," Oscar said.

"If not, this would be a good time to start," Leo retorted.

"How do you think Landon and Knox are going to do against FDR?" Alvin asked.

"Now, that's a question comin' at us out of left field," Leo said.

"Just thinking," said Al. "It's been a couple weeks since the Republican Convention, and I haven't heard much about those two. Politics, that's where Laurence shines. I value his opinion."

"All I know about the Republican ticket is that Frank Knox is a colonel sixty-two years old and Alf Landon is a governor," said Oscar.

"Governor of Kansas, and Knox is that newspaper publisher," Leo chimed in. "New Hampshire and Illinois, I hear."

"They got the nomination by unanimous declaration," said Alvin, "but I doubt they can upset Roosevelt. He's pretty well entrenched, I think."

"Depends. Depends what kind of platform the Republicans come up with," said Oscar.

"There is that, and I'd just like to know more about those two," said Alvin.

"Well, don't depend on our neighbor to fill you in," Leo said, and then shut his eyes, cupped his hand over his mouth, and rubbed his jaw. The rasp of his whiskers against his kneading fingers was loud in the room.

Oscar and Alvin ignored Leo's careless words and his obvious embarrassment over them. They had no illusions about Laurence's chances, but preferred them unspoken.

"Dad-blamed politicians anyway," Leo grumped.

His comment put paid to Alvin's aborted attempt to divert attention from the slow progression next door. With that conversational gambit closed as final as an overdue bill stamped with a last payment, each man settled down to his own devices.

Alvin chose to read. He still hadn't completed *The Last Light*, which he had started the first of the month. Not much left to go, but he had neglected it on the advice of Gillis, who warned him about the strain holding a book could have on his lungs. Today he would make an exception. Oscar chose to nap. Leo sank back into his pillows with the radio now tuned just for his ears.

It was after a dinner of potato soup and mystery meat sandwiches that Phil poked his head in the door to ask, "What do you hear from next door?"

"We were counting on you for the answer to that," Leo said.

"All I know is, his parents are here, and they're spending the night. His mother seems to be taking it better than his dad. Dad's been walking the halls," said Phil.

"Seen that," said Leo.

"Flora let drop that Laurence is fading, but still talking. I asked if I could go in one more time, but she said better not," Phil added.

"She's right. Better not. It's family time," said Oscar.

"Well, Phil's one of them peas in the pod. Should be able to go in and say goodbye, if he wants to," snarled Leo.

"I'm a what?" asked Phil.

"Never mind. Just go in, if you want to. You gotta right," Leo advised.

"No...I think I'll listen to Flora. I'm not so good at goodbyes, anyway. Best this way, like she said. But this waiting...gets to a man!" Phil turned abruptly and left.

The gloom was thick enough to cut with a knife.

"To hell with this!" Leo exploded. He jumped out of bed, threw on his robe and careened out of the room.

"Probably out of smokes," Oscar said, with a weak laugh.

Leo did not come back to the room until the lights dimmed, and patients were bedded down for the night. When Flora made her rounds, she had not even asked where he was. *Good thing since we didn't know.* Alvin figured Flora and Gillis were making a few allowances this evening, maybe more for the near neighbors of Laurence, who could not be kept completely unaware of what was transpiring on the other side of the wall.

It wasn't long until Leo's snores were ricocheting around the room. Oscar, a much quieter sleeper, finally followed suit. Alvin lay in bed, tense, eyes wide open.

Wednesday, July 1. 2:30 o'clock this morning marked the death of one of the patients. Laurence Tilton aged 27 years. Marshall, Calloway and Hennessey local "funeral home" owners and operators took the body away at approximately 4:32.

Frances Potts

It is now 5:00 o'clock.

"For he who much has suffer'd, much will know."—Homer

Chapter 64

Frances did not go to the san Wednesday afternoon to visit Alvin. Instead she was dripping chloroform onto a mask over Frances Pearl's face while Dr. Campbell worked with a lancet on her neck.

Their Tuesday appointment had resulted in this surgical procedure in the doctor's office after he diagnosed the child's problem as an abscess. Frances was surprised, and not too pleased, when she arrived at his office to find herself enlisted as his assistant.

"I'll open her up and we'll let the abscess drain," the doctor explained shortly.

His instructions were just as concise and brief.

"Put these on," he said, handing her a pair of rubber gloves.

Frances rolled the gloves on, smoothing each limp finger down around each of her own, following the doctor's example.

"Hold this," he instructed.

Frances cautiously took the chloroform bottle he handed her.

He placed a sterile drape over Frances Pearl, leaving the left side of her neck exposed.

Frances looked down at her lethargic child, lying still as she had been told to do.

"You're just going to go sleepy-bye for a little while. Mother Dear will be right here," Frances said.

"Drip it slowly onto this," said Dr. Campbell, settling a mask over the child's face.

Frances pressed a gloved finger over the mouth of the bottle and shook loose a drop to fall onto the mask, then another, and another. She watched Frances Pearl's eyes close sleepily as the sweet fumes rose above her.

She did not want to watch as the lancet sliced into the soft, swollen, little neck that was such an angry red. Still, her eyes could not escape the thin line of blood that followed in the path of doctor's instrument. It was as if they were drawn to the sight. She was surprised at how little blood there was. Dr. Campbell mopped it away with only a small pad of gauze.

The lancet was laid aside. Dr. Campbell grasped a pair of scissors with strange curved ends instead of points. When he inserted the blades into the wound he had made, Frances gasped. Ignoring her, he spread the lips of the incision aside, and pus gushed out in a thick, yellow stream.

"Oh, I feel woozy," said Frances. Her face, if she could have seen it, was the color of the gray modeling clay she had recently bought to entertain the baby.

"Well, lie down on the floor. I don't have time for you," snapped the doctor.

She sank to the floor without another word. Her ears filled with a noise as of rushing water, and her world turned gray, then black.

Dr. Campbell continued to work on Frances Pearl above her mother's unconscious form. His fingers flew, gauze pressed into service to force the abscess to expel its poison. He caught some of the drainage in a vial and set it aside.

Frances first became aware of the bright light overhead, then the cold linoleum on which she was lying, as consciousness slipped back. She took silent stock of herself. *Not dizzy now. Just don't think about what is going on up there. Just lie still here where it is cool.*

Dr. Campbell did not give her that choice.

"Are you all right?" he asked.

"I think so," was Frances' weak answer.

"Well, then, come back up here and help me!"

She got unsteadily to her feet, and took the chloroform bottle he offered her.

He was still coaxing matter from the wound, and then, to Frances' horror, he began to stuff a length of gauze into the now clean, but gaping, hole in Frances Pearl's neck. He used the scissors to tamp in length after length of the gauze. Surely no more could fit into that little neck, but still he pressed in more material.

Finally, he fitted several thick pads over the top of the incision and taped it into place.

"There! We got through that all right," said Dr. Campbell.

He explained that the vial of putrid matter he had taken from the child's neck would be analyzed for the presence of tuberculosis.

"And you must bring her back every day or so, and we'll extract that gauze stuffing inch by inch as it absorbs more drainage. When it is completely drained, I can stitch it up," he further explained.

When Frances Pearl began to stir, the doctor helped Frances carry her out to the Ford she had borrowed from Murray. They settled her on the back seat, where she drifted back to sleep.

"She must be kept quiet. No running, no crying. Keep the operation site clean and dry. We don't want it to get bumped. Baby her, if you have to, until we're over this, but keep her quiet," Dr. Campbell advised.

It was evening before Frances left the child's side. Ida came in to take over for her so Frances could visit Alvin. It was good to have her mother to talk to, to describe the unexpected role she had played today in her child's care.

"Didn't think I'd ever be doing something like that," Frances concluded.

"We can do a lot of things we don't think we ever could, if we have to," Ida said.

One of the things Frances knew she was going to have to do now was keep this from Alvin. That might just be more difficult than the ordeal she had gone through in Dr. Campbell's office.

Oh, she would tell Alvin about the operation, just not her part in it. Definitely she would not tell him of the tuberculosis testing, not until the results were in anyway.

The threat of TB seemed to always be hanging over the family in some form or another, but Frances knew they weren't alone. The beds that were never vacant at the sanatorium were proof of that, although the number of contagious diseases in the county continued to drop. Frances knew the health department had reported one hundred fifty-seven cases of TB in the county last year, with only one case of the dreaded smallpox. Measles were still a common disease. More than 400 cases last year, Frances recalled. *Measles, I think, we'll always have with us.*

She yearned for the day when illness or the threat of it was not always uppermost in her mind. Frances had no idea of the bad news that awaited her that evening.

Alvin told her of Laurence's passing in a few brief words.

Frances had known Laurence only slightly, but, looking at Al's somber face as he told her, Frances ached for all those touched by the young man's death. That included her own husband, whose face spoke more than the few words he offered.

She had come to intimately know this man of hers in the short time they had been together, and now, in addition to sorrow, she saw a new awareness etched on Al's face.

One could not live with virulent poison inside one and not have misgivings, but, when the Grim Reaper walked in the door and stopped so near to one's own bed, it was often the chill grip of fear he left behind. It was this fear Frances saw on Alvin's face, and she did not know how to deal with it. Speaking of it might be the wrong thing to do. Ignoring it seemed cold and uncaring. She settled for stroking his hand, and hoped he would understand.

When Alvin told her he was concerned about Leo's wife, and would like Frances to visit Alta and ask her to do a little 'mother-henning,' Frances was happy that she could do something to please him. "But I won't be gone long," she said as she hurried away.

Alta produced a bright smile when she saw her sister-in-law. Alta was obviously her usual happy self, in spite of treatment in which one of her lungs had been collapsed to allow it to rest. She told Frances she had undergone artificial pneumothorax.

"And isn't that a mouthful!" said Alta, explaining that she was glad to have escaped the more invasive thoracoplasty in which a portion of the ribs would have been removed to permanently collapse a lung.

"In my treatment they introduced air into the pleural cavity under enough pressure to collape the diseased lung."

"What effect does that have?" Frances asked.

"The tissue in that lung ceases to expand and contract with my every breath. It's an odd sensation," said Alta.

She told Frances that the procedure involved tubing attached to a complicated, glass apparatus that supplied the air pressure.

"They inserted the tube right into an incision in my side," she said, pulling aside her hospital gown to show Frances.

"They say it's just like splinting a broken leg," said Alta, grinning.

"Sounds like an understatement to me," said Frances.

Frances got around to Alvin's request by relating the story Alvin had told her about the day Ruby was admitted. "Very frightened she was, is what Alvin said."

"I'd say so!" said Alta. "We could hear her all over the place when they brought her in. I believe it was last Friday, Thursday or Friday. They put her in with little Susie McCloud. Susie is a quiet sort, but a good listener. Any newcomer would be in good company, if they draw Susie. So, why does little brother want me to be Ruby's mother hen? Why does he think she needs one?"

"Al says that Leo sort of adopted her when she was just a kid, married her and then took care of her right up until he had to come in here. He is a lot older than she is, and he's worried about her, and Al is worried about Leo, so he hoped you could make her stay here more tolerable. I don't think Alvin knows that you are on complete bed rest like he is," said Frances.

"I would be glad to help out, but, as you see, I am tied up at the moment," Alta said with a teasing smile. "I'm sure your Ruby isn't walking around yet either. Usually the new ones aren't allowed to be up and around for awhile."

"Well, then, there isn't much that you can do for her."

"Oh, sister, I wouldn't say that. I have some fashion magazines that have been passed around here. From what I hear of our newest patient, they might offer a pleasing distraction. Why don't you carry them to her on your way back. Hers is the second door on your right as you leave here."

"All right. I will stop to see her, but, before I go, I want to ask you something. Why do you think it is that Alvin isn't getting the kind of treatment you had, if it helps to heal?"

"I don't have the answer to that, but the doctor here told me treatment can be different for different patients. He said the rest cure is often enough, but sometimes surgical treatments are advised. The way I understand it is that we come in, get a lot of rest and go home cured. Maybe Al will even go home before me!" said Alta.

"I'd be grateful if you both walk out the door at the same time," said Frances.

Frances took up the magazines Alta indicated. They pressed cheeks in their usual farewell gesture. "Be sure to tell that brother of mine I said hello," said Alta. "But let's not tell him about this," she added, touching her side.

Alta's secret to keep from Al.

As soon as she walked into Ruby's room, Frances thought she could guess some of what Alta had been hearing about this new patient in the women's wing.

Ruby was sitting amid a puff of pink feathers, polishing her fingernails. The feathers adorned an elaborate, lavender, satin bed jacket tied at the neck with a huge pink and white bow.

"You look about ready to fly out of here," Frances said before she thought.

"You can say that again, kiddo! Would if I could, would if I could!" Ruby responded.

"My sister, well Alvin's sister, sent you these magazines. She's a patient, just down the hall from you. She thought you might like them."

Ruby glanced at them, at first without much interest. Then she saw their subject matter and flipped through them excitedly.

"Gosh yes! These are keen. All my favorites, too. Aren't you just the fairy godmother tonight!"

"My sister...Alvin's sister, Alta. She sent them to you. She would come in to see you, but she's confined to bed."

"Me, too. It's a lotta crap. I could get out of this bed just as easy as lyin' here. Easier, in fact. This eating and sleeping in bed doesn't make for anything but crumbs and wrinkles. I'm gonna look like a prune before I get out of here!"

Frances laughed.

Ruby looked affronted. Then, seeing that Frances wasn't laughing at her, she joined in. "Pruney, wait and see!" she added, giggling.

"Are you headed down to see your husband?" Ruby asked.

"I am."

"Well, tell my old man...tell Daddy I said howdy-do and I miss him, will you?"

"I can do that. I know he misses you, too. If you want to write him a little note, I could come get it on Sunday and deliver it to him for you," Frances offered.

"May do, may do just that," said Ruby. She already had her nose buried in a magazine.

"Oh Ruby, your bed jacket really is elegant, and you look swell in it," Frances said, pausing on the threshold.

"A present…from an admirer," Ruby admitted with a wink. "But keep that to yourself, OK kiddo?"

Another secret.

When Frances finally told Alvin that Frances Pearl had been operated on that very day, his easy, almost casual, acceptance did not bother her as it would have before she had the talk with Nita. Now she could more easily understand how the reality of everyday life outside the san did not always penetrate the self absorption of institutionalized patients. Still, she did not mention to him the test for TB.

And that's my secret.

When Frances got home that evening, Ida asked how things had gone.

"I feel like our electrical box when it blows a fuse—overloaded!"

"Don't give up yet, little girl," Ida advised, giving her a quick hug.

Ida had no more than left when Frances heard whimpers of discomfort from the bedroom. Remembering Dr. Campbell's words of caution, she went in, scooped up Frances Pearl, along with all her blankets, and settled into the rocking chair pulled up next to the crib. Soon the squeak of the rocker contended with the sing-song of Frances' voice as she attempted to lull the child: *"Bye Baby Bunting, daddy's gone a hunting, to find a little rabbit skin to wrap his Baby Bunting in…"*

Chapter 65

*Thursday, July 2. It sure was
hot today. It has cooled off
and is a little better now.
Frances was out for a while
last evening. Baby had to be
operated on. Sure hope she
is better.   Daddy.*

Alvin's conscience was pricking him like a sharp thorn. With all this time on his hands, thoughts rotated through his mind like a gilded steed on a merry-go-round. Over and over, the same thoughts, and now this prick, prick, prick.

Every time he thought about how he had jumped to a hasty conclusion, a wrong one as it turned out, when Leo was called to Dayton to deal with trouble at home, he flushed hot with embarrassment. *Why do I have to be so quick to latch onto a negative? Damned if I know.*

Alvin had thought for sure that Ruby's flirtatious ways had come home to roost in a way that had sullied her nest. He could not have been more wrong. *Oh, Lord, was I ever wrong!* For a minute, he had even fretted that Murray might be involved until Frances assured him that whatever fire there had been had gone out. *Thank God for that.*

Alvin had been beating himself up about his mistake, *unspoken thank the Lord*, ever since Leo returned with Ruby as a patient. He had read and re-read the meditation for that day. Friday, July 26. He wouldn't soon forget that date. It was Socrates who was quoted: *"O, beloved Pan, and all ye other gods of this place, grant me to become beautiful in the inner man."*

Well he wasn't feeling very beautiful inside. It did not matter that only he knew what a twisted turn his mind had taken as soon as Leo said "trouble at home." That he had thought badly of Ruby at all ate at him. And how arrogant he had been to pat himself on the back for having a faithful wife. *Not to say that isn't so. It is. Frances is the most faithful, most loyal mate a man could have, but, oh, my arrogance!*

Alvin had no idea when, or if, the gods would ever rework his inner man. And certainly had no idea how he could accomplish it himself. The whole idea of gods, singular or plural, was just another gaudily painted figure revolving on the merry-go-round of his mind, but appearing as more of a fire-breathing dragon than a horse with a flowing mane.

He could not seem to wrap himself around the concept of a supreme being who had to be placated in order for one to win a heavenly reward. Death Chant Harry, with his fire and brimstone, seemed to have no doubts at all about the here-after. Nor would the easy-going Father Gallagher, Al supposed.

Talk about extreme opposites, but both headed for the same place and intent on dragging as many with them as they could rope in. If religion refused, like a ferocious dragon, to be tamed, it also offered, contrarily, a vague hope that there was more to life than what had been served on Al's plate. When he was in a particularly optimistic mood regarding his Catholicism, Alvin signed not only his given, middle and surname, but also his baptismal name, Peter, and the one he had chosen at the time he was confirmed, Patrick.

As painful as his struggle with wavering faith was, the dishonor his mind had inflicted on Ruby was by far the more harrowing of the two. Alvin rode both of these hobbyhorses to exhaustion, then with an effort banished them, only to remount them when they swirled around again.

It was regret and shame that had driven him to ask Frances to try to help Ruby come to grips with a challenge she seemed ill equipped to meet alone. A stack of fashion magazines might not be much, but far more than he could do from where he was lying. Frances had also good-naturedly offered to carry messages between Ruby and Leo, which might give both of them some comfort, Alvin thought.

Even sleep did not allow Alvin respite from these knots that defied untangling. Always elusive, when sleep did come, it swarmed with dreams that manifested themselves through grim images of death in a variety of forms. One night, after hearing Ruby's description of Graybill's swimming pool, death was presented as a drowning in crystal clear water that bubbled continuously from an underground spring. *That one wasn't so bad.* The dreams that were filled with black shrouded figures, buckets of blood, and cheap, charity coffins made of cardboard covered with felted wool left him drenched in perspiration and gasping for air when they frightened him awake.

> *I don't feel so good as I*
> *would like to. My mind*
> *wanders to thoughts I don't*
> *care to think of. I have*
> *such awful dreams. I*
> *wish I were home.*

Alvin wrote that in his diary on July 6, a Monday, after awakening from a particularly bad nightmare in which dirt clods rained down to smother, not only him, but his wife, baby, Alta, Pearl, and, strangely enough, Ruby, all gathered together in a trench that seemed to be a smaller version of Mill Creek's river bed. *And it was cold, so deathly cold.*

That dream had been preceded by two extremely pleasant visiting days, one unexpected visit from Frances on the Fourth of July, which fell on a Saturday, and then the usual Sunday visit. The extra hours on the holiday were coveted because Frances was finding it difficult to squeeze hours away from the care Frances Pearl's illness demanded. There were the frequent appointments with Dr. Campbell to ensure the abscess drained properly, and many hours in which Frances rocked her daughter or played little games with her to keep her quiet and occupied. It was taking several soda baths a day to keep her temperature down.

It all took time, time that Frances was forced to steal from Alvin. She often missed the afternoon visiting hours, but always showed up at seven-thirty or eight o'clock Wednesday and Sunday evenings. Her hair had still not been marcelled, but she had added a snappy leather belt to the new pink dress, which emphasized her tiny waist. "A gift from Angie," she said. It seemed that Frances' sister was intent on building a bridge over the troubled waters of the past.

Alvin marked the Fourth of July holiday with a Catholic prayer and a special inscription of his own in his diary:

> *Saturday, July 4. May the Souls*
> *of the Faithful departed*
> *through the mercy of*
> *God rest in peace.*
> *Amen.*
> *Independence Day.*
> *May God bless him who fought*
> *and gave his life that we*
> *may have this wonderful day.*

He followed it with a plaintive entry on July 7:

> *I sure wish I could*
> *see things in a different*
> *light. If I could only be*
> *a true believer. It seems*
> *I can't believe anything*
> *anyone says. I trust no*
> *one. I am unhappy. Al*

"We are slow to believe what if believed would hurt our feelings."—Ovid

Chapter 66

The toll of burning her candle at both ends finally caught up with Frances. She came down with a raging fever and a sore throat that felt as if a cheese grater was at work.

When she first felt the onslaught of illness, she called Miss Gillis to get permission to stop in for a short time on the morning of July 8, knowing that the Wednesday morning visit might be her last for awhile. Although she would rather be in bed, she had news to share.

Dr. Campbell had given her the result of the test done on the matter from Frances Pearl's abscess. It was a great relief to her to learn that no tuberculosis was present. She wanted to tell Alvin, even though he hadn't even known testing was being done.

She found her husband still preoccupied with the weather. The heat of the Fourth had blended into the cooler weather he liked, and had brought some rain with it. He always felt better on the mild days, and this day of seventy-six degrees had him smiling.

She disliked telling him about her own health, or lack of it, but just being here at nine-thirty in the morning told him something wasn't right. She was glad he was feeling better. If he was having one of his bad days, it would have been more difficult to tell him not to expect her company until she recovered from whatever this was.

Usually she wanted to wring every minute out of the short hours they had to share, but this morning she was anxious to leave, needed to leave. She felt smothered under the mask she had been given to wear over her mouth to avoid spreading her germs. She wanted nothing so much as to be at home in her own bed. With Ida's help, she was going to be able to do that as soon as she could get home.

Four days later, Alvin earned a trip home the hard way.

Frances' condition had worsened, to the point Dr. Campbell recommended to Ida that she try to arrange for Alvin to come into town to see her. The doctor had made house calls every day, starting on Thursday, and by Saturday night he advised Ida to call Miss Gillis and secure the necessary permission.

"Take the baby out of the house, and get Mr. Potts in here for a few hours, at least," Dr. Campbell said. "I think she is going to be all right, but she has me worried."

Gillis took the call Saturday evening, and notified Alvin that Ida would be out to pick him up first thing Sunday morning. Alvin cringed inside when he heard himself tell Leo and Oscar, "There's trouble at home. I'm going into town for a few hours tomorrow."

When he arrived at the house on Poplar Street, he found Frances in bad shape, and it frightened him. Heat radiated from her body, yet she was buried under a stack of covers and still shivering. Her eyes were wide and glassy in her narrow face, and her legs moved restlessly. When he tried to still them with a smoothing hand, she complained that ants were crawling up and down her legs. He brushed repeatedly at them in an effort to appease her, but the hallucinations continued to plague them both. He soaked wash cloths in the cold water Ida brought him, wrung them out and wiped her burning face. He moistened her cracked lips, then coated them with a thin layer of Vaseline. He left her side long enough to take the ice pick to a block of ice in the icebox, making chips small enough to feed to her. Still, she continued to fidget and moan in her delirium.

He drew one of her arms from under the blankets covering her, poured a little Johnson's baby oil into the palm of his hand and began to smooth it over her hand and along the length of her arm. As he did, he began to whistle.

He chose no known tune, but one that seemed to escape from his past. The lilting notes spoke of violets peeking from the grass in April, the summer sunshine he had run through as a kid, the wind he had heard blowing through the pine trees in far away Daisy. When the sound of a bubbling, clear spring come forth from his parted lips, the twitching of Frances' limbs stilled and her eyes closed. He tucked her arm back under the blankets, moved to the other side of the bed and withdrew that arm, and began to massage it with oil, whistling all the while.

From her seat at the kitchen table, Ida recognized a new tune Alvin was whistling, and sang along quietly under her breath, *"Little old lady, passing by…"*

Frances' eyes fluttered open, focused on Alvin and she smiled. "My precious," she murmured, and raised her hand to touch his right cheek. Her hand felt hot against the puckered skin of his scar. Her eyes closed again.

The sun was sinking in the west when Frances finally fell into a deep, but natural, sleep. Alvin smoothed back the hair that now lay damp on her forehead, a sure sign that her fever had broken.

"Time for me to go back," he told Ida, looking at the watch cupped in his hand.

"And isn't that just the damnedest shame," Ida said, lumbering to her feet.

For the first time, Alvin was truly convinced that his mother-in-law fully accepted him.

> *Sunday, July 12. My wife is sure*
> *plenty sick. I went to town today*
> *to see her. She has a sore throat,*
> *a mighty high temp. Sure am glad*
> *to be able to cheer her. Anything*
> *I can do for her sure makes me*
> *feel happy.   Her Hubby. Al.*

"The main object of study is to unfold the aim; with one who loves words, but does not improve, I can do nothing."—*Confucius*

Chapter 67

Monday, July 13. I feel about the same.
after my trip to town. Have a pain in
my back—pleurisy. That is nothing
unusual.

Alvin returned to a room Sunday night that no longer held Oscar.

"Gillis moved him out of here not long after you left, but it's not what you might think," Leo quickly informed Al.

"Then what is it? Why is he out?" Alvin asked.

"He had a coughing spell, some blood. Gillis said she could do more for him if he had a room all to his self."

"Did you swallow that?" Alvin asked, skeptically.

"Hook, line and sinker. Because Oscar isn't too bad. Was feeling good up to the time he started coughing so hard. Seemed to feel just fine when he wasn't coughing, and, you know, he wasn't on total bed rest so he can't be too bad off.

"Yeah. Yeah, I trust old Gillis," Leo added. "Oscar'll be back with us before long. He's just gonna get extra rest and some extra attention, like maybe some ice packs on his chest."

Alvin wanted to believe that Oscar, who had seemed to be in the best shape of the three of them, was going to be back with them soon, but the Doubting Thomas in him was itching to be heard. *Why do I always have to be so negative?*

Oscar and Alvin had forged a link in the hours after lights out and after Leo's snores cut him out of the conversational loop. With beds side by side, Oscar and Al had slowly begun to share snippets from their pasts.

Al had learned that Oscar was a happily married man, who had never been blessed with children, an especial hardship for his wife but not so much for Oscar. "The wife was enough for me," Oscar claimed. "Her and my old hound dog," he'd said, making Al laugh. Their night time talks stretched into realms they might not have touched upon in the light of day. They spoke about what they would do when they returned to their homes and families. They asked themselves what they would have done if they hadn't settled down and married. Then they answered the question by exploring the possibilities open to those they knew who were free to roam the world. They discussed the touchy subject of religion, which often caused arguments in the ward but never between them in their one-on-one in the middle of the night. It seemed those conversations, at least for now, were at a stand-still.

"Let's hope Gillis knows what she's talking about. We need old Oscar and his Frenchified bonnet back in here," said Alvin, referring to the black beret Oscar pulled on over his bald head whenever the weather cooled down.

Alvin had returned with an ache of his own. "Stabbing pains in my back, probably just pleurisy," he told Miss Gillis when she came around to make bed checks just before lights out. "Is there anything you can do about it?" he asked her.

She put stethoscope to his chest and back. "You understand, Alvin, this isn't serious, but we can give you some relief from what I am sure is an uncomfortable annoyance," Miss Gillis said. "I'll see to it first thing tomorrow."

It was the new ward clerk, whom Alvin had presumed would be "so dumb," who arrived in his room after breakfast Monday with a bath towel and alcohol, prepared to massage his back, as ordered by Miss Gillis. A relaxing alcohol back rub at bed time was not an unusual occurrence, but starting off the day with one was always treatment.

"It does feel better," Alvin admitted to the 'new girl' when she finished. After having Rose's cool fingers walk up and down so effectively on his spine, Al unbent so far as to tell her of the illnesses of his wife and baby.

"My wife was too sick to have our baby at home with her, so I didn't see her yesterday when I was home," he added. "She'll be two next month, and she is getting so she likes her daddy and knows him better. She can say almost anything. Last time she said

'Daddy, come home.'

"Wish I could go home for a month or two," Al confided. "Wishing gains one very little," he added before realizing that he was doing all the talking.

"I hope that helped," said Rose, all business as she capped the alcohol bottle. But she gave his arm a brisk pat before she left the room.

As the pain in his back eased, Alvin began to change his mind about this new girl. *She might not be such a dumb bunny, after all. But I still prefer Flora.*

With Oscar removed from the room, Leo still his new taciturn self, and Alvin recovering from a full day out of bed, Monday and Tuesday passed uneventfully, except for a quick message from Phil, the ward's news monger.

"It seems Miss Sanders and her favorite patient disregarded the advice from on high and tied the knot this weekend," Phil reported. "Yep, our Miss Sanders is a married woman now."

"Guess Lucky really got lucky!" Leo said. "Is he still a patient?"

"Nope! Went home same time he got himself a missus! And she won't be back to work for a week," Phil said.

"Good for them. Time somebody around here was happy," Alvin said.

Phil's newscast was the only highlight of two quiet, but extremely hot days, and even Wednesday offered no respite, neither from the high temperature nor boredom…until eleven o'clock at night when their world began to shake itself apart.

Alvin was lying flat on his back when a tremor intruded obscenely and abruptly into the soles of his feet and snaked through his body like a thick, quivering rod. By the time the invasive sensation reached his chest and exited through the top of his head, he felt totally helpless and violated.

"What the hell was that?" Leo called out in a hoarse voice filled with sleep.

The windows chattered. Leo's bed slammed into the door, and Alvin's skitter-danced sideways before coming to rest against Leo's night stand. The sound of smashing glass joined the thud of books flying around the room that was still dark. Glass sprayed onto their beds with a hiss like falling sleet. In the faint light from the windows, Al thought he saw the exterior wall bow and sway.

"Jesus Christ, it's a 'quake!" Leo screamed.

All along the hallway, shouts were raised by patients jolted from sleep. The crack of glass, muffled thuds and unexplained crashes added to the din.

As quickly as the tremor had come, it was gone, leaving in its wake total confusion.

Even through the noise, the click of Nurse Gillis' shoes could be heard, but instead of her usual stately gait, the steps were now rapid fire as she raced along. Her voice, however, held its usual calm, authoritative tone.

"Gentlemen! Gentlemen! Keep your heads and keep to your beds!" she ordered, her words loud, clear and demanding obedience.

"Boys, stay calm and stay in your beds!" She repeated the message over and over again as she moved along the hall.

The sound of running bare feet proved that not everyone was heeding her advice.

Her voice was joined by Flora's saying, "It's over now. It is all over. The lights will be on soon. Just stay calm, please."

"Please stay in your beds! There may be glass on the floors. Stay in your beds!" Nurse Gillis demanded. "We will get around to all of you just as soon as we can."

Their pleas and instructions were beginning to take effect as they moved from room to room, pausing just seconds at each door to make a speedy check.

"I've got to get to Ruby, Curly," Leo said in a voice that shook. "She's gonna be scared silly. I've got to get to her."

Alvin was gripped in a silence as tight as the hold he had fastened onto the iron posts of the head of his bed when it had first begun its dance.

"Curly! Curly, you there? Al, you OK?" Leo's voice cut through the darkness, panic in every word.

"Here," Al was finally able to say, embarrassed now in an aftermath that left the room so steady it was almost impossible to believe it had been rocking only seconds before. There had been no time for coherent thought, and still wasn't. Instinct had cut through the terror and moved him to hang on and ride it out.

He slowly unwrapped his fingers from around the posts, flexed them and hid them under the blankets, hearing the tinkle of glass as it sifted to the floor.

"I think we better do what they say, stay right here, in our beds. The women will be doing the same thing in their wing, Leo. Let's just wait it out."

Alvin's calm advice belied his inner turmoil. A grunt was Leo's only answer.

Staff that had been sleeping on the second floor could be heard easing down the stairs and cautiously entering the rooms to join Flora and Gillis in ascertaining the condition of each patient.

As more helping hands arrived, order was slowly restored. When the maintenance men had the lights up and running, the full extent of the damage done by the earthquake to the interior of the rooms could be seen. The sight of cracked and broken windows, shards of glass from these and fractured drinking glasses sparkling across the floors, and beds and furniture toppled had a two-fold effect. It quickly quieted the patients, who had expected to see even more serious damage, and discouraged them from leaving beds that suddenly seemed the safest place to be. The ones who had fled barefooted were rounded up and returned to their rooms.

Even Leo accepted that others were better equipped than he to look after his wife.

Al chalked up another point in Rose's favor when she came in with an orderly to clean up the debris, but first told Leo that she had checked on his wife and, not only was Ruby just fine, but was being "a tower of strength" for her roommate.

"Now ain't that somethin'! Imagine, Ruby being a tower," Leo said. He grinned and, with some of his old flippancy, added in an aside to Alvin, "And here I always was worrying she might turn into a pillar...of salt."

Leo's irreverent sally poked a hole in the tension in the room, but could not dispel entirely the apprehension that hovered. If the earth could shake like that without warning, who was to say it would not happen again at any moment.

As hard as Alvin looked, the exterior wall he thought he'd seen buckle seemed just as sturdy now as it had been before the earthquake. Could that be? Could a solid wall undulate and return to its original shape?

Wednesday, July 15. At about
11:07 o'clock this night we
experienced an earthquake.
The first one I ever felt and
I hope the last.

July 16. We are still having
a few tremors. I sure hope
they stay mild. The one
main one last nite turned
chimneys completely
around and cracked some
brick walls.

Friday. Between 1:17 o'clock
and 1:20 we had three small
shocks or tremors. We
will probably have a good
big one before we are through
with them. I had a letter from
my wife today.

"Nothing has such power to broaden the mind as the ability to investigate systematically and truly all that comes under the observation in life."—Marcus Aurelius

Chapter 68

A second letter from Frances reached Alvin on Saturday. In it she promised to visit him Sunday. The week since his trip home had brought her to the edge of a recovery not quite complete, but she would not go another day without seeing him. Jenny offered to stay with the baby, and Murray offered to drive her so she felt up to making the attempt.

Murray left the house early Sunday morning, but assured her she would see his face just before two o'clock. "You can count on me, Sis," he'd said.

He pulled up in the Ford just when she was getting anxious. She liked to walk through Alvin's door on the stroke of the hour. She knew he watched for her. It looked as if she would be late today, but not by much.

Murray dropped her right at the door.

"You go on in, Sis, I'll park and then drop in to see Alta for a bit. Catch you at Al's."

Frances didn't see him reach into the back seat and take out a huge bouquet of yellow roses wrapped in a cone of the dark green, waxy paper Fiedler Florists used for cut flowers. But Al, watching from the window, did. He recognized their origin. He had once bought Frances a bouquet from Fiedler's when he was courting, a much smaller bouquet, true, but still wrapped in Fiedler's signature paper.

Frances was muffled to the chin in a wooly scarf, her face appearing wan and peaked above it. She wore a sweater, around the front of which she tightly wrapped her arms. It was one hundred degrees outside and hotter yet inside the room, in spite of a slight breeze that wafted through the open windows. Obviously, she was not fully recuperated.

She was content to sit silently in the chair beside his bed, close enough to hold hands, while he carried the conversational ball. He gave Nurse Gillis full credit for dispelling panic during the earthquake and restoring order with the help of Flora. "It was some ordeal," was the closest he came to telling her how he had felt when the tremor had made its strange, and frightening, way through his body.

She had already told him in her letters how she had coped with the 'quake's damage. One broken window and a cupboard of smashed crockery was the sum of the damage at their house. Murray had repaired their window and two more at the house of the landlord, who had paid him a quarter to do the job. She had written of how she was rocking Frances Pearl when the first tremor hit, and how glad she had been to have her child safely in her arms. If it had been even four hours earlier, Frances Pearl would still have been at Ida's, but she had begged Ida to bring her over to at least spend the night since Dr. Campbell had just stitched her incision up that day.

It was nearing four o'clock, almost time for Frances to leave, when Murray sauntered into the room. Alvin looked him over. Every curl in place, slacks stylishly hanging loose, starched shirt neatly tucked in, shoes shined. Never a slob, Murray still had taken pains today. When Murray reached over to shake hands, Alvin pulled him closer and quizzed him in an undertone, "Flowers from Fiedler's?"

Murray winked and answered his question with a question: "Wouldn't you say our sister's worth it?"

"Sister, my eye!" Alvin rejoined.

"Let's leave it at that," Murray said in a voice that brooked no argument.

"I'm joining the Army, brother. It's all set up for next month," said Murray.

"When was this decision made?" Al asked.

"Been thinking about it for some time now. You know I thought about the Navy. Why not see the sea I says to meself, like Popeye the sailor man, but the Army recruiter caught me instead."

Then he turned serious and said, "I've been looking for work, Al, and just can't latch onto anything more than odd jobs and caddying at the golf course. Roosevelt's New Deal is stretching only so far, and the days of making fly-proof privies with covered lids for the CWA are over. I need more than that, and this—the Navy—could be an opportunity for me. Will is thinking about joining up, too."

Alvin offered no opinion on Murray's decision. He could see that he was not looking for advice. His young brother's mind was made up, and Alvin felt that he was now dealing with a man, not a boy.

"Is this a for-sure thing," he asked.

"Signed, sealed and to be delivered in August."

"Then good luck to you."

A chime signaled the end of visiting hours, and Murray held out his hand to help Frances from her chair. Pressed cheeks and a firm handshake were the extent of their goodbyes to Alvin, until Murray turned back just as he was walking out the door.

"Oh yeah, brother, 'sis' said to be sure to give you her regards." He flipped Al a mock salute as he left.

"A half-million," Leo mumbled from where he sat propped up in his bed.

"A half-million what?" Al asked.

"A half-million of those fly-proof crappers is what the workers for the Civil Works Administration produced," said Leo. "And they say they saved lives by getting rid of disease. I built a few of them myself in 1934."

Even at his most reticent, Leo was good for a laugh, Al thought.

Frances and Murray were well out of sight when Alvin remembered Frances had not asked and he had not told her about Oscar.

> *Sunday, July 19. My Darling Wife*
> *was out to see me. She looks*
> *lots better but she doesn't*
> *look any too well yet. I shall*
> *sure be glad when she is*
> *entirely well. It was 100 degrees*
> *today. Al*

Chapter 69

*Monday, July 20. It has been
another hot day. It is awful
since being so nice and cool.
It was 104 degrees today. We
can expect about a month
and a half of such weather
as this.*

*Tuesday. Sure are having
some fine hot weather
but I'll be plenty glad
when it cools off.*

*"My concern is not whether God is on our side; my greatest
concern is to be on God's side, for God is always right."—Lincoln*

*Wednesday, July 22. My Dearest
Wife was out to see me today.
Oh! God how I love that little
wife of mine. She sure is of
the finest. She is a self made
woman and a mighty swell
one too. Her Man Al.*

*Thursday. It is 6:45. 6:20 o'clock
marked the Death of one of the
patients, Oscar Lodi. He was
from Prosser and a very good
friend of mine since coming
here. May his soul rest in peace.*

"If there were no God, it would be necessary to invent him."—
Voltaire

"Danged if Gillis didn't pull the wool over our eyes."

"What's that?"

"Just talkin' to myself."

"You don't want to be doing that too much, Leo, or…you'll be just like the rest of us around here," Alvin said.

Chapter 70

The empty space that divided the beds of Leo and Alvin was a constant reminder of Oscar's death, which seemed to be the final blow in a month of confusion and catastrophe. They had not recovered from the stunning loss of Laurence on July 1, before the earthquake struck on July 15.

Although the staff had been quick to return the ward to its normal appearance after the 'quake, more damage had been done than met the eye. In the days that followed, the patients were jittery, unsettled and restless.

The same uneasiness was felt throughout Walla Walla among those who had experienced the five jolting tremors on July 15 that toppled several chimneys and sent pans, pictures and dishes flying in homes across the city. Leo's confusion and the pandemonium exhibited by some of the patients were typical reactions. Theatre audiences had fled into the streets, while other residents, who had been sleeping, trooped outside in pajamas to try to discern what was happening. One man grabbed his dog and leaped from a window. Perhaps not an unusual reaction, but probably not one appreciated by the wife he had left behind to fend for herself. The huge clock on the Whitman College Chapel stopped at 11:08 p.m., a reminder of the unusual event.

It was the first earthquake in Walla Walla since 1872, so the response of unprepared citizens was not unreasonable. The '72 earthquake, the first felt in the county since it was settled by whites, also struck at night. This one that had pulsed its way through Alvin in such a shocking manner had made itself officially felt at 11:08. The following tremors came at 11:15, 11:25, 11:40, 11:55 and, finally, the first of another series on the 16th at 12:10. Mopping up was still being done throughout town on July 23, the day Oscar died. Clean-up was especially heavy in nearby

Freewater, Oregon, which bore the brunt of the damage. The light tremors on the two days following the 'quake kept people on edge, not knowing what to expect, but expecting something.

That sense of anxious waiting was still prevalent in Ward One, and it had gone a long way toward making a pessimist of Alvin when Leo had insisted that Oscar would return to their room. Even so, Oscar's death took not only Leo by surprise, but also Al. Leo especially felt betrayed by Nurse Gillis. He had believed her, maybe because he so much wanted to believe. Leo sank into a sullen silence.

Alvin faulted Gillis not at all. If she had deliberately given them eleven nights free of sleeplessness, he could only be thankful. He was even willing to give her the benefit of the doubt, and accept that even Gillis had not foreseen Oscar's death.

But he would not bet on it.

Alvin consciously set his mind on a more positive course, finding simple delight in fresh fish served for the main meal on Friday instead of the tuna fish sandwiches for which, he told his diary, *I certainly have no use for.* Saturdays still reminded him of the big day farmers had in town once a week when they trooped in to spend money, window shop and parade the streets with their best girls or wives on their arms.

He still yearned to be one of them, to be home with his wife, to be a normal man with normal desires that could be fulfilled, not fought shrouded in tangled, lonely bed sheets. Most of the time, even without saltpetre, he could control the strong sexual emotions that plagued him, but a visit from Frances could fan the ashes and set the fire to blazing again. Then he could make them both miserable with wishes, spoken and unspoken.

He tried for a light touch when he wrote in his diary on Saturday, July 25: *The farmers' big day in town. I sure hope they enjoy themselves. They probably will in their poor, innocent, ignorant sort of way. Oh! I forgot I am a farmer myself.*

He clung to thoughts of getting well. If bed rest is what it would take, then rest he would, but, Jesu Christus, as Oscar would say, four months in this place seemed like a lifetime, and there was no guarantee that he would be here only four more.

Sunday, July 26. My only "love"

*was out today. She sure loves
me I know. Some day she
will be repaid for this
kindness. I love her and baby so.
I am going to get well just
for them.   Al*

*Monday. If anything should
happen to my wife and baby
I wouldn't stay here for
myself over night. I am
going to fight for them
and get well for them.
Oh! Sweetheart I love you so.*

                              Al

*"This above all: to thine own self be true, And it must follow
as the night the day, Thou canst not then be false to any man."—
Shakespeare*

Chapter 71

A meal of salmon that skirted the edge of rotten did nothing to improve the mood of the gentlemen in Ward One. Alvin was the chief complainer when his stomach rejected the fishy fish.

Even the good news of a weight gain the first of August could not outweigh an ear ache and a nose bleed that attacked him simultaneously at three o'clock on the morning of the third. His pessimism burst into full blossom with the onslaught of the earache, causing him to write *I sure would hate to lose one of my ears.*

The sad part of the notation was that he was not being humorous.

"This outfit resembles a bunch of sheep," Al grumped to Leo after his miserable night.

"Yeah, I suppose we could use a good shearing," said Leo. "How long has it been since the barber trimmed us up?"

"It is thirty-one days today since we had hair cuts. We're having the barber out today, and it's about time."

"Guess you'll be glad to have that tangle of curls tamed in time for your wife's visit tomorrow."

"It's either that or start learning to bleat."

"You really dote on her visits, don't you?"

"I wouldn't say 'dote'. I don't think I'm excessively demonstrative, but I like her company, that's for sure."

"You're such a damn stickler for the English language. Why is that? Dote is dote. Means you like someone, doesn't it? Means you count on them, doesn't it?"

"In common usage, I suppose it is taken that way, but to me a doting husband would be a guy you see hanging around his wife's neck even if the whole world is watching. You know, the kind of fellow who is foolishly in love and makes a big show of it."

"Well, I'd *dote* on Ruby, if I had the chance, let me tell you!"

"What do you hear on the grapevine? Is she settling in, doing all right?"

"Your Frances brought me a note from her Sunday, remember? She didn't sound too happy, but said her roomie is a swell gal. Ruby's teaching her how to put on rouge and all that eye gunk. Said it gives her something to do. Ruby is a do-er, not a sitter, you know. That makes this place kind of tough for her."

"Maybe Gillis will arrange a visit for you two. Think so?"

"I ain't about to count on Gillis. I plan to meander down that way before long on my own. Maybe even today, after the barber spiffs me up."

"Oh we are going to be two handsome gents this afternoon, aren't we?" Al teased in a lame effort to interject some levity.

His attempt fell flat. They lapsed into silence until Rose delivered their breakfast trays, which were welcomed for more than the food on the plates.

Leo and Al always found something to talk about over breakfast. Usually the conversation centered around the news Leo gleaned from the *Union*, Walla Walla's morning newspaper. This morning all Leo offered up was old news, and gloomy news it was too. He wanted to re-hash the drought in the Midwest where grasshoppers, chinch bugs and beetles had invaded homes in mid-July when they couldn't find food in the parched fields. It was not a subject Alvin cared to explore. Sounded too much like Death Chant Harry's prophecies. So this time Al was the one to cut the conversation short.

Instead, he turned to the meditation in his Diary and Daily Reminder, looking for inspiration in the proverbs. Today, it was a maxim from Mencius. He wished he knew who all these fellows were that were quoted in the book. Marcus Aurelius he knew had been a Roman emperor. Shelley and Byron, of course, were poets. Dickinson an author. Some names everyone would know, such as Lincoln, Shakespeare and Plato. But this Mencius was a stranger.

Alvin read his words for today with interest. *"The virtues are not poured into us, they are natural: seek, and you will find them; neglect and you will lose them."*

To think that there were standards of moral excellence lurking inside everyone *was* interesting. *Pulling them out of one's self might be the tough part.*

It was always easy to admire virtue in someone else and even easier to see their flaws, than it was to see into one's self. Alvin thought you would really have to open yourself to introspection to dig out the truth about yourself. *Well, I've certainly got the time.* He decided to give it a go.

He leaned against his pillows, closed his eyes, let his arms go limp. He assumed this was the appropriate posture for self examination, or was that for meditation?

Damn! His nose itched. He brushed at it briskly, opened his eyes and sat up.

All right. He'd take stock of himself. *I'm not a bad looking chappie, barring the scar. A bit taller than the average fellow. Eyes are a good color. Not as blue as Frances', but still a clear blue. Second toe is longer than my big toe. I like that. Hair the color of honey in the comb, mother always used to say. Can't see it myself. But curly! Curly hair doesn't count for anything, except with Frances who is crazy about it.*

Well, hell, this wasn't introspection! It was nothing more than looking in a mirror.

Interior. Interior. What's inside of me?

He flopped back down, closed his eyes and waited for the virtues promised by Mencius to reveal themselves. Tangled sheets immediately sprang to the fore. His tangled sheets. His sheets that too often in the morning showed the struggle he had undergone in the night. The struggle to put to rest tempting thoughts of bare legs, soft breasts and hot kisses, temptations that threatened to lead to actions too vigorous for his own good. Most nights he was successful, but it was always a battle.

Gillis, Flora and the doctors ruled the patients with so much discipline it left little for patients to do on their own, but, Al conceded, he was not a stranger to cracking down on himself. *Self discipline, maybe I can count that as my first virtue. And I have the temper tantrums under control, too!*

So, what else? What else was buried inside?

Even with his eyes closed, nothing came to mind. Nothing…except rippling wheat fields, golden in the sun. He could almost smell the dust that had arisen behind the combine and feel it as it coated what little of his skin was left bare to the weather. So little was left exposed that all of his body was milky white, except for face, neck and forearms that the sun branded with the tell-tale farmer's tan. He had spent months under that sun, sweating and working in fields from sun up to sun down.

No one could accuse him of being a slacker in the fields. When it came to work, he had always been one of the first in the fields, and never called it quits until the job was done. But, if he was being honest in this soul searching—and he was—Alvin decided he would have to admit to the joy he derived from being the first to tromp out to the field, the first to examine the beard on the wheat, the fullness of the head. Just running his hand across the wheat stems caused them to bow before him. A farmer could feel like a god when he walked his fields alone in the early dawn.

I'm not sure it is a virtue to play God.

But they were not his fields. He was only a hired hand, paid a dollar a day to help grow another man's crops. He had been taught by Emerson that a job worth doing was worth doing well, and it was not only a lesson he stuck by, but one on which he thrived. Every weed he hoed loose from the soil, every field he irrigated, every crop he helped bring in were his. He had felt the same way when he worked at St. Mary's. Whether it was carrying away a bed pan, mopping a floor or stocking the supply closet, it had been a labor of love.

Was doing a job the best you could less virtuous if you did it because you loved what you were doing? Al decided that a strong work ethic was a virtue, no matter what prompted it. *So that's number two.*

He felt as if he was standing at the crap table at Lutcher's, with the dice coming up winners. *I'm on a roll.*

A third virtue immediately presented itself for his consideration.

He had denied to Leo that he doted on Frances. It was true that he would not like to be called a doting husband, if that did mean one who fawned over his wife in public, but he was loyal.

Never would step out on my wife. Faithful that's me. Virtue number three!

Alvin was now entering enthusiastically into this mental game.

I have a sense of humor, but sometimes I use it to tease the ladies. Would that be a virtue or a venial sin? God knows I am a negative soul, and there's no virtue in that. Patience? That's a matter of opinion.

Then the ear ache, whose throbbing he had ignored to this point, kicked in with stabbing pains, as if to test his store of patience. He clapped a hand over the offending ear, and wrapped the other hand over the top of his head. *Jesu Christus, Oscar, I don't have any patience with this G.D. earache.*

The pain drove him out of his self contemplation. All thoughts of Mencius and his proverb vanished from his head, except for the cautionary advice that he might lose these few virtues he had rooted out today if he neglected them.

It was then that a gleeful Leo slipped into the room looking like nothing so much as a robber completing a successful heist.

"I dood it, kid, I dood it!" said Leo, coming over to crouch beside Alvin's bed.

"Why are you hunched up down there? You hiding from someone?" Al asked.

"They're out lookin' for me, that's for sure, but I have eluded them!"

"Well, no one has been in here looking for you, Leo, so why don't you cozy down in bed where you belong. Then, if they look for you here, you'll be right where you belong."

"Good idea. Why didn't I think of that myself!"

"Now, what is it you did?"

"I snuck in to see Ruby!" Leo said, rising up slowly from his hiding place.

As Leo's head came even with Al, a pink feather fluttered from where it was caught in his hair.

"Looks like you're molting, Leo!"

Leo picked the feather up, tucked it rakishly behind his ear, and climbed into his bed. "I've been robbing the henhouse," he said, grinning. "Got close to a couple really warm little eggs, but the ward coppers got on my trail and I had to fly the coop."

"Was it Flora or Gillis? Are they still after you?"

"I did not see who the snooper was. I was...let us say, I went under cover, but I believe it was that soft spoken Rose I heard. Ruby gave her some song and dance. I was near fit to bust with laughin'. Ruby kept a pinchin' me to hush me up! She hiked her knees up, and I was tucked in under them. Nearly smothered! But what a way to go!"

"Leo, you are going to be in some kind of trouble for sure. You want your can kicked out of here?"

"Love it! Just purely would love that, Al, my boy. But a fellow in my state of health ain't going to be let go, no how, no way, no sir!"

"Still, if you don't abide by the rules...well, I don't know what they could do."

"Aw, Al, a fella's gotta have a little fun. And it didn't hurt anyone. Maybe Rosie won't say anything about it. Heck, she isn't even really sure anyone was in Ruby's room. She may have her suspicions, but she did not see me! I know that for sure. As soon as Rose left, I hightailed it right back here. I know for dang sure no one saw me leave."

"Leo, you are nothing but a big, overgrown kid. You better hope Mrs. Gillis doesn't found out about your little foray."

"I didn't have time to 'foray'," said Leo, tugging the feather out from behind his ear and passing it slowly under his nostrils. "*That's* one thing I promise you I did not do, but it damn sure was the best half-hour I've spent since I came into this joint."

Monday, August 3. I had an ear
ache and a nose bleed at 3:00
o'clock last night. My ear still
aches. I sure hope this medicine
they put in it does some good.
Al

Chapter 72

A specialist, Dr. Rooks, was called in to examine Alvin when his earache continued. Rooks found a tiny opening in the ear drum. "Evidently caused a long time ago," he told Alvin. When he left, it was Alvin's understanding that the doctor intended to try to heal it. Rooks left some medicine with the nurses, and it seemed to ease some of the discomfort.

I do seem to be an unlucky fellow that unfortunate things keep happening to. Maybe that old gypsy fortune teller was right.

He was recalling a winter when Emerson had set up a tent camp in the northern woods of Washington for the family so he could cut ties for the railroad. Their large, canvas tent had been given extra protection from the cold with a surrounding wall of boards that extended about three feet from the ground. A wood stove provided the heat. Theirs was one of several camps in the area set up by others engaged in the same work.

One was a camp that sported a gypsy wagon instead of a tent. It was a source of curiosity for Alvin, Alta and Murray, who could only guess at what luxuries it might contain. Just seeing smoke rise out of the skinny chimney that sprouted from its roof led them to believe the gypsies were living warmer than they were.

When unfamiliar, but tantalizing, odors from the gypsy wagon drifted their way at meal times, they were pretty sure the gypsies were not dining on the likes of the beans, bacon and cornbread Alta put on their table every day. Curious they were, but it was no longer a curiosity embedded in fear. The Potts kids had outgrown their fear of gypsies a long time ago, recognizing Emerson's threats as just one more thing grown-ups used to keep the tadpoles in line. Still, Emerson told them to keep their noses to the grindstone here in the woods and out of other people's business. Even though he did not issue it as an order, they knew he meant they were to stay away from the gypsies and their alluring little house.

It was a directive Alvin could not fail to disobey.

The opportunity came one evening after supper when Emerson wandered over to another tent to play a few hands of cards with the fellows living there. Alvin wasted no time in making his way through the trees to the wagon that set off by itself.

He approached it cautiously, but not in a sneaky manner. If he saw any sign that he was not welcome, he would not go any further, but he was carrying an armload of firewood and thought that might earn him a ticket in. He was still debating whether to knock at the door or just hail the house, when the door opened and a tiny woman stepped gingerly down onto the trunk of a tree that was serving as a step.

Without thinking, Alvin dropped his load of wood and hurried forward to offer her his arm. Showing no surprise, she accepted his help as she took the last step that put her safely on the ground. Then she looked up at him.

Her eyes were black marbles in a cocoa brown face seamed with such deep creases Al could not begin to guess how old she might be.

In spite of looking as if it had been molded from a piece of good leather, it was a pleasant face. Laugh lines crinkled the corners of her mouth, as if she had found much to be amused about through her years of living. A kerchief patterned in bright green and yellow framed her face and covered hair that seemed to be coal black except for a white blaze that swooped back from her forehead. There were tremendous smells, perhaps of roasting meat, swirling out the door behind her.

That was Alvin's introduction to his gypsy neighbor. It was the first of many clandestine visits he made to the wagon, always, after this first one, in the afternoons when the men were at work and Emerson did not need his help.

He learned the little lady was Rosarita Sabatini, and even she did not know how old she was.

"But many, many years," she said. They always talked outside, she perched on the tree trunk that was her stairway to home and Alvin squatted beside her, a position that put him face to face with her, but also shielded him from anyone passing by. She shared with him the freedom her family experienced as they traveled from place to place, their home pulled along by a team of horses and the seasons marked by wherever they happened to find themselves. Alvin confided to her that, when he and his brother and sisters were little and had misbehaved, his father had threatened gypsies would run off with them.

"Why would we want such naughty children!" she exclaimed, laughing.

Always the visits were outside, until the day Mrs. Sabatini stood at the door and silently waved him in.

Heavy velvet curtains were pulled across the small windows. Alvin thought they probably were hung to keep out the cold, but they also darkened the interior of the wagon until it became a cave. A cozy cave packed tightly with the accouterments of living. Al was disappointed to see that there was not as much space in this wagon as they had in their tent.

And the air was not as fresh. Closed more tightly against the winter wind and cold, the wagon held the musky odor of the press of bodies that filled it in the evening and through the night. Lingering now in the daylight, it was not an unpleasant smell. It was mingled with a tinge of tobacco, the sharp bite of yellow soap, the tang of sage and rosemary…and something wonderful simmering on the stove.

But there was no mystery here. Just things people needed. Blanket-covered cots and pots, pans, coats, hats, all hanging on the painted walls.

Mrs. Sabatini urged him onto a stool pulled up to a table hinged to the wall. She set before him a mug of steaming liquid she dipped from a kettle on the stove. He saw flecks of meat floating in it, and the sheen of fat glossed the surface. A rich, heady aroma arose from the cup, reminding him of something he could not quite remember.

She pulled a stool up next to his and, for the first time, touched him.

He was startled to feel her tentative touch on the sleeve of his shirt, and sat very still to see what she would do next.

She slid her hand down to his and turned it over slowly. He could feel her eyes on him, but he hesitated to meet her gaze. She gave his hand a little shake, as if, he thought, to ask permission.

He raised his eyes to hers, and saw the same question there. His head gave a slight nod, almost without his own volition.

Mrs. Sabatini then grasped his hand firmly in hers, as if they had sealed a bargain, he thought.

She bowed her head over his hand, cupped now in hers, then straightened it out on her own palm, and ran a finger firmly over the lines his hand revealed to her.

"I have lived a long life, but you have lived many lives. I see you, far back in the ages, stitching, stitching, sewing by hand. A very good tailor you were then. You sewed a tight, but flexible, seam, chose good materials, did fine work. That is what gives you the ability to recognize fine clothing today."

She laughed as she leaned over and fingered the rough cloth of the shirt he wore. "Ah, you might not wear it now, but you *know*. You know, in here," she said, tapping him on the chest. "You know a good garment when you see it. Yes?"

Alvin was puzzled, but not frightened by her strange talk. It was true he had always been taken with the cut of a good pair of trousers and admired a vest that fit close to the waist without wrinkling across the chest. Some day he intended to wear clothes like that. No, he wasn't frightened. He wanted to hear more.

"So? You are not going to fly away like the leaves before the wind? Maybe, you think, this old gypsy lady is not completely daft?" Her wrinkled face crinkled into a smile. She turned her attention again to his palm.

"You understand? You understand that this life you find yourself in now is not the only life you have lived? Once, many years before you sewed clothing, you were a writer. You wrote not with words, but with symbols you scratched onto clay tablets. You wrote, and you traveled over water at times to do this work. You wrote words about things you did not particularly like, but you wrote them because it was your job, your duty. These words were important to others. They were used to keep records."

She peered at him with her bright, black eyes.

What she saw caused her to continue.

"You like to run?" she asked, tipping her head to one side to signal her expectation of an answer.

"Sure. I guess. I ran a lot in Daisy. I was the one mother sent to carry notes to grandma, who lived across Huckleberry

Mountain. I did like running over the hills."

"Those messages between daughter and mother were not the first you carried. Once you were a runner with a strong body and strong legs that could carry you fast over the miles. Even before your life as a scribe, you were the skilled runner chosen to carry important messages from one place to another. Often these places were far apart, and you would cover the distance with ease. You ran like the wind."

She paused, stroking his hand thoughtfully.

"Many lives. In this one here…," she said, putting her forefinger delicately on a short line that started strong and faded into nothing, "…in this one I see that a little more than two hundred years ago you wore a crown. It was a royal life, but a depressing one that was not good for you. You suffered much. Miserable illnesses were inflicted upon you. It was not a good life for you, and you left it when you were only a young man."

A sad look stole over her face. She ran her fingers over his palm, folded his hand into a fist and held it tightly.

"You are an unlucky young man, my little friend. An unlucky man to whom unfortunate things keep happening. Could it be you are a slow learner?"

Then she gave his fist a brisk shake, dropped it, and said, "You have a good heart, and I like you very much. Now drink. Drink!"

She thrust the mug into his hand.

"That is broth of the deer, and it is very good for you."

The next morning the gypsy wagon was gone from the camp.

"Hey, Al, you sure been quiet this morning. That ear still actin' up or are you just in a fog?"

"Leo, do you believe in reincarnation?"

"You mean dying and coming back in a new body?"

"Yeah, like that."

"I still ain't comfortable with the thought of dying and going to heaven!" Leo said. "But guess one would be about as easy as the other. What do you think?"

"The way I understand the theory is that living over and over again gives you a chance to rub the raw edges off your character, sort of like a diamond cutter takes what looks like a rough stone and nips away at it until the brilliance is exposed. When we get to the diamond stage, then it's so long-oolong for good."

"Wonder how many lives it'd take to get down to the good stuff?" said Leo.

"That'd be anybody's guess. I had a lady tell me once that I have lived other lives, a lot of them. Sometimes it seems I can almost remember some of those lives. Reincarnation would explain a lot of the things that happen to us in this life, don't you think? I mean, when we meet someone who feels like an old friend. If you had met them in a life before this one, that might explain why they seem familiar."

"Yeah. And what about when you walk into a place like Lutcher's and some cowboy jumps up in front of you and you just know right away that you and he ain't gonna get along a'tall? Ever have that happen? He could just be sittin' there, doin' nuthin', and you know im-medj-i-at-ly that you don't like him one bit. Don't like him right then, never gonna like him ever, and you got no idea why. Reincarnation would sure explain that situation. Right?"

"I guess. But there's an awful lot of people I've seen at Lutcher's that I knew right away it was better not to get tangled up with."

"OK. Maybe Lutcher's was a bad example. A pool hall does lend itself to some unsavory characters at times. But I've had that feeling happen to me when I've been other places too. And that attraction you talked about. Look at me and Ruby. Couldn't get her out of my mind once I saw her. Even when I was a young buck and she was a little kid sittin' on my knee, I felt drawn to her. Oh, nothin' sexual then. Just a powerful need to take care of her, make her happy, see that the world treated her right. Do you suppose her and me shared a life somewhere along the line, afore this one?" Leo asked.

"I don't know, Leo. Reincarnation may be one of those big mysteries we never figure out, but I'd like to think there could be another chance, if this time didn't pan out the way we hoped. Don't they say all things are possible on god's green earth...or something like that?"

"Yeah, I can see me and Ruby living another life before this. Now we got this one here, which sure ain't what it's cracked up to be. Yeah, I'd like another chance, but not one without my Ruby girl."

"Or maybe," Al said, "it would be good to just get it right this time around so a body could sleep in peace."

Chapter 73

Her baby fingers plucked at the puckered scar on her neck as she sat on her mother's lap. Frances either held the child's fingers still or gently brushed them aside without comment.

Alvin watched with growing irritation as Frances Pearl batted away her mother's hand, and squirmed on her lap in an attempt to get down. Mother and daughter had been visiting for a half-hour, and, all through the visit, the child had whined, demanded attention and generally was an all-round irritant. "No" was a prominent word in her vocabulary, and she had exercised it repeatedly.

"Looks to me like your daughter is getting out of hand," Alvin said. "What's happened to her in this past month to make her such a pill?"

It was the first time Frances had brought their daughter to the sanatorium to visit since the baby's operation. She had hesitated to bring her today because it was true that the post operation care had put a serious crimp in the kid's behavior. The extra attention required to protect the incision in the first few weeks had extended for several more to keep the area free of infection.

The 'babying' Dr. Campbell had mandated had taken a toll on discipline, and it made for a trying visit now. Frances explained, and not for the first time over the past weeks, why the passive child Alvin was accustomed to was now far less than perfect. Her explanation today that Frances Pearl had come to have unrealistic expectations during the painful process that required frequent rocking and constant entertainment was falling on deaf ears.

"Seems like she could just straighten up and be her old self," Al complained. "Have you ever seen such a spoiled brat, Leo?" he added, drawing his roommate into the conversation.

Leo, who had studiously been avoiding the visiting pair, but had certainly heard the whines and whimpers, gave Al a look that asked *"Why drag me into this?"* But, taking the bull by the horns, Leo grasped his chin in his left hand, screwed his face into a parody of a man deep in thought, and looked Frances Pearl up and down.

"Wal, now…," Leo drawled, as the child kicked her ankle-high shoes against her mother's legs, "it 'pears to me this here child, this child with the big, blue eyes, this child with that mass of golden curls, that child what looks like an almost certain replica of her own dear daddy, this child right here…," he continued, flinging an arm out to point dramatically at Frances Pearl, "this here child is…a diamond in the rough!"

Wednesday, August 5. I had my Wife and baby out all during the first visiting period. The Baby sure is cute but awfully spoiled. That's because she has been sick. Frances will bring her out of that all rite after a time.   Daddy

Thursday, August 6. To my Dear little wife and baby. Your daddy is feeling fine today. All except his ear. The Dr. said it was only a minor ailment. He said it would take some time to get completely well. Al

Friday, Howdy folks. We had fish for dinner. Ha ha. What did you have? Tuna fish at that. I'd rather have liquor for mine.

"Clean your fingers before you point at my Spots."—Franklin

Saturday, August 8. We weighed
today and I gained 1 ½ lbs.
I had a letter from Frances
today and she had a lot of
good news for me. I will
get to see her tomorrow.
Thank God.   Al

Sunday, Frances was out
to see me. Lily and Pearl
were out also. Sure was
glad to see the girls.
I am always glad to see
my wife. She sure is
good to me.

Monday, August 10. Just
another nice cool day.
We surely are having
nice weather for August.
It is hardly ever over
92. We had some hot
weather during July.
I like this cool weather.

"Self conquest is the greatest of victories."—Plato

Tuesday. It is cloudy and
cool. Today is bath day.
I feel fine this morning.
I would like to have
about "three fingers" in
a bathtub of "Loganberry
Highball". I think I need
a stimulant.   Al

Chapter 74

Frances did not repeat the visiting fiasco of August 5th. Whenever she went to the san in the next week, she parked her child at Ida's where her fussing got lost in the frenetic atmosphere. The excitement and tension in the house were being repeated all across the county as the folks of Walla Walla geared up for its centennial celebration.

This year of 1936 marked the one hundredth anniversary of the arrival of Marcus and Narcissa Whitman, missionary pioneers, to the Walla Walla Valley. Their settlement on the banks of a creek in what, for centuries, had been Indian land came to be acknowledged as the founding of the city of Walla Walla. So, the celebration scheduled for August 13th through the 16th served the dual purpose of observing the centennials of both city and mission.

When Ida had enthused to Alvin about the covered wagon ride she, Jenny and Frances Pearl would be taking with Docey in the centennial parade, she was talking about the end result of an elaborate publicity production started by a new men's group, which had organized in April. The group called itself The Wagon Wheelers, and its purpose was to pump some fun and games into the celebration, before and during it, to give it widespread recognition. Forty-four men signed on as charter members, but every man in Walla Walla was eligible to join in the antics, if they were up for an initiation ceremony on the main street of Walla Walla that could include a dunking in a horse trough that had been hauled into town just for the event.

As a charter member, Docey missed out on the public humiliation, but was an enthusiastic participant at the kangaroo courts that 'welcomed' new members. "It's all in good fun and for a good cause," Docey told Ida, who often stood by to watch the proceedings. As early as spring, the Wagon Wheelers had begun taking their act on the road, visiting neighboring towns to publicize the coming August event. They were on hand, with their covered wagons and a medicine show, to help enliven Dayton Days on June 6. They staged feuds, one with Walla Walla's mayor, to gain newspaper publicity and spread the word of a celebration the entire city was intent on making one of its biggest and best.

The most expensive step had been taken when the centennial celebration was still in the talking stage between Walla Walla's Chamber of Commerce and Whitman College, the prestigious institute which bore the name of the missionaries. It became apparent that the local merchants were enthusiastic about having a celebration on their commercial doorstep, but their vision extended beyond that. They wanted to see the original mission site of almost thirty-eight acres restored and become a national monument. When the idea was pursued, it was found that the owner of the land would sell it for ten thousand dollars. A corporation was formed to petition the United States Congress to give national park status to the site, and the ball started rolling. The committee turned to the public for the money to purchase the land and shoulder the cost of the centennial through private donations and fundraising.

Plans for a four-day celebration quickly took form. In addition to parades, it was decided to have an outdoor historical pageant and programs every morning to honor the Whitmans, who had come to be considered missionary martyrs after being killed by Indians eleven years after their arrival. The celebration this year would be the second dedicated to the Whitmans. In 1922 Whitman College organized a pioneer pageant, labeled *How the West Was Won*, to commemorate the anniversary of the deaths of the missionary pair on the 29th day of November seventy-five years before.

It seemed that everyone wanted on the band wagon for the August hoopla this year. The Oregon Trail Memorial Association, the Daughters of the American Revolution, the American Medical Association and the Presbyterian and Congregational churches took over organization of the morning programs. Not to be outdone by the men of The Wagon Wheelers, a group of women united under the name of The Spinning Wheelers to handle hospitality for the great number of invited, honored guests and to sponsor a contest to choose a Pioneer Mother.

Ida thought her own mother, Caroline Kalmer Hempe, who had come west when they earned a homestead in Union, Oregon, would be a good candidate for Pioneer Mother, but the pioneer train that had brought her family and their belongings west had been a locomotive and wooden railroad cars, not a prairie schooner.

"I think they are looking for someone who bumped over the range in at least a stagecoach," Ida fretted to Docey.

"Or on Dr. Baker's rawhide railroad," Docey opined.

"Whatever that was!" Ida said.

"It was, my dear lady, the first railroad into Washington Territory."

"Believe my German forebears were a few years behind that train," Ida said. "And don't mind me. I'm just spitting sour grapes."

If Ida anticipated starring roles in the celebration would go to names that graced the more prominent buildings downtown, she did not let pessimism mar her own endeavors to contribute to the success of the four days. In addition to the finishing touches she thought up to add to the completed pioneer costumes for herself, Jenny and her grandchild, Ida was working on four outfits for friends, whose skills with a treadle Singer sewing machine did not match her own.

The floor and table at her house on Chestnut Street were covered with their paper patterns and yards of material as Ida rushed to complete these last minute sewing projects. It had become natural for her family to see Ida crouched on the parlor carpet with a mouthful of pins, adjusting a pattern to fit one or another of the women who took turns balanced on a stool before her.

She would shove all the work aside whenever Docey stopped by to see how their combined sales of Wagon Wheelers buttons had progressed. They would put their heads together to tally the receipts and count the cash they had accumulated. The buttons, along with souvenir novelties being sold by other groups, were part of the public effort to financially support the centennial. Ida had made it her mission to tap all her friends at the Eagles and in the neighborhood, as well as any stranger who appeared willing to buy a button.

Together, Docey and Ida were pulling in the bucks. Docey was able to report to her that the Wagon Wheelers had collected almost two thousand dollars in button sales, with just two days left before the big event.

Frances Pearl played in and around the chaos of Ida's home, gradually reverting to the contentment her own company had provided her before. A cigar box full of buttons Ida gave her provided hours of amusement. Frances Pearl threaded a darning needle, whose big eye made it easy for her fingers to do, and strung buttons into long strands that Herbie tied off into necklaces and bracelets for her. She also sat quietly and nodded off almost to sleep while Herbie brushed her curls, over and over again, much as a mother cat grooms her young.

Jenny had tried her costume on so many times that Ida decided it needed to be re-ironed to freshen it up. She assigned that task to Jenny while she carefully folded the last finished dress into a box with the others she would deliver to her friends. She would leave the starching and ironing of those to the ones for whom they had been made. She called Ray in from outside and told him to round up Herbie and Frances Pearl.

"I'm taking you all for a ride through town so you can see the fixings that have been going on," said Ida, urging Jenny to finish ironing so they could leave.

The log cabin that had been moved to First and Main Streets to serve as headquarters by The Wagon Wheelers was the hub of centennial operations. Four or five men climbed onto its roof several times a day to hold the kangaroo courts that attracted so much attention. That is where Docey and the other men coerced passersby into buying the bulk of their buttons. The roof they stood on was a flat extension to the original cabin. Held up by posts, the roof was shade as well as stage.

Ida thought she could give the kids a glimpse of Docey and the other Wheelers at work, along with the store fronts of some merchants who had decorated them in pioneer fashion. The Model Grocery, also known as the Red & White Store, at Three South First Street was the first store, and best in Ida's opinion, to decorate. The store's front had been given a completely new facade of rough hewn logs, and fresh fruits and vegetables were displayed in twin openings left in the logs on either side of an open doorway. She wished she had enough money to take the kids for Wimpy burgers at Mitchell's, which had been given a surround of log posts supporting a pseudo balcony and renamed *Fort Walla Walla Eaten House* for the centennial.

Ida expected the altered appearances of Walla Walla's businesses to be lost on young Herbie and his even younger niece, but Ray and Jenny would get a kick out of it. Just a ride in the Ford would be a change for them. With the cost of gasoline hitting ten cents a gallon, Ida thought twice before tooling around on joy rides.

For herself, Ida wanted to stop in at Woolworth's and see how the pioneer costumes of the employees there compared to the ones she had sewn. Ida's daughter, Miriam, who worked at Wards and had looked in on the competition, said the floor-length dresses were real similar, but at least one of the clerks had a pretty print dress that came only to her calves so a pair of ruffled, lace-trimmed pantaloons could show. Pantaloons were something Ida hadn't thought of, but wished she had, at least for Frances Pearl's outfit. The men, Miriam said, were dressed like cowboys, cowboys with shiny, black oxfords for footwear. Woolworth's was only one of many stores that promoted pioneer wear for their employees during the month of August, so there would be lots for the children to see.

Ida wanted to see for herself. She had been put off by some advertising the centennial committee produced. Seems like some slicker advised them the media would be a lot quicker to give them promotional space if they used pretty girls in their ads. The result had been a mixed bag, as far as Ida could see. She had no quarrel with the sedate photograph of the Pioneer Mother—a mighty young looking pioneer mother, Ida noted—posed seated at a spinning wheel in a long, cotton gown with puffed sleeves, but she certainly did take exception to another picture used to promote the centennial. That one was of another young, but obviously curvaceous, girl dressed in western boots and hat and not much else.

"That dress covers no more than a Jantzen bathing suit does, and those new suits are a shame in themselves," Ida had proclaimed when she showed the ad to Docey. "And the gun and holster she has strapped around her waist only points up her nekkedness, as far as I'm concerned."

While she was throwing her full support behind this once in a lifetime event, Ida just was not buying into all of it. Truth was, she was angry at herself for the green-eyed monster twinge she had felt when Docey had picked up the newspaper to take a second look.

Chapter 75

The weight of Docey's thigh pressed against her hip, and she was aware of the spread of his legs as he braced his feet against the pull of the team. The buckles on the harness creaked and jingled as the horses shifted from foot to foot, waiting for Docey to give the signal to move out.

It was a tight space he and Ida shared on the seat of the prairie schooner, much narrower than she had foreseen. Jenny and Frances Pearl were seated on one of the two benches that ran the length of the wagon because there was room for only two on the driver's seat. The young ones would still be seen by the crowds lining the parade route, but they would not be as obvious as Ida and Docey would be on their forward perch.

The canvas covers on all the wagons were rolled up on both sides and tied to the ribs, exposing the interiors with their occupants, all friends or relatives of the 'Wheelers and all in dress appropriate to the 1836 era. The ladies in the lead wagon wore broad brimmed hats, more in keeping with go-to-Sunday-meeting fashions than the poke bonnets Ida had created.

Ida noted with satisfaction that poke bonnets outnumbered any other kind of hat in the rest of the wagon train.

A team of eight oxen were being held in check by the lead driver. His team was made up of stocky, horned critters with no two alike. Three were dappled in various colors, three solid colored and two that looked as if their hides had been painted on in two precise, but different, patterns. Docey's four horses were as near a matched team as one could hope for. And they were stamping in their eagerness to get underway.

Ida swiveled in her seat to look at Jenny and the baby and the line of wagons behind them. The shift moved her nearer to the heat generated by Docey's overall-clad leg. For just a minute she let herself enjoy the contact. Then she pulled her own leg away, and said, "This is surely going to be a once-in-a-lifetime event for Jenny. I think I'll let her sit up here with you so she can see and be seen better."

She avoided looking at Docey as she said it.

Instead of descending from the wagon, she turned impetuously, drew her knees up at the same time, and kicked her legs over the seat until her feet rested on the bench below in the bed of the wagon. Then she slid, landing on her well padded hind-end in a flurry of skirts, an awkward position for any female, but especially lacking in dignity for the fifty-year-old woman Ida was. With a little more grace, Jenny, at her mother's urging, took her place next to Docey.

Ida was still adjusting her bonnet and ignoring the stares of her fellow passengers when two aerial bombs burst overhead to signal the start of the parade promptly at one-thirty on this sunny Thursday afternoon.

Fort George Wright's Infantry band was the first entry to step out from the staging area on Main Street in front of the County Courthouse. In spiffy uniforms, the band members announced themselves with fanfare and drum rolls that set a festive mood for the horse and buggy that followed. It carried the parade marshal, Dr. H. R. Keylor, a pioneer physician who had often traveled to serve his patients in a similar buggy during earlier years in Walla Walla.

When the oxen team ahead of Docey's maneuvered into the 'Wheelers position in the parade, Docey gathered the reins tightly in his outstretched, gloved hands and, with a soft "ge-upp" and a flick of the reins, set the wagon to rolling. His was not the first, nor was it the last in the line of sixteen wagons the 'Wheelers had entered.

Ida craned to see what floats were falling into place ahead and behind them.

She pointed out Safeway Grocer's float to Frances Pearl, but the small pointed pedestal depicting the tall monument that stood on a hill at the mission site meant nothing to the child. The horses that milled around waiting to enter the line-up were what caught Frances Pearl's eye, and she clapped and waved to them, in imitation of Ida.

"She sure is gonna get a work-out if she waves to all the mounted entries," said an elderly man seated farther along the bench where he leaned on a cane he had propped between his knees.

"I hear tell there's hundreds expected to ride today," he added, shifting his top hat until it tilted flirtatiously over his right eye. The stout lady next to him linked arms with him, and reached over to straighten his tie.

Ida, who was active in the Eagles Auxiliary and her church, was surprised that she did not see a familiar face among her fellow passengers. Docey had told her that he had not invited anyone outside her family to ride with him, but there was no lack of kin among the 'Wheelers anxious to fill a seat, so he was assured of a wagon load.

Ida saw that all aboard were primed for a good time.

Their costumes ranged from the old gent's shiny top hat and spats to cuffed jeans and cowboy hats.

A group of horsemen that overtook Docey's wagon drew all eyes as they rode up in a clatter of unshod hoofs. The riders on their blanketed horses jockeyed into parade position, easing, a little late, into a stately line that stretched from curb to curb on Alder Street. The bronze-skinned riders, wearing feathered head-dresses and fringed buckskins, reined their horses with left hands that also held hand drums on which they beat cadence with their right hands as they rode.

It was a dignified group, but, as it made its way along the parade route, it became apparent it was being viewed not just with curiosity and sidelong glances but, in some cases, outright hostility. Applause that welcomed entries ahead of them petered out or was cut short as the Indians rode past. The men maintained stoic expressions and their own silence in the first few blocks. After that, every now and then, the rider in the center of the group would give out a series of high pitched, sharp yips. His unexpected and startling demonstration often caused a nervous flutter among the crowd that made Jenny smile.

"Blood curdling, huh, Mom," she whispered, leaning her face into Docey's shoulder to hide her grin. She thought these muscular men on such well trained horses were by far the most interesting and colorful entry she had seen yet.

In stark contrast to the Indian riders, a replica of Baker's first engine on his rawhide railroad that had opened the west to a polyglot of serious settlers plugged along Alder Street, to cheers and shouts from the viewers. Docey pointed it out to Ida, calling over his shoulder, "Ida, that's the rawhide railroad I was telling you about."

Ida nodded her understanding, even though Docey could not see her bobbing head from his perch without twisting around.

They had gone just four blocks and were at Fourth and Alder when Jenny spotted Frances and Herbie in the crowd. They were standing with Nita and Carl Spence in the shade of a hotel's marquee.

Ida tried to point them out to Frances Pearl, but she gave no indication that she recognized her mother or any face among all the others, until her seven-year-old towheaded uncle broke free of Frances and dashed toward the wagon. Frances Pearl laughed and clapped then, calling out "Momma" over and over, as Frances sprinted after Herbie. He was too quick for her, and leaped onto the step at the rear of the wagon before she could catch him.

A woman seated next to the tailgate reached out, grabbed Herbie by the scruff of the neck, and held him steady until a man with a long reach boosted him in.

"Does this belong to any of you?" he asked, laughing, as he dangled Herbie and swung him to and fro. Seven was too big to be man-handled, but Herbie dared not object beyond looking peevish. He knew he was on shaky ground or, in this case, up in the air, after his daring deed.

Ida claimed him, amid laughter. She reeled him in and settled him—not too gently—onto the seat beside her. Docey pulled a red bandanna from his hip pocket, twirled it in the air, motioned to his own neck, and tossed it back to Ida, who tied it around Herbie's neck cowboy-style. Wasn't going to be anyone riding in this wagon train unless they wore the proper gear.

The entire parade route from lower Main up to Palouse and back was crowded.

The crush of spectators packed both sides of the streets. As they rolled slowly along, Ida was kept busy waving, and helping Frances Pearl wave at the people who hooted and hollered to show their appreciation of the big show.

As Docey guided his team into the turn at Palouse Street where a crowd was gathered on the steps of a stone church with an impressive tower, he glanced back over his shoulder, and threw a wink in Ida's direction. The turn gave them all the opportunity to see the entries that trailed behind them. Lewis and Clark in a canoe with Sacajawea pointing the way over a sea of fringed crepe paper floated along behind them. Jenny, with the better view, related to Ida that a sign on it said the local Dental Association was the sponsor of the entry depicting the history-making expedition.

Ida got a better view of a float featuring a miniature grist mill that had won first place for the Marcus Whitman Grange in the Whitman Story division. The replica of the missionaries' grist mill included real rye grass like that which still grew alongside the creek at the mission site. When Ida saw the reeds waving in the breeze, she thought of the massacre survivors, children, who had hidden by the creek, concealing themselves in rye grass, to escape the slaughter. The widespread killing on a quiet morning at the Whitman Station could be laid on the doorstep of cultural differences and Indians suspicious of the outbreak of measles that had taken so many Indian lives after the Whitmans' arrival at the place the Indians called *Waiilatpu, the place where four creeks meet*.

Ida thought these facts could not be far from anyone's mind as first the Indian riders and then the grange's float passed by.

She did notice that the Lions Club entry of an Indian village peopled with pale faces received hearty applause and cheers.

Lively marching music was provided by five bands interspersed throughout the parade, and, when they made their stops at intersections to perform, the shuffle of the hoofs of Docey's halted team seemed to keep time to the music. At first, it seemed a coincidence, but, when the team 'performed' every time the band performed, it was good for a laugh from all on board and attention from the crowd.

The cream white, glazed terra-cotta façade of the Liberty Theatre was as much an attraction for those on the floats as the parade participants were for the crowd. The theatre, built in 1917, looked band-box new, and its chalet-type roof line and alpine window boxes showed the influence of its German architect,

Henry Osterman.

"Oh look, Mom. The feature is starring Bing Crosby and Frances Farmer. Can we go? Can we go tonight?" Jenny asked. When she saw the expression on Ida's face, she added a plaintive "Please, Mom."

"We'll see," said Ida.

"That usually means 'not likely'," Jenny said.

"Pretty girl, and smart too," replied Ida.

Docey pulled the team to a halt for inspection in front of the reviewing stand at South First Avenue and Main Street. His horses did their little dance again, and earned a round of applause from the dignitaries.

Ida had her eyes on the waters of Mill Creek that flowed from under the street in a deep channel at this intersection. The creek's rolling presence seemed incongruous downtown, surrounded as it was by sturdy, brick buildings with their fancy crenellations and curlicues, some, like Baker-Boyer Bank in the next block, rising to seven stories.

The creek provoked a disturbing thought for Ida.

She pushed away the image of Alvin working in the cold and wet of its channel just five months before. She was intent on making the most of this day that was supposed to be festive.

As they approached lower Main Street and the end of the parade route was in sight, Ida wondered if she had missed seeing her kids. Will had said he and Murray would take Ray and Agnes with them to watch the parade, and would be sure to look for them and wave. So far, she had not picked them out. She stood behind Jenny, and rested a hand on her shoulder for balance.

"Have you seen the kids, yet?" she asked.

"I'm looking, but haven't seen them," Jenny replied.

The words were just out of her mouth when Docey lifted his whip and pointed off to the right.

There were the three boys and Agnes, standing in front of Lutcher's Pool Hall. Will was waving his hat overhead to get their attention, and Ray, forgetting his almost grown-up fifteen-year-old status, was jumping from one leg to another and waving both hands over his head, shouting, "Ma. Ma. Here!"

"Ask and ye shall receive," Ida said, waving back. She lifted Frances Pearl up, had her wave, too, and made room for Herbie, who pushed his way in until he was squeezed onto the seat between Docey and Jenny.

When Ida tried to pry him loose, Docey said, "Aw, let him be. We're almost to the end now." Docey caught Murray's eye, and made a come-along gesture toward the courthouse with his whip. Murray flipped a finger salute to signal message received. The boys would help him unharness the team.

Frances was waiting for them when the parade dispersed back where it had started. She was watching a group of square dancers, who had performed along the route, but were still promenading and do-si-doing right in front of the courthouse steps to the accompaniment of a banjo strummed by a picker. The music-maker was sitting comfortably, as if at home, on a chair obviously his own. The square dancers' western wear was a mixed lot, Ida noticed, with one woman even wearing a pair of riding britches, puffed at the hips and tight to the legs.

"Not something I could wear, but on her it looks good," Ida said, coming up behind Frances and gesturing toward the dancer in question.

Frances looked over her mother's generous figure, soft and rounded in her gingham dress, and eyed Jenny's gangling, but budding, seventeen-year-old body.

"You all look great," said Frances, "you and Jenny, the baby, Docey, all of you...and you, you little imp..." She grabbed Herbie by the straps on his overalls and gave him a shake. He gifted her with a gap-toothed grin, and wriggled out of her grip.

"Let's just wait here until Docey gets the horses taken care of," said Ida.

Agnes sidled close to Jenny and whispered, "If I had known that little snot Herbie was going to be riding in Docey's wagon, I would have let Mom make me one of those old dumb dresses and a crazy hat that looks like a coal shuttle so's I could ride along, too."

"You know you didn't want to ride along. You told Mom there was no way you were going to dress up like this," said Jenny, fanning her skirt out to the side.

"I might have! I would have if I'd known..." Aggie started to protest, but Jenny interrupted her.

"Anyway, Herbie was an after thought. No one planned on

him hitchin' a ride."

"Just the same. He's only seven, and a brother six years younger than me shouldn't get to do things I don't."

"Things you *could* have done, if you hadn't been such a brat," Jenny hissed.

Jenny and Agnes were careful to modulate their voices so their conversation did not carry to Ida. Although neither girl could strictly be called a child, both still operated under their mother's axiom that children should be seen and not heard. Children might squabble and tiff among themselves, but, it was understood, such behavior was never conducted in the presence of adults. It was also understood that children's quarrels were to be settled by children, among themselves. No tale-bearing was allowed in Ida's home, and she never spent time on settling childish arguments that would be forgotten in an hour, if left alone.

Jenny now took the role of peace-maker, wrapping an arm around her younger sister as she said, "Now, Ag, Herbie's got nothing to do with today. You know you wanted to go with Will instead, and you got to do that. Bet you had a better look at all the floats than we did anyway."

Agnes was easily placated. And it had been interesting, standing on the sidelines in among all those people. Especially after Will herded them away from in front of Jackson's Sporting Goods Store where all those old, dead deer were hanging up. Real deer, and all dead. Three hanging up with their white butts stuck up in the air, and as many more lying right on the sidewalk. Even a couple of heads with their horns attached. Antlers, Will said they were, and who cares. It was better on down the street where Will found them a spot in front of Lutcher's.

Agnes had gotten a good view as the parade went by, but there were some strange sights right on the sidewalk. She had never seen anything like what that old guy did. He squirted a stream of tobacco juice right out of his mouth and into the street, almost under a horse's hooves. Now that was a sight Jenny probably had not seen, even from high up there next to Docey. It was pretty funny, too.

Before the parade started there had been a cowboy, leaning up against the front of Lutcher's like he owned it. She had watched him pull a cloth sack of tobacco from his shirt pocket, pry its puckered top open, and tip a stream of tobacco out into a cigarette paper neat as you please. *And rolled it up, using just one hand.* No one she knew used just one hand to build a cigarette. The cowboy had seen her watching him. He had watched right back at her with his sleepy eyes. When he used his teeth on the strings to pull the sack closed, and then stuck out his tongue and pulled the paper slowly across it to make the seal, she got a crawly feeling deep in her stomach.

She had not liked that feeling. She had moved closer to Ray, and quickly turned her attention to the street where a band was approaching.

"Here it comes," said Ray. "It's starting now…"

And then Agnes could no longer hear her brother because the drums were loud. They were so loud they beat that creepy feeling right out of her gut. She was glad it was gone. It was so gone, it was forgotten even before the line of Indians clip-clopped past. She heard words behind her, words she did not understand. *Siwash, teepee-creepers, barn-burners, squaws.* She had not turned around to see who was speaking, but leaned over to Will and said, "What are they talking about?" He had hushed her with a finger placed on his lips, then bent over and whispered one word into her ear: "Injuns."

If one of the words had been papoose, Agnes would have recognized that. She had seen Indian babies tucked snugly into cradle boards, and had admired the way the mothers had hung beads and trinkets on the curved part to give the babies something pretty to look at. "Very creative. Stimulates their thinking process." Ida had said.

Yes, standing on the sidewalk had been interesting. Jenny was probably right; she had probably seen more from there than she would have from Docey's prairie schooner.

The banjo player was really getting a second head of steam, and the square dancers' feet were flying. Jenny linked arms with Agnes and they did a little toe-tapping, which set both of them to giggling.

"It is music that makes you want to dance," Frances noted, calling Ida's attention to the girls.

Frances felt a tug at her skirt.

"Why is that guy wearing frilly drawers?" Herbie asked.

Frances looked to where he was pointing.

It was a monument to Christopher Columbus that had his attention. And, to a boy's eyes, the statue might look as if it was wearing ruffled underpants. Frances herself could not put a proper name to the short, pleated and puffed trunks worn by the replica of the Italian explorer, which was also garbed in tight leggings and a tunic that fell to its ankles. Really, Frances thought, it was a very impressive sculpture the way Columbus' hand rested on a globe of the world.

"That man lived a long time ago, and that is the kind of pants some men wore then," said Frances. She squatted down beside Herbie, deciding to take a few minutes to give him a short history lesson on the discovery of the Americas. When she finished and he was still curious about why this statue was on the front lawn of the courthouse, she took him by the hand and walked him around it. She showed him the names of 97 Italians, who had spent a thousand dollars in 1911 to honor 'Italy's illustrious son'. She read off a few of the names to him. "Guglielmelli, Torreta, Columbo, Alessio, Basta, Spagnuolo, Elia…"

"What does lustrious mean?"

"*Illustrious*…means dignified," she said.

Frances would have liked to tell Herbie how the sagebrush and bunch grass on Walla Walla's flat-as-a-pancake valley had been turned into orchards and truck gardens full of onions, carrots, spinach and all kinds of produce by early Chinese immigrants and later by a growing Italian community, but his curiosity had been satisfied and she could tell she no longer had his attention.

They rejoined Ida in watching the dancers. When Docey returned with the boys, he motioned to Ida to step away from the rest. When Docey had her somewhat alone, he said, "How 'bout all of us mosey back up Main and have us a feed of Wimpy burgers, my treat?"

"That sounds like champagne talk on a beer budget," Ida replied.

"Actually, I sold a hog a couple days ago, so I'm flush."

Ida turned a shoulder, presenting her back to him, and did not answer. Docey put a hand on her arm to turn her to face him.

"It's not a lot I'm asking. I think you could let me do this much."

Ida's gaze was directed at the ground. She shuffled a foot against the sidewalk. Her heavy sigh hung in the air between them.

Finally, Ida lifted her head. With eyes still closed, she wiped her left hand across her forehead in a tired gesture.

"Oh, have it your way then, Do-si-do."

His hand slipped from her arm, and he pranced over to Jenny, hooked elbows with her, and swung her around in time to the music that was still flying off the banjo strings.

"Do-si-do and away we all go for Wimpy's!' he chirruped.

That night seventy-five hundred people gathered at the Walla Walla fairgrounds to watch the *Wagons West* pageant, a highlight of the centennial. All of the Wagon Wheelers, including Ida and Jenny, were there to add their canvas-covered prairie schooners to the show. A cast of more than three thousand, backed by a chorus of three hundred voices and a symphony orchestra, acted out the few years the zealous missionaries had lived in this land. It was a scene that was to be repeated every night of the four-day celebration.

A novelty in the pageant, incidental to the Whitman story but mystifying to most in the audience, was a Hammond electric organ that didn't even need pipes to produce its tones.

> *Friday, August 14. Here it is Fish*
> *Day again. These days sure come*
> *close together. We are having*
> *a mighty fine big Centennial*
> *in Walla Walla—Here I am in*
> *bed with a big celebration*
> *going on.*
> *Alvin*

"In every work of genius, we recognize our own rejected thoughts; they come back to us with a certain alienated majesty."—Emerson

Chapter 76

*Saturday, August 15. We just
weighed but I haven't found
out yet how much I weigh or
gained or lost. I haven't
been feeling very well this
week and don't expect to
gain very much if at all.
Al*

*Sunday, My Wife and Baby
were out. I sure enjoy
seeing my girls together.
They sure look fine together.
So much alike and have a
good time together. I
wonder how the three of
us would look in one picture.*

*"He who has conferred a kindness should be silent; he who
has received one, should speak of it."—Seneca*

Chapter 77

There was no doubt about it. Alvin felt left out of things. The world was passing him by, and he could not run fast enough to keep up with it. This bed rest was for the birds!

"Hey, Leo, what's new?" Alvin felt like stirring up a little trouble, but pumping Leo for news before he finished his morning paper was the best he could do.

Leo refused to take offense at being pulled away from his regular morning entertainment.

"Says here Mitchell's sold more than ninety thousand Wimpy burgers during the centennial. That's a lotta beef...or B.S., depending on how much you can believe in newswpapers."

"Frances must have been one of those ninety thousand. She said Docey took her and Ida and the whole clan out for burgers after the parade Thursday. Must have cost an arm and a leg. I wouldn't mind having a big, old Wimpy right about now. With lots of fried onions."

"Isn't our toast and gruel good enough for you?"

Alvin ignored Leo's gibe. "What else does it say in there?"

"If you just hold your horses, I'll pass the paper over to you when I finish reading it."

"I'm fresh out of horses. I want news!" Alvin demanded.

This was a new Al Leo was seeing, and he cocked a quizzical eye at him.

"You're just a tad on the cantankerous side this morning, seems to me," said Leo. "Well, let's see...sure is a lot writ up about the centennial. You'd think it was something that happened only once every hundred years."

"Funny. Har-de-har-har."

"OK. Remember how they had all that folderol over the centennial people trying to get the postal authorities to issue a stamp with the Whitmans on it and had to settle for an Oregon territory one? Well, says here, Walla Walla sold more than two hundred fifty-seven thousand of those stamps on the first day they come out, more than any of the other cities in the Northwest. It was sorta a contest, says here.

"Here's more centennial crap," Leo continued. "But this happened on the first day of the thing. Our beloved Governor Martin was taken to court…"

"To court? For what?" Alvin asked, perking up at this hint of trouble.

"That mock court those Wagon Wheelers held downtown as part of their hijinks. They claimed the suit and white collar the gov was wearin' were not the proper western attire. Also got him for instigating that goldang state sales tax they hung on us last year. Now *that* I'll go along with. Whoever thought it up ought to be hauled into court. A real court! Say, isn't Docey one of them Wagon Wheelers?"

"I don't want to hear any more about a celebration I didn't even get a sniff of," Alvin grouched.

"Well then don't ask me to be your news boy," Leo grumped right back at him.

If Al's mood was on the downside, his sister's was just the opposite. Alta had been given permission to sun outside in a lounger on the lawn, and the fresh air put her in good spirits.

The sun felt good on her face, and she tilted her head to receive more of its warm kiss on her skin. Now if she could just dig her hands into the warm earth, plant a seed, and see it grow, she would be a happy woman. Alta had a natural green thumb. Folks said she could coax a dry twig to sprout. In fact, if they but knew it, she had. Today, the green of the trees and the bright flowers blooming in the beds along the driveway filled her with a peace she had not felt since entering the sanatorium. She longed for the garden she had left behind. The pot of wandering jew Elwin had brought her added a homey touch to her room, but she was missing a spot of bright color.

Alta's eyes were drawn to the flowers just steps away. So bright, so alive with color. *Maybe I'll just saunter over for a closer look.*

Zinnias and asters glowed in deep oranges, rich reds, bright blues and purples. *Truly, God gifted the world when he granted it flowers.* She snapped off a few dead heads, stuffing them into her pocket to discard later. She wandered down the row, picking off dead leaves she let fall into the soil. *Good mulch.* She ran her fingers through the feathery petals of an aster, cupped the stiffer, spiky bloom of a zinnia in the palm of her hand. *So many flowers, such a bountiful display.*

Almost reverently, Alta dug a sharp thumb nail into a stem, severing it. She touched the plucked flower to her nose. *Roses smell better.* She picked another and held them together, intent on the tiny details of petals that combined to form the beauty of these two flowers on this very day, just for her. She lifted the blooms to her lips and felt a light dusting of the golden pollen brush onto them. She licked it off. *Tasteless.*

An image of Frances came to her, an image from a time she had accompanied her to Mass at St. Pat's, Frances kneeling at the communion rail, eyes closed, head tilted back, tongue resting passive on her lower lip, ready to receive the hard, thin, white wafer the priest held delicately between two fingers. Alta wondered if her practical sister-in-law really believed that the— what had she called it?—the *host* was a piece of a man's body. And not just a man, but God himself. Kneeling there like that Frances had looked as if she believed.

This day, these flowers, this pollen are the food for my soul.

"Just what do you think you are doing, Miss?"

The harsh words jerked Alta from her reverie as sharply as a slap across the face.

"I asked you, Miss, what are you doing?"

What am I doing?

"Walking," a stunned Alta answered. It was the first thing she thought of, the only fault of which she might be guilty. Walking, instead of lying quietly in the sun like a good patient.

"Do you call this 'walking'?" Nurse Gillis asked in a tone heavy with sarcasm. She pointed to the flowers, now forgotten by Alta, but still clutched tightly in her hand.

"No, M'am."

"Oh, you don't? Then what do you call picking flowers that do not belong to you and that are not meant for you?"

Alta was speechless, and that did not please Nurse Gillis

either.

"Here!" Alta quickly held the flowers out to the supervisor in a conciliatory gesture. Gillis waved them away.

"You have not abided by the rules, and you, Miss, shall return to your room *now*. You may deposit your ill-gained goods in the dust bin on your way in. Such a waste!"

'It was a waste,' Alta thought, as she dropped the blooms into the first waste receptacle she passed. She blinked back tears, tears of humiliation at being a twenty-seven-year-old married woman subjected to a public scolding. She wondered how many out on the lawn had witnessed it. She would not give Gillis or anyone else the satisfaction of seeing tears fall.

She swiped at her eyes with the sleeve of her dressing gown, and marched down the hall with head held high. She was racking her brain to see if somewhere in there was lodged the rule against flower-picking, when she heard someone sobbing as if their heart had just broken. The misery was coming from behind the door to the room Ruby Pritchard and Susie McCloud shared.

Alta debated whether to enter or leave well enough alone. The door was ajar. She decided to just take a quick peek inside.

She saw Ruby sitting cross-legged on her bed, arms folded so tightly her fists were wedged into her armpits. Her face was distorted by a frown wrinkling her forehead and a mouth pulled into a taut line by teeth that were grinding together. Displeasure was exhibited in every line of her body. This was the ebullient Ruby at her finest, the fiery Ruby the ward had come to know over the past seven weeks.

Across from her, Susie huddled on her own bed, trying to cry her eyes out of her head, if appearances meant anything.

Alta's cautious retreat from the room was halted by a blast from Ruby.

"Did you ever in all your life hear of anything so silly?" Ruby screeched.

"Are you speaking to me?" Alta asked.

"You'll do! You may know something we don't! I asked you if you ever heard of anything like what's going on in this room?"

"And…that would be…what?"

"Crap is what it looks like to me, but it could be any number of things. Susie has just been given the word that she's being moved out of here any minute. And no one will tell us a G.D. thing. No why, wherefore or go to hell. And we want to know why!"

Alta had been hospitalized a month longer than Ruby, but surely Susie, who had been here longer than either of them, knew what a move could mean. It did not *have* to mean isolation and all it stood for. It could just be a change of rooms and roommates for the sake of change. Alta knew she did not want to be the one to offer an explanation. She might guess wrong. This move could just be the result of another rule with which she was not familiar. Who knew how many other rules were hidden away to be trotted out on any given day. She decided to offer sympathy, but no advice.

"There, there," she crooned to Susie. She came back into the room and crossed to Susie's bed, sitting so she could rub her shoulder in what she hoped was a comforting way.

"That ain't going to work. I already tried that. Even offered to remove all the polish on her toes and fingernails, and give her a whole new do with this shell pink. She ain't buyin' nothing but an answer to why they're hauling her ass out of here," said Ruby, quickly adding, "Pardon my French."

Alta continued to draw easy circles over Susie's back, lingering on muscles that felt tight beneath her hand. These she kneaded as she would a batch of bread dough, gently but firmly. The sobbing stopped. Alta had a feeling for yeast dough, much as she had a special touch with all growing things. She pulled and pushed at the muscles just as she pushed and pulled the dough to pop free the air bubbles. The skin warmed beneath her fingers, and knots began to unravel. Alta continued to gently massage.

When she felt the last of the tension ease away, she switched to a smoothing stroke, the one she used to spread freshly churned butter lightly over the top of a raw loaf before setting it to raise.

"And rise we will, little Susie, rise to the occasion we surely will," Alta said, giving her a final pat.

To Ruby's astonishment, Susie pulled her head out of the covers, rolled over and sat up. Her face was blotchy, eyes swollen and red. Mucus dripped from her nose.

Alta pulled a handkerchief from her pocket, not noticing the dried flower heads that fell from it onto the floor. "Here we go," she said, holding the hanky to Susie's nose. "Blow!" When Susie responded with a big honk, Alta praised, "That's the way. Now I think you could use a nice warm cloth on that pretty face. Don't you think so, Ruby? Could you see about getting her one?"

"Well damn me all to hell," Ruby muttered.

But she went away and came back with a wet cloth that still retained some heat. Rosie, sitting up and working on a smile, took it and scrubbed away.

Alta had worked her way almost to the door when Ruby caught her by the arm and hissed, "We still don't have any answers, but, by gawd, I intend to get some!"

It was early evening when Phil slipped into their room and announced, "The Grapevine's buzzing tonight. You guys hear the news yet?"

"Phil, you know we live for only *your* pronouncements. Shoot!" Leo said.

Phil led off with the fiasco over the flowers, keeping it short and to the point out of respect for Alvin, and offering the opinion that the patients who were on the scene thought Al's sister had got the short end of the stick. He then gave them a longer version of Susie's emotional outburst and Ruby's irate reaction to Gillis' transfer order. Phil was not content to just tell about the tantrum Ruby threw after Susie's crying fit, when Gillis still refused to give her any information about why a move was necessary. He used gestures, bobbing and weaving, flailing his arms and kicking his legs almost up to his head.

Phil's acting was so good Alvin could almost see Ruby throwing her weight around. He wondered if her kick had really been as high as Phil's and what she was wearing at the time.

"When Gillis and Flora wheeled the McCloud girl away, that redhead was swearing and crying, cussing up a storm that would make a gandy-dancer blush. She was carrying on in a way you wouldn't believe," Phil said as he wound up his story.

"Oh, I'd believe it all right, Phil. The redhead, if you recall, is my wife."

Phil's mouth flapped shut. His eyes swiveled left, then right, as if looking for a way out.

"Are either of you related to Deven Forster?"

Alvin and Leo assured him they were not.

Phil relaxed and said, "Well, you'll never guess what he did! He got up a petition today and started passing it around. Said he was going to put a stop to all this spoiled salmon the kitchen's been fobbing off on us. He was collecting the signatures like crazy until Gillis caught up with him. The man has been confined to quarters, and I don't mean maybe. But, from the rumbles rolling down from above, he just may have done us all a big favor."

Just before lights out, Leo called across to Alvin, "Looks like you weren't the only one woke up on the wrong side of the bed, Curly."

Alvin didn't grace his remark with a response. Instead he reached for his red book.

> *Monday, August 17. Boy did we*
> *have a big upset out here today.*
> *Over just a few of the things*
> *that happen in a place of*
> *this kind. I do think it will*
> *help the conditions somewhat.*
> *I hope so.*

Chapter 78

Alvin awoke to whispers. Furtive whispers. Behind his back. In the dark.

He lay very still, listening.

"I can't take no more, Daddy."

It was a plaintive sound, just above a whisper.

Was that Ruby? Here? In the men's ward? In this room? In the middle of the night?

Leo's gruff voice was just a mumble.

"I mean it. I've had enough crap to last a lifetime."

More than a whisper. Definitely Ruby.

"Shhh, baby. Don't want to wake Curly, do we?"

"I feel like wakin' up the whole damn place. Feel like screamin' it right down."

"Sure. Sure. But let's keep it down or we'll have Gillis in here."

"That's somethin' else I've had enough of...that Gillis and her stupid rules. Wasn't enough she dragged Susie right off from under my nose, but I heard she jumped on another patient just for picking a G.D. flower. Did you hear about that?"

Ruby's voice was getting louder, and now Al started to worry that Gillis really would come in. Leo must have thought so, too, because Alvin heard him hushing her.

"Don't be hushing me, old man. If it weren't for you, I wouldn't cven be in this predicament." Her angry tone made *'old man'* sound like an insult.

"Ruby, now Ruby, you aren't being fair," Leo protested, forgetting to keep his own voice low.

"Fair has nothing to do with this, Leo," Ruby answered, dropping her voice back to a near whisper. "You dumped these germs on me, and you dumped me in here. Now I'm getting out."

"Baby, I think you better hightail it back to your bed. We can talk about this tomorrow."

"I'm through talking, Leo. I just wanted to let you know I've had enough of this place. I can't take it." Resignation had replaced anger. "I won't take it, and that's that."

"Aw, Baby…"

Alvin heard scuffling, then silence.

"I'm sorry, Daddy. Real sorry." The whisper was so low, so throaty, that Alvin could not be sure he had heard it right, but it was followed by the softest of footsteps out the door.

Al tried to breathe in a normal sleeping way, but then realized he did not know if he should take quiet, shallow breaths or long, noisy ones. He had never heard himself sleeping. Leo was a noisy sleeper. Frances a quiet one. The question became moot when he heard something from the next bed that he would never in a hundred years have expected to hear. If tough old Leo was crying, he had to believe Al was asleep.

Chapter 79

No one looking at Leo in the light of day would ever guess the scene that had transpired in the middle of the night. Alvin watched Leo prop himself up, slap open the *Union*, and latch onto the cup of coffee he had just poured from the pot Rose had brought them. If Leo did not want to acknowledge the night's doings, neither would he.

Alvin poured coffee into his own cup, added a dollop of cream and a spoonful of sugar. He did not really like coffee, but, doctored up, it was passable.

The smell of perked coffee in the morning was an aroma he had grown up with, and one he associated with family gathered around the kitchen table. It was his mother who always had the pot waiting on the back of the stove when Emerson hauled himself out of bed. His dad was an early riser, but Al's recollection was that Ora made it her business to be the first up. And she was always quick to pour a big mug of coffee for Grandma Potts when she would stump into the house, whether it was before breakfast, the last thing at night, or anywhere in between.

Alvin was still drinking warm milk when Ora moved out of the cabin and into Colville. It was his dad who started mixing hot coffee into his milk. Alvin had never had the heart to tell Emerson he did not fancy it that way. He really preferred the tea Ora had always brewed when Grandma Kennedy came over the hill of an afternoon. His mother would slide a nugget of brown sugar into his cup, and, when he was at Grandma's house, he would sometimes have a thin slice of lemon in his tea. But that was a seldom treat. Lemons did not often find their way through the piney woods to Daisy. Even though the afternoons over tea with his mother and grandmother were his favorite childhood memories, the aroma of tea never had the strength to invoke them like perking coffee did.

Al wondered what thoughts were floating through Leo's head this morning. He certainly did not look upset. He looked…normal.

I would not be looking normal if my wife roused me out in the middle of the night. That girl was mad as a wet hen. Wonder how it's going this morning.

Al did not have to wonder long.

Rose was just clearing away their trays when Ruby showed up.

She was dressed in the same violet dress in which she had arrived under protest such a short time before. That was not a good sign. She should be in a hospital robe like the rest of those confined to bed. Alvin did not think these outdoor clothes signified an official release from bed rest.

"I think I'll just mosey on down the hall for awhile," Alvin said.

"There will be no 'moseying' for you Mr. Potts. You know the rules," Rose said, scooping up the last of the dishes and heading out the door. "I will be right back," she cautioned, throwing him a look over her shoulder.

"Leo, I do think I'll just sneak out for a little walk, give you two some privacy."

"Don't you be a damned fool, Curly. No use you runnin' off and getting yourself into trouble," said Leo.

"This here isn't apt to take very long," he added, looking at Ruby when he said it.

Her only response was, surprisingly, a blush. The rosy flush of embarrassment sat strangely on the cheeks of the intrepid Ruby, whose high cheek bones more often wore angry blotches or the dewy patches she painted on to compliment the batting of her eyes.

This Ruby looked like a butterfly emerging from its cocoon, slightly damp around the edges and vulnerable. Gone were her exaggerated movements, the flouncy bounce, the flirtatious toss of her head. She stepped close to Leo, laid her head on his shoulder, wrapped an arm around his neck. She whispered something into his ear. The sides of his mouth turned up, but it was a sad imitation of a smile.

Al turned his back, trying for invisibility.

There was a lot of quiet coming from Leo's side of the room.

"Well, now!" Ruby finally broke the silence. "We don't need all this gloom and doom. Put on a happy face."

"What's your plan, little girl?"

"My immediate plan is to hop into the taxi cab that should be here pretty soon, and take me a train ride home to Dayton. Then, this 'little girl' is going to make a serious stab at growing up."

"That's a mighty tall order. You up to it?"

There was no judgment in Leo's voice, maybe some concern, but mostly it was logic that came through. Anyone hearing his terse statement would have to question how much cash the lady had tucked away because taxi and train fare did not come cheap. If she were looking for an argument, she might be able to scrape one up over the gentle challenge he had flung at her.

But this morning Ruby was not in an argumentative mood. She had fired her last salvo during the night. The answer she gave him was in the form of a question, and, when she gave it, her voice was as practical as his had been.

"We'll find out if I'm up to it, won't we?" she asked.

Alvin was relieved to see that it really was a taxi that was wheeling into the drive. This was not the day for Hudsons.

Ruby stepped to the window, waving a handkerchief to let the driver know she was aware he was there. "Guess it's time to go, Leo," she said, returning to his side. He reached out a hand, as if to hold her back, then dropped it back to the counterpane. "Guess so," he muttered.

Alvin wished himself a million miles away.

"Gillis know you're leaving?" Leo asked.

"She does, and she tried to stop it. We had a set-to this morning. Now she can like it or lump it," Ruby said, her voice flat, devoid of animosity.

Suddenly, she reached over, flung her arms around Leo's neck, and squeezed him to her breasts. Her cheek rested on the top of his head, his face tucked into her neck. Her eyes squeezed shut to hold back tears. Then she pushed Leo away, tilted her chin up, and strode over to Alvin's bed.

"Well, this is so-long, Curly," she said, sticking out her hand. "Take care of yourself. And, if you ever find out what's up with Susie, don't tell me!"

She gave him no time to respond, just whirled away. Her skirt flared out and up, revealing what, Alvin recalled, she had once described as 'ringless chiffon hose'. If this was the same pair, they had held up as well as she had predicted. She paused, rested one hand on the doorjamb, put the other on her cocked hip, and turned to look at them over her shoulder. A toss of her head sent her red hair flying in the old familiar way, and she gave them a deliberate wink. Then she was gone.

"That's my Ruby," Leo said.

"She's my same old Ruby," Leo insisted on a note of desperation, as if Alvin had argued the point.

Alvin thought the lady *had* made a strong effort to leave them believing she surely was the same old Ruby.

"She's the same Ruby, right, Al?" Leo said, pleading for reassurance.

"You said it, Leo." *The same Ruby, but without the joy. Joy, that's what's gone right out of her, for sure.*

> *Tuesday, August 18. I am feeling*
> *fine after a good hot bath. I*
> *have been feeling pretty well*
> *here lately. My ear bothers*
> *me some. It discharges quite*
> *a lot and it is sore.*
> *Mrs. Pritchard went home*
> *today after an argument.*

"How dull it is to pause, to make an end, To rust unburnish'd, not to shine in use!"—Lord Tennyson

Chapter 80

Ruby's departure had an immediate and devastating effect on Leo. If he had looked to be an old man when he brought Ruby into the san as a patient, that old man now looked as if he had been dragged through the back woods—briars, brush, brambles and all—tied to the back end of a runaway mule. He seemed to grow gaunt within the first hour of her leave-taking, and had not improved overnight.

What scared Alvin even more was the way Leo seemed to embrace his misery.

There had been only glimpses of the old irascible Leo since Oscar died, but Alvin had hoped for a comeback, that Leo would again be the outgoing, witty roommate he had enjoyed before. Now, he would settle for grumpy.

Alvin had not expected Leo to be talkative after Ruby left, but neither had he expected him to grow deaf and dumb. Alvin had not plied him with questions, nor offered much in the way of conversation, but, what little he did pass Leo's way, was chaff before the wind. Leo just blew it off, as if Alvin had not said a word. Even gentle Rose was unable to get a response. Leo ignored his breakfast and lunch trays, lying, eyes closed, on his bed.

To look at Leo now was like looking at a corn husk with the cob removed.

Alvin had never seen such a sad sack.

He was glad it was Wednesday, a visiting day. Visitors might help. Alvin would welcome other voices, other bodies in the room. Out of common courtesy Leo would have to acknowledge them.

The hours dragged, and two o'clock was slow in coming. When the magic hour finally struck, Al was still waiting. He waited. And waited. Rose finally brought him a message that had been called in before breakfast, she said. His wife had telephoned to say she was doubtful that she would make it out today. Frances was not the only one unable to help pass the time or raise spirits this Wednesday afternoon. No visitors entered their room.

> *Wednesday, August 19. I spent the*
> *afternoon all alone. No company*
> *and was I lonesome. I am waiting*
> *for my wife now. I don't expect*
> *her but I am watching and waiting*
> *for her anyway. I love her and*
> *baby so much. I want to be with*
> *them all of the time.*

In the middle of the night, Leo began to moan. It was a soft sound at first, one that Alvin could ignore, one actually that a good roommate should ignore, but it increased in volume until there was nothing to do but call for a nurse. It was Flora who answered. She came with that soft patter patients dreaded hearing in the dark hours. It was much better if halls were quiet until the sun peeped out of the east and turned the low slung hills rosy. Dark hours here were notorious for bringing trouble.

This will be another bud sprouting on the grapevine.

Alvin raised up to watch Flora, who was fussing over Leo, taking his blood pressure, listening to his chest with her stethoscope.

"Mr. Pritchard," said Flora, a question in her voice. "Mr. Pritchard, can you hear me? Are you all right?"

When she received no answer, she called again, a little louder, more urgent, "Leo. Leo?"

He had not quit moaning since she entered the room, and moans were the only response he gave her now. She bent low over him, talking directly into his ear. Alvin heard Leo mutter, but could not make out the words. Flora patted Leo's shoulder, and straightened up.

"There is nothing wrong with him, Mr. Potts," Flora said, not looking at Alvin. "But I am going to give him a sedative. He just needs to sleep, poor man. This has been a strange and difficult day for him."

*Thursday, August 20. I am left alone with
Pritchard. He won't be here long
considering his condition. He
may move back to Dayton.*

*"He prayeth well, who loveth well both man and bird and
beast."—Coleridge*

Chapter 81

*Friday, August 21. Just a good
hot day. I am expecting my
wife out today as she couldn't
come out visiting day.*~~~~

It was not Leo that made a move. Rather, a new patient was added to their room late Friday morning. His name was Brannigan, and he was everything that Leo and Alvin were not. Brannigan was not only spiritually inclined, he was religious, and, what's more, Rose announced, Brannigan was a priest.

Alvin had to smile to think what kind of reception Brannigan might have received if Leo were in top form. As it was, Brannigan moved in without fanfare. He was ensconced in a bed Rose and Flora moved between Leo and Alvin. The introductions were brief, and Leo took no part in them. Seemingly he was unaware that someone else was sharing the room.

His shoes were the first thing Alvin noticed about Brannigan. *Looks like a size five. Maybe a seven.* In addition to being very small, the priest's shoes were highly polished. *No shortage of beeswax.* Even his bones were on the small size. Bird bones that made for delicate wrists, on one of which a watch flopped loosely, as if there had been a recent weight loss. His nose came to a sharp point, adding to the bird-like image. As he unpacked his few possessions, his mouth squeezed into a moue that gave him a prissy look.

Alvin had no time to get to know Brannigan before Frances slipped into the room. Since she had been unable to visit Wednesday, she had been given permission to, once again, steal in on a non-visiting day. She arrived alone, and she came with a proposition.

"Murray will be leaving for the Army the end of this month, and he is going to sell his car. What would you say to me buying it?" she asked Al.

"My first thought is that I wish he would keep it for himself for awhile. I would be hesitant to have you try to drive it. It needs a lot of work. It doesn't sound like a good idea to me."

If Frances was disappointed, she did not show it. She turned the talk to Frances Pearl's birthday, which would fall on the coming Sunday.

"What should we buy for her gift?" she asked Alvin.

"Not just one gift. Pick out two or three, but make one a doll," he replied. "I want to see what she will do with a doll baby of her own."

"I could bring her and the presents out Sunday, and you could give them to her. Would you like that?"

"That would be *tremendous*," he said. And they both laughed at his use of his favorite word.

They planned the impromptu party they would hold Sunday in his room. Frances said she would bring cupcakes for everyone. She flicked a finger toward the other beds when she said it. As she did, she realized Leo was not sleeping, as she had thought, but seemed to be in a daze. She raised a questioning eyebrow at Alvin, and nodded toward Leo.

Alvin shrugged. Then he yielded and said very low, "Ruby went home without permission. He is taking it pretty hard."

Husband and wife were being scrutinized. Evidently, Brannigan had not yet learned the patient's technique of ignoring visitors just steps away from one's own bed. His pointy nose pointed relentlessly in their direction. He obviously expected an introduction.

Normally Alvin would have extended the courtesy when Frances first entered the room, but he had not, and, for some unexplained reason, he resented the priest's assumption that he was due an introduction. His hackles were up, and he did not know why.

The fellow did not look like a priest. Or maybe he did, but a priest without one of those stiff, white collars crowding his Adam's apple. And what was a priest doing in a county-operated hospital? Alvin was pretty sure the Catholic Church would not stick one of their own in a ward with a lot of charity cases. No way. Al had seen that beeswaxed parlor and all that fancy furniture. He figured it was par for the course at all Catholic rectories. No way would a priest be turned out of those kind of trappings and plopped in here.

Alvin gave the introduction grudgingly. And was ashamed of himself as he did. He should not assume that every man of the cloth was a Bible-thumper or fire and brimstoner, but it just did not feel right to have one with him in the same room.

Frances was here and we
had an awfully nice time.
I surely love my Wife.
Al

Saturday, August 22. I am
Looking to Sunday already.
Those are the only days that
are to be enjoyed out here.
I weighed today and I weigh
about 133. I haven't gained
any the last two weeks.

"It is a wise father that knows his own child."—Shakespeare

Chapter 82

The grapevine produced its own doubts about Al and Leo's new roommate. Within a few days, the tentacles of gossip had Brannigan defrocked, a tippler and a renegade.

In passing on the word, Phil could give no concrete basis for any of the accusations. *"They said"* was the strongest attribution he offered. That was not good enough for Al. He had his own doubts, but he was not about to justify them based on rumors.

As for Leo, he still was taking no notice of the new roomie or much of anything else for that matter. He would sit up to start the day with his morning cup of coffee and newspaper, but now he did both in total silence. When Leo completed his perusal of the paper, he tossed it across to the next bed, which meant that Brannigan read the news before Al laid eyes on it. Try as he might, Alvin could not read any malice into Leo's insouciance. It was not just Al who Leo brushed off. It was the entire ward. Leo roused only to take in food. Between meals he remained rolled in his blanket, back to his mates. No one and nothing grabbed his attention. Leo slipped through each day, like a pebble dropping into watery depths, never causing a stir.

Al would have liked to discuss Brannigan with Leo, but that was not an option. So he kept silent and watched and waited. Up to this point, Brannigan had done nothing more questionable than spend an excessive amount of time reading in a black book. Al could tell the book was not a Bible, but it still looked to be of a religious nature.

Al was glad that the expected sermonizing and Bible thumping had not materialized. There was not an inordinate amount of conversation either, which made for boring days. Al had to admit that perhaps his own reticence had led to the lack. For now, he was content to leave it at that. There was still something about this

Brannigan that rubbed him the wrong way.

All thoughts of the priest—if he was a priest—were swept away when Frances, Murray and Elwin crowded into his room Sunday afternoon. Al knew Elwin was here mainly to visit his wife, but, again, Alvin benefited from having his sister as a fellow patient. Having two in the Potts family hospitalized definitely meant more visitors for both.

A visit from Elwin always meant that Alvin would be brought up to date on farm news. Elwin was a dyed-in-the-wool farmer, and belonged to the loose network that kept those of like interests in contact with each other. It was Elwin who had pointed him to the roustabout job with Kent when he sprung loose from the sanatorium in 1932. Alvin was surprised that Elwin had not been able to steer Murray to a job. Perhaps he hadn't tried. It was a moot issue now that Murray was signed up with the Army. The connections Elwin had meant that Al heard not only about Elwin's crops, but how farmers and ranchers in general were doing. Farming was an iffy business. A man had to keep his nose to the grindstone.

The ruddy face of Alta's husband attested to the hours he spent in the fields. Al envied Elwin his farmer's tan. His own had faded months ago.

Murray took a back seat in these confabs between his brother and brother-in-law. He knew he was still the kid of the family, as far as Elwin was concerned. Murray propped his butt on the window ledge, and kept his mouth shut while they talked market prices for peas and wheat. Murray had taken his turn in the fields, but he knew Elwin wasn't interested in hearing his opinions. He still had to prove himself, and he was well aware of that. Wait until the Army got hold of him. He wouldn't be sitting around Walla Walla for long. Sweating from sun up to sun down in the dust kicked up by a combine might be the hand he'd be dealt if he stayed around here, but it wasn't one he was interested in playing out. Murray expected to see something of this old world before he was through.

Frances, too, stayed out of the conversation. She had nothing to offer when the men talked farming. Her experience with harvest crews was confined to the food she had helped put on the table. If the talk got around to the hours spent in a steamy, farm kitchen peeling spuds, husking corn, roasting hams and frying steaks and eggs in a continuous round from breakfast served in near dark to supper after dark, she might find something to say. Today her daughter's birthday was her main concern. The frosted cupcakes waited at home. She would bring them and Frances Pearl out this evening. The gifts and wrapping paper she had with her. When Elwin left to visit Alta, she would show the presents to Alvin and then wrap them. She wanted him to see the doll she had chosen for him to give Frances Pearl for her second birthday.

Frances became aware of Leo huddled under his covers. She wondered if he were really sleeping or only pretended sleep to provide them with privacy.

Frances noticed that the new man did not try to hide his interest. His eyes went from Elwin to Alvin, and swept the corner where she sat and Murray perched. He seemed to take it all in, but, like Murray and herself, Brannigan said nothing.

Chapter 83

Brannigan's curiosity during Al's Sunday afternoon visit with Murray, Elwin and Frances had not gone unnoticed by Alvin. It was just one more perplexity. He wondered why this little man so disturbed him.

As soon as his visitors left, Al took out his diary to record their visit.

> *Sunday, August 23. Frances was out this afternoon. Murray came out with Elwin. Baby's birthday is today. Frances has some presents for her. She is going to let me give them to baby.*

As he wrote, Al saw that Brannigan was also deeply engrossed in a book, the same black book he had been reading since Friday.

I really should make an attempt to be sociable.

The thought did not spur Al to action. He took refuge in the rest period, for once succumbing to inactivity in a way that would have made Miss Gillis proud.

Brannigan sat upright, back propped against his pillows and knees drawn up to serve as props for the book he held. Rose, looking in on them, thought he looked like a book himself, caught between two bookends, flanked as he was by Leo and Alvin.

They were each rolled in their blankets and turned away from Brannigan. Rose knew she should stop and encourage the reverend to put his reading aside and take full advantage of this rest period, but, seeing how intent he was, she hesitated to break his concentration. After a moment, she passed on by.

Leo only nibbled at the sandwiches and canned apricots Rose brought them for supper. He ignored her pleas to eat more, and slumped silently back into his blankets. Brannigan left the room as soon as Rose cleared away the supper dishes. Al settled down to wait for the birthday party to begin.

Always waiting for something. Why isn't the moment enough?

"Why is that, Leo? Why isn't the here and now enough for me?

He hoped for, but did not expect, an answer.

"You don't have to talk to me, if you can't, Pritchard, but I do expect you to sit up and eat a cupcake in honor of my two-year-old's birthday. All right?"

Al was relieved when Frances finally showed up.

Frances Pearl wore Shirley Temple ringlets and a frilly dress with a ruffle that skimmed just below her underpants. Her pudgy legs carried her in a duck waddle over to her daddy. With upraised arms, she begged to be picked up. Al could oblige only to the extent of stretching out a hand and ruffling it through her hair. He coaxed her to climb onto the chair pulled up to his bed. From there, she could wiggle onto the bed beside him.

Frances set out the cupcakes she had brought. Devil's Food with thick, chocolate icing topped with a curl of pink. "Very fancy," Alvin pronounced them.

She placed each one on a square of waxpaper, and put two on each man's table.

Frances added a pink candle to the center of Frances Pearl's. Just as she was lighting the candle, Brannigan entered the room.

"What's this? A party?" he asked, taking note of the cakes on his table.

When Al told him it was his two-year-old's birthday, Brannigan dug in his pocket and pulled out a nickel. He held it out toward Frances Pearl. He beckoned to her with the shiny coin.

"Here's a present for a pretty little girl," he said.

"Oh, that isn't necessary," said Frances.

It was an awkward moment, but Brannigan brushed aside their protests. He waved the coin again. This time he called Frances Pearl to come and get her gift. There was nothing for it, but to lift her down from the bed. She stood with her thumb tucked into her mouth. She was a shy little girl, still a momma's girl. It was obvious that she knew the nickel was for her, but she was too reluctant to go after it. Frances prodded her toward the gift-giver.

With that encouragement, she made her way around the end of Alvin's bed. As she did, Brannigan stepped back until he was standing between his bed and Leo's. His move increased the distance between them, and she hesitated to take the extra steps. His laughing voice coaxed her onward, and she sensed it was a game. She entered into the spirit of it, and was laughing herself when she reached him.

Brannigan squatted down beside her, and then it was only the top of his head and the child's that Alvin and Frances saw. He seemed to be getting along famously with their shy girl. They watched as his hand held the coin delicately between his thumb and forefinger. He held it up. They saw Frances Pearl's head tip back as he showed her the nickel. With a flip of his fingers, the coin disappeared. They heard Frances Pearl giggle. Brannigan's hand lifted one of her curls. His fingers slipped under her hair, and he whipped the nickel out, holding it high for her to see again. More giggles.

Even with his limited view, Alvin could tell it was adroit sleight-of-hand Brannigan was performing. He wished he could see it better. Leo was in the perfect position to watch this impromptu entertainment, but he seemed to have his eyes closed to it.

Al watched entranced as Brannigan's dexterous fingers repeated the coin trick, lifting the nickel aloft, flicking his fingers, then...poof! Gone! The hand dipped into the curls again, rummaged around, and withdrew the coin with a flourish that brought fresh squeals from Frances Pearl.

Alvin and Frances laughed along with their daughter, as much because of her obvious enjoyment as at the trick that had turned her birthday into a real party.

On the far side of the bed, the raised hand stroked the top of the little, blonde head, and then it, like the coin, disappeared. Again all that could be seen were the tops of both their heads, his bent close to hers.

Brannigan's voice was just a murmur of baby-talk. There were no more giggles.

It made Frances uneasy. She never used baby-talk with Frances Pearl. She felt it best to speak clearly and properly so a child would learn the correct way of speaking, but she supposed it wasn't worth making a fuss about this once.

Suddenly, the Shirley Temple curls jerked away from Brannigan's sleek head, and a fretful whine replaced the giggles.

At the same time, Leo erupted from his blankets.

The unexpected appearance of Leo reminded Frances of a broody hen disturbed on her nest.

"What kind of party is this?" Leo barked.

Now it was Brannigan's head that bobbed backwards, and the man quickly rose to his feet. Frances Pearl, whimpering, ran to her mother.

"About time to eat cupcakes, ain't it?" Leo grumbled.

Al laughed, relieved to see that Leo had finally joined the party.

"Past time," said Al. "I think the kid is getting tired, and she hasn't opened her presents yet."

As if to prove her daddy right, Frances Pearl, still whimpering, climbed into her mother's lap. She wiggled closer, and tugged fretfully at the ruffle on her dress. Frances helped her free a corner of it that had rucked up into the edge of her panties. The child hid her face against her mother's breasts, which muffled the whimpers that were not quite sobs.

Frances Pearl's whimpers faded, but she still lay coiled on her mother's lap. Frances had to coax her to try a bite of cupcake.

By the time the doll was unwrapped, Frances Pearl was willing to leave her mother and sit beside her daddy on his bed. She grasped the doll baby in a tight hug, and released it only to hold it up to his lips to beg a kiss from him.

"You were right about a doll for her present," said Frances. "She couldn't be more pleased."

The last crumb had been wiped away, and Frances and baby were out the door when Alvin saw the nickel lying forgotten on Brannigan's table.

Chapter 84

*Monday, August 24. Murray is
going to sell his car. I wish
he would keep it for awhile.
Frances talked like she
wanted to buy it, but I
know she couldn't drive
it. It needs work done on it.*

*Tuesday. It has been real
cool today. In fact rather
cold. I sure like the days
when I have to cover up to
keep warm. I can rest and
sleep so much better. I also
had a real nice bath. I also
washed my head. One isn't
supposed to do that, but I did. Al.*

*Wednesday. I had a lot of
company today. My wife,
my sisters Lily and Pearl.
my brother Murray and Mrs.
Spence. I really enjoyed myself.
I am waiting now for my
darling wife. She will be
here in just a few minutes.
I love her! I love her! I love her!*

*"Under the wide and starry sky, dig the grave and let me lie.
Glad did I live and gladly die."—Stevenson*

Chapter 85

Alvin had hoped for a further display of Brannigan's dexterity with the coin, and, perhaps, even other magic tricks he might have in his repertoire, but none had been forthcoming in the three days since the birthday party.

It was not for lack of hinting.

Al had told Brannigan he enjoyed the show, and thanked him for entertaining his girl on her special day. When the compliment had not produced the desired results, he resorted to an outright request for any "hocus pocus" Brannigan might like to offer.

After throwing a quick glance in Leo's direction, which Al couldn't understand at all, Brannigan begged off, and that had been the end of it.

"It's a shame to let all that talent go to waste when he could be providing us with some sport, don't you think, Leo?" Al asked when they were alone.

His question was directed at a blanket-covered lump from which a stalk of hair protruded. He got a grunt for an answer.

"I got the idea he thought you might object. Maybe if you ask him?" Alvin persisted.

"Believe I'll pass on that, Curly," Leo said from within his den.

Alvin, with regret, gave up on the idea of being entertained by Brannigan. Their roomie was choosing to spend most of his time buried in his black book, almost as silent as Leo. Yesterday when Al was reveling in the conversation of five visitors, Brannigan had left the room, and Leo opted to den up.

Alvin felt almost guilty as visitors crowded his room, and none came for Leo or Brannigan. He could not imagine coping in this place without the comfort of family and friends like Nita Spence. There were other friends who had gone the T.B. route, but, once out of here, were in no great hurry to return, even just to visit. Mrs. Spence had proved to be different. She was a good friend to Frances, and now to him, too. He liked her lighthearted ways.

With Leo snugged down as usual and Brannigan off somewhere, Al was at loose ends. Thursday was always a draggy sort of day, coming as it did on the heels of a visiting day. Nothing could match a Wednesday, especially when it brought so many different opinions as it had yesterday. Pearlie had been apprehensive, but also excited, about the pending trip to Spokane in September for leg surgery. Ironically, it was her good leg that doctors would operate on. They would shorten it to try to make it equal to the length of the leg that had been stunted by tuberculosis. Al could not quite grasp how this would be accomplished, but Pearlie seemed to have faith in the doctors, who had already examined her and said it could be done.

Al was giving this some thought when a row broke out down the hall.

Some hard language was being tossed around at a level that easily reached their room. Al slipped out of bed when it sounded as if fisticuffs were involved.

"What's up?" Leo asked, rising up on an elbow.

Alvin stood at the door, looked both ways, but saw nothing.

Leo joined him at the door, and they both edged down the hall toward the sounds of battle.

Just then a chair skittered out of Rooney's room into the hall. They hurried to the door. Al was astonished to see Rooney, a quiet family man, pounding on Brannigan's head.

Brannigan was back-pedaling, a move that put him out of Rooney's reach, but brought him up short against Rooney's table on which sat a coffee pot and cup. Brannigan blindly grabbed the tin pot. He tossed it in a side-arm throw without taking aim. It whizzed harmlessly past Rooney's ear and crashed against the wall.

Rooney roared and plunged forward, hot on the attack.

Brannigan scooped up the cup and let fly. It, too, missed Rooney, but shattered on the floor in a spray of glass. The shards slowed Rooney down, which gave Brannigan his chance to escape.

He took off running down the hall, squeaking in fright as his little feet slipped and slid over the linoleum. Brannigan headed not to their room but toward the office, Alvin noted.

"Let's get the hell out of here," Leo said, tugging on Alvin's arm.

They were disappearing into their room as orderlies and nurses converged on Rooney's room.

"No use us getting mixed up in that," said Leo. "Least-wise not when we're supposed to be bed-bound."

They heard no more about the fracas. Brannigan wasn't seen the rest of the day.

> *Thursday, August 27. We had a lot of*
> *excitement out here this morning.*
> *One of the patients socked one of*
> *the other patients on the noggin.*
> *The insulted one threw a coffee pot*
> *and cup at the other but missed.*
> *The Dr. has put us on restrictions.*
> *No visiting.   Al*

Brannigan re-entered the room in the dim, gray light of dawn. Alvin heard the closet door open, and the rustle of clothes. It sounded as if Brannigan were dressing, but Al did not open his eyes to look. The drawer in Brannigan's table snicked open and then closed with a click.

There was the soft patter of feet, and then silence.

Chapter 86

Al seldom could sleep once he was awakened, but Leo did not suffer from that particular failing. His snores were soon sawing the air after Brannigan's departure. They told Al that Leo, too, had been awake during the underdog's early morning return. He guessed it was embarrassment that kept either of them from speaking to Brannigan after his ignoble defeat.

Al was asleep when Rose came with the towels and basins of warm water at six a.m. He did not remember falling asleep, but knew he must have slept well, in spite of the early awakening, because he was so rested.

Rose pulled his table with the water close to the bed. He spread the white towel across his lap and set to work with soapy cloth. As he was patting his face dry, he saw the nickel.

The coin was sitting atop a black book next to Alvin's basin. It had to be Brannigan's book, but what was it doing here?

Rose had no answer for him when she returned to collect the basins. But she could put a name to the book.

"It's a breviary, full of prayers and psalms and hymns, like that," she said.

"All Roman Catholic priests have one, and have to read in it every day," Rose explained.

"Well then, Rose, will Brannigan be back with us?"

"Oh no, the man's gone for good, that's for sure."

"I suppose then he forgot to take the book with him."

"No, Mr. Potts. No fear of that. If he put it on your table, it's meant for you. Patients' tables are sacrosanct, as you well know. No one touches another's belongings in here. Miss Gillis wouldn't have it. The breviary is yours. The why of it, I couldn't say, but, for sure, the man handed it over to you."

"Now, isn't that mysterious?" Alvin asked Leo after the first cups of coffee were behind them. He gestured at the book with the nickel crowning it.

"This whole damn world is a mystery to me, so what's one mystery more or less?" was Leo's ironic reply.

> *Friday, August 28. It is beginning*
> *to get warmer again. I am feeling*
> *pretty good now. My ear hurts*
> *like the dickens. I haven't had*
> *any medicine in it for a week.*

"Observe good faith and justice toward all nations; cultivate peace and harmony with all."—Washington

> *Saturday, August 29. The Dr. Rooks*
> *is coming out to look at my ear. I*
> *sure hope he does something for it.*
> *Dr. was here. He left a prescription*
> *to have filled out. I was weighed*
> *today—gained ¾ of a lb.*

> *Sunday, August 30. My Darling wife*
> *was out. She will be out again*
> *this evening. I can stand a*
> *lot of her company. Murray*
> *was out also.*

"Praise from a friend, or censure from a foe, are lost on hearers that our merits know."—Homer

> *Monday, August 31. We have two*
> *new patients on our side. Both*
> *fairly young. One of them came*
> *Friday. The other came Sunday.*
> *Tomorrow is bath day. It seems*
> *we are always dirty.*

> *Tuesday, September 1. Bath*

day and the first of our fall
months face us. It will
soon be that I have seen six
of them come and go. It
doesn't seem that long. I
wonder would four years
seem long? A.E.P.P. Potts

"If you wish to remove avarice you must remove its mother,
luxury."—Cicero

Wednesday. It seems to
be about the beginning
of our rainy weather.
Anyway we are having
some very fine rain.
I suppose it will end
up nice and hot.
I sure dread cold weather.
Al.

Thursday, September 3. We
are having some very much
needed rain. One can surely
sleep fine when it is raining
and cool. I didn't awaken
once all night last night.

"Do good with what thou hast or it will do thee no good."—
Wm. Penn

Friday. Fish day and what
a rotten batch of salmon
we did have. I sure hate
to have my fish all
greasy and fried crisp.

Chapter 87

Saturday, September 5. Weigh day
and the last day of the Fair. This
is one year during the Fair that
I stayed sober. I gained ¾ lb.
this week. Not much but better
than losing that much.

There was a lot Al could have written as today's diary entry, but the terse note was all he could manage. If he pulled any more words out of the seething cauldron of thoughts stirred up by this year's state fair in Walla Walla, it would take a book to hold them.

He remembered the first time he had a snoot full of fire water at the fair. He was seventeen, just two years younger than Murray was now. He hadn't intended to go to the fair at all. He had a big night planned with a girl named Louise.

A honey of a girl with a mass of black hair, Louise was several years older. She waitressed at the Coffee Cup, and it had taken a dozen cups over several weeks before she stepped out with him.

There had been walks in the park, then movies, and finally she agreed to the big weekend he had planned. The family was camped out up at Kooskooskie, as was usual during the summer months. Al wanted to take Louise up to meet his family, and stay overnight before they closed the camp for winter.

It was not a hardship camp. There were two large tents, one with a wooden floor and sidewalls with a regular screen door. That one was the roomiest. Their woodstove for cooking was in there, along with cots for Alta, Lily and Pearl. There would be room for Louise to bunk with the girls. Al's dad had strung a canvas tarp alongside to provide cover for the wooden picnic table he had thrown together out of scrap lumber. Alvin enjoyed eating out in the fresh air, and was anxious to share a meal with Louise in the woodsy setting. There were a lot of places to be alone.

It was going to be a tremendous weekend, and the fair in Walla Walla held no interest for Alvin at all.

He had arranged a ride for himself and Louise with a rancher whose spread was a mile from the camp. The walk up from the ranch was everything Al had hoped it would be. Accidentally on purpose, his swinging hand found hers, and she didn't pull away. They walked like that, hand-in-hand, crunching through leaves that were beginning to fall. Louise was a happy sort of girl. Chatter came easily to her, and he didn't have to do much talking.

They were singing a silly song when they came in sight of the camp. She had her head tossed back, and was really belting out the tune. Maybe more than the song called for, he thought, but still it was good fun. His dog, Pup, interrupted the singing as he raced toward them and threw his enthusiastic furry body against Al's legs.

It was the first introduction to his family that Alvin made. Louise acknowledged it with a pat on Pup's head. The second introduction came minutes later when Emerson stepped out from under the shade of a tree where he had been standing, watching their approach.

His eyes raked over the girl clinging to Alvin's hand. He seemed to take her in at a glance, from the top of her ebony hair to the flirty swing of her skirt to the sensible shoes she had chosen for this weekend in the backwoods. Alvin knew that look. His father had a way of quickly summing up anyone he met. Al called it making snap judgments. Emerson said first impressions don't lie. Alvin wished Louise had not been singing quite so lustily as they came up the road.

Emerson stood in front of them with his hands tucked into his back pockets as Alvin introduced his girl. His stance pulled his loose coveralls snugly against his body. That, along with his uptilted chin, gave Alvin's dad a cocky look.

"Well then..." Emerson said, looking directly into her eyes.

Louise blushed under his scrutiny, but she politely held out her hand.

Emerson clasped it in the briefest of handshakes.

"Come meet the girls, Louise Bertinelli," he said, and turned on his heels.

Alvin and Louise followed him into the camp. Lily and Pearl were waiting at the door of the cook tent to greet them. This was a big occasion. Alvin had never brought a girl home before. It was also seldom that visitors came up here, and even less often that the girls went to town. They were wide-eyed with interest, but Alta came forward as if she played hostess to Alvin's young ladies every day.

The first thing she did was draw Louise into the tent to show her the corner she had arranged for her for the two nights she would be with them. A sheet had been thrown over a makeshift line to shield a cot so Louise would have some privacy.

Next to the cot was an upended apple box which held a twig of crimson leaves in a jam jar full of water. Pearlie, who would be eight years old at the end of this month, darted in to place a huge pinecone next to the jar. She looked up at Louise with shining eyes and a whispered, "For you."

Alvin was pleased with the reception his sisters had given Louise. Now, he took her in hand to show her the rest of the camp.

A fruit jar, also filled with colorful autumn foliage, centered the picnic table, which had been laid with a red and white checked oilcloth. "Here's where we'll eat tonight," he told her.

"Alfresco," she said.

Al looked puzzled, but Emerson came to his rescue. "In the fresh air," he offered.

"We have a grape arbor at home, and most of our meals in good weather are alfresco. Very pleasant," said Louise.

Al looked to his dad for a high sign that it was all right to show Louise into Emerson's tent. Getting the nod, Al escorted her into the other large tent. This one had only a flap for a door, and its floor was hard-packed dirt, covered in places with tightly braided rag rugs. The cot here was larger than those in the girls' tent. A green and brown Pendleton blanket covered it. Again, an apple box served as a bedside table. On it was an oil lamp, its chimney polished and its wick trimmed. A rocking chair sat in the far corner, a steamer trunk pulled casually up to it to provide a foot rest. An orange crate stood on its end, the divider in the middle formed a shelf that was packed with books. Pegs hammered into the tent supports at each of the four corners held items of clothing, a jacket, a hat, a pair of overalls.

"This is dad's lair," said Alvin.

"If we get a heavy rain storm, Murray and I drag our bed rolls in here, but we prefer sleeping in our own lean-to over here," he added, leading her outside.

The boys had fashioned a place for themselves under a cluster of small pines. The trees acted as a natural wind-break, but they had stretched canvas on three sides for added protection.

"We have a roof we can put up, too, but we like to asleep *alfresco*, so we can look at the stars," he told her, grinning.

Cooking odors drifted their way. Smelled like cornbread. Nothing new about that. Cornbread and beans were staples here. But tonight Al thought he caught the heady aroma of chicken and dumplings. Oh, how he hoped his smeller was working right.

But Al intended to serve his surprise *before* the meal.

He had planned this entire weekend around a walk he would take with Louise just before the evening meal. It was camp policy for someone—usually Alvin or Emerson, but sometimes Alta—to take the rifle and walk through the woods in search of a plump squirrel for Pup's supper. While he would do that this evening, the main purpose of the stroll tonight was to get Louise alone in the woods.

Al had noticed on previous walks how the setting sun cast long and graceful shadows over the forest floor. Since meeting Louise, he had often imagined them walking the paths arm-in-arm and stopping in one of those dark shadows to exchange a kiss.

He had forced himself to not think beyond that kiss, but the soft bed of moss around a freshwater spring teased him every time he walked by. He was anxious now to start that walk so he and Louise would have plenty of time before dinner was ready.

"Now I'll show you the best part of this camp, Louise, if you will take a little walk with me." Alvin said.

He walked over to a tree where the rifle hung on a nail by its trigger guard. He carefully lifted it free, tucked it under his arm with the barrel pointing to the ground, and turned to take his girl's hand.

Emerson stepped up, slid the rifle from Alvin's grasp, and said, "Let me do that, Son. I'll get Pup's dinner tonight."

"But it's not just the squirrel, Dad. I want to take Louise…well, the paths are real pretty and I thought I'd show off the woods."

"Now, that's a good idea. A real good idea. Come on, Louise, I'll give you the grand tour while Al lays in some more firewood."

Alvin watched helplessly as his father offered his arm to Louise. He noticed his dad had changed into his go-to-town clothes, but he didn't seem in a hurry to leave.

Emerson stepped closer to Louise, gesturing with his elbow until she reluctantly tucked her arm through his. She threw a confused glance at Al as she was led away.

The cornbread was getting cold when Emerson and Louise emerged from the woods. Empty-handed, Al noticed. No squirrel for Pup tonight. Louise's cheeks were rosy red; it must have been a long walk.

Alta and Lily carried the food from the cook tent to the table outside. They were sitting down to eat when Murray trudged in, dusty from a job he had been doing for the rancher down the road.

"Wash up and sit," Emerson told him.

The little group waited in silence at the table.

Murray quickly rubbed his hands with yellow soap and splashed water over his face and neck at a basin sitting on a rough board table next to the cookhouse door.

"Be quick about it," Emerson ordered. "Supper's getting cold."

It was only the cornbread that was cold. The chicken and dumplings were still bubbling, but the dumplings were a little dryer than they would have been if served as soon as they were done. No one reminded Emerson that it was he who had delayed supper.

Emerson made a production of filling Louise's plate first.

"You must be ravenous after that long walk," said Emerson in the teasing, low voice he used on Pup when brushing him down after a run in the woods.

A rosy blush blossomed on the soft skin exposed by Louise's low cut blouse and rose up the column of her neck to stain her cheeks a bright red.

"We're all hungry, Dad. Pass the cornbread please," Alta said brusquely.

Emerson grinned across the table at his eldest daughter, and winked.

Throughout the meal he continued to press second helpings on Louise, and even forked a good sized piece of chicken from his plate to hers. When Alta brought blackberry crumble to the table for dessert, Al felt as if his family was really going all out for his guest, who was looking mighty pretty with a wild rose nestled behind her ear. Al thought all the flowers in the woods would have faded by now.

He was still feeling disappointed over his failed plan for the walk, but no use ruining the whole evening.

He found himself alone with Louise after dinner, when Emerson secluded himself in his tent and Alta insisted she and the girls needed no help with the dishes.

"So, how did you like my woods?" Al asked, trying to sound Louise out, to at least get a second-hand impression.

"Very…woodsy."

She looked pensive, then added, "You and your father look enough alike to be twins, with him the more mature version. He even has the same wavy hair."

"Darker than mine though."

"True, but you look so much alike. Except for that scar of yours, of course," she said, adding, "Your father is very handsome."

Well, he knew with the scar *he* would never be handsome, but he hadn't expected her to put it into words. He could think of nothing to say. The silence hung heavy between them.

Then she relented, saying, "The walk might have been better if you had been along." She pulled the flower from her hair and threw it on the ground.

Alvin beamed.

He could live with those words. Next time he would be along for sure.

And he had another plan up his sleeve. The fire had died down to a nice bed of coals, just right to roast marshmallows. He settled Louise into a camp chair by the fire, and went into the kitchen to get the marshmallows. He sent Murray out to sharpen sticks. Soon they were all gathered around the fire, laughing and singing. This time Louise's voice was not only modulated, it could scarcely be heard. Still, she *seemed* to be having a good time.

The moon rose and was still hanging low when Alta pronounced it bedtime for Pearl and Murray. "I think we'll go along, too," she said, tapping Lily on the shoulder.

Alta and Lily never went to bed this early. Al knew she was making an opportunity for him to be alone with Louise. But Louise pushed up out of her chair to stand beside Alta.

"I think I'll also retire. I seem to be working up a headache," she said.

Al thought her voice sounded as if there *was* an ache behind it, so he tried not to show how disappointed he was. He walked her to the door, and said he would see her over flapjacks in the morning.

Alta had already shown Louise the outdoor convenience, a two-holer set back a ways behind the tents. All four girls trekked to it before the light in their tent was extinguished. Murray had been unusually quiet tonight. Alvin thought his thirteen-year-old brother had been awed by having a strange girl in the camp. So much so, that he had avoided the privy and took off into the woods. It was only after the girls were all safely inside that Murray came back and crept into the lean-to without any coaxing.

When Louise first entered the tent, Alvin heard her ask Alta if she could have a basin of water. He sat alone in the dark now, watching the coals turn ashy and thinking about Louise in the tent, in the dark, cooling herself with a cloth dipped in that water.

A harvest moon angled through the trees, but added little illumination to the black shadows that stretched over the clearing. There was still a dim glow from Emerson's lamp, which cast his giant shadow on the tent walls as he moved about the room. When he lit a candle and blew out the lamp, Alvin knew his dad wouldn't be going into town. It looked as if Emerson were settling down for the night, too.

Al decided to turn in. He kicked his boots off outside the lean-to, stripped down to his skivvies, and crawled into his bed roll. He wasn't sleepy at all, so he propped himself against one of the pine trees that formed the back of their nest, and watched the play of the dying embers. An owl hooted nearby, and night birds called in the distance.

The woods were not a quiet place. There was always something rustling—the wind, an animal searching for food.

Sometimes a skunk wandered through camp, and the boys were always careful to remain very still so they didn't rile it up. They had never been sprayed yet, but they always knew when a skunk was passing by. Its natural musky odor was a dead giveaway. They had learned the hard way not to leave food scraps out after a porcupine waddled into camp one night to sample a scrap of bacon left wound around a stick on which Murray had cooked it. It had taken some serious coaxing to get the prickly visitor to leave the scene.

It was not quiet, but it was peaceful. Soon Alvin's eyes grew heavy and his head nodded. The harvest moon had lost its orange glow and hung high overhead, a yellow globe. The candle flickered out in Emerson's tent.

Alvin didn't know what awakened him, but he was immediately alert. Still propped against the tree, he swept his eyes over the clearing.

Nothing seemed out of place. All black shadows, but nothing stirring. Then he saw a red glow centered in the black triangle of the opened doorway made by the tied back flap in Emerson's tent. His dad was having a smoke.

Al settled back, ready to drift back to sleep when he heard the faint squeak of the screen door.

A moon beam found the figure poised hesitantly behind the screen, half in, half out of the tent, as if undecided. The girls were never so quiet when they made a midnight run on the outhouse. They never eased the door shut. They just let it whack behind them with never a care as to who it might disturb.

The figure slid from behind the screen. The door settled back into its groove with only a whisper. But Al heard it.

A cloud passed over the moon and the clearing was cloaked in black again.

Al saw the ruddy end of his father's cigarette as it prescribed an arc through the air. *Like a beacon.* The gesture was repeated not once, but three times.

Then Alvin heard a sound that chilled him through and through. The soft patter of bare feet crossing to Emerson's tent.

He listened to the rasp of canvas on canvas as the dark triangle fell into place. He did not want to think about what was behind that tent door, but he could not ignore the twinkle of firelight as a candle was lit inside the tent.

Alvin watched the small, dancing flame perform against the canvas. It seemed like hours before it dwindled to no bigger than a firefly. Finally, it flickered out.

He spent the rest of the night awake, staring into the darkness.

Before first light, he heard a bow string being plucked and knew it for the twang of the screen door. As if it were a signal for which he had been waiting, Alvin eased out of the lean-to. He skinned off his underwear, stepped into new, and covered it with clean trousers and shirt. He took his hoard of folding money from a cache deep inside the lean-to, tucked it into his wallet, and shoved it into his back pocket. He set aside his boots in favor of a pair of oxfords and dress socks. His jacket and felt hat were added to the mix.

He seated himself in the camp chair beside the dead fire and waited.

Alvin was the first thing Emerson saw when he emerged from his tent.

He ignored his son, walked to the wash basin and scooped water over his face. With his back to Alvin, he toweled his face and arms, taking his time. Then he turned, tossed the towel over his shoulder, and stepped to Alvin over the cold ashes.

"Well, let's have it then. What's on your mind?" Emerson said.

"You know damn good and well what's on my mind. What I want to know is what the hell you've got on yours."

"Watch your mouth, Alvin. This is your dad you're talking to."

"Some dad!" Alvin was dismayed to hear his own voice crack.

"Listen, boy. That girl just wasn't right for you. She's got a weak streak in her, and you might as well know it now as later."

"You don't even know her!"

"I knew her the minute I laid eyes on her. What I did, I did for your own good. I did you a favor, son."

"Bullshit," Alvin said in a voice devoid of emotion.

Before his father could react, Al strode away from camp.

He was passing under the tree where his father had stood to watch Louise's approach the day before when Murray caught up with him.

"Can I go with ya, Alvin?" Murray said, trotting along beside Al.

"Not this time, little brother. Not this time."

Murray finally had to run to keep up with his brother. Then he dropped back. He stood watching until Alvin was out of sight.

Alvin passed the ranch owned by the man who had given him a lift the day before. The county road, where Al hoped to catch a ride into Walla Walla, was a mile beyond. Al had reached that road when Emerson's truck, with Louise in the passenger seat, passed him, and pulled onto the shoulder just ahead of him. Al stopped dead in his tracks. He did not want to see her, and he surely did not want to speak with her.

Emerson stepped out of the truck, walked to the rear, and called out. "Come on. Hop on board."

"No, Sir."

"What are you going to do?"

"Hitch a ride to town."

"Coming back to camp?"

"Later."

"All right then." Emerson got back in the truck, and drove off.

That was the first night Alvin got drunk at the fair. He tipped a few home-made brews with some fellows he met up with, then, behind a barn filled with cows, he drank deeply from a bottle one of his new friends pulled from his hip pocket. That drink of hard likker was followed by more than he could remember.

He awakened in a heap of damp and smelly straw with what he believed was the worst headache anyone ever had. He thought his stomach would empty itself then and there, but, from the looks of his shirt, his stomach had already had that pleasure.

He stripped off the shirt and threw it on the straw pile. He raked his fingers through his hair, gave it up as hopeless, pulled on the jacket he had evidently been using for a pillow, and headed out.

After that, drowning his sorrows became routine.

Celebrations were a cause for getting pie-eyed. When Frances came into his life, Al tempered his drinking. He exchanged the beer and the hard stuff for loganberry wine laced with soda water.

But at every fair since his marriage, he had been just as able to tie one on with loganberry flips as he had with that first taste of moonshine.

Yes, this fair of 1936 was the first that Alvin had managed to get through sober. Of course, he could not claim it was to his credit. He had not even attended the fair, and no one here at the Blue Mountain was serving anything remotely like a loganberry flip.

Resolutely he drew out his Diary and Daily Reminder. There was something in it that he wanted to look at again. A quote from that Quaker poet. Oh yes, here it was.

"Our common sorrow, like a mighty wave, Swept all pride away, and trembling I forgave!"—John Greenleaf Whittier

Chapter 88

Sunday, September 6. Visiting day.
My wife and Baby were out.
Murray took the baby back home
but Frances stayed. Baby sure
is getting sweet. She talks a
lot more than she did. She
looks better too.

Monday. Labor Day and also
visiting day. It is 2:25 and I am
waiting for my wife to come.
I slept this morning so
wasn't sleepy this afternoon.

"Let us have faith that right makes might, and in that faith let
us, to the end, dare to do our duty as we understand it."—
Abraham Lincoln

Tuesday, September 8. We had
a bath this morning, now it
is 6:50. I wish it was time to
go to bed. It sure is a long
time until nine. Maybe I can
think of something to do.

Wednesday, Company day.
Frances was out to see me.
She seems to be feeling
pretty well. She went to
the Clinic a few days ago.

Dr. Cox said she was O.K.
I thank God with all my
heart.   Al

"Heard   melodies   are   sweet,   but   those   unheard   are
sweeter."—John Keats

Thursday, September 10. We
had a dinner of nice fresh
salmon today. Mr. Linderman
caught it. His wife is a
patient out here so he
made us a present of it.
Sure was fine.

Friday. We had a fine, well, extra
fine, dinner of fresh Olympic
oysters. They are better than
ever. Here comes Docey looking
for grass. He was here last
evening and got some. There
isn't any tonight.   Al

"The greatest of faults, I should say, is to be conscious of
none."—Carlyle

Saturday, September 12. Just the
last day of the week. A big day
for the farmers. I don't mind
Saturday because it is our
weigh day and I gained
1 ½ lbs. today.

Sunday. I really enjoy this day.
You know why. I shall see
Frances and maybe my baby
will be out to see me~~~
Frances and Lily were here.

"Ill fares the land, to hastening ills a prey, where wealth accumulates, and men decay."—Goldsmith

Monday, September 14. Old blue Monday. Pearlie has gone to Spokane to have her leg taken off and made shorter. She sure is a game kid. Frances took her to the bus.

Tuesday. We are having some darn cool weather. The thermometer stays around 40 or 50 all the time. I have caught a fine cold, feel like the dickens.

"Earth's crammed with heaven And every common bush afire with God."—Elizabeth Browning

Chapter 89

"My gosh, that Charlie is a handful, but he is the loving-est little kid you ever saw."

"So who is this Charlie?"

Frances and Alvin were in the middle of their Wednesday afternoon visit when the unfamiliar name slipped into her conversation.

The look on her face told him he had stepped in it. Or maybe she had.

Frances' hand flew to her mouth.

After some probing on his part and reluctance on hers, it came out that Frances had been working for the past week. Charlie was one of six children of a widower, who had offered her a job as housekeeper. It was quite an undertaking, with a two-story house to clean, laundry for a big family, and lunch and dinner to prepare, as well as riding herd on three young children not yet in school. The widower's father-in-law, who lived with the family, was also part of the package.

"It's an all day job five days a week, but I can take baby with me. I didn't want to tell you until I had my hours worked out," said Frances with an apologetic smile.

She knew Alvin was angry or hurt or both.

Her husband was fighting a cold and was not in the best of moods anyway. This surely was not the time to tell him about taking a job when he had been so explicitly against her having any job. She had not intended to tell him today, but now the cat was out of the bag and she had no way of stuffing it back in. She would just have to explain and hope he would understand.

"Our time together is so important to us that I wanted to be sure I could handle the job and still visit you twice on Wednesdays," she said in the face of his silence. "And it is working out, Sweetheart. It really is."

"It's Murray's car, isn't it? You want money to buy that wreck of a car."

Frances could not deny that she would like to have transportation of her own with Murray leaving any day for the Army, but that was not what motivated her to accept the job offer that had come like a gift from heaven. She was feeling the pinch of hard times. It was getting increasingly difficult to supplement the staples from welfare and come up with the few dollars she gave to Alvin now and then to purchase small things not provided by the sanatorium.

This motive she damn well was not going to share with her husband. She knew how helpless he felt, lying there day after day unable to assist his wife and daughter in any way. She had no intention of increasing that feeling. She wanted her husband strong, not weak.

"Alvin, the Wilson family needed help. I'm in a position to provide that help."

"Did you *forget* that I don't want you working?" His tone was sarcastic and biting. He knew very well she had not forgotten. What possessed her to go behind his back!

"Don't be angry with me. It will work out fine, Al," she pleaded.

The stubborn set of his jaw spoke more plainly than words. Alvin was not about to be persuaded that *her* decision, made by herself alone, was a good one.

"Mr. Wilson's two oldest girls have been trying to run the house. They're still in school, and it's too much for them," she said, still trying to reason with him.

"But it's not too much for *you*, is it?"

She chose to hear his snide remark as a request for more information.

"It's a lovely old home with all the bedrooms upstairs. The girls keep that part of the house in order, except on Wednesdays. We've worked it out so they cook the dinner that night in exchange for me doing their upstairs work. That way I can be with you for evening visiting hours. Grandpa watches the little ones for the few hours I'm away on Wednesday afternoons."

"And where does *our* baby come into all of this?"

The hours she had spent arguing—no, *discussing*—jobs and kinder care with welfare were not up for discussion today. The welfare worker had tried her best to get Frances to place Frances Pearl in kinder care while she worked. Frances was not about to let control of her child slip into government hands. She had been determined to take no job where she could not have baby with her. That is why the job with the Wilsons seemed heaven-sent. Mr. Wilson had assured her he had no objection to her bringing her child along.

It really was working out nicely for everyone, if only Alvin would be reasonable.

She offered her husband her last excuse.

"I thought I could use some of the money to get my teeth fixed. This one here...," she said, hooking a finger around her back tooth, "...is crumbling all apart."

Alvin looked at his wife perched on the edge of her seat, her mouth agape, eyes on him anxiously.

He wanted to pull her finger out of her mouth, wrap her in his arms and kiss away all their troubles, but he could not erase her duplicity from his mind. How could she go to work and then sneak in here to visit, leaving him in the dark? She had excluded him, hadn't given his wishes a second thought. Betrayed him, that's what she'd done.

The rest of the visit limped along, and both were relieved when it ended.

Leo's radio was crooning *Say It Isn't So* as Frances left.

> *Wednesday, September 16. Frances*
> *was here but I didn't feel very*
> *well so we didn't have a very*
> *good time. She accidentally*
> *made a slip and then she had*
> *to tell me that she had been*
> *working a whole week without*
> *me knowing it.*

> *Thursday. I try not to think about*
> *Frances working but "no go".*
> *It wouldn't hurt half so much*

*if she had told me she was
going to. She wants to get
her teeth fixed. If she would
have told me that, it would
have been O.K. with me for
her to work for awhile.*

*Friday, September 18. She
can laugh and have a
good time now. Oh! What
a big fool I made out of
daddy. It is easy to pull
the wool over a man's eyes.*

*Saturday, September 19. I
feel better this morning. I
have a pretty bad cold but
it seems to be more loose
this morning. I have
weighed but don't know
what I did. I don't care
very much either. ~~~
I gained ½ lb.   Al*

"The use of money is all the advantage there is in having money."—Benjamin Franklin

Chapter 90

The long awaited notice, addressed to Murray, finally hit Frances' mailbox. *The paperwork is finished. Pack your bags, boy. You're in the Army now.*

Murray had been on tenterhooks since the first of August. He expected to be on his way before the end of August, but he was learning the Army operates on its own schedule. It had turned out to be a flexible schedule for sure. Now that he had notice to report in hand, he felt a few butterflies fluttering around in his innards. The unknown was always…well, unknown. He had hoped Will would buddy up and join, too, but Will and Esther were getting pretty serious. Murray could practically hear the wedding bells.

Better Will than him. He wanted to see something of the world before he settled down. Heck, he hadn't gotten any further from Washington than Oregon. The Army was going to change all that.

This being Saturday night, Murray decided to take a run down to the pool hall. Let the boys get a gander at his car. Shined up, it looked pretty good. Runs a little rough, but can't expect much if you aren't paying much. Too bad Al wouldn't let Frances take it over. Probably better for Sis that she doesn't though. Its little idiosyncrasies might be too much for her. Let one of those wrench-happy boys buy it tonight. He could use the cash.

Lutcher's was hopping by the time Murray arrived with Will in tow. He had coaxed him along on the promise that they would pick up Esther and drop in on a house party later.

The pool tables were all in play, but there was room at one of the poker tables. "Haven't got the money for that!" Will said. "Let's not lose sight of why we're here," he added, when Murray ambled over to the table.

The gambler in Murray was drawn to the cards. Put a pool stick in his hand with a quarter on the table and he was a happy man. Give him a hand of cards, preferably with a pair of any kind in it, and he could not be budged from the game until his last dollar was gone. And it always was. He was a gambler, yes, but a winner, no, or at least seldom. His big brother had told him many times that a poker player needed three things: ability to read the other players, to know what cards were still out, and to know the odds. "And, of course," he always added, "you need patience." "And luck!" Murray would add, just to get Al's goat.

Murray's failing was that he could never figure the odds. He played the game as if the odds were always in his favor. Will knew that, and wanted to steer him away from a losing game tonight when they were here in hopes of selling a car and making a few bucks. Besides, Esther was waiting.

"Let's steer clear of the moochers; stick with the guys with the dough," Will said, feeling somewhat like a cattle-driver with all this herding he was doing. Sometimes being with Murray was like sitting with a baby. Will would never tell Murray, but he thought the Army might be the best thing that ever happened to him. Murray was the kind of guy who would benefit from having a set of rules and a sergeant who would enforce them.

Will figured Esther was enough to keep him in line. He knew himself well enough to know he needed direction, positive direction. He and Murray always had fun together, but sometimes they walked a tightrope. There had been a couple times they had just narrowly missed getting into serious scrapes with the law. That they hadn't...*that* had been their luck, Will thought. He was through with all that now. He was sticking to Esther from here on out. That was his good luck charm now. He counted on the Army being Murray's.

Will and Murray spied an Ebding and an Erdman at the same time. "Now boys from those families usually have a dime to spare," Murray said. "And that one there, Buddy Ebding, does love cars, even though he's a motorcycle man," Will added.

They soon had both men kicking tires, opening and closing doors, and revving the engine of Murray's car.

"Out of tune," grunted Ebding.

"Nothing you can't fix," Murray rejoined.

"At the price he's asking, it's a steal," said Will.

Ebding cocked an eyebrow inquisitively at Will.

"No. No," Will protested. "It's his car, free and clear."

"Take it for a spin?" Ebding asked.

"Have at it!" said Murray, waving them off.

He and Will stood around scuffling their feet waiting for the two prospects to return. When they did, Ebding had money in hand, and the car was his.

"Now that's one trip into Lutcher's where you came out a winner," said Will.

"Nothing to keep me here now. Let's get to that party," said Murray.

Chapter 91

Alvin was completely wrong. Frances was not laughing and having a good time thinking she had made a fool out of her husband. She did not—in any way, shape or form—think he was a fool or that she had fooled him. She intended to show him that she was what she had always been with him—faithful, true blue and considerate of his desires.

She had taken the first step in that direction as soon as she left the sanatorium Wednesday afternoon. She used the Wilson's phone to make an appointment. Today Alvin would see the results.

Frances took special care in dressing for this Sunday visit. Her wages did not yet stretch to accommodate the store-bought dress Alvin had urged her to buy in June, but she had found the wherewithal to purchase a frilly blouse. She slipped it on, tucking it into a slim, black skirt Ida had cut down from one of Miriam's cast-off dresses. Then, she pulled on a pair of the new Chardonize knee-high hose, being careful not to snag the twenty-five-cent bargain with her newly painted nails.

The nail enamel had been Nita's idea. "No reason not to gild the lily," Nita had said, when she heard about the beautification project. She even offered to loan Frances some polish. She had her choice of poppy red or petal pink. When Frances chose the pink, Nita had laughed and said, "Why am I not surprised?"

Now, with her newly polished finger tips, Frances smoothed her skirt down over the hose. Good. The skirt was plenty long enough so no one would know that she wasn't wearing full-length stockings, which certainly were not in her budget now and probably would not be for a very long time. She stepped into her wedgies, also newly polished. No stickery heels for her, even if she could afford them. She just knew she would fall right off a pair of those. The belt Angie had gifted her with at the beginning of summer was the last thing Frances added to her outfit.

She inspected herself in the mirror. Her lips were such a vivid rose that adding lipstick would be redundant. But her pale eyelashes and brows were almost invisible. She wet a lead pencil with the tip of her tongue and drew it lightly over her brows. Better. Not much, but better.

Now she took a bold step, one the beauty operator had told her would do wonders for her looks. She put the curved instrument the girl had given her up to her eye. It was a strange looking thing, like a cross between tweezers and scissors, but it had no cutting edge. "Honestly. It can not hurt you," the girl had assured her, "Just clamp the little cushion over your eyelash and squeeze the handles together. You'll have the curliest lashes ever."

First one eye, then the other, underwent the treatment with the eyelash curler. Sure enough. Curly lashes resulted. Pale lashes still, but curly.

Frances opened her eyes wide. Blinked. Blinked again.

Now she was ready to show her husband he had a wife he could depend on.

Alvin had been mentally practicing how he would greet Frances. The edge of his anger had dulled since their last meeting, but he was still unhappy with her. And he wanted her to know it. He was no milksop, and she darn well better recognize that. He was debating whether it was better to go with his first idea to give her the silent treatment or set her down firmly and lay down the law, when Frances walked into his room, baby in hand.

"You got your hair marcelled!" a startled Alvin exclaimed.

"Cut *and* marcelled!" he added.

"About time, don't you think, husband of mine? I believe you put your order in three months ago."

She swiveled, so he could get the full effect of her new short, wavy hair.

The do ended just below her ears.

"It looks great. It looks great on you. Just like I knew it would," said Alvin. "Come here and let me see it."

She walked into his arms, and baby was forgotten, along with all of the anger he had stored up for her. "It's tremendous," he whispered in her ear.

Sunday, September 20.
My Darling little wife and baby.
This has been a pretty good
day. Tomorrow is bath day.
Oh my cold is no better. I
put in a bad night last
night. Coughed a lot and
such.

Monday, September 21. I
certainly enjoyed seeing
Frances and Baby yesterday.
Frances left me a picture
of baby. Sure is sweet.
It is about 8 inches by 10 inches.
Alta was over today. Sure
looks fine.

"One may lead a horse to water, Twenty cannot make him drink."—Christina Rossetti

After he wrote in his diary, Alvin contemplated the picture of his daughter. She, too, had his curls, but they were a softer version, not so tightly coiled. He thought that was all to the good. Hers would not crimp up in the rain.

His eyes were drawn back to the diary entry. Why hadn't he been able to express himself in Sunday's entry? Why had he taken refuge in a description of his health? There was so much he wanted to say, to do, to feel.

He was glad the misunderstanding between him and Frances was over, put to bed. He would like to put *her* to bed, right alongside him. Beneath him. Over him. *Oh to feel her warm, naked body next to his once again.*

He might as well be a eunuch for all the good he was to her. Oh, she did look mighty fine Sunday. From her head right down to her shoes. *Those shoes.* His fashion sense told him his little wife still clung to the plumage of a wren. But on her it was so becoming!

A thought pricked him. *One may lead a horse to water, but*

twenty can't make him drink.

True, he had been stubborn in the face of Frances' independent decision. He had dismissed the very reasonable explanations she had used to lead him to see her point of view. Yes, he had been like the stubborn, balky horse in today's *Daily Reminder*. But Frances had got him to the water, finally.

Alvin admitted he had even swallowed her argument, and found it refreshing. Obviously, not one of the twenty who could not get the horse to drink, was a loving blonde wife with a marcelled hair-do and a new blouse.

Chapter 92

Rossetti was the name of not one, but two, English Victorian authors. The Rossetti in whom Alvin was interested was Christina Georgina, born in 1830, died in 1894. She it was who had penned the *horse to water* lines.

Al was learning about her now because his curiosity had prompted him to search out an encyclopedia. The meditations in his red book had become crutches on which Al leaned daily. As often as he recognized the authors of these words, he just as often had no idea who they were. This Rossetti was one of the unknowns, until he got his hands on the encyclopedia.

Her work, it seemed, spanned a range from fantasy to religious poetry. Where the stubborn horse fit in, Al was not sure. The lady's older brother, Dante Gabriel, was the second Rossetti mentioned in the encyclopedia. Love sonnets were his forte, but he also had been noted for paintings of languid, mystical beauty…so the book said.

If Gillis did not catch him holding up the heavy tome, Al might be able to spend some interesting hours immersed in the encyclopedia. As a trial, he poked his finger randomly into the pages. It lit on *Germany: History of—Although Rome conquered the left bank of the Rhine, the Teutonic tribes of central Germany were never brought…*

Well, maybe he would tackle Germany some other time.

Al was too nervous to concentrate right now. It was the nature of the disease, but that did not make the creepy, crawly, ants-in-the-pants and everywhere else sensation more bearable. Added to it was a change that had been foisted on Ward One: An old maid who could benefit from a new pair of ears, Al thought. He had learned, after his reluctance to accept Rose as a ward clerk, that pre-judgment was not an accurate art. *But when you had to scream to be heard...*

It was true that this new clerk, Annie, tried the patience of the patients. This addition to the staff seemingly could hear nothing that wasn't delivered like a blast from a whistle on a steam engine. Al and many others were hoarse from trying to communicate with her. Annie's skill at bed-making also fell short of Alvin's expectations.

"As long as Flora helps her make the bed, we get by. Alone, she is a fizzle," Al complained to Leo.

"What are you, the Princess and the pea?" Leo shot back.

Al was surprised to hear Leo talk at all, and more surprised when he chose a fairy tale to use as a squelch.

"What do you know about fairy tales?"

"I know enough about them to know that a pea under the hiney of a girl proved she was a princess."

"The pea was not under her hindquarters, Leo."

"Was the way I heard it," Leo snapped.

"The pea, my misinformed roommate, was placed under a stack of mattresses upon which the gentle maiden tried to sleep," Al corrected.

"Heard it was her hiney," Leo muttered.

"It was a mattress, lots of mattresses, and it was her sensitivity to that tiny, dry legume that proved she was of royal blood...But what does that have to do with the wrinkles Annie leaves in my bed?"

"Proves you're too sensitive, Curly!" Leo crowed triumphantly.

Alvin collapsed in a fit of giggles, joined shortly by Leo.

It was the first laughter the two had shared in a long time, too long.

They also shared a good midday meal of fresh trout, brought in by the friend of another patient. Laughter and food put both of them in a good mood. It pleased Alvin to have Leo back to his more normal self, and Leo, too, seemed relieved to regain some of the energy that had drained away since Ruby left.

"Do you want to talk about it?" Al asked after they had chatted the afternoon away on topics of no more importance than the price of a Hupmobile Sports Coupe they'd seen advertised in the paper for a hundred-seventy-five dollars.

Leo did not duck the question. He had been expecting it. It was what he had been hiding from under those covers, but what it was now time to confront.

"Wouldn't say 'want to', might say 'have to'," Leo said.

Over the next several days the two talked.

They talked about Ruby alone in Dayton, the helplessness Leo felt not being able to protect her, his guilt that maybe he was the cause of her illness.

They talked about Ruby, maybe not alone in Dayton, the pain that thought caused Leo, and the guilt he felt for being so selfish as to deny her company when she really needed it.

They talked about Frances working, about Baby growing up without her daddy, and the guilt Alvin felt for letting them down.

They talked about Phil, Oscar, and the half-dozen other men they had watched die in this place, and the sorrow they felt at their passing, and the heavy load of guilt they felt because they were glad it was not them.

They couldn't get away from the guilt.

"That's what eats at me," said Leo. "That's what's killing me!"

None of their talks were conducive to healing. At least, they had been told repeatedly that peace of mind was as important as rest was to their bodies.

It was true that they had not pursued peaceful topics, but both Leo and Alvin slept well during those days of talks. Oh, there were still wrinkles in their beds. They both still had colds. They were both told they had gained weight, but were not sure they believed it. Frances still came to visit, and Ruby did not.

Finally, they were talked out. Leo now slept both night and day.

On Monday, September 28, a Dr. West made a special trip out to see Leo. After a bedside examination, he gave the nod to Miss Gillis to transfer Leo to a room of his own.

Gillis murmured her usual platitudes to Leo, and told Alvin he would have a new roommate by the end of the day. She and Flora quickly stacked Leo's table on the end of his bed and prepared to roll him away. Leo motioned them to wait.

"Just for a minute," he said.

He reached a hand to Alvin, who got out of bed to take it.

Joined by that handshake, unashamed tears formed in the eyes of both. They were past the point of pretending.

"It's been good," said Leo.

"That it has."

"I've got just three words for you, Curly," Leo said, squeezing Al's hand.

"Don't feel guilty."

Chapter 93

*Monday. Dr. W was out this
morning. Leo Pritchard is
pretty bad so they are
moving him into a room
by himself. We are here alone
just us two, Booze and I.
They moved 4 of the fellows.*

*Tuesday, September 29. We have
finished our bath and I feel fine.
That is the reason I am catching
up on my writing. I have my
carrot plant all prepared
and hanging by my bed. I
shall enjoy watching for it
to sprout.   Al*

*"A single conversation across the table with a wise man is
better than ten years' mere study of books."—Chinese maxim*

*Wednesday. Visiting day and
Pearl's birthday. I hope our
presents get to her in time.
I know she must be lonely.
Frances was out and did we
have a good time. She
brought me a lot of things.
She sure is good to me. Al*

Thursday, October 1. We have
had a very quiet day so far.
Alta was over for 45 minutes.
We had a very nice visit. She
sure is jolly. One would never
think she was ill. It is well to
be that way.   Al.

"*For sweetest things turn sourest by their deeds; Lilies that*
fester smell far worse than weeds."—William Shakespeare

Friday, October 2. We had no
heat today. The furnace is
undergoing a few repairs.
It sure was cold taking a bath.
Just warm water and no heat.
We had oysters for lunch. I
wanted six but only got 4.

Saturday, October 3. Weigh day.
It is just a stand off which way
the indicator will go.~~~ Well
I found out that the indicator
moved up ¾ of a lb. It is still
moving upward at a slow pace.
*   Al.*

"*Tis hard for an empty bag to stand upright!"—Benjamin*
Franklin

Sunday, October 4. Here it is the
best day of the week. The Sabbath.
I wish I were able to go to town
to Mass. Pray dear God let me help
celebrate at least one more Mass.

Monday, October 5. It has turned
pretty cold. Friday night at 11:17
marked the Death of one of the

patients. Leo Pritchard. He was
from Dayton and spent about
4 months in this room with me.

"God divided man into men that they might help each other."—Seneca

Chapter 94

Alvin held himself together through the four days it had taken Leo to die. With great effort, he held himself together during the following three days. Through it all, he struggled to be true to Leo's request not to feel guilty. When Sunday came around and he could not even go to Mass to pray for Leo's immortal soul, he wasn't so sure this time that he *was* glad that he was not the one to die.

Even being a survivor wasn't easy in a place like this.

The furnace that stopped spewing heat the day Leo died was still on the fritz four days later. The patients huddled under their Pendleton blankets in an effort to keep warm, many of them fighting colds. Alvin declined to brave the icy hall on the Tuesday bath day. *Already have a cold and don't want any more,* he scratched in his diary. The heat was still off when the next bath day rolled around on Friday, October 9. It had now been nine days since he had sluiced water over himself and he was feeling kind of gritty.

Remembering the advice Leo had given him the first day he entered the hospital, Alvin made his bath run through the cold halls as early as he dared. He was rewarded with hot water. He would have liked to stand under the hot spray until his bones thawed out, but, in consideration of those still to come, he used it sparingly.

Unfortunately, his partner was not one of the lucky ones. Booze reported that he had bathed in cold water. "And damn quick, too! Scarcely got my wienie wet," he said.

Al laughed. And surprised himself in doing so. Crude language—even mention of someone's wienie—he could do without, but coming from Booze this morning it struck him funny. Maybe because he remembered how his own *wienie* had protested the cold and tried to retract as far into its fuzzy nest as it could go before warm water coaxed it out.

Booze was not Leo, but they were doing OK together. One of the first things Booze had told Alvin when he moved into his room was how to pronounce his name.

"Contrary to what you might surmise, I do not imbibe to excess nor am I named after the family's pet dog. The name is not Booze or Bowzer. It is *Bow-zay*. Since my given name is René, it is clear that my parents cherish the idea of a Frenchman cradled in the limbs of our family tree. We contribute the concocted and slightly idiotic *Booze* to have occurred when an ancestor, perhaps a French Canadian or even a froggy from across the big pond, passed through the immigration gates and was registered by an officer confused by the foreign tongue of this ancestor, mythical or real.

"However..." Booze paused impressively. "However, I am not averse to answering to whatever you would like to call me, so long as we can be friends."

Booze was a man with a lot of friends, so their room looked like a train station on Wednesdays and Sundays with all kinds of visitors passing through bundled up in overcoats, scarves and hats. Alvin was pleased to be able to express his thanks to Booze's friend who had brought the string of trout that had provided him and Leo with such a good dinner the last week they were together. In turn, Booze seemed to be entranced with Ida and not fazed at all by her sharp tongue. Unlike Leo, Booze was not afraid to join in conversation with any and all who entered, whether they came to see him or Alvin. It made for some lively hours.

The furnace repairs were completed on October 13, and, as things warmed up, the men began to venture out from their rooms. The bath water was nice and warm, the halls were tolerable, the rooms almost toasty. Phil made an appearance after a long hiatus. The news he brought was lackluster, all about coughs and colds and general malaise among the patients.

Al and Booze listened halfheartedly to Phil's run-down of patients, room by room. Al thought they could have added their own health report for Phil to carry to his next stop. But how interesting would his cramps of indigestion after Saturday's 'craut and wieners be to fellow patients? Damn his reticence at belching in front of visitors, a scruple not shared by Booze, who declared it was unhealthy to keep all that explosive gas inside.

"Much better to let fly, Potts, than to lie there and suffer," Booze had said after Al suppressed his desperate need on two visiting days.

"It seems too crude with my wife in the room," Al protested.

"Next time, give me a signal, and I'll let loose with a big one so you can use it for cover. Wouldn't want you to spontaneously combust," Booze teased.

The red-tinged tissues that had been coming away from Booze's lips this past week and the bloody geyser that had erupted from Al's nose before breakfast were also health issues they kept from Phil.

"Nobody's damn business," Booze said without rancor when Phil left. For emphasis, he spat another splash of blood into his sputum cup and fastidiously pressed a tissue to his lips.

Phil's drop-in, news deliveries usually had the ability to lift spirits or, at least, to provide a diversion, but today's offerings put a damper on the day. If things were not going so well in their room, Al was not selfish enough to wish the same luck on others trapped by this disease. But, if bad luck abounded, he preferred not to hear about it. Al was just like a sponge, soaking up the atmosphere around him. Just as he had felt better after Alta's cheerful forty-five minute visit, he was soppy with gloom and doom after Phil's.

If I should lose Frances and baby I would never stay here one more night, he wrote in his diary after Phil stopped by. *I am living only for my wife and baby. I love them with all my heart. I pray I can go home to them* he confided to his book, writing by only the light of the harvest moon beaming in his window.

> *Friday, October 16. A TB patient*
> *lives only to be able to go home.*
> *It is hard to be compelled*
> *to die so young. There is so*
> *much to see and do. What*
> *a beautiful time I could have*
> *with my Wife and baby if I*
> *were home now. I have*

learned an awful lesson. Al.

He lifted the pencil from paper, then set the point back and squeezed in one more sentence although he had already used up the nine spaces provided on the page for Friday's entry. *Today is 7 months for me here, he wrote.*

Alvin was told that he had gained twenty-one pounds in the seven months of his hospitalization. That put him at one hundred forty pounds. While many patients were released when they reached a hundred forty-five, Alvin was pretty sure it would take more than five pounds to earn a ticket home this time.

His temperature continued to hover just under a hundred degrees. Indigestion clawed like a cat in his gut, while a twelve-pound dog sat on his chest. When his head wasn't floating dizzily a foot above him, it was sitting like a cannon ball atop his slender neck. Just when Al grew accustomed to all these symptoms, a good day would come along and brush away the cobwebs, aches and pains. Instead of being grateful, he viewed the improvement with suspicion, remarking in his diary *Maybe just a lull before the storm.*

Too often that skepticism proved to be reality.

The roller coaster was in full swing during October, sending him to the heights of nervous anticipation when Frances was expected and to the valleys of despair when the scale refused to swing his way. His diary was his secret weapon. In it he could record his lowest depths without apology to anyone. *I don't mind staying here if I feel well and gain. If I start losing too much weight, I shall take to the bushes. I couldn't stand to lie here and die.*

Death was a constant companion as the holidays approached, even though the Grim Reaper had to stand aside momentarily when Al sat in the barber's chair or plunged into the warm shower. Stand aside, but never truly disappear, the reaper was always a threat. Alvin felt Death's bony hand even as he conjured up a smile for Frances and baby. If he were truly getting better, surely they would let him go home for Thanksgiving. Alta had said she might be allowed that privilege. Alvin had not heard a word about such a reprieve for himself.

Al had to laugh when Alta made a surprise visit to Ward One

on Halloween. His sister and a friend from the women's wing paraded through the halls wrapped in sheets.

The live 'ghosts' made a nice change, Al thought, from the ones that clanked through his nightmares these days.

Chapter 95

On November 8, Alta was granted a two-day leave to go home. Elwin came to pick her up, and they were a happy couple as they waved goodbye to Alvin from the driveway out front.

Seeing them leave, arm-in-arm, and knowing they would soon be in the privacy of their own home turned Alvin's thoughts to his own wife. *I certainly need my wife now if a man ever did,* he wrote. *This sure is "hard" to take.* With his physical desire still unquenched, he poked fun at himself when he wrote *Frances was out to see her "Man" ha ha!* And then he added a plaintive note *Oh well he could be a man if "fate" so wished.*

He made them both miserable during a Sunday visit when he could not hide his longing for Frances and home. He brought her to the verge of tears with demands she was in no position to meet. As much as she, too, desired it, she could not pack him up and take him home, nor could she crawl into the bed beside him and give him the physical comfort he craved. Pushed to her limits, she finally burst out with a threat that it might be best if she stayed away, if her visits caused him so much frustration.

It was an unhappy Al who put pencil to paper the next day.

> *Monday, November 16. Thy Will be*
> *done. Please dearest Wife forgive me,*
> *an old sick man, for making you*
> *so very sad and unhappy. Oh God*
> *dear girl you will never know how*
> *it hurt me Sunday and now*
> *to think of what you said*
> *and were going to do.*
>
> *Tuesday. It seems God is*

not being very good to me.
I am ready to give up now.
I have honestly tried to
make a good stand for my
life. I have been fighting
as only a man can fight
that knows that he has
lost in this old world.

Wednesday, November 18. Oh
Dear God if it wasn't for Frances
and little Frances how easy it
would be to~~ ~~~ ~~~~?
I can't say it. But it is so.
Please Frances try and
always think kindly of me.
Maybe I am a coward and foolish
but I am also awfully tired.

"The pressure of a hand, a kiss, the caress of a child will do more to save sometimes than the wisest argument even rightly understood."—George McDonald

Thursday. I have always
hoped that I might die at
home but I know now I
will wind up the long trail
right from here. It probably
is better but I always dreaded
dying in a charitable insti-
tution. Even for such
untouchables as I am one of.

Friday, November 20. Frances
I have enjoyed the last years of
my life more than all of the others
put together. Be happy and know
that you and Baby have made it
easy for me. I pray that you are

well repaid between here and the end.
Black clouds ahead are all
I can see for myself.

"To the untrue man the whole universe is impalpable. It
shrinks to nothing in his grasp."—Hawthorne

Chapter 96

Of course, Frances did not curtail her visits. She did plead with Miss Gillis to try to wring a Thanksgiving leave for Alvin, but no soap. The supervisor did relent to the point of offering Frances the use of the recreation room so they could dine together in privacy on Thanksgiving Day.

With that prize in hand, Frances bearded her own special lion in his den. She thought the smile he turned on her looked as if he was trying too hard, but his blue eyes reflected none of the misery he had scrawled in his diary. Unaware that he had already given up, she set about to give him something to look forward to.

She painted glorious pictures for him of the holiday they would share. She would bring baby and his favorite pumpkin pie with that good, rich whipping cream from Duff's Dairy. Their meal would be provided by the hospital, but she prodded him to think of extras she could buy to make the dinner special.

"Olives, dill pickles, carrot sticks?" she suggested.

"You, you and you," he said, drawing her close.

This time his grasp on her was loose, undemanding, and she comfortably cuddled against him.

She shared with him the letter she had received from Murray, who was training at Fort McDowell on Angel Island in California.

"He seems to like it," she said. "Says he might as well be in the Navy since he's surrounded by water. The island is in San Francisco Bay. Listen to this. *We can see Alcatraz Island from here where they started penning up all the big bad criminals a couple years ago. Angel is just another rock like Alcatraz, but we're the good guys over here, just like the name says.*"

"Bet that's one 'angel' that's seeing some night life in the big city," said Alvin.

"He said he has been to San Francisco. He calls it *'Frisco.*

This next part is especially for you: *"Brother, you wouldn't believe the bridge they're building at the entrance to the bay. There's two towers over seven hundred feet high, and a span between them that's over four thousand feet long. And that's only part of it. Construction on this Golden Gate Bridge should be finished up next year. It's something this little country boy never thought he'd see the likes of, let me tell you!"*

"It's a big world out there. I'm glad Murray is grabbing a piece of it. Me? I'd settle for warming my toes in front of our wood stove."

When Alvin saw dismay begin to register on his wife's face, he hastened to add, "No. No, sweetheart. No more carping. I promise. I'm a turned leaf."

When she left, Frances thought Alvin seemed in better spirits than when she had arrived, that he was looking forward to their private Thanksgiving celebration and not minding too much that he could not be at home with her and Baby.

She would have been disappointed if she had read the diary entry he penciled in that evening.

*Wednesday, November 24. I
asked to go home for Xmas
but I reckon I am doomed
to stay right here. After all
they are awfully good to
me—Miss Gillis and Miss Sanders.*

*"It is the cause, and not the death, that makes the martyr."—
Napoleon I*

Chapter 97

Wednesday, November 25. Here it is
visiting day again. I always have
some very swell company on
Wed. and Sun. My Wife and Baby
are the best company I can have.

Thursday. Thanksgiving Day. My
Wife and baby are coming out
this morning. They moved me
down to the Rec. ~~~The Baby
came inside and was she
glad to be with her dad again.

   "Let not thy mind run on that thou lackest as much as on what
thou hast already."—Marcus Aurelius

   Outwardly Alvin presented a calm and accepting demeanor,
but his handwriting began to show the toll stress and depression
were exerting. The point of his lead pencil, which he always kept
sharp, no longer pressed heavily against the pages of his diary.
The words floated fairy light in a gray haze upon the paper, as if a
breeze could lift them free and send them sailing. Where he used
to fit as many as six words to a line, he now sprawled out as few
as two.

Friday. I was tired
last night but feel
fine tonite.
We sure had a
fine time yesterday.

The baby can
say anything.

Saturday, November 28. My sis
Alta went home
for good Thursday.
She sure was
a happy girl.
She is entitled to
a break for a
change.
"For to cast away a virtuous friend, I call as bad as to cast
away one's own life, which one loves best."—Sophocles

Sunday, Company
again
Frances and
Baby were here.
I wish they were
here all the time.
Or better let me
go home.

Monday, November 30.
Bath day
I should be
plenty clean
after a good
bath.

"Our country is that spot to which our heart is bound."—
Voltaire

Tue   s   d   a   y ,

Chapter 98

Leo would have known Alvin abandoned his diary on the very day he did, but Booze had not yet taken notice of the daily ritual. Even if he had seen Alvin let the pages fall shut without writing in the book on this first day of December, it is doubtful Booze would have mentioned it. It would have seemed a small thing to him. If he had recognized it for what it was, he still would have ignored it as he and Alvin had not yet reached the stage where prying could be accepted as concern.

It was Flora who found the book where it had fallen unnoticed under Alvin's bed.

She came upon it in the middle of the night. Although she was no longer assigned to Ward One, she still visited the rooms in the wee hours "just in case," she told Miss Gillis when questioned about her zealous work habits. She had been curious about 'Alvin's little red book' for some time, and was surprised now to see it on the floor.

She picked it up, was tempted to open its pages, but resisted.

The way Alvin reached for it first thing in the morning and last thing at night had led her to believe it had great importance for him. It had appeared to be leather-bound, but, now that it was in her hands, the wine red cover proved to be a thin veneer over very stiff paper. Still, it could be a leather veneer. Difficult to tell in this dim light. In the past eight and a half months her favorite patient's hands had rubbed all the color from the spine. The soft brown exposed beneath very well could be leather. She could feel as well as see a grain in it.

It was an attractive book with an ornate cover. A gold seal embossed in the center held the words *Diary and Daily Reminder* in fancy red script. The ornamentation did not end there. Raised scroll work encircled the seal and ran from top to bottom. Even the edges had raised patterns.

She might just open the first page.

Flora was astonished. Even the end pages were elaborate. Alvin had himself a very expensive diary here. She tipped the double page she now held open before her toward the light from the hall. It featured a sketch of a globe of the world on one side and a feathered quill in an ink bottle on the other. A streamer of calendar pages circled the globe and stretched across the feather of the pen. All this was overlaid on a faint hatch design. Very nice. It wasn't like Alvin to discard it so carelessly. Perhaps he had fallen asleep before he could put it away.

Flora snapped the book shut. She would hate to be caught poking her nose in where it should not be.

She laid the book on Alvin's table, and left the room.

Alvin opened his eyes, reached over and swept the book into the drawer.

He let his mind play over today's meditation, which he had memorized before he let the book slide to the floor.

It was from Emerson. Not his father, the poet.

How did it go?

Though we travel the world over to find the beautiful, we must carry it with us or we find it not.

Those words had hit home. He doubted he would ever hike through snow drifts in the Austrian Alps, row with Frances over a tranquil lake in northern Italy, or even be treated to a tropical sunset. Heck, he probably wouldn't even get as far as Angel Island. And, if he had to carry beauty with him to have it, that probably wasn't going to happen either. At this point, with the end of the year rushing at him, Alvin felt the load he already carried was more than he could bear.

"Oh, Leo." The moan seeped into his pillow. Then he wept.

Chapter 99

Snow drifted down in puffy flakes that caught on Frances Pearl's curls and gave her a sparkling cap. She looked like a haloed angel in her new blue snowsuit, Frances thought, as she reluctantly brushed the snow away and covered the child's cork screw curls with a scarf.

They were standing on the corner of Third Street to watch Santa come to town. Kids fourteen years of age and under had been invited to visit with him, and Frances held three of the one thousand tickets that had been distributed for a free show at the theatre. A block on West Alder, from Third to Second, was roped off, and every foot of the block was swarming with kids and parents awaiting Santa's arrival.

The tip of Frances' nose was red from the cold. She tucked a blanket in closer around Frances Pearl, where she huddled in the wicker buggy, and flipped the hood of the buggy over the child to shut off the snow fall. She looked for Herbie's towhead in the crowd. He had resisted every effort she made to keep him quietly at her side. Every time Frances let go of his hand, he darted off to disappear among the squash of people, only to reappear so she could attempt to corral him again.

Herbie was determined to be the first to catch a glimpse of the jolly man who was getting him into a Saturday movie free. He had no illusions that this same fat guy was going to put presents under a tree for him. He was wise to that caper, but, at his sister's insistence, was willing to pretend for his little niece's sake.

The kid was pretty smart, but Herbie thought the chances were slim that the two-year-old even knew who Santa was supposed to be. He bet when Frances Pearl saw his red suit and all that hair on his face she'd cry up a storm. He remembered the first time he'd been dragged into Monkey Wards to see the department store

Santa. Those big black boots had about scared the pea-waddin' out of him. The old guy had not brought Herbie the pony he'd asked for that year, so he hadn't really trusted him since then. Herbie just hoped Santa wasn't going to cop out on the movie tickets. Frances had assured him repeatedly that she already had them in her purse, but he hadn't *seen* them.

This outing was as much for Frances' entertainment as for the children's. The Christmas spirit had not stirred within her yet, and she was anxious to prod it into existence. She loved the feeling of good will that the Christmas season always seemed to bring, when you could walk down a street and everyone you met wore a smile for you. It was miraculous how you could be walking around in an ordinary body one minute and in the next be filled with the kind of bubbly effervescence you saw when you shook a bottle of 7-Up. It was that exhilaration she hoped to ignite this afternoon. She knew that once the Christmas spirit entered her, it was apt to last clear through to the New Year. Maybe looking for it as early as the fifth of December was too much to expect.

They had passed a lot filled with Christmas trees on their walk downtown. There were some beautiful, tall, shapely trees for sale, but they cost a dollar and a quarter. She would have to make her choice from the ones for two-bits, if she bought one at all. Docey had mentioned something about driving up to Kooskooskie to cut their own trees. If they did that, she could have a nice, big bushy one to put in her front window, and it wouldn't cost her a dime.

"Here he comes!" Herbie shouted, racing back to her and pointing at a red figure pressing through the crowd.

Frances grinned when she saw where Herbie was pointing. It definitely was a red-clad figure, but it surely wasn't a roly-poly Santa. It wasn't even a man.

"Hey there, Ruby," Frances called.

And Ruby it was.

A diminutive red-headed Ruby, wrapped in a bright red, wool coat that reached her ankles and covered the tops of shiny black galoshes. It was all that red that had fooled Herbie.

Ruby approached Frances eagerly, with a gloved hand extended.

"Well, as I live and breathe, if it isn't Curly's wife!" she exclaimed.

"Are you here for the movie, too?" Frances asked her.

"Not hardly! You wouldn't catch me in with all those screaming little meemies. Present company excepted," she added, grinning at Herbie, who was still looking chagrined at the mistake he had made.

"I was so sorry to hear about your husband's..."

Ruby interrupted Frances with a quick chop of her hand.

"Over and done with. Water under the bridge." She paused, then turned a bright smile on Frances and asked, "How have you been? How's Curly doing?"

"Everyone is well. And you? You're looking good," said Frances, noting the high color on Ruby's cheeks and the brilliant shining eyes so often produced by a high fever.

"I'm good. Real good! Long as I stay out of that pest house, I'll be just fine,"

Frances heard defiance in Ruby's voice. Time to change the subject.

She tipped back the buggy's top. Pulling the scarf off to reveal the baby's curls, Frances said, "Here's our meemie. I don't think you've seen our baby, have you?"

Ruby leaned over the buggy, poked and praised halfheartedly, and then looked over her shoulder at Frances and asked, "How is Murray?"

The relationship, if there had been one between Murray and Ruby, had never been openly acknowledged. As was her way, Frances chose not to do so now.

"Alvin's brother joined the Army. He writes us that he likes it."

"So he's a soldier boy, is he?"

The question confirmed for Frances that Murray had put paid to whatever he had shared with Ruby. She could be more generous now, knowing they had not been in touch recently.

"He's stationed in California on an island in San Francisco Bay. He's taking in all the sights. I think the big city has taken hold of him," said Frances.

"Well, let's hope it doesn't corrupt him!" Ruby said, laughing.

She took a pack of cigarettes from her purse, tapped one loose, and stuck it between her lips. She handed a chrome lighter to Herbie, showed him how to spin the wheel on it, and demanded,

"Light me up, little buddy."

Delighted at the attention, Herbie held the flame to the cigarette's tip, eyes intent on Ruby as she drew in deep breaths that set the tip to glowing.

Frances smiled. Even the little fellows were putty in her hands.

A shell burst overhead, followed by cheers and applause. Santa had arrived. Frances made a frantic grab at Herbie. She caught him up by a fistful of jacket, and held him fast. In the crush, she did not notice Ruby slip away.

When she thought to turn and look, Ruby was only a distant, red flash among a welter of winter coats.

Chapter 100

Docey followed through on his idea for a winter outing to the foothills in search of trees. He told Ida he would break out the big truck he used to haul trash and lumber, throw some hay bales in the back, and would be ready to take whoever wanted to brave the winter weather in the open bed of his truck.

"All you have to do is set the date," he said.

Ida settled on the second Saturday in December.

It was unthinkable for Miriam to be one of the party. She was expecting her first baby any day. She elected to keep Grandma Hempe company, an offer that left Ida free to accept the invitation. While Grandma was not obviously ailing, she was no longer left home alone.

"Grandma's getting to a ripe, old age," Herbie said solemnly to Frances when they were discussing who would go with Docey. She hid a grin, but thought the adults had better start paying attention to which 'little pitchers' were listening before they spoke.

It was decided that Will would ask Esther, and Ray, Herbie, Jenny and Agnes would round out the party. Frances declined because she did not want to miss visiting hours with Alvin. Besides, a day in the winter air would be too much for Frances Pearl.

When the day came, Ida handed over the keys to her car to Frances so she could drive out to Blue Mountain while they were away. Frances reciprocated when she leaned into Docey's window and handed him a large sack of home-baked cookies.

"These should go good with the hot cocoa and coffee Mom's taking along," said Frances.

"We're going to make it a real party," Docey said, showing Frances a bag full of buns and wieners he had stashed on the floorboards. "But you won't miss out, because we'll bring you back a humdinger of a tree!"

Frances loved driving in the country. She especially loved the Kooskooskie area where her family and friends gathered to play softball and splash in the river on summer Sundays. Those outings were just a few of many things she had missed out on this year. The Saturday house parties with their music and midnight suppers were also a thing of the past for her. Now she stayed home while others danced the night away. She had even given up the Saturday night ambles up and down Main Street. Without Alvin, it would not feel proper. Nor would it really be much fun to go to town without her husband. Truth was, nothing was very much fun without Al. The nights before she started working at the Wilson's had been endless and restless. Now, tired as she was by the end of the day, sleep came quickly, but the empty pillow was a constant reminder of better nights. And those she missed most of all.

When all was said and done, there really was nowhere she'd rather be than at her husband's side, wherever and whenever possible.

And today, with the use of Ida's car, it was very possible.

She wondered in what kind of mood she would find Alvin today.

This husband of hers had turned as broody as an old hen. For the past two weeks she had found him either hunched into his blankets like a biddy on her nest or as fractious as the same bird fighting off predators. She was never sure which Al would be waiting for her beyond those gleaming windows.

It was so unlike Alvin to be moody. He had that spell some time back that caused her to speak to Nita about him, but this now seemed to be something else. It was not so much that he was self-centered these days, but more as if he were detached. Detached from what she hadn't decided yet. It better not be from her, that much she knew.

The Dalles-Military Road was rutty beneath the Ford's thin tires, mostly mud. Winter was still young. What snow had fallen had quickly melted away, leaving this slush behind. While it did nothing for the looks of the car, slush was better than sheets of ice or drifts of snow. She didn't look forward to months of driving or, worse, walking in that in the months ahead. The steering wheel jittered in her hands as the tires grabbed for purchase.

"Oh, my kingdom for a car," she sang out. She really did intend to bring that subject up again with Alvin when she felt the time was right...maybe after she had a few more dollars saved toward the purchase of one. Oh yes, she did have a plan. But would he go for it?

As soon as the twin, white wings of the san came into view, Frances' heart began to pound. It was always like this. Had been since the first day she drove into that circular drive and knew Al was on the other side of a window watching for her. Her heart fluttered like crazy whenever she knew she would soon have his hands on her and hers on him. She wondered if every wife felt this wild exhilaration coming into the presence of her husband. Or was it true that absence makes the heart grow fonder? She dearly loved this bean pole of a fellow. Would love it even more when he blossomed out to the hundred and seventy he weighed when they married. Oh, how she wished him well and strong again...and home.

Inside his room, watching the window for her arrival, Al's thoughts were traveling along the same road. He had never expected to be so deeply in love. He had never expected to put his trust and faith so completely into the hands of a woman. That kind of thing made one so vulnerable. While he would have it no other way, now that he experienced it, it still frightened him. If he didn't have Frances...and now little Frances...he would be alone in the world.

At one time he considered that an ideal situation. A single man could roam just about anywhere in the world he wanted to go. Just pack a bag and take off! Catch a tramp steamer. Hire out on a cattle boat. Grab a ride on a freight train. The possibilities were endless, even if one did not have cash in the pocket. Be like Murray. Join the Army or Navy, if you *had* to. Al didn't have anything against his country, but wearing a uniform and going where you were told to go wasn't exactly the kind of freedom he had in mind when he daydreamed about the single life.

If he removed Frances from the equation, the single life still sounded good to him. If he had never met that blonde-headed gal at the poorhouse...or, if he had met her, but hadn't gotten to know her, his life might be different today. It might have been him, instead of Murray, packing that bag.

Oh, he could imagine a life in a place like Hawaii, or even in a cabin in the Rockies, but now it wouldn't be much of a life without Frances.

That he could not imagine. She was part and parcel of him. They went together like salt and pepper, sugar and cinnamon, tea and lemon slices. He dearly loved his girl, but, oh, how he would have liked to have seen something of the world before his light flickered out for good.

And it appeared to be flickering, all right. What else could Gillis' refusal to let him go home for Christmas mean? Meant he was on his last legs, that's what it meant! What else was he to think? Heck, even Booze, who was still spitting blood, was granted a few days away from this zoo. He, Alvin, was supposed to be content with the promise of Christmas day in the rec room alone with his wife and baby.

Well, wasn't that magnanimous of Old Lady Gillis. Golly, gee whiz, forgive me for not being grateful.

Outwardly, Alvin still turned a calm face to the world...well, at least to his ward and the people in it, as many as he could see from his bed. But Frances had been right when she thought he seemed detached. He *was* detached. Well, not *completely* yet, but he was working on it. He had held on by the skin of his teeth through these long months. No more. He was letting go. Isn't that what life was all about? Accepting what you could not change? Well, he sure as heck was not going to change anything in here.

Alvin was so caught up in his gloom and doom outlook that he missed seeing Frances wheel the Ford to a stop out front, so her entrance into the room took him by surprise. Before he knew it, she had her cold nose buried in his neck. She was a chilly armful as she wriggled in for a hug.

For a minute there was no one in the world but the two of them. Eyes closed, they rested in the comfort of each other's arms.

Then Frances broke free to pull off her coat and scarf. She draped them over the chair. She whirled back to him, waving a sack. "Guess what I have in here?"

"Cookies!" Booze exclaimed.

Al's roommate was not shy about putting in a claim on the oatmeal cookies Frances often brought. It was a big sack, and it was a good thing because the room soon filled with Booze's friends, who were invited to share. Frances surreptitiously slipped a smaller sack into the drawer of Alvin's table. "For later," she said, winking.

Visiting hour quickly turned into a party as Booze's visitors also passed around snacks they had brought. Frances could not keep all their names straight, but several stuck in her head.

There was Trina, a small dark woman, who unwrapped a plate of crispy, brown Italian cookies. "Dipped in honey," she said, explaining that these were a traditional Christmas treat. "Lots of work to make, so only once a year!" she said, laughing.

Lars, a big man with a hearty laugh, was another whose name Frances caught and held. He was so vigorously healthy! She thought he looked like a Viking, with his shock of thick blonde hair, broad shoulders and arms and legs like tree trunks.

A tall slender woman wrapped from neck to toe in a sleek black coat with a rich ruff of fur for a collar was the last of Booze's guests to enter the room. She was accompanied by a gentleman in a wool overcoat that flapped open to reveal a dark suit and a tie the color of ripe grain. A slender tracing of deepest green threaded through the gold. A large pearl tacked the tie to his shirt. He slid the woman's coat from her shoulders. She emerged from it like a butterfly from its cocoon, sleek in form-fitting crimson. Frances had never seen such elegance.

Booze had such interesting friends. The men who had come to visit on Wednesday looked as if they were just off the farm, dressed in overalls and boots. This group was an entirely new experience.

The elegant lady was named Crystal. Her voice tinkled crisply and clearly when she spoke. She was well named, Frances thought, entranced at first by the music of her words rather than the words themselves.

"…can you believe? Did you dream he would actually abdicate his throne to marry that divorcee? And an American!"

"And why not an American, my dear?" asked her escort, as if upholding his end of an ongoing argument.

"Why any divorcee is worth a throne is the question," she retorted.

"Now you have to elaborate for us shut-ins," Booze said. "We are uninformed chuckleheads here in our little world." He threw a broad wink in Alvin's direction.

"I believe, René, you know very well that King Edward VIII has been dallying with Mrs. Wallis Warfield Simson. Less than two weeks ago he threatened to give up the throne of Great Britain to marry this woman. And now, this past Thursday, he actually abdicated. His father must be rolling over in his grave!"

"He has had a short reign. It hasn't been a year since King George V died. Some time in January of this year, I believe it was." Booze offered.

"I see no good coming of this. His abdication could be the beginning of the end of the monarchy." Her words cracked like the sharp ping of a goblet struck by the silver tines of a fork.

"And would that be such a loss?" Trina quizzed.

"A new voice heard from!" exclaimed the Viking. "Of course, it would be a loss. If England lost its monarchy, thousands of years of rule would be erased as if they had never been. And think of it—all those beheadings would have been for nothing!"

Lars' last remark met with groans and snickers.

"Shame on you," said Crystal's escort. "The real conundrum would be the difficulty in which the housewives of Great Britain would find themselves."

"What do you mean by that?" said Crystal, puzzled.

"No pictures of royalty to put on their walls!" he rejoined.

Laughter greeted his sally.

"I do think all this royalty is a to-do about nothing," Trina persisted. "Absurd, when you think about it. When the old king died, he had a string of titles as long as my arm," she added, stretching out her small limb and flapping her hand dismissively.

"King of England and Ireland, right?" Booze asked.

"Officially, *King George by the Grace of God, of Great Britain, Ireland and the British Dominions Beyond the Seas King, Defender of the Faith, Emperor of India.*" Crystal reeled off.

Her words were met with stunned silence. Then the room erupted in laughter.

"How would you know that?" sputtered Booze.

"Leave it to Crystal to *know*. But how did she remember it?" her companion said.

"That proves my point," said Trina. "Absurd, totally absurd."

Later, looking over the gay gathering with its far reaching interests and diverse opinions, Alvin leaned close to Frances and said, "It might be nice if we told Gillis we would like to invite another couple to share the rec with us on Christmas day."

Chapter 101

The tree was a marvel. Its tip brushed the ceiling. Its branches spread out to touch both walls of the spacious corner in which it was ensconced. Its colored lights gleamed dimly in the winter sunshine that streamed through the windows of the recreation room.

Alvin took Frances Pearl by the hand and led her to the tree Docey had brought back from Kooskooskie especially for the sanatorium. Into her hands he put an ornament. "Let's put Santa on the tree, shall we?" he said.

The tree had already been decorated by staff members and patients after Docey trundled it in and set it up the day after the Kooskooskie trip. Several volunteers from the tuberculosis league had used Docey's donation as an excuse for a holiday punch and cookie affair for the patients. Alvin had not gotten in on the decorating party because he was still confined to bed rest, but the volunteers had showed all the patients how to make ornaments from materials they distributed.

Alvin had tried his hand at making a Santa from red yarn, tissue paper and cotton. It was this little figure that he handed to his daughter. Under his guidance, she attached it to a limb. A few presents were scattered under the tree. Frances had brought several for the baby and Alvin. Lou and Mary, who would share the room with them today, also had gifts under the tree. The couple to whom Miss Gillis had extended their Christmas day invitation had no children, so it would be just the five of them. They would have all day together, with the holiday dinner to be served by the staff at noon. Frances and Mary had both brought extras to go along with the meal. Mary's offering was a dozen oranges, a bargain, she confided to Frances, that she had found at Red and White for twenty-four cents. Frances Pearl had never had an orange, and

Frances looked forward to seeing her reaction to it.

Frances had made cinnamon rolls that she was going to serve with coffee as soon as Rose brought Lou from his room. Lou, like Alvin, was bed-bound, so both men would spend most of this day, like all the others, resting in their beds. Since a little movement was allowed them today, they might all sit at the table to eat later, but coffee and rolls would be eaten from a tray in bed. It was clearly understood by both Lou and Al that they were to avoid exertion.

"That means a very quiet day for us, but a very sweet one," Al said, drawing Frances to him with one arm while holding their daughter with the other. "This is what I live for," he said to his wife. "This—you and baby," he said, squeezing both of them.

The loudspeakers piped Christmas music throughout the rooms. Miss Gillis had been in earlier to test the volume in the rec room. "We can tone it down, if it gets to be too much," she had said. Then, seeing Al silently mouthing the words to a song, she pointed a finger at him and said sternly, "No singing now, Alvin. Promise?"

It was difficult for him not to open his mouth and let loose in song. Music came as naturally to him as breathing. Whistling was his first choice for release, but singing was also second nature.

There had always been music in his home. His mother's contralto, Emerson's tenor and the children's voices in various ranges and pitches had often been raised in song. Not often together, true, but each had used songs to make short work of their chores. He and Frances, along with their friends, learned all the new songs and sang them together at the weekend parties, which had been so much a part of their lives until this past year. His favorite this year was *It's Been So Long*, a Benny Goodman number. He didn't particularly like Fred Astaire's singing style on *The Way You Look Tonight*. A little too affected, he thought, but it was a super tune. He'd like to wrap his own tonsils around that one. Not that he thought he was competition for old Fred, but just to have the pleasure of feeling his lungs pump out those wonderful lyrics. Maybe someday.

Today he had promised Gillis he would be good, and good he would be. No singing.

When the breakfast snack was finished and gifts opened, Lou

suggested a word game.

"That wouldn't be too strenuous, would it?" he joked.

"Not if we avoid funny words that make us laugh," Alvin said, remembering the belly laughs Leo had inspired before Gillis removed him from their room.

They devised their own game and rules to go with it. The women were allowed three guesses if the men posed a sports question, but only two if the answer could be found in general information.

It took Mary only one guess to name Jesse Owens as the American who won four gold medals at the Summer Olympics in Berlin, but no one, not even Alvin, could answer Lou's question as to who the Heisman Trophy winner was in 1936. "We need Phil here for the tough ones," said Al, conceding defeat so Lou could provide the answer. "A Yale man, Larry Kelley," Lou informed them.

"What's the Heisman?" Mary whispered to Frances, who just shook her head in bewilderment.

The baby played quietly beside the tree, turning the pages of a picture book that was one of her gifts.

Frances was first to answer "Volkswagen" when Alvin asked them to name the car Hitler had introduced to Germany that year. "How did you know that?" asked Mary. "If you are married to Alvin, cars are one thing you hear a lot about," Frances said with a grin in her husband's direction. "Guilty," Alvin agreed.

Mary and Lou were not old friends of Alvin's or Frances'. In fact, Lou was a relatively new patient to the san, which may have been why Gillis had chosen them to be the couple to share this Christmas day with Alvin and Frances. The game was giving them an opportunity to get acquainted, as well as acclimating Lou to his new environment.

When it was Mary's turn to ask a question, she said, "What is transparent, keeps out germs and can be reused, if you remove it carefully?"

"Cellophane!" all three chorused.

"Oh, phooey," said Mary, disappointed that they had found her question too easy.

"You could have asked what company makes the Cellophane wrap, and that might have stumped us," suggested Lou.

"Dupont!" Mary, Frances and Alvin said simultaneously.

"Guess that shows the power of advertising," said Lou.

The oranges at lunch were a big hit. Alvin scored the rind of his twice with a knife, making cuts in two directions. He then inserted a teaspoon into a cut, bowl side curved into the fruit, and folded back a quarter of the rind, all in one piece. He separated the orange sections, and fed them, one by one, to Frances Pearl. Juice ran down her chin, and she elicited smiles as she lapped at it with her tongue.

The first half of the day certainly had not tired the women, but Al and Lou gave Annie no argument when she announced the rest hour. They were ready to stretch out. Annie snapped off the lights as she left the room with their dinner dishes. Mary settled into a chair beside Lou's bed, her feet resting on its edge. Frances put the baby down for her nap across the foot of Alvin's bed, and then she lay beside him.

"This has been a tremendous day," Alvin whispered contentedly to Frances before he fell asleep with her hand in his.

The lights from the tree threw a soft, colorful glow over the dim rec room. The only sound was a muffled snore from Lou's corner of the room.

If Al had turned to his red book tonight, he might have learned from Marcus Aurelius, the Roman emperor noted for his stoicism, why today had been so pleasing to him. The excerpt from Aurelius' *Meditations* read: *"The happiness of your life depends upon the quality of your thoughts; therefore guard accordingly."*

But Alvin had not opened his *Diary and Daily Reminder* since last month.

Or had he?

Chapter 102

The best thing about Christmas this year was that it fell on a Saturday, which also gave Alvin and Frances the following day together. Again the room was filled with Booze's friends, which always made for a sprightly time, as far as Alvin was concerned. Frances would have enjoyed her time with him just as much if they had been the only two in the room. They did bring some interesting snacks though.

Today it was goat cheese.

A wizened little fellow with a face like a shriveled apple was the bearer of the crumbly treat.

"I make myself," he informed them as he passed around a thick cake of it from which he carved off thin slices with a wicked looking knife he withdrew from an inner pocket of his leather vest. Booze's other guests today were of the same ilk as the little man. The women—and there were three of them—wore long, black woolen skirts with white blouses and vests. Two of the vests were embroidered with colorful designs. The third was made of bright scraps of patchwork with intricate embroidery outlining each piece. Leather boots laced to their knees completed their unusual outfits.

They reminded Alvin of Mrs. Sabatini, from his youthful days in the piney woods. Perhaps Gypsies, maybe Basque. He never found out just who or what this quartet was.

Booze never explained his guests. And they just kept coming.

Now Alvin never knew what Wednesdays and Sundays would bring. He began to look forward to the diverse parade. The conversation equaled the exotic foods they brought. It seemed if Alvin was unable to venture into the world, the world was coming to him. It was a stimulating change.

And Flora presented him with a provocative New Year's day

gift.

She plopped it down on his table, unwrapped. It was a stack of pages about two and a half by three inches wrapped in cellophane. Next to them she placed what looked like two miniature croquet hoops hooked together. It took Alvin only a second look to identify Flora's gift. It was a 1937 desk calendar. A very small desk calendar. Flora lingered only long enough to accept thanks from Alvin and Booze, to whom she had given a pack of stationery.

When she was gone, Alvin examined his present. The small, loose pages were punched with two holes, and were intended to be threaded onto the metal hooks. The top page, a stiff brown cover, was labeled *Daily Reminder 1937*.

Alvin unwrapped and opened it. Calendars for the years 1937 and 1938 were printed on the first and second pages. The third and fourth pages listed the main holidays, month by month, for 1937. The only holiday this month, other than New Year's Day, was Benjamin Franklin's birthday on January 17. *By gosh, we'll have to celebrate that one.*

Every page thereafter was imprinted on the back with the day of the week and a small calendar of the current month. The face of each page was blank.

The entire two and a half by three inches, blank.

What a writing surface. Filling one of those sure won't strain my brain.

Alvin laughed—a scoffing, mirthless sound—when he saw the pages assigned to the weekends. One little page to be shared by *two* days.

Al doubted that he would use the calendar for anything more than marking time.

But when afternoon visiting hours ended and Frances was not due back in the evening, the room seemed extraordinarily empty, and it wasn't long before Alvin found himself threading the calendar onto its small holder. From there it was just a step to once again putting pencil to paper.

Temp 99. Spenditure 20 cents, he wrote.

Maybe he would just jot down his temperature each day. A record of that would be helpful. He already tracked his progress by the fluctuation of his body temp. A high temperature usually brought a splitting headache, a low one sometimes a pain-free day. The more low temps he could record, the quicker he would be out of here.

Oh yes, he was determined to walk out of here a free man. Accepting any other premise was for the birds. He had been crazy to give up. He had as good a chance as any one of these patients, and he was seeing one or another of them leave every week. Well, *almost* every week. One day, and he bet it wasn't that far in the future, he would be the one walking down that circular drive, getting into a car with his wife and driving away. That would be a tremendous day.

Without thinking, Al drew the stack of calendar pages closer, and began to write on the face of the one marked Friday, January 1.

> *Frances was out*
> *all day today.*
> *She couldn't*
> *come out tonite.*
> *I talked to her and*
> *baby over the*
> *phone. Baby*
> *said, "Daddy*
> *come home."*
> *I am soon I hope.*
> *Daddy*

Al dug in the drawer to find his red diary. He leafed through it until the page for December 6 lay open before him.

"Tis the mind that makes the body rich."—Shakespeare

He read the line, then re-read it. Yes, that's the way he remembered it. Words to live by.

He closed his diary, and packed it away in the Mars candy box, repository for all his treasures. He slid the Mars box back into the drawer. The 1936 diary was no longer timely, but he would save it and take it with him when he went home. Those empty pages of December would be reminders of the days he had let depression rob him of making any entries at all. Those days were behind him. This was a new year.

Chapter 103

January 2-3
Saturday and Sunday
Sat. Temp 97.6 98.6
Just waiting
for visiting day to
come. It is sure
cold today.
I gained ½ lb.
Sun. Temp 97.6   99.2
Frances was out
today. She doesn't
feel very well.

January 4
 Monday
Temp. 97.4 a.m.
Temp. 99 p.m.
This was bath
day otherwise
it has been
rather quiet.
We had some
rain and wind.
It is lots warmer.

January 5
Tuesday
Temp. 97.4
"   99.2
We had a real

blizzard today.
It snowed about
4 inches on
the level. It
sure was drifting
around here.
A regular old
norther. The
night nurse's
home burned
down night before
                    last.

January 6
Wednesday
Temp. 97.6
"   98.8
It is plenty cold at
7:00 clock in the
morning and that
is what it is.
Visiting day and boy
what a day, the
snow is sure drifted.
Frances was here
but won't be back
tonight. We had a
nice time. I'm in
love with her. Al.

January 7
Thursday
Temp. 97.4
"   99
It is still real
cold and I am
plenty tired of it.
I am ready
for summer.

Although I feel
like a young
stud horse.
I am ready for
visiting day too.
I love Frances
and baby. Al.

Chapter 104

Alvin had to laugh at his new 'diary'. He had been recording in it for a week, and his fingers cramped with the effort to fit even three words across a page. Booze had noticed and offered to scare up a real diary for him, but Alvin's stubborn streak kicked in. The lilliputian pages were now a daily challenge.

"I don't have much to say," he told Booze as he refused his offer.

He actually had a river flowing through his brain, but he was learning to compress his thoughts into these tiny words on these tiny pages. At first he resorted to squishing the numerals denoting his temperature into whatever space he could get them to fit. He refined that so each morning and evening temp now had its own slot. Condensing a day into three inches or less had become a competition with himself. He was reluctant to give up.

Alvin viewed the 1937 Daily Reminder as *Flora's Dare*. He recalled the night Flora had secretly skimmed through his 1936 diary. This New Year's present from her was such an obvious antithesis of his leather book that Flora must have had a specific reason for choosing it. Until he figured that out, he would continue to log his days in it.

He had plenty of time. The winter weather was taking a toll on Frances' visits.

Snow drifts and icy roads forced her to relinquish the evening hours. Since Booze's friends had never visited in the evenings, Alvin and Booze had to rely on each other to enliven the hours after dinner. World and national affairs provided ample fodder for discussions. Together, they read in the *Union-Bulletin* about the widespread strikes and shutdowns plaguing the automotive industry.

"The United Automobile Workers of America claim the jobs

of a hundred thirty-five thousand men are imperiled," Booze read. "It says the strikes stretch from Michigan to Ohio, Georgia and Missouri where Chevrolet and Buick assembly lines are tied up."

"Workers are getting restless...and tired of working for peanuts," Alvin commented.

"The guys in the know—the industrial leaders, bankers and economists—are predicting there will be more unrest this year and even a shortage of skilled workers in some areas," Booze noted.

"We don't feel the impact in here, but, generally speaking, the depression seems to be pinching a little less," said Alvin.

"Lars said that's what business is reporting. Actually, he said 1936 is supposed to be the first good twelve-month period for business since the depression," said Booze. "With it, will come higher prices, I'm betting."

Alvin thought of the dozen oranges Mary had brought to their Christmas dinner. She said she paid twenty-four cents for them, and he saw in today's paper *two dozen* were on sale for thirty-three cents. Maybe Booze was wrong. Maybe there was going to be a silver lining in these gray clouds.

Or maybe these were December's oranges that had to be sold before they rotted.

Chapter 105

The wind whistling along the walls of the sanatorium whipped the falling snow into frenzied flurries that flew in all directions. The windows, thrown open by Gillis an hour ago, funneled the weather to the pillows of Ward One. Alvin and Booze handled the chilly day each in his own way. Al's solution was to pull the covers over his head after asking for extra blankets. Booze was more direct. He heisted himself out of bed, tromped off determinedly, and returned with not one, but a stack, of the wool blankets that were parceled out reluctantly.

By now Alvin had concluded Booze came from richer stock than he. The variety of Booze's guests and the delicacies they brought him provided a clue to his background. The man obviously was accustomed to the out of season fruit, the pâtés and cheeses, and the specialty breads and crackers visitors brought. But it was Booze's demeanor that cinched it for Alvin. Booze was always polite and gentle spoken, never demanding, with the staff, yet he took as his due any courtesy they extended him.

Today, it was blankets. Where Alvin considered an extra blanket a boon, Booze took it as his right, and came back with more than enough for both of them. Al was nursing a sore throat, and the extra warmth felt especially good today.

When Al speculated on what brought a man like Booze to a place like this, his guess was that Booze had fallen on hard times. But he couldn't be sure.

In a place of this kind, the code of the Old West was alive and well.

One just did not ask questions. You waited for a man to even tell you his name, and you sure didn't dig into his past. So far, Booze wasn't talking.

But, if Booze were flush, he would not be in a county-operated hospital. The gents with money received care at one of the private tuberculosis sanatoriums at either St. Mary's or Walla Walla General Hospital. Still, Al would bet Booze, at one time, could have afforded a place where the salmon served on Fridays did not stink.

Snow was still flying when an apparition blew into the room as if ejected from the storm.

A tall, skinny man wrapped in layers covered by a flimsy, cloth coat was followed by Annie, who dragged him forward and introduced him to Booze and Alvin as Tom Riddle.

She announced, "He will be sharing this cozy room with the two of you. Make Mr. Riddle welcome, please." As Annie said this, she brushed snow from Riddle's garments in much the same way a proud mother slicks down the cowlick of a son she is presenting for a teacher's inspection.

Alvin and Booze did not disappoint her. They certainly inspected this surprise addition to their room. They gave him the once-over, then subjected him to closer scrutiny. Welcoming a newcomer was always an ordeal. You never knew what you were going to get. Whatever it was, you knew you had to live with it day and night. So, both men eyed him carefully.

Their first impression was of a bag of bones wrapped in rags. A closer look showed them a man on the verge of collapse.

Pain had etched deep lines across his forehead that gave him a scowling, angry look. His mouth hung slack as if it would take energy he did not have to close it. A pinched nose and pursed lips painted him, perhaps unjustly, with a miserly overtone.

This Riddle tugged off a wide-brimmed, felt hat. He knocked the snow from it, and tossed it onto a chair. His hair, which could use a good cropping, sprouted up from his head in unruly peaks. Annie helped him peel off, first, the black jacket and a long gray scarf, both soaked from the snowfall. A coarse, gray sweater that had to be pulled over his head was next. It, too, was wet.

Under the gray sweater was a finer knit, but obviously old, blue sweater that buttoned over a vest in a bold red and black, window-pane plaid. Under the vest the collar of a dingy shirt could be seen. And under that, yet another. These he left on.

Riddle gave an abrupt nod to acknowledge Annie's introductions.

She soon had a bed and table brought in for him. Although it was a Thursday and not a bath day, she gave Riddle a pair of pajamas and a robe, and hustled him off to the showers.

"As Lars would say, another voice heard from," said Booze. "We'll have to wait and see how this pans out, won't we?"

"Poor chap looked as if he was going to pass out," said Al.

"Well, Annie will have him snugged down in his own nest of wrinkles before long. A hot shower will do him good."

"And some food," said Al, remembering back to his first day here.

"Such as it is," lamented Booze. "But, if staff does not come through with something edible this evening, I believe we can enhance the menu with a tin of sardines and some crackers." He rapped a knuckle against the drawer in his table.

Al swore to himself that he was not going to be quick to judge in this case. He had learned his lesson with Ruby, calling a pot black when it was unwarranted. This Riddle didn't look like a prize package, but he might be an all right fellow. They would just wait and see.

Chapter 106

The stormy day of Riddle's arrival had followed a series of decent days in the first two weeks of January in which Al had felt well. His temperature, duly recorded each day in his gift, had fluctuated from a low of 97.2 to 99, a high that had made him unhappy. The sore throat had come and gone, and his weight was holding steady at a hundred and forty-one. *I would like to gain 81/2 lbs. more. Then~?*, he had written on January 10.

Riddle had become a patient during the snow storm of January 14, and, while Al certainly was not blaming the newcomer for it, his temperature had soared to 99.6 the next day. It worried him. *It seems my temp is rising. I feel kinda like I had the flu*, he wrote in his tiny book.

His jotting this evening seemed to annoy Riddle.

"What's that you're writing there?" Riddle demanded of Alvin.

Taken aback by Riddle's tone of voice, Alvin said simply, "Not much."

"What kind of answer is that?" said Riddle, further startling Al and catching Booze's attention.

"It's just my record of how the days go," Al elaborated, hoping to avoid trouble.

"So how do you say today went?" Riddle persisted.

Al's grip on his pencil tightened.

"Fine," he said between clenched teeth.

"When they weighed us, I heard the old bag say you didn't gain any weight this week. You're coughing up a storm, and the food tastes like garbage. You call this a fine day?"

Riddle had been with them only three days. Like most new patients, he had slept away most of the first two days. This was the first time he had really taken notice of his surroundings.

Apparently, he did not like what he saw.

Alvin was stumped as to how to handle Riddle's rude questions. His first reaction, not surprisingly, was anger. But he would be damned if he'd give in to that. Nor did he intend to tell Riddle what he had actually written tonight.

His glance caught the page he still held in his hand.

> *Have a cold.*
> *Sure am*
> *lonely for my*
> *dear wife. Boy*
> *oh boy do I*
> *love her. I*
> *know she is all*
> *good. Too good*
> *for me I know.*
> *But I love her*
> *and want her*
> *all the more.*
> *daddy*

It was none of Riddle's business how much he missed his wife or how much he was looking forward to seeing her tomorrow or even how badly he felt right now. But Alvin knew that adjustment came slowly in a place of this sort. It was up to him to make allowances for the new fellow.

So, Alvin turned a cheerful face to Riddle, and said, "Some days here are better than others. You'll see."

"A real *Pollyanna* is what we got here," Riddle sneered.

Alvin decided his best bet was to ignore the man.

Which he did.

Until Riddle pushed himself upright, leaned over as far as he could toward Alvin, and, while deliberately looking into Alvin's eyes, spat into a napkin he held in the palm of his hand at a dangerous distance from his own mouth. The sputum sprayed through the air and landed in a wet glob, which Riddle crushed into the napkin with a squeeze of his fist.

When Gillis had taken away their sputum cups on January 11 and instructed the patients that now they were to spit into napkins and place them in sacks pinned to their beds, Alvin had been among the dissenters. He did not like change, and this particular change irked him no end. Spitting out the sputum that could lead to intestinal tuberculosis, if swallowed, was a necessity. Alvin had grown accustomed to spitting into the little cups provided for that purpose. In comparison to using napkins, the cups seemed, to Alvin, to be the more sanitary method of collecting the sputum that had to be burned, the only way to assure the tubercular germs were destroyed.

The sputum cup process, while disgusting to Alvin, was tolerable. Holding a napkin into which he had to spit was loathsome, but endurable if done discreetly. To have Riddle put the abhorrent act into practice right in front of Alvin in such a deliberately offensive way was the last straw.

The color drained from Al's face. His fists clenched.

Booze carefully swung his legs out of bed and rose to a sitting position, silent but watchful.

Riddle's thin lips assumed a mocking grin.

Anger surged through Alvin in such hot, heavy waves that he became lightheaded. He was riveted to his bed even as filthy words clawed at his throat trying to get out. Al's fury robbed him of speech long enough for him to recall the promise he had made to himself years ago. He took a deep breath.

Alvin began to count…slowly to himself…with his eyes on Riddle.

The man sat, head tilted back at an insolent angle, whiskery chin jutted out. With his shaggy mane and dressed as he was, in washed-out, hospital-issued pajamas, Riddle presented a ludicrous figure.

The anger drained from Al as quickly as it had come.

The poor fool. He doesn't know any better.

Alvin saw Riddle in a new light. He recognized his roommate for the crude bumpkin he was, a dolt who had not yet caught onto accepted behavior in this strange place. *Why, Riddle was a victim, not an aggressor!* This then, this obnoxious manner of his, might be the only weapon Riddle held against a scourge not of his making. *Poor fool, he doesn't realize that none of us here have a defense against this plague.*

Al uncurled his fists. He relaxed into his pillows. He looked steadily at Riddle…and he smiled.

"You should have been here when we spit into cups. That might have been more to your liking," said Alvin.

"Those were the days," said Booze.

The bed springs creaked under Booze's weight as he settled back into his bed.

"You can say that again," said Al before he turned away, pulled the blanket over his shoulder, and prepared to sleep.

Tomorrow was Sunday, and his wife would be with him. This had been a fine day, but tomorrow would be better.

Chapter 107

Sunday morning Booze stepped into the breach, giving Riddle no time to even think of taking up where he had left off the night before. Booze laid claim to Riddle's attention while he was still rubbing sleep from his eyes.

"Slept well, did you?" quizzed Booze, without waiting for a reply. He formed and reformed the question as to how Riddle had spent his night in so many different ways that Rose delivered breakfast before Booze had exhausted the topic. As soon as Riddle swabbed the last bite of egg up with his last crust of toast, Booze led him into a conversation about snippets he culled from the morning paper.

Booze turned an advertisement for a movie into a discussion of the acting talents of Barbara Stanwyck, who was appearing as the sharpshooter Annie Oakley in a movie of the same name at the Capital Theatre. Seemingly not content with seeking Riddle's evaluation of the actress, Booze proceeded with an in-depth history of Oakley, who, he concluded at the end of thirty minutes, "was perhaps the most misunderstood female of her time and a consummate showman in her own right...and only five foot tall. She was called Little Sure Shot, you know. Married to Frank Butler; don't hear much about him, do we? No. She's the one whose name history remembers. Died just ten years ago."

Al wondered how much of Oakley's history had been dredged up from Booze's imagination.

Another advertisement, this time for a grocery store, captured Booze's attention and sent him off in another direction. Alvin listened with amusement as Booze pretended an avid interest in the price of pearl tapioca, an ingredient, he noted, that was essential to the pudding they sometimes found on their dinner trays.

"When made with a delicate hand, tapioca pudding can be a delight," Booze informed Riddle, adding seriously, "And it can be had this week at only twenty-five cents for three pounds of the cassava starch."

When Riddle wrinkled his brow at Booze's use of the words *cassava starch*, Booze took it as an invitation to enter into a long explanation of the derivation of tapioca. He described in detail the 'tropical spurge' that made possible the creamy pudding with its transparent specks of tapioca, familiarly called 'little frog eyes' by the patients.

Riddle questioned the word *spurge*, which elicited another monologue from Booze that did not end until Riddle yawned hugely and said he believed he was ready for a little shut-eye before lunch.

Booze cast a look in Al's direction as Riddle stretched out and closed his eyes.

"More than one way to skin a cat," said Booze.

If Riddle thought Booze's comment was anything more than the introduction of a new topic from the *Union*, he gave no evidence of it.

"I had yet to touch on 'Gorilla' Jones' victory over the N.B.A.," said Booze. "Very interesting how the association finally lifted the ban on the former middleweight champ and will allow him to fight for his title against Freddie Steele. More interesting still is the news media's anachronism by referring to Mr. Jones as the *Akron Darky*, don't you think, not to mention the 'Gorilla' moniker hung on him?"

"Well, they can't very well call him the *Brown Bomber*. Louis already has that title," said Al.

"I respectfully ask you to refrain from using either of those terms Wednesday evening when I introduce you to some special company in whom I think you will be very interested…and, no, dear fellow, do not ask me to elaborate at this time. I believe I have talked enough this morning."

Booze knew how to leave a guy in suspense, but Al loved a good mystery and was content to wait to see what surprise Booze would spring on Wednesday. He picked up a book to fill the hours before lunch. Let Riddle sleep now; Al would reserve his own nap for after the meal. Booze was right. There *was* more than one way to skin a cat.

Both methods employed by Booze and Alvin succeeded in maintaining peace in the room right up to the two-thirty visiting hour. Frances was first to arrive and, while Riddle noticed her entrance and Al's failure to introduce her, he said nothing. She took a place close to the window on the far side of Alvin's bed. Situated as his bed was at the far end of the room, the married couple thus had a semblance of privacy.

As Booze's animated friends filtered in, they became the center of attention, and Alvin and Frances were soon overlooked. Crystal was again among the quartet clustered around Booze's bed. Her three companions today were men, none of whom had visited before. Booze greeted all as one would longtime friends. While they were still sloughing off their winter wraps, a silver flask was handed to Booze.

Riddle watched as amber liquid spilled into Booze's toothbrush glass. His tongue slid across lips in thirsty anticipation.

Booze cocked his head at Riddle, raised an eyebrow, and drew a finger across his lips. Riddle's answer to the unspoken question was a nod, his silent promise that he would not give Booze's game away. With that slight assurance, Booze signaled to one of the men to pour a generous libation into a glass on Riddle's table. Then the flask was slipped discreetly under Booze's pillow.

Crystal rummaged through a large, leather bag and extracted several containers. From them she prepared a feast of gherkins, olives, pearl onions and finger sandwiches of thinly sliced beef. She distributed plates to everyone, even Frances and Al in their isolated corner. Riddle did not question this unexpected windfall, but, wide-eyed, simply accepted.

After peering around to be sure he was unobserved, Booze waved his flask in Alvin's direction.

In a flash, Alvin tasted the sharp bite of scotch, a sensation that was followed by the mellow flow of sweet wine redolent with the flavor of berries. And he was...*repelled.*

There was no other word for it. Alvin felt like gagging. He knew he would just as soon stuff a chunk of the greasy, Friday salmon into his mouth as to take a drink of whatever liquor it was that Booze offered. *Might even prefer it, by god.*

This aversion to an offer of alcohol was a complete reversal for him. Al was more than surprised. He was shocked. Drink had been nectar of the gods to him for eight years. Not only had it been nectar, but necessity on too many days. He realized with a start that he had not craved a drink since September. And, if today's reaction was any indication, he never would again.

He reached for Frances' hand. Her deep blue eyes met his lighter ones. He saw a world of understanding in that look. He thought he had hidden his weakness from her since their marriage. He could see now she had not been fooled when he used any occasion, any celebration, as an excuse to mix the loganberry flips he wanted so desperately. His need had been clear to her all along. It was all there in her eyes, lifted so trustingly to him.

In their depths, he saw reflected nights when she had gently removed the car keys from his hand and slid behind the wheel, the times she topped his glass with 7-Up when he had held it out for a refill, the mornings he awoke in their bed still clad in his trousers.

God, I have so much to make up for. Please just give me the time to do it.

He snapped out of his reverie to decline Booze's offer with a casual wave of his hand before using the same hand to squeeze Frances'. She seemed to recognize the pressure as the pact he intended it to be.

"Having a woman for president is not an outrageous idea," Crystal was saying to her cohorts.

"Nor did we say it was," said the taller, leaner man by her side.

"There is a precedent for such a choice," chimed in a rotund, bespectacled gentleman.

"And, Rodney, that would be…?" questioned another.

"More than sixty years ago, in 1870 I believe, the premise of a female in the highest office of the nation was put forth. Within two years, there was actually a lady candidate for president of the United States."

"Now, Rodney, you wouldn't be pulling our leg, would you?" asked the tall man.

"It's true, Geoffrey. Her name was Victoria Woodhull, a real trail-blazer in her time. The women of her era did not take too kindly to her, but she was definitely a man's woman. Nominated by the People's Party."

"I recall hearing of that political party," exclaimed Crystal. "It was also called the Equal Rights Party, wasn't it?"

"Indeed!" Rodney replied, happy to have substantiation.

"I find it difficult to believe any woman could even have been thought qualified for such a responsibility, let alone to have one rise so high in political circles in 1870. I can't see that happening today or at any time in the near future," said the third man.

"You have a narrow outlook, Toby," Crystal chided.

"That's as may be, but it is an outlook shared by many, I wager," Toby responded.

""Did this Miss Woodhull have a running mate?" asked Geoffrey.

"Of course she did," said Rodney.

"What brave soul ventured into that maelstrom?" Booze said, entering into the discussion for the first time. He wore an anticipatory smile as he waited for Rodney's answer.

"A reformer," said Rodney. "A Negro reformer, Frederick Douglas, was nominated for vice president."

"No!" Toby exclaimed.

"Don't sound so shocked, Toby. It's unbecoming," said Crystal, casting a fierce eye on Toby, who stood a good inch shorter than herself.

"Not shocked. I deny the charge. Startled. That's all. Startled."

"Much the same, startlement and shock," murmured Crystal.

"Dear Crystal, there is no such word as startlement," Geoffrey pointed out.

"That is totally beside the point, Geof. You know what I mean," said Crystal. "Toby's bias is always all too apparent whenever our talks expand beyond the lily white. We must dissuade him."

"Tell us about this Frederick Douglas, Rodney," Booze encouraged. "What sort of man not only joined forces with a female, but allowed her to take the leading role?"

"His nominator set the stage for the combined campaign of a female and a Negro when he placed Douglas' name in the running," said Rodney. "*Oppressed sex/oppressed race*, the nominator said."

"Ah yes, but how did Frederick Douglas view the arena from which the presidential candidate was chosen?"

"Are you asking what Douglas thought of women's suffrage?" Rodney asked hesitantly.

"Just so," said Booze.

"Obviously, Booze, nothing gets past you. The vice presidential candidate stated for the record that women's right to vote was of no consequence."

"There! What did I tell you? Impossible in 1870 for a woman to garner the confidence of the men casting the votes. According to Rodney here, her own running mate had no confidence in the ability of females to even vote intelligently," said Toby.

"Or perhaps this Frederick Douglas only meant that a female was such an *obvious* choice for president that the vote of men alone would elect her to the highest office in the land," said Crystal.

"You think perhaps?" said Booze.

"Well, if that was the intent of his words, he was wrong. She did not succeed, nor, in my opinion, would she have even if all the women in all the nation could have voted. Nor would any woman succeed in such an endeavor today," said Toby.

"Don't be too sure of that, Toby. Let another Victoria Woodhull come along, and the outcome just may be different. Women are becoming a force to be reckoned with. We've had the vote since 1920, you know," said Crystal, jabbing Toby playfully in the ribs.

"A woman maybe, some day," Toby relented, "but a darky never!"

"There's that word again," Booze called over to Alvin.

"And it is a word that we must help our poor, backwards brethren eradicate from his vocabulary," said an irritated Crystal. "I beg of you, join me in forcing enlightenment upon Toby, if he will accept it in no other way. I am beginning to despair of him."

Laughter fell upon a sheepish Toby, whose hair was vigorously knuckled by Geoffrey while Rodney buffeted his shoulders. "Enough, enough," Toby cried, as Booze fell against his pillows helpless with laughter.

In the confusion, Alvin leaned close to Frances and said, "Aren't Booze and his friends the most interesting people we know?"

"Well, they are a well-informed lot," Frances replied.

"They are that, but what they don't know, they still argue about!" said Alvin, admiration in his voice. He grinned, leaned even closer and whispered, "And their food is tremendous."

The ongoing gaiety gave Frances the opportunity to slip a package into Alvin's hands unobserved by the others. When he opened it, he found she had brought him a watch. She strapped it onto his right wrist, watching his face to judge how the gift was being received. He held his arm out at full length to admire the time piece. He slowly drew it back until the watch was against his left ear. He listened to its tick. He lowered his arm until it encircled her shoulders. He drew her close, placing the watch next to her ear. Together they listened to the watch click off the minutes.

"Very nice," he said, and planted a kiss on her cheek.

That night, just before lights out, Alvin lifted *Flora's Dare* from its resting place and smoothed down the tiny, blank half-page for Sunday, January 17.

He glanced apprehensively at Riddle, but his attention was elsewhere.

Al gave the page another smoothing touch.

> *Temp. 97.6*
> *"   99.4*
> *Expense 15 cents*
> *My Frances was to see*
> *me and did we have a*
> *mighty fine time. We*
> *always do. She brought*
> *me a watch but I sent*
> *it back. Toomuchmoney.*
> *She sure is a sweet kid.*
> *She needs somanythings. Al*

Alvin flexed his fingers. By scrunching and writing very small, he had managed to fit in most of what he wanted to say this evening. But it had been a chore, especially limited as he was to using a pencil and one whose lead just would not pare down to a point this evening.

If he had another inch of space, he thought he might have mentioned just how nervous those tiny ticks of the watch had made him. Bad enough to have these tiny little pages counting off his days so slowly.

Chapter 108

January 18
Monday
Temp 98
"   99.4
It has snowed all day
I think I am getting
sinus trouble back
again. I can feel it
coming. I hope
not. I wish my
wife was coming
out again tonight.
We always have a
good time together.
I shall see my
baby just as soon
as it gets warm.
God bless them and
keep them for me. al.

January 19
Tuesday

Temp 98
"   99.4
Don't feel too hot
tonight. It has
been thawing
most all day.

January 20
Wednesday

Temp 97.8
"   98.6
Frances was here
to see me. We had
a nice time.
She was going
to call if she
couldn't come back
but she didn't
come or call.
I hope nothing
is wrong. I pray
to God that all is
well.   Al.

January 21
Thursday

Temp 97.4
"   99.6
It sure is plenty
cold. I feel not so
good. It is snowing
a little just now.
My wifie called
me and told me
why she didn't
call last night.
I talked with
baby a little too.
I sure love the
girls~~~my girls.
Be good to them
dear god.   Al

January 22

Friday

Temp 97.2
"   99
It snowed most all
day but has been
fairly warm. I have
read all day. That
is the best way to
spend the time.
Tomorrow is weighday.
I enjoy that. I have
been taking some
Holiver Oil tablets.
Mabe I can gain
a little more weight.
Al

January 23-24
Saturday
And Sunday

Temp 97.4
"   99.2
We are still having a
mighty big snow
storm. I hate it.
Tomorrow is my day.
I know she will be
here to see her man.
Temp 97
"   99.2
Frances was here
both times to see
me today. 8:35
She just left here.
We had a mighty fine
time all of the time.
I love her and baby. Al

Chapter 109

As positive as Alvin was that alcohol's stranglehold on him was forever broken, he was equally as sure that he needed to speak to Frances about it.

So far, his struggle had never been put into words between them. He felt the need now to acknowledge the craving he had tried to hide, but, more important, to give voice to his appreciation of the forbearance she had shown. He also knew that such a talk was completely unnecessary.

In three short years of marriage, the two of them had become as one. She could read him as easily as he read the book he held in his hand. The look they had exchanged when Booze offered him a drink a week ago really had said it all. She knew. Still, he wanted to open himself to her in words, even if those words were so much less than the strong current that flowed between them.

He felt so irrevocably entwined with his wife that to separate them would be like trying to remove a fishhook deeply embedded in the thick wool of one of the Pendleton blankets he used to stave off winter's chill. 'I'd like to see anyone try that', he thought, 'Neither the blanket nor the hook would be worth a tinker's dam afterwards.'

These past three years of married life seemed like a lifetime to Al, and he was sure it was the same for Frances. She had come to him a young, and, yes, a naïve girl, although twenty-one when they married. He was beginning to see some changes in his young wife, a growing independence. From the beginning she had dedicated herself to him and their happiness. That was still true, but there had been little things, and then her decision to take a job without considering his wishes had signaled a major change in the girl who always had left all decisions up to him. At first, this had bothered him, mostly because he doubted her motives. Now, he viewed her emerging self-reliance as a tool that might come in handy in the future. He had also learned to trust her.

The effort she made to trudge through all kinds of weather just to spend a few hours with him had not been lost on him either. He knew she lived for him, and he, literally, lived for her. If he didn't have Frances, he would not stay tied to this bed. These were some of the things he wanted to put into words for her. Of course, she *knew*, but he wanted to be sure she knew *how much* she had come to mean to him.

Al made a promise to himself to get her alone soon and tell her. It wouldn't be easy to do with two others sharing his room.

Right now he wanted to tackle Booze. The enticing company Booze had promised for last Wednesday had not been forthcoming. "Not cancelled, merely postponed to the twenty-seventh," Booze had said.

The evening Booze's surprise guest had been expected was the night Frances had been unable to come out, so Alvin had limped through the hours between dinner and lights out with only the briefest of remarks to avoid a conflict with Riddle.

Alvin couldn't quite peg Riddle, who seemed to use bickering as daily recreation. So far, he and Booze had been able to ignore most of it. He didn't know how long their evasive measures would last. Booze had finally given up trying to out-talk Riddle. He now diverted him with food.

"If he is masticating, he can not be agitating," Booze explained to Al when Riddle was out of the room.

As for himself, Al was getting fed up with pretending to sleep just to get Riddle off his back.

Chapter 110

January 26
Tuesday
Temp 97.6
"   99.2
We had our heads
washed this morn.
I feel just fairly
well. Nothing extra.
There is a big
snow drift out in
front in the highway.
The bulldozer came
down tonite. Maybe
it will be open by
morning. Well I
am anxious for
2:30 tomorrow—you
know.   Al.

January 27
Wednesday
Temp 97.4
"   98.6
Good old visiting
day. I had my
wifie to see
me. She sure
is most loving.
I do love her with
all my heart.

*Maybe I can go
home some day.
I sure hope to
be of some good
to her some day.
I love her. Al.*

"Tonight's the night," Alvin said to Booze.

"I hope you haven't built this up too much. I don't want you to be disappointed," Booze warned.

"I'm looking forward to meeting your mystery guest, but any distraction is welcome on a night when my wife isn't going to come calling," said Al. "I'll be glad when winter is over and the roads are dependable. Do you think your friend will be able to get out through the snow?"

"The snow fall since this afternoon hasn't been too heavy. I am sure he will be here. In fact, I phoned earlier to verify, and the visit is definitely on. I expect him momentarily."

"I'm on tenterhooks," said Al, only half joking.

"His visit—yes, it is a male—should go swimmingly now that we have the room to ourselves," said Booze, pointing his thumb in the direction of Riddle's bed.

"How did you manage that?"

"Miss Gillis was only too happy to accommodate my polite request to allow Mr. Riddle some privacy with his own guests in the recreation room this evening. Especially in light of the fact his brother and sister-in-law have driven a goodly distance through this awful winter weather."

"You are being secretive about this guest of *yours*. Any particular reason?"

"I did not intend to be, but, yes, it is wiser to have a limited audience tonight."

"Would you rather I not be here?" Alvin asked, startled by Booze's serious tone.

"No, no. I especially wanted you to hear what my friend has to say. From the conversations you and I have shared, it is evident you have a great interest in affairs outside these walls, affairs beyond our fair city, far beyond. As you have pointed out, there is really nothing that can be done from within here to affect what goes on out there, but I believe it is still important for us to be *aware*, especially aware of worldly affairs…and that is what I hope my friend will bring to us tonight, an awareness."

Booze's guest was a surprise, although Alvin had been expecting something out of the ordinary when Booze had cautioned him, unnecessarily, about avoiding epithets involving color.

The stocky man who entered their room promptly on the stroke of seven-thirty was certainly a man of color. *Brown Bomber* or *darky* would hardly do justice to the ebony countenance that shone in gleaming radiance above the folds of a scarlet scarf of wool so fine as to resemble silk. He was all eyes and teeth. The whites of those sparkling black eyes gave him a wide-awake look, and the square cut of his extremely white teeth was revealed by a broad grin. His handshake, when he took Al's hand in his, was firm, calloused and cold.

"Alvin, this is my friend, who requests we call him Teddy to avoid embarrassing ourselves by trying to wrap our American tongues around an Ethiopian name. Al Potts, Teddy."

Ethiopian!

"Come, sit here where we both can hear," urged Booze, pulling up a chair.

He settled himself and Teddy next to Al's bed, and placed a package within easy reach.

"What is this? Pettit fours, my decadent American friend?" Teddy asked in lightly accented English.

"A gift from a friend taking pity on my reduced circumstances. Tonight, for your enjoyment," said Booze with a laugh. Then more seriously he added, "If it is appropriate to indulge while we speak of war clouds."

"Clouds portend a storm. America is watching and waiting to see to where these war clouds will break loose, but the storm with its poisonous clouds has already destroyed my country."

"And it is that sad fact of which we want to be informed," said Booze.

The Ethiopian bowed his head over his joined hands as he rubbed them together. He removed his hat. His scarf and coat already were draped over a chair. With the removal of the hat, the light fell fully on a face that at first glimpse could have been mistaken for a chubby cherub's. A second look revealed the strong bone structure beneath the fleshy padding over brow and cheeks.

His age could be anywhere from twenty to forty, Al thought. As Teddy fussed with his hat, it was apparent he was not anxious to begin, although Alvin was sure he had come to see Booze for this purpose alone.

Booze gave Teddy some time to collect himself, filling in with mundane pleasantries. Finally Booze said, "Please, Teddy, whatever you care to tell us."

"Where do I begin, that's the question. How do I help you to understand what is happening on the other side of the world when bombs are not falling around you? While your president dedicates himself to peace and induces other American republics to join in pacts to keep your hemisphere quiet and neutral, Italy runs rampant over my country." His voice was hoarse with anger.

"Of course, you know that from your newspapers," added Teddy.

"We know what we read. Tonight, we would appreciate hearing it from your lips," said Booze.

Teddy cleared his throat. He laid a fist on the table, and used it to beat emphasis as he began to speak.

"It did not take the fascist dictator long to crush us. Mussolini's campaign of '35 and '36 was short-lived. He brought his Italian boot across the Mediterranean and kicked our collective ass. Cudgels and fists are no match for planes and guns and poison gas.

"I tell you, Booze, it was a brutal conquest." His fist gave one last thump against the table top.

"Truly, we were so ill-equipped we might as well have been ducks sitting on the waters of Lake Tana. You remember them, Booze? How squawks and flight were their only line of defense? Easily picked off. So were we. What happened in Ethiopia was slaughter of the most extreme. We had our losses, all of us. My eldest brother fell. You knew him. And then the youngest we called Telfi. Both dead. Our home gone. The dead and dying all around us," said Teddy.

He rubbed a hand across his forehead and swiped it across his eyes, but not before Alvin saw the glitter of unshed tears.

"And the League of Nations stood by and let our country be slaughtered. The League called it a border dispute and claimed surprise when Benito refused to accept the proposals it put forth to settle these 'disputes'. The League is a weakling, a cripple hobbling on crutches. It did nothing to halt Mussolini's aggression. It merely voted economic sanctions against his precious Italian boot. Much he cared!

"I think Benito Mussolini must have been laughing at his great coup as he left the league, and went on to forge a new empire for himself. You know where he launched this campaign from, Booze?"

"Somalia."

"Yes, Somalia and *Eritrea*! We should have rooted the Italians out of Eritrea in 1896 when we defeated them at Adowa. But, no, they dug their long toenails into Eritrea, and held on. Now, forty years later they jump off from there and crush us. So, the war is over now. Ethiopia is Mussolini's, crushed under his boot. I spare you the bloody details."

"You blame us…America, for not coming to the aid of Ethiopia?" asked Booze.

"Why should one of the most ancient kingdoms of the world expect a young, upstart nation to jump into the fray when turmoil has been our middle name since our former kings claimed descent from the son of King Solomon and the Queen of Sheba?" Teddy asked, his voice heavy with sarcasm.

"What do you foresee in the future?"

"You think our Emperor Haile Selassie left me his crystal ball?" Teddy sneered.

"I would prefer *your* educated guess," said Booze in a conciliatory tone.

"I recognize your American diplomacy at work," said Teddy, struggling to regain his composure. "I beg you not to judge me too harshly tonight, friend Booze. Our war has just ended, and I am still raw. The future you ask about. So then, I will do my best.

"No crystal ball tonight. At any rate, I think Selassie must have taken it with him when he got the boot." There was no humor in Teddy's voice when he said this.

"Mussolini, while perhaps Ethiopia's greatest problem, is not the only problem. While your president Roosevelt has his foot on the war brake, he is not one of the three who hold the controls. Whether the world will see the spread of war will depend on Premier Benito Mussolini, Joseph Stalin of Soviet Russia and Reichsfuehrer Adolf Hitler. Trust me, that one has his eye on Poland, if Russia doesn't beat him to it," said Teddy.

"There is nothing better the three of them would like to do than divide the world between them. And, if they accomplished that, then you may be sure they would fight each other, like dogs over a bone.

"These three with their dictatorial powers are already spreading long fingers. Last year it was Mussolini in Ethiopia and Germany reoccupying the Rhineland; just this month the Nazis seized a Spanish ship. Whether there will or will not be a world war is in the hands of these three men. Wherever I have traveled— and I have traveled to places and in ways you could scarcely believe in these past months—I have seen world powers arming themselves on land, on sea and in the air.

"Do I think Ethiopia will regain her freedom? My friends," continued Teddy, looking solemnly at Booze and Alvin, "I do not see that happening soon, and never without outside help. We are truly ground down under the boot. In the meantime, President Roosevelt petitions his legislators to proclaim the neutrality of the United States. I, personally, see no help for us coming from that quarter."

"But our president is desirous of keeping arms and supplies from reaching warring countries," said Booze in defense of a president he admired.

"Which means very little to my countrymen at this time," said Teddy, resignation in his voice.

Through all of this, Alvin had listened intently. It was one thing to glean world happenings through the pages of the *Union* and *Bulletin*, but quite another to hear them first-hand.

"Mussolini has been on the march for so many years, I fear he can not be halted," said Booze.

"You are right there, my friend. Mussolini knew exactly what he was doing when he split with the socialist party to advocate joining the allies in the Great War. He was smart. He enticed many of his countrymen with his Fascist group. That blend of nationalism and socialism was a sure-fire attraction. He has always worked both sides of the fence. He wrested his premiership from the king when his Fascist military marched on Rome in '22, and then seven years later signed the Lateran Treaty with the papacy. The old boy knew what he was doing. That agreement with the government established Roman Catholicism as Italy's state religion and Vatican City as an independent sovereign state."

"In your travels did you get a feeling for this Hitler?" asked Booze.

"The little dictator? Oh yes. I saw the man in action."

"Your impression?" said Booze.

"I found him to be a coarse, unstable, ugly little man, who, like Mussolini, knows exactly what he wants and is dedicated to getting it. A great orator, gentlemen. No one can fault him on that. You wouldn't believe how people fall under his spell. He stomps and screams, and they cheer him on. To see him in action is to see what power really is.

"Hitler has had a meteoric rise, as you know. And it is my belief he is only beginning. Think of it, all this from a man who has had no formal education beyond the age of sixteen! The man is intent on restoring what he calls 'the greatness of Germany'. I believe he will not stop until he has forced himself down the throat of every country that stands in his way or until he is dead."

"That much of a threat?" said Booze.

"And more," said Teddy. "His brown shirts thunder down the streets unchecked. Jews have been ousted from the work place, but more disturbing, they disappear overnight and no one questions it. To be a Jew in today's Germany is to fear for your life. And no one really knows who will be next."

Teddy rose from his chair, walked to the window, and gazed out at the snow-covered landscape. His finger tapped nervously on the windowpane.

"Stalin? Have you gathered an opinion of him on your way here, Teddy?"

The Ethiopian turned back.

"What I know of that man is only what I hear. No more, no less than has come to your ears. He is another from humble beginnings who quickly climbed the golden stairs of opportunity. This son of a village shoemaker was intended to be a priest, you know. If he had followed that path instead of tying his kite to the tail of the Russian revolution, he would be pope now! But I know nothing personally about him beyond what we have all heard. There were his purges in 1935 in which he spared no one, neither his family nor political associates.

"To know that is probably to know all about him," Teddy concluded.

Booze heard the increasing agitation in his friend's voice, and acted accordingly.

"Let us change the subject to something more pleasant. Tell us, Teddy, about your homeland. Not the war ravaged country of today, but the land of your childhood. Please," coaxed Booze.

Teddy looked at Alvin to see what his interest level might be.

What he saw was the eager, questioning face of a man to whom all this was new. So Teddy reseated himself and began.

"Ethiopia is like a jewel held closely in its setting between three lands, one of which is Somalia that lurks in the east and may have dubious intentions. Ethiopia's open face is kissed, sometimes gently sometimes stormily, by the Red Sea that laps at her from the north. Nature has had its turn in playing roughly with this sultry gem, tossing her about over centuries until she lies rumpled like bed linen after a night of love."

Teddy paused, grinned impishly at Alvin and asked, "Do I sound like a geography teacher?"

"None I ever had, and I'm sure I would remember if anyone had ever told me about rumpled countries," replied Alvin, making no attempt to hide his lopsided smile from Teddy.

"Rumpled may be too tame a term for the forces of nature that pushed up the mountainous highlands of Ethiopia, cut her spectacular river gorges and flung out her great plain. Her highest peak is more than fifteen thousand-feet, which is higher than your Mt. Rainier," Teddy noted.

Teddy's voice dropped to a throaty throb as he continued to speak.

"My country is a land of scarlet suns and black velvet nights where cooking fires of many cultures perfume the air and her winds carry the voices of myriad tribal languages. Its lowlands are tropical, and…" Teddy's voice changed yet again, losing its dreamy quality. "…if it weren't for the stinging, biting pests, I would call these lowlands paradise! Still, I think you would like it, and, some day, my new friend, if the gods will it, it would be my privilege to show it to you," said Teddy.

"How big is this little jewel?" Alvin asked, still eager for information.

"So, it *is* a geography lesson you want? Very well. Ethiopia, as you know, is in eastern Africa. I call it a jewel because she is not large, but she could easily contain your states of Washington, Oregon and even Texas, and still have room for thirty or so of your Rhode Islands. As I have already mentioned, we are a land of diversity. The Tigri and Amhara, of which I am one, have been historically and politically the most important peoples in Ethiopia.

"If you don't believe that, look it up," said Teddy, smiling broadly as he tapped a finger on the encyclopedia lying on Alvin's table.

"Yes, if you wish to broaden your horizons, young man, you must visit Ethiopia. I think you would like it. But, perhaps, not today."

Booze offered the packet of finger-sized, iced cakes to Teddy, and urged him to try one of each. The offer was a deliberate distraction that drew Booze and Teddy away from Alvin's bedside in an unobtrusive way. The remainder of Teddy's visit was carried out in low voices in a two-way conversation in which Al had no part, but from which he in no way felt excluded.

The visiting hour ended abruptly when Riddle sauntered back into the room and jolted to a stop at the sight of Booze's guest. He took a few stumbling steps, as if to pass by Booze's bed, then jerked to a halt again.

Al stifled the laughter he felt, but Riddle did look funny, standing there with his mouth hanging loose and just staring.

Finally Riddle snapped his mouth shut, only to open it as if to say something. Before he could, Booze hurriedly shoved a petit four into his gaping maw and another into his hand.

Teddy took the opportunity to say a hasty goodbye to Booze while flicking his hat in a salute to Alvin. His white-toothed grin was as wide when he left the room as it had been when he entered.

Alvin, watching from the window, saw Teddy pull on his coat and settle his muffler about his throat before entering a bright red car that Al recognized, in spite of its heavy dusting of snow, as a Nash Ambassador.

Sleep did not come quickly to Alvin. The experiences related by Teddy were so far out of Al's realm of reality he was having trouble grasping their full scope. Teddy's opinions were easier for Al to relate to as he had drawn some conclusions of his own.

Although he had never seen Hitler in the flesh as Teddy had, Al had spent many a rest period puzzling over what was happening in Germany. Grandma Hempe still had relatives there, and Alvin had often wondered how they were dealing with the man who had so suddenly, or so it seemed, come into power.

The letters from Germany had stopped more than a year ago, according to Ida. The ones that had come to them before had implored Caroline to send whatever she could in the way of food and clothing. The only means Caroline had at her disposal was a small nest egg from the sale of the Hempe homestead in Union, Oregon. The farm, with its unusual eight-sided barn, had been sold when Caroline's husband, Francis, died, and Caroline had been taken into the shelter of her daughter's home in Walla Walla. Still, even with their limited resources, Caroline and Ida had managed to send packages across the ocean to help out relatives they had never seen.

It troubled Alvin to think that these same people might be turning into oppressors of the kind that had overrun Teddy's country. Surely, Caroline's Catholic relatives would not fall into step with Hitler's plan of aggression. It was difficult for Alvin to conceive that *anyone* would.

When Booze and Teddy spoke of the possibility of a world war, it caused Alvin to think of Murray, whose last letter had been mailed from Honolulu, Hawaii. His brother had sent a short note to inform Al of his new duty station. Murray had said not to expect much news from him because there wasn't any, and he was still trying to adjust to a tropical climate where it rained almost continually from November through March.

As he lay in bed with all these thoughts running rampant, Al decided to write his brother first thing in the morning. Maybe lob some of Teddy's conclusions at him. See if the soldier boy had anything to add.

Chapter 111

The halls of Ward One were silent, only a snuffle or cough here and there. In the room occupied by Alvin, Booze and Riddle the only sound was the snow sifting off the eaves outside their open windows. That slight noise was not enough to keep them awake. They, like the rest of the patients in Ward One, were deep in slumber.

The rooms and halls were never completely dark, nor were they now although it was well past midnight. Faint illumination filtered from a green-shaded lamp at the nurse's station and strategically placed lighting along the halls.

A form moved silently through these pools of light, more shadow than substance. When it reached the room where Alvin slept, it paused, then glided into the room. The shadow, a silhouette now against the shine of the moon on the new fallen snow, stopped at Alvin's bedside. Cool fingers gently, but firmly, grasped Al's wrist. As the figure bent over the bed, the rustle of a starched skirt identified the shadow as a nurse.

It was not unheard of for the night nurse to check pulses as she made her rounds. At first, the nightly visits had broken Al's sleep, and, once awakened, he had difficulty falling back into it. The insomnia that accompanied tuberculosis made sleep such a precious commodity that Al had trained himself over the months to ignore the nightly check-ups. The pulse-taking took only seconds, and now he usually slept right through it. Tonight the cool grip rested on his wrist long enough to enter his dreams, which caused him to smile in his sleep and snuggle into a blanket that somehow had become tucked under his chin.

When Al awoke in the morning, the dream that had been so pleasant the night before was illusive, as most dreams are in the light of day. He was left with a vague memory of a cloud of wild, black hair and green, green eyes. He felt slightly guilty that apparently a female other than Frances had walked into his dreams. His conscience—in a formative, but irritating, Catholic stage—was appeased when he realized his member was as flaccid as if he had been imbibing saltpetre on a regular basis.

One can not help what one dreams, can one?

Still Al was grateful not to be saddled with a physical manifestation on this morning after.

Annie's appearance with the morning wash water was a surprise. When the night nurse's home was destroyed by fire earlier in the month, Annie and her wrinkles had been assigned to the night shift until, or if, the regular nurse returned to work. Phil had circulated reports from 'a most reliable source' that the night nurse had moved in with relatives out of town and would not be returning to Blue Mountain. It was thus assumed, and put out on the grapevine as gospel, that Annie was relegated forever to night duty. Yet, here she was. Shades of the princess and the pea! Al already could feel the creases from wrinkled sheets forming on his back.

Riddle clarified the situation for all when he snarled, "Whatcha doin' back here?"

Annie turned a happy smile on Riddle.

"I've been replaced by a new hire on nights. You lucky men have me back again," she said.

"Some luck!" growled Riddle.

Annie giggled.

Annie never took offense at anything Riddle said or did. He had been a favorite of Annie's from the beginning. She fawned over Riddle as a mother would a child although she was younger than he, and she shrugged away his grumblings whenever they focused on her. Annie consistently refused to be dragged into his quarrels with Alvin and Booze, when she observed them. She either tut-tutted at Riddle or laughed, as if he had made the greatest of jokes, no matter how cantankerous he became.

Al wondered if there were anything Riddle could do that would upset her. He doubted it.

Annie now took the opportunity to place a new bar of soap beside Riddle's wash basin. Al noticed that Riddle hadn't even used up all of his old bar.

Al pushed aside his own wash basin, and dug out stationery. He just might have time to write that letter to Murray before breakfast. If he finished soon enough, it could go out in today's mail. Last night's meeting with Teddy had set the old gray matter churning. Times like this is when he really missed Laurence and his penchant for delving into politics.

Alvin recognized his limitations when it came to assessing the information Teddy had shared last night. His experience was so limited, both in travel and politics. But it didn't seem so bad to him that Roosevelt was for keeping peace.

Chapter 112

January 29
Friday
Temp. 96.8
"   99
Just another 12 hours.
Nothing much to
record. I am anxious
for Sunday to come.
I always am.
They are my only
days. Sun. Wed.
Tomorrow is weigh
day. I love my
two girls. They
are my only real
true pals and
friends. I surely
love them. Al.

January 30-31
Saturday & Sunday
Temp 97.2
"   99
This was weigh
day but no go
for me. I neither
lost nor gained.
Temp 97
"   99
My pal Wifie

was out today.
She called me
this evening
and we had
a chat. Baby
was asleep
so I didn't
get to talk
to her. May
God keep them.

Februrary 1
Monday
Temp 97
"   99.2
Monday you know
is our bath day.
We have had
our bath and
am feeling fine.
Boy Katie sure
is a rotten cook.
I missed two
meals this afternoon.
I am sure to
lose weight
this week. I
feel pretty good
outside of being
hungry. Maybe
I can get some
eats tomorrow.

February 2
Tuesday
Temp 97.8
"   99.8
It has been
snowing most

*all day. I
haven't felt
very well today.
Altho I was feeling
fine yesterday.
My stomach
is all upset
from yesterday's
eats or lack
of eats. Al.*

**February 3
Wednesday**
*Temp 98.4
" 99.6
My Faithful
little wife was
out to see her
cranky old sick
hubby. How in
christ's world
she can love me
is more than I
can tell. May she
be well loved
some day for
all her goodness.
Alvin*

**February 4
Thursday**

*Temp 98.4
" 100
I believe I am
on the verge of
getting the flu.
Miss Gillis is
going to doctor*

me for a bad
cold and flu.
I hope I feel
better by Sunday.
Al

February 5
Friday

Temp 97.6
"   99.2
I feel some
better tonight.
Sure hope I
continue to
improve. I want
to be able to
visit with my
wife Sunday. I
don't get to
see her often
enough to feel
badly when she
is here. Al.

February 6-7
Saturday & Sunday

Temp 98
"   99.2
Not a bad day
but I don't feel
very well. My
heart is jumpier
than I like to
have it. It probably
will go flooey
one of these days.
Temp 98

”   99
I am just
waiting the
arrival of my
wife. I think
she will be
here this
evening.

February 8
Monday
Temp 99
I am feeling
a bit better
than I did.
I mabe will
be alrite after
my stomach
gets more
settled. It has
been better today.
Miss Sander
brought us in
a fern and a
stand for it. Al.

February 9
Tuesday
Temp 97.6
”   99
It has been
cold all day.
This cold winter
weather is
getting mighty
tiresome if
you ask me.
I don't like it
too hot out

neither do I
crave this cold
damp weather. Al.

February 10
Wednesday
Temp 97.6
"   98.6
It is after supper
and also after temp
time. I feel
pretty well, but it
is awfully cold.
Frances was out
this afternoon. We
had a darn nice
time. She sure is
a mighty swell pal.
Different from most
women. True that's her. Al

The first weeks of February were not particularly kind to Alvin.

Snow and ice painted a pretty winter landscape outside his windows, but those same windows were flung open every day to let winter wrap its chilly embrace around the tubercular patients. The thickly woven wool blankets were all that stood between them and the frigid outdoors. If the wind blew, it blew relentlessly across their beds. If it snowed, flakes found their way indoors. And the air was always cold.

Visitors huddled in their coats and scarves to keep warm when they came to visit. Booze's loyal friends still drove through the drifts to be among the first for afternoon visiting hours, but they thought twice about staying until the end when they could see their breath floating in the air. Indeed, few of them stayed for more than half an hour. Their conversation lost its scintillation, centering more on road conditions than on controversy. Even their gifts of food and drink tapered off.

Frances would have happily tolerated the chill of the room

afternoons and evenings just to be with Alvin, but Ida was reluctant to loan the car when passage depended on snow plows. Afternoon visits between husband and wife became the norm, but she always stayed as long as allowed.

The curtailed evening visits left Alvin with hours to fill as best he could. The new night nurse proved to be a surprising distraction Thursday on an otherwise dull evening.

Annie had provided no information about the new hire, beyond giving her name and saying that Christina's supervision at night had freed her to return to the wards during the daytime. While the patients were aware of the change, it meant little to them. The new nurse came on duty long after they had slumped into slumber. Some of the more sleepless or restless might have caught glimpses of her as she made her quiet rounds. Al was not one of them. He had slept well and deeply these past weeks. As far as most of the patients, including Al, were concerned, Christina was still an invisible entity.

That was about to change.

The supervisor rescheduled the shifts. The adjustment Gillis made would allow both day and night workers to travel the difficult roads earlier in the evening. To the men on Ward One, it meant that instead of Annie rearranging the wrinkles in their beds before lights out, the new hire would be responsible for their comfort.

Phil was the first to pop into their room with the news.

"New woman on deck, fellows. Out with the old, in with the new," he caroled after reporting the first sighting at the early shift change on Thursday, February 11.

"Does this mean nightly wrinkles are a thing of the past?" Booze asked.

Phil wiggled his eyebrows, snapped a wink at the room in general, and said, "She can put wrinkles in my bed any time!"

His comments and the leer on his face were so unlike the gentlemanly Phil, Al fell to laughing. Riddle, brought upright by Phil's remark, snickered. Their reactions were for entirely different reasons, but Booze did not discern that. He was surprised at Alvin's. Not what one would expect from a fellow who thought it too crude to belch in front of his own wife.

In spite of Riddle's apparent interest, Phil did not stay around to elaborate. He hurried off to spread the word before the new nurse made her appearance.

She did not keep Booze, Riddle and Al waiting long. Theirs was one of the rooms nearest the nurses' station. They heard the crackle of her starched uniform and the soft tap of shoes before they saw her.

Alvin was stunned when Christina walked into the room. It was as if an illusion had become reality. That cloud of dark hair and those green, green eyes.

Thus it was that Al met the woman who had invaded his dreams.

Embarrassment lit a slow burn that traveled uncomfortably through his body.

The young nurse's professional demeanor as she introduced herself, straightened the sheets on each bed, refilled their water jugs and tidied the room helped alleviate an emotion, which was, after all, illogical. Christina had not really shared that dream with him.

Unlike Riddle and Booze, Al had climbed out of bed while she tugged his sheets smooth. He remembered the feel of those slim, cool fingers on his wrist and wasn't about to push his luck. It was easy to understand how her brief contact in the middle of his night's sleep had propelled her image into his subconscious, but he still wasn't taking any chances. But, by the time she finished, his equilibrium was restored.

In the short time she spent in their room, Christina, in spite of her extreme beauty, proved herself to be just another nurse intent on providing the care that would pave the way for patients to heal and go home. Even Riddle's nasty-sounding snicker when she finally asked if there was anything else she could do for them was met with professional disdain that discouraged such behavior now or in the future. Yet, she tarried at the door to exchange a few friendly remarks with all of them about the weather, what books they might like to read, and to remind them she would make rounds during the night.

"But I will try to enter and leave your room quietly so your sleep will not be disturbed," she said. She flipped off the light as she departed.

In her wake, she left a respectful silence and smooth...very smooth…sheets.

Chapter 113

Booze was out of bed, which he should not have been, but it put him in a good position to see a car swing into the driveway Friday afternoon. The hour for visiting was right, the day was not, so Booze watched with curiosity the approach of a man with the gait of a farmer, a pleasantly plump woman, and a stunning young girl with the most angelic face he had ever seen.

"Who have we here?" Booze queried, without taking his eyes from the trio advancing to the front door. "An angel disguised as a mere human," he offered to the room at large.

Riddle peered out from his blankets, but angels seemingly held less interest for him than nurses because he did not move. Alvin, on the other hand, was much interested in anyone who could assault the 'fortress' on a non-visiting day.

"Are they coming in, Booze?"

"That they are, my friend, that they are," said Booze, watching the little party enter the front door. He then moved across the room to peer down the hall from their doorway.

"Marching right along, coming our way," he sang out.

"Won't be anyone for me," Riddle mumbled from within his den.

"It's an emergency visit of some sort," said Alvin.

Booze had taken up a deliberately casual stance at the doorway, positioning himself so he could glance either to the left or right, which opened the entire hallway to his view. He was now in a position to see which room the visitors entered and report to Riddle and Al.

The plump lady was in the lead. She walked determinedly along as if she knew exactly where she was going, so it startled Booze when she came to a stop right in front of him. Now that he was almost nose to nose with her, Booze could see that she was still in her twenties, but deserving of the title of matron with which he had already labeled her. The gold band on her left hand probably tied her to the stalwart fellow bringing up the rear. Booze was pleased to see he had been right about the girl sandwiched between the two. She was definitely angel material, but young, a school girl.

"You must be Booze," said the leader of the pack.

And she pronounced the name correctly! "A point to you, Madam," said Booze, even as he wondered who these visitors might be. Someone who knew him, it seemed.

When it was apparent they intended to enter his room, Booze stepped aside, and welcomed them in with a sweeping wave of his hand. And the matron led the way right to Alvin's bedside.

Alta threw her arms around her brother, exclaiming all the while at how fat and sassy he looked. Although those were coveted words, Al knew she spoke with a forked tongue. No way could his pitifully thin frame be called fat, but mentally he thanked her for her subterfuge. Elwin and Pearl crowded in around Alta to greet him. It had been a long time between visits. The greetings were barely over when Alta, with reluctance, told Alvin she and Elwin had to run errands, but would leave Pearlie to visit for an hour.

"However, brother mine," Alta chirruped, "Pearl and I will be staying with Frances until Sunday, so will have the opportunity for a good long visit before we have to leave town."

She cast a quizzical eye on a pot of chrysanthemums she had left with him when she left the hospital at Thanksgiving time. "These look in need of some tender care, Alvin. I believe I should take them with me and revitalize them. What do you think?"

"Good idea."

Elwin and Alta, with plant in hand, were gone almost as soon as they arrived, and Al was left looking at his youngest sister, who was sitting in the corner she favored.

"So, how is my sister doing?"

Pearl knew Alvin's question was not an idle one. He had received letters from her relating the extent of what the surgery on her leg had accomplished, but she had not given details beyond reporting that she was fine. Now, he wanted to know how she *really* was.

For some reason, Alvin had it in his head that her leg had been removed, made shorter and reattached. *That* would have been some miracle. The reality was almost, but not quite, as drastic. The physicians had been able to shorten the bone in her good leg to match the height of the leg that had been stunted by tuberculosis. The surgery had alleviated her lopsided, lurching walk, but it had also left her leg frozen in an unbendable condition. She had known in advance what the results of the surgery would be, but had chosen to pursue it as the best of her options. The two legs, now evenly matched in length, gave her a smooth carriage, and long skirts concealed most of her legs.

The stiff leg was noticeable only when she sat and had to stretch it out before her or rest it on a chair, as she did now. It made Al's heart ache to see his young sis so afflicted. It was to Pearl's credit that the leg was the last thing one noticed about her.

Pearl had brought Al a surprise, a letter to her from Murray.

"I'll leave it with you to read and share with Frances. Then she can mail it back to me," said Pearl, as she handed over an envelope.

The hour with Pearl passed quickly, but, with Murray's letter in his hand, it was easier to say goodbye to her when she had to leave. He slipped out of bed to watch his two sisters drive away with Elwin. It made him feel good to know Frances would have their company for the next few days. And he had this letter from his brother.

He settled down with it as soon as Elwin's car was out of sight. *Honolulu, Hawaii* was the postmark. Al saw that it had been sent just after Murray had written to him to tell him about his new duty station. But, unlike the short note sent to him, Pearl's letter had some heft to it. Nothing Al liked better than a nice long letter. He slid two pages from the envelope and began to read.

Co. C 27th Inf., Schoffield Barracks, Hawaii

My Dear Sister:

I don't know who's turn it is to write, so I'll take the bull by the horns and make it my turn.

As you can see I'm not at McDowell any more. I left there Jan. 8. We were on the boat for 5 days and a half. I got seasick about two hours out from Frisco and got over it about two hours after we landed at Honolulu. Not bad do you think so? (ha ha) So you can see about how much I enjoyed my trip. For myself I can't see much to have enjoyed about it.

We left San Francisco at 1:00 o'clock p.m. Jan. 8 and got here 9:00 a.m. Jan. 14 and we averaged 14.83 m.p.h. So you figure it up how far I am away then write and tell me. It's too deep for me to figure out.

Alvin paused in his reading to do the arithmetic.

One hundred forty hours on the open sea. What an experience that must have been. Now his brother was more than two thousand miles from home. Blast the boy for not doing his own ciphering. Murray wasn't a numskull. He knew how; he just waited on others to do it for him.

Al smiled to think of the many times Murray's coaxing grin had elicited help from him. The kid was persuasive, that's for sure. Well, if Pearl didn't forward the figures to Murray, he would. When he realized what he had just committed himself to, he laughed out loud, drawing a look but no comment from Riddle.

Al shook loose the page and continued to read.

We have quite a climate over here. The temp stays between 70 and 80 degrees all the time, but I can march a quarter of a mile (which I do very often, grr!!) and I'm soaking wet with sweat. I guess it's the humidity.

Hot? Murray had written to him that it was raining all the time. That was a contradiction. Kid was creating more questions than answers.

The country is very pretty. I'm going to try and buy a Kodak and get some good pictures. If I do I'll send you some. The part of the country I'm in is very rugged and covered by a small bush like tree. Which makes it very pretty.

We're about 25 miles from Honolulu and come from there to here by train. I wish you could have seen it. The engines and cars are about half or a third as big as the ones back there. The track is about 1 ½ feet across, and it was so crooked that we were always meeting the engine coming back from a turn. (If you can see what I mean.)

No doubt Murray had ridden on a narrow gauge railroad. Alvin recalled seeing one himself up in mining country, and, at the time, thought it looked mighty like a toy.

The country we came thru was all swampland raising rice, higher land sugar cane, pineapples and bananas. The bad part of it here is there is a fine of $50 if you are caught swiping a pineapple or a banana. (Boo Hoo).

So, another myth squashed. No free pineapples dropping into hands anywhere!

Our sleeping quarters are called barracks. They are large two storied cement buildings. In the quarters I sleep in there are about 28 men. It is on the top floor of one of these buildings and consists of about 1/6 of the top floor. The room is about 120 feet by 50 feet, so you can imagine the size of the whole building.

He's doing it again. Leaving the measurements to Pearl's imagination instead of doing the figuring himself.

Our mess hall is on the bottom floor right underneath of us and is about 2/3 as big as our sleeping quarters. There are nine tables which are set for 16 men. Our chow must be fairly good as I've gained 11 lbs. since I've come over here. I weighed 147 when I came here, so get your 'rithmetic book out and figure out what I weigh now.

Maybe he's setting up some problems for Pearl on purpose, but she's a sharpie and could whip right through those grade school tests he's setting. Wish our chow was better and I could put on some poundage.

Our work now consists of drill with rifles from 8:00 to 11:30 and common labor from 1:00 to 3:30. That work is quite easy. I've worn three blisters on my hands since I've been here. One for each hard days work with pick & shovel.
The natives over here are inclined to riot, and us rifle men are sent out to quell them. There has been five deaths since I've been

here. That's just the 27th infantry.

That sounds serious. I wonder what the natives are rioting about, and who died? The natives or soldiers? At any rate, it sounds dangerous. Al tapped the pages with a stiff forefinger, and then returned to Murray's writing.

Well, Pearl, excuse me to the rest of the family for not writing to them, as you see my time is very limited and will continue to be for about four more weeks. For that period of time I will get up at 6:00 o'clock, eat at 6:30 and at 7:45 will take my rifle, which is 43.69 inches long and weighs 8.112 lbs., and which I clean until it shines between 6:00 o'clock and 7:45 and will march one third of a mile (are you keeping up with me) and "drill" until 3 in the afternoon with a half an hour for noon. Then I have to shine it and my shoes until time to go to bed (which time it is right now). In other words it is 9:00 o'clock p.m.

Well, I'll be seeing you Dec. 15, 1938 so will close with

Lots of Love, Murray.

Alvin folded the pages together and carefully inserted them into the envelope. He would be sure to get them back to Pearlie. This was the kind of letter that brought the world a little closer to the stay-at-homes. It was well worth a second read.

Chapter 114

February 13
Saturday
Temp 97.4
"   98.8
This was weigh
day and I
gained 1 ½ lbs.
this week. Not
bad. I hope I
feel as well
tomorrow. I
am looking
forward to my
company. Al

Alvin had written that diary entry last night with more than the usual anticipation at seeing his wife. Nineteen days ago Alvin had resolved to have a sit-down with Frances to lay out for her the whole sorry mess he felt he had made of his life by giving strong drink the highest priority.

He had not done that yet, but not because of procrastination. Temperatures that dropped below zero had forced Frances to miss almost all of the evening visiting hours, which cut in half Al's opportunities for a serious conversation. Privacy in a room shared by three people made such a conversation difficult at best, if not impossible, but Al was determined to have that talk with Frances today. He had petitioned Gillis for use of the recreation room. Recognizing that home issues sometimes had to be conducted behind closed doors, Gillis had agreed, so Al was all set for this afternoon.

He had no qualms about broaching the subject with Frances. He had finally realized his thirst would be no revelation to her. The complete absence now of that long-held desire might be. It was that—and his sincere sorrow that he had not been all he could have been to her since their marriage—were what he wanted to talk to her about today.

Al was watching at the window long before Frances could possibly arrive. Hers was usually the first car to turn into the drive, but today several emptied out visitors before Ida's Ford wheeled into a parking space. Al was dismayed to see that Ida was the driver.

Alvin really enjoyed his mother-in-law. In fact, when he was courting Frances and found her not at home on a Saturday night when he had unexpectedly called on her, it was Ida instead of Frances who had accompanied him to town. He took a lot of razzing from his buddies after they saw him strolling Main Street with her, but Ida had been good company. Any day, except today, he would have welcomed her presence and the caustic comments that tickled, rather than annoyed, him.

He saw that his wife had their daughter in her arms as she got out of the car. It was the first time in many weeks that he had seen the baby. He knew he had the Chinook wind that was blowing warm today to thank for her appearance. Another mixed blessing on a day he hoped to have his wife all to himself.

Alvin rushed to the entrance to meet them. He pulled Frances into the circle of his arms, resting his chin on the top of her head and snuggling baby's curls to his cheek.

The three-way hug mingled their fragrances, talcum powder, violets and minty after-shave. Al stood with eyes closed, inhaling, just inhaling, the aroma of family.

When he opened his eyes, he caught Ida looking at him, a fond expression on her face, an expression she quickly erased.

"What a lot of folderol," Ida sniffed.

With one arm around the shoulders of his wife, Al flung the other around Ida's waist and propelled them rapidly toward the rec room. Ida tried to curb his advance and raised her voice in laughing protest, while the Baby, perched firmly on Frances' jutting hip, laughed aloud. Alvin was pale and panting at the end of the short rush that carried them into the room where he had planned to have his tete-a-tete. He released the women, and sank into a chair.

Frances looked alarmed to see her husband in such stress after so little exertion. Ida stepped to her, linked her arm with Frances', and swung her around so Frances was no longer facing Alvin.

"What a devil you are, Alvin!" Ida exclaimed as she pushed Frances into a chair and situated the child on her mother's lap. With her own back to him, Ida set to pulling off Frances Pearl's snow suit. Her diversion gave both Frances and Alvin time to recover, so Frances was soon able to turn a smiling face to him. The smile he returned was the feeble result of a strong effort.

The shock his physical condition had given both women created opposite reactions. Frances retreated into silence. Ida grew extremely talkative.

Ida bombarded Alvin with details of Ray's winter camp-out with a group from church, Herbie's latest shenanigan in which he had painted a white stripe on the neighbor's black cat and tried to pass it off as a skunk, and her own efforts to get the teen-aged Jenny to quit sucking her thumb in times of stress.

"Because, sure as I'm standing here, that girl is getting buck teeth!"

"Well, that won't do at all. What will people think?" said Al.

"She does hide it. I'll give her that much," Ida said grudgingly. "She puts her thumb behind her fingers, cups them over her mouth, and sticks her old thumb right in. If you didn't know what she was doing, you *wouldn't* know."

Alvin wondered what kind of stress was driving Jenny to a childish habit. It reminded him of the fights he had waged in Daisy in lieu of solutions he was incapable of providing for a problem so big it was never mentioned. He trusted Ida to be wiser than his parents and Grandma Potts had been.

Ida's last piece of news was the startling announcement that Will, who had just turned twenty, was going to marry his Esther.

"I'm awfully afraid this isn't going to be a church wedding since she isn't of our faith," said Ida.

"We don't know that for sure, Mom," Frances interjected.

"No. Not for sure. But, if it isn't to be, I won't be the one to fight it," her mother answered.

Alvin thought about the strict church law that tied Ida to a non-Catholic husband, who, at last word from California, had just married a widow lady with a nice little farm in Bakersfield.

Before they took up another subject, Ida announced her intention of driving into College Place. "I'll leave you to visit, and pick you up on my way back, Frances."

Al brightened at her words. It appeared he was going to get to make use of the rec room in the way that he had planned.

When they were alone, Alvin put a picture book in Frances Pearl's hands. He had learned from Frances that theirs was the kind of baby that could entertain herself for hours with a book or a set of blocks. He took a seat next to his wife.

"I want to talk to you about something," he said, taking her hand and stroking the fingers one by one. His touch lingered on the gold band on her left hand.

"About my drinking…" he began.

Frances jerked her hand out of his, and placed a finger across his lips to shush him.

"Let's not talk about that now," she said.

"We have to. *I* have to, sweetheart. It's been ignored too long. Ignored to the point I refused to call it a problem."

"It wasn't! It isn't!"

Her head wig-wagged an emphatic denial.

Al retrieved his wife's hand and held it firmly even though she tried to pull free. He caught the other hand that was fluttering like a wild bird and snared it too. With both hands gripped tightly, he forced her to face him. Although her eyes darted around the room, refusing to focus on him, she could not fail to see the rapid rise and fall of Alvin's chest and hear his labored breathing as he struggled to capture her attention.

With that sight before her, she stilled.

Her hands lay limp in his. Her gaze met his.

Slowly, Alvin sank back in the chair until his head rested on the cushioned back. He closed his eyes, concentrating on his breathing until it returned to normal.

Al sighed deeply. *How to make her understand?*

"It goes a long way back," Alvin began tentatively.

"I started drinking early. I was never a falling down, rip-roaring, mean drunk. Those kind are easy to spot. But I had a thirst inside that wouldn't quit."

He forced those last words out. This was harder going than he had expected.

Reluctantly he told Frances about what had led up to the first time he drank himself into oblivion on firewater. The telling took some time. He was surprised when the old memories of Emerson and Louise no longer stung. He remembered, and told Frances, how he had hated the taste of the fiery brew, but loved the way it had blotted out betrayal. When he saw sympathy begin to creep across her face, he raised a hand, palm out. It was unclear whether he meant the gesture as a stop signal or as a solemn pledge.

"No excuses," he said.

He hurried on to tell her that first drunk, no matter who or what drove him to it, was in no way the last. He reeled out for her inspection the rowdy weekends with rowdy friends and the solitary bouts with any bottle he could come by.

"All with no one at the steering wheel, but me, myself and I."

Doubts crept across her forehead and left worry wrinkles behind.

Frances was having trouble believing, but he drove home the truth. "There were plenty of mornings I woke up and couldn't remember the night before, and I'm sure not proud of that."

He commiserated with her difficulty in seeing him as he was before he met her, but he pushed on. He revealed the conscious effort it had taken to control the drinking when she came into his life, the tricks he used to try to fool—and also hide—the awful craving that gripped him. "Drink wine instead of the hard stuff, add 7-Up to dilute it, call it a highball to make it seem more acceptable. Anything to disguise that damnable craving for something stronger that was always there, even after seven, eight, nine, ten—I don't know how many—loganberry flips.

"I wasn't fooling you, was I?"

He looked, as well as spoke, the question at her.

Blue eyes to blue eyes, she held his gaze. Then reached out her hand to him.

"I never saw a great problem. You've always been a hard worker, the best of husbands and a good father to our baby," Frances said simply. "We had fun at those Saturday night parties. You were always happy and laughing."

"I *was* a happy drunk, wasn't I?" Alvin said, grinning at her.

"I wish you wouldn't call yourself that!" she protested.

"Sweetheart, thing is this," said Al, his grin fading as he cupped her hand in his. "I controlled it to some extent, but the craving never stopped. Even when I didn't have a drink, I wanted one. A man should put his wife and family first. For me, what came first was old John Barleycorn. I wanted to be with that demon every day. I wasn't. But I *wanted* to be! *That's* where I wronged you."

Alvin stopped talking. He stared at the floor. Gave a disbelieving shake of his head. Looked up at his wife. Cleared his throat, and continued.

"Now I wouldn't give two cents for a drink. Craving's gone, dead and buried. Don't know why. Don't care. Just grateful for it. These past months I've had nothing to do but think about where I went wrong. I've been a damn fool, Frances. I'm as sorry as can be, but I can't ask you to forgive me. Some things are just too big to forgive."

"There's nothing for me to forgive, Al," Frances insisted.

"Well, that's where we differ, Sweetheart," said Alvin. He stroked her fingers, again lingered on the gold band, then wrapped his long, thin fingers around her delicate wrist and gave it a gentle shake.

"I can't even promise I'll make it up to you." A vague wave of his hand that took in not only the room in which they were sitting, but seemed to encompass the entire tuberculosis sanatorium spoke volumes about the uncertainty of outcomes in a place like this.

He lifted her hand to lips he kept carefully closed.

"But, Pal of mine, I love you with all my heart."

Frances bowed her head to hide the tears that sprang unbidden.

They sat in silence, joined together by the tight grip of their hands, until Frances Pearl tired of her picture book and claimed their attention. They spent the rest of the visiting period absorbed in their child, Al making cat's cradles from twine twisted around his fingers and Frances prompting the baby to show off her ever increasing vocabulary.

That night when he drew out Flora's Dare to record the Sunday hours, he thought long and hard before making an entry. He concluded that just as some things are too big to forgive, other things are too big to consign to paper.

February 14
Sunday
Temp 98
" 99
My girls were
out to see
their daddy. I
moved to the
rec. Baby and
I had a swell
time. Ida was
out with them.
I sure had a
fine time.

Chapter 115

February 15
Monday
Temp 98.2
" 99
St. Valentine's
day has come and
gone. I am sure
glad to see this
snow leaving so
quickly. I am
getting so I
hate snow.

February 16
Tuesday
Temp 97.8
" 98.8
I haven't been
feeling any too
well today.
Kinda upset. I
hope to get
straightened out
in a short while.
Most of our last
four inches of
snow is gone.
It has been
Chinooking all
day. I like to see

this snow
disappearing. Al.

February 17
Wednesday
Temp 97
"   99.2
I had my dear
little wife to
see me today.
We had a swell
time. We always
do. She is surely
good to me. I
pray I can go
home and be of
some use to her
and baby some day.Al

February 18
Thursday
Temp 98
"   98.8
It has been
rather cold
today to my
notion. I got
my third 50 of
Holiver Oil
capsules. I do
believe they
are doing me
a little bit of
good. If I can
only gain another
10 lbs. I will be
pleased.   Al.

February 19

Friday
Temp 97.6
"   99.4
We had some
very bad fish
for lunch today.
It really didn't
taste good at
all. Some they
had in cold
storage for a
month or two
I suppose. I get
along pretty
well nevertheless.
Al.

February 20-21
Saturday & Sunday
Temp 98
"   99.8
It is weigh
day and the
weighing is
all over. I
gained 1 ½ lbs.
I am very
pleased with
myself. Al.
Temp 97.4
"   99.4
I didn't have
any visitors
tonight. I
guess my wife
couldn't get
the car. She
is a lot of
comfort to me.

I really needed
her to talk
to me. I love
her. Al.

February 22
Monday
Temp 97.6
Temp 99.6
Frances was
out to see me.
You see it is
W.B.Day. All
holidays are
visiting days.
We surely had
a good time.
She even came
out tonight. I
didn't expect her.
I am not feeling
very well. Al.

February 23
Tuesday
Temp 97.6
"   99.2
I am feeling
a bit better
this morning.
Altho that is
none too good.
My lungs haven't
hurt so much
this afternoon.
They sure were
sore yesterday.
I rubbed them
good with

camphorated oil
last night—so.Al.

February 24
Wednesday
Temp 97.6
"   99.2
It was visiting
day and I had
a fine time with
my wife. We sure
played hard. In
fact I am almost
all in. I hope
to be more
rested after
supper... Here is
my wife again
and I feel fine.
She sure is full
of the devil. Al.

February 25
Thursday
Temp 97.4
"   99
I think spring
has come at
last. I sure am
tired of the
snow and cold
weather but I
suppose the hot
weather will be
worse and more
of it.

February 26

Friday
Temp 97.6
"   99.4
I don't feel
any too good.
My heart is just
about to get
the best of me.
I wish I could
feel good enough
of the time to
notice it. One
has to take the
bad with the good
but darn so much
bad.

February 27-28
Saturday & Sunday
Temp 97.5
"   98.6
I have weighed
and lost a little.
I am not feeling
so good. I sure
have a beastly
headache. Maybe
I will feel better
after I eat.
Temp 97.4
"   99.4
The fog is about
as thick as it
could be and
still be able to
see. We had a
nice day yesterday.
I feel pretty
well today. I am

waiting for my
wife. Baby was
here for a
minute. Al.

Chapter 116

March 1
Monday
Temp 97.6
"   98.6
It has been a
dismal day but
I have felt very
well, thanks to
our dear God. Al.

March blew into Walla Walla like a lion, and the uproar reverberated into a room that was threatening to close its walls around Alvin, Booze and Riddle. While the wind hurled itself against the window screens like a maddened beast clawing to get in, at least one of the animals inside was on its own rampage on this second day of the new month.

Riddle had blown as much hot air during Sunday's visiting hour as March stirred up cold the following day. His behavior had not gone over well with Booze, whose trio of visitors had been forced to tolerate the vocal Mr. Tom Riddle.

From the get-go Riddle had been at his most obnoxious, asking them "Whad ya bring to eat this time?" as if he had a right to know. A hot flush of shame had rushed over Al at even being in the same room with Riddle.

Booze had simply looked irritated.

He swatted his hand through the air as if shooing flies, a motion that had not fazed Riddle in the slightest. Before they even shed their coats, Riddle bombarded the elegant Crystal with more questions calculated to reveal what was in the satchel she carried. A paper sack with its neck screwed tightly around what was obviously a bottle also drew his attention, and Riddle lost no time in trying to learn its contents. The man holding the sack was Rodney, who, on a previous visit, had been so forthcoming with information about the first woman to run for president of the United States and her Negro running mate. He had not been so quick Sunday to throw light on the sack and its contents.

Their party was rounded out by Toby, whose prejudices had been challenged by Crystal on that first visit; challenged, yes, but not in the abusive way of Riddle's verbal attack. Toby ducked the onslaught by squeezing into a chair near the door, as far from Riddle as he could get.

As Riddle had continued to build up a head of steam, Alvin wished that the burly 'Viking' had been among Booze's visitors. Lars of the tree trunk legs surely could have deflected Riddle. Snide remarks from Riddle had punctuated the conversations Booze attempted to hold with his friends until Booze finally capitulated and resorted to pushing food at Riddle.

In an aside to Alvin, Booze had muttered, "I've created a monster," even as he dribbled a fine white wine into a minuscule glass Crystal produced from her portmanteau.

The "dismal day" Alvin recorded in his diary on Monday, following the Sunday fiasco, had little to do with the weather and much to do with Riddle's continued behavior.

Instead of improving, Riddle had found fault with anything and everything.

Alvin refused to be goaded. Booze maintained an aloofness that only served to irritate Riddle. But Booze drew the line. No more food passed from him to Riddle. When night finally drew a curtain on Monday, it was a nervous Al that sunk his head onto his pillow. He felt certain they had not heard the last from Riddle. After relegating the first day of March to his calendar/diary, Alvin had offered up one of his rare prayers, begging God to let up on the disturbing gusts, both inside and out.

That prayer, like most of his others, went unanswered, and he knew it as soon as he opened his eyes Tuesday morning. The March wind was howling around the building, wrapping it in shrieks and moans as it whistled across the roof and under the eaves. As if having it batter at the windows wasn't enough, Annie hurried through to release the catch and throw open every window in their room. She then sped away to offer the same dubious benefit to the rest of the ward, leaving in her wake a flurry of papers uprooted from trays and tables by the wind and sent flying across the beds.

The paper storm elicited from Riddle snarls worthy of a cornered bear. Al was determined to ignore him. He thought he might get in another hour of sleep, if he covered up his head.

It was a false hope.

Riddle abandoned his animal snarls for barely smothered curses and took his act on the road. Like a man possessed, he stomped around the room, tossing papers about without a care as to where they belonged. When he grabbed a handful of papers from under a weight on Booze's table, it was Booze who came out of bed like a bear on the attack. Booze ripped the sheaf of papers from Riddle's grasp, placed the flat of his hand on Riddle's chest, and pushed him towards the door.

"Go! Get out! Take your mangy hide to the showers and scrub the meanness from your soul before you come back in here," Booze ordered.

Al, whose head was now sticking above his blanket watched in disbelief as Riddle backed from the room. He paused there in the hallway, looking as if he might raise a protest, but thought better of it. He turned, without any clean clothes or toiletries, and went in the direction of the shower room.

"Wonder what's got into the fellow?" said Al.

"I have no idea what got into him, but I know what he is going to get into," Booze responded.

"What's that?" Al asked.

"That man who causes us nothing but grief is going straight into a *hot* shower. And it's all my doing. I wager he won't leave us a drop of anything but icy cold."

They exchanged looks, Booze's wry and Al's full of chagrin.

It was not a subdued Riddle who returned to their room just in time for breakfast. Rather, Riddle swaggered in, the chip on his shoulder barely clearing the doorjamb. Annie was first to see him. Her simper welcomed him into the room in a way that Booze and Al were not yet ready to do. Annie was pouring coffee into Alvin's cup, but, in her rush to do the same for Riddle, she sloshed coffee onto Al's table. She did not even notice the spill, but Riddle did. A warped grin sprang to his lips, and Riddle snickered as he watched Al use a handful of tissues to mop up.

Annie's flutterings as she bustled around Riddle's bed, pouring his coffee and lifting the covers from the dishes on his tray, only widened the sneer on Riddle's face. Annie's efforts on his behalf were met with obvious contempt to which she was immune.

Al tried to get interested in the morning eggs, even though they sat in a puddle of congealing bacon fat. On his side of the room, Booze was doing the same. Riddle, from his bed between theirs, began to pick at Annie. First he blamed her, in no uncertain words, for the quality of the food on the tray. Everything he said about it, from the greasy eggs to the almost burnt toast, was true, but Annie was not the cook and could do nothing about it. Through his tirade, Annie kept a smile on her face and busied herself straightening Riddle's dishes and rearranging his silverware as if that would appease him.

When he saw that he had not made a dent in her composure, Riddle turned to sarcasm. In unctuous tones, Riddle complimented Annie on her hair, which lay in a mousy brown wad under a thick hairnet, on her nails that were bitten to the quick, and, finally, in an even more syrupy voice, on her skillful bed-making. The beaming smile, with which Annie had greeted the first kind word from the patient on whom she doted, gradually faded to timorous and finally was replaced with apprehension. Even good-natured Annie could not believe in praise heaped on a task for which she had so often been reprimanded by Nurse Gillis.

Alvin had watched Riddle's attack with silent dismay. Booze, from his perch, had done no better. Nor did they now. This was Annie's ball game. They waited to see what she'd do with her turn at bat.

If Riddle had expected tears or recriminations, Annie disappointed him.

Through lowered eyelashes she looked at him as one would at a wayward child, slightly disapproving, but mostly disappointed. Her tongue clicked sharply against her teeth twice before she turned away. Without a word, she took with her the offending breakfast tray. Riddle was left without even a cup of coffee.

"Well done, Tom," said Booze, employing sarcasm of his

own.

Booze snapped open the pages of his newspaper, pushed aside the plate that bore only a smudgy trace of egg yolk, and hoisted his coffee cup to his lips.

"Ahh, it's a delicious beverage we have this morning, the piece de résistance to this meal, wouldn't you say, Al?"

In his mind's eye, Alvin again saw Annie's raised hand gently patting the thick, black mesh of her hairnet and the brilliant smile she had bestowed on her tormentor.

"Excellent," said Al.

Together they tipped their cups in a toast to each other and drank deeply of the tepid, bitter brew.

"S'pose you think it's funny that I'm left without a bite to eat!" Riddle snapped.

"Leave well enough alone, man," said Booze.

"Wouldn't hurt you to turn loose of some of that grub you keep in that there drawer," said Riddle, pointing to where Booze might or might not have something stashed away.

"Store's closed," Booze said curtly.

"Well, I say open it," Riddle demanded.

"Lost the key," rejoined Booze, still trying to keep the peace, but adamant about not giving in to Riddle's unreasonable demand.

"Think you're so high and mighty with those highfalutin friends of yours, their fancy foodstuff and their cock-and-bull talk. Well you ain't so much," retorted Riddle.

"I will ask you, kindly, Mr. Riddle, to keep your tongue away from my friends. I take exception to you calling them prevaricators. If there's any cock-and-bull going on in this room, it stems from you, and I, for one, have had just about enough of it."

"Whatcha gonna do about it, Frenchy?"

"Let's just say that whatever it is, you will be on the receiving end of it."

Booze and Riddle, sitting like tightly wound springs on the edges of their beds, confronted each other across the short distance that separated them. Before the hot words could be followed by action, Al strolled between them.

"Things are getting a little out of hand here, fellows. Let's all just settle down," Al said.

"Make him gimme a bite to eat," Riddle whined.

"There's no making anyone do anything in this room," said Al.

"You against me, too?" Riddle said, his voice harsh with anger.

"No one is against you, Tom. In a place of this kind, we're all in it together," Alvin said.

"So says you! I'm the one without a cup of coffee," Riddle said belligerently.

"Maybe we can do something about that," said Al.

At the same time, Booze countered with, "Whose fault is that?"

Raising a pacifying hand to the bristling pair, Alvin made another attempt to bring peace .

"We all have to get along, fellows. We have to pull together…," said Al, and then, without thinking of the consequences, added "…and, Tom you're not pulling your share."

Riddle threw himself off the bed and made a grab for the would-be peacemaker, but Al ducked out of his way. Booze grabbed Riddle from the back and pinned his arms in a bear hug that held the lanky man firmly in place.

"Do us a favor, mon ami, and fetch us a nurse," Booze said to Alvin over Riddle's shoulder.

After Nurse Gillis and two orderlies escorted Riddle from the room, Booze clapped Alvin on the back and said, with a grin, "I thought for a minute there, my friend, you had him won over."

March 2 Tuesday

Temp 97.4
"   98.6
I am feeling
fit as a fiddle.
Boy oh Boy
did we have
a fine big fight
or rather an
argument.

Chapter 117

March 3
Wednesday
Well the argument
is over and I hope
for better days.
Booze and I are
alone. I think it
will be O.K. this
way. I think
Frances will be
out tonite although
I forgot to ask
her. I hope so.Al.

For eight, blessed days the thermometer Annie pressed between Alvin's lips twice a day registered the first normal temperatures he had enjoyed since coming to the Blue Mountain. He recorded them faithfully each morning and evening—97.2, 98.6—but, superstitiously, he wrote not a word about them in his diary. No use jinxing them.

He wrote instead about the *good feed* of sardines he filled up on for supper, the sunshiny day that made him feel *a lot better*, and then the day when he admitted *I love myself and want to get well.*

Finally, on March 8 the lead in his pencil pricked out the painful words *I went off the 'normal standard'*. That was the day his temperature rose to 99. The triple digits that followed day after day elicited the terse diary notation *my temp indicates my feelings*. He blamed the rising temperatures on *about as bad a cold as a person could have.*

The cold clung tightly to his chest, squeezing his lungs until they burned and forced air out in short, sharp bursts that felt like hammer blows. It was no wonder he was scribbling *The cold still runs wild. I feel like hell if I must say so* on his calendar on the day a priest new to the St. Patrick parish stopped by for a visit.

Pieter Verhoeven had a warm smile and a handshake that gripped firmly. His correct clerical black with its stiff white collar gave him a dignified air, and Alvin liked that, but what made him sit up and take notice was the confidence the priest exuded. Self-reliance was in every line of the way he carried his tall, lean body, and the forthright way he reached forward and offered his hand, but, more important, that trust in himself seemed to extend to the person on the other end of the handshake. That initial grasp felt like a bond.

Al liked Father Verhoeven immediately.

This priest was a totally different prospect from the verbose Father Gallagher and, for that matter, from Alvin's own hearty, Irish grandfather. As the two, joined by Booze, wound their way through the usual small talk that opens the pathway between people meeting for the first time, Al discovered in Father Verhoeven an affability that led to deeper discussions and made exchange of ideas easy. After they had covered many topics and laughed far more than Gillis would have liked had she known, Al ventured to ask about the Pope's recent open letter to all Catholics in Germany.

"I know it has the world buzzing, and astounded even German Catholics," Verhoeven said in his serene voice, and then offered the disclaimer that he probably knew nothing more than they did, if they had been reading the *Walla Walla Union*.

"Basically, this letter accused the Nazi regime of violating the German-Vatican concordat of 1933 and encouraging anti-Christian movements, as you probably already know," said Verhoeven.

"The letter was read on March 14 by the bishop of Berlin, Count Konrad von Preysing-Lichteneggmoos, at the cathedral there."

Alvin saw an expression he did not recognize cross Verhoeven's face when he carefully pronounced the mouthful that was the German bishop's name.

'The church hierarchy starts from already lofty heights across the ocean,' Alvin thought. In trying to catch Booze's eye to see if he had spied the same expression on the priest's face, Alvin met with a speculative gleam. It looked as if he and Booze might have something further to discuss when they were alone.

"The pastoral letter was delivered to German parishes secretly by automobile messengers," Verhoeven continued. "Catholic men's societies were warned beforehand to be prepared for an open fight with the Nazis. It was a shocking situation."

The priest fell silent and looked thoughtful as if considering what impact his next words might have.

"It is my opinion—and it is only my opinion, you understand—that the message from the Pope was sorely needed, but perhaps was a *reaction* rather than the decisive action for which it was taken. You see, it coincided with the Protestant opposition's fight against general synodical elections, which Hitler insisted—no, ordered—be held. The removal of a pro-German from the Austrian cabinet was also at issue. As for the Catholic grievances against the Nazi regime, as outlined in the Pope's pastoral letter…was it a case of the tail following the dog or coincidence?" Verhoeven shrugged.

"Or perhaps," Verhoeven said with a wistful laugh, "it was a calculated effort on the Vatican's part to join forces with our Protestant brothers in Christ."

The priest dusted his hands together in a dismissive gesture and rested his hands on his knees in preparation for pushing up from the chair in which he had lodged himself.

"It has been pleasant, gentlemen, but I had best be on my way," said Verhoeven, leaning once again over Alvin's bed to clasp his hand. "Until another time," he added.

After the priest's departure, Al and Booze mulled over the skimpy bit of information that had floated across the ocean, but it sounded ominous, coming as it did, on the heels of the warnings shared by Booze's Ethiopian friend.

Al wondered when he could expect an answer to the letter he had written to Murray. If there *were* war clouds on America's horizon, surely some word would have trickled down to a soldier.

Fever still had a hold on him as night fell, and Al dutifully pulled the little calendar out to complete the notation he had been entering when Verhoeven arrived.

" *100.4*
Father Verhoeven
was out today.
I sure like him.
He surely cheers
me up. Alvin Ezra
Peter Patrick Potts.

Today=One year for me.

Chapter 118

March 17
Wednesday
Temp 97.6
As you may see
yesterday was
"one year" here
for me. I have
tried to be a
fair patient but
I am afraid I
haven't succeeded
very well.

The laughter he had indulged in yesterday with Booze and Father Verhoeven weighed heavily on Alvin's mind this morning. He knew he really should make a stronger effort to comply with the rules—give the old lungs a rest. He had been told often enough that the road to recovery was complete rest.

But try that sometime and see how far you get.

Whenever any patient moaned about the necessity of lying passive day after day, Gillis was heard to ask rhetorically, "Do you want to get well? Of course you do, but are you willing to pay the price?"

After a year of trying to pay, Al felt bankrupt.

There was no hiding the cough that racked his body, and the glitter in his eyes and high color on his cheek bones did not go unnoticed by Booze either.

"Still not feeling so well?" he asked Alvin over their morning coffee.

"I think I'm feeling some better than I have been," replied Al.

"My cold seems to be a little better although it is still quite tight. It bothers me that there is nothing being done about it. I sure hope it improves by afternoon. I want to be able to enjoy my wife."

Booze rubbed his forehead thoughtfully. He seemed about to speak, then, apparently, thought better of it.

They finished their meal in silence. When Annie came to remove their trays, Booze asked her, "How's Riddle doing these days?"

Annie's lips parted, then moved soundlessly, as if, Alvin thought, she was being manipulated by a voiceless puppet master. She snapped her mouth shut, then moistened her lips with the tip of her tongue, paying extra attention to the corners of her mouth. She rolled her lips against each other as if working kinks out of them. Finally all these oral exercises seemed to loosen her tongue.

"Mr. Riddle is now the roommate of that nice Mr. Schmidt. Although their room is not on my rounds, I hear they seem to be getting on very well together," Annie said.

"I don't believe I've met Mr. Schmidt, but he must be a very patient man if all is going well with him and Riddle," Booze said to Alvin when Annie left.

"I don't know about patient," Al said, "but Hymie Schmidt is as deaf as a post."

Then the two of them engaged in a bout of illicit laughter.

It was a sleepy-eyed Al who greeted Frances when she arrived at two-thirty. A hearty lunch of smelt—and good little fish they were—had lulled him into a deep sleep.

He was still groping his way out of dreams when she kissed his cheek.

"Here's something for you," she said, handing over a cigar box.

"Smokes? For me?"

She cut her eyes at him and grinned. "Not likely, husband of mine. I thought you might use it to store things in. It has a nice, hinged lid."

Al inspected the box that had held Certified Cremo cigars, according to the design with which its top was decorated.

"It's certainly colorful," he said, tipping the box so Booze could take in the picture of a dandy holding a sheaf of tobacco in each hand and wearing a flaring yellow hat, a blood-red shirt and green striped pants bloused into knee-high, shiny brown boots.

"Cremo, the cream of the tobacco, it says," Al pointed out. "Three for ten cents. How about that?"

"I wouldn't mind having myself a stogie about now," said Booze. "According to that picture with all the blue waves and sailing ship, it looks like they were shipped across the ocean."

"Back here," said Al, tipping the box upside down, "it says these cigars are from Factory No. 117 District in South Carolina."

"Well, that's hardly across an ocean, but I'd still welcome a Cremo wherever it came from. You ever smoke?" he asked Al.

"Nope. That's one habit I never had," said Al, casting a conspiratorial glance at Frances.

It wasn't long until Booze had a visitor of his own. Today, it was just one, but it was an extremely pretty one. Their private conversation gave Al and Frances privacy too.

Frances used the rare opportunity to show Alvin something she had been waiting to surprise him with since the last day of December. She placed a blue folder in his hand, and looked expectantly at him.

"What have we here? Baker-Boyer National Bank. Now what business would you have with them?" Al said, playing along.

He knew a bank's savings book when he saw one. But when he opened to the first yellow page where the name of the account listed *Mr. or Mrs. Alvin E. Potts*, a film of tears blurred his vision. He knew how frugal Frances was, and expected his wife to have tucked away a little something from her earnings, maybe a few silver dollars in a fruit jar, but nothing like this. Nothing like an account in which she had included him, as if she really believed he would be coming home, would once again be the head of their household.

Frances tapped the first deposit figure with her pointer finger. Al noticed the nail was coated with a pale pink enamel. He very much liked the look.

"I've been saving up a little from every paycheck since September, but I didn't open the account until December 31 because I wanted to have a nice round figure to deposit," she said. "Are you surprised?"

"You bet I am," said Al, blinking away tears that threatened to embarrass him. Then he got a good look at that first deposit figure and was really surprised. One hundred dollars! And another twenty-five at the end of February and yet another twenty-five this month! Frances was saving half her wages every month.

"At the rate you're going, you'll be driving one of those Nash LaFayettes before you know it. Heck, maybe even the Ambassador Eight," he kidded her.

"I'd settle for a Ford, if it would get me out here twice on every visiting day," said Frances, referring to the lack of transportation that had kept her away more than she liked.

"Is it a car you're saving for?" Al asked seriously.

"It's just our nest egg for now. We'll wait and see what hatches, OK?"

She dug a Mars candy bar out of her coat pocket, flipped open the lid of the cigar box, and popped it in.

"Now Mr. Booze isn't the only one to have a food stash," she whispered.

Her hot breath against his ear tickled, but, before any reaction to it could set in, Alvin began to cough.

Chapter 119

March 18
Thursday
Temp 97.2
I feel fair, not
good. My cold
still prevails~~
Time out for
business purposes.

Al had hurriedly scrawled that last line after Gillis bustled into the room yesterday and told him he was to go immediately to x-ray. "Doctor's orders," she had said.

The x-ray technicians were on site, so it had been a quick trip down the hall. It had been the rest of the day and the night that seemed long, filled with wondering what all the rush to take x-rays had been about. Al had no heart for taking up pencil again to complete the aborted entry.

He was waiting now for Dr. Smith to arrive and tell him the results of his chest x-ray. Alvin had tried to get Booze to speculate why an x-ray order would come out of the blue the way this one had, but his roommate had only encouraged him to list his questions and try them out on Dr. Smith when he arrived. Booze had also been mum on the subject of the cold that Al griped was "hanging on longer than was decent, and still no one doing anything about it."

The morning seemed to drag, but, wouldn't you know it, Doc arrived just as the lunch trays were being trundled down the hall.

"Not very good timing on my part, is it, Mr. Potts?" the doctor commented. "I hear you are having sandwiches for this meal, so I am sure the ward clerk will be happy to accommodate you when we are through."

Turning to Booze in the next bed, Dr. Smith said, "Will you drop a word to her to hold Potts' lunch?"

In that offhand manner—and with the addition of Gillis appearing in the doorway behind Dr. Smith—Alvin learned that he was not in for the casual bedside chat he had been expecting from the doctor.

Gillis and Dr. Smith escorted Alvin to one of the examining rooms where Dr. Smith prodded, poked, palpated and, in general, began giving Alvin a thorough physical examination. Al was pleased with the attention. He wanted an end to this cold, and it looked as if someone had finally heeded his repeated requests for relief.

This was not a hasty exam, and each new poke or pry at first brought a question to Al's lips. Smith waved them all aside. "Wait. We'll talk when I've finished," he finally said curtly.

Al went through the rest of the routine in silence. He balanced on one leg and then the other, touched his nose with the tip of his finger, bent and squat, gave up his urine and some of his blood, and read with ease one of the very smallest lines on the eye chart.

Through it all he could not see how all this related to his cold.

Except when Doc Smith asked him to cough. That would have been the easiest part of the entire exam to comply with, if it hadn't hurt so dadblamed much.

Only when Al was again clothed in pajamas and robe did the doctor slap the black sheets of film into a holder in front of a light box.

"X-rays are nothing new for you, Mr. Potts. As you know, we have taken them on a regular basis, always comparing your progress. Now I want to show you where we are at the end of a year.

"Here," Smith said as he pointed at the first picture. "This is one of the pictures we took of your lungs yesterday, Alvin."

"You remember, do you, that the lungs show up as dark shadows with the shadow of the ribs in white over the lungs?"

Seeing Al's nod of assent, the doctor continued. "See this light, mottled area here, here and above the heart shadow?" Smith asked, using a pencil as a pointer. "In a healthy lung those whitish areas would be black or very dark. Now take a look at this x-ray.

This is a picture of your lungs when you arrived here a year ago. You see the extensive mottling?"

Al looked at the first x-ray, shifted his eyes to the second. He discerned no difference. He admitted that to the doctor.

"That's because there is no visible improvement."

Smith laid the words down with a lack of emotion. Alvin didn't think he could have stood it if the doctor had shown any sympathy.

Alvin turned away from the black and white images.

"Now," said Smith, slapping his leg for emphasis, "now for some better news.

"You came in a mere shadow of yourself at 119 pounds. Now you are a strapping 144!"

When Al gave a derisive snort, Smith's face colored and he added, "Twenty-five pounds may not seem like a lot, but, generally, Alvin, your physical condition is better."

"With this cold I don't feel better. I feel like the very devil, but, even with it, I might call myself strapping, if I topped out at 170," said Alvin.

"All in good time. Don't get discouraged," said Smith. He slipped the x-rays from their hangers and shuffled them into their envelopes. "Your lunch should be waiting for you in your room," he added.

The consult was definitely ended. *And not one word about this insufferable cold.*

A return to his room and the company of anyone, even good-natured Booze, held no appeal. Al wanted to be alone. He made a quick detour into the room to pick up his lunch tray, and, without asking permission of Gillis or Annie, took it to the recreation room where he settled into the darkest corner. With any luck, he could eat in peace before he was discovered.

Booze in the meantime was undergoing an exam of his own. Smith made a few perfunctory taps here and there on Booze's broad chest and back before asking, "How's it going, René?"

"Not too bad, Robert. Better with me than with my young companion," said Booze, nodding in the direction of Alvin's bed. "I'm worried about him. He frets over that 'cold' of his. Have you talked to him about it, told him the nature of it?"

"I have deliberately avoided all talk of it. The symptoms of tuberculosis need not be spelled out for him. He knows them well enough—the feel of the flu upon one, the dry hacking cough or the loose one that brings up sputum, the chest pains, the fluttering of the heart, the poor appetite, night sweats. I'm sure they are his constant companions.

"Today we looked at his x-rays, the ones taken yesterday and the ones from a year ago. We discussed the comparisons he saw with his own eyes. But, René, at this juncture, it is easier for him—and perhaps better for the morale—to just deal with this persistent 'cold'. He's bright. Subconsciously he knows what his body is telling him. He will come to it in time."

"Such a fine young family man. So many nice young men here in this dismal place," Booze remarked.

"And you, how about you, my friend? Is there anything I can do that would make you more comfortable here?"

"See if you can get us a new cook!" Booze laughed.

"I am afraid that is out of my jurisdiction," Smith said, ruefully.

"René, tell me, does Potts know that you are a physician?"

"No, he does not and I don't want him to know. Nurse Gillis knows and perhaps one or two others on staff, but the fewer who know, the better. And that's *was*, Robert. I *was* a doctor."

"Once a physician, always a physician," said Smith.

"Ah, Robert, there are those who would disagree with you. Without that paper I am nothing," Booze said.

"Pulling your license like that was a damn shame. You did not deserve that!"

"They were totally justified and you know it. I knew what I was doing, and I knew the risk, but I did it. And, to be honest, Robert, I'd do it all over again," said Booze.

"That is, if I were able," Booze added, tapping his chest with his thumb.

"You only did what most of us are too cowardly to do. You saved the lives of many women…"

"Let us not talk of it, Ronald. It's over and done with. Nothing can be gained from revisiting that old moral issue."

"Still, it is a damn shame. And now tuberculosis, too…totally undeserved!" said Smith.

"René, I may be unable to secure a new cook for this

establishment, but I can bring you a delicacy now and then. Anything in particular for which you have a craving?" asked Smith.

"Really, Robert, I am doing fine in that department. Old friends and former patients are taking very good care of me. I've even been gifted with a Madeira, if you can believe it, to go with one of those sponge cakes for which Trina is so well known."

"Well, old son, you are eating better than I am," laughed Smith.

"Now and again. Now and again," Booze agreed.

The two took leave of each other, and Booze was deep in a book when Alvin returned. They passed what was left of the afternoon in silence, stretched out at rest At one point Booze heard Al, in direct violation of the rules, singing softly. The song was *Stormy Weather* first sung, and so beautifully, by Ethel Waters in 1933, the year Alvin walked away from the hospital at the County Farm weighing 170 pounds.

March 19
Friday
Temp 97.6
"   98.8
Not much of
a day. We
don't get to
weigh tomorrow.
Only once a month.
Baloney. Al.

Chapter 120

March 20-21
Saturday & Sunday
Temp 97.6
" 98.6
Not much of a day.
I feel just fair~~
What I really need
is about 20 years
at home—now—Boy
for my girls I sure
would be happy.

Temp 97.6

Excitement was high and mounting higher as the Sunday afternoon visiting hour approached. Yesterday Booze had announced his intention to host a small party in the recreation room. The occasion was an annual tradition, Booze said, he had started years ago, a welcome to Spring party.

"I have the total cooperation of our Miss Gillis, and Crystal and her gang of thugs are standing in my stead since I am incapacitated this year, so to speak. You and your Frances must come join the revels," said Booze. "Of course," he added, grinning, "the reveling this year will be tempered to Gillis' standards, but it will still provide diversion."

Booze's excitement was understandable. It was his party. While Al loved a party of any kind, what had flushed his cheeks, brightened his eyes and set his heart to pounding was the anticipation of a few minutes alone with Frances. It was so seldom that they had this room all to themselves. But, of course, they would not miss Booze's big affair. It was all he and Booze had talked of this morning. As Alvin understood it, this Spring fling thing was what Booze did instead of observing Easter.

"Celebrating the rites of the Spring goddess, just like a pagan," Booze had laughed. Alvin hadn't been able to tell if he was joking or not. But it sounded like fun, and he and Frances surely would be there.

Now if she would just get here. Al checked his pocket watch, and not for the first time.

Last night, after Booze issued his party invitation, Al had made his way to the telephone, dialed 3583 and hoped that Frances would be at her mother's. She had been, and he was able to give her Dr. Smith's report.

"No visible improvement in my x-ray, but he says my physical condition is better, so that is good news, isn't it?" said Al.

"Of sorts," Frances had answered.

"Of sorts? What does that mean?"

"We'll have all afternoon tomorrow to talk about it," she had replied.

Alvin had hurried on to tell her about Booze's invitation. Frances promised she would be right on time, maybe early, because Ida was loaning the car and keeping baby with her.

So where is she?

Al checked the time again, and, then, there she was. Or more correctly, there was Ida's car. He was sure Frances was the one behind the wheel. And she was, skipping out of the car like a school girl, but deliciously all woman, which her just-to-the-knee skirt and low-cut blouse did nothing to hide and a lot to reveal. Oh, his wife did look extremely good to him today. And it was a beautiful day. *Such a hot damn, dog doodly, wonderful day!*

"Hello, wifie," he called unceremoniously out the window. Yes, he had taken the liberty of excusing himself from the mattress. A wife like that deserved the effort of a special greeting on this wonderful Spring day. Look at her sweet little smile. God *bless her, and God bless this cold, and don't let me cough for the next two hours.*

Then she was in the room, and in his arms. And all the x-rays in the world had no meaning for them at this moment.

Al became aware of Booze looking on with amusement.

"I assume we will see you two when we see you," Booze said, ready to leave.

"Oh, you'll see us. Just a few things to discuss before we begin to revel," said Al.

Frances had not moved out of the circle of his arm. Nor did they separate after Booze left, closing the door quietly behind him.

It was some time before Al reluctantly let her go, but then only to guide her to a chair, where he seated himself and pulled her onto his lap. She sat rigid as a lollipop stick.

"Al, do you think this is a good idea? Suppose someone comes in."

"Let me hold you just for a minute."

The few words were enough to melt her. She cuddled close. "How nice it is that you are so much taller than I am. I feel so protected, surrounded all around by you."

Al willed himself to behave decorously. He had brought tears to his wife's eyes on too many visiting days by voicing the desire that burned inside him whenever she was near. The frustration on those days overwhelmed both of them and added a sour note to the visits. He did not want that to happen today, so he was careful where he put his lips and fingers, but could do nothing about the increasing pressure a certain portion of his anatomy was exerting against her inner thigh.

She cuddled closer. What could it hurt if he ran his finger just once around the rim of the neckline that skirted the tops of her small breasts? The skin there was so cool and silky. He stroked gently, then dipped into the valley that was dewy and warm from the spring sunshine. Her back curved over his arm until her breasts were raised for his touch. He put his lips to the taut skin and then laid his cheek against their smoothness. Her fragrance, violets and talcum powder, enfolded him...and he breathed it in.

His erection prodded more insistently against her, and Alvin clutched her tightly. Every part of her he could reach was now pressed against his body, lips to neck, curls tangled with marcelled waves, breast to chest and, oh god, his penis thrusting against the warmth of her womanhood. His breathing, which had been no more than a gentle sigh, grew hot and harsh in her ear. "I want you so much," he groaned.

It took him a moment to hear the frantic "no, no, no" she was whispering into his ear. Her voice was edged with anxiety.

With an effort, he stilled his hands.

"It's all right, sweetheart, it's all right now," he said, easing his hold on her. He held her loosely cradled. He smoothed her hair and straightened the ruffle of her blouse. "I'm sorry, so sorry," she said. Tears sprang to her eyes, forming dewdrops on her lashes.

Al's knuckles brushed them away. "It's all right," he repeated. But they both knew it really wasn't.

Al was still struggling to gain control of himself, but he tried for a light touch. "It's about time we went to that party, don't you think?"

"Past time," she said.

She stood and did the things Al had noticed all women do before they present themselves before others. While Frances' hands were busy pulling her skirt into alignment, tucking her blouse into its band, and patting powder over her reddened cheeks, Alvin settled for pushing his still unruly member flat against his abdomen under his pajamas and covering the offender with his robe, which he belted tightly.

When they opened the door, sounds of the party drifted to them from down the hall. Someone was playing the piano, and a fine baritone was singing the old melody *In a Shanty in Old Shanty Town*. It looked as if the entire ward was present and listening to the elegant dresser who had accompanied Crystal on a visit to Booze, but whose name escaped Frances. His tie again held the pearl that had caught Frances' eye.

"I believe Booze called him Griffin," Al said when she leaned over to inquire. "I don't know if that is his given or surname. Whichever, he's doing a first-rate job on that song."

The recreation room was festive with huge bouquets of hot house flowers, and tables that bore platters of fresh fruit, a variety of cheese, and tea sandwiches cut into fancy shapes. There was also a many-tiered cake that blossomed with a baker's idea of a spring garden. It sprouted frosting replicas of tiny violets, blue forget-me-nots, lilies of the valley, deep-throated golden daffodils and lush red rosebuds.

Iron chairs had been brought in to accommodate the patients, who added a bizarre note to the setting, dressed as they were in pajamas and robes. Most wore the blue and white striped numbers the sanatorium provided, but others, like Alvin and Booze, wore their own robes. Al's matching set of rayon had been a Christmas gift from Frances. He felt very spiffy in them until he spied, as had Frances, the pearl tie tack and also the tonsorial splendor of this Griffin, whose perfect haircut almost outshone his extremely well cut suit. In that moment, as he appraised the singer's perfectly turned out appearance, Al remembered the gypsy woman telling him that he understood style because he had been a tailor in another life.

"I can almost believe that," Al muttered under his breath, as he sent another appreciative glance Griffin's way.

Crystal, looking beautiful in a dusty rose gown over which she wore a dove gray bolero, came over to greet them.

"Say hello to your official hostess," chirped Crystal, placing a long, slim hand in Alvin's while she reached to give Frances a comradely pat on the shoulder. Trina, a petite contrast to the statuesque Crystal, appeared at her side to offer her own welcome to the late arrivals.

"René gave us so many years of festivity, it is only right that we should step into the breach," said Trina in response to the thanks Alvin and Frances had extended.

"All of us...," Trina added, sweeping her hand around to include Lars, Toby, Geoffrey and a handful of Booze's other unnamed friends who were clustered about the piano, "...all of us are enjoying so much doing this for our friend and his friends here at the Blue Mountain. We are so glad to be with everyone here today."

At the piano a sprightly girl in bright yellow was tinkling out tunes. The group around her sang along for the patients' enjoyment as she segued from one air to another.

When she entered into another old song from his courting days, *Night and Day*, Alvin wished with all his might that he could be up there singing with them. Instead, he leaned over and whispered to Frances, "Night and day, you *are* the one." She blushed, but tucked her hand in under his arm.

The iron chairs soon grew too hard for the ambulatory patients who had been allowed to fill them for this rare occasion. They drifted away but not until only crumbs were left of the elaborate refreshments. The party ended when the pianist thumped out a rousing chorus of *Happy Days are Here Again*.

Booze later told Al that cake had been sent to all the patients confined to bed. "My friends were very generous to us today. One would never know from their bounty that we are still in the throes of a depression. Although, from all appearances, things are looking up. Consider ourselves lucky!" he said when the party voices were stilled and they were back in their room.

Al was exhausted, and rest period had never looked so good. But he had some unfinished business. After Annie came around to take temperatures, he took out the calendar and added to his morning entry:

> "   98.8
> *Frances will be*
> *back out to see*
> *me. I am always*
> *making her unhappy.*
> *I am sorry. Al.*

He made a solemn promise to himself that he would be on better behavior when she came back for the evening visiting hour.

Chapter 121

Blue Mountain's rec room had never before seen the likes of the kind of party Booze had put on, and with just spring as an excuse, the patients marveled. Usually the iron chairs came out for a rare movie or a variety show when a troupe of performers could be cajoled into bringing its act out as a public service to the patients. Even then, refreshments never surpassed the obligatory bowl of red punch and a plate with enough brittle cookies on it for everyone, if no one took more than one. The repast Booze and his friends had provided was a minor miracle to men who had come to consider a bowl of tapioca pudding the epitome of cuisine.

"Residual benefits," Booze had commented when Phil showed up days after the party to report that chatter about it and the jovial hosts was still providing entertainment for the ward.

After such a show, Easter Sunday, with its lone Easter lily displayed at the sanatorium's entrance and bowls of tapioca on every tray, was anticlimactic.

Some patients, like Alvin, received little extras from friends and family members. The most common offerings that marked the religious occasion were Easter baskets filled with artificial grass and chocolate rabbits. The one Frances put together for the baby to give her daddy also contained colored, hard boiled eggs, which Al and Booze sprinkled with salt and pepper and consumed with gusto. Booze's friends, who had not stinted on the Spring observance, turned a benign eye on Easter. However, neighbors of Ida's, Chet, Eunice and Art, brought gifts for his roommate as well as for Alvin, a shaving set for Al and stationery for Booze. Their gifts reminded him of the Saturday night get-togethers at which neighbors eventually became extended family members. *They sure are fine people*, Al inscribed in his diary after they left.

Frances' Easter visit was the fourth time she had been out

since Booze's party, if one counted her evening visit on the day of the party. During all the visits, Alvin had kept the promise made to himself to exercise restraint. The fickle March weather that could not decide whether to cast down brilliant sunshine or rain and hail gave them safe topics to talk about. The screen on the door at home had been ripped off in the wind storm that had almost blown Al out of bed the day after the party. The new street being built from College Avenue to Sumach to open up Stadium Park to the northeast section of Walla Walla had churned into mud, and Ida had mired her car on an equally muddy strip of road south of town. It took Docey's team of horses to pull it out.

Yes, March was having its way with Walla Walla and the surrounding country side, Alvin had agreed in his most agreeable manner. And, he had kept his hands to himself. But he did ask Frances to take his ice cold feet into her warm hands. They had been cold all week and even a shower had not thawed them out, he told her, probably because there was no heat in the building.

Will and Esther had married on March 24, which was a Wednesday, but Frances had still squeezed in two visits with Alvin on that day. There had been no wedding cake to bring him because the ceremony was held before a judge at the courthouse, sandwiched between the end of Will's shift at the Ford garage and the start of Esther's at the Green Lantern tavern. "Maybe later," Frances had said of a reception.

Yes, Alvin had behaved himself through all four visits with his wife, and it was darn dull going, but far less frustrating for both of them. At least this way, no one felt guilty.

March 30
Monday
Temp 98
*   "   99.6*
I have a "bad"
headache and
when I say bad
I mean it hurts
like hell. Vulgar
of course. Well
tomorrow is

my very esteemed
Birthday. Or date.
I surely feel
plenty ancient.
26 years to be exact.

Chapter 122

Angie had made a tentative visit to her brother-in-law while
Leo was still a roommate of Al's, a visit she had intended as a
bridge over the waters she had roiled when she and Roy snatched
the ranch jobs away from Alvin and Frances. Even though Al had
been cordial during her hesitant peace mission, Angie had not
attempted a repeat, nor had Alvin heard from Roy, now married to
her.

That was about to be remedied.

Al had his usual attentive eye on the window when the hour he
waited for all week approached on the afternoon of his birthday,
which, glory of glories, fell on a regular visiting day this year. His
wife would be with him, and that would make a special day more
special. He watched for either Ida's Ford or Frances on foot. His
window gave him a good view of the drive up to the entrance, but
he had to stretch the rules somewhat if he wanted to see her
walking on Dalles-Military Road.

He made that stretch, and stood at the window looking
expectantly at the arriving cars, when he saw she was nowhere in
sight on the road. But there was no sign of Ida's car among the
line forming around the circular drive. He was concentrating so
intently on Fords, that he did not recognize his wife when she
stepped from an unfamiliar Plymouth.

Not until Frances waved the baby's hand repeatedly at him did
he recognize her. A package was clutched under one arm and she
held the child balanced on her hip, but still was able to direct
Frances Pearl's gaze toward the window where, the child was told,
her daddy waited for them. Alvin had eyes only for his blonde
wife and even blonder baby, both now waving at him. *Oh they are
a peach of a pair all right, my girls.*

He waved back and, at Booze's sudden urgent admonition to

get back in bed, slipped under the sheet just as Gillis entered the room.

"I trust *everyone* here is ready for company today, and prepared to adhere to the rules," said Gillis with a stern eye cast in Alvin's direction.

"No singing, no laughter, no excitement. That's a promise," said Al, grinning.

"And...resting in bed. Understood?"

"Understood," said Al, adding, "From this moment on."

His hasty departure from his station at the window prevented Alvin from seeing Angie and Roy, whose Plymouth had delivered Frances, so he received a jolt of surprise when they followed Frances into the room.

A black cartwheel hat Angie wore at a sophisticated tilt that cast the left side of her face in shadow partially hid Roy, who appeared to be taking advantage of the concealment. It wasn't until they were clustered around his bed that Al had an entire view of this brother-in-law of his. Roy, a rural product of Missouri, wore a sheepish grin when he finally poked his head out from behind Angie's hat.

"Howdy," he said. A nervous shuffling of feet and a slight flush on Roy's already ruddy face made it obvious that this reconciliation was pushing him in over his head.

Alvin took in Roy's narrow face with skin stretched tautly over bone.

Roy's broad shoulders were built to carry more weight than was on them today, and his torso slimmed down into faded denim jeans washed to the softness of a cotton hanky. Al noticed that Roy's cowboy boots were worn, but polished.

"Good to see you, Roy, and you, too, Angie," Al said, as he extended a hand to Roy.

From that point on, the birthday party Frances had planned around these surprise visitors proceeded as frivolously as she had hoped. Past differences were set aside as Frances handed Al a present, and Angie served the cupcakes Frances had baked. Whenever an awkward silence did fall, baby was a convenient topic. It was apparent to Alvin, as Roy jostled Frances Pearl on his knee, that she was the apple of his eye and the child was equally enamored of this uncle. The affection shown to Frances Pearl by both Angie and Roy and her ready acceptance of their attention told Alvin more clearly than words that these two were not strangers to his daughter. *Frances has been mending fences.*

Conversation that had been stilted flowed freely after the cupcakes were eaten. Why is it, Alvin wondered, that sharing food dissolves constraints that might exist between people. The simple act of breaking bread... He left the thought unfinished as Roy inched his chair forward.

"How about this boom year the wheat farmers are having?" said Roy.

"I heard prospects are really bright."

"Dollar a bushel for wheat that hasn't even been harvested yet. That's a deal and a half, I'd say."

"How much has been sold at that price?" asked Al.

"Dealers aren't about to say, but they do say several contracts have been signed in this county for a little above or a little below a dollar, with it still three months to harvest."

"I remember three years ago it was a common practice to sell a third of each year's crop before harvest, but the government frowned on it and that little wrinkle put a stop to it," Al recalled.

"It's different now. The farm board and government has let up. The export business, millers and speculators have free reign."

"This buying ahead by these fellows is all guess work," Al said.

"Sure is. A lot of the wheat that's being bought up is bought by speculators, who are gambling that wheat prices will be even higher in three months."

"Whether millers buy wheat the day they sell flour to avoid the risk in price fluctuations or whether a speculator takes the risk by buying ahead, wheat *farming* is always gamble," responded Al.

"But them farmers still make a pile, don't ya know," said Roy, bobbing his head in agreement with himself. "They're the ones livin' in these fancy, big houses that look like castles."

"And there are ones that go through some tough years, too. Some that aren't living so high on the hog. You know that," said Alvin.

"Reckon that's so. I've worked for some of them. Prefer it, too, to tell the truth."

"I've heard crop prospects in Walla Walla County may be at

an all-time high. You hear that?"

"Yeah, fields are looking good. Those spring rains sure helped out," said Roy.

"From what I see and what I've heard," Roy added, "the crops gonna be a bumper, bigger than any since '28, what's I heard."

What about up in the Inland Empire? What's going on up there?"

"According to a couple fellas I was talking to down at Lutcher's that's been up that way, contracts in Spokane are payin' ninety cents a bushel, and the carry-over from last harvest is the smallest since the World War. That's bound to boost prices, don't you think?" Roy speculated.

"All around, it sounds better than fair. I hope these good prices come Elwin's way. I haven't heard from him or Alta about this year's crop. I believe he's farming on shares with Zebediah."

"Shares is the way to go, if you aren't big enough to go it alone. Better than working for someone else…if you can avoid it," said Roy.

"I wouldn't know. I always worked for someone else. But, you know, Roy, I can't complain. I've been treated real good by people like the Kents and Meliahs. Good people. Real good," said Alvin, realizing that their talk was coming dangerously close to the employment situation that had fractured their friendship two years ago. He steered the conversation to a silly item he had read in the *Union* a few days before.

"Hear about the hen that knew when it was Easter?"

"Don't believe I heard that one," said Roy, grinning in anticipation.

"This isn't a joke. It's the real thing. This hen over in Boise laid an egg on Easter that was seven and a half inches long and nearly as wide. Article said the owner couldn't figure out which hen had left her the surprise."

"Probably the one that was limping," Roy said wryly

On that note, the talk became general and even spread over onto Booze's side of the room, where, as usual, he was surrounded with visitors willing to share opinions.

March 31

Wednesday
*Temp 98.2
"   99.2
I am 26 years old
today. Baby and
Frances were out
all afternoon. She
brought me new
slippers and new
dressing robe. Sure
is keen. She is going
to exchange it for
a different color.
I am looking for
Frances now. I
sure hope she
doesn't walk.*

Chapter 123

It was April Fool's Day, and the cartoon Al received in the mail that Thursday afternoon showed him that his wife had a sense of humor.

The cartoon, cut from the Union and labeled *Quite a Help*, featured four people—a pert and comely nurse with shapely legs sitting at a bedside holding the hand of a male patient, a bearded doctor and a bespectacled old nurse. The doctor was pictured saying, *"I brought you a new nurse, Mr. Potts. You need complete relaxation!"*

Al showed it to Booze, and they both had a good laugh remembering that Frances had twitted Al after meeting Christina when the attractive nurse had arrived for duty during one of the evening visiting hours. "When you told me you had a new night nurse, you didn't tell me she was so pretty," Frances had said, sending a sweet sly smile at him. "Oh is she pretty? I didn't notice," Al had answered with mock innocence. The remark had earned him a swat on the arm.

Both men had enjoyed Frances' teasing and easy acceptance of a beautiful woman involved in the personal care of her husband. The truth was that Frances had been pleased to see the slipshod Annie replaced by a nurse so obviously dedicated to the wellbeing of her patients. Good care could only help send Alvin home quicker.

The cartoon and a letter Frances put in the mail after Roy and Angie dropped her off at Ida's were intended to brighten Al's Thursday, after Frances was forced to disappoint him Wednesday night. Ida's car and baby care were not going to be available to her for the evening visitation, so Frances was doing what she could to make up for it. She knew how he doted on their brief time together. Well, she did, too, but a missed visit wasn't the catastrophe to her that it was to him because she had so much to occupy her time. There was the job at the Wilson's, of course, but the care of her own home and baby also had to be squeezed in. Trundling the laundry to Ida's every week was almost an all day chore, and a trip to the grocery store was made difficult without the use of a car.

Even when Frances was unable to visit her husband, she felt connected to him through the many errands she ran for him. This week that would include returning the navy blue, birthday robe for a maroon one, a color for which he had expressed a preference. She intended to make the exchange so he could have the robe Wednesday evening, but without someone to watch Frances Pearl, the mile walk to the sanatorium was out of the question so shopping could wait.

At Ida's invitation, Frances and Frances Pearl stayed for supper so Frances could call Alvin that evening from Ida's phone. "A phone visit is better than nothing," Ida said. Frances Pearl was delighted that they were going to eat with Grandma. "I love dinner on a plate," she said. In answer to Ida's raised eyebrow, Frances said, "I guess we do eat a lot of sandwiches." They smiled over the head of the two-and-a-half-year old. "She does have a vocabulary," Ida said. "And a mind of her own," said Frances.

April 1
Thursday
Temp 98
" 98.6
As you may see
the temp. is down
some. Frances
called last night
and I went to
the phone. I also
talked to baby.
I also received
a letter from her
today. She is
plenty sweet to me.

The first week of April passed in a blur. It was a whirlwind of activity that turned the whole week bleary for Frances but, for Alvin, the seven days were engulfed in boredom so dense it was like a fog that made one day undistinguishable from the next. He refused to let the days pass without note, no matter how dull they were. There was always a temperature to jot down. *God knows that is ever changing.*

On the second day of April he tried to be optimistic, even when his temp had to be recorded as 99. *I seem to be a little better than I have been,* but in the next sentence his mood darkened and he wrote *I expect to lose about 3 lbs. I haven't eaten very well the last month.*

Optimism, he confided in Booze, did not come easy to him in this place. "Buck up," Booze encouraged him, but the fog that was obscuring his days seemed to be seeping right into his head. *Too darn confusing to even try to figure out this life.*

Weigh day proved disappointing, but only because his weight remained the same as the month before. Highlights, of course, were the visits with his wife. *I couldn't possibly do without her,* he noted on the calendar he still called Flora's Dare. One of these days he would figure out why the ward clerk had gifted him with such a tiny time marker.

When nausea and headache overcame him, he gave them short shrift in his diary. *Not a god day,* he wrote as pain split his head and his stomach roiled. He did not notice his bad day was missing an "o".

But, just as April's unpredictable weather fluctuated, so, too, did the state of Al's body. His temperature did a drastic switch, starting one morning with a 99.2 and receding to normal by evening. *Now what does this mean?* The mercury in the thermometer outside his window dropped and continued to drop. He knew what that meant, with the windows flung wide open. *It is too cold to get from under the covers to read or anything so am very dull* he reported.

Sarcasm cropped up in the diary at the end of that first uneventful week. *It has been a very big day! Oh yes, every day is immense when one has to stay in bed. And of course one must stay in bed and recuperate.* He used the caustic words like someone else might use curses. As far as he knew, sarcastic remarks did not have to be confessed.

Diversion finally came, in the form of two people.

The patients waiting for long, overdue haircuts on April 12 were introduced to a woman as tall as she was wide. Her broad face bore a web of wrinkles finely drawn over time by worries, laughter and too many hours in the sun. Astigmatism and nearsightedness had scored two vertical lines between her eyebrows, giving her a perpetual look of puzzlement. This, the patients were told, was Maud Davis who would wash their hair after they were clipped.

The shearing had turned out well, but Al was not looking forward to a shampoo. Other head washers had proved a bust, either drizzling soap in his eyes or rinsing with water cold enough to set his teeth on edge.

When it was Al's turn at the basin, Maud Davis first ran her thick fingers through his curls, lifting them away from his scalp as if weighing them. The touch from this massive woman was light and feathery. She slowly worked in lemon scented shampoo, carefully guiding the lather away from eyes and ears.

Al's eyes drifted shut.

As her fingers massaged circles into his temples and the base of his neck and the thick pads of her hands loosened the pain that had gripped all week, Al began to think of Maud Davis as 'Ma'. She finished the job with a spray of warm water, and avoided the brisk rub that had in the past been used to dry his curls. Maud's gentle pat-down did not turn his hair into a frizzy mop.

"Ma Davis is a good head washer and she is a pretty good scout, take it all around," Al passed on the good word to Booze, who was waiting his turn.

After Booze underwent Maud's ministrations, he said he had never had such tonsorial attention, even when he was paying for it. Alvin, whose headache was a thing of the past, said he had always washed his own hair, never thought of paying anyone to do it, but, if he had to pay, this woman would be worth it. They were satisfied, shorn men when they returned to their room.

The second diversion was there waiting for them.

Chapter 124

Not another new roommate! That was Alvin's first, but unspoken, thought when he saw a third bed rolled again into place between his own and Booze's.

He and Booze had been getting along pretty good together, just the two of them, since Riddle had vacated their room. Al's second thought was that throwing a third man in with them could be like tossing a monkey wrench into the works. Alvin had once seen what an engine looked like after that mishap, and the thought crossed his mind that it was something he had better work to avoid. People were not pieces of machinery.

The new patient had missed out on the haircuts and head washings, but he looked pretty dapper, for all of that. *This one comes to us already shorn.* Al noted that he was neither old nor young. *This is sort of an in-betweeny we have with us.* Like most newcomers to the ward, he looked as if he had seen better days, way better. He was a sort of washed out gray, which didn't bode too well for him, but he had plenty of meat on his bones, judging from the barrel-like shape under the blankets. The patient lay limp in his bed, eyes closed. If he was awake, he didn't care enough to let them know it.

It was up to Booze and Al to take the bull by the horns and introduce themselves. This patient had been settled in while they were down the hall being spruced up.

Booze exchanged a questioning look with Al. *Do we disturb him or not?*

Silently, they made the decision to let well enough alone. After all, there was time enough to make introductions and welcome him into their den. Time was something that wasn't in short supply around here.

This man in the next bed was not the only new patient to the san. Alvin recognized one moving into the room next door. Pete Jensen and Al had worked on farms together, shared a bunkhouse, and always hit it off. Alvin wished it had been Pete assigned to his room. Even though Pete was just in the next room, he might as well be as far away as the moon. Without the run of the ward, a patient had little opportunity for visiting. Alvin and Frances had enjoyed their Christmas day with Mary and Lou, but the only glimpse he'd had of Lou since then was at Booze's party. Al often thought of his room as an island unto itself, and himself a castaway. He guessed it could be worse. He could be in here completely alone. His first few months here had been freedom months, if he had only recognized them as such. *Guess you don't know what you've got until you lose it.*

Irvin Woods turned out to be a pleasant surprise for Al and Booze. When he finally woke up, just in time for dinner, Woods' big moon face came up off the pillow smiling. "Call me Irv!" he said, and smiled through their introductions. He smiled at Annie delivering his tray. "What's a pretty lass like you doing in a place like this?" Woods joshed.

The cliché caused Annie to blush and fumble the dishes until the entire dinner almost spilled into his lap. Irv just smiled, wiped up some splattered coffee, and continued smiling as he happily downed salmon fried crisp and greasy. Al noticed that Irv's smiles even reached into his eyes, where they twinkled mischievously, as if he thought a TB san was the greatest place to be.

Al found himself smiling along with Irv. There was no way one could not return those smiles. Even if one had to ask what the devil this fellow had to smile about. And Al sure was asking. Because Irv not only smiled, he laughed. Big old belly laughs that set his stomach to jiggling until the blankets danced.

Al had to admit he couldn't ask for a more cheerful roommate.

The following day gave Alvin no reason to change his mind. Woods oozed positive attitude and smiles right up to Tuesday's bedtime. Even the cold shower he had been subjected to that morning hadn't dampened his spirits. Al heard him singing even as he came down the hall to wash away his own weekly accumulation of flaky skin and bed lint. He debated whether to advise Woods of the 'no singing' policy, but decided against it. The song bird would be silenced quick enough when Gillis got within warbling range. Until then, a song in the shower was rather refreshing.

Al was a little hesitant to draw his pencil and calendar to him just before lights out, remembering Riddle's belligerent reaction to his record-keeping. So far, this new guy had been easy-going, but, from past experiences, Al suspected there was going to be something to set him off. Al hoped it wouldn't be his scribbling.

> **April 13**
> **Tuesday**
> *Temp 97.8*
> *"   98.8*
> *My darling wife*
> *and baby. I love*
> *you both just*
> *this much. O.*
> *There is no end*
> *to my love for*
> *you. I am looking*
> *forward to*
> *tomorrow. I know*
> *it will be a*
> *wonderful day*
> *for me. Al.*

The last thing Al heard when he turned out the light was a hearty chuckle from the depths of Woods' bed, followed by a snort of laughter from Booze.

'My god, it's contagious,' Alvin thought, smiling to himself.

Chapter 125

Alvin himself was all smiles Wednesday. His darling would be here in…let's see…two minutes. She was never late. Often early.

It would be interesting, too, to see if the newcomer received visitors today and, if Woods did, of what ilk they would be. God knows his roommates were welcome to reap any amusement they could from his own visitors, although he was sure none of his stacked up to the entertainment value of Booze's varied lot.

And here she was! His little brown wren.

He tied the belt of his maroon robe tighter around his waist. Frances had delivered the robe the Sunday following his birthday. He liked the feel of the satin swish of it around his calves, and the slippers fit perfectly. He thought he looked well in his new outfit. Frances had told him so, and Christina had even commented on it. "Such a good color on you," the nurse had said. He was glad he had asked Frances to exchange the blue one. Blue was surely his wife's color, but, for himself, he thought this wine red much better. It was such a cheery color too. When Al had put the robe on today, Woods had cast an eye on it and exclaimed in that exuberant voice of his, "A dandy! We have a dandy among us. Doesn't Al look super, Booze?"

Woods' voice had been full of admiration, without a trace of envy, even as he settled his hospital-issued robe over his paunch and belted it loosely around his generous waist. Then he had launched into an anecdote about a spats-wearing dandy who wore a monocle in his eye and the trouble the eye-piece had gotten him into. Before he ever got to the punch line, Al and Booze were doubled over with laughter. *This has got to stop or Gillis will be hauling someone's backside out of this room. But, dear lord, this Woods really knows how to tell a joke.*

As usual, Frances was the first visitor through their door. She always tried to squeeze in every minute of the allowed time, first to arrive and last to leave even when she had no transportation except those size four tootsies of hers. *My wife is some lady.*

Woods seemed to agree with Al's unspoken words. He did everything but kiss Frances' hand when Al introduced her. And, for a minute there, Alvin thought that was exactly Woods' intention when he raised the back of Frances' hand almost to his lips. But, no, he was merely examining the gold band on her left hand.

"Just my luck," Woods said, "This fair lady is already taken!" He tapped her ring, but the chuckle that rolled off his lips as soon as he spoke prevented any offense from being taken.

Al didn't blame Woods. He thought his wife was looking her best today. Those marcelled waves still intact, and he could see she had used a dab of powder and rouge. She was wearing a cotton print, cherry red sprigged flowers on an ivory background, that he had not seen before. *And looking mighty pretty in it.* Al also caught a gleam in her eye that, before his incarceration in this place, had usually meant she had something up her sleeve, something that could portend either trouble or pleasure for him.

Al had never been sure which until Frances sprung whatever it was on him. The anticipation had always been half the fun, and so it was today. He grinned at her, and she knew full well that he had caught her out. Yes, she did have a surprise for him.

The room quickly filled. Booze's company today included a new face, a woman so petite she made Trina look tall. Her body and mode of dress proclaimed her a young girl with no more curves than a 12-year-old, but her face bore the deep wrinkles of a very old woman. Today, the group clustered more closely around Booze and their conversation was muted, though not noticeably solemn. Alvin did notice that Booze was taking a more active part. Usually Booze was an intent listener, only occasionally injecting a comment here or there. Today he seemed to be doing most of the talking.

Woods also had a visitor, a frazzled looking woman a head taller than Woods. She wore a nondescript dress that hung on her like a sack, and she looked very tired. Woods did not introduce her, but took her gently by the arm and led her from the room.

Evidently, he was not confined to bed as most new patients were or, perhaps, he was not above breaking a rule. From the ashen looks of Woods on his arrival, Alvin had expected him to sleep for several days before getting itchy feet.

Al wasn't sorry to have his corner of the room to himself and his wife. It gave them a chance to talk, and he liked having her hand in his, even if they couldn't snuggle. He wasn't big on showing his affection in public, but a little hand-holding, especially with the others ignoring them as they were, suited him just fine.

"So?" he asked.

"So what?" Frances teased.

He jiggled her hand. "So I believe my wife has something to tell me."

"I can't keep anything from you, can I?"

"Your eyes, my dear, give you away. Besides, I know you *want* to tell me. So give!"

She reached into her purse, removed their bank book and handed it to him.

The blue book with its yellow pages was encased in a tan envelope of cardboard. Before he removed the book, he turned the envelope over and over in his hands. He still couldn't understand how she was able to support their household, buy him gifts and have money left to put away. This wife of his was a wonder.

"I see we are account number 11798. That just may become my favorite number," he joked.

"Go ahead. Open it!" she urged.

It was obvious she had squirreled away even more money since she had told him about the account in March. Yes, here it was. This month Frances had deposited fifty dollars, twenty-five more than each of the previous two months.

This time it was pleasure she was springing on him.

"You have two hundred dollars," he said, letting the tone of his voice tell her how impressed he was.

"*We* have two hundred dollars," she corrected.

He put the book back in its envelope, placed it in her hand, and then grasped both her hands in his.

"Are you skimping on yourself?" he asked. "I don't want you skimping on food or clothing for you and baby."

She laughed, thinking of baby telling Ida she liked dinner on a plate.

"We are doing fine," she assured him.

"Baby may think we eat too many sandwiches, but she has plenty of milk, canned fruit and raw vegetables," Frances said, and then told him about the night they had eaten at Ida's and how baby had made them laugh. "She gets her cod liver oil, too, and, I hope you noticed, this is a new dress, store-bought," she said, smoothing the skirt of her cotton print.

"I think it's keen that you are saving, but I don't want you penny-pinching, sweetheart."

"Don't you worry. We aren't doing without," Frances said.

Alvin thought he just might have a word with Ida next time she came out. Find out if she thought his wife was spending too much on him and too little on herself. He could depend on Ida to lay it on the line for him. She didn't mince words.

They spent the rest of their time together exchanging news. He had Ma Davis and Woods to tell her about. She filled him in on her family. Will and Esther were both still working and had a place of their own. Miriam would like to take her baby and join her husband, who was stationed on the East coast with the Navy, but he wanted her to stay on at Ida's, at least until he could come home on leave. Agnes loved having Miriam's baby to play with after school, but Jenny was balking a bit at having to share a bed with Agnes to make room for Miriam. Ray was delivering newspapers, and even Herbie was earning his own spending money, collecting bottles and turning them in for the refund.

John? "Well, we don't hear much from him," said Frances. "We think he's down with Dad in California. But wherever he is, John will be all right. He's one who can take care of himself."

Then Al noticed Frances had that gleam in her eye again.

What's she springing now?

"Oh by the way, Lily would like to come live with me," Frances said casually.

Bingo!

"Just like that? My sister wants to come live with you and you are just now telling me?"

"Asking is more like it," said Frances. "She just brought it up this week, and I said I'd mention it to you. You know she's been with Alta and Elwin on the farm, but I think she'd rather live in Walla Walla where she won't be so isolated. It's up to you, but I don't mind, if you don't."

"I suppose you told her that."

"No. I told her I'd mention it to you. It's your decision. She's your sister."

"Are you sure it won't be too much for you? Can we afford it?" Al asked.

"I think she would want to look for work, but, even so, we could manage," said Frances. "I think she could be a help, just like Murray was."

"Well, Lily isn't Murray. She's a whole different kettle of fish. She wanted to work at the cannery that year I was at the County Farm, but I tipped Alta to it and asked her to steer Lily clear of it. She's too delicate for that cannery crowd. I'm not too sure just what sort of work she would be suited for. She could end up being a big responsibility for you. Any idea what she has in mind?"

"Alvin, Lily isn't a little girl. She's almost as old as I am. I trust her to do what is best for her. She's welcome to share our home, but I don't feel I'd have to shelter her from the world."

"Still, has she given any indication..."

"Al, please. Where she works, or if she works, has to be up to Lily."

"It just seems to me we need to know more about her plans," Al persisted.

"Honey, I feel as if your sister is my sister, but I can't be her mother. She's welcome to come live with me and baby, if you want her at the house. But I'm not about to lead her around by the nose. You decide."

Lily, as fragile as the flower for which she was named, had always been the timid one in the family. When arguments between their mother and Grandma Potts had raged overhead in their log cabin in Daisy, it had been Lily who had crept quiet as a mouse down the stairs to the chalk cellar, following in Murray's footsteps to scratch pictures into the walls until the house grew silent again. When Grandma Potts died and the children had only their father to turn to, Lily became Alta's shadow, always hovering near the elder sister who became a mother figure in the family. While camping out in their summer tents had been fun for the rest, Lily had cringed at every trip to the outhouse, holding her nose and turning as pale as the moths that fluttered against their kerosene lanterns at night. A walk through the woods was agony for Lily, who was sure every clump of grass hid a snake, every tree a bear, every bush something that would either sting, bite or gouge her. She was so often right, that it did them no good to try to reassure her.

Now Alvin's Lily wanted to move out into the world, and he wasn't sure that she would fit into it any better than she had in the woods. But he also saw the wisdom in his wife's reasoning, even though Frances' indomitable stand, so foreign to her usual passivity, had come as a surprise. This wife of his, and perhaps the times, were changing.

"If this is what Lily wants and if you are willing, let her come," Al said.

Looks like it wasn't just Frances who had something up her sleeve this time.

When visiting hours were over, Alvin felt as if he had been rode hard and put away wet. Working through knotty questions these days seemed as tiring as a full day in the fields. Al was glad to pull a sheet over his head, put thoughts of everyone out of his head, and sleep until dinner time. But by evening, he was ready for another visit from his wife.

This time they avoided talking, a decision reached by mutual—although unspoken—consent. Frances had brought a magazine, from which she read to Alvin while he lay quietly. Booze, who had no company this evening, busied himself with letter-writing. Woods had again taken his lone visitor, this time a woman younger and more lively than his afternoon caller, out of the room.

Gillis poked her head in midway through the visit. Taking in the quiet scene, she said, "Now this is what I like to see—my boys behaving themselves. Keep up the good work!"

"A dollar says I've been so good my temperature tonight will be under 99.5," said Alvin.

"You're on!" said Gillis before she whirled out the door.

Frances was taken aback to hear Alvin so casually lay a whole dollar on a bet. She was not a gambling person, and could not really understand the attraction of risking hard-earned money. Ida had drilled into all her children that anyone who bet might just as well throw their money down a well. All her kids to date had heeded her warnings, except Will, who helped support Lutcher's from time to time, but only in a small way. Frances just couldn't see the sense in it, but she knew Alvin liked a good wager now and then. She gave him what she called "pin money" to spend on incidentals, which she thought were things like stamps, envelopes, and an occasional treat from the hospital's hospitality cart. She hadn't realized he might bet with some of the money she provided.

When she saw him looking at her, and realized a frown was creasing her forehead, she made an effort to smooth it away and tossed him a wink.

But she hadn't fooled him. He leaned over and whispered in her ear, "I only bet when it's a sure thing, sweetheart."

Just as Frances was leaving, Christina came around with thermometers. "Want to wait and see if I won?" Al asked, waving the thermometer in Frances' direction.

"Another time," she called back, making a pistol with her finger and thumb and pointing it at him.

Alvin laughed and ducked his head as she pulled the 'trigger'.

After Christina tugged the wrinkles out of his sheets and smoothed the blankets, Al settled against his cool pillows and propped his calendar into writing position.

April 14
Wednesday
Temp 98
" 99.2
I bet a $ on that
temp and won.
I bet it would
be under 99.5
and so it was.
My darling wife
was out. We sure
had a beautiful
time. I sure love
Frances. She is
so good to me. Al.

Chapter 126

Ultraviolet treatment—it was a new hope Dr. Smith threw out to Alvin like a lifeline cast to a sinking sailor. The treatments began April 15, a panacea for the stomach pains Alvin had been experiencing. He was scheduled to lie beneath the lamp three times a week.

On that first Thursday, he lay with eyes closed, imagining the rays sinking into the deep-seated pain that gnawed at his innards. He believed he could feel the warmth absorbing—or was it melting?—the ache. He so wanted this light to have the healing power the doctor had hinted at, but had not really promised. At least, the cold that had permeated his room all day was held at bay under the lamp's circle of light in this cubicle.

He forced himself to try to forget that his body was bared except for the area covered by his white briefs. *Thank god Gillis is supervising the treatment and not Christina.* Soon, Alvin forgot his body. His self-consciousness faded under the artificial sunlight, and he basked in its warmth, drifting on the edge of sleep.

He was beginning to imagine wind through pine trees when Gillis' strident voice announced the end of the treatment. Back in his drafty room, shivers that rattled his teeth pushed out all other thoughts.

It was not until morning that Al realized he did not feel the improvement he had expected. He was still wearing a long face when Annie came in with the breakfast trays. Along with the hot coffee, she had a message for Alvin.

"Miss Gillis said to tell you she would be in soon to speak to you about your request for a dental appointment."

"Now that's the news I've been waiting for," Al said to the room at large.

Booze knew that, along with the ache in his stomach, Alvin's teeth had been sending out shooting pains for weeks. He had encouraged Al to ask for an appointment, which took a special dispensation to go into town since dental care was not available at the sanatorium. Booze had an appointment scheduled, and he told Alvin maybe they could make the trip together.

With the good news that an answer was in the offing, Alvin tackled breakfast with unusual gusto. He made short work of his stack of flapjacks, even while musing aloud as to how the cook could fry salmon to a crisp but send bacon out lying limp in a puddle of congealing grease.

"This kind of cooking takes special talent," said a smiling Irv, holding up his own strip of flabby bacon. He curled it around his forefinger, and, using tongue and teeth, skinned it off into his mouth. He munched it up, jaws working mightily, swallowed ostentatiously, and then smacked his lips loudly.

"Yes sir, takes a mighty creative cook to come up with a piece of pig like that," Woods said, chuckling. His exaggerated performance had even Annie grinning.

Alvin was finishing his second cup of coffee when Gillis came in. He greeted her with an expectant smile.

Without fanfare, the nurse stood at the foot of Alvin's bed and delivered a terse sentence that had the impact of a bombshell. Stunned, Al could only stare at her. She turned on her heels and left the room. Al pushed his breakfast tray away, eyes blinking back tears.

Booze and Woods could not pretend they had not heard Gillis, but neither did they comment. Their silence wrapped around Al's until the room was quiet as a tomb.

Al retreated into his cocoon of blankets, and emerged only when evening shadows began to filter across the counterpane.

April 16
Friday
Temp 98.2
"   99.2
Well I don't feel
so good today.
Miss Gillis told
me Dr. said I

            couldn't go in
            and have my
            teeth fixed. Just
            the same as saying
            it wouldn't be
            worthwhile. Sure
            have a lot to
            build my castle on.
            Much.   Al.

Booze knew better than to try to put a positive spin on Ron's refusal to allow Alvin to receive dental care. There wasn't much one could say when news like that was handed out, but he couldn't help wondering if Alvin really understood the purpose of the ultraviolet light treatment. Al seemed to think there was going to be an overnight improvement, and that it was being given solely for the pain in his belly.

Booze was torn between keeping his mouth shut and telling his roommate the facts of life. The stomach pain, the pleurisy, the coughing, the headaches were all derived from the TB that apparently was running rampant. The lamp treatment was just concentrated sun rays given in the small hope that the ultraviolet rays would dissipate the tubercle-bacillus. Booze knew the treatment was sometimes beneficial and also knew it would not do any damage to the patient, barring burns from too lengthy exposure. Nurses exposed to the ultraviolet rays over time as they administered treatments were more at risk. The rays had been known to damage retinas.

Most nurses considered the risk to their eyes a professional hazard, and wouldn't think of refusing to carry out the treatments. Not one at Blue Mountain had ever shirked the assignment, but some walked through it with eyes at half mast, hoping for the best.

For all his experience in presenting bad news to his own patients, Booze had not known how to deal with Alvin yesterday. It seemed callous to remain silent after Gillis' announcement, but offensive to intrude on the meager solitude available in a three-bed room. And Al had given every indication that he wanted to be left alone. So, in the end, that is what Booze granted him.

Although today was another day, Booze did not foresee a

pleasant Saturday in this room, although the sun was out and the wind, for once, was not stirring things up. Al looked punky, and only picked at his breakfast. He had skipped two meals yesterday. Booze thought Al was a tad too sensitive, letting his emotions rule when he should be concentrating on eating well, gaining weight and maintaining a state of repose. Ron was an adequate doctor, but he was no hand-holder. What Al needed was a morale booster. He was always in better spirits after a visit from his wife. Too bad that little lady couldn't be out here seven days a week. *The man would probably be up and out of here in less than a month with her egging him on.*

Booze knew, in theory, that his roommates were not his problems, but it was difficult to separate the man from the doctor. He had better take his own advice. Mind his own business. Think peaceful thoughts and concentrate on regaining his health. Maybe Smith was right. Maybe Al was not as unaware of his condition as he appeared to be. Anyway, it was better to keep hope alive, wasn't it? Booze had seen the desire to live overturn several of his diagnoses. And he certainly hadn't ruled out a complete recovery for this particular roommate. Why, he hadn't even seen Al's x-rays.

April 17-18
Friday & Saturday
Temp 97.6
"   99.2
Just another Sat.
Nothing to say
only I don't feel
very good. It was
a nice day. I pray
my wife is over
her cold tomorrow.
Temp 98
"   99.4
My Frances is here
and I am waiting
for her. She is my
lovely wife and
sweetheart. I love

her all there is
and more too—honest.al.

April 19
Monday
Temp 98.2
" 99
Old blue Monday.
I look forward
to this day. We
have our bath
and violet ray
treatment. My
temp is going up.
They probably
will discontinue
it on me. I hope
not. I want its
help on my tummy.

April 20
Tuesday
Temp 98
" 99.4
Booze went to
the dentist today.
Maybe I will go
in a week or so.
It all depends on
my temp.

Chapter 127

April 21
Wednesday
Temp 97.6
" 99
This of course
is visiting evening.
It is also my very
wonderful wife's
Birthday. She is
25 and very sweet.
I love her.

Alvin had his gift for Frances in hand, waiting for her to arrive at seven o'clock. Her work at the Wilsons had prevented her from visiting this afternoon, so he had to wait to celebrate her birthday.

She was twenty-five years old today. He was only a year older, but there had been a time when Frances seemed so much younger than him, just a young girl he had almost been afraid to take into his arms. Now, somehow, his wife seemed to have surpassed his years. While he was worrying over the condition of his "tummy" like some child, she was earning a paycheck, banking money and buying him gifts that would have been extravagant, no, *impossible* purchases for them a year ago when a chicken was a luxury.

Frances had become the bread-winner. There was nothing like a birthday to drive home that point. *And she does it with such grace and such style that it hasn't even been a bitter pill for me to swallow.*

Al wondered at that. How could a little slip of a woman accomplish so much and still make her man feel like a man when, god knows, he had not performed as a man for more than a year? Yes, sir, Frances was some woman. And he couldn't wait for this wife of his to arrive.

She was not the first one in the door tonight. Woods' woman, the pert one, bounced through first, threw herself into his arms, and went off down the hall arm-in-arm with Irv, both of them laughing fit to be tied. Al had not yet learned just how these two visitors of Irv's were attached to him, but he was thinking this one tonight was probably his wife, while the sad sack was an unhappy sister. Opposites do run in families, Al thought, as he mentally compared his happy-go-lucky brother, Murray, with their highly responsible, older sis.

Booze, as usual, had enjoyed a large group of visitors in the afternoon, but was solo tonight. When there were just the two of them in the room during company time, Booze considerately ignored Al and his wife. Lately, he had taken to playing his radio softly while Frances talked with Alvin. It reminded Al of Leo's attempt to cut himself out of the conversation by tuning in a station when visitors were present. *God, it seems Leo has been gone forever.*

Alvin tried never to think of the ones who had come and gone in this place. Not even the ones who had *walked* out the door. He thought those who had escaped with their lives probably did not do too much thinking of the ones they left behind either. He knew his own sister, Lily, avoided visiting him, as if the plague in this place would hop aboard again if she returned. Of course, Nita did maintain a friendship with Frances, and dropped by with her now and then. *Nita was good folks. Not afraid of much, that one.* He wondered if he would be quick to come back in here, if he were ever turned loose. He would like to think he would visit Phil, bring him some sports sheets, maybe treat Hymie to a German sausage from that butcher shop, and pick a handful of those apples off Docey's trees when they were at their crispest. Wouldn't Booze like those, if he were still here? Heck, buy a whole bushel from Docey and pass them out to everyone in the ward!

That's what Alvin would like to think he would do, if he were ever turned loose. But maybe he would be like all the others who flew the coop for good. Maybe he would never want to come back.

He spent a few minutes thinking about what he would have

bought Frances for her birthday, if he had money. She wore a school pin attached to the collar of her blouse in the graduation picture that he kept on his bedside table. Maybe a pin. Maybe that's what he would buy, a gold pin, maybe with a little diamond in it. Or a ring. Maybe a pearl. Fresh-cut flowers, for sure. They were such an impractical buy for folks without folding money in their pockets. Yet Al liked the thought of buying hothouse flowers, their blossoms rich and full one day but soon gone. He had bought Frances a gloxinia plant once; she had it still. She nursed its fuzzy leaves and exotic-looking blooms from one season to the next. She had put so much care into the plant, he knew she would hate to see it die. That was the thing with cut flowers; there was no bother to them. You just enjoyed their short-lived beauty and *expected* them to die.

Al shrugged his shoulders, shedding thoughts as well as kinks.

He had no money for a gift, so no use wool-gathering. Instead, he held in his hand the card Christina had purchased for him from the dollar he had won from Gillis. He couldn't have been more pleased with the card, if he had selected it himself.

It was almost square, a half-inch wider than high and it felt like silk in his hands. A cut-out design of ivory overlaid a silver paper sandwiched between the ivory papers that made up the card. An apple green ribbon was threaded through one corner, tying the silver paper to the ivory. It was the color of the paper and ribbon that pleased Al mightily.

He knew Frances would see the significance of those colors. Apple green and ivory had been her class colors, as she had often told him. Centering the cut-out were three flowers, two red and a pale yellow, surrounded by the words *Birthday Greetings to My Wife.*

The verse was just right. He had told Christina he wanted a sincere message that would convey the love he had always had for Frances. The card she chose read:

Just the same old Happy Birthday
Just for you, Dear,
And it bears
Just the same old fond, sweet message
Someone loves you,
Someone cares

Al underlined "you" in the second line, and at the bottom he added: *You, My Dearest, and God alone, will ever know how much "he" cares.*

He dated it and signed it *Alvin and Baby.*

He had fun writing her name on the front of the envelope. *Mrs. Frances Caroline ("Kerr") before* and then his own name under hers: *Alvin, Ezra, Peter, Patrick Potts after.*

Oh, yes, he did love this little girl he had taken as a wife, and he loved the woman she had become even more, if such a thing were possible.

Chapter 128

April 22
Thursday
Temp 97.6
"   98.6
I went over and
answered the
phone this eve.
My wife and baby
entertained me
nicely. I sure
enjoyed myself. I
stayed and played
quite awhile. I
love Frances and
Baby all there is.

April 23
Friday
Temp 97.4
"   98.8
We had our
treatment today.
8 min. My
stomach feels
pretty good. I
hope it stays
alright. We are
only going to
have them twice
a week instead

*of thrice. I think
I burned my
stomach. It feels
that way. .. ..*

**April 24-25
Saturday & Sunday**
*Temp 97.4
" 99
I have been
rather nervous
and quite fidgety
all day after a
"hard" night.
Tomorrow is "my"
best day. Al.
Temp 97.4
" 99
My sweet wifie
bought her a new
coat. She sure is
sweet. I like her
to have nice
things. Al*

**April 26
Monday**
*Temp 97.8
" 98.6
It has been a
nice day, I think.
I have felt very
well. My wife
sure was sweet
to me Sun. She
looked fine in
her new coat.
I love her. All
my heart will*

stand. al.

April 27
Tuesday
Temp 97.6
* ”   98.8*
It has been
rather a cold
day. I sure hope
we have a nice
day tomorrow.
As you know it
is visiting day.
I know I will
see Frances if
she isn't hurt
or sick. I shall
be looking
forward to seeing
her. We are the
best of pals, real
pals. We belong
to each other.

Chapter 129

April 28
Wednesday
Temp 97.6
"

My wife is here
and it is 15 "minits"
early. I suppose she
will have to wait.
She sure is a mighty
fine girl. Just as
true as the day is
long. I love her
with all my heart.
She has been mighty
good to me. She
sure is a swell
little mother. al.

Frances' arrival always stirred Al up. His heart, seldom an organ content to thump monotonously in his chest, fluttered more wildly when he knew he would soon be with his wife. Today, knowing she had already entered the building but was not allowed to walk the few yards down to his room, practically made him a nervous wreck. This is where Flora's Dare proved its usefulness. If he couldn't see his wife right away, he could at least write about her. He was better at squeezing more words onto one little page.

Of course, now there was no room left to write anything this evening, except for the after dinner temperature. Al was more or less satisfied with the temps he'd been running lately. *Anything under 99 is good-o.* Al was still trying to figure out what Flora was thinking when she gave him this miniature calendar/diary. *Maybe she figured this would improve my penmanship. Pete's sake, it does make me work at it.*

Keeping written records was a habit in the Potts and Kennedy families. Alvin's mother and his sisters called their records 'diaries'. He and Murray had referred to their books as 'logs', if they called their notations anything at all. "My log" is what Emerson called the book in which he had tracked his sea voyage to Alaska long before Alvin was born, and Alvin was sure that was where he had picked up the name. In here, in this place, Al's jottings became 'the diary' when he entered because that is what was inscribed on the cover of the red book Alta had given him when she coaxed him to sign himself in. This year, he was more apt to refer to his notes as 'the calendar' since more space on a page was devoted to the day's date than was left for him to write upon. Alvin still kept last year's red book near. He found it interesting to look back and see what was happening at the same time a year ago. He paged through it now to while away the minutes until Frances was allowed to come in.

Unlike Alvin, Woods did not sit by and wait for his company. He was up and out of the room as soon as Al spied the tired woman and told Woods she was entering the building right behind Frances. Of course, Alvin did not refer to her out loud as 'the tired woman', but her worn countenance mentally conjured up the title every time Al saw her.

"I would have an extra fifteen minutes with my wife, if I could get out of this bed," Al groused to Booze as he listened to Woods' footsteps hurrying to meet his visitor.

"That you would because your little lady is always early. My guests are always fashionably late, don't you know?" Booze said. "But oh! When they do arrive!"

Booze laughed. He knew that his roommates had to be curious about the variety of those who came to see him. Booze's closest friends—Crystal, Lars, Trina, Geoffrey, Rodney and Toby—were pretty much cut from the same cloth, but his patients ran the gamut of society. He thought Alvin had shown considerable restraint after the visit of the child with the crone's face. Not once had he questioned who she was or what was wrong with her. In fact, Booze was not sure that Alvin realized she *was* a child. Booze knew he could not expect a lay person to readily recognize Hutchinson-Gilford Progeria, the rare and fatal condition that was accelerating the aging process in his young patient. She was often mistaken for an old woman.

Sybil was a dear child, so accepting. Such a little optimist, even though she knew her life was on the fast track, like a race horse running all out. Her body would wear out soon. That was one of the reasons for her recent visit. Her mother had brought her to see the doctor who had tended her from birth, to seek even a shred of hope from Booze, who could offer none. Advice he had aplenty; hope was in short supply. Booze did not believe in gilding a lily, especially when the lily was fast fading.

Yes, Booze had been grateful for Alvin's reticence.

Al's unquestioning attitude was one reason Booze did not hesitate to welcome his former patients to this room. When Riddle had been in with them, it had been awkward. Booze never was quite sure what the man would say or do. He and Al may have just lucked out on this latest roommate, though. So far, Woods had not hung about, but Booze had no doubt that, even if he did, there would be no muddying of the waters.

The clock in the hall chimed two-thirty. Visitors began to saunter down the hall.

Frances, again, was the first through the door. In fact, she and Al had a quarter of an hour to themselves before Booze's friends began to wander in. He had quite a crowd today. Lars and Toby made up the advance guard. Others came and went during the two hours allotted, none staying long. Several brought packages, but none were opened and there was no sharing of food today. Frances promised Al she would bring applesauce cookies this evening, enough for the three roommates.

"Oh. I almost forgot. You have a letter from Murray," she said, digging in her purse to pull it out.

"Is it in answer to mine? Remember I told you I wrote him to ask if he thinks there's anything to this talk of war?"

"I remember, but I haven't opened it. It's addressed to you," said Frances.

"What's mine is yours, sweetheart. Open it up!"

Frances removed a fingernail file from her purse, slid the point of it under the flap of the envelope, and glided it along carefully so the glue separated from the paper without tearing. As she inserted two fingers in to remove the letter, which appeared to be rather thick, Alvin noticed she was again wearing a pearly pink polish on her nails. His wife was beginning to be quite stylish with her painted nails and new coat.

When Frances would have handed the letter over to him, Al stopped her and asked, "Will you read it to me, please?"

But Al did take the envelope from her. He thought holding this envelope with its exotic postmark might be the closest he would ever get to Hawaii.

Frances looked around the room. Booze and his group were deep in conversation.

She unfolded the letter, showing Alvin the multiple pages before she began.

"Good! A nice long one," he enthused.

"Are you sure you want me to read this out loud?"

"Fire away!"

"All right. He has his address right here at the top. See?" Frances said, tilting the page so Al could read it along with her. *Co. Hq. 27 Inf. Schoffield Br'rk. Oahu, T.H.*

"Whatever that means," she said. Her smile would have fit well on an imp, Al thought.

"I'd say it means Company Headquarters, Twenty-seventh Infantry. And, according to the envelope, little brother just butchered the spelling of the barracks he's living in. The postmark reads *Schofield*, but Murray has given it an extra letter. The T.H., I think, stands for Territory of Hawaii."

"So now we know exactly where he is," said Frances, laughing and extending her arm southward.

Al reached over and adjusted her aim. "I think it's more like that. South-west."

"I looked for it on the globe. It's just this speck in the ocean."

"Bigger than it looks on the globe, though. Read on!"

*"My Dear Al...*See, it isn't written to me. Wouldn't you like to just read it yourself?"

"Just read. If you come to any racy parts, you can whisper them in my ear."

"Oh you! All right then. Here goes.

"My Dear Al: Excuse me for not writing sooner, but I've been

quite busy lately. There was a war declared over here…"

"What!" Al exclaimed.

"…and it lasted 15 days. It was a 'mock' war between the Army & Navy."

"Now why didn't you say that right away?"

"Al, why don't you just read this yourself, and I'll read it later."

"No. You're doing fine. Go ahead. It just startled me there for a minute."

"…It was a 'mock' war between the Army & Navy. There were 12,000 soldiers against 39,000 sailors. Who do you think won? I'll tell you when I find out. (Ha Ha) This happens every year. The whole regiment goes out and we pack everything we expect to use in a pack. We sleep on the ground and eat our meals out of what you call mess-kits. It's quite a lot of fun.

"The only thing is, they keep getting you out of bed at all hours of the night. It's just like a real war in all ways, but they give us blank ammunition. I counted at one time 65 airplanes flying in formation. It sure is some sight. I also saw the entire naval fleet, that's some sight too. I saw one ship that they said could carry 1000 airplanes. I don't know whether they were exaggerating it or not. But it was a large ship.

"We are going to fire the rifle on the range for a month, beginning in May some time, so I don't suppose you'll hear from me again until late in June. I'm still figuring on making 'expert' which will mean another $5 a month. (Here's hoping.) Did you ever fire an army rifle with a standard shell? It's a Springfield .30 calibre. It kicks about 4 times as bad as a twelve gauge shot gun"

"He knows I've fired a shotgun, but where does he think I'd find an army rifle?"

"I think Murray was asking what's called a rhetorical question. He doesn't expect an answer."

"No. I didn't think he did. And neither did I."

"Oops," Frances said, grinning. "Well, your brother goes on to ask another question. This one he may be interested in having you answer." The impish look was back, accompanied by a rolling of the eyes. "So, to continue:

"Did you ever hear of Waikiki beach? It's about 2 miles out of Honolulu, and is the one that the movie stars go to for a sun tan. I

was down there during the war (the war was called off for Sat. & Sun. Ha Ha) and it sure is a nice beach. I'm going down again sometime when I have some money, and rent a surf-board. There is a wonderful surf there. You can ride on it for about ¾ mile.

"In about two months I'm going to the Island of Hawaii. It's about a 24-hour boat ride, and the government gives you one month out of every six over there on full pay. It's supposed to be a prettier place than it is here.

"This sure is an easy life over here. Five days work a week, and the work is easy. To tell you the truth, I've done just 3 hours work this month. I weigh 165 already. I'm afraid to think what I'll weigh when I leave here. I'm liable to be quite fat. (ha ha).

"How's Frances & the baby & yourself. I hope fine. I haven't heard from Lily for seven months. I guess she has forgotten all about 'lonely little me'. After all it is quite lonesome over here. I don' know what I'd do if it wasn't for the little Hawaiian girls."

"Sweetheart, get your lips over here on my ear. We're getting to the racy part," Al teased.

Frances laughed, waved him off, and continued to read.

"I'm going to be able to send you some pictures before long. Up until now I haven't seen very much money. In fact not hardly any. Tomorrow is the big day, 'payday'. I might have a dollar left after I pay my bills. I have a company bill of 12 dollars and owe some more besides that. I guess I'm due to stay home and be a good boy."

"I'll just bet he's broke because he's been rolling the dice and gambling at cards," said Al.

"Hmmm. Maybe. Maybe not. Then he writes:

"How is Pearl now? I never could find out if her operation turned out a success or not. Everybody has been sort of vague about it. Does Alta seem to be getting along alright? Is Frances still on West Poplar?

"Well, Alvin, I guess I'd better start closing before you go to sleep reading all this 'gab'.

"Be seeing you in 1939.

"Best wishes, Murray.

"P. S. My address is changed to Co. Hq. instead of Co. C. I transferred about a month ago and I'm sure glad of it. It's a lot better place.

"And that's the end," said Frances, refolding the letter and handing it to Alvin.

"Sounds as if he's living the good life, but I wish he could hold onto his money."

Alvin's voice was fretful. Frances recognized it as the tone that crept in when problems her husband couldn't control frustrated him.

"He's still young, Al. Murray just hasn't learned how to save for a rainy day, but he will. He really is a good kid," said Frances. "I miss having him around the house."

"I can't say his letter answers the questions I had. They don't seem to be taking this war talk very seriously, so maybe there's nothing to it. Playing at war just once a year doesn't seem as if this country is getting ready for any big threat. All his talk about surf boards and a month off out of every six. That doesn't sound like war to me. He makes the army sound like a little slice of heaven, doesn't he?"

"He does seem to like it, even the camping out."

"At least we know he's being fed good and has a roof over his head. That means a lot in times like these," said Al.

"Think I'll hang onto this and read it over again later," Al added, tucking the letter under his pillow. "See if I can read anything between the lines, you know?'"

Chapter 130

April 29
Thursday
Temp 97.4
"   99
We have had
a mighty busy
day. I put that
responsible for
the rise in temp.
Bath day, hair
cutting day and
treatment day.
After my treatment
my temp was 98.4.
I know that doesn't
bother my temp. I
am looking forward
to Sunday and my
wife. She is sure to
be here. She always
comes to see me.

April 30
Friday
Temp 97.6
"   99
It has been a
very nice warm
day. Rather quiet.
We had a new

patient in last
nite and another
one this morning.
I wish I could give
my place to
someone. Not
hoping anyone
TB. Tomorrow
is weigh day. I
wonder- - - - Al.

May 1-2
Saturday & Sunday
Temp 97.4
"   99.4
My Darling wife.
I love you so much.
and I didn't gain
for you. I stayed
just the same.
Honey Girl I want
to get well so bad
for you. It looks
so hopeless but I
will always be
fighting. Al.

It was a triumphant Frances who laced her arm through her brother John's, and escorted him to Al's bedside on Sunday.

"Look who we have here," she announced, pushing John forward.

What she had looked like a human version of Lewis Carroll's dormouse. John, clothed head to toe in a rumpled brown suit and a shirt with a too-large collar that bunched around his neck, looked as if he had just stepped out of the pages of the *Alice in Wonderland* tale. This brother of Frances' was all of one piece— from head to toe John was a stubby oval seemingly with no parts that moved independently within the clothing that wrapped him. Fur and whiskers were all that was needed to complete the picture.

His hands clasped in front of him and a worried frown creasing his forehead, John looked as if he were about to squeak, but instead he nodded a silent hello to his brother- in-law.

Alvin had never met a gentler creature than this brother-in-law of his. And he was the shyest man Alvin had ever known. If past experience was any criterion, there would not be much conversation issuing forth from this man today. But it was good to see him and to have this wandering relative home and not have to wonder where he was.

Ida and Agnes trailed into the room, so Alvin knew details would be forthcoming, even if John remained true to form. Sure enough, between the two of them, with a few monosyllables from John, their wandering father, for whom John had been named, was pegged down in Bakersfield where he was still hunting the illusive strike, panning the Sacramento River for whatever gold the rush had left behind and picking away at quartz rocks up in the hills.

What caught Al's attention and stirred up a mixed bag of memories was Agnes' enthusiastic, second-hand description of the living quarters inhabited by their father.

"John says Dad has a tent bigger than our two bedrooms, and it has a wooden floor and windows made out of screens and canvas that roll up and down to let the light in. Clean as a whistle, too, John says," Agnes rattled off, adding, "I sure would like to see that. Set up in the woods, John says, where it's all cool and piney-smelling, and John brought back a big, old boulder dad gave him. It's filled with so much quartz it sparkles just like diamonds."

"Your father also found fifty cents worth of gold just lying on a rock right in the middle of the river, isn't that so, John?" said Ida.

She was looking to her son for something more than confirmation, Alvin thought.

"Didn't see it," mumbled John.

"Think of that! Gold lying right out in plain sight. That must be something," said Agnes, eyes shining and looking as if she were ready to pack her bags and hunt down her elusive father.

"John?" said Ida.

Refusing to meet her look, John set his gaze on his feet. He worked his upper lip over the lower, a movement that set his nose quivering slightly. His eyes blinked sleepily. He shuffled sideways until his elbow jostled Agnes.

"Home's best," he said, nudging Agnes gently.

"I sure would like to see gold shining in the river," said Agnes, peering intently at her eldest brother through her wire-rimmed glasses. "And I sure would like to see Dad fire up that stove and cook me up a mess of bacon and eggs like he did for you, and then eat it right there outdoors. Fifty cents—just lying on a rock waiting to be picked up. Think of that!"

"Can't live on half a dollar," said John in what was, for him, a long speech.

Agnes' face that had been alive with expectation a moment before stilled. Puzzled, she looked from her brother to her mother, and, finding no answers on either face, she turned to Frances.

"Wouldn't you like to go visit Dad and see his camp and the river full of gold?" Agnes urged.

"Remember that story about the goose that laid golden eggs?" said Frances, not waiting for a reply.

"When we find that goose, little sister, then we will go looking for a river of gold."

"But geese don't lay gol...oh...," said Agnes.

"Dad never was content to just dream for himself," Frances said to Alvin later. "He always stirred up dreams in us kids. That's what took John down to California in the first place, Dad's get-rich stories. When John found out he had to buy the bacon and eggs if there was going to be anything for Dad to cook for breakfast, he quit dreaming. He stayed on, helped Dad prospect for awhile, but John said he knew from day one that he would be coming home. It's good to have him back.

"You know, Alvin, with Will married and not about to chase rainbows, I think we may have heard the last of Dad."

Chapter 131

May 3
Monday
Temp 97.4
"   99.4
*This is our third hot
day this year. It was
88 by the window at
my bed. I am going
to have an electric
fan. I never noticed
the heat so much
today as the first
two hot ones. Just
two more days till
visiting day. I love
that day. Al.*

May 4
Tuesday
Temp 97
"   98.6
*Just a freak of a
day. It is so darn
cold I am about
frozen. One day
it is so hot one
can hardly stand it.*

May 5
Wednesday

Temp 97
" 98.6
Hello wifie! How are
you tonite? I feel
fairly well. I am so
glad to see you
because I love you
so and you are so
good and cheerful.
You are my angel
girl. I can't begin
to tell you how
much I love you.
Your Al.

May 6
Thursday
Temp 97.8
" 99
It has been a fair
day. Warm and a
slight breeze. I
am feeling some
better today.

May 7
Friday
Temp 97.8
" 99.2
It is a nice enough
day. I hate to stay
inside. Especially
if I have to stay in
bed. If I knew I was
getting well, it
wouldn't matter so
much. I could stay
for years.

May 8-9
Saturday & Sunday
Temp 97.8
"   99
The only good thing
about Sat. is only one
more day before I
see my lovely wife.
She called me tonite.
I love her so much.
Temp 97.2
"   99
(Mother's Day)

Al begged a lined page from a notebook Annie had tucked into the pocket of her uniform, and, when she had carefully torn it out and passed it over to him, he set his freshly sharpened pencil on the first line and began to compose a greeting to the wife who would soon be with him.
(Mother's Day 1937)

Dearest Mother,
Most Precious Wife,
Darling Pal and playmate. Please accept this small token as my sincere appreciation of your love and kindness to me.
Your loyalty to me is unsurpassed.
I love you "Little Mother".
                           Daddy Alvin

Still no money for rings, pins or flowers, Al made do with what he could find at hand. He knew he was lucky to have a wife who would be satisfied with so very little.

May 10
Monday
Temp 97.4
"   98
Oh God Frances
You were so sweet

last night. You are
"so" good to me.
This is Monday and
I feel so much better
It has rained all day.
Just a slow drizzle
but mighty steady.
Not one let up. I
feel pretty fine
today. All on account
of my sweet wife. I
went to confession
and received communion.
I am all ready for Wed.
now.   Al.

May 11
Tuesday
Temp 97.8
"   98.8
Just another day.
Nothing to do or say
just tomorrow and
the day I am always
glad to see come.
Father Verhoeven was
in for a few minutes.
I enjoy talking to him.

Although the purpose of Father Verhoeven's visit to Room 102 was to see Alvin, he tossed a friendly greeting to Booze and Woods as he strode in. This visitor was a favorite of Alvin's, and, with Murray's letter in mind, Al took the opportunity to ask the priest his opinion of an army that practiced warfare only once a year.

"Does that sound to you like a country expecting trouble?" Alvin asked.

"Doubtful. Doubtful, and perhaps with good cause. Germany and Russia are busy elsewhere. America is so far removed from the troubles they are stirring up, the ocean would wash out a threat before it reached our shores," Verhoeven offered. "If the Yellow Peril takes a notion to get involved, it is my opinion that it is the countries to the south of Japan that need to be on the lookout, not us. Wars take oil and lots of it. The Dutch East Indies with its ready supply of petroleum would be a tempting target. And let's keep in mind, Alvin, that our president is set on steering a peaceful course for America."

Verhoeven did not stay long because he was making pastoral rounds, but his reassurances, added to the lighthearted tone of Murray's letter, eased Alvin's mind.

As he took his leave, Verhoeven cast a glance in the direction of Alvin's roommates, and asked them if there was anything he could do for them.

"I'm not of your flock, padre," Woods said, beaming his big round smile at the man in black.

"Oh I don't mind tossing a little fodder to the strays," Verhoeven joked. When both assured him there was nothing they needed, the priest tipped his black hat to them, snugged it onto his head with a sharp tug, and was gone as quickly as he had arrived.

Al decided he had to get his hands on a world globe. Nothing was more exciting than seeing how the world was put together. He could picture the Dutch colony at the edge of the Indian Ocean, but he would like to pinpoint its location more exactly, determine exactly how far it was from Japan. 'Just in case,' he thought.

May 12
Wednesday
Temp 97.4
"   98.6
I am waiting for my
darling wife. She was
out all afternoon.

When Frances came in that evening, she had their baby with her as well as Roy, Angie, Ida and Agnes. It had been a long time since Alvin had seen his daughter. Phone conversations had kept him up to date on her increasing vocabulary, but he wasn't prepared for the physical changes he noticed now. She was losing her baby fat and he thought she seemed to be turning into a fairly decent looking specimen. A far cry from the battered thing she had been at birth.

"I believe I see a personality emerging," Alvin said to Frances as he played patty-cake with Frances Pearl.

Frances told him that the others were there just to say hello and goodbye before taking Baby home to bed. "But I'm staying," she hurried to say when she saw disappointment cross his face.

Ida left Alvin with a thick heel of freshly baked bread she had buttered and wrapped in a cotton cloth. Later, the yeasty aroma mingled with the lemon fragrance Alvin's nose discovered when he buried it for a stolen moment in the soft waves of Frances' hair. He believed these two, heady scents were the most sensual he had ever experienced, and he clutched his wife's hand tightly, even as he pushed her gently away.

> *Roy brought Baby, Angie,*
> *Ida and Agnes out. So I saw*
> *and talked to my baby.*
> *They came after Frances*
> *about 8:15.*

> **May 13**
> **Thursday**
> *Temp 97.8*
> *"   98.4*
> *It sure is a long*
> *time until Sun.*
> *That is all I have*
> *to look forward to.*
> *My visiting days are*
> *my whole source of*
> *recreation. My wife*
> *is so good to come*
> *and see me as*
> *regularly as she does.*
> *Some day she will*
> *have her reward.*
> *Maybe I will get to*

go home. Al.

Chapter 132

This Friday night in the middle of May brought a torrent of dark dreams to disturb Al's sleep. He leapfrogged from one nightmare to another.

He would be released from fiery images of soldiers and sailors, ships and planes only to be plunged into another filled with pale, pajama-clad patients stumbling in an ever-widening circle that took them nowhere. Just when he thought the worst nightmare was over, another and then another would take its place until he wrenched himself awake, sweating and shivering.

He fought off sleep, although his body was crying for rest. He forced himself to stay awake, even as he tried to push away the frightening memories that became only bewildering tangled threads in the dim light that filtered in from the hall. In time, the frantic beating of his heart slowed, his body cooled in his sweat-soaked pajamas, and loneliness tugged at him as remorselessly as a persistent tide. *Oh God, let me be home with my wife.*

Dawn was painting pink strands through a leaden sky when Al lost his battle and fell asleep. This time the dream that emerged from his subconscious was of a gentle nature that stroked his libido, first with sensuous fingers, then with breathless demands.

He awakened to frustration and clammy sheets tented over his erect penis.

May 15-16
Saturday & Sunday
Temp 97.8
"   98.4
Just one more
day and I shall
see my wife.

Of course she
is my sweetheart
too. Oh Dear God
I love her so.

Sunday dawned clear and the sky remained cloud-free all day. Sundays were always good days for Al, even if the weather was not to his liking. Having his wife for company colored every Sunday rosy, but today really was a beautiful day.

When Frances arrived, the sun was tilted just far enough so the young trees out front cast spindly shadows across the drive. She parked her mother's Ford in the scant shade of one. As Frances descended from the car, she rested one foot on the running board, shaded her eyes with an upraised hand and faced into the sunshine. Alvin thought he had never seen anything quite so precious as her sun-washed countenance.

A slight breeze, stirring from the west like the rays of the sun, pressed the cotton of her skirt against her legs. For a moment, the material molded itself around that upraised leg. The vee between her legs was little more than hinted at, but it was enough to make Al's breath catch in his throat. He watched Frances modestly bat the wind from her skirt and settle her foot on the ground, and he was reminded of Friday night's dream and his rude awakening.

Beyond Frances a woman was plodding up the driveway.

Alvin recognized her as the woman Irv had not yet introduced.

He saw that Frances and the woman he thought of as Irv's sister would reach the entrance at the same time.

He was curious to see if they would speak, and, if they did, what the drab little woman could possibly have to say beyond hello. However, the vestibule quickly enveloped them, cheating Alvin out of seeing their meeting and giving him only a glimpse of Frances' back clothed in bright blue as she followed behind a dull brown coat.

Frances was no longer trailing when she came into the room. It was Irv's sister who was lagging. She stood at the door, half in the room, half out, as if she could not make up her mind to enter. Irv settled it for her. He moved to join her at the doorway, giving Frances a cheery grin as he side-stepped to let her pass by. With a hand under the lady's elbow, Irv escorted her from the room without a word to either Booze or Alvin.

"Do you know who your roommate is?" Frances asked, as she leaned over to kiss Alvin on the cheek.

"In addition to being Irvin Woods?"

"Yes. In addition. *Your* Mr. Woods is related to *my* Mr. Woods! Your roommate is my landlord's brother. You haven't met Art Woods, but, when you do, you'll see a family resemblance."

"Oh, your Mr. Woods is a charmer, is he?"

"I was referring to his heft, not his disposition," said Frances.

"How did you come by this information?"

"When I went over to tell Mr. Woods that your sister would be staying with me for awhile, the talk just drifted around to you and the san. He told me his brother was here. We finally figured out his brother was your new roommate. That's how."

"Small world," said Al.

"Mr. Woods owns another house right behind ours that the wife of your Mr. Woods moved into. She said it needs a lot of work, and I told her maybe John could help fix it up."

"You met Irv's wife?"

"Arlene and I have talked over the fence. She seems awfully sad, don't you think?"

"Irv's wife? Sad? I wouldn't say so. They have a barrel of laughs when she comes in here."

Frances looked puzzled. Then it clicked for Al.

"The woman that came in same time as you today...that's Irv's *wife*?"

"Why, of course. Who did you think she was?"

"His sister?" Al said, hesitantly.

"A barrel of laughs...?"

Al just wagged his head slowly from side to side, and they dropped the subject.

Booze, who had been studiously ignoring them, belted his robe, and stepped past Irv's bed until he stood within their circle.

"Geoffrey and Crystal have gained permission for an impromptu picnic on the back lawn so you will have to do without my presence for the next hour or so," said Booze, a grin lurking at the corners of his mouth. "Think you can manage that, Potts?"

Several hours alone with Frances. *Can I ever!*

"It'll be a struggle, but we'll manage," said Alvin.

Booze was scarcely out of the room when Al urged Frances to perch beside him.

Her hands, bird bone thin except for her work-enlarged knuckles, were warm in his. He intended to keep this visit on the up and up. No sending a frustrated or guilty wife home today. He began to tell her about the two women who were regular visitors of Irv's, the one he now knew was the man's wife and the perky little evening visitor he had mistaken for his wife.

"I can't figure out why he hasn't introduced either to us," said Al. "Not that he has to, but it's something we usually do. He never visits with them in the room; always takes them away. He seems to get a big kick out of the younger one. They always go off laughing. His wife...Arlene?...does look sad or maybe she's worried. We see a lot of that in this place. I thought maybe she was sick, too, the way he handles her so carefully."

"Carefully? How is that?"

"Gentle may be what I mean, like she might break. When I saw him escort her from the room the first time, I thought of those china cups your grandma keeps in that glass cabinet in the sitting room. The ones so thin you can see right through when you hold them to the light."

"Well, I can tell you Arlene is no china cup! She may look frail, but you should have seen her yanking out weeds. That's all her back yard was, weeds! She has it all cleaned out and I'm giving her some flower seeds from mom's garden. Arlene and I are talking about putting in a vegetable garden together. She has enough room for both of us, she said."

"You're right. She doesn't sound like china cup material."

After they had explored all the possible plantings for the combined garden and the repairs that John might do to Arlene's rental, Al asked Frances how Lily was settling in.

Al had no driving need to know what Lily was or was not doing, but he was anxious to keep his wife talking. So far he had kept his baser instincts under control, and hoped to do so through this final visiting hour, but the play of fabric over Frances' breasts as her torso twisted to and fro was not lost on Al. The neckline of her dress was cut just low enough so a hint of creamy curve was revealed as the material pulled this way and that. He felt himself hardening.

"Tell me what new words Baby has learned?" he said in a frantic effort to take his mind off what was happening below his non-existent belt.

"Well, at dinner last night, Frances Pearl asked for a second wiener and, when I told her they were all gone, she pointed to one on Lily's plate and said, 'No they aren't. There's one!' Lily and I had a good laugh over that."

Al smiled appreciatively. Then, as the front of Frances' dress took another dangerous dip, he quickly asked, "And Herbie? What's that little devil been up to?"

Unfortunately, Frances' kid brother had been on his best behavior. Thinking quickly, Al had only to ask "How are you making out with the Wilsons?" to get Frances started on little Charlie Wilson's latest lark.

The drone of his wife's voice was background to the thoughts of stickery nettles, thumbs being smashed with hammers and chalk screeching across a blackboard that Al conjured up for more dire distraction. When her raised voice finally caught his attention, he realized Frances was fuming over the latest demand made by Charlie's grandpa.

"First that old man wanted me to wash out his spittoon and now he wants me to clean his dentures after every meal. I think that's going too far."

Frances' voice was spiraling upward as she grew more agitated.

"I know I get paid to take care of the household, but there's a limit, don't you think?" She did not wait for an answer.

"That's a big old house with a jillion windows to be washed inside and out, and there's a bathroom around every corner that needs swamped out every day. I mop and wax and cook and dust, and I iron everyone's clothes. If that isn't enough, Mr. Wilson comes along and wants all the silver that no one ever uses polished to a tee, and then Grandpa decides I'm just the one to polish his set of ivories!

"It's hard, Al. It's so hard!"

"How hard is it?" Al said without thinking, his voice harsh with pent-up emotion.

"Is it this hard?" He grabbed her hand and thrust it against his erection that was rooted so deep inside him it was a physical pain and had been for the past hour.

Her eyes widened in shock. Blotches of red bloomed on her cheeks, and she bit her lips to hold back tears.

Al could not believe what he had done. The shock he saw on her face he felt in his bones. *Ah, what a dirty dad I am.* He became aware of the tight grip he had on her wrist. Slowly, he released her. Just as slowly she pulled her hand away.

"I don't know what got into me, Pal. Can you ever..." He broke off in the middle of his apology as Irv entered the room alone.

Ignoring his roommate, Alvin reached to Frances, but she slid off the bed, keeping her back to the room as she dabbed at her face. When she turned back, her eyes were brighter than usual and the color higher on her cheeks, but Alvin didn't think Woods noticed anything amiss. He motioned for her to come back to his side, and was grateful when she did. He laid his hand, palm up, on the sheet.

After a bit, Frances laid her hand in it, and he closed his fingers gently around hers. She bent to kiss his cheek.

"I'm sorry, sweetheart," he whispered, with his lips smothered in her hair. "Can you forgive your dirty dad?"

Her brow bumped against his shoulder. He felt that the small gesture was more than he deserved.

> *Temp 97.7*
> *"   98.6*
> *Please Dear God*
> *forgive me for*
> *being so unkind*
> *to my lovely*
> *Frances. She is so*
> *good to me and*
> *then I do her the*
> *way I do. I am*
> *heartily sorry. Al.*

Chapter 133

Al spent all of the next morning castigating himself for his selfish behavior of the day before.

His greatest sin, he felt, was the way he had totally brushed aside the struggles Frances had finally confided to him. Yesterday's complaints were the first she had ever raised about the life she was living without him. And he hadn't listened. He had allowed his petty needs to override his good sense. He wouldn't blame Frances if she never came back to visit him.

God knows, the livelihood of his family should be his responsibility, and yet his wife had shouldered that responsibility without a murmur...until yesterday. He could kick himself for his insensitivity. But there was nothing he could do about it now.

What's done is done. Yet, he had to live with this burning knot of embarrassment and regret that was twisting like a knife into his gut. *What a fool I am. What a damn fool dirty dad.* He did not need this gnawing at his vitals to remind him of his stupidity, but he welcomed it as a flagellant accepts the whip, reluctantly, but recognizing the necessity for penance. He did not expect to hear from Frances today or tomorrow, and he would be surprised if she showed up on Wednesday. He was pretty sure there would be no letters.

May 17
Monday
Temp 97.2
"   98.2
My Darling Frances
I love you and beg
your forgiveness for
making you sad and
unhappy. I am always

sorry and wish I
could die. I really
don't want to die. I
want to come home
to you. I am coming
home very shortly.
I am very lonesome
for you all the time.Al.

Frances did not place a call to Alvin Monday or Tuesday, and she thought long and hard before making the complicated arrangements that were necessary for her to take three hours off in the middle of her work day. But when Wednesday came Baby was safe in Ida's keeping, the stay-at-home Wilson children were napping under their grandpa's watchful eye, and Frances was bumping her way out to the sanatorium in Ida's car.

She had their bank book with her. She had taken advantage of the two hours Baker-Boyer was open on Saturday to make the latest deposit, but had forgotten to show it to Alvin on Sunday. Frances had been pleased to learn their account had already earned seventy-nine cents in interest, and even more pleased with herself that she had been able to deposit another fifty dollars this month.

Frances also was bringing Alvin a fan she had bought to cool his room, and a book Lily had offered to send to him after she had declined Frances invitation to come along. In spite of Lily's reluctance to visit Al in the san, which irked Frances, she did think their living arrangement was working out fairly well. While Frances could make a bed or wash dishes in half the time it took Lily, she appreciated that her sister-in-law was willing to do her share.

Frances had given some thought as to how she would approach this visit with her husband. Lily would have made a nice buffer. With his sister along, it might have been easy to pretend nothing had happened Sunday. On her own, Frances felt a different tack would have to be taken. Some acknowledgement would be necessary.

Frances regretted that she had complained to Alvin, but only because she knew there was nothing he could do to change things. She did feel she had a legitimate gripe and he could at least have listened to it. Well, she had aired it, and it went right over his head.

Remembering what she had expected of her husband and what his reaction had really been, she couldn't help but giggle.

It was kind of nice that he still felt that way about her. But his behavior had startled her, and it was a really crude thing for him to do. Grabbing her hand like that and putting it *there* in broad daylight when anyone could have seen. That wasn't like Al at all.

She giggled again, a nervous giggle, thinking how it would have been if Mr. Woods had come into the room just a minute sooner. If he had, and if he had seen what Al was doing, she didn't know if she would ever have had the courage to go back into that room.

But he hadn't, and here she was! *Going back into the lion's den with the hungry animal.* Frances giggled again. Gosh, couldn't she and Al have a good time together if he were well enough to go home! This old sex thing was getting tiresome…for both of them. She didn't quite understand how it was for a man, but Al's urges seemed stronger than hers. She knew that she had yearnings, and sometimes they *were* pretty strong, but she could always work them off—scrub the floor, wash the windows, or tackle the ironing.

Frances thought maybe she should consider her work in the Woods household a blessing instead of complaining about it. By the end of the day she was pretty well tuckered out. Ida said men had to work off a lot more energy than women did before the urge for *that* left them. And even then, Ida said, men still didn't quit *thinking* about it.

Since exercise is out of the question for Al, he's kind of caught between a rock and a hard place. Frances giggled again, and was promptly ashamed of herself for making light, even mentally, of a predicament that was causing so much frustration for her husband, for both of them really.

Now that she'd had time to think about it, Frances came to the conclusion that Sunday was nobody's fault. She and Al had just been on different engines running on the same track, head-on into each other. Her job today was to put them on the same train, heading in the same direction. If she could do that, she just knew their way would be smooth from now on and he would be home with her soon.

May 19
Wednesday
Temp 97.4
"   99
Today has been
a very nice visiting
day. Frances and I
had a swell time
together. She is
plenty sweet to her
old daddy. She visits
so nice. She brings
me just anything
I ask her for. It
seems I ask for plenty.al

May 20
Thursday
Temp 97.4
"   98
This idea of taking
temps at 3:30 is all
hooey. After a sleep
of about an hour and
a half or two hours
one's resistance is
too low to run even
a normal temp.
Sometimes I think
they are completely
nuts around here. Just
an experiment station.
We are the experimentation.

May 21
Friday
Temp 98

" 99
I don't feel very good
tonight. Have rather
a cold in both head
and lungs. It has been
pretty hot today. I
had a nice long talk
with wife and baby
last night. Tonight I
should say. I love them
with all my heart. Al.

May 22-23
Saturday & Sunday
Temp 97.2
" 98.6
I feel just a little
better tonight. I
will feel better when
I get to see my darling
wife tomorrow.

"I don't know why I can't go see Alvin. Everybody else gets to. It isn't fair," whined Herbie.

Frances did not have time for a cranky kid brother. She was hurrying through chores so she could leave for the san as soon as Ida returned from cleaning the KUJ radio station, a job she usually tackled on Saturday nights but which Ida had to postpone until this morning because a going-away party for a staff member had been held there last night. In exchange for riding herd on Ray and Herbie and preparing the Sunday meal at Ida's, Frances would get the use of her mother's Ford this afternoon and tonight.

Frances was anxious to walk into Alvin's room right on time. So far she was on schedule. Ida was due back in fifteen minutes, and Frances figured that would be just enough time for the boys to skin out of their muddy clothes and change into something dry. They had spent the morning playing in the creek that cut through Chestnut Street at the end of the alley, and they looked it. Frances had pies cooling on the kitchen counter and a pot roast in the oven, browning nicely in its nest of potatoes, onions and carrots. The baby was down for her nap, so all she had left to do was whip off her apron and run a comb through her hair. But Herbie's whining, which had escalated to an insistent demand, was threatening to throw her schedule out of kilter.

"You can not go, so straighten up, behave yourself, and get out of those wet clothes," Frances ordered.

"Not fair," he muttered, but she let Herbie have the last word because she intended to make sure that it was his last word.

The boys peeled off their soggy coveralls, dropped them in a heap on the porch, and pushed and shoved their way into the house, oblivious to their near-naked state.

When Ida drove up, Ray and Herbie were standing on the porch, shiny faced and dressed in clean coveralls. Frances was already hurrying down the sidewalk to meet her mother at the curb.

"Looks as if you have everything under control," Ida said.

"Dinner's in the oven, pies on the counter, Frances Pearl and Grandma are napping," said Frances, accepting a quick hug from her mother.

"Well, what have we here?" Ida asked, peering over Frances' shoulder.

Herbie was staggering toward them, bowed under the weight of a dishpan he was carrying in his arms.

"I got a present for Alvin," the youngster said.

Water sloshed onto Herbie's bare feet as he extended the pan for their inspection.

It was covered with a wire screen. Peering through the mesh, Ida and Frances exchanged looks, Frances' dubious and Ida's verging on laughter.

"Oh yes, Son, I know Alvin is going to be thrilled with this gift," said Ida.

Frances nudged her mother in the ribs with a sharp elbow and said, "Sure, Mom, Alvin is going to think this is just *tremendous*." In spite of her misgivings, Frances opened the car door and placed the pan on the floorboards where it would be less likely to spill.

Temp 97.4
"   99 Expenditures $1
My wife was here and

we had a wonderful time. She brought me a lot of things. She always brings me whatever I want. She is all good. Al.

May 24
Monday
Temp 97.8
"   98.6
It is warmer today. Just about 85 not too hot nor too cool. I enjoy just right weather. My wife brought me some tadpoles, pollywogs, or baby frogs. They have two legs and are keen to watch. Al.

Chapter 134

"We've been over this ground before. No matter how many times we plow it, it's never going to produce for us."

"Now what kind of talk is that?" said Docey.

He directed his words to the back of Ida's neck, which, in his opinion, was just as stiff as it had ever been when he tried to talk turkey to her.

"Plain talk! Straight talk! Sensible talk! Take your pick, Docey, but get it through your head once and for all there is never, and I mean never, going to be any more between us than there already is. Friends! That's what we are and that's all we are ever going to be to each other."

She stamped her foot for emphasis, poised at curbside with her back still turned to him.

"Now, Ida, you know we've got more than that going for us," he wheedled.

She whirled to face him, as ruffled as a barnyard hen.

"I don't know any such thing! And if you think we do, then have another think!"

"Well, girl, I sure as hell would like to have something more. Wouldn't you?"

"No! I am not about to break up anyone's home, and you shouldn't be thinking of doing anything that would make that happen," snapped Ida.

"What home?"

"Don't be giving me any of that. You've got a home. You've got a wife."

"Some home. Some wife," Docey grumbled.

"All that's left is for you to tell me she doesn't understand you. Then I'll have heard it all."

"Oh, she understands me all right. I can't claim she doesn't. If she doesn't, it wouldn't be for my lack of telling her what makes me tick. I've always been up front with her, Ida. I told you she just plumb doesn't care what I do or who I do it with, as long as I don't do it with her. We have nothing in common. Never did. And don't ask me why we got married because I couldn't tell you if my life depended on it. The only thing she asks of me is that I sit in front of the radio with her on Saturday nights and at the dinner table on Sundays, and it's getting so she isn't that particular about Sundays."

Docey was a picture of dejection as he slumped behind the wheel of his truck, fingers tattooing nervously on the steering wheel.

Ida took a reluctant step forward.

They had just returned from Milton-Freewater, the small town over the Oregon state line, where Docey had picked up some alfalfa seed. It had been a pleasant enough drive until Docey had raised an age-old question Ida thought she had settled long ago. She really did not feel like re-hashing it today, but she knew she had to put paid to it or say goodbye to this friendship that had come to mean so much to her.

A few halting steps brought her to within reach of the truck.

Ida gripped the edge of the door where Docey had the window rolled down, and let her weight fall back until her arms were fully extended. She swung there, her face drawing close to his where it was framed by the door, then away. Back and forth, until he finally raised his head. Their eyes met. She gave him a smile and held it until his brow unfurrowed. He forced a grin.

"You're sure? Just friends?"

"I'm sure."

"You won't change your mind? Even if she'll let go?"

"Sure as shootin'."

"It is what it is then, isn't it?" Docey said.

"That it is."

"Well shit!" He thumped the steering wheel with a clenched fist, and slammed his forehead into an upraised hand.

His fingers rubbed through his hair in frustration, pushing his felt hat backwards off his head. Ida caught it as it fell. She smoothed his rumpled hair with a quick hand, and tipped the hat back into place.

"There you go, my friend," she said. "Off with you!"

Ida rapped her knuckles briskly against the door, and turned away. She was nearly to the porch when Docey called out, "I have to pick up some pullets tomorrow. Want to ride along?"

She turned and stared at him in disbelief.

He grinned.

"As friends. Just as friends. Promise! Scout's Honor!"

They were both laughing as he drove away.

"I think this may be the start of a beautiful friendship," Ida murmured to herself as she entered her house, being careful not to slam the screen door behind her.

Chapter 135

May 25
Tuesday
Temp 97.4
"   98.6
Of course tomorrow
is visiting day and
I love to think of it
as <u>my</u> day. I love my
wife and baby.

May 26
Wednesday
Temp 97.6
"   99
My wife and baby
Frances were out.
Baby for just a
short while and
Frances for all
afternoon. We
couldn't seem to
be able to think of
anything to say. We
love each other so
much we don't have
to say anything. We
are very happy when
we are together.

As he finished that entry, Al wondered if he was trying to

convince himself. There *had* been a few awkward silences this afternoon.

May 27
Thursday
Temp 97.8
" 98.8
It was warmer
today than it
has been lately.
Docey was in to
see me. I am
already lonesome
for my own Frances.
She is good to me
and loves me. I
sure appreciate
that. I will always
know she has been
true to me.
Her husband. Al.

Al could think of no good reason to tell Frances that Docey had sneaked in to see him on a non-visiting day, and, furthermore, he had no intention of telling her what had been bothering the would-be Romeo.

May 28
Friday
Temp 97.2
" 98
I pray that I can be
with my Frances
this time next year.
Two years is so long
to have to stay away
from the woman you
love. I sure love her
and need her with

*all my heart. Why
can't we be together?*

May 29-30
Saturday & Sunday
*(Memorial Day)
Temp 97.4
"   97.6
Just one more day
until I can see my
Frances. I called my
darling on the phone
this evening. Al.
Temp 97.2
"   99
It won't be long
to wait now. I
love my wife and
baby girl. They
are so good to
daddy. Al*

May 31
Monday
*Temp 97.2
"   97.8
This is also a
visiting day. My
Frances is coming
out to see me tonight.
I told her not to come
out this afternoon.
She has to work too
hard to come out in
the afternoon unless
she has the rest of
the day off. I love
her and want her
all the time. She is
my idol. Al.*

"Hey, Booze, what does it mean when your temp won't even reach normal?"

"Ask your doctor, Potts. Ask your doctor."

Chapter 136

"What? You don't like raisins in your tapioca pudding?" Woods asked, laughing.

He had just removed the cover from his lunch meal, but Booze and Al were still batting at the flies buzzing around their trays.

The screens on the windows were not doing their job. Room 102 was thick with the fat, black, dive-bombing insects. Long coils of brown, sticky flypaper dangling in front of the windows and over the doors had trapped a number of them, but their frantic buzzing and bodies thrashing in the last throes of death were doing nothing for Al's appetite. He had already ordered a flyswatter, but Annie had not yet brought it to him. Booze was doing what he could with a rolled up magazine, but Woods was accepting the attack as if it were the joke of the season.

"Darn things are about a foot deep over here," Al complained.

As Booze and Al whacked away and neglected their food, Woods' fork dipped rhythmically in and out, gathering up mashed potatoes and gravy interspersed with forkfuls of liver and onions. His right hand did not miss a beat as the left continuously swished away flies. Chuckles accompanied the choreographed moves that would have made a dance team proud.

Al never lifted the lid from his food, just shoved the fly-laden tray away in disgust.

Booze pushed his away, too, and got out of bed. He belted his robe around him as he marched out of the room.

"Looks like our partner's going on the war path," remarked Woods, still shoveling and swishing.

Remembering the stack of blankets Booze had brought back the last time he left the room in a huff, Al hoped for the best, but didn't expect more than another strip of the loathsome flypaper. He resigned himself to doing without lunch.

The flies had followed the food, so Al had his bed pretty much to himself as he settled down with the calendar. He fingered the minute pages and again tried to guess Flora's intent at presenting him with such a small writing surface. So far, it had forced him to express his emotions and daily events in the briefest way possible, perfect a handwriting style that, while cramped, was still legible, and, above all, keep the lead in his pencil razor sharp. But Al suspected Flora had something beyond these things in mind when she chose this calendar for him to use as a daily reminder. He would get to the bottom of it sooner or later.

In spite of the fly infestation, Al felt pretty good today. Annie had recorded a morning temperature of 97 degrees for him, and, with the thermometer outside his window registering just 88 degrees, this Tuesday was shaping up to be one of the better days, *if* Booze brought back some fly relief. Al inscribed his below normal temp on the calendar page for June 1.

"If it doesn't get any hotter than this, I could stand the summer all right," Al said, tossing the words out even as he wrote them down.

"How about you, Irv?" Al asked.

"I'm with you on that. But whatever we get, we'd better take because it's all we'll have," said Woods, scooping up the last of his pudding.

Alvin wasn't sure if Irv was talking about the weather or the food he had just consumed.

Whichever it was, Al thought Woods had the right attitude. At least he had some nutrition under his belt, while Al only felt hollow along his belt line. No matter. He just could not eat while fighting off flies. He saw that they were still buzzing around the dishes, a repulsive sight, but better than having them flutter into his hair or walk across his nose.

"I admire your attitude, Woods," Al said. "I wish I could be as cheerful as you are all the time."

"Any man who has a wife as pretty as yours should be smiling all the time. Never saw such a blossom of a woman. You're one lucky man, Potts!"

Al examined the words to see if offense was intended. There wasn't a hint of a leer on Woods' face, only a smile that Al couldn't read. He thought Irv's expression could signify appreciation, or, just as easily, a gentle reproach.

"I could do with a lot more of her company, that's for sure," Al said.

"Well, we all could! She just lights up the room when she comes in. A sunflower, that's what the little lady is, a veritable sunflower among us weeds!"

How did Frances get into this? Al did not feel comfortable with the direction the conversation was taking. He sought to change it.

"What's the philosophy behind all those smiles, if you don't mind me asking?"

"Don't mind at all. It's beauty! Strictly beauty, Potts. That's it in a nutshell."

"How so?"

"Think of beauty like it was rain. Just like a thirsty tree soaks up the rain and flourishes, I soak up beauty. I thrive on it. And it's easy to come by. Why, it's everywhere and it's free for the taking. You *might* find it in a cloud, a flower or a bright yellow, harvest moon. But you'll darn sure find it in a woman. Why, I've found even an ugly woman doesn't disappoint. If she has a face that would stop a clock, look at her ankle, I say. If the ankle is thicker'n a fence post, check out the wrist. You keep looking and I guarantee there will be a spot of beauty somewhere that will lift your spirits."

"Are you pulling my leg?' Alvin asked.

"Skeptical, are you?" Woods said.

"I think you're having fun with me," said Al.

"Try it! Try it for yourself and see if you don't get a rise."

Al shot a suspicious look Irv's way. Innocence shone on the man's face.

"Perhaps a poor choice of words there, Potts. Meant nothing by it, I assure you. All I'm saying is that when one is surrounded by beauty, life becomes beautiful. You asked, and I'm telling you. Beauty is what motivates me, what keeps me happy."

A burp exploded from Woods' lips as if in punctuation. He looked surprised, and then laughed. After a second, Al joined in.

"Glad to see someone thinks something is funny around here," said Booze, returning to their laughter. "Think this will solve our problem?" he said, holding up a coil of flypaper.

"Beautiful, just beautiful," Alvin said, still laughing.
"Well, you can't win 'em all," Booze said.

The following day was the hottest of the year so far at 93 degrees. Frances came in wearing a sleeveless dress, and Alvin found much to call beautiful, not the least the soft curve of her shoulders. He was glad Woods had scurried out of the room again with his wife. *Let him soak up whatever beauty he finds there, and leave my wife to me.*

"When you are here, I don't want anyone else around," Al whispered to Frances as Irv and Arlene exited the room. "I don't ever want anyone anyway. I don't crave company," he added, looking over at the group around Booze's bed. "They are such a bore," he said, as heated opinions from that quarter flew thick and fast about a recent stockyard strike in East St. Louis, Illinois. But when Rodney passed around a photograph he had taken of a tractor mired in a newly seeded alfalfa field at Lowden, just west of Walla Walla, Alvin stretched out a hand for his turn to take a look.

"I know this place," he said, turning to Frances. "This farm gets its water from the Burlingame Ditch."

"Right-o! And it was a plethora of that irrigation water that sunk the machine," said Rodney, pushing his eyeglasses higher on his nose. "You should have seen them trying to extricate the monster from the mud. Fence posts and planks shoved in with the hope of providing a solid footing splintered like toothpicks and were completely buried in the mire. It was quite a sight. For two days people from town trooped out to watch them do battle. They finally got wise and turned off the water and let the ground dry out overnight."

"Never would have happened if Dad was still on the job," Alvin commented.

When Frances left, Al watched her skirt flutter around her legs as she walked to the car. The same gentle wind that lifted her hem began to stir through the trees. By evening the trees were bending under its increasing force, and the flies had abandoned the room.

Alvin's temperature, which was 97.2 in the morning, finally reached normal by the time Annie recorded it for the second time. He noticed that his temp always seemed slightly elevated after a visit from his wife. Even though they did nothing strenuous, he always felt as if they had played hard.

June 3
Thursday
Temp 97.8
"   98
The wind is blowing
pretty hard today. We
sure are having a fine
dust storm. I think
most of Wallula has
blown by and am
expecting to see the
Columbia River Gorge
go by most any time
now.   Al.

The ward came awake with a jolt Friday morning. Al had been awake an hour before the earth quaked at six-thirty. The beds jiggled, water glasses tinkled, and window shades rattled. Alvin, now an old hand when it came to earthquakes, turned over and went back to sleep. That evening he gave the quake only passing mention in his diary.

June 4
Friday
Temp 97.2
"   98
The wind is still
blowing. We felt a
small quake here
about 6:30 this
morning. Of course
I am looking forward
to talking to Frances
this Eve. She didn't
say she would call
but I know she loves
me and wants to hear

me say hello pal. Al.

"Booze, that shaking up didn't do a thing to my temperature. Annie said it is still six points shy of normal. What do you make of that?"

"Ask your…"

"I hear you, Booze. I hear you."

"You two are a hoot!" said Woods. His laughter started deep in his throat and spiraled until it became a witch's cackle that set off Booze and Al.

"Someone's going to be hauled out of here if this keeps up," said Al, when the laughter died down.

June 5-6
Saturday & Sunday
Temp 97.4
"   98.8
I had a nice long talk
with Frances and baby
last night. I am so lonesome
for my sweetheart.
Temp 97.4
"   99
Frances was out all
during visiting hours.
She wasn't feeling well.
I hope she is taking
care of herself. She
sure is the sweetest
wife a man ever had. Al

June 7
Monday
Temp 97.6
"   98
The wind is blowing
plenty hard. It almost
blew me away during
rest period. Mr. Noel

left to go home this
afternoon. It was kinda
a forced departure. The
sheriff came after him.
Also county nurse.

"Daddy, I 'melled somesing."

"You what?"

"I 'melled somesing not nice."

Alvin held the telephone tightly to his ear, trying to understand what his baby was saying to him. He enjoyed these calls from Frances. In addition to being a part of his family for a few minutes, the calls gave him an excuse to leave his bed. Tonight she had put their baby on the line to tell him about the circus they had gone to that afternoon, but Alvin was not understanding her at all.

"Frances, what is she trying to tell me?" Alvin asked, knowing his wife had her ear pressed next to the telephone.

Laughter came softly over the wire. "She's telling you she *smelled* something. And she knows what she's talking about!" Frances said, breaking into laughter again.

"When the elephants paraded around the ring, one of them deposited a steaming surprise right in front of us. *That* is what she is telling you. She smelled something."

June 8
Tuesday
Temp 97.4
"   98.4
I had a very fine
talk with my two
Franceses this evening.
Lily had a word or two.
Frances didn't sound
as if she felt very well.
I pray to Our Dear God
that she will be all right.
They went to the circus.

Al smiled to himself as he wrote the last line. God, what he wouldn't give to be out in the world, even if it meant getting a whiff of elephant shit.

Chapter 137

It was surprising to see how much beauty was around, if you took the time to look for it. Since Irv had outlined his philosophy, Al had been taking his advice to heart. If Woods was just having fun at his expense, so be it. The fact was, this search for beauty seemed to be working.

Take today for instance. It was a visiting day, sure, and Al knew his spirits were always high on that day, but even breakfast became more appealing when Al concentrated on the curl of steam rising from his coffee cup. The faint trail of moisture through the still air began to waver in waltz time as it was stirred by the slightest of breezes. Immediately Alvin felt the pressure of his wife's fingertips on his shoulder, a pleasant memory from their dancing days. Maybe that's what Woods meant. Maybe this beauty hunt led to more than what was right before your eyes.

With strains of the *The Merry Widow Waltz* floating in his head, Al eagerly scooped up his scrambled eggs.

This morning's coffee was not the only bit of beauty that had hit Alvin in the eye this past week. At first it was a shadow cast on the wall by the sun filtering through the window screen, then the speckles on Herbie's burgeoning frogs, and, late one night, the moonlight silvering Christina's hair.

The list was endless.

Keeping an eye out for such innocuous things gave a purpose to Al's days that was missing before. He wondered if Frances would be wearing that sleeveless dress again. In her telephone call last night she said she would be here both afternoon and evening. But there were hours to get through before he could expect her. A good read and lunch would take up the time. Then, of course, there was always rest period. Annie would be in to draw the shades and remind them that they were expected to sleep for a good hour at least before visitors descended. Sometimes Al could sleep, but often not when worries he could do nothing about plagued him. Nothing felt as good as sinking quietly into darkness unencumbered by dreams. And nothing felt worse when that release eluded him.

Frances was not wearing the sleeveless dress when Ida dropped her off. Instead, a flounce of lace on her blouse edged a mere suggestion of sleeves that barely cupped her shoulders. With the floral patterned top she wore a slim white skirt that brushed her calves, a length that Alvin thought had gone out of style. Alvin thought it looked so well on his wife that the style should make a come-back. Her tiny waist was emphasized by a gold-buckled pink belt that picked up one of the colors in her blouse. No effort here to look for beauty. It was spread from head to toe.

"You are becoming something of a fashion plate, Sweetheart," he said as he drew Frances into his arms.

It was an embrace that would be seen only by Booze, if he had been looking.

That was another good thing about having Booze as a roommate. He knew when to fade into the wallpaper. Booze became near invisible when Frances arrived. Woods, of course, had disappeared as usual, which was also convenient.

Booze's visitors began to straggle in. There were no faces familiar to Al among this bunch, he saw, but, beyond that Al took no more notice of Booze's company than his roommate did of him and Frances.

The hum of conversation from that corner of the room only lent a more private aspect to his tête-à-tête with his wife. As they held hands, she filled him in on their afternoon at the circus, and they laughed again at the embarrassment their child had caused Frances when she had loudly declaimed her stinky discovery for everyone seated around them to hear.

"I can laugh now," said Frances, "but it wasn't funny yesterday. I was praying no one would understand what she was saying, and you should have seen Lily trying to pretend she wasn't with us. Poor girl. I'm sure she will never go to another circus with us!"

Alvin told Frances how he had been practicing Irv's

philosophy and how much he was enjoying himself. "Do you think he was just pulling my leg?" he asked her. They mulled that over for awhile. As they did so, Alvin carefully refrained from mentioning Irv's comments about finding beauty in women. That was one aspect of his neighbor's philosophy better left alone. If Frances even *thought* she was under Woods' inspection when she entered this room, she would be a reluctant visitor.

Alvin was sure Woods' motives, in regards to Frances, were pure, but he did not care to defend them either.

They exhausted one topic after another, until Al noticed *that* look.

Something was up. But what?

"Something on your mind, Sweetheart?" he asked.

"It's just that I've been thinking…"

"Yes?"

"The cannery is hiring."

"Oh, Frances, no. I don't want Lily working there."

"I wasn't thinking about Lily, Al. I thought I might get on a night shift. Lily could stay at home with Frances Pearl."

"Sweetheart! If I don't want Lily working at a cannery, I surely do not want my wife in that environment. The cannery is no place for a lady."

"Al, the way I look at it, a lady can go wherever she wants, as long as she remembers she is a lady. Anyway, I know lots of women who work there and no one ever bothers them. The cannery isn't as bad as you make it out to be."

"Well, you already have a job. What about the Wilsons?"

"Working for the Wilsons is steady work. I wouldn't give that up. I thought I could just work a season at the cannery. You know, maybe through peas and carrots or spinach. If I could hire on to a night shift, I could still work at the Wilsons during the day."

"And when would you sleep?" Alvin's tone was dry, just short of sarcastic.

They spent the rest of the visiting hour batting around Frances' plan. Al used every argument he could think of against it, but they had settled nothing by the time Ida marched through the door. And it *was* a march that Ida was doing, dressed in her full drill team uniform.

"Where's the parade?" Alvin quipped.

"Down at Fourth and Alder on Friday night, Smarty Pants!"
Ida shot back. "I got all duded up today just for you. This is a little
preview. Our Eagles Auxiliary's drill team is going to march and
perform in the softball parade before the city league's tournament
at the stadium. What do you think?" she asked, turning around so
he could get a look at her from all sides.

"Pretty snazzy," complimented Al.

Ida did cut a fine figure in her uniform. The crisp lines
flattered her generous proportions, the cut of it making the most of
curves while minimizing what Grandma Hempe would call her
heinie.

Alvin started to put his thoughts into words. "Ida, you are
truly…"

"A fine figure of womanhood we have here! What's the
occasion?" The interruption was Woods, who entered the room
and began to walk an appreciative circle around Alvin's mother-
in-law. Instead of standing passively, Ida rotated herself so she
continued to face the little man, who was smiling from ear to ear,
face flushed and eyes shining, as they stepped off their circular
dance.

Oho! Now the fat's in the fire.

Alvin waited for the eruption he was sure would follow Irv's
searching look.

Ida's forefinger shot out like an arrow from its bow.

"Now you hold it right there, Mister!" she said. Her finger
pointing directly at his chest anchored Woods as solidly in place
as if she had nailed him to the floor.

Woods shook his own finger at her, much in the fashion of a
mother warning a naughty child.

"Whoa, yourself!" he said. "What right do you have coming in
here looking like a million dollars, getting our hopes up, and
knowing you'll do nothing but break our hearts?"

Ida burst out laughing, and Woods fell upon her, alternately
hugging and then shaking her like a rag doll.

"They know each other," Frances said, laughing at the look on
Alvin's face.

"All Eagles are feathered friends," Woods said.

"We are old friends," Ida said, explaining that she had met
Arlene and Irv at an Eagles convention, and had competed against

Arlene's drill team in past contests.

"Arlene and I are going to go to the parade together Friday. The Walla Walla Girls Drum and Bugle Corps will march in it along with the softball teams, and, of course, we want to see Mom's team drill," said Frances.

"Now that's going to be something to see!" enthused Woods, giving Ida another squeeze. "Arlene told me she would like to get on the drill team here after she gets settled and whenever there is an opening."

"We'll be lucky to have her," said Ida.

'Well, small world,' Al thought, and wondered what Irv's little sad sack of a wife would look like in a drill team uniform.

When Frances came back for evening visitation, they resumed their talk where they had left off, debating the pros and cons of a young mother holding down two jobs while her husband lay idly by. When she left the san, Al was still not sure what, if anything, had been decided. He relegated his feelings on the subject to his diary.

June 9
Wednesday
Temp 97.6
"   98.6
My true love was
here and I played
so hard. Still I
didn't have a temp.
Do you suppose
Frances that I am
really getting better?
I pray to god to be
with you before I die. Al.

June 10
Thursday
Temp 97.8
"   98.2
We have a very fine

day. It has rained most
all day. I hope we have
some more tonight. I
think my Frances is
going to work at the
cannery. I wish she
wouldn't. I love you
my true pal. Al.

Chapter 138

June 11
Friday
Temp 97.8
"   98.4
I am fine and lonesome
for my lovely wife.
Dear God bring me
to her. I need her.
I need my mate.
Just as she must
need me. I thought
I would get to talk
to her tonite but
I guess she is gone
to work. God have
mercy on her. I love
her. Al.

The house was quiet, save for the ticking of Frances' alarm clock and baby's breath sighing rhythmically in and out. Frances Pearl still slept in a crib, and it was an arm's length from where Frances lay, trying to fall asleep.

If she could manage that right off, she could get in four solid hours of sleep before she had to get up to go to work at the cannery. Baby was accustomed to going to bed by 6:30, but Frances wasn't. She was determined to get used to it, though, and quickly.

The alarm was set for 10:30. Everything was ready, lunch packed, clothes laid out, including rubber boots, hair net and rubber gloves. She had already sprinkled baby powder in the gloves, so they would slip on easily. The walk to the cannery shouldn't take her more than fifteen minutes. It would not do to be late her first night on the 11 to 7 shift.

Frances was still mentally running down her to-do list, when sleep descended.

Her Big Ben jangled her awake, pulling her from a dreamless sleep. It took her a moment to remember why she was waking up in the middle of the night, but, as soon as she did, she was raring to go. She was anxious to start this second job, but she had not expected the adrenalin rush that made getting up in the dead of night so exciting.

Frances straightened the covers around her, so they were in place when she crawled out. All she had to do was give the bedspread a tug and plump the pillows.

On her way to the bathroom, she set the coffee pot on the still-hot wood stove. She had timed it just right. By the time she dressed, pulled the bobby pins out of her hair, brushed out the pin curls and settled the results neatly under her hair net, the coffee was ready. She poured a thermos full, removed her lunch out of the ice box, and tip-toed in to cast a last glance on her sleeping daughter. She settled a blanket closer around her, and pulled the bedroom door almost closed. Cracked open as it was, Lily would hear Frances Pearl if she woke before morning. In their small house, Lily's bed on the davenport was only a few steps away.

Frances fastened her jacket close around her as she stepped out of the house into the brisk breeze that was sweeping the darkened street. West Poplar, overshadowed with trees that were as old as the city, lay ahead like an unknown trail through a forest. The wind-flicked trees swayed overhead and played hide-and-seek with the halos of dim, yellow light from the street lamps. Frances hurried along the sidewalk, plunging in and out of the deep shadows, the only pedestrian on the street. She was glad when she came to the busier, more traveled Ninth Street and could put the dark street behind her. She still had a ways to go, but the blocks seemed to melt away along this brighter route. As she drew near the cannery, she was no longer alone on the street.

Frances recognized several women. Unlike her, they walked in pairs. Cars were also wheeling into the parking lot, either dropping people off or pulling into spaces. While some men and women streamed into the cannery, others were gathering around the office door. She knew those people were waiting until the shift changed in hopes of being put to work if employees did not show up for work on time. Frances had been lucky. On her first visit to the office yesterday, she had been hired for this graveyard shift.

Sorting peas turned out to be a wet job, but not particularly messy. With a few quick words, the floor lady, looking like a nurse in her white uniform, introduced Frances to the sorting process she would use to remove pebbles, dirt and nightshade from the freshly picked peas that passed before the sorters over moving belts. There was nothing complicated about the job, the floor lady told her, but the sorters were expected to keep their hands moving and their fingers picking so the peas would be free of debris by the time they reached the end of the belt.

"And no sleeping on the job!" she warned.

Frances wondered how anyone could fall asleep with that mass of green moving so rapidly along in front of them and cold water dripping down in a steady stream.

Thank God for the rubber apron, gloves and boots.

Frances intoned the words as a sincere prayer while the cold bit into her hands and feet. Tomorrow night her socks would be wool ones.

Women were stationed on both sides of the belt, facing each other. The idea, Frances quickly learned, was for belt partners to share the sorting of peas in front of them, with each taking care of the peas from the center of the belt to their own side of it. Easier said than done when one was not even five-foot tall and had a limited reach. When Frances' partner saw her stretching on tip-toe and still failing to reach the peas passing along the center, she swept a load over her way. At first, she pushed them over with a big grin, then a smile, then with a face that grew blanker as the night drew on. After their first break, Frances' partner no longer was moving peas to her side of the belt, and Frances could only watch as peas she should have sorted slid rapidly out of sight.

The floor lady assigned to their belt was diligent. She was soon tapping a drum beat on Frances' shoulder.

"What seems to be the trouble?" she snapped.

Frances could feel embarrassment pushing heat into her cheeks. She shrugged, reached out as far as she could, which squashed the bib of her apron against the belt, and let the floor lady see the problem for herself.

"If you can't do the job, you'll have to go home."

Frances felt as if every eye was on her. A quick look up and down the belt proved her wrong. The women were intent on their own jobs, but Frances was not completely wrong. One pair of eyes had been watching.

Just as Frances was preparing to give up and step away from the belt, another tap on her shoulder stopped her.

"Try this."

A hand scooted her over to one side and a man plunked a wooden stand down where her feet had been.

"Step up on that."

Frances did, tentatively.

"Sturdy enough?"

Frances moved from one foot to the other. No wobble.

"Will that work for you?"

Frances reached out. Her hands, now well in the center of the belt, began to move rapidly back and forth over the peas. The floor lady turned away with a satisfied smile as Frances scooped nightshade and pebbles right and left.

"This is fine. Great. Thanks so much," Frances called over her shoulder, never taking her eyes or hands from the work in front of her.

"Looks like you've got a guardian angel," said Frances' partner, winking at her.

The 'angel' was right behind her when Frances stepped off her stand when it was time to break for lunch. To Frances he was just a man in denims and a flannel shirt. Her eyes had been riveted on the stand, not on the man who placed it at her feet.

"Did that work out for you?" he asked, falling into step beside her.

"Did what...? Oh, are you the one who gave me the stool?"

"The stand, yeah. Was it OK?"

"It was great. Gave me just the height I needed. Thanks so much."

The location of the lunch room had been pointed out to her, and Frances headed toward it now.

A half-hour lunch was going to go by quickly, and she was

ready for a cup of coffee. The past hour had made her aware of how easy it might be to fall asleep while standing up. Coffee would remedy that.

"Smoke?"

The 'angel' still kept pace with her. An unlit cigarette dangled from the corner of his mouth, the match to light it grasped between the forefinger and thumb of his right hand.

"Smoke?" he repeated, flicking a thumb toward the exit door.

"Thank you, but no. I don't smoke," Frances said.

"Would you like to take your lunch outside? Fresh air would be a welcome relief after being in here."

The heavy, green, warm smell of peas, not particularly unpleasant but certainly in a class by itself, gave weight to his offer.

Frances thought a nice warm lunch room sounded better than the chilly night air, and she was not about to go outside with a stranger, but she wasn't sure just how to discourage him.

She began rolling her gloves down over her fingers.

She felt the rubber material catch on her wedding ring. Of course, he hadn't seen her ring. A tug released her hand from the concealing glove. She made sure her ring was in plain sight as she flipped the glove around to force air into the fingers and straighten them right side out.

"I believe I'll eat in the lunch room where it's light enough so I can write a note to my husband."

Disappointment was plain on his face, but he recovered enough to ask, "Is he out of town?"

"Oh no, nothing like that." Frances used a laugh and a flip of her second glove to end the conversation. "Well, thanks again," she added, moving swiftly away.

She left him standing there looking after her.

A pale wash of gray was pushing night toward morning when the crew was released for the second break. This time Frances headed for the exit, along with her partner on the line, Sal, a leggy brunette, who at five-foot eight appeared to tower over Frances.

Frances was expecting nothing more than a glimpse of the early morning sky and a breath of fresh air to chase the cobwebs out of her head, but the two women became the center of attention as soon as they stepped outside.

"Well, if it isn't Mutt and Jeff," a voice crowed.

Sal laughed and placed a finger under her nose, mimicking the tall, mustachioed character in the comics to whom she was being compared.

The heckler was among a group of fellows resting on their haunches and lighting up smokes. The long night had rubbed away whatever inhibitions they might have had and they were in a teasing mood. As they catcalled and wolf whistled, Sal linked arms with Frances and pushed their way through, heading toward a bench beyond the group.

"Never mind them. They're just slap-happy after working all night," said Sal.

The ribald laughter of the men sailed like a blue cloud in their direction. Alvin's misgivings came to mind, but Frances settled on the bench and unwrapped half a sandwich left over from lunch. Sal strolled away to get a drink of water from a nearby fountain.

She had no sooner moved away than one of the bolder men in the bunch came forward, propped a foot on the bench next to Frances, and leaned an elbow on his upraised knee while he let his eyes roam over her.

"Yep, Mutt and Jeff. And how is little Mutt doing today?"

The stance he had taken put his crotch at Frances' eye level, and he laughed at her obvious discomfort. He blew a smoke ring over her head, and looked to his cronies to see if they were catching his act. A ripple of laughter was his answer.

Frances folded the waxpaper back around the uneaten portion of sandwich, and moved to the opposite end of the bench. She kept her face turned from him, and wished Sal would hurry back. The joker persisted, moving down the bench until she could feel the heat of him on her back.

She jumped up, and took a few quick steps to put distance between them.

"What's the matter? Don't you want to get acquainted, little lady?"

Before Frances could move, a voice was raised from among the loungers.

"Put a sock in it, Charlie."

"What's it to you?" grumbled Frances' pursuer.

"Close your yap and get back over here. Leave the ladies alone. They're entitled to a little rest."

As the man dubbed Charlie sidled reluctantly away, Frances sent a fleeting, grateful glance at the whiskery fellow who had moved the pest along. She pulled her gloves out and began working her fingers back into them as she hurried into the cannery.

Sal joined her at the line just as the buzzer blared its back-to-work warning. The break had given Frances and Sal their second wind, and their hands flew over the mass of peas that never quit flowing by. They finished their shift in silence.

When the buzzer announced quitting time, Frances was the one to link arms with Sal and steer her toward the exit through which the sun was now shining.

"I'm ready for a little shut-eye. How about you?" Sal said.

"I believe this *lady* can't wait to get home to get a hug from her baby," said Frances.

Chapter 139

June 12-13
Saturday & Sunday
Temp 98
"   99
Just one more day
and then I can see
my Frances. I am
so lonesome for
her. I hope I may
go home.

Frances rang up Alvin as soon as she awakened Saturday afternoon to let him know the first night of work was behind her.

"And, yes, it went well," she reassured him. "After I gave Frances Pearl her breakfast this morning, Lily took over and I just woke up after five wonderful hours of sleep. I'll work tonight, and then we'll be together all day Sunday."

With that promise ringing in his ears, Al was not too unhappy when they had to end the call. Not long after, Frances hurried to town. She had something she wanted to buy.

Temp 97.8
"   99
My true love has
been with me all
the visiting time
today. She brought
me the loveliest
pajamas I ever hope
to have. I love her.

all there is. Al

"Hey, Potts, what is this? The luck of the Irish? You not only got yourself two visits from your wife today, but a pair of spanking, brand new pajamas in the bargain! Some fellows just have all the luck," said Woods.

"What can I say? It's a beautiful world, Woods, simply beautiful."

Woods chuckled. "I won't even try to argue with that, Potts."

Frances had sacrificed sleep to share the Sunday evening visiting hour with Al. She hoped the nap she had squeezed in between the two visitations would tide her over. Of all the things she definitely did not want to do, falling asleep with peas for company was at the top of the list. She felt a bit intimidated knowing that her next chance to crawl into bed would not be until Monday evening. But she had asked for this, and, by golly, she would make it work.

June 14
Monday
Temp 97.8
"   98.6
We are having
a little rain. Looks
like it is going
to set in for a
day or two.

"Hear that Booze? Annie says I finally have a normal temperature. Maybe this rain is good for more than the crops."

June 15
Tuesday
Temp 97.8
"   99
Just one more day
to wait to see my
lover. I always look
forward to that. She

is my life and my
love. I love her
devoutly.

June 16
Wednesday
Temp 97.6
"   98.8
My Darling Wife
and Sweetheart was
to see me. That is
Frances. She is my
everything. We both
love my beautiful
pajamas. I believe
I even look well
in them. They sure
fit me well. I love
you. I love you. I
love you. I love you.
I love you Frances.
Your Al.

June 17
Thursday
Temp 99.6
"   98.4
I am fine today
My Frances. Of
course Dearest I
love you more
than anything or
anyone in all the
world. You are so
beautiful and lovely
I cannot help but
adore you. You are
precious to me my
loved one. Al.

June 18
Friday
Temp 97.6
"   98.4
I haven't really
had a decent meal
for two or three
days. Rotten liver
and onions for
dinner tomorrow.
I guess there is no
let up. It is O.K.
but not this poor
grade of stuff we
get here. Always
the cheapest. Al.

Al was having difficulty in finding anything beautiful in what had been appearing on his dinner plate lately. The menu for tomorrow offered no relief, if past servings of liver were any indication of what he could expect. Irv's smile never wavered, even when faced with food Al could not stomach. Peas cooked to a mush, tasteless cabbage and greasy fried potatoes failed to erase Woods' perpetual good nature.

Alvin could not understand it. No farm boy worth his salt could call this hospital food real cooking. Maybe that was the answer. Maybe Irv was not raised on fresh grown, home-cooked grub. Perhaps the kind of food that the Meliahs and Kents had served up on their harvest tables had spoiled Alvin for anything else.

Dinner time here could easily serve as the penance Al was sure the priest was going to pile on him at his next confession. Now that would be a penance really hard to swallow. He might just suggest it when father started handing out the Hail Marys and Our Fathers, which came nowhere near to sticking in his craw like the liver and onions did.

June 19-20

Saturday & Sunday
Temp 97.6
"   97.8
It has been a very
dismal day. Rain all
the time. I had a
letter from my lover.
It sure was sweet of
her to write.

Sal had taken to teasing Frances during lunch hours when she
hunched over her sandwich and coffee with a tablet, writing, she
said, to her husband, who lived right here in town.

"I think you're just trying to avoid your guardian angel," Sal
teased. "He's just waiting for you to show some interest, you
know."

Frances never rose to Sal's bait. She just smiled, and kept
writing. She felt somewhat guilty that she had chosen sleep over
an evening visit with Alvin last Wednesday.   She intended to
bombard him with letters on the days she could not be with him.
She would do it so he would be less lonely, but the letters made
her feel closer to him, too.

She also liked trying to describe her co-workers to him. Sal
had been no challenge; she had told Al to just imagine a female
Jeff from the comic strip, only prettier and without the mustache.
And Gina, the floor lady, was just another Flora with galoshes
on…and, perhaps, just the slightest tinge of a mustache. The
fellows who smoked and cat-called were more difficult to write
about. Frances did not want to worry Alvin, so she skipped a
description of the razzing she had taken the first night. Since then,
not one of the men had stepped out of line. She settled for
mentioning a new thing they had begun, singing—harmonizing
really—during the last break while the sun was still struggling to
rise over the distant hills. Listening to them as they sang, it was
difficult to believe they were the same lot that had made her so
uncomfortable such a short time ago. Still, she had not returned to
sit on the bench outside. She could hear them well enough through
the window of the lunch room, if she wanted to hear them at all.

A lot of the things that happened at the cannery she could

write to Alvin about. But there were things she did not write about, too. What good would it do Alvin to hear how her eyes grew so heavy along about two o'clock in the morning she nearly had to prop them open, or how the cold seeped into her bones and wouldn't shake loose until she could get home and soak in a hot tub, or how Frances Pearl started sobbing the minute her mother arrived home, as if she had saved all her loneliness up for just that moment? No good; it would do Al absolutely no good to hear any of that.

And there was something else Frances had not yet seen fit to write about. She had made no mention of the man Sal called her guardian angel.

(Father's Day)
Temp 97.2
" 99
My Sweetie and I
had a swell time
today. I love her
and know just how
much she loves me.
I want to be with
her all the time. Al.

Chapter 140

June 21
Monday
Temp 97.4
"   98.2
I was supposed to
receive Holy Communion
this morning but broke
my fast. Dear God please
forgive me. It was done
without me knowing
or thinking anything
about it. I am heartily
sorry.   Al

June 22
Tuesday
Temp 97.6
"   98.2
I received Holy
Communion this
morning. I feel
fine. I am looking
forward to tomorrow.
We are going to
listen to the big
fight tonight. I sure
hope the champ
wins back or retains
his crown. Al.

Phil had been making the rounds of the rooms, unofficially booking bets and talking up the fight that would be piped throughout the ward tonight. While the men were looking forward to hearing Braddock defend his heavyweight championship against Joe Louis, the match wasn't generating the excitement the Schmelling-Louis fight had a year ago.

Phil was finding it tough going trying to get anyone to match the dollar he was willing to put up himself, but he had helped several patients put their quarters on the line.

"Can I put you down for two bits to cover Hymie's bet?" he asked Alvin.

"Hymie is sure to be backing Braddock, and I'd like to see the champ keep his crown, too, so I believe I'll pass. In fact, I don't plan to make any wagers tonight, Phil," Alvin responded, thinking of the effort Frances was making to add to their bank account.

"You are going to be missing out," Phil warned. "You know this is the first time Braddock has defended his title, so he isn't going to let go of it easy."

"I'm counting on that, but I'm not betting on it!" Al said, laughing.

Booze took a pass, too, and Woods said he couldn't care less who won, so Phil, seeing that he couldn't stir up any business in Room 102, went off to try his luck elsewhere. Alvin wondered if the lack of enthusiasm was endemic to this room, or if the entire ward was infected with it. He was sure anticipation over the bout would be higher if Leo and Oscar were here to kibitz. But they weren't, so he would just have to make the best of it.

The fight started right on time.

Alvin listened intently as his favorite took a pounding in the first round. The one good hit Braddock got in did put Louis on the canvas, but he bounced up so quickly there was no count on him at all. The announcer related a fast second round that left a cut over Braddock's left eye.

There was no conversation among Booze, Alvin and Woods between rounds. In fact, Woods got up and strolled out of the room at the end of the second round.

"Louis is entering the ring at a run!" The surprised sportscaster screeched in excitement at the start of round three, and Al couldn't help the groan that passed his lips.

"Want to put a quarter on the outcome, Al?" Booze teased, but his heart wasn't really in the offer.

Al perked up during the fourth round as Braddock boxed *"beautifully,"* according to the announcer. Al grinned, pleased to see the champ finally show some fight, but also at the idea of anyone finding *beauty* in a boxing ring.

As if to put the lie to that image, both fighters were bloody at the end of round five, Louis with blood pouring from his nose and the cut over Braddock's eye streaming blood. Louis used the sixth round to inflict heavy punishment, pounding away at Braddock until he was reeling and blood gushed from a split lip. Al felt his muscles tensing as if the Bomber's blows were aimed at him. The taste of that indescribable bloody mix of salt, iron and something almost sweet was sharp on his tongue.

Braddock's not a quitter, that's for sure. Al did not speak the words aloud. It was obvious that Booze and Woods, who was wandering in and out of the room, did not really care about the battle being aired. But Al couldn't help admiring the fighter, who, the announcer said, was driving the Brown Bomber around the ring in a last ditch effort to hold onto his championship. *"His legs are wobbling, his face is bloody and bruised, but the champ just put two hard punches to the Bomber's head...and there's the bell!"*

The roar of the crowd and the announcer's staccato announcements were in sharp contrast to the silent room where Al lay. *"Braddock's handlers are in his corner working furiously over him, and there's the bell to start Round Eight,"* the announcer screamed.

Alvin felt his chest tighten up as Joe Louis' punches to Braddock's face were relayed over the wire to his bedside. *"A straight left, both hands to the face, lefts to the body, and there's a sharp left hook Braddock tries to sidestep and runs right into it!"*

And then, after a minute and ten seconds into Round Eight, it was all over, Braddock down in a bloody heap after Louis rammed home a terrific right to the side of his head.

The announcer, screaming over a frenzied crowd that milled into the ring, informed his listeners that the badly beaten Braddock couldn't make it back to his corner under his own power. His handlers carried him.

Alvin listened to the wrap-up as the Associated Press score card gave Louis four of the first seven rounds. Braddock was given the edge in rounds two, four and five. The twenty-three-year-old Louis, at one hundred ninety-seven and a quarter pounds, was the new champion, the second Negro to hold the U.S. heavyweight championship. Braddock took home fifty percent of the net receipts, and the new champ garnered seventeen and a half percent. The gate was estimated to be as high as three hundred thousand dollars.

Later that night, lying in the dark and reliving the fight, Alvin wondered what he had ever found exciting about a sport that left men battered and bloody and the loser richer than the winner.

Chapter 141

June 23
Wednesday
Temp 97.2
"   98.6
Frances just left. It
seems as if I were
left alone in the
world. We had a
fine time. I pray
to God that I can
go home for an
afternoon soon. I am
so lonely I just can't
seem to be able to
figure it all out.

June 24
Thursday
Temp 97.4
"   97.8
I felt rather punk
this morning but
feel better now.
Father Verhoeven
was in for a few
minutes. He looks
as if he were
suffering a lot.
Today is a nice day
about or just 70

*degrees—about 75
is just right. Al.*

It shocked Alvin when Father Verhoeven was admitted to the sanatorium. He had always looked so healthy. The priest would have been the last one Al would have suspected of having tuberculosis, but that had been the message he carried to Alvin's bedside this morning before Gillis ushered him away to a bed of his own. Today the priest looked like Al felt on one of his worst days. Al hoped for the best. He really liked this man, and now would miss his occasional visits.

**June 25
Friday**
*Temp 97.6
       "   98.6
It has been plenty
warm today. I am
waiting patiently for
Sunday to come. I
feel as if I would like
to go home for a
year or two. All
anyone would have
to do would be to
say boo and I'd go.
       Al.*

**June 26-27
Saturday & Sunday**
*Temp 97.4
       "   98.4
Father Gallagher
was just in for
about 40 seconds.
I wish it was my
wife. Tomorrow
boy oh boy.
Temp 98*

"   99
My lovely Bride was
out and did we have
a fine visit. I took up
about half an hour
with a nose bleed.

When blood started gushing without warning from Alvin's nose, Frances grabbed the first thing she could lay hands on. The cotton scarf from around her neck was quickly saturated, but Annie, summoned by Booze, scurried in with a stack of towels. Frances saw they were so tightly woven as to make them absorbent-resistant, but Annie pressed them, one by one, into service. Alvin's head was soon tipped back and ice packed under his neck, but the blood continued to pour forth.

Through long experience, Alvin had found a finger clamped forcefully beneath his nose sometimes staunched the flow. He tried that, but this time the trick did not work.

He was more concerned about the effect this bloody display was having on Booze's company than he was about the nosebleed itself. But, as he should have known, Booze carried it off with aplomb, herding his guests discreetly out of the room, even as Annie erected a screen around Al's bed.

Frances Al did not worry about. He knew his wife. She could cope with anything. And she was. As quickly as the almost useless towels were soiled, she had a new one in place, and used a cloth, dampened in a basin Annie provided, to swab Alvin's face clean. Annie cranked the bed to lower Al's head to an acute angle, and finally the bleeding stopped.

He felt limp as a rag when it was all over.

Frances held his hand in hers through what was left of their time together.

When it was time to leave, Frances gingerly picked her scarf out of the wastebasket where Annie had tossed it, wrapped it in a newspaper and took it home where she put it to soak in cold, salt water. Then she hurried off to work.

June 28
Monday

Temp 97.6
*   "   99.2*
Boy it sure has been
plenty warm. 98 degrees
to be exact. I hate to
think of it getting
warmer. I was lonesome
for a time last nite but
feel more better tonight.
I love my Frances so much.
I do love you my sweet.Al.

June 29
Tuesday
Temp 97.2
*   "   99*
I talked with my Frances.
She was lonely. I am also,
for her.

June 30
Wednesday
Temp 97.6
*   "   99.2*
Frances my Sweet. Your
Alvin is sure waiting for
you. Of course that is
all I have to do. I love
you and like to think
that I am waiting for
you and am all yours.
I am glad you didn't
go out in the dust
and rain. Your Al.

Frances could not get the use of Ida's Ford on this Wednesday afternoon, so she was left with a dilemma. She had a choice between walking to the san, which would leave little time for visiting, or going out in the evening, which meant she would not get any sleep today. A look through the window pane she was washing at the Wilson house convinced her. Ugly weather!

She telephoned Alvin to let him know rain and circumstance prevented an afternoon visit, but she would be there at seven o'clock on the dot. So what if it meant another day without sleep; she would manage.

Work at the cannery was going well. She had another fifty dollars she would deposit at Baker-Boyer tomorrow. She planned to kill two birds with one stone. The Wilson children and Frances Pearl would enjoy a walk downtown, and she could make her deposit at the bank before it closed at three o'clock. The key to working two jobs was organization. Frances felt she had a handle on both. Four hours of sleep a day were plenty for anybody. Why, she had energy to spare! And, if she did flag, a visit with her husband always re-energized her.

Lily was also turning out to be a big help. In addition to staying with Frances Pearl at nights, she had the child bathed and dressed and breakfast waiting when Frances arrived home each morning from the cannery. She also had taken over packing a lunch for Frances to take to work in the evenings. Lily was good about ironing her own clothes, too, and sometimes even did some ironing for her sister-in-law. All around, it seemed to be working out nicely. And Frances loved to see the balance in the bank account grow. Why, with the deposit tomorrow, she and Alvin would have three hundred and seventy-nine cents! You could buy a Kroehler, custom-made, mohair davenport and chair for a hundred and fifty dollars. Not that she had any interest in spending their hard-earned money on furniture. What they had was plenty good enough.

No, this nest egg was intended for something really special. She and Alvin hadn't figured out yet just what that would be. But they had a nest egg. Frances liked the sound of that.

Chapter 142

News of yesterday's storm was plastered all over the *Walla Walla Union* Thursday morning. Until he read about it, Alvin had not realized exactly what Frances had ventured out in the previous night.

From the pages of the newspaper he learned that the drastic drop in the 100-degree temperature he had enjoyed the day before heralded the thunder and lightning that destroyed a house in Lowden, several miles from nearby College Place, just about the time Frances was fighting the wind on her way home from the Wilsons.

"This article reports that a Lowden family's house was set ablaze by a lightning bolt yesterday," Al said, reading aloud for the benefit of Booze and Woods. "Says they had *'little more than time to scurry from the burning structure'*.

"We could see the storm was a rough one, but I had no idea how rough," Al added.

As Al continued reading, Annie summoned Booze to the telephone where a call was waiting for him, she said.

"Now there's a coincidence. That was a friend of mine, a minister who lives on Russell Creek, reporting on the storm," Booze said when he returned. "JayDee said a cloudburst dumped more than a half-inch of rain out there yesterday in just half an hour. He said his cellar looks like a swimming hole, but luckily, the creek didn't overflow. Filled right up to the banks, but that was it."

"The paper says Mill Creek took a hit, too, with the rain pouring down just like a water spout," Al responded. "Paper also reports fears of flooding with all that rain pouring out of the mountains into the creek, but I believe Mill Creek will hold. I know first hand there's some sturdy revetment work in it. Some wheat's been lost, but it says it's too early to say how much."

"This Walla Walla County is a strange one," Woods observed. "First we were treated to the granddaddy of all dust storms and then nearly washed away. I didn't know what I was getting into when we moved here."

"How's that, Woods? You didn't find yesterday's storm *beautiful*?" Al ribbed.

"Now I did not say that. I said 'tis a *strange* place in which I find myself."

The frown that had creased Woods' face as he talked about the complexity of rain and dust in the same storm smoothed away and was replaced with his jolly jack-o-lantern smile. "Remember, Potts," he added. "Mother Nature is a *woman,* and you know my philosophy about the feminine gender."

"Mail call!"

Annie bustled in with her hands full. She gave several envelopes and magazines to Booze, passed a single envelope from the bundle to Alvin, and then took her time delivering a small package to Woods. Before she handed it over to Irv, she waved the package through the air in a teasing motion meant to tantalize. Irv made several ineffectual grabs at it, which drew giggles from Annie. Al was aware of their banter and laughter, but was too busy slitting open his letter to pay further attention.

The letter was from Frances. It was the kind he liked—nice and long. Her cannery stories always entertained him, but he thought she painted some of those guys too white.

Woods kept the contents of his package a mystery, but neither Booze nor Alvin expressed interest in it any way. However, Woods was more than forthcoming about who sent it to him. Indeed, he could hardly wait to inform his mates that it was from his young, female evening visitor. Estelle, Irv called her, a grin creasing his face from ear to ear.

Booze apparently had no interest in this Estelle either, at least none that was in evidence. Instead, with a new stock of magazines in hand, he declared his intention to share his old ones with other patients. "Maybe your priest friend would enjoy one of these," said Booze, flourishing a handful as he left the room, taking advantage of recently being released from complete bed rest.

Although Woods had not fired up Booze's curiosity, Alvin

had to admit to a curiosity of his own about the woman he had first taken to be Irv Woods' wife. If not his wife, who then was the lady with whom the jolly Irv shared such abandoned laughter every Sunday and Wednesday evening?

"Yes sir, it was my cheery nightingale, who sent me this," Woods said, interrupting Al's reverie. He stuffed the package in his nightstand, and turned to face Al.

It appeared that Woods was about to enlighten him.

"Now there, Potts, is a female to delight the heart! Always cheerful, always a sweet smile upon her soft lips, and never a care in the world. And have you noticed? Estelle has not missed an evening yet! Why, she is almost as faithful as your own honey! I do believe Estelle would visit twice each visiting day, too, if she had her way. But that wouldn't do." He paused delicately. "No. It would not do at all," he added.

"It wouldn't?" Al used his question to coax open a door.

But even as he asked, Al felt a stab of guilt for being such a nosey parker. He wondered if it was obvious that he was deliberately drawing Irv out.

Woods grinned. He knew he was the one baiting a conversational trap. And Al was taking that bait nicely. Irv had been longing to talk about Estelle with someone, anyone, but especially with his roommates who had seen her come and go on such a regular basis. He had enjoyed whetting their interest by whisking her away without introductions, making a mystery lady of her. He had hoped to have both Booze and Potts as his audience when he finally broached the subject of Estelle, but Potts alone would do nicely. A young man like Al could easily appreciate the wonder that was Estelle.

"A fair blossom, the fairest of the fair, that is what my Estelle is," said Woods, happy to at last wrap his tongue around her name. "Yes, I am a fortunate man to be the object of her affection. Can you believe, Potts, that the fair damsel followed me here to Walla Walla when she knew I was to be confined for an unlimited time?"

"At first, I assumed she was your wife," Al admitted, slightly embarrassed by such flowery words.

Woods chuckled.

"An understandable mistake. But, no, and neither is she a sister or a relative of any kind. It would be difficult to put a name to her place in my life, except to say I hold her in high regard. I do not question why she followed me here any more than I question the pink blush on a rose. She seems to be content to share my company when and as she can, which, now, isn't all that much. To be with her even for a minute is pure delight!"

Woods smiled his way all through this speech, and ended it with a roll of laughter.

"You know my philosophy, Potts! I am a lover of beauty in all its guises."

"But your wife, Woods," Al said hesitantly.

"Ah, yes, and what about Arlene? She's a wonderful lady. We've been together many years without the benefit of children, thank the lord. She understands me, she loves me as I do her, and she accepts my philosophy. Arlene knows beauty keeps me happy and laughing. If only it would do the same for her! No, what tickles Arlene's fancy and keeps her going is a nice little plot of garden, a tidy house and a husband who doesn't let beauty interfere with her home life.

"Oh, and let's not forget her drill team. That's essential to Arlene's peace of mind. Put my wife in a uniform and..." Irv's face radiated a look of genuine appreciation, and, to complete his comment, he bunched his fingers together, touched them to his lips, and flicked away a kiss with a continental gesture reserved for the best of the best.

Woods fell silent, and settled down to gnawing at his thumb.

The silence that enveloped them stretched out, long and awkward. Al was sorry he had ever wanted to know anything about Woods' visitor. He thought Booze was well out of it. This is what he got for being a nosey parker. *Serves me right!*

"I can't help it, Al," Woods groaned, throwing himself onto his bed. "Estelle is such a pretty little thing. Such an innocent little flower. How could you not love something as pretty and as innocent as that?"

Startled, then overcome by the outrageousness of Irv's helpless plea, Al started to laugh. At first it was only a few embarrassed spurts like water trickling through a crack in a dike, then Al's laughter swelled until it poured out, unrestrained, unleashed, in a flood like water crashing over a dam. Once started, he could not stop. Alvin's laughter flowed out until Woods was caught up in it. Shoulders heaving, beds shaking, they whooped uncontrollably. Bordering on hysteria, their wild laughter rolled around and out of the room...until Gillis poked her head in the door.

The supervisor's arrival was as effective in cutting off their hilarity as if she had doused them with a pitcher of ice water.

Under Gillis' stern eye, they wiped tears of laughter from their eyes, swabbed their noses, and tried to look innocent. They failed horribly, and, in no uncertain terms, Gillis told them so. They were not innocent. They had broken a cardinal rule of the sanatorium. They were *laughing*! And not just ordinary laughter, but a riotous, damaging display she would not excuse.

"And don't think you've heard the last of this!" Gillis warned as she stomped from the room.

From the metallic taste rising at the back of Al's throat, he thought there might be worse things than Gillis' well-deserved wrath. He touched a tissue to his lips, spat carefully, and surreptitiously wadded the bloody tissue into the bag attached to his bed.

July 1
Thursday
Temp 97
"   99
Frances Sweetheart. You
are my everything. I love
you beyond words. That
was the loveliest letter
I ever got today. I was
also so surprised. You
surely are the sweetest
person in all the world.
I adore you. My true love.Al

Chapter 143

July 2
Friday
Temp 97.4
"   98.6
My own lovely precious
beautiful adorable perfect
little wife and sweetheart.
I had the most beautiful
letter from you today and
then you call me up. You
are so good to your daddy Al.
I love you.   Al.

July 3-4
Saturday & Sunday
Temp 97.4
"   99.5
Hello love. I weighed today
and gained 1 ½ lbs. That
is all for you. I will see
you Sunday. I love you.
Temp 97.6 (Independence Day)

The marcelled hair-do was a thing of the past. The structured beauty school waves had succumbed to the alternating chill and moist heat of the cannery and reverted back to Frances' own natural curls. Today they framed a face that bore light touches of rouge.

There was a look of expectancy on the rosy face and the same anticipation twinkled in Frances' eyes as she approached Alvin's side. Her husband did not disappoint her.

"Well, looks as if I am about to have a visit from my very own firecracker," Al teased. He ran an admiring hand over the sleeve of the bright red frock she wore. It was obviously a new dress, and well suited to her, he thought as he admired the way it hugged her hips without revealing too much. Frances lifted the skirt an inch and waggled a red-shod foot at him.

"New shoes, too! You angel, you! Finally you are taking my advice and buying something for yourself."

He noticed that the white piping on the shoes and the subtle matching white trim on her dress kept the red from being too bold a statement. He thought she looked very spiffy, although the red bow tucked into her hair just over her ear might be a tad too much. As she leaned over to kiss his cheek, he plucked the ribbon from among her curls. When she drew back and cocked an inquisitive eyebrow at him, he said nothing, just drew the ribbon through his fingers to smooth it out and then wrapped it in a tidy coil around a finger. Slipping it off the finger, he handed it to her.

"Tuck that away in your purse for now, Sweetheart. When your hair grows longer, you can tie it back with this bright ribbon when we go on a picnic," he said. As she took the strip from him, he raised her fingers to his lips and gave them a chaste kiss followed by a wicked wink.

Booze, watching the exchange from his side of the room, wondered at the way the removal of a simple, childish bow from a female's ensemble could turn the wearer into a sophisticated lady. He had little time to dwell on the vagrant thought as his own company began to filter in from the hallway, but Alvin dwelt on his wife's metamorphosis at length.

He not only praised Frances for her taste in clothes, but also complimented her on how well she wore them. "And it goes without saying you look grand today. This is a far different look from the pink and blue prints Ida whips up," he said. Quick to read the expression on Frances' face, he hurried to add, "Not that there is anything wrong with the dresses Ida sews for you, sweetheart. I'm just saying that with this new outfit you have found your particular style.

"And I love it," he said, pulling her close enough to place a kiss on her cheek.

The slight exertion set his chest to pounding, and he sank back on his pillows. Sweat broke out on his brow in tiny beads that Frances blotted away with her handkerchief. He smiled apologetically.

"I'll talk. You rest," she said, laying a restraining hand against his shoulder when he made a move to sit up.

Her quiet voice began painting pictures for him, and slowly he relaxed. She made him see the orderly rows that defined the garden Arlene and she had laid out, rows that were producing lettuce and beans and beets. Her words also brought to life the Italian floor ladies at the cannery as she described how they vied to out-do each other with their pristine white uniforms, carmine lips, plucked eyebrows and hair black as midnight piled in intricate coils. "They make the rest of us look like drowned rats in our rubber boots and aprons and hair nets," Frances said, not realizing she had resurrected for Al a memory, buried these past months, of another black-haired, Italian girl whose al fresco dining had been just one of her exoticisms that had charmed an impressionable boy.

It was a painless memory that faded almost as quickly as it had formed, and Frances' next words had Al's full attention. She was telling him how much easier it had been to sort peas after a man had provided her with a stand that gave her a few extra much-needed inches.

"I think the floor lady was on the verge of giving me the axe because I am so short, when he came up with the stand. Sal calls him my guardian angel, but I don't know that I'd go that far, even though the lift is a big help," Frances said.

"Guardian angel? That sounds…significant," Al said, trying to keep concern out of his voice.

Frances did not even pretend not to hear the nuance in her husband's words.

"*This* is significant," Frances stated. She flashed her ring finger right in front of his face.

"Sal may call that fellow an angel. I don't call him anything, but, if I did, I believe 'gentleman' is the tag I'd hang on him." She flipped her hand with its wedding band in a dismissive gesture, and patted Alvin on the shoulder.

"Sweetheart, you and the man who helped me are two of a

kind. I know, if the shoe were on the other foot, you'd do the same thing to help a lady keep her job.

"And..." she added in an exaggerated western drawl. "...I'd be *mighty* proud of you for doing it."

Frances' unexpected stab at humor scattered any dark thoughts that might have been forming in the recesses of Al's mind. As for Frances, the dread she had fought down in order to raise the subject of her 'guardian angel' was replaced with relief that it was now over and done with.

An inconsequential matter, the man's unsolicited help somehow had taken on a worrisome importance by not being mentioned to Al before. Now it was relegated to its proper place.

> *My Darling Pal. You were*
> *so extra lovely today.*
> *Your new clothes looked*
> *very nice on you. Your Al.*

July 5
Monday
Temp 97.8
"   99
Lover girl. I wish I could
be with you every day.
You are so good and true.
Oh God, Frances, I love
you so much it makes my
heart ache. I want you so
bad and know I can't have
you. Mabe some day I
can—huh? Al.

Al should have been in seventh heaven. Two visiting days in a row, with visitors also welcomed on Monday because Independence Day fell on a Sunday this year. Instead, the Monday hours with Frances had stirred him to an impassioned fever pitch again. At least, he consoled himself, he had behaved himself this time. But, damn, without any effort on her part, that woman sure could send even his temperature over the 98.6 limits of normality.

July 6
Tuesday
Temp 97.4
"   98.6
Visiting day yesterday
visiting day tomorrow.
That just suits me.
Honey precious, I
received the sweetest
letter today. I wasn't
expecting it either.
They are surely fine
when one isn't
expecting them. Your Al.

On Wednesday Frances staggered into Al's room under the weight of a bulky radio that left only her head, white-knuckled hands and legs exposed. Irv was the first to reach her. He pried the radio from her determined grasp, and placed it on the nightstand next to Alvin's bed where it sat like a crown jewel waiting to be admired. Booze and Irv quickly did the honors, commenting favorably on the radio's gleaming wood cabinet and its shiny dials marked so clearly with the stations it could reach. The radio stood there, its knobs ready for Alvin to turn to tune him in to the world beyond his windows.

This radio was the same Montgomery Ward's model that had squawked and squealed at the beginning of President Roosevelt's speech on the night Alvin had proposed to Frances. The radio the likes of which Al had vowed never to own. And here it was, sitting on his nightstand, a generous gift from his overly generous wife. The problem was Al knew exactly which radio model Monkey Wards had that he would like to own. It cost $18.95, had a shortwave band, and the reception was guaranteed to be top quality. And it was not this radio.

July 7
Wednesday
Temp 97.8

"   99.4
Lover girl, I am so
sorry to be such a
worry to you. I know
I am too particular
but I hate to spend
that much money
without good results.
You are so good and
I love you so much. Al.

The radio had gone home with Frances to be returned to the store. But she had another plan up her sleeve.

Chapter 144

The early days of July passed relentlessly for the patients at the Blue Mountain Sanatorium. The thermometer Al could see from his window snagged just below three figures and hung there for days, sending hot blasts of air into Room 102. The thermometer Annie stuck under his tongue in late afternoon followed suit, and it was rare when Alvin was not forced to record 99 for his personal temperature.

"Just another hot day" became a mantra in his diary as if the frequent use of the words would negate the uncomfortable results of hot summer days with a fan on the fritz that pumped only hot air into the room. Booze and Woods were also feeling the effects, and Alvin noticed Irv's laughter now sounded forced except when his Estelle visited.

It was too hot for Alvin to do more than lie among his pillows and sweat, and, truth to tell, the sweating took more energy than he felt he had in him. As much as he craved to hear Frances' voice, the nights she telephoned tested his strength. By the time he reached the telephone on those nights, he was a trembling figure of a man. "Some man!" he would mutter to himself as he lifted the receiver to his ear with a shaky hand.

He did his best to hide his increasing weakness from Gillis and Annie. No way did he want those phone calls curtailed. They meant the world to him.

> *Sweetheart darling I was*
> *so happy to hear your*
> *dear sweet voice. I love*
> *you Frances. You are so*
> *good and pure. You are*
> *so dear to me. I love you*
> *I love you I love you. Your Al*

It was after he answered her phone call of Friday, July 9, that he wrote those words in his diary. The few lines were no idle expression of devotion. They spoke to a growing obsession. It was an obsession that not only wrapped itself around the fervent love he had for his wife, but also dug into the desperate desire he had to be with her.

His preoccupation with Frances colored every day until doubts began to seep in. When she was with him, he felt secure in her love, but alone…well, he wondered. He tried to reassure himself with his penciled words, words like: *You are so good and pure* and *I love you and know you love me* and even, on a particularly insecure day, *I honestly know that you love me and are true to me. Because you are you. Honest to God.*

While Al used words to stave off his suspicions, Frances used words to maintain the tie between them. She wrote letters that reached him on the days she could not visit. If she did not have time to write to him during the day, she used her lunch hour at the cannery in the middle of the night to fill at least one page she posted to him on the way home. When he became frustrated with his weakened state, lost his temper, and made hash of their Sunday afternoon visiting hours on July 11, Frances shrugged it off even though he offered no apology. It would be a long time before she got a glimpse of his diary entry for that evening and learned of his remorse:

We weren't feeling
well today was I pal.
I know you have
forgiven me for being
such a dirty dad. Your Al.

She had no idea that missing the evening visiting hour on that same Sunday would throw him into a terror that caused him, when it became apparent she was not coming, to frantically write in his diary the next morning:

Sweetheart, why haven't you
come out or called? Is
everything alright. I pray

that you are well. If I felt
better I would have called.
If anything happened to
you Oh! God I couldn't
stand it. Pray God save
and protect her for me.
                                    Al

Everything *was* all right. Frances had just been unable to borrow Ida's car.

She explained that to him in the letter she wrote at the cannery Sunday night. She did not mention how good it had felt to add four hours of sleep that night to the extra hours she had clocked that morning.

Alvin received her letter on Tuesday, and, when she visited Wednesday afternoon, she brought him a pair of pajamas he immediately dubbed "lovely". She also surprised him when she told him she had put an order in at Montgomery Wards for the shortwave radio model he preferred. "It should be here soon, maybe next Wednesday," she told him.

While he looked forward to having that really nifty radio, on Thursday he was still compelled to tell his diary *I hope my baby wife is alright and doesn't get too tired working. She is a fine girl. I love her.* This being a dependent husband was sometimes a confusing load to bear.

July 16
Friday
Temp 97.4
"   98.8
It was 90 degrees today.
I am very lonesome for
Sunday to come. I have
a new radio coming or
I think it is coming. I
expect it next Wed.
Frances is of course
my communicant in
the deal. I love you. My
pal.   Al.

July 17-18
Saturday & Sunday
Temp 97.4
"   98
It is 94 degrees today
which is plenty hot.
The fan pumps just
hot air. No good. I
had a letter. Al.
Temp 98.2
"   99.4
Frances honey, I can't
stand to see you leave
me on visiting nights.
Please know I love and
trust you. Your Al.

July 19
Monday
Temp 97.8
"   98.6
My own precious pet.
I pray you are well
rested and happy. I am
not too unhappy. I try
to be your good little
boy. You are so good
to me. I sure was a
bad boy yesterday.
I am sorry. Please
forgive me, will you? Al

Chapter 145

July 20
Tuesday
Temp 97.8
"   97.8
Precious Pal. I was
glad to hear your
dear sweet voice. I
am sorry you have
a bad cold. I always
think it is

"Squiggle, squiggle, squiggle. What do you find to write about every day, Potts?"

There was no animosity in Irv's voice. In fact, Al thought, the man did not even sound that interested, but these dull, dog days of summer had all of them scrabbling for diversion. Non-visiting days were especially trying with only the same old faces for company.

Annie had just made the rounds to take late afternoon temperatures, and a long evening now stretched out before them. Al decided to take Irv's question seriously.

He tapped his pencil against the calendar on which he had been writing. "This was a gift from Flora at Christmas time. She gave Booze stationary and me this calendar, which I use as a sort of diary. In it I record a few things as reminders," Al explained.

"Reminders of what?" Irv questioned.

"Oh, what the temperature is—inside and out," Al said, smiling and pointing out the window and then at himself. "And other things, as I think of them."

"That thing is a mite small, isn't it, for recording much of anything?"

Booze joined in. "I offered to provide him with something more equitable to the little book he kept last year, but he clings to Flora's gift."

"You mean you kept a record all last year, too?" Irv said, astounded.

"Keeping a log is second nature to me," said Alvin. "I grew up in a family of scribblers. I think we got the habit from my dad. He kept a log when he sailed to Alaska, and we enjoyed hearing him read from it. None of us had as fancy a book as he kept then. We used about anything we could find to write on."

Irv shook his head in disbelief that anyone would take the trouble, let alone find enjoyment in doing so much writing.

Seeing Irv's reaction, Alvin added with a grin, "Why, one of my sisters even wrote on the cellar walls of our cabin."

"Now that's going some," Booze said, laughing.

"Well, it was a sort of game," Alvin said. "Our house was built over a vein of chalk, and the walls in that cellar were white as could be and just right for scratching on. Lily would go down there and draw and scribble away to her heart's content. Actually, all of us, at one time or another, took our turns scratching into those walls when we were kids. We'd come up out of there covered in chalk and looking like ghosts."

"Well then, this little calendar of yours is quite a come-down for a boy who once had entire walls to write on, isn't it?" Woods said, giving Al one of his widest grins.

"These days I probably don't have as much to say as I did then," Al said, returning the grin. "Maybe that's what Flora was thinking when she gave me this," he added, flourishing the calendar on its metal spindle. "But, like Booze said, I have grown accustomed to this baby. I cherish its little pages," he mocked, holding it to his chest.

"And, you know," he said seriously, "I do believe Flora was trying to tell me something with this." Again, he waved the handful of pages, which were getting a little dog-eared from the daily use he put it to.

"I just haven't figured it out yet. But, give me time. Give me time, gents, and I will!"

Booze ran his fingers through his hair, ruffled it and then

segued into a massage in a performance that somehow indicated Al puzzled him. Woods' reaction was more direct. He erupted in chuckles, taking the whole thing as a huge joke.

Before Al could get back to his writing, Phil poked his nose in the door.

"Got a minute, Al?" he asked.

"Two or even three, if you like."

Phil edged his way past Booze, nodded a hello, and sidled on by Woods' bed, leaving the same greeting in his wake. Al thought the ebullient Phil was strangely on the quiet side tonight. It did not appear that he had come in to give them the sports news this evening. But he obviously had something on his mind. And whatever it was, he apparently did not want to share it with the entire room. Al waited to see what Phil was going to spring on him.

When Phil reached Al's bed, he continued on around it until he had his back in the corner, up against the wall, just as far from the others as he could get.

Al watched as Phil fidgeted. He not only rocked from foot to foot, but gnawed at his lower lip until his face was twisted into a mask of indecisiveness. *Was the inevitable bell tolling again? And, if so, for whom?*

"We're friends, right, Al?" asked an anxious Phil.

"Sure," Al said, surprised.

"So you won't take offense, if I speak to you about something that came my way today?"

Al did not respond quickly, but his mind was racing. He wasn't sure he wanted to hear what Phil was so reluctant to tell him. He finally said, "Out with it."

Phil bent over the bed until he was so close Al could feel his breath on his cheek. It carried a faint odor of the tomato soup that had been served for dinner. Then, in tones only Alvin could hear, Phil told him one of the hospital handymen had brought him a story about a fracas that had happened at Walla Walla Cannery the night before.

"Dodie's brother works there, and he told Dodie two guys got to scrapping. He told Dodie these two were fighting over a blonde dish...uh, woman." Phil ducked his head as he said it. Then he added in a whisper so low that Al almost didn't hear it. "Dodie's brother said the woman was your wife."

Phil drew back and avoided Al's eyes, obviously embarrassed at being the bearer of such news.

"And this happened *last night*, that right?"

Phil snapped his head around, surprised at the hint of laughter in Al's voice.

"Last night. Monday," Phil confirmed.

"Two guys. Fighting over Frances. That right?"

"That's what Dodie's brother told him. He said the brawl started when Fr...the woman went into a car to eat lunch with one of them and the other guy got mad. I thought you'd want to know." Phil was still nervous. This was not the kind of news he liked to carry.

"Guess who telephoned me this evening?" Al asked.

"Frances," Al said, supplying his own answer. "My wife called to tell me the cold that kept her home from work *last night* was a little better today."

When Phil offered no comment, Al grinned and said, "Tell Dodie I think he better stick to hauling garbage, not spreading it."

As soon as Phil shuffled from the room, Alvin pulled his calendar over to finish the diary entry he was writing when Irv interrupted. Let's see, where was he? He read over what he had already written:

> *Precious Pal. I was*
> *glad to hear your*
> *dear sweet voice. I*
> *am sorry you have*
> *a bad cold. I always*
> *think it is*

He picked up his pencil, sharpened the tip with his pen knife and finished the sentence he had left dangling.

> *think it is my fault.*

Smiling to think what a blessing it had been to hear his wife's voice, especially in light of Phil's visit, he added a closing line.

> *My how the lies*

thrive here. Al.

July 21
Wednesday
Temp 98.2
"   99.6
Frances, Pal girl.
You are all mine
and I am surely
all yours. I love you
my dear good friend.
You are my friend
aren't you, Frances?
I love you and am
positive that you
love me. Al.

July 22
Thursday
Temp 98
"   98
An extra warm day. I
am thinking of you my
true love and am
lonesome for you and
your arms. You were so
lovely Wed. I surely
love you my pal. Al.

July 23
Friday
Temp 98.4
"   98.2
Sweetheart, Little Pal.
You are my everything.
Honest to God. Your Al.
It was 95 degrees today.
You were surely sweet
over the phone tonight

Frances. You didn't
hang up on me. Ha Ha!
Your Al.

It was a new Al that emerged from that awkward talk with Phil.

The rumor Phil had carried to Al's bedside could have shattered a man already filled with doubts, but it had the opposite effect. It was as if Alvin had steeled himself to hear his suspicions proved true. When finally faced with words he had been dreading—even expecting—he heard them ring false, knew his wife was incapable of deceiving him, and recognized his own insecurity as something born of past disappointments and more then a year of what amounted to captivity. While it had been reassuring to have in hand Frances' own words to present to Phil to put lie to the rumor, Alvin had not really needed them for himself.

Al recognized that Phil had done him a favor, although not, perhaps, in the way Phil had intended. Since their talk, Alvin had felt a new resolve flowing into him. Part of it was based on his love for his wife that deepened with each passing day and that emotion did not surprise him, but the trust it was giving birth to, trust of which he had never thought himself capable, did surprise him. The peace it brought was a welcome relief.

But even as this new strength filled him, he could feel his physical strength draining away. As usual, his only bright spots in a week were visits from Frances. He longed to see his child, but those visits were a rarity. Too risky to expose a child to the germs floating around here.

Alvin spent the remaining long, hot days of July in increasing torpor.

Chapter 146

August 2
Monday
Temp 97.4
"   98
Honey Girl. I wish I
could be of some use
to you. Do you think
perhaps mabe I will
be well some day and
be able to help you.
Meantime I shall help
you by being a good boy.
Your Al.

Booze watched his roommate with the concern of a physician, but spoke with the words of a friend. He noted that Al's spirits seemed high, higher than usual, and his smile quicker to respond to Irv's optimism, but he was too quiet. It was the noisy, rowdy patient one expected to see the back of as he took that final walk out the door of the sanatorium with bag in hand. The quiet ones were the ones to watch.

No, Booze did not like what he saw. A quiet Al, content to lie abed, mostly with eyes closed, did not please the physician that still lurked within Booze. He did not think it a coincidence that Gillis began visiting their room more frequently.

Try as he had, Alvin could never get an answer to what a less than normal temperature might mean. He continued to watch the mercury rise to only 98 day after day, the elusive six-tenths always out of reach of the silvery thread. He preferred the lower temps to the ones that had nudged 100 degrees and brought headaches with them.

He felt so dependent on the little ball of mercury that twice daily marked his progress that, when Flora brought him a vial with a ball of the metallic chemical element in it, it was like being given a familiar toy. Often when a thermometer broke, a nurse or ward clerk would scoop the slippery mercury into a vial, take it home for a child of the household to play with or give it to a patient, who could while away a good deal of time fiddling with it. Tonight, it was Al who was handed a vial.

As he tipped it out into the cup of his palm, Irv came over to see what was up.

"What's that you've got there?" Irv asked.

"Hold out your hand."

Irv complied, presenting a flat surface to Al, who shook his head and, with his free hand, squeezed Irv's hand until the palm formed a nest into which he slid the ball of mercury. As the pellet glided to and fro, Al laughed at the surprise on Irv's face.

"Feels funny, doesn't it?" Al asked.

"Sure does! It's slippery."

"Now, press on it…but gently, gently."

Irv pressed and, of course, the mercury separated into two pills, each finding a crease on Irv's hand to slide into. Al reached over and mashed a thumb carefully over both pills, and Irv's hand was filled with multiple, tiny dots of silver.

"You broke it!" Irv's dismay was so comical Booze and Al broke into laughter.

Again Alvin squeezed Irv's hand to bump the tiny flecks together so they reunited into one gleaming, silver ball. Using the lip of the vial, Al divided the mercury again and scooped half back into the vial. "When you're tired of playing with that, we can put it back in here," he said.

Alvin placed the vial on his bedside table, rolled over, closed his eyes, and was soon asleep.

August 3
Tuesday
Temp 97.6
" 98
The temperature has

*gone up a bit. It is
still not bad. As long
as it stays below 90
degrees I feel fine.
Tomorrow is my big
day. Phil left the San.*

Phil was released into the bright sunshine early on Tuesday morning. He had made the rounds before he left, shaking hands left and right and promising to come back to visit. Alvin did not put much faith in that promise. He had seen too many patients walk out the door in the past year and a half and never look back.

As he watched Phil walk to a waiting car and toss his bag into the back seat before climbing in next to the driver, Alvin mentally wished him well. At the same time, he admitted to a wish that he was the one going home. Strictly speaking, Al should not have been out of bed and standing at the window, even for the few minutes it was going to take to see this friend off. That onus upon Al only emphasized for him how far he was from being released. Phil had been walking the halls for months before he received the coveted ticket home. Alvin had not yet earned the right to abandon his bed.

While Alvin could crank up his generosity to the point of smiling and even waving a farewell as the car with Phil in it rolled down the drive, yesterday he had been able to allot only four terse words in his diary to Phil's leave-taking.

August 4
Wednesday
*Temp 97.4
"   99.6
We sure had a swell
time today didn't we
honey girl? Gee Pal
I love you all to pieces.
I sure love you because
you are so good and
sweet.   Al.*

When Annie took temps after visiting hours, Booze noted the rise in Alvin's. No matter how quietly the young man rested, his wife's presence never failed to raise his temperature. It worried Booze that Al appeared to be so exhausted after so little effort. He had heard Alvin mention that he had *"played hard"* when, in actuality, Al had done nothing more during the visit than sit upright and carry on a conversation. However, Booze thought it was a good sign that a visit from Frances always raised Alvin's spirits. He might be a tired man after a visit, but he was a happy one. Booze also noticed that Al usually did justice to the evening meal after a visit from his wife. On other days...well. As a doctor, Booze hoped for a better appetite for the man who had become a favorite of his.

While Phil's departure had stirred some interest on a lazy August day, the ward fairly bristled with excitement on Thursday. The word was out. A show would be held that evening in the recreation hall at seven o'clock sharp. And every patient would attend.

"Wonder what we can expect?" Irv asked the room at large.

"Maybe a choral group, or some fiddlers," Booze suggested.

"What? No chance of a girlie show?" Irv joked.

"If Phil were still here, he'd have all the details," Alvin commented.

"Well he isn't, so I guess we take potluck," said Irv.

'Potluck' turned out to be a trio of jugglers, a lass whose kilt left enough bare leg to elicit a satisfied comment from Irv, a squealing bagpipe that accompanied her highland fling, and a dog act that made the animals seem smarter than some humans.

Because the beds of patients confined to them were usually rolled into rows in the rec room for events like this, Alvin had been surprised when Annie told him he would be ambulatory for the evening. When the show was over, and he was once again ensconced within his blankets, he reached out a long arm, dragged his calendar within writing distance and recorded his impression of this festive night out.

August 5
Thursday
Temp 97.4

"   97.4
We had a big show
and party this evening.
I wish it was you and I
together some place
all alone. I sat 1 ½ hours
in an iron straight back
chair.

The wind started whipping up at midnight. The shades at the windows of Room 101 stuttered a noisy alert. Al, Booze and Woods—all jolted wide awake—were joined by Christina, who came in to check on the racket. She released the shades from their anchor and raised them to let the wind blow silently into the room.

"As long as the wind is going to come in, it might as well do it quietly," she said softly, as she made the adjustments. She kept them company for a few minutes, then left with a whisper of her soft-soled shoes.

The wind continued to blow all day Friday. Al found it—and the cooler weather it brought—a pleasant change. There was something about a wind he found comforting. He had fallen asleep to it many nights under his tarp with Murray at Kooskooskie. Today it soothed him into slumber on and off throughout the day.

During one waking spell, he uncorked his vial of mercury and tipped its contents into his hand. The bead seemed smaller than when he had shared it with Woods. When he brought that to Irv's attention, his roommate gave a sheepish grin and admitted he had mushed his ball of mercury into so many bits that they had slipped out of his hand and become lost in the sheets.

"Couldn't get the slippery little devils all back together," Irv said.

As Al rolled the pill around in his hand, he noticed that his wedding ring had lost some of its luster. It could stand a good polish. He looked at the shiny ball of mercury, and then, tentatively, he rolled it around and over his gold wedding ring. He fully expected a gleaming gold band to be the result. Instead, his gold ring turned silver right before his eyes. *Criminey! Now what have I done?* He tipped the mercury back into the bottle, shoved it aside, and scrubbed at his ring without effect.

That night in his diary he buried his confession under a weather report.

August 6
Friday
Temp 97.8
"   99
The wind is blowing
and it is nice and cool.
It has been pretty hot
lately. Pal honey I
shined our ring with
mercury and it turned
silver. I sure hope
it wears off.   Al.

Al closed the diary and slipped it into the drawer. He rubbed his ring against the lapel of his pajamas in another futile effort to restore it. Then he took the vial of mercury off the stand, shook the bottle vigorously and watched the silvery sphere splatter apart. Without waiting to watch the mercury reform itself, he dumped the vial in the wastebasket.

Chapter 147

August 7-8
Saturday & Sunday
Temp 97.8
"   98.6

Alvin could not scare up the energy to do more than record his temperature on Saturday. Although it had finally reached normal, he spared no celebratory words on it. He was also unaware of Booze's continual watchful gaze.

Frances had nothing to say about Alvin's 'new' silver ring that was showing more tarnish than silver when she arrived Sunday. Her concern, like Booze's, was focused on the listless form of her husband. She hoped to coax some vigor from him with the radio that had finally arrived, but even the cat's eye on its dial that widened with an eerie green glow as they tuned it to the shortwave failed to stir much interest in her husband. Booze and Irv lavished praise on the radio, perhaps in the hopes of igniting some spark in their roommate.

The child Ida held in her arms did bring a smile to its father's pale countenance, but raising a hand to pat his daughter's head full of curls was the most strength Alvin could muster. Seeing his fatigue, Ida cut her visit short and took Frances Pearl home.

Frances stayed on through the afternoon, silently holding her husband's hand as she watched him sleep. Several times her own worried glance across the heads of Booze's company caught an equally concerned look from him. When it was time for her to leave, she kissed Al's cheek gently, which caused him to open his eyes and smile drowsily at her. With no more notice than that, she slipped away.

Although Ida questioned why Frances would return to the san

that evening when Alvin was apt to again sleep away their time together, she did agree to loan Frances the car to make what she considered a wasted trip. It was true that Alvin did not stay awake the entire two hours, but he was more alert than he had been in the afternoon.

"Everyone is entitled to a sleepy day," Frances told Alvin when he apologized for giving her such "a boring time".

"I like watching you sleep," she said, stroking his hand and ducking her head shyly.

She could not bring herself to tell him about the lonely, hollow feeling that had crept over her as she watched his breath flutter in and out in painful puffs through his slightly open, dry lips. Even his long eyelashes fanned vulnerably across the rise of his cheeks had sent fearful quivers deep inside her.

They did little talking, but listened to music on Alvin's new radio. Alvin made his fingers do a two-step in time to Eddy Duchin's *It's De-Lovely*, and Frances tapped hers back at him until they were 'dancing' together across his nightstand. When they said goodnight, it was Benny Goodman who serenaded her out the door with *Goodnight, My Love*, but it was Al who threw her a kiss when she turned back for a last look at him.

With great effort, Alvin opened his diary and made his mark for Sunday.

> *Temp 97.4*
> *" 100*
> *My radio is fine. Frances*
> *Baby and her mother Ida*
> *brought it out. I seem to*
> *have soared in temp. I*
> *feel sorta sickish in my*
> *stomach.*

Chapter 148

August 9
Monday
Temp 97.4
"   98.2
I don't feel very
well, I hope
to feel better
by visiting day.

August 10
Tuesday
Temp 97.8
"   98.8
I feel like hell.
I think I have
the flu.

"Does anyone else on the ward have this flu?"

Booze looked at the wan face turned to him. The appeal on Alvin's face was clear.

"I suspect quite a few have the same thing you do, Al," said Booze in a voice meant to convey comfort.

Irv, standing at the window out of Al's line of sight, raised a questioning eyebrow, but Booze chose to ignore it. Irv wagged his head, swiped a hand across his face as if to wipe off the solemnity etched there, and pasted on one of the smiles for which he had become noted. On the way out of the room, he paused at the foot of Alvin's bed where he playfully grasped Al's ankle. Giving it a gentle shake, he said, "I'll just meander down the hall and survey the troops. See who is and isn't feeling up to snuff today. You hold the fort here until I get back with the answers. Maybe I can scare up some hot lemonade for that cold of yours, too."

Irv's words brought a faint smile to Al's face, but he lapsed back onto his pillows before Woods was out the door.

August 11
Wednesday
Temp 98.4
"   100
I still feel like
hell. No relief
in sight.

August 12
Thursday
Temp 98
"   100
I feel no
better. Still
no relief in
sight.

August 13
Friday
Temp 98
"   99.2
I believe I feel
some better
today. Haven't
such a headache
as I had yester
day.

August 14-15
Saturday & Sunday
Temp 97.4
"   98.5
Hello Love. How are
you this even? I

feel about the same
as yesterday. Al.

Temp 98
"   99.2

Chapter 149

The touch of Ida's hand jerked Frances awake just an hour after she had stretched out to grab a few winks before heading off to work the night shift. Still half-asleep in the darkened room, she tried to make sense out of why her mother was bent over her. To add to her confusion, she saw Lily hovering in the doorway, silhouetted from the light in the kitchen.

Ida, being Ida, spared no words.

"The san called. Alvin's had a hemorrhage and they want you out there right now."

The words had no meaning for Frances. She had just left Alvin. He was fine.

"Get dressed. I'll drive," Ida snapped as she switched on the bedroom light. "I've already called the cannery and told them you won't be in to work tonight. Lily will stay with the baby."

When Frances did no more than sit up on the edge of the bed, Ida grabbed a dress from the closet and threw it onto the bed.

"Come on, girl, get a move on," said Ida.

Numbly, Frances began to react, pulling on whatever clothes came to hand.

Questions whizzed through her head as wildly as race cars on a dirt track that obscured more than they revealed in the confusion of speed and dust. *A hemorrhage? Al? She had been visiting with him just...when? An hour or so ago? And wasn't he fine then? A hemorrhage? What did that mean?* Around and around the words flew dizzily, posing question after question, none of which had answers.

And where are my damn shoes?

On her knees, Frances clawed frantically under the bed for the elusive oxfords. Lily, watching from the door, came to her, took her arm and urged her to a sitting position on the bed. She knelt in front of Frances, retrieved the shoes and fitted them, one by one, onto her feet. She pulled the laces taut through their eyelets and tied them into sturdy bows. "Don't worry about Baby. We'll be waiting for you here." Lily grabbed Frances by the elbows and hoisted her from the bed. She stuffed her sister-in-law's arms into a sweater, and gave her a gentle push toward the kitchen where Ida was waiting.

The push from Alvin's sister seemed to be the start Frances needed. She and Ida were at a run by the time they reached the Ford.

Ida, hunched grimly over the steering wheel, had nothing to say as she pushed the Ford to its limits down Poplar, onto Ninth Street, and finally onto the home stretch of the Dalles-Military Road. Frances' lower lip was gnawed raw by the time Ida pulled up to the Blue Mountain Sanatorium and screeched to a halt in a splatter of gravel.

Gillis met them at the door.

Frances anxiously searched the supervisor's face for a clue as to Alvin's condition. She saw nothing there but steely determination. And what that portended, Frances had no way of knowing.

Whether Ida did or did not see more than Frances, something moved her to reach a hand out to her daughter. So, hand-in-hand, they started to follow Gillis down the hall. Before they had taken more than a few steps, the nurse turned to them and stopped.

"Normally, we would move Alvin to a single room to give him and his family *privacy* at a time like this."

The way Gillis pronounced the word *privacy* stuck in Frances' head and rattled around in there, pushing all else out. Frances was sure she had never heard *privacy* pronounced without the sound of a long i. *Priv*-acy, as if the word was related to a *priv*-et hedge. Maybe, she marveled, she had never heard that word before. *Privacy. A room for privacy. Like the one Alvin's neighbor, Laurence, had been moved to before...Oh God, no! Not Alvin. Please, no!*

"...which is why we decided to let Mr. Potts remain with his roommates," Gillis said, obviously concluding a thought Frances' ears had missed.

Recognizing that Frances had no idea what Gillis had said, Ida whispered to her daughter, "She said Mr. Booze helped Alvin when the hemorrhaging started, and he and Irv Woods want Alvin to stay with them, so that's where he is."

"One more thing, please, ladies," Gillis said, laying a restraining hand on Ida's arm.

"Alvin is not to talk, even if he is able. He is to stay completely quiet, completely still. He must not move at all. Is that understood?" She stood firm until Ida and Frances each nodded agreement. She turned then, marched to Room 101, and threw open the door.

The room was blocked from view by a screen of white, pleated material that had been erected across the doorway. Gillis stepped around it, and they followed her.

At first glance, the room seemed packed with people, and Frances could not see Alvin at all. Christina's was the first face upon which Frances focused. The dark-haired nurse was standing on the far side of Alvin's bed. She acknowledged their entrance with a brief nod. Across from her was a white-coated figure, a man whose back was to the door. He turned, and Frances recognized Dr. Smith. Booze stood at his shoulder. Another screen, which was meant to close Al's bed off from the rest of the room, stood folded back. Irv stood at the edge of the screen. He came forward as if he had been waiting for them.

He took Ida's free hand, and patted it with a trembling one of his own. His chubby face held no smile tonight, only an expression that bordered on fear. Ida unclasped her hand from Frances', and nudged her toward Al's bedside. As her daughter moved forward, Ida took both of Irv's hands in hers. She set to stroking and petting them in much the way someone, more gently inclined than Ida, would comfort motherless kittens.

Frances approached Al's bed hesitantly, looking for direction from Dr. Smith. In her world, doctors and priests were next to gods. It would not do to presume.

The doctor waved Frances forward. Christina stepped aside to make room for her.

"I think I've done all I can do for now," Dr. Smith said to Gillis, turning away from the bed. "It's up to you now." To Booze he gave a pat on the back, and said, "Good job" as he left. "Clear away," Gillis said to Christina, and followed the doctor from the room.

Christina maneuvered Frances closer to the bed, even as she scooped up supplies and debris that littered the floor and table tops. Frances was unaware of the nurse's departure and Booze's quietly watchful presence. Her eyes were on her husband.

Alvin was a shrouded figure, blankets pulled neatly to just under his chin, his bloodless face an exposed, pale halo framed by those unruly curls. Frances reached a finger to coil one back into its proper place. She let that finger rest lightly on his temple, afraid to disturb him, but anxious to see a breath of life or feel a pulse. His eyes remained closed, the lids a pale lavender outlined by honey-colored lashes. His lips were dry and cracked, the lower one flecked at the corner with a dab of crusted blood.

Frances could detect no breath escaping from him at all.

She placed a tentative hand on his chest, and was shocked to feel it stone hard and icy cold beneath the warmth of her palm. Of its own accord, her hand flew up in reflexive protest and she stumbled back a step.

"It's only ice," Booze said quickly.

Frances turned a dazed look upon him.

"There is an ice pack on Alvin's chest. That is what you felt," Booze said. "We want his lungs to rest, and the ice helps them do that."

"What's happening?" Frances asked.

Booze deliberated before answering. *How much does this wife really want to know? How much can I ethically tell her?*

"You've been told that Al's lungs hemorrhaged, correct?"

"Yes. Well, they told my mother when they called. We don't have a phone, so she took the message for me. But no one has told me exactly what a hemorrage means."

Ah, the joys of medical procrastination. Booze was not about to do the job of Dr. Smith or Gillis, but the doctor within could not leave Frances completely in the dark.

"A hemorrhage is bleeding. A hemorrhage can be severe or light. Understood?"

"I think so," Frances said uncertainly.

"We've all had hemorrhages at one time or another," Booze continued. "I'm sure you have had a bruise. You get bumped, your skin darkens where you were bumped. That coloring is from bleeding under the skin. That is a very light hemorrhage. In Al's case, the bleeding was from the lungs. Of course it was not caused from a bump; It was caused by the tuberculosis, as I'm sure you know."

"Severe or light, Alvin's hemorrhage?" Frances asked

"That is a question for Dr. Smith," Booze responded. Then he relented and added, "I believe your husband is at rest, Frances. Christina gave him a powder that will make him sleep soundly for awhile, and rest is exactly what Alvin needs now."

Ida abandoned Irv, whose hands had steadied under her stroking, and went to her daughter.

"Come. We'll just sit here next to Alvin." Ida pulled chairs up for them, and settled Frances close so she could rest her hand on the counterpane.

Irv faded away behind the screen that hid his bed from them, but Ida heard the springs creak under his weight. It would be good for everyone if things could return to normal as quickly as possible. *'Though I have my doubts as to what normal can be for this son-in-law of mine,'* she thought with Alvin's unnaturally still body stretched out before her.

Chapter 150

Frances pushed her bank passbook and six bills, a twenty and five ones, under the wicket. The teller meticulously entered the amount of Frances' deposit in the passbook with a fountain pen held elegantly in long, slender fingers that bore an ink smudge on the forefinger. With a practiced smile, she slid the book back under the grille.

"Thank you, Mrs. Potts, and good day to you."

The night before at Alvin's bedside had passed in a daze, and Frances was still moving in a fog today, but she was moving.

Frances wanted to have the passbook with its new total of $325.79 ready to show Alvin on the off chance he would be alert enough today for it to mean anything. She had earmarked fifty dollars for savings this month, but that was before she purchased the radio. Still twenty-five dollars *was* twenty-five dollars. With last night's wages lost, tonight's still uncertain, and with the cannery season winding down, there was no telling when another deposit would be possible.

Ida and Frances had stayed at the san last night until Alvin awakened. "Cold, so cold," had been the first words he uttered when his eyes blinked open. He had repeated them over and over in a hoarse whisper until Ida fetched Christina. The nurse brought an extra blanket, but she was unable to make Al understand why he had to be packed in ice. However, he seemed to recognize his wife, and he ceased to call out. When Christina left the room, Frances dampened a tissue in water and sponged away the dried blood from his lips, and then slipped a hand under the blankets so she could cradle his chilled hand in hers.

As soon as Alvin's eyes had closed again, apparently in a deep sleep, Ida insisted they leave.

"You need to get a few hours sleep yourself if you're going to be in shape to work at the Wilsons. You won't be any good to Al, if you get sick, too," Ida scolded, using the one argument that could draw Frances away from Alvin's bedside.

Today Ida had offered to take Frances' place at the Wilsons for the afternoon so she could get back to Alvin, but Ida insisted that Frances leave Frances Pearl with Lily. "It won't hurt that girl to keep the baby for you. You'll have enough on your plate today," Ida grumbled. This was a sore, but old, subject with Ida, who thought that Lily was not carrying her weight.

"Oh, Mom, Lily is always willing to help," Frances protested. And, indeed, Lily happily accepted the new duty, anxious to help in any way she could, short of going out to the sanatorium.

So, alone in Ida's Ford, Frances made her way from the bank to the Blue Mountain. Again, Gillis approached her as soon as Frances stepped through the entrance.

"Remember, Alvin must not talk, and he must stay as quiet as possible." Gillis' reminder, although not prefaced by a greeting, was innocuous enough, but the curt voice in which it was delivered reminded Frances of the snip-snap of garden shears. It was difficult to talk to a woman with a voice like that, but Frances wanted to know how her husband was doing before she saw him. So, hesitantly, she posed the question. Gillis frowned in irritation, tipped her head at a haughty angle, and sniffed as if she smelled something bad.

"As well as can be expected," she snapped.

"That's what I need to know," Frances persisted. "What can we expect?"

Surprisingly, Gillis capitulated. "The worst seems to be over, but we can only wait and see," she said.

When Frances would have spoken again, Gillis raised a finger sternly in her direction and, jabbing with the finger to punctuate her remarks, she said, "Sometimes, in some cases—and this is one—it is better not to speculate.

"Go," Gillis added, holding the door to Room 101 open. "Go in, Frances." The ice in her voice thawed perceptibly. "Sit with your husband. Talk to him, if you like, but, remember, it is in his best interests to remain absolutely quiet and still. Your job is to see that he does that."

Frances saw no change in Alvin. He could not have been more

pale or lifeless if he had been a corpse. The image made a shiver run up her spine. Then she saw that Alvin was shivering too, shivering in earnest, and she heard his teeth chattering. A hand on his chest told her the ice was still in place. *'What are they trying to do, freeze him?'* It was a fleeting thought, but who was she to question authority? So, she did not.

The passbook stayed in her purse, and Alvin's eyes remained closed.

Alvin's chest was encased in ice for seventy-two hours. When he was able to speak again, Alvin told Frances he felt as if he would never be warm again.

"Just wait until I get you home, sweetheart. I'll heat you up," she said, cupping his hands and holding them over her heart.

Chapter 151

The exodus of visitors left the Blue Mountain's halls dark, empty and quiet. The only sound was the shuffle of crepe-soled shoes as the nurses and ward clerks moved from room to room preparing the patients for the night ahead.

Frances, still under the preferential umbrella that had given her free access to Alvin these past three days, had left long after the last stragglers, but the light in Room 101 still burned. Christina, pulling sheets taut and tucking in edges on Booze's bed, was almost finished. As she plumped the pillow and wedged it back into place under Booze's head, she followed up with a quiet question.

"How do you think our boy is doing?" Her head dipped toward Alvin, asleep now after his brief return to consciousness.

"Every day beyond the hemorrhage is one day closer to recovery," Booze responded.

"Are you hedging, Doctor?"

Irritation flared briefly on his face. "Christina, dear child, let's not forget that I am *not* the doctor on this case. Nor on *any* case, for that matter."

"Point taken, *Mr.* Booze," Christina said, smiling.

She smoothed the counterpane with a quick swipe of her hand, and left the room, switching off the overhead light as she went.

Alvin's recovery moved slowly. Irv and Booze were the best of roommates as Al struggled to regain the ground he had lost.

Irv, playing the part of court jester, became an even more eager proponent of beauty, pointing out to Al anything from which Woods felt even an iota of admiration could be squeezed. Irv's choices ranged from the sublime to the outrageous. His soliloquy on a double rainbow seen from their windows brought a weak smile of appreciation from Al, as much for the speaker's poetic and dramatic rendition as for nature's colorful offering. But an especially noisy and juicy fart to which Irv treated the room and then looked comically 'round for approval, drew a disgusted wrinkle of the nose, which only caused Irv to burst into peals of unrestrained laughter. The laughter and the roly poly man who produced it with generous gestures of hilarity did provoke a reluctant smile, which, obviously, was the jester's intent.

Booze provided a steady stream of delicacies in an effort to tempt Al's appetite. Too often the fragrant slice of cheese, finger of roasted meat or ripe peach remained untouched on his tray. Booze knew nausea was Al's constant companion, making even the suggestion of food repellent. When he could not feed the body, Booze set out to provide food for thought. Remembering the interest Alvin had shown when Phil made his rounds to spread the latest sports news, Booze scanned the pages of the *Union* for interesting items. He thought the report of three musical cowboys riding a bull from Idaho to New York had possibilities, but Al fell asleep during the reading of it.

Booze skipped over a story about the world cup yacht races, judging that a contest involving crafts that cost $500,000 would have little interest for a dollar-a-day laborer. He did not know how wrong he was. When Booze announced that Joe DiMaggio, who was clouting a home run on an average of every 25 innings, had a good chance to come within shouting distance of Babe Ruth's 60-homer mark for a season, Al perked up his ears, but the item led to no further conversational exchange.

Booze and Irv could not have been more considerate. They kept nosey ward-walkers at bay, allowed no disturbance during rest periods, and took their cue from Al each morning. On the rare occasion when he felt well enough to talk, they accommodated him with non-controversial subjects. If he stayed rolled in his blankets seeking the oblivion of sleep, they tip-toed through the day to give him every chance at what was so elusive for all TB patients.

When these two had asked Dr. Smith to leave Al in the room with them, they had taken him on as a project. Booze had urged Smith to agree because he knew being moved to a room alone could have an adverse psychological effect on a patient who had seen it happen, with unfortunate results, to other men. Woods had blindly agreed to it, but he was no less dedicated to providing support. It was what he would want, if he were in Al's place. In pleading their case alone with Smith, Booze had argued that his presence in Al's room would be as good as, or better than, a nurse who could not be with a lone patient twenty-four hours a day. With that argument before him, Smith had been easily persuaded. The two men took their role in Al's recovery seriously.

Their goals were to help staff keep him contented, rested and fed. In spite of their efforts, they were discouraged by what they saw as August slid slowly into September.

Chapter 152

"I want to go home."

Alvin placed a pleading hand on Frances' arm.

The knuckles were knobs, the veins prominent, his arms like sticks. He no longer told her how much he weighed, if he even knew. Pounds and temperatures no longer had meaning for him in this place.

He repeated himself.

"I want to go home, Sweetheart."

His eyes glittered like mica struck by the sun. The signs of fever were also painted in a rosy flush across his cheekbones in a face that had narrowed in these past weeks as the flesh fell from his bones. Tiny beads of perspiration stood in bold relief on his forehead, dampening his curls but refusing to roll away.

To Frances, a sweaty brow following illness had always been a good sign, a sign of a broken fever. Tuberculosis was re-educating her to its own idiosyncrasy in which fever co-existed with oily sweat as the body worked to expel poisons from a body made clammy by the effort.

She wiped away the perspiration to buy time as she searched for a response.

Alvin's eyes had never left her face. He was doing more than making a statement, and he wanted her to realize that.

Frances took a deep breath. She decided to try a little side-stepping.

"I want you home, too, Sweetheart. Maybe when you gain a little…"

Alvin's hand gripped her wrist. "Frances, *I want to go home.*"

The date was September 1. Al's hemorrhage was exactly two weeks, two days and seventeen hours behind them. Frances had counted every one of those hours while she watched for a sign, any sign, no matter how slight, that her husband was regaining strength. That sign had not appeared. He still had no appetite. He was skin and bones. Although he tried to hide it from her during visiting hours, Gillis had told her Alvin could not walk without the support of an orderly. Frances could see for herself that even sitting up in bed without the bolster of pillows was beyond him.

She finally let her eyes meet his. In the depths of his clear blue eyes, beyond the frantic feverish shine, lay a calm resolve. In that determination was reflected strength and faith and trust and, yes, the spark of life. A sense of peace stole over her. She recognized it as the peace that comes from making a decision when a decision is the last thing you want to make.

"Let me see what I can do," she said.

Alvin raised her hands to his lips.

At that moment Frances prepared for battle.

Gillis would be the first obstacle. The supervisor had to be won over, if Alvin were to receive permission to leave the sanatorium and come home. The decision would not be hers to make, but they would need her on their side.

This was going to take some planning before it could even be presented as a question to the powers that be. Frances knew just the hard-headed, practical person to consult. Ida.

When Frances left the san, she drove directly to her mother's. The Wilson children could wait their turn.

"Alvin wants to come home, Mom." Frances eased the screen door closed behind her.

"Well, hello to you, too," said Ida.

Frances laughed.

Their talk did not last long. It couldn't. Frances had to rush back to rescue Grandpa Wilson from children who would be waking from naps, if they weren't already out of bed and driving him crazy. In just a few minutes Frances convinced Ida that the only thing she could do was bring Alvin home.

"How to do that is where I need your help. We have to think of every possible reason they will come up with to say no, and then have all the answers that will give us a yes."

"Oh, is that all?" Ida's mingling of sarcasm and humor brought just the right amount of levity to the situation that was needed. They agreed to put their heads together that evening.

"It will be quieter at your house. I'll come over after supper," Ida called to Frances as she raced out the door.

The first thing Frances did when she arrived home from work was open the pantry. She wanted to reassure herself, and the jewel-like jars filling the shelves did just that.

She surveyed with satisfaction the rows of Economy and Kerr canning jars packed with a colorful array of fruits and vegetables. The pears, peaches, apricots and Italian prunes had been canned from the windfalls she and Ida had collected in orchards after the harvest. The string beans, tomatoes, beets, carrots and cucumbers came from the garden she and Arlene had planted. Because Frances did not trust herself to can a decent batch of vegetables, Ida had put them up, taking a share for herself for her trouble. They had picked the cucumbers young so Ida could use them for pickles. There were also smaller jars of jams and jellies, made on the evenings rain had washed out a cannery shift and given Frances a few extra hours at home. A bushel basket held a gift of winter onions Docey had planted in the spring and just pulled. He said he would bring a bushel of potatoes when he dug them after the first frost, and told her he would have apples for her before that. She planned to make applesauce and apple butter from some of those, maybe dry some for pies. Alvin loved her homemade apple butter.

"We have enough fruit and vegetables here to see us through the winter," Frances announced to a puzzled Lily, who stood with Frances Pearl's hand clasped in hers waiting for a greeting.

Frances slapped herself alongside the head for her thoughtlessness in ignoring them, and scooped her daughter into her arms, thanking Lily all the while for taking such good care of her girl. Frances still took her daughter to work with her, but Lily had begged her to leave her home on Wednesdays, saying she would enjoy the company. It did make visiting day at the san easier for Frances.

Frances Pearl was the center of attention in the remaining hours before her bedtime, but the inventory of the pantry was not far from Frances's mind.

A pot of coffee was waiting for Ida when she arrived. They settled in at the kitchen table with paper and pencils. Ida had been doing some thinking, and, as she fired off the protests they could expect, Frances jotted them down.

You won't be able to work. How will you get by? was the first on their list. Frances had anticipated that one, and it had led to her inspection of the pantry's hoard. The money from her last check at the cannery was knotted into the toe of a sock in her dresser drawer. That and whatever she earned at the Wilsons between now and the time Alvin came home could be used for living expenses. The money in the bank would be their emergency fund. She would swallow her pride and ask for welfare, if it came to that. They had done it once, they could do it again.

They wracked their brains, refilled the coffee cups again and again, and built arguments against every objection they could think of. When they thought they had covered every base, a quiet question from Lily caused Ida to drop her head into her hands, and Frances to slowly lay down her pencil, prop an elbow on the table and rest her cheek against a fist.

"Will they let Alvin come home if the baby is in the house?" Lily had asked.

Well, of course they would not since the child was no longer even allowed to visit inside the sanatorium. Probably Lily's presence in the home would also keep Alvin away. It was an obvious stumbling block, but Ida and Frances had overlooked it.

Frances pushed away from the table. She stood erect. With arms dangling at her sides, she rotated her head in slow circles, three times to the right, then three times to the left. As her head sagged forward, rolled around, and then lolled back, her neck protested with little noises that sounded like gristle grinding.

Finished, Frances shook her hands as if flicking off water, then rested them on the table and leaned toward Ida and Lily.

"We'll have to give this some more thought, but, thanks to Lily, they won't catch us by surprise. I say we've done enough for tonight. Who wants a cookie?"

Chapter 153

"I believe I'll be going home."

Booze looked up from his newspaper. Alvin nodded. "That's what I want, and Frances is looking into it for me."

"That would be something, wouldn't it?" It was the kind of noncommittal remark Booze felt he could stand behind. Anything more might stir up hopes that really had no chance of developing into anything. Too many rules and regulations stood in the way was what Booze was thinking.

"You see, René it's not just a matter of wanting to go home. I *have* to go."

Booze could not recall Al ever addressing him by his given name. It sounded strange now to hear it. Alvin's casual use of *René* imparted a confidential note to his simple statement. At least it sounded that way to Booze. If he was right, Alvin had picked a good time for confidences. They had the room to themselves since Irv was out prowling the hallways looking, as he said, "for something more beautiful than your two mugs."

Booze felt the lines of his face falling into the listening mode that had coaxed embarrassed matrons into revealing physical ailments they considered to be too intimate for discussion, but that were only all too commonplace to the doctor.

"That so?" he added as further encouragement to Alvin.

The receptive but non-judgmental countenance, the ear tipped as if to catch every word, and an attitude that indicated Booze had all the time in the world worked on Al just as it had on the most reluctant of Booze's patients.

"Ever since I walked through the doors of this place, it's been on my mind that my life could end in a charitable institution." Al paused, but Booze did not interrupt. "I've seen it happen to others," Alvin said doggedly.

"I know you have."

"Well, I just don't have the stomach for that." Anger and defiance tinged the comment. After a pause, Al added softly, "I really don't, René."

"I can understand that, Alvin. I'm sure we would all like to be somewhere other than where fate has placed us."

"Oh, don't get me wrong, Booze. If I were sure I was going to get well, I could stay here for years. But it sort of looks like the cards are stacked against me. And if that proves to be the case, I want to be home," said Al.

"You've had a set-back, yes. But you aren't letting that get you down, are you?"

"Haven't thrown in the towel, you mean? I don't think so. I believe I can still go a few rounds." Al grinned. "And, who knows, the cure I need just may be waiting for me at home."

"You aren't pinning your hopes too high, are you? About going home, I mean. There's a lot of bureaucracy between here and your front door," Booze warned.

"It's going to happen. I know it," Alvin insisted.

In the face of Al's determination, Booze could almost believe it would.

Still, Booze thought it prudent to offer an argument for the establishment.

"You know, Al, the medical care here is as good as, or better than, you'll find anywhere. The doctors and nurses know what they're about. The patients are their main concern, and they will continue to give you the best of care, if you stay holed up here with us."

"I know that. But, René, it really is time for me to go home."

"Then we'll say no more about it!" said Booze, slapping the bed. "Now, you tell me when you are going to start writing again in that diary Flora gave you."

The animation that Booze had been pleased to see return to Alvin's face in the past few days faded away now. It was replaced with a faraway stare as if Al were seeing through the walls and beyond to the distant Blue Mountains that had loaned their name to this institution. His gaze was bleak, as if he did not like what he saw.

"I'm not up to that," was Al's brief reply when he came out of his trance.

The diary, with its calendar pages untouched, remained out of sight in the following days, but Al's appetite seemed to have returned. It was a rare day when a tray of his went back to the kitchen with much more than bones on it. If he had to stretch out flat immediately after a meal in order to keep it down, he did not comment on it, but it did not escape Booze's notice. The soft white bread spread with liverwurst or calves-foot jelly that Booze had specifically ordered his friends to bring seemed to go down more easily. Booze was pleased to see that these treats, probably more nutritious and certainly more digestible than what had appeared on their dinner trays, did not go to waste.

While it could not be said that Al turned into a picture of health in the one short week since he and Frances had come to an agreement, he was able to pull himself up in bed to sit without the aid of a pile of pillows and even walk about the room without assistance. At times, he made rather shaky progress as he maneuvered between their beds, but he kept at it, and every day he walked a little longer than the day before. Irv watched the daily parade in silence, and tossed over a towel whenever sweat fell into Al's eyes.

Booze thought rest would be the better road for Al to take, but he knew Al was physically preparing himself to go home. He hoped he would not be disappointed.

Booze still read snippets from the *Union* each morning over coffee. Now Al stayed awake through all of them. Booze, who was always looking for something unusual, felt he had a winner with an article on the front page of the September 7 issue. It was a story about a vicious dog threatening a Walla Walla woman.

Irv and Al listened with half an ear when Booze first started reading. A crabby dog and an upset woman seemed small potatoes.

They began to suspect something more when Booze read that the officer answering the call was armed with a pistol that had been confiscated from a prisoner.

"That must have been some vicious animal, if they had to pack a gun along," Irv commented.

"Well, just listen," said Booze. He went on to relate that the woman's would-be rescuer found the dog holed up under the house and, when he crawled in to rout him out, was confronted by a snarling animal with more than escape on its mind. "He raised that pistol and he pulled the trigger, but nothing happened. Not just once, but twice."

"That'd be a tight spot for sure," said Irv.

"It gets even tighter. Listen," said Booze, who went on to tell how the gun, on the third try, gave a little pop and a bullet rolled out of the barrel. "Real slow," said Booze.

"Just rolled out? Migod! Never heard of that," said Irv.

"That's what it says. Just rolled out. The dog was still on the attack, so he fired the pistol again, and what do you think? Another bullet just *dribbled* out."

Irv guffawed, and Alvin wore a broad grin.

"Well, this was a persistent fellow that they'd sent out with that confiscated pistol," Booze continued. "He fired a fifth time and this time there was a tremendous explosion...that explosion not only killed the dog, but it *blew him to pieces*."

Booze looked at his stunned audience and then delivered the last line: "It says when officers examined the gun back at the police station, it was found that 'the cheap affair' had faulty mechanism and was entirely out of commission."

"Well, not *entirely*," Irv gasped through his laughter.

Booze considered the next article he intended to read to them an even riskier choice than a dog blown to bits, if reading was meant to raise their spirits. There was no humor in it at all, centered as it was on Japan's invasion of China. The article detailed Japan's advance and fighting over a two-thousand-mile war front with savage fighting on the Shanghai front and eight Chinese divisions trying to hold back sixty-thousand more Japs south of Peiping. *What a nightmare!*

As Booze scanned the rest of the article, the physician in him recoiled at the report of cholera now exposing millions in Shanghai to grave danger. This was an article better left unread this morning. He folded the paper and pushed it aside.

"Can I pour anyone another cup of coffee?" Booze asked, as Al wobbled his way on one last pass around the room.

Chapter 154

Frances and Ida had been no less busy than Alvin in preparing for his return home. While he was trying to regain strength, Frances had found an alternative home for Lily in the event they actually received permission to bring Al home.

All it had taken was a phone call to Alta the day after their pow wow around the kitchen table. Alvin's sister had been dismayed when she first heard the news of his hemorrhage, and it had taken no persuasion at all for her to accept that home would be the best place for her brother now. "Of course, Lily can return to us, if it will help bring Alvin home. Elwin and I will be glad to have her. We never really wanted her to leave," Alta had said.

Now Ida and Frances were tackling the problem of what to do with Frances Pearl should her daddy come home. Frances was not willing to turn the child over to just anyone. As they sifted through the possibilities, it was quickly apparent there was only one choice. Frances Pearl had come to know Angie and Roy through their frequent visits to town, and was as fond of her aunt and uncle as they were of her. If they were agreeable, they were the ones to whom Frances would entrust her. But, in this instance, a phone call would never do.

"We'll have to drive out to the ranch and talk to them," Ida agreed.

They chose the first day they did not have to work, which was just three days after Al had set the ball to rolling. It was Ida's idea to make a picnic of the Saturday outing.

"We may as well have some fun along with the work, and it's always easier to have a good talk over food, don't you think?"

Frances saw the wisdom in that. They added Lily and Agnes to the party, and they sat in the back seat surrounded by hampers of food and thermoses of coffee and buttermilk. When Agnes pointed out that she did not drink coffee and did not like buttermilk, Ida said, "Well, Roy does!" and that ended the complaints. Even Agnes understood there were ulterior motives for packing food along.

The women could have saved themselves the trouble. Both Angie and Roy were quick to fall in with their plans. And that was even before Ida cut into the raisin pie that was Angie's favorite. Married now, Angie and Roy would have welcomed a child of their own, but it had not happened. They were still working at the ranch in the positions to which Alvin had inadvertently led them. A house of their own had been part of that deal, and they showed Frances the alcove in their bedroom that could be used for Frances Pearl's crib. As Frances looked it over and listened to Angie's excited plans for her daughter, tears stung at her eyes, but she refused to let them fall. It was no time to cry when you were getting what you asked for.

The ten miles back into town gave Ida and Frances time to plan their next step.

"It's time to talk to Miss Gillis," Frances said. "She's such a stickler for rules, how can we get her to go along with this?"

"Leave that one to me," said Ida. "I'll beard the lion in her den."

Although Alvin was full of questions when Frances arrived on Wednesday, she kept all the details from him, telling him only that she was making headway. If she could bring this off, then would be time enough to tell him how she had done it. Right now was so confusing it produced only headaches. He had no idea that Ida was closeted with Miss Gillis trying to unravel one of those headaches right now.

"Be patient," Frances said, patting Alvin's hand.

She did regale him with a description of all the canning that had been done and all she would be doing. Without telling, he would know how important those glass jars would be this winter. Alvin, in turn, did not tell Frances that he flaunted the rules and slipped out of bed behind Annie's back because he was determined to be strong enough to walk from his bed to the car on the day Frances came to take him home.

Ida's visit with Gillis produced mixed results.

"We can't look to Miss Gillis for a lot of help," Ida told

Frances on the way home. "She isn't in favor of it, but she said if we can get the approval of social services, she won't stand in our way."

"Why do social services have to be involved?" Frances asked. The go-rounds she had with a social worker when she was trying to find work and get off the welfare rolls had not yet faded from Frances' memory. She had resisted every effort that had been made then to get her to take a job where she could not have her baby with her, but it had been a struggle.

"Since you and Alvin were receiving help from the government when he went into the san, social services are part of the picture, Gillis said, whether we like it or not," Ida said. "And she gave me a name for you to contact. Miss Gillis said to call and make an appointment to talk with this Frieda Pickens. Do you want to come to the house and call now?"

The place smelled of sweat and smoke and garlic, and the line Frances stood in wound halfway around the crowded room, which was painted a depressing shade of gray. Frances was in the welfare office waiting for her appointment with Miss Pickens, who had told her on the telephone Wednesday afternoon that, if she could not be there the very next day, she would not be able to see her for two weeks. The social worker had said it as if it pleased her to make Frances quickly hop at her command. She had no idea how eager Frances was to jump at anything that would hurry the process along. Now it looked as if she would still be here a week from today, unless they pushed these people through like sheep through dip.

Frances had no idea where that thought had sprung from. She knew nothing of sheep, but supposed the memory of bleating animals being herded through a ditch filled with nasty looking water was a leftover image from some cowboy show. Now that the thought was in her head, the raised voices tangled around her reminded Frances of the senseless bleating of sheep. And they were all in a row, standing as passive as sheep waiting to follow a leader. Frances did not like feeling like a sheep, especially when she wasn't sure where this was going to lead.

She waved away a cloud of cigarette smoke that had floated into her face from over the shoulders of a man in front of her.

"Some people got no manners."

The comment came from a tall, rawboned woman directly behind her in line.

"Just as lief smother you as look at you, them smokers would," said the woman.

Frances was embarrassed that a gesture of hers had prompted the remark. She hoped the smoker had not heard it.

Her embarrassment must have been noticeable to the woman because she laughed and said, "You don't have to worry about offending that one. Most smokers are deaf, don't you know?"

The bony shoulder in front of Frances swiveled, but just enough to allow the smoker to blow another cloud of smoke out of the corner of his mouth. This time the smoke sailed past Frances and bumped against the woman's gray cardigan where it gradually sunk into the wool.

"There's a fine how-de-do," she said, flapping the front of her sweater. "My old man will think I've been hanging out with some rapscallion instead of crossing swords with Picky Pickens."

A woman clutching a baby inched closer to the woman in gray.

"I called her Fearsome Frieda when she was my social worker, but this time they gave me a really nice one. Try to get your case switched to Ruth Roman. She's a lot easier to get along with."

"Trying to get out of Pickens' clutches once she's got a grip on you would be like trying to fight the heavyweight champeen. Guess I'll just make do. What about you?" she said to Frances. "Whose been assigned to your case?"

"This is just my first visit. My appointment is with Miss Pickens."

The women cast sympathetic eyes on her. The woman with the baby clucked her tongue. "Well, maybe she'll go easy on you."

"Dream on, little ladies, dream on. Pitiless Pickens takes no prisoners," the smoker said under his breath, but still loud enough for them to hear.

The gray-sweatered woman gave a great honking laugh. The mother giggled.

They fell back into sheep-like silence, and the line shuffled forward another foot. Frances really did not like feeling like a sheep, and even less so now that she had heard the leader called

Picky, Pitiless and Fearsome.

When Frances was finally seated in front of Miss Pickens, who was barricaded behind a gray metal desk stacked with file folders, all of her carefully planned presentation flew out of her head. She could only look into dark, piercing eyes magnified by thick lens in horn-rimmed glasses and say weakly, "I want to bring my husband home from the Blue Mountain."

It was not a good beginning. Pickens waved the words away as if they were of no consequence whatsoever. What she was interested in, she said, were the facts. The 'facts' for Miss Pickens consisted of filling out forms. And there were many forms to be filled. Just when Frances thought there could not possibly be anything more she needed to know, Miss Pickens whipped out another form. She seemed to have an endless supply. Most revolved around money; money the family had, money the family did not have, money the family owed or expected to owe. When Frances tried to explain that she was not asking for any money at all, those words, too, were brushed away by Miss Pickens, who accompanied the gesture with a look that would have turned a tornado from its path.

And Frances was not feeling anything like a tornado. She was perfectly capable of working eight hours washing, scrubbing and tending kids at the Wilson's, grabbing four hours of sleep, and then getting up to put in another six or eight standing on her feet at the cannery, but she crumbled in the face of authority. In fact, Pickens had taken all the wind out of her sails.

Frances had no idea how to get the interview back on the track that would lead to Alvin's release. She sat with lips pressed tightly shut, and willed herself not to cry.

"Come back next week, same time, but on Wednesday," Pickens snapped, bringing the session to an abrupt halt.

Frances had no idea why she would be coming back or what, if anything, Miss Pickens intended to do about her request.

"I didn't get anything accomplished," a deflated Frances reported to her mother that evening as she helped Ida with Grandma Hempe. The little lady, who was showing her age, had taken an early supper of potato soup and was on her way to bed. Ida had invited Frances to supper so she could hear firsthand how the appointment had fared.

Ida, Lily and even Jenny and Agnes grew somber as they listened to Frances' description of Pickens and the forms that seemed to have nothing to do with Alvin. Herbie and Ray, who were not enthusiastic about spaghetti, pushed the food around on their plates until Ida said they could be excused. Frances Pearl seemed to be the only one enjoying her 'dinner on a plate'.

"Wouldn't you know the next appointment will be on a Wednesday? That means I'll miss visiting Alvin in the afternoon because I'll have to use my lunch break to see Pickens, and I don't know if even an hour will be long enough. I had to wait more than that today just to get in to see her, and Grandpa Wilson was not a bit happy when I got back late," said Frances.

"Lily and I will work out something with the Wilsons, won't we?" Ida asked.

Alvin's sister seemed surprised to be consulted, but she nodded in agreement.

No matter how much the three of them picked at what had happened in the meeting with the social worker, no one had unraveled any sense in it by the end of the evening.

"She never once mentioned Alvin," Frances lamented.

"Well, we'll just have to keep on keeping on," Ida said.

Chapter 155

Frances flicked a drop of water onto the flat iron. When it sizzled, she ran it across the pillow case on the ironing board. The Wilson children and Frances Pearl were down for naps, and an afternoon of ironing stretched out before her.

When she wasn't feeling like a sheep these days, Frances felt like a woman split in two. Half of her was tied up in the routine of keeping house for Mr. Wilson and his family. The other half was called into battle whenever Miss Pickens snapped her fingers. The Wilsons were the easy part. Every day there had its own schedule. As long as she kept to it, the work was effortless. Of course, now and then, young Charlie threw a monkey wrench that put her out of kilter, but he had such a charming smile that any little peccadillo of his was easily overcome and forgiven. And he played so nicely with Frances Pearl, sharing his toys and being as gentle with her as could be. He was a fine little fellow and she was going to miss him, if she had to quit this job.

It was squeezing in those visits to the welfare office that were tearing Frances apart. She had faced Pickens over that desk three times now, and she still did not feel any closer to reaching her goal than she had on that first awful visit. Miss Pickens had finally gotten around to talking about Alvin. Frances almost wished she hadn't.

Frances had not anticipated a problem in caring for Alvin at home, but Pickens raised all kinds of concerns. Frances thought she was making mountains out of molehills. She guessed she knew how to take care of a sick husband. Just give her the chance and let her do it! Pickens was also trying to get Frances to agree to let Frances Pearl become a ward of the state. She refused to listen to the plans Frances had already made for her daughter.

Pickens had pounded on that issue at the last two meetings. In stating her case, Pickens was unvarying from one visit to the next. It was always 'if this' and 'if that'.

"*If* your husband were to come home, you could not keep that child in the house." That was the signal for Frances to resume her argument that a temporary home was already waiting for Frances Pearl. As if she had not heard her, Pickens would launch into another if. "*If* a tubercular patient were allowed out of a hospital setting and into a home, I am not at all sure it would be in anyone's best interests." To that, Frances always answered patiently, "My husband thinks it would be in his best interests." That only earned a snort from Pickens, who would charge on with her ifs. "I said *if* it were allowed, and that is a big *if*, the child would be better off as a ward of the state, which would place her in a good, safe, healthy home."

Frances was sick and tired of Fearsome Frieda, Picky, Pitiless Pickens and her godawful *ifs*, but she was afraid of her. Pickens held the key to the door Alvin wanted to walk through. Their future was in her hands. That had scared Frances into submission, but now the threat of having her child taken from her had put Frances' back up. She would never allow Frances Pearl to become a ward of the state. There must be some way to get Pickens to hand over that key without letting her take away the baby.

A good thing about having a basket of clean wash to iron was the time it gave one to think. As the iron steamed over shirts and blouses, Frances racked her brain to come up with the justification that would convince Pickens to change her mind when she met with her next Wednesday. Alvin hoped to be home before the end of September, but it was already the twenty-third and chances looked slim. It was getting more difficult to face him and stay positive when things seemed so hopeless.

Frances unrolled another piece of ironing and set about smoothing out the wrinkles.

Booze had years of experience in reading the expressions, often conflicting, on the faces of the patients who consulted him. Paying attention to his patients' faces, the way they entered his office, and the language spoken by the movements of their bodies had revealed as much or more to him than what they said to him. So when Frances and Ida entered Room 101 for the Sunday afternoon visiting hours, Booze found it natural to do a little facial reading.

In spite of the cheerful smiles they presented to Al, Booze discerned a tension that both seemed to share. All Al wanted to talk about was going home, and Booze received a definite impression that Ida and Frances were giving carefully worded answers when he questioned them about when that was going to happen.

If they were being evasive, as Booze thought, Alvin seemed not to notice. His color was high, as it usually was when his wife was with him, and the excitement this talk of home had aroused in him two weeks ago still punctuated his conversation. In the last week, Booze had urged him to take it a little easier, to stay abed more, and stroll around the room, if he really felt he had to, just once a day. Surprisingly, Al had heeded his advice. Booze thought he even seemed relieved to take it; Al may have found those strolls were a little too much for him. He slept a lot, but still roused up to listen to Booze read the daily news and still ate almost everything Annie brought at meal times.

Booze also noticed an increase in Alvin's visitors. His sister and her husband, only infrequent visitors before Al suffered his hemorrhage, came in at least once a week now. A short, jolly-looking man, who had little to say, had taken to accompanying Ida on some of her visits, which also had become more frequent. Booze had noticed that Frances's last two Wednesday visits had been limited to the evenings, and he wondered about that. Al's wife had been such a steadfast visitor. There must be a good reason why she had not shown up in the afternoons.

Booze himself had no visitors today, so he gave his curiosity free rein. At one point, when Alvin asked how Frances' meetings with the social worker were progressing, Booze saw the glint of tears in her eyes before she buried her face in a handkerchief and coughed unconvincingly. At least, it did not convince this doctor. Yes, for sure, something was going on here. Booze, without visitors to distract him, thought he just might attempt to find out what.

When Ida stepped aside to make room at Alvin's bedside for Alta and Elwin, who came in mid-way through visiting hours, Booze saw his chance. With Ida blocking him from Al's view and her arm within convenient reach, Booze drew her attention with a tap on that arm.

A slight nod of his head toward the door when Ida turned to look caused her eyes to widen in surprise, but she casually turned her back to Booze again.

Certain that Ida had intercepted his message correctly, he slipped out of bed, thrust his feet into slippers, and went out the door, wrapping his robe around him as he went.

It was a perplexed woman who found Booze waiting for her outside the door of the recreation room. He motioned Ida to follow him in, and shut the door behind them. They had the large room to themselves.

"Is our young man going home or isn't he?" Booze asked.

His direct approach, accompanied by the bedside manner that had stood him in such good stead as a physician, soon had Ida telling him about the snags Frances had run into with Miss Pickens. It was not a short story she had to tell. It took time for Ida to relate to this compassionate man all the plans they had made and the barriers that Pickens had thrown up against each and every one of them.

"Now with this Pickens trying her best to get hold of Frances Pearl, it seems hopeless," said Ida when she had finished the telling.

"When does Frieda Pickens next meet with Frances?" Booze asked.

"Wednesday, the 29th," said Ida.

"There should be something that can be done. Let me think on it," said Booze. "But let's keep this little talk just between ourselves."

Ida did not question Booze's interest or his faint hint of help. Her hopes were raised no higher, but she felt relieved to have shared a burden that was beginning to weigh too heavily.

As they left the sanatorium, Frances and Ida met Dr. Smith entering. He brushed past them, ignoring Frances' greeting, and hurried down the hall.

"Now there's a doctor who could take a lesson from that roommate of Alvin's," said Ida. "René Booze looks and acts more like a doctor than that fellow. Smith always looks as if he's sucking lemons."

Chapter 156

"Sign this, and this, and this," Miss Pickens ordered, pushing paper in front of Frances the minute she sat down.

Frances was not about to sign anything she had not read, and she said so. She prepared for a fight, but was surprised when Pickens just said, "Of course."

Before Frances had read even a sentence, Pickens' cold voice interrupted.

"Your husband will be discharged from Blue Mountain this Friday, October 1. Can you have your home ready to receive him?"

Frances was stunned. She could not believe what she had heard. Was Alvin really coming home in two days? It was all she could do to nod.

"The sanatorium will tell you what time to pick him up. Do not be late. Understood?"

Frances nodded.

"A health nurse will be assigned to visit him weekly or more often, if needed. She will be at your home Friday afternoon to see that you have settled him in correctly and to answer any questions you or your husband may have about his care. Understood?"

Another nod.

"One last thing. Have that child and your sister-in-law out of the house before Mr. Potts arrives home. Is that understood?"

Frances bit her lip, cocked her head, and stared directly into Pickens' beady eyes made ridiculously large by the thick wedge of glass in her spectacles.

"I understand," said Frances. With great effort, she added, "Thank you for your help, Miss Pickens."

"No need to thank me, Mrs. Potts. I think this is a very poor plan. I have no doubt you will be begging the sanatorium to take your husband back before the year is out."

Frances was halfway down the block before she realized she had not signed the papers.

Chapter 157

In fifteen short minutes Alvin had been granted his freedom. Frances forgave the sharp tongue that had announced it because Pickens had left her enough time to go out to tell Alvin the news. She couldn't wait to see his face when he heard.

There were a million things she had to do before he came home, and she had only today and tomorrow to do them in. Well, she would manage.

Frances fairly danced her way to the car, and she was still prancing on tiptoes when she burst into Room 101. Booze grinned from ear to ear when he saw her. *Old Smith's influence must have done the trick.*

She flung herself onto Al's bed and wrapped her arms around him.

"You're going home, darling! You're going home!"

She felt tears on her cheek, but didn't know if they were hers or Alvin's, but when he lifted his head her husband was smiling.

"I knew you could do it, Frances. I never doubted for a minute you would get me home," Alvin said, hugging her close again.

Pressed against her husband, Frances' own smile faltered. She had persisted, but she could think of nothing she had done that would have made Pickens change her mind.

Her troubled glance caught the grin that still spread over Booze's face. What she saw there now was more than delight. Self-satisfaction, that's what it was. Definitely self-satisfaction. And where had that come from? Sunday afternoon came back to her in a flash. Booze leaving the room. Ida disappearing shortly afterwards to be gone much longer than a visit to the restroom would take. Then Ida reappearing, but seeming more at peace than she had been for days. For the first time, Frances wondered just who René Booze was.

The frost-tipped grass sparkled under a thin golden haze that marked a perfect Walla Walla autumn morning. They couldn't have asked for a better day for Alvin's homecoming, Frances thought, as Ida's Ford crunched through fallen leaves on the sanatorium's circular driveway. It was just eighteen and a half months ago that she had brought Al out here, but they had been the longest months of their lives. She was glad to see the end of them.

Gillis opened the door for her, and waved her in.

"Someone is up, dressed and anxious to be away," Gillis greeted. "I bet you're anxious to have your fellow home too, so I'll just give you this list of suggestions for Alvin's care, and we can go to his room."

Frances took the several pages handed to her; pages, she saw, that were filled neatly with spidery penmanship. *Complete bed rest* were the first words she read.

"You'll have no problems I'm sure, but, if you do or if you have any questions, any at all, at any time, just telephone us. We'll be happy to help." Gillis surprised Frances with a quick hug. "Now, let's get Alvin bundled up and out of here," she said.

The satchel Frances had brought Alvin the night before stood by the door. She had helped him pack most of his things in it then, but he had wanted to keep it with him to add some last minute items, he said. His winter coat, also delivered to him the night before, hung on the back of a chair. The only hat he had was a battered felt with a sweat band that spoke loudly of hours in the field. Alvin had made her take it back home. "I seldom wear a hat unless I'm working," he'd said.

The room filled with people. Sanders came up from the lab to say goodbye. She gave Al a green sprig planted in a clay pot. "Try your luck raising peanuts," she said. Annie and Flora crowded in, too. Christina was right behind them. "Can't let our prize patient leave without our good wishes," Christina said, when Al teasingly asked if she was now working two shifts. Christina picked up his bag. "I'll just put this at the entrance for you," she said to Frances.

It was a small procession, led by Gillis, that followed Christina from the room. Booze and Irv walked on either side of Al, their arms looped in his. Frances thought they might be supporting him, but they were so casual about it, it could as easily be just friends saying farewell. She couldn't hear what they *were* saying, but Al was smiling and nodding his head.

Annie and Flora trailed behind Frances, until Flora stepped up beside her. "Let us hear from you. Give us a call from time to time," Flora urged.

"I will. Thank you," said Frances.

"We'll be counting on it," Flora said.

At the door, Frances took the satchel and stepped outside. The little group milled around Alvin, and Frances watched with a smile as he became wrapped in their embraces.

Then he broke free. The door closed behind him, and his arm linked with hers.

"I should be carrying that bag," he said.

"Don't rush things, mister," she said, poking her elbow gently into his side.

Alvin kicked his way through the leaves, enjoying the slight breeze that cooled his fevered cheeks and brought a tangy aroma of apples to his nose. He inhaled deeply.

"Smell those apples! Ummm. That's the thing about a farming community, there's never a doubt about what's being harvested," he said, pressing Frances' arm tighter to his side.

Al pulled her to a halt. "Look there," he said, pointing down the driveway to where it met the road that led to town.

"What?" asked Frances.

"The open road."

Freedom washed over him. He was free to walk to the end of that drive, free to take that road to town and beyond. The wind stirring through the trees, the crisp whisper it made of the blowing leaves, even his whipped about mass of curls made him feel like a young stud. He took several strides toward that open road before his legs began to tremble.

"We'll leave it for another day," he said, and turned to the car.

When Frances braked at the end of the drive and would have turned right onto Dalles-Military Road, he stopped her with a hand on her arm.

"Remember that homemade apple cider we used to buy at that little stand in Milton-Freewater? Let's drive over and get some!"

"Maybe we should get you home to..."

She stopped talking when she felt his grip tighten on her arm.

"I think a jug of cider is just what we need!" she exclaimed. "We're on our way." She wheeled the car left toward Oregon.

"It won't take long either, five miles at the most. We don't have to go clear into Freewater. That stand's right on the state line," said Alvin. "If it's still there," he added.

Booze and Flora stood companionably side by side in his room, watching Ida's Ford until it was out of sight.

"It must have taken some string pulling to get permission for Alvin to go home. Would you know anything about that, Doctor?"

"All it takes is cooperation, Flora, cooperation."

"All right. Have it your way. I didn't expect to get a straight answer."

"Seriously, Flora, that is a straight answer. If more people learned the art of cooperation, there would be no end to what could be accomplished. But now I have a question for you," said Booze, with a twinkle in his eye.

"Did you have anything special in mind when you presented our Mr. Potts with the calendar at Christmas?"

"What a queer question? Special in what way?"

"Well, Al spent some time speculating as to why you gave him that particular calendar. You know he used it as a diary?"

"I would have thought the calendar would be too small for that," she mused. "He had a lovely leather diary last year. But yes, I do remember why. The stationer the sanatorium does business with sent us several extra items at the end of the year. The calendar was one of them. I knew Alvin liked to track the days so I passed it on to him."

"No other reason then?" Booze persisted.

"Why, Doctor, what other reason could there be?" a puzzled Flora responded.

Chapter 158

The drive into Oregon had always been a favorite of Al's when he was courting Frances. Today the road unrolling under the Ford's wheels did not disappoint them.

The warm colors of autumn were all around them, and they rode with the windows down in spite of a breeze with a bite. With the chill came the smoky scent of burning leaves as they passed a fellow raking even more onto a smoldering pile, and then, as the Ford rattled past a herd of cows, the acrid odor of fresh manure drifted into the car.

Alvin sniffed as enthusiastically at one as at the other. Frances mimicked him, and laughed.

"But it's been such a long time!" he protested.

When the spicy aroma of apples began to circulate, Al said, "Smell that? Orchards! That old stand is still there." Then he turned his sniffs into snuffles to tease her.

Al humored her when they reached the stand. He agreed to sit in the car while she bought an acorn squash and their jug of cider and another for Ida. It was obvious that he was tuckered out. He drifted off to sleep before they were even back in Washington. For Frances the drive home seemed to take longer than the trip over had. She drove it with the windows rolled up.

Frances nudged Alvin awake just before she turned off Ninth Street. She wanted him to rouse up before they reached the house. This was his homecoming and she wanted to share it with him.

She thought the house looked nice from the outside, especially in the golden autumn light. The windows gleamed from the washing she had given them inside and out. Ida had sent Ray over last night to rake up the leaves. He had bagged them, and the gunnysacks stood neatly at curbside waiting for Docey to take them for mulch. Frances had kept one for the compost pile she and

Arlene had started.

Frances tapped out a shave-and-a-haircut on the car horn. It brought Ida to the door. *Understanding mother, I've got. She let me go alone to pick up Al.*

Now Ida hurried out to the car, calling out a welcome as she came. Before Alvin could open the door, Ida flung it wide.

"Well you laggard. It's about time you got yourself home," she said, beaming.

"It's a wonder you didn't have the F.B.I. out after us. We took your old Ford across the state line," Alvin joshed.

"So that's where you've been. Did you do any good?"

Al cocked a thumb toward the back seat.

"There's a couple of jugs back there, and one of them's yours."

Ida peered in, saw the satchel, and hauled it out. "Frances, you grab the rest, but don't you dare take my cider. Is that Freewater cider? Bet it is!"

They made their way into the house where Al was met by the fragrance of apple pies. The pies Frances had baked early that morning were lined up on the counter where she had put them to cool. She had sent two of them along with Alta, who had not only picked up Lily this morning, but had also taken Frances Pearl out to Angie and Roy. While one pie would do for each of those families, Frances had made an extra two for Ida's larger household. There wasn't much she could do to repay the help they had given, but she did what she could. And anyway, everyone likes apple pie.

Frances turned down the covers on Alvin's side of the bed, and motioned him to crawl in.

"I think I'd like to sit up awhile," he said.

His raised hand stopped the protest she had been about to make.

"The house looks swell. And it smells good too!" The compliment coaxed a smile from her, just as he intended it to do.

Ida pulled the wicker rocker closer to the woodstove. Al offered no resistance when Ida motioned for him to sit. She flopped the oven door open.

"Kick off those shoes and hike your feet up here," she ordered. "You look like you need warming up."

Frances came out with a quilt and wrapped it around his legs, tucking it in at his waist. "There now. How's that?" she said.

"You girls are going to spoil me, I can see that," said Al.

"Well, it'll soon be lunch time at my house, so I'm going to skedaddle. You'll have to settle for whatever spoiling Frances is up to doing for you," said Ida, pulling on a sweater.

"I think we'll have our lunch right here in front of the fire," said Frances.

Ida put on a good show of surprise when Frances handed her the pies. "Fresh baked pies, the first of the season. If that isn't spoiling, I don't know what is," she said.

The house was awkwardly quiet after Ida left. The crackle and snap of the fire sounded loud now that they were alone. Frances pulled a chair up next to Al's, but did not sit. Alvin began to hum and then softly sing a new song, *They Can't Take That Away From Me.* As he sang, Frances pouted in mock dismay, "What's wrong with the way I wear my hat." To the next line he sang, she nodded an emphatic *yes* in time to the tune and said, "I admit I do sing off key." Al was fighting laughter at her responses to the lyrics, but he continued through to the last line at which her finger wagged a *no-no* at him.

"Memories. So many memories we'll always have with us," he said, reaching out to grasp her hand. She let it rest in his for a minute. Then she withdrew it to lift the lid of the stove's firebox. She poked at the burning sticks and settled them in a flurry of sparks. She added another stick, and replaced the lid.

"Maybe I'll just bring in some more firewood," she said. But she made no move toward the back porch where the wood was stacked.

She wore a soft pink sweater over the black skirt that Al thought brushed her ankles so becomingly. Her hands smoothed and tugged self-consciously at the sweater and skirt.

"Is my wife nervous?" Alvin asked.

"Nervous? Of course not!" denied Frances, but her busy fingers said otherwise.

"Come here, Love. Come to me."

She moved closer. He reached up and gently drew her down into the chair beside him, close enough so his cheek could rest against hers.

"It is a little strange to have your old man home again, isn't it?"

Her head nodded against his.

"Before you know it, you won't even remember that I've been away."

"Oh, Alvin, I don't think I can ever forget all those days and nights without you. I've been so lonesome," she said, grabbing his hand and holding on tightly.

"Me, too, Love. Me, too."

"I don't know why I'm feeling…"

"Kind of shy?"

"I guess. I guess that's it," she answered.

"Well, we've got all the time in the world now, Love. All the time in the world."

Chapter 159

From the *Walla Walla Union* issue of Nov. 15, 1937
> **POTTS**— Alvin Ezra Potts, 26, died at his
> home, 902 West Poplar, Sunday, Nov. 14,
> 1937, after an illness of about a year and
> a half. Funeral services will be at 9:30 a.m.
> Tuesday at St. Patrick's Catholic Church.
> Remains at Marshall, Calloway &
> Hennessey Funeral Home — (Paid notice)

Frances cut the obituary notice from the paper and placed it carefully in Alvin's red leather diary. She laid the book aside, and took his tiny calendar diary into her hands. She opened the fragile pages and looked for the last entry he had made. There it was:

> **August 15**
> **Sunday**
> *Temp 98*
> *"   99.2*

She sharpened a pencil, touched the lead to her tongue to dampen it, and added:

> *Al had hemorrhage Aug. 15.*
> *Came home Oct. 1 until Nov. 14*
> *at 10:30 o'clock when God*
> *took him from us. God help*
> *baby and me.*

Frances let the tears fall, then brushed them from her eyes. She stood, shrugged into her coat, pocketed their bank book and headed for Baker-Boyer to close out their account. The day had come to spend the special fund. She thought it might stretch to cover some flowers for the coffin, too.

AUTHOR'S ACKNOWLEDGEMENTS

First and foremost, let me be clear, that without the diary kept by my father, Alvin Potts, for seventeen months in 1936 and 1937 this novel would not exist. I am also indebted to my mother, Alvin's sisters and his niece, Barbara McLay, for sharing family history with which I took complete liberty, with their blessings, to twist and turn to add flavor to the narrative.

I shamelessly borrowed beloved, family names for some of the characters in *The Diary*, but, once the ball was in their court, those characters ran with it in fictional directions entirely of their own making.

I owe a debt of gratitude to psychic reader Aris (Dee Dee) Diaz whose insight triggered something more than my imagination; Vernon and Velda Jordan, who own the site in Walla Walla, Washington where this novel begins and graciously introduced me to it; and my internet surfer Victoria Hardesty, who came up with some vital tidbits for me.

I am sincerely thankful to those who served as readers of the manuscript. Nora Hernandez and Patricia Mattison read several of the first chapters and urged me to continue writing. The entire manuscript was read by Bob Story Jr., managing editor of the *Daily Sun News* in Sunnyside, Washington, who was the first to read and edit the completed version. Sunnyside Library branch manager Dr. Francisco Garcia-Ortiz read, critiqued, and offered encouragement. Valuable input was also given by Eileen Bussell, school teacher; David Taylor, information and technology architect for a Fortune 100 Company; and Linda Logan, the self-proclaimed, ornamental center of the universe who suggested that I open the story with a prologue.

Their opinions and comments were extremely helpful and much appreciated. Daddy and I thank one and all.